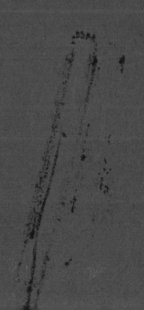

QUEEN'S ROYAL

By John Quigley

KING'S ROYAL
QUEEN'S ROYAL

QUEEN'S ROYAL

JOHN QUIGLEY

Coward, McCann & Geoghegan, Inc. New York

Copyright © 1977 by John Quigley
All rights reserved. This book, or parts thereof, may not be reproduced in
any form without permission in writing from the publisher. Published on the
same day in Canada by Longman Canada Limited, Toronto.

SBN: 698-10756-X

Library of Congress Cataloging in Publication Data

Quigley, John.
    Queen's Royal.

    Sequel to King's Royal.
    I. Title.
PZ4.Q65Qe3   [PR6067.U4]   823'.9'14   76–45786

PRINTED IN THE UNITED STATES OF AMERICA

To Betty

Author's Note

In the closing years of the last century it first became possible for speculators to make money by investing in casks of Scotch whisky. Ever since, men have dreamed of "cornering the market," or a vital part of it. One of the earliest attempts—that by Pattison Ltd., of Breadalbane Street, Leith—ended in financial disaster for the syndicate behind it.

QUEEN'S ROYAL

1

Although the spring of 1897 was slow to open, it lingered on until, suddenly, after a few hot days at the end of April, the blossom of two seasons flared across the Central Lowlands of Scotland in an unprecedented profusion of scent and colour. Along the shores of the Clyde and its many craggy inlets the very late and the very early mingled in disconcerting novelty. Dusty lanes from which snowdrops had hardly faded were all at once adorned with butterflies and droned over by bees. Birds nested amid cascades of pear and apple blossom while the fragrance of honeysuckle gathered sweetly at the doors of sheltered cottages. In the parish of Row, in the county of Dunbarton, the grounds of the big houses had been aflame for weeks with rhododendron and azalea, crocus and bluebell, tulip and daffodil, primrose and broom, magnolia and camelia—a vibrant glory not seen for perhaps a century, according to the old gardeners at Castle Gare.

Fiona King had enjoyed the short drive from the castle. As she gazed across the shimmering Gareloch to the low green hills of the Rosneath Peninsula, she blessed her father-in-law for his discovery of this idyllic place only an hour from the dirt and din of Glasgow. Four generations of the family now spent much of each summer here.

The village itself was hardly more than a dot beside the pier, but the parish, straggling on up the loch, contained some fine mansions. In winter most of them, including Castle Gare, were locked and shuttered until their owners reappeared from Glasgow at Easter. The visitors came then, too. There had been a great many this year. Lured by the amazing weather, they came to Helensburgh by train from the upper, industrialised stretches of the Clyde and then walked the stony road to Row. Their movements were predictable. They would sit at the shaky tables among the poppies and lupins in Granny Reid's cottage garden, drinking her twopenny tea and eating her halfpenny scones and pancakes. Then, refreshed, they would either take the ferry over to Rosneath or ramble on toward Shandon. Few disturbed the peace.

But now, as Fiona walked toward the marquee where, as chatelaine, she was to open the annual Daffodil Fair, the torpid still of the afternoon was broken by a hoarse cry. As she turned, a Spider phaeton came rocking into the village, the driver almost standing as he urged the horses on. It was a carriage designed for outings in parks or city streets but it was being handled now like a Highflyer. The light frame, intended to be drawn by one horse, had been harnessed to a pair of black high-spirited animals which seemed to be enjoying their sensational shattering of the village calm.

Yellow dust rose from under them and billowed over a wedding party leaving the ivy-covered church. Even above the clattering hooves and grinding wheels Fiona heard cries of dismay. But the Spider pounded heedlessly on, the driver bracing himself to take a bend along which some sale-of-work stalls had been erected. Two women in feathered hats shrank back, clutching the flowers they had been arranging. Others scattered, dropping eggs and vegetables.

As the carriage raced past, Fiona glimpsed a wild dark face lit by a smile of savage concentration. Beside this demon a girl sat, her hair streaming in silken strands, her expression a study in reckless exhilaration as she swayed to the mad dance of the slender springs.

Fiona clenched her hands in anger, then held her breath as a cart laden with milk cans slithered to a lopsided halt at the water's edge, the yokel in charge furiously waving his whip after the Spider, which, clear now of the village, was plunging faster than ever up the twisting lochside.

From where Gordon King lay in the boat he could see the girl moving slowly along the shore, treading a delicate way between clumps of sea pinks and marsh marigolds. She walked with a tall, swaying grace, almost as if barefooted, one arm pressing to her breast a bouquet of wild flowers.

Occasionally she broke a twig or bent to pluck a daffodil from among the grey rocks and the rough, sea-washed grass. As she stood on tiptoe, reaching for the rhododendron blossom thick above her head, the loose sleeve of her dress fell away, showing a suntanned arm with bracelets of gold or silver glittering on her wrist.

She was a stranger, but as Gordon watched, the ache of guilt and aimlessness that had lain heavily on him all that day began to roll mysteriously away. He realised that from where she stood he was invisible. The dinghy, to which he had come to sun himself and hide from his father, drifted gently, two or three hundred yards out. Probably she imagined the boat to be moored. Clearly she thought herself alone.

Her dress, a simple high-necked garment with little adornment, was yellow, and in the breeze that came softly down the Gareloch from the high mountains beyond Arrochar the material fluttered and gathered behind her like a train. For a moment he fancied he could hear the cloth rustling. As he strained toward the imagined sound, she bent and placed her flowers carefully on the pebbles. Then she turned her face to the sun, her shoulders tilted slightly and her arms stretched wide. He was startled by the almost pagan pose. He held his breath and stared, fascinated, at the tumble of shining brown hair and the tightly stretched bodice of her dress.

His ribs ached where the narrow seat dug into them, but he thought, *I mustn't move; if I do, she will see me and go away.* If she went away he might never see her again. He was filled with an unreasonable anxiety, and for a moment he glimpsed the extent of his discontent and lonely lack of purpose.

For a long time the girl stood as if hypnotised by the sun. Suddenly her arms fell and she turned as if startled by some sound from the direction of Castle Gare. After a moment Gordon heard it. It was a voice, muted by distance, but seemingly raised in anger.

The girl lifted her flowers and began to walk back along the shore. She went slowly because of the pebbles, and still with the light-footed grace that made him think of petals floating weightlessly away from a flowering tree. To one side of her the ground went up through rocks and grass to a dusty road, bounded by a drystone wall and shaded a little by trees that enclosed the castle grounds. From among the tangle of shrubbery behind the wall flame-tinted azaleas shone. Their perfume hung in the still air and he could smell it even out on the boat. On the other side of the girl the loch glistened smoothly to another shore, perhaps two miles away on the Rosneath Peninsula, before opening out into the wide estuary of the Clyde.

Once, she stopped briefly to watch a paddle steamer with black and red funnel manoeuvre out from Row pier and begin thrashing its way up the loch toward Shandon, Mambeg and Garelochhead, the seagulls that circled it diving suddenly in a screaming mass as a pail of scraps was dumped from the galley. Then she was gone, a glimmer of fresh yellow disappearing quickly now down a dark green glade that marked the twisting line of the road.

Frantically he struggled from his agonised position, flung himself onto the seat and seized the oars, rocking the boat wildly in his desperate haste. Momentarily, reason stirred and then died as he ignored the warning of the onset of one of the strange and sometimes frightening impulses that played such a part in his life, leading him into actions that ended in quarrels with his father or the inflicting of pain on his mother. He must see where the girl went. He pulled mightily for the shore and jumped out when the water was still a foot deep. The tide was in and he had to drag the boat only a few yards over the warm pebbles to beach it above high-water mark.

He bounded up the bank, jumping over rocks, the wet trousers clinging to his legs. The road was empty except for a pony trap clattering past with two giggling servant girls perched on either side. They stared after his dripping figure, shrieking to the driver to slow and have a look, but in Gordon's mind they hardly registered. He was too hungry for a glimpse of yellow dress or tumbling brown hair. He passed the castle gates and rounded a bend by a humpbacked bridge over a burn that had shrunk to a trickle between parched rocks. In a wood at the side of the road a cuckoo called, and from an open stretch came the scent of bog myrtle. But of the girl there was nothing. There were houses into which she could have gone, many twisting little paths she might have taken to the shore or to the bracken-covered hills.

He passed Ardfern, his grandfather's turreted house where as a child he had known happiness, and the long, creeper-grown cottage of his great-grandmother. Today he had no thought for them. He ran to the next long, straight stretch and stared disappointedly along it. His wild dash from the boat had been for nothing. The road was empty except for an old man carrying rubbish to a fire on the shore. Gordon turned. There would be a quarrel when his father saw him, for he should have been at business in Glasgow, but there was nowhere else he wanted to go now but home. He couldn't hide all day.

As he walked to the castle he tried to formulate some sensible explanation of his irrational behaviour. Although he had already had several furtive adventures, his interest in the other sex was sporadic. It had never gone beyond the casually physical. If a girl became available when he was on the spree with his city acquaintances, he took her. If not, he got on with his other interests.

He felt hot, limp and strangely breathless, not just from his headlong race along the road but from the force of the whole unnerving experience. He had never felt such a compulsion to possess any girl, let alone one to whom he had not spoken and whom he had seen only from a distance for a few speeding minutes.

* * *

14

In his study at Castle Gare Robert King put as much cool mockery into his voice as he could dredge from the anger he was struggling to control.

"Oh do please for God's sake sit down, Dunbar," he said.

"Thank you, but I'll stand," Douglas Dunbar roared at him.

"Suit yourself, but all this ugly spleen can't really be good for you. Or for the peace of the neighbourhood. The window is open and you must be disturbing the whole of the Gareloch. You're liable to give yourself something nasty."

Dunbar clenched very large fists. "I'm liable to give you something nasty, you jumped-up toff," he said, with a ferocious scowl round the long panelled room. "Your damned castle doesn't impress me, you know."

"Oh, doesn't it? Well, don't let that worry you. Some people have no taste for these things."

Robert's lean, clean-shaven face had an expression of relaxed insolence but he was tense and wary, ready to leap from his chair if the bulk of the dangerous dark-skinned man looming over his desk became any more threatening.

Douglas Dunbar's temper had led him into more than one violent incident, and everyone in the whisky trade knew it. At thirty-eight he was still tough and unpredictable, standing at least two inches over six feet and wide to match. The keen dark eyes that glared at Robert from under ragged eyebrows were set in a head like the top of a totem pole. Behind the good looks of a savage and the frame of a circus wrestler Dunbar had a cunning business brain and a flair for publicising himself and his brand of blended Scotch whisky.

Robert, six years older and three inches shorter, had for a long time known the man as a formidable whisky salesman and a dangerous competitor. But he had been shocked in the previous spring to find that in some of the best hotels and restaurants Dunbar's Special was ousting his own King's Royal. A grim year's battle for trade had followed, but, to his consternation, the loss of custom to his belligerent rival had not only continued but had accelerated alarmingly.

Dunbar's weapon was the discount. To get business, he cut his price ruthlessly, and when Robert matched him he cut again. It was a suicidal process that could lead only to bankruptcy. The terrifying thing was that Dunbar seemed fanatically ready to accept ruin as long as he took King & Co. with him.

Robert watched him mop his glistening forehead with a handkerchief of sparkling white linen. It was a contradiction in Dunbar's character that despite his often violent and uncouth manner, his dress and his personal grooming were fastidious and even fancy. His clothes were fussily cut from the best broadcloth, and two or three gold rings glittered incon-

15

gruously on hands that even careful manicuring hardly made less murderous. His thick dark hair was lightly Macassared, too lightly to stay in place during his enraged pounding of Robert's desk. As he mopped his brow he tossed back the locks that had fallen across it.

"Perhaps all this heat and sunshine is upsetting you," Robert suggested as Dunbar carefully folded away his handkerchief. "We're not used to such a long spell of it, especially so early."

"Damn the heat and sunshine. You're the chiel who's upset me."

"A pity, but I really don't see why. I simply indicated I would be interested in buying your business. Some men would take that as a compliment."

"It's not just what you asked, King, although that was bad enough. It's the damned cheek of the way you asked it."

He tore a piece of paper from a pocket and, leaning forward, shook it in front of Robert's face. "I don't have to tell you what this is, for you sent it."

"It's a telegram, isn't it?"

"Aye, a telegram, by God. An impudent bloody telegram of four words for the work of a man's life." He looked ready to strike.

Robert shrugged without taking his eyes from Dunbar's nearest fist. "If you didn't like my suggestion, you could have written to me in a civilised manner. You didn't have to come ranting and raving down here. I'm supposed to be having a few days' holiday. I conduct business from my office in Glasgow."

"The pages would have taken fire, King, from what I have to say to you."

"Really?"

Dunbar brandished the telegram again. "Aye, really," he sneered. "Man, your head will burst open if it swells any more. It's delusions of grandeur you must be having to send me a wire like this."

He held the telegram to the light, peering at it shortsightedly, as if the words were not burned on his outraged mind. "'How much your company?'" With a grunt he tore the paper and scattered the pieces about the room. Then he shouted the offending words even louder, emphasising each with incredulity. "'*How much your company?*' The bloody gall!" He smashed the desk with a fist like a boot. "Do you imagine a man like me would sell his business to a man like you?"

Robert lifted a paper knife and put it out of sight in a drawer. "I credited you with being a businessman. I thought if the price was right you might consider it."

Dunbar shook his head fiercely. "I wouldn't sell to you at any price, King. If there's anybody that'll be selling, it's you, when I'm done with you. And that's what I'm here for. I wanted to ask you a question. I couldn't wait till you got back to Glasgow. I wanted to ask you today, to your face."

He stepped back from the desk as if to give himself more room for some strenuous manoeuvre, stretching and bracing shoulders like carriage doors. "'How much your company?' That's what you asked and you paid for a reply. Well, here's your reply: how much *your* bloody company? Tell me that, King, and I'll buy it." He stopped, swaying slightly, his great chest heaving.

Robert rose with a short laugh. He had shown the strength of his nerve. He could afford now to stand. He walked to the window and stood looking down on the loch. When he turned his expression was solemn.

"You're a successful man, Dunbar, but not that successful. I don't think you could afford to buy my business. I had the advantage of inventing blended whisky. I've been selling it for twice as long as you."

"But your days are numbered, King, and you know it. I'm going to wipe the floor with you and your King's Royal. By the time I'm finished with you you'll be glad to get back to your father's grog shops."

Robert fought down a hot flood of anger. "If your whisky is even only half as crude as you are, Dunbar, I pity your customers."

Dunbar pretended to be taken aback. "Oh, my. Don't tell me I've put my foot in it? Are the grog shops forgotten now that you've bought yourself a castle? Are you ashamed of them?"

"No, I'm not ashamed of them, and I don't know what this infantile sarcasm has to do with the matter in hand."

But Dunbar was still engaged with his vision. "Aye, you'll be lucky to get your King's Royal even into the wee back-street corner shops."

"For God's sake, don't be so damned stupid. We're both busy men. If we're going to talk, let's talk sense."

A twisted smile spread across Dunbar's glistening face.

"I'm talking sense. You're frightened, King, and well you might be. You were cock of the walk for a long time. You got used to throwing your weight about because you had a head start on everybody else. For a long time you didn't know what real competition was. Now you're up against me and you want to withdraw from the contest. Or rather, by God, you want me to withdraw. Well, you're going to have to stand and fight. Douglas Dunbar is not for sale."

Robert lifted a chair, put it down close to one of Dunbar's massive legs and stood waiting. After a long hesitation Dunbar sat down with a look of sullen disgust.

"It will be a very painful fight for both of us," Robert said, walking again to the window and sitting on the broad stone sill. "But King and Company must win. In your heart you must know that. We are more

17

firmly established than you. We have more money at our command. Our sales are worldwide. No matter what punishment you inflict on us in the United Kingdom, we can subsidize our home trade from our overseas profits." After Dunbar's long tirade he could not resist a jab of his own. "Besides, our whisky is better than yours."

Dunbar growled some incoherent rebuttal but refused to rise to the bait. "Get on with it," was all he said.

"There isn't much more to say. You wouldn't find us difficult or cheeseparing. If you were sensible and sold out to us now, you could save us both a lot of suffering and at the same time show a good return on your invested capital."

"Maybe. But where would I hide my face?" Dunbar's voice was acid with scorn.

"There's nothing dishonourable in selling a good business for a fair price. Where will you hide your face if you bankrupt yourself? Have you thought of that?"

Dunbar began to rise, then seemed to think better of it. "God, don't push me too far, King. Every month my sales creep up on yours and you've got the nerve to talk about me going bankrupt. Douglas Dunbar's whisky is booming. Have you not heard?"

"Oh, yes, your sales are booming. It couldn't be otherwise with the methods you use. But I've heard differently about your profits. You're cutting your price so recklessly you're in danger of leaving yourself with nothing."

"Don't be taken in by everything you hear." Dunbar's expression was confident enough, but Robert detected a note of bluster. He had hit the mark and he followed the blow quickly.

"I'll be perfectly honest with you. You are forcing us to offer bigger discounts than we are happy about. We are in business to make profits and your tactics make that very difficult. Both of us are suffering because of your desire to be top dog. Why don't you sell out or be content with the market you can get by selling your whisky at a sane price?"

Dunbar stared at him oddly for a few moments. "For a very simple reason, King." His voice was quiet and his anger appeared to be under control. He looked suddenly tired.

"When I came into blended whisky you were already an established company. You must have been well on your way to being a millionaire. One more blended whisky would have made no real difference to you. You could have ignored me. But for some reason you got it into your head I was a threat. I was an outsider working too hard, doing too well too soon, I suppose. You sent your travellers round to my customers offering discounts if they would drop my whisky."

18

Robert rose quickly from his seat at the window. "That's a lie! What we did was perfectly honourable. They were our customers, not yours. You were the interloper. And the discounts we offered were normal commercial inducements, not the foolhardy bribery you are indulging in."

"Dress it up anyway you like, King." Dunbar's voice rose. "The fact is, for two years I damned nearly starved. And so did my wife and daughter. A dozen times I nearly went under. But I struggled on. And eventually you got tired of cutting your price. You decided to let me be. I swore then that one day I would knock you out of top place. I've worked for that, night and day, ever since. And, by God, I've almost managed it. And I will manage it, for I'm big enough now to finish the job by using the methods you taught me."

The raw, quiet hatred was more upsetting to Robert than the earlier threatening fury. "You're poisoned, Dunbar," he said.

"Aye, and it was you who poisoned me."

"Anyway, your considered answer is no?"

"That's what it sounded like to me."

"I take it you know my reputation?"

Dunbar gave a contemptuous snort. "Do you mean with the women?"

Robert didn't flinch. "With anything. I always get what I want."

"And I hang on like hell to what's mine. That's *my* reputation."

They glared at each other till Robert walked to his desk and pulled a silk tassel hanging on the wall behind it. When the butler came Robert said, "Show this visitor out, Miller. Then bring me tea in here."

He turned to Dunbar. "I have to be in Glasgow early this evening for an important meeting. You'll understand if I don't offer you anything."

"It would choke me," Dunbar snarled.

He rose, casting his chair violently aside. It crashed into a table, scattering ornaments and tumbling a vase of flowers. With hardly a glance at the mess, he stalked thunderously out with the elderly butler running after him.

Gordon King was almost home when he heard again the angry voice that had disturbed the girl in the yellow dress. It was louder now but still too blurred and blunted by rage for him to be able to hear the furious words.

He stopped to listen, halfway up the avenue that curved steeply between the trees, astonished that the row should be taking place inside the castle. Servants would not dare behave like this; therefore, his father or his mother must be involved. He hurried on up the long incline. Above the trees he could see the battlements of the central tower and the lion

19

rampant flapping listlessly at the masthead. Gardeners raked the driveway smooth every morning but there were new wheel marks on it.

A moment later he went through the arched entrance to the courtyard and saw the girl. She sat very straight and alone behind the monogrammed door of a dusty but expensive-looking Spider phaeton, still clutching the wild flowers to her yellow dress. Almost at the same instant, the impassioned voice inside the castle went silent, leaving her enshrined, it seemed to Gordon's wondering eyes, in the sudden stillness.

Sun slanted over the courtyard wall, touching the high gloss of coachwork and harnessing. A horse moved slightly and the silvery sound of jangling metal echoed pleasantly from the old walls.

The girl was staring at an open window on the first floor. When Gordon coughed she turned, but without surprise. He smiled confidently as he walked to the carriage.

"You look lonely, sitting there all by yourself," he said.

She was older than he had thought: perhaps twenty. She had a wide mouth and restless dark-blue eyes that were examining him with interest. Her skin was fair and smooth.

"I'm waiting for my father," she said, moving as if to sit even more erect.

"May I sit with you until he comes?"

She looked at him suspiciously but did not seem offended by his boldness. She appeared to consider the suggestion. "Who are you?" Her voice was calm, almost amused.

"My name is Gordon King. I live here. My father is Robert King, owner of this castle."

As they looked at each other a faint breeze from the loch sent the perfumes of the garden across the courtyard. He was thinking that she was even more attractive than she had seemed at a distance when, to his consternation, he realised her expression was changing. The line of her mouth had hardened and her eyes were blazing. To his astonishment she almost spat at him.

"You may *not* sit with me. If you are one of the King family, my father would forbid it."

Indignation overcame his surprise. "Would he, indeed! And why would he forbid it? I'm sure I don't know your father. Who is he? Who are you, come to that?"

Her chin had a defiant tilt. "My father is Mr. Douglas Dunbar. I am his daughter Anne Dunbar."

Her whole attitude irritated him now. "And where is this father of yours, who would be displeased if I sat with you?"

20

"He's in there." The tone of her voice and the way she nodded to the house suggested contempt.

"Was that his loud, ugly voice? I heard it down on the shore. He's a peculiarly noisy brute, if you don't mind my saying so."

"How dare you call my father a brute!" In her fury she had risen and he saw again the slim loveliness of her figure. The flowers she was holding quivered. "Your father has made him very angry. It's no wonder he raised his voice a little. He's been insulted by your father."

"Raised his voice a little!" He gave a derisive laugh. "He was going on like an out-and-out madman. I'm amazed the horses didn't bolt. But perhaps they're used to the sounds of the gutter."

He was so breathless and confused by this inexplicable rage between strangers that before he knew what she intended, she had stepped quickly from the carriage and lunged at him. "You're an impertinent beast," she cried. "Father was right about you Kings. You're an arrogant, hateful lot." She hit him on the face with her flowers and then threw them over him.

He jumped back, shaking the petals and broken stems from his hair. "You must be a very violent family, Miss Dunbar," he gasped. "I'm glad your flowers weren't in a vase."

She had started to climb back into the carriage, but paused to glare at him anew. "That wouldn't have stopped me. You would have had the vase about you as well."

He stood studying her, noting the suggestive turn of her hips, the wild mouth and passionate eyes. "I like spirited women," he said with quiet calculation, striving to hold her gaze. "Couldn't we perhaps forget our fathers and be friends?"

Her fury had subsided into a wary watchfulness at the blatancy of his interest.

"I would be honoured if you would dine with me some evening, Miss Dunbar. But what did you say your first name is?"

She almost shook herself before turning and throwing herself into a corner of the carriage. "Go to hell, you silly boy," she said witheringly, her eyes studiously turned to the loch and the low green hills on its other shore.

"I'm eighteen," he said indignantly, bracing his shoulders and stretching to his full five feet ten inches. "Almost nineteen." It was a lie by almost a year.

The carriage rocked and the horses reared as she sprang to her feet. "I don't care what age you are. Go to hell and stop annoying me." It was almost a scream.

"My God, Miss Dunbar," he fumed, "you are not a lady."

21

He turned and rushed up the worn steps to the front door of the castle. At that moment it swung open and her father burst out. He crashed into Gordon, glared at him and then, without a word, went lumbering down the steps and over the gravel like the fish train from Mallaig.

Gordon stood uncertainly in the raftered hall, staring unseeingly at the paintings as he wondered where in the castle to seek refuge. He could go to his room and sit there with nothing to do except watch the steamers and pleasure yachts on the loch, or to the library and try to find a book that would put the infuriatingly tempestuous Miss Dunbar out of his head. He kept seeing her face, distorted with extravagant anger, the eyes dangerous and unrestrained.

The old butler, who had stood dumbly at the door watching Douglas Dunbar drive his daughter madly down the avenue in a shower of flying gravel, came in shaking his head, white-faced and shocked.

"I'd like tea in the library, please, Miller," Gordon said, and ran quickly up the curving staircase past two paintings by his uncle, James King. Before he had the library door half open he heard movement inside, but it was too late to withdraw. His father was standing in a pool of sunlight by the window in the otherwise shady room.

Robert smiled and closed the book he was holding. "One day I must engage someone to index all this information," he said, looking round the tightly packed shelves. "I can never find anything I want."

Gordon thought he saw a chance to leave. "Then I won't disturb you, Father," he said breathlessly. "I can get what I'm after anytime."

"No. Come in, Gordon. I'm looking for *Munro's Parliamentary Handbook*. You might be able to help me find it. It's a fairly small volume, bound, if I remember correctly, in dark blue. You certainly won't be disturbing me." He laughed softly as he turned back to the shelves. "That's already been well and truly attended to by an expert."

"You mean your rowdy visitor? He made enough noise for a regiment. I thought the servants were rioting."

"I imagine it must have sounded like that. Perhaps I should have closed my study window. Which reminds me: I asked Miller to bring me tea along there. I only slipped in here to collect this damned book." He looked over his shoulder. "You could hear him outside, then?"

"I heard him down on the shore. He must have been kicking up the most awful din. I didn't know you mixed with people like that. What is he? A mobile foghorn?"

Was nervousness making him too smart?

"He's a business competitor. I'm sure his name must be well known to you: Douglas Dunbar."

Gordon realised that to confess ignorance of the name would be another damaging sign of his lack of interest in the affairs of King & Co. Perhaps his father was already aware of this and trying to trap him. He glanced worriedly at the healthily handsome face, but there was no sign there of guile.

"I do recognise the name, of course."

"Then mark it well. Dunbar is a rough, tough man fanatically determined, apparently, to be a thorn in our side. His awful voice is the gentlest part of him, I'm afraid."

"I can say the same for the virago he had with him. She said she was his daughter and then attacked me with a bunch of flowers because my name is King. She ended up almost having hysterics. And it was all about nothing."

"Yes." Robert nodded as if from a Dunbar such behaviour must be expected. "He has a daughter who is said to be every bit as wayward and uncontrolled as he is. They have the reputation of being a wild and unpredictable family. I can't remember the girl's name. She's married, of course. Craig, I think, is her married name. Her husband is a stock and share broker."

"That must be another daughter. This one isn't married. She introduced herself as Anne Dunbar." He laughed. "Just before she hit me."

"There is only one girl."

"I think you must be wrong, Father. She wasn't wearing a wedding ring, either. She had an armful of jewellery but no wedding ring."

Robert hesitated. He did not normally gossip, least of all to his children.

"It's the same girl, all right, Gordon. Apparently her marriage is not altogether happy. I think her husband is rather older than she is. I don't know what their trouble is or who is to blame but I've heard they have frequent separations. She storms out of the house and goes back to live with her father. Like him, she does nothing by halves. She drops her husband's name and insists on being known again as Anne Dunbar." He shrugged. "She probably discards her wedding ring as well."

Gordon wrenched himself from a memory of the girl as he had first seen her on the shore, her arms bare and brown, her graceful walk carrying her along with her fine face turned to the sun.

"She's beautiful," he said. "With golden brown hair like mother's."

"So I believe, but I've never seen her."

"Despite her foul temper she looked . . . like a lady . . . not a bit like him. It just shows you can't go by looks."

"Her mother was a lady. She was Ethel Anderson, one of the shipping family. According to the stories, there was an awful row when she took up with Dunbar. Old William Finlay Anderson almost had apoplexy.

23

Apart from the fact that they were both very young, he had a long line of better-connected men in mind for his daughter. I believe he finally gave them his blessing, though, and despite the inauspicious start I don't think Dunbar ever gave him cause to regret it. The marriage was always looked on as a happy one. Dunbar's a widower now, of course. Ethel was drowned in the Clyde, not far from where they live. It was a terrible tragedy. It's since she died that Dunbar's become a real menace. He has no home life at all now, so he can devote all his waking hours to business and to his insane quest for our ruination."

Robert stopped, realising that his face had distorted at the unwelcome return of Dunbar to his thoughts, but also because he had become aware of questioning intensity in Gordon's eyes.

"Why do they hate us, Father? What have we done to them?"

"We haven't done anything to them. That's what makes it so absurd."

"They can't hate us for nothing."

Robert hesitated. "It's as good as nothing," he said tonelessly. "Dunbar bears a silly grudge from years ago. It's only a matter of business, but he's a dangerous man."

"Can he hurt the business?"

"Yes, he certainly can. And does. He is also a danger to my pride."

"I suppose you'll be able to stand that."

He could have bitten his tongue, for although the remark was innocent, it could, in the permanently delicate state of their relationship, be misinterpreted.

Robert looked into his son's eyes for a piercing moment, then returned thoughtfully to his search of the bookshelves.

"Where do they live?" Gordon asked.

"They have an estate on the banks of the Clyde, just this side of Glasgow. It's quite a romance. Dunbar was born in one of the farm labourers' cottages. Now he owns the big house. You see it quite clearly from the train when there are no leaves on the trees. In a way I greatly admire Dunbar. He had none of the advantages of money or a good education." He stopped and looked reflectively at his son, remembering Dunbar's gibe about humble beginnings. "Rather, in fact, like your grandfather."

Gordon made a face. "I can't imagine a brute like that getting a title from the queen, as Grandfather did. And I'll wager he's never read a book since he was at school—if he ever was at school—or given more than a glance to a painting or any of the other fine things Grandfather loves. I'm sure he's not like Grandfather at all."

"His voice did make a bad impression on you," Robert said with a surprised smile. "I only meant that he resembled your grandfather insofar as they are both self-made men."

"Well, Grandfather made a better job of himself."

They were still laughing when the butler came in with the tea tray.

"If Miller takes that along to my study, we can have tea together," Robert said. "I can get what I want here some other time. I must leave for Helensburgh soon to catch a train for Glasgow shortly after six o'clock. I'm afraid I'll be very late home tonight. You'll all be asleep." He turned to the butler. "You can leave me something, Miller. A sandwich will do. Here, in the library, I think. And don't forget to put a jug of water with the decanter."

Gordon made another effort to escape. Soon it must dawn on his father that he should be at business in Glasgow. He would have realised it already if it hadn't been for his lingering preoccupation with Dunbar's brawling visit and then the hunt for the missing book.

"If I stayed here," he said, "I could look for the book you want while I have tea. I'm sure it must be important to you."

"No. Just some figures I wanted to check." He turned brightly toward the door. "Come along, Miller! Lead the way."

In the study his joviality soon faded. After a few minutes he had little to say. "Excuse me, Gordon," he said after a long, withdrawn silence. He took a sheet of notepaper from a Buhl writing set on his desk and, frowning slightly with concentration, began to scribble, as if making notes.

Gordon edged quietly to the window, where he drank his tea in quick, almost furtive gulps, returned his cup quietly to the tray and began to retreat stealthily to the door. If Robert had forgotten he was there, the movement reminded him.

"Oh, Gordon?"

"Yes, Father?"

Robert had the end of his pen gripped tightly between his teeth. His eyes seemed to come reluctantly into line with his son's. He took the pen from his mouth.

"Something struck me a little while ago. I feel I can't let it pass. Why aren't you in Glasgow, at work?"

Gordon flushed. "It has been such beautiful weather, Father, I thought I would take advantage of it."

"But this is Monday. You have had the whole weekend in which to relax and enjoy the sunshine."

"I know, Father, I have no excuse, really, except that there is a sort of holiday feeling in the air. The cruising steamers are packed, and two or three charabancs have gone past with trippers and . . . and I knew you yourself didn't intend going to business today."

"Good heavens, boy, that has nothing to do with it. You know very well I'm just back from a long and tiring business visit to Canada and the United States of America. That's why I'm here rather than in Glasgow.

25

But, even so, I haven't been idling. I have been at my desk all day. How have you spent your time?"

The atmosphere in the room was suddenly suffocating. Gordon felt his face hot and his legs weak. "This morning I climbed the hill to Glen Fruin and after that I took the dinghy out."

"I daresay that must have been very pleasant, but it can't possibly have furthered the affairs of King and Company or the progress of your career in it. You know, Gordon, when I was your age I started work at eight o'clock in the morning and finished officially at six in the evening. But most nights I worked on when everyone else had gone. I was ambitious. I wanted to show my father I was as good a businessman as he was. Now, I don't expect you to work as hard as I did. I want you to have fun and enjoy the advantages the business has brought us. But since you had no interest in study or in an academic or any other kind of independent career and freely chose to join King and Company, I expect you to keep normal business hours. Is that too much to ask?"

"No, Father. I'm sorry."

"I accept that you're sorry, Gordon, but there is another point. Did you ask Mr. Paterson's permission for this day off?"

Gordon felt his face go scarlet, but with anger this time. "Paterson is only a clerk." His voice was shrill.

"He is the head clerk."

"But I am your son. I shouldn't have to bother about Paterson."

"That is where you are wrong. In the offices of King and Company you are still only a junior clerk of very little experience. Andrew Paterson is your superior. You cannot take time off without consulting him and obtaining his permission. Please don't do it again. It's bad for office discipline. You are undermining Mr. Paterson's authority. I presume you don't want to do that?"

"No, Father." His brief resistance collapsed into sulkiness as he realised he had no defence. "I suppose it was thoughtless of me. Do you want me to apologise to him?"

"I'm glad that has occurred to you. I think it would be the proper thing to do. You won't always be under Paterson, you know. One day he'll be the one who has to consult you. He'll have more respect for you when that day comes if you give him his due now. Anyway, in another two or three months I'll move you out of the clerk's room. Learning to be a distiller might be more to your liking. I don't think you'll find the work at Lochbank so humdrum."

Lochbank was the company's distillery on the eartern shores of Loch Lomond, near the clachan of Balmaha. It had been in the family of Gordon's mother for almost seventy years, until King & Co. bought it on the death of her father.

"You would have to live locally, of course, except at weekends; but you'll have Jack Hoey for company."

Gordon's spirit had begun to rise but it drooped again at this mention of his cousin. "I suppose I will."

"McNair tells me Jack is doing exceptionally well. He's taken to the business like a duck to water. He's interested, hardworking and quick to learn. I think he's going to be an asset to us. McNair was telling me that only last week Jack handed him a drawing for a new type of copper junction tap that should allow us to fill the casks with a saving of about fifteen minutes in every hour. I don't know where Jack got the . . ."

He stopped as Gordon, his face white and his eyes blazing, turned and tore the door open. "Blast Jack Hoey! Blast his brains and his copper junction tap! I don't want to hear about him or them. I'm tired of hearing how clever and hardworking he is; what a credit and an asset to King and Company he is. Oh, what a failure I am in comparison to Jack Hoey. It's a pity, Father, you hadn't him for a son instead of me."

He ran from the room with tears of rage and humiliation stinging his eyes, furious that once again he had recklessly put himself into a position in which a quarrel with his father had been inevitable.

In the corridor he passed his mother without responding to her smile or her cheerful enquiry about where he was off to, knocking heavily into a massive Dutch marquetry display cabinet in his anxiety not to be detained. For several moments a fine collection of delft ornaments swayed precariously in his wake, glass doors rattled and flowers trembled.

Fiona King stared after her eldest son for a few puzzled seconds, then turned thoughtfully and went along the corridor that led to her husband's study. Robert looked up, white-faced and distracted, from his desk as she opened the door.

"Oh, it's you, dear. I'm just working on some notes." He pulled out his watch. "I'll have to remember my time. I did tell you I was going to Glasgow tonight and that I'll be late home?"

"You did, Robert. I don't want to detain you, but Gordon passed me a moment ago looking terribly upset. I wondered if he'd had another disagreement with you?"

Robert moved his notes about impatiently. The prospect of trying to justify himself to Fiona was not a pleasing one.

"You could put it that way," he said in what he hoped was a discouraging tone. "It has not been a very pleasant afternoon for me, I'm afraid."

"What a shame!"

The words were oddly lacking in feeling and he looked at her uncertainly until she said, "Well, aren't you going to tell me?"

27

He sighed and put down his pen. "First, I had Douglas Dunbar in here raving like a madman and threatening to destroy us. You must surely have been out or you would have heard him."

"I was down at the village. I had to open the Daffodil Fair."

"Ah, yes. I had forgotten. Well, I had no sooner got rid of the mad Dunbar when I became involved in a quite unexpected scene with Gordon. We came in here to have tea together, but before I knew what was happening he was practically at my throat." He stared at her almost accusingly. "There are undercurrents in his nature I find quite alarming."

In the sunlight a few strands of grey shone in the brown halo of Fiona's carefully dressed hair. Her summer dress was startlingly white and feminine against the faded brown of hide armchairs and antique mahogany furniture. She sat down, her back very straight and her hands clasped on her lap. Diamonds shone on her fingers.

"Can you spare a few minutes to tell me exactly what happened?"

"Of course. It was all shatteringly simple. He objected to me pointing out that this is Monday and that he should be working in Glasgow instead of lazing about here. He had to agree with me, of course, that he had done wrong, and he said he was sorry. Then I quite innocently mentioned how well Jack Hoey is doing over at Lochbank and he went into a tantrum. He seemed to take it that I was having some sort of dig at him."

She unclasped her hands and put them flat on his desk as if for emphasis. "Of course he would think it was a dig. They don't get on. I thought you knew that."

"Good God, I don't go about remembering all the adolescent squabbles my children have had. Anyway, it wasn't about that. It was about his not taking his job with the company seriously."

"He seems to me to have been working quite conscientiously lately. And you have to admit it's very boring work you've got him doing."

"It's only for a limited time. He's got to start somewhere. It won't always be boring work. But the more he malingers, the longer he'll have to sit on a stool under old Paterson's eye, checking invoices."

"Really, Robert!" She rose quickly and walked to the open window. The fat buds of a climbing rose tapped on the glass and the scents of the garden stole into the room on a warm breeze. "I'm sure he's not malingering. You're far too hard on him. He's only a boy."

Robert moved a hand in exasperation, almost knocking over his ink pot. "Well, I want him to stop acting like one. He insisted on leaving school and absolutely refused to go to the university. He told us he was a man, and he's certainly big enough to be one. When I was just a little older than Gordon is now, I was badgering my father to let me start my own business."

"Perhaps when Gordon is a little older he'll do the same."

"I very much doubt it. Not the way it looks at this point."

"We can't all be geniuses."

The mockery was too obvious this time to be ignored. "Is that sort of remark really called for? Or helpful to Gordon?"

She smiled an apology. "No, it's not, Robert. I'm sorry. But I'm sure you misjudge Gordon. I'm quite certain he'll take his responsibilities to heart in due time."

"And meantime?"

"Just try to be a little more tolerant. You have no idea how much he admires you or how hurt and humiliated he is by these quarrels. Strange as it may seem, that's why he fights with you so often and so bitterly. There are times when he knows you are displeased with him, and he sees that to some extent it is his own fault. On those occasions he becomes distressed and unhappy at having let you down again, and the whole thing blows up into one of these awful rows."

He sighed. "How complex he must be."

"Human beings are complex. Today's disaster probably began quite innocently. To begin with, he would see nothing wrong in the chairman's son having a little more freedom than an ordinary employee. Then, as the day went on, he became guilty and frightened."

He rose and went over the room to stand in front of her. "My dear, your diagnosis may well be accurate, but it doesn't remove the root of the trouble. Even if it were true that he should have more freedom than other employees, it would still have to be properly arranged. It's Gordon's selfish thoughtlessness I'm really worried about. If he simply strolls in and out as he wants, it will undermine the discipline and routine of the whole office."

She straightened his cravat. "Oh, your precious routine!"

He put his hands lightly on her waist, thinking that she had changed little in twenty years, except that in some ways maturity had improved her. "I'm sure you would be upset if your domestic routine were to be ignored."

Her expression hovered between protest and fondness. "You blow in and out of our lives, Robert, like a whirlwind, shattering the peace I've carefully built up when you're away. It's not good enough, and I'm not going to have it."

His face darkened, but before he could speak she forestalled him. "Now don't get ready to explode, because you know perfectly well what I'm saying is true. You have left it far too late to start taking a close interest in Gordon. Since the earliest days of our marriage you have rarely been at home for longer than three months at a stretch. You have gone off and left me with four children to look after for as long as a year at a time. They have never been terribly accustomed to a father's influence. It would really be wiser to leave it that way."

He walked away from her. "My God, you make it sound as if I had abandoned you all instead of keeping you in luxury."

"Despite the luxury, you've hardly been a doting father."

"Fiona, I admit I may well have devoted too much of my life to business, but what else could I do? You can't have a worldwide organisation without travelling. I had no option but to leave the children to you. They are what you have made them and I do not complain about that. They are fine children, but it would be unnatural of me not to give Gordon perfectly proper fatherly advice. Because I am away from home so much, I fancy I can see him a little more objectively than you."

As he began to pull out his watch again, she went to the door. "I'd better see what he's doing." She stood holding the handle. "By the way, what colour is Douglas Dunbar's carriage?"

"I haven't the faintest idea. Why?"

"When I was in the village, a dark-green carriage came through at a disgraceful pace. There was a man and a girl."

"It could have been Dunbar and his daughter, I suppose."

"Would he be driving himself?"

"It's more than possible."

"If the horses had been flying, they wouldn't have been going fast enough for him. You could see him willing them on."

"That would be Dunbar. Apparently he does everything like that, living life at a gallop. He'll burn himself out. And the sooner, the better."

"He looked like an apparition. Especially with that rough dark complexion."

Robert looked balefully at the panelling, as if overcome by unpleasant memories. "In the trade he used to be known as the Black Douglas. Not that there were many dared call him that to his face."

2

Next morning James King came out of his father's house at No. 3 Park Place, Glasgow, and stood on the grey sandstone steps looking down on the city of St. Mungo. Although it was not much after nine o'clock, the air was warm and full of the promise that Clydeside was this year almost beginning to take for granted. Above the wide river the air shimmered slightly, creating the illusion of cranes swaying gently over the skeletons of half-built ships. Heat seemed to radiate from the shiny slate roofs of the new tenements grouped around the shipyards and the iron works.

A faint perfume came to James from a cherry tree trailing delicate pink necklaces over the grassy banking opposite the house. At least on this residential hill there was a breeze. Below, it would be still, and later, James thought, too hot for comfort in the studio.

After his last painting expedition to Ardfern on the Gareloch he had returned to a city more Continental than Scottish, with some of his artist friends sitting on stools at street corners, recording the boisterous passage of parasols, fancy waistcoats, outrageous hats and boas.

James had noted with sardonic amusement that even King & Co. had twice abandoned an important meeting of its directors, an unheard-of concession to private pleasure. James, technically in the business to please his father but in fact excluded from its vital workings by his temperament, sensed that for these other, business Kings, weather and mood happily coincided. Rarely, it seemed to him, had the family's powerful sense of destiny been so strong. In twenty years Scotch whisky had shot from the doldrums of parochial appeal to huge international success. In the past twelve months one hundred and fifty booming distilleries had produced no less than thirty million gallons of whisky, much of it because a simple idea had come to Robert King, his elder brother: the idea of blending malt whisky with a proportion of grain spirit to produce a more palatable whisky taste. That had been in 1875 and it had taken the Kings from being prosperous Glasgow publicans to what they were now: the best-known name in Scotch whisky. The family was experiencing, James felt, the same thrill of creative achievement that came to him when he worked on a painting good enough to satisfy his restless striving—like one of that sensationally acclaimed series he had exhibited after his visit to the South Seas. He remembered with a stab of regret that many months had passed since he had painted anything that he could honestly regard as fine.

There were times, these days, when he felt stale, squeezed empty by the demands of city life. A picture came to him of the house he had in the previous year bought for himself on the Solway Firth. He sighed regretfully, remembering the visits to that sheltered retreat that he had promised himself and had never made. Success could make too many inroads on a man's time, and on his talent.

He was saved from the onset of further sombre thoughts by a rattle of wheels. He turned, hoping to see the carriage that had earlier taken his father into town, but it was only a corporation watering-cart laying the dust. Slowly his sense of family and business involvement drifted back. This was the year of the queen's diamond jubilee. The nation, still untroubled by ominous developments in the Transvaal, was preparing to rejoice. King & Co. proposed commemorating the great occasion by marketing a new whisky of superior age and smoothness. That, James remembered, had been Fiona's bright idea. Some of the best schemes came from her, although the male members of the board usually managed to claim them, a process to which, he noticed, she submitted with good nature.

For months now Peter Ross, the director in charge of blending, had worked in secret at the brief he had been given: to produce a blend of unparalleled quality, a whisky fit for a queen. Tomorrow they would all meet to pass judgement on the result of his labours. It would be an important day not only for King & Co. but for Ross himself. Because of this lavish new venture, the company's fortunes were, to a large extent, in his hands. James felt a stir of sympathy for Ross. He remembered his brother's manner the day the decision had been taken. There must, Robert had said gravely, be no mistake; they were after the ultimate. For this new super-whisky was not only to be a golden tribute to a great monarch, it was to be a major advertising event designed to restore to the Kings the sales leeway they had recently been losing under the assaults of other aggressive blenders. Robert always spoke the names of these menaces with respect, acknowledging worthy, though dangerous, rivals: Dewar, Buchanan, Dunbar, Walker.

James looked up the street again, but the sound came this time from a man pushing a barrow laden with milk cans. As he turned his face back to the sun, the family came again to his mind, dominating him in a way he had only recently become aware of, making the half-formed idea of an escape to his house on the Solway seem almost imperative. His involuntary musings went on. However the various Kings were enjoying the freak weather, they would all have to converge tomorrow on the long mahogany-lined boardroom in Seabank Lane, the cobbled alleyway behind Trongate where the deceptively small and unimposing headquarters of their empire was sited, within sound of the steeple bells of Glasgow Cross.

In an effort to drive them all from his mind he shook his Glasgow *Herald* open and glanced at the front-page advertisements. Pettigrew & Stephens, after "electrifying the community with a series of the greatest gifts and bargains ever known or heard of in the wide world," were about to make "a final and sweeping sacrifice" by "simply giving away" pure hair mattresses at twenty-five shillings each, bedsteads at twelve shillings and sixpence each and Ayrshire blankets at four shillings and elevenpence each. Paderewski had written to J. Marr Wood & Co. Ltd., of Buchanan Street:

Gentlemen—
   I desire to order another Pianola for use in my residence. Will you kindly select an instrument in rosewood, and have it packed with rolls of music, and shipped via steamer.

The Anchor Line's new third-class fare to New York was five pounds ten shillings.

As he opened the newspaper, the carriage he was expecting came along the street and stopped at the high step on the pavement edge opposite the house. James went stiffly across the pavement, a tall, dark and, the coachman always thought, cheerfully reassuring figure, despite the sadness of disability and the sometimes wistful expression in the wide grey eyes.

"Another grand morning, Paton." James nodded toward the golden cockerels gleaming on many church spires, and toward the yellow river beyond.

"Aye, it is that, Mr. James. That's why Ah'm a wee bit late. The town's awful busy. Sir Fergus was beginning to champ a wee bit. Ye know, worried about his appointments."

James smiled as he manoeuvred himself into the coach. His father had been "champing a wee bit" about something or other for as long as he could remember.

"Well, I'm in no desperate hurry," he said. "Take me the long way, through the park." He handed the man a paper bag. "You can stop for a minute at the Kelvin and throw these crusts to the ducks. My mother—"

"Aye." Paton nodded understandingly as he pushed the bread into a pocket. "Her ladyship never misses a chance to feed the birds."

As the carriage moved off, James glanced back at the house and waved to his mother, who was at one of the first-floor windows. For seventeen years, since a street accident had led to her younger son having his right leg amputated, Rita King had never failed to "see James off," as she put it. She still worried that he might fall going down the steps. The year he had spent sketching and painting in the South Seas had been a torment to her, the distance and totality of their separation being almost as great as that produced by death itself.

James's studio was at 134a West Regent Street, about a mile from Park Place. As usual, he passed the journey sketching, but only for amusement. He did not paint grey streets or frock-coated lawyers, even in sunshine. His vision as a painter was of children in an idyllic world of heady, flower-filled landscapes, fringed with blue water or blossom-hung woods. It was a world carpeted with bluebells, blue flax and seashore roses.

A critic had recently written,

> In a James King painting, it is always spring; the springtime not only of the year but of life. There are no adults to introduce lost innocence. No noisy boys to climb the stylised trees or frighten the statuesque swans; only Mr. King's slant-eyed little maidens in smocks, pinafore frocks or kimonos, fondling lambs, gazing tenderly into birds' nests or reclining among those miraculous King flowers that never fade or die; the whole confection redeemed and sometimes made marvellous by this artist's powerful and unfailing sense of colour.

Sometimes, recently, the critics had been snide, wondering when the artist would widen his horizon, pointing out that merely to alternate Polynesian girls with Scots girls was not progress. But James's paintings had wide popular approval, and this, his father comforted him, was what annoyed the critics. Some were even failed painters themselves, and jealous that James could make money from his pictures. James doubted if it was as simple as that. Certainly, all his exhibited work sold and he had regular commissions from public galleries, not only in Britain but abroad, at four hundred guineas for large canvases. But was that the real test? For many, his had been the most original talent of the startling but short-lived Glasgow School, that sudden flowering of beauty that had risen for a little while from the industrial wasteland, to charm not only London but the artistic sophisticates of Munich, Amsterdam and Paris. Had the talent, like the school itself, run its course, its end hastened by too much commercial success? Was his finest work already accomplished?

As he looked out at the warm stone of the sunlit city, James was startled by a sudden sense of time—precious time—hurtling past, his life speeding on at a headlong rate. Good God! It was thirteen years since James Guthrie had inspired them all with "To Pastures New" and seven since George Henry had scandalised academics and men-in-the-street alike with his "A Galloway Landscape." Where were the masterpieces now? Who in Glasgow was painting them? In a strange surge of agony James wondered if only repetition lay ahead. He dare not believe it. But in that instant of fright he made his decision to leave the smothering comfort of life in Park Place. He would escape from the family and the family business to his house in Fleetside and there, in the lush Galloway countryside, find himself again, recapturing the fresh originality of work that had earned him the reputation on which, in this luminous moment, he could see he was beginning to rest.

Sir Fergus King, first baronet of Ardfern, in the county of Dunbarton, came out of the Crown salerooms in Sauchiehall Street and turned west. There had been nothing at the auction preview to excite his discerning eye, even though the estates of two or three substantial citizens had been involved. He cast his mind back over the badly displayed jumble of furniture and porcelain, deciding again that there hadn't been a stick of it good enough even for Gwen, his daughter, to buy as stock for her antique shop. People had no taste now; that was the trouble. There was no elegance anymore. They made their money out of ships, iron or coal, built themselves mansions and stuffed them full of ugliness, and when they died it was all bundled into Morrison McChlery's and sold for a few pounds, which was all it was worth. All that velvet and horsehair, all that modern red mahogany, heavily carved, French-polished and factory-made, depressed Fergus. He was grateful that he and Rita had started collecting when they were young, in the days when good eighteenth-century pieces, made by men who cared, were still plentiful and reasonably priced.

He looked at his watch and decided he would have time to call at Gwen's shop, in Blythswood Street, and tell Miss Murray, her assistant, that he had viewed the sale. In weather like this Gwen would be glad not to have the bother of it. They would all have enough of indoors tomorrow when they met to discuss their Dunbar-inspired troubles and to taste Ross's new whisky. He realised, with a twinge of complacency, that he was facing the launching of this new brand with more equanimity than should have been possible in a man of his age.

For a moment he allowed himself to dwell with wonder and gratitude on his remarkable sense of physical well-being. His hair was snowy now, but there was plenty of it, and his beard was as fiercely bushy as ever. In damp weather he suffered twinges of rheumatism in his arms, and uphill his breathing wasn't as good as it once had been, but if this was old age, then he was willing to suffer it for a long time yet. Of course, he had never abused his powers, except by way of hard work, and even then it had been in steady plods through sixteen-hour days rather than in outbursts of frantic activity that could only upset and unbalance the body. Above all, his home life had been as rich and stable as Rita could make it, and despite the worries Robert had heaped on them and the tragedies of James's accident and Gwen's twice-shattered life, their love for each other had never altered. Rita had been his great support. Of all the treasures life had given him, she was the priceless one.

That was the only doubt he had about all this energy—that it might not be fair to Rita. It was all right for him to go on like a youngster, but she might prefer to take things easier, even though she was eight years his junior. He blew reflectively into his beard. He didn't know! And there was no way of finding out; for even if Rita had thoughts of a quieter life, she was too staunch to admit to them when she knew he wanted to go on as he always had.

The odd thing was, when he was in his late fifties he had felt his active life was coming to an end, imagining that by sixty he would be retired from business, moved from the noisy bustle of Glasgow and installed with Rita at Ardfern, with walks along the rocky shores of the Gareloch to punctuate the long, restful days. Never had this seemed more certain or more desirable than in the terrible autumn of 1880, when Gwen's husband had died in Dublin of a Fenian bullet, the firm's first distillery had been mysteriously destroyed by fire and the malt distillers' long vendetta against King & Co. had culminated in the disgrace of Robert's being dragged into the sheriff court as a contaminator of whisky and in the King's Royal blend's being denounced as a fraud on the public.

Instead, each year had passed with him as involved as ever in all his varied affairs, and now, his seventy-third birthday only four days away, thoughts of retirement rarely came to him, except in a vague way, as today, when prompted by concern for Rita's feelings. Those worrying years from 1874 to 1881 had receded into a mist, lost in the renewed exhilaration of an endlessly burgeoning business, the satisfaction of his charitable works and the fascination of watching five grandchildren grow: Robert's daughter and three sons and Gwen's dashing boy, the child born six months after Tom Hoey's death.

Poor Gwen, Fergus thought. And yet, brave Gwen, fighting her way back from the ashes, rearing her boy and at last allowing Colin Lindsay to lead her in his tranquil, almost absentminded way into the haven of a second marriage that had mercifully suited them both. Lindsay was a romantic and a dreamer, of course, but responsible and well enough off now since the death of his father, who had owned a busy brass foundry in Dumbarton. After their marriage Colin had even given up the silly business of schoolteaching, into which idealism, plus an aversion to business, had led him when he was too young to know any better. Now he pottered prettily but amateurishly with oil paints and composed poetry that occasionally, to his own admitted surprise, had a flash of fire in it.

With Gwen he dabbled in the antique shop, which she had opened a long time ago as a deserted wife, to give her life a purpose, and which she kept on now as a hobby and a habit, and to keep Miss Murray in a job.

At the corner of Hope Street Fergus lifted his stick in recognition of Hannay, his shirtmaker, who was dressing his shop window. A few steps farther on he was saluted by Ferguson, "bootmaker to the gentry," whose footwear was sold with a guarantee of "no leaks, no squeaks." At Millar's Family Hat Warehouse he stopped, his eye caught by a large green notice pasted to the window:

For years past the complaints made against Black Felt Hats have not been without cause. That they frequently break and do not retain their original colour none can gainsay; the atmosphere of the city makes them faded and brown-looking—the sun and sea air bleaches and makes them quite green.

We have over and over again brought these facts under the notice of our various Makers, and from all we get the same answer, viz., that owing to demand they are not allowed to make and finish these goods as they ought to be made and finished. In addition to this, the Makers allege that more complaints against Felt Hats reach them from Glasgow than from all the other large towns in Britain put together; and it is the opinion of scientific men that our atmosphere, at all times strongly impregnated with deleterious chemicals, is very prejudicial to the wear of any material, especially of a dark colour. WITH THIS KNOWLEDGE, we have taken every precaution to avoid these complaints by having our Felt Hats Dyed, Proofed and made up in the dull season, when the Makers' Factories are not overtaxed with work.

Fergus glanced surreptitiously about him before removing his hat. It did have a faint brown tinge at the crown, and in the sunshine the brim had an undeniable hint of green. He frowned and replaced it quickly, thinking the hatmakers had their nerve blaming the good air of Glasgow for the shoddy impermanence of their goods.

Despite his bulk, and eyesight that was at last beginning to fade, he crossed the street quickly, dodging nimbly, with flying coattails, between the flow of handcarts, private carriages and clattering trams. As he arrived, almost breathless, at the other pavement, he felt a hand on his arm and heard a voice say, "My word, King, I wish I could skip about like that."

It was Bilsland, chairman of his political-party association, portly and red-faced in the heat, his coat hanging open to reveal a waistcoat draped with a gold watch chain.

"If this traffic gets any worse," Fergus said, smiling cautiously at Bilsland's compliment, "we'll all end up having to have policemen see us across the streets. Dear knows! Where does it all come from? This weather brings people out, I suppose."

Bilsland nodded, his pink, clean-shaven jowls quivering. "It's not just that. Every man in business for himself seems to have his own carriage, these days. I feel quite deprived travelling by train and public bus."

Fergus waggled his beard. "I don't know where the half of them get the money from."

"Well, times are good. You know that, surely, in your business."

"Good?" Fergus looked at him carefully, wondering for a moment if Bilsland had heard that for the first time in fifteen years King & Co. were not having things their own way. "I suppose they are."

"Let's hope we can keep them that way."

"Is there any reason to doubt it? This city gets bigger and busier all the time." He looked along the street, his eyes suggesting a distance that the tall buildings did not allow. "I remember—not so long ago, either—when we thought of ourselves as living in the outskirts at Park Place."

"I'm not thinking of Glasgow so much as the country as a whole. There could be war in Africa soon. These damned Boers are getting above themselves."

To Fergus, foreign affairs were foreign.

"We'll have to face that if it comes," he said. "So far, it's only a faraway shadow. The queen's jubilee is a reality. Sixty years! It's wonderful. For the next twelve months business is going to be good."

He spoke with certainty, looking with the appearance of proprietorship at the prosperous shops and the people hurrying in the sunshine. This was a city built on the sound and lasting foundations of hard and well-directed endeavour. He had grown and prospered with it, since

38

opening his first public house in 1844 with a few pounds borrowed from an aunt. Although he was the son of a Highland crofter, his feeling for these grey streets, the skyline of smoking chimneys and far-off hills, was almost mystical. His generation had consolidated the vision of men who had passed this way earlier in the century. Bilsland, sensing his confidence and drawing comfort from it, said, "Well, you've always had a name for seeing ahead."

Something in the remark deflected Fergus's thoughts. He said, "That was a shock about Russell Mathieson. I knew he wasn't well but I hadn't thought it was anything serious."

"I don't think anyone realised how far gone the poor chap was."

"How long had he been in Parliament?"

"Close on twenty years."

"I remember during his first election campaign one of the halls he was speaking in was set on fire by a rabble. To show his contempt he went on with his speech until flames were coming out of the platform and the only audience he had was the fire brigade." Fergus chuckled at the memory. "I hope you've got another fighter to follow him."

Bilsland's amusement at Mathieson's grand dismissal of the mob became tinged with surprise. "You don't know?"

"Know what?"

"You can't have seen your son today."

"I had breakfast with James, as usual."

"Not James."

"Robert?"

Bilsland nodded, smiling slightly.

"No, I haven't seen Robert today," Fergus said with sudden irritation. "Why?"

"We've offered Mathieson's seat to him."

Fergus stopped. "To Robert?"

"He addressed the selection committee last night. The decision was unanimous."

Fergus looked confused.

"You seem very surprised. Didn't you know Robert was interested?"

Fergus ignored the question. "Has he accepted your offer?"

"Not formally, but he will. It's one of the safest Tory seats in Glasgow. I can't remember Russell Mathieson's majority—something like fifteen thousand, I think. We could put a monkey up and it would win. Apart from the formality of polling day, your son is the new member of Parliament for Whitehill. No mistake about it!"

"But Robert doesn't have the time for that." Surprise and puzzlement made Fergus's tone abrupt.

Bilsland brushed the implied protest aside. "He spends much of his

39

time in London, anyway, doesn't he? At least that's what he told us last night."

"That's on business. At our office in St. James's."

Bilsland shrugged. "The House sits outside of business hours. Ninety percent of the members have other interests. After all, being a member of Parliament is hardly a full-time job."

"No, but being a whisky blender is."

Bilsland slowed and looked at him uneasily. "I say, King, we're all rather keen on Robert. We're built up on him. I hope you won't do anything to dissuade him?"

Fergus saw two women step from a cab. He raised a hand to attract the driver. "If you'll excuse me," he said, "this is what I've been watching out for."

He climbed hurriedly into the cab without another glance at the surprise flopping about on the loose folds of Bilsland's perspiring face.

"Claremont Row," he said, slumping back into the leathery shade, angry that this startling revelation about Robert should be made to him without warning in a public street.

The yellow tints in the stonework of No. 1 Claremont Row were strong in the clear light. Nearby houses, built a few years earlier, were already dulling with the black deposit of Glasgow's grimy prosperity. It was ironic, Fergus often thought, that the fashionable West End of the city suffered most from smoke and soot because the prevailing wind passed over so many works and shipyards before reaching the elegant houses. Eventually, the prosperous merchants and professional people, who had started moving here from the old town some thirty years ago, would move on again.

It was Fergus who had gone excitedly to Robert and Fiona when this fine house, designed by Gilbert Scott, architect of the new university on Gilmorehill, became vacant.

"Buy it," he had advised. "It's elegant and convenient. You'll never find a more suitable town house."

It had been part of his pleasure in the last seven years to help them collect furniture and paintings appropriate to the proportions and atmosphere of the house. As he turned from paying off the cab, he paused to admire Fiona's flower displays at the main windows; whatever his hurry or preoccupation, beauty always touched him. Fiona had been tutored in the art by Rita, of course, and this and the arranging of furniture and ornaments had become a strong bond between two otherwise dissimilar women.

"You're lucky to find me here, Grandfather," Fiona said as she came

40

smiling into the room to which the maid had shown him. "We've been at Castle Gare for the last two weeks. I only came to town this morning to see my dressmaker. I want to wear something new at your birthday party on Friday."

Fergus had almost forgotten the party they were giving for him at Castle Gare. No doubt Rita would have all the details noted down. Despite the agitation that had brought him hurrying here, he found himself slipping into his customary admiration of his daughter-in-law's bountiful attractions. The sculptured sweep of her hips and breasts had delighted his eye for twenty years. The vitality of her features, the healthy colouring that still, in her late thirties, held the bloom of a twenty-year-old—these were among the pleasures of his life; simple, guileless and free. That cool green dress she was wearing would do well enough for the party, he thought, and for a moment almost told her so. She was a picture in it, standing there in an unselfconscious pose between a huge gilt mirror and the window, with the sun streaming in on her hair. In this bright airy room there was a wholesome freshness about her that made him think of flowers, wild and breeze-blown, and of clear mountain streams singing happily to the sea.

In Fiona's presence Fergus's thoughts often became lyrical. She had the same quality of unfathomable beauty as did some of his paintings, impossible to pinpoint or satisfactorily explain, but, once seen, the image lingered on. When he was confronted by it, his heart never failed to lift a little or his blood to quicken with pleasure. Even all those years ago, when he was meeting her for the first time, he had thought she was the only "big" girl he had ever seen who could also be described as pretty. She had been wearing a dress so tight he had thought it quite immodest until Rita, in her kindly way, had put it in perspective by saying, "You must remember the poor child has no mother to guide her now." And not all that many years later she had been left with no father, either, when old Roderick Fraser had died at last of his excessive weight. There was a time when Fergus had feared that stoutness must run in the Fraser family, but Fiona had fined down wonderfully, despite carrying four children. She was too tall, he supposed, if one had to admit to any fault in her, but softened by the delicate blush of her skin and the deep brown lustre of well-brushed hair. Her sudden, reckless smile suggested that underneath the undoubted lady there lurked quite a lot of the milkmaid. Over the years he had noticed it was a combination—or a contradiction—men found interesting.

He kissed her cheek and then watched her pour two glasses of sherry.

"I'm sorry to burst in on you like this, my dear," he said, "but I've just been given the most extraordinary news about Robert. Has he told you he's going to stand for Parliament?"

41

She gave him a glass, took the other herself and opened a door that led into a small garden behind the house. "The first I heard of it was at breakfast this morning," she said as she went down two steps to a terrace. "I am as surprised as you appear to be. Even yesterday afternoon he didn't give me the slightest hint. Apparently it all happened last night. It was after midnight when he arrived back at the castle from Glasgow. There had been some sort of meeting."

"But, damn it, doesn't he know where his first loyalty lies?" Fergus's temper flared at last as he followed her into the garden. "He doesn't have the time for Parliament. Our sales are facing fierce competition from that dastardly man Dunbar. This is no time for Robert to neglect the business. Anyway, what does he want to go dabbling in politics for, at his age?"

A bee drifted from a cloud of pink clematis on the wall of the house. Fiona moved a bare arm slightly out of its way as it droned toward a shrubbery alight with the tints of azalea and rhododendron.

"I asked him more or less the same question." She smiled at the recollection. "He said it was the only way of becoming prime minister."

"Prime minister!" Fergus's amazement exploded down a leafy glade. "Is he remembering he's forty-five years old? He'll be nothing but a damned backbencher, starting in politics at his time of life."

Fiona laughed at his exasperation. "He was joking, of course, Grandfather. Robert is too much the realist to have illusions like that."

Fergus gave her a shame-faced glance. "I suppose so, my dear. I shouldn't have lost my temper, but I've been bottling it up since Bilsland took me by surprise, making me feel a fool in the middle of Sauchiehall Street."

She took his arm and walked him across some paving carpeted with scented thyme. He complained as they went, his head shaking a little with the wonder of it. "Robert should have told us of his intentions." He turned to her, his expression of concern deepening at a new thought. "It's damned inconsiderate that he didn't even confide in you. I don't understand him." And never did, he reflected. "Dear knows!"

They sat down on a bench above which honeysuckle trailed, and they put their glasses on a slatted table. Fiona bent to lift a spray of blossom that had been broken from a lilac tree. "Robert quite often doesn't confide in me."

Before he could sort out the undertones, the moment had passed.

"I'm afraid there's nothing to be done about it," she said. "He obviously feels deeply drawn to the idea of sitting in Parliament."

Fergus had left his hat in the house and the sun was hot on his head. The glare had the pleasing effect of cutting off the nearby houses. They could have been in the garden of a country cottage. He leaned into the shade of her parasol.

"As soon as Bilsland told me, I couldn't get here quick enough. I was anxious to know what you thought."

He had grown accustomed to wondering what she thought, had even consulted her—as he had never done any other woman, not even Rita— on business matters. It was hard to remember that once he had thought of this warm and reassuring woman as too high-spirited and rebellious, one of that "wild yachting crowd on the Gareloch." That was how he had regarded the sailing friends of Robert's youth, a youth that had been burned out all too early by the boy's obsessive ambition to found a business on his newfangled blended whisky. It still could make Fergus un- comfortable when he recalled how fiercely he had opposed his son's con- suming dream. And now, here it was, an empire, and he, who had never wanted it, complaining that the founder was neglecting it!

Fiona slanted her parasol to cut a beam of sunlight that played annoy- ingly on his eyes. "If you want to know what I think, Grandfather, all I can say is I'm not surprised. The truth is, Robert does not seem to be as dedicated to business as he once was. He has developed other interests. In London he has made friends who have opened new avenues to him."

His head tilted. "Avenues, my dear? What kind of avenues?"

"Social. Outlets for entertainment."

Fergus closed his eyes. "Is it true he goes gambling and drinking with the Prince of Wales?"

A bird sang among the fattening buds on a rose rambling over the wall of an outbuilding. She listened to it for a few moments before replying. "I don't think he has reached quite that exalted level, just yet."

He was surprised and uneasy to note that her expression was serious. He said, "Yet?"

"He will probably arrive there eventually. Some of his new friends seem to be close to the prince."

"You don't sound all that enamoured of the prospect."

She knew he was drawing her on and sympathised with his curiosity in the doings of this son with whom he had never been at peace for long.

She tried to speak lightly. "Perhaps it's because it is a closed world to me. You see, it's very much Robert's own life. He is away from us so much. He never invites me to join him in London. It might be at the oth- er side of the world." She laughed quietly. "Perhaps he thinks me still too much the country girl. That's what he used to call me, you know."

Fergus grimaced, silently appealing to her to desist from what sound- ed to him like self-punishment.

"This latest business of wanting to be a member of Parliament is all part and parcel of the same thing," she went on. "The House of Commons is the best club in London. Being a member carries a lot of cachet. To understand what is happening to Robert, you must see it through his eyes. He has a worldwide business, a great deal of money, a castle in the country, a town house in Glasgow, an apartment in London, offices in Glasgow and London. One day"—she touched Fergus's arm in gentle apology—"though may it be a long way ahead, he will be the second baronet of Ardfern. In the meantime, he is plain Mr. Robert King. The letters MP after his name could be very useful to him."

Fergus took her hand and held it between his own in a gesture of comfort and concern. "My dear, you sound almost bitter."

She shook her head. "Not really. And I may be absolutely wrong in my reading of the situation. Perhaps I am doing Robert an injustice. Perhaps he simply wants another excuse for being away from home."

Fergus was aghast. "What on earth do you mean, Fiona?"

"Isn't it obvious to everyone?"

"No," he said in dismay. "What is it?"

She hesitated. She had not intended this but there was no retreating now. "I sometimes think Robert has lost interest in me as well as in business. It's a process that started a long time ago. And the fault isn't all his."

It was too preposterous for him to be as alarmed as he had been prepared to be. "What nonsense, Fiona. Robert loves you. We all love you." He thought he saw a way of raising a smile. "Even your mother-in-law."

She did smile, but remained silent.

"Why do you think we all lean on you so often for support and advice? Why do you think it was you I came running to this morning when I heard about Robert? What would James do if he didn't have his weekly drive with you?"

She said, as if he had not spoken, "Robert is changing, Grandfather."

Fergus lowered his eyes and toyed with a medallion on his watch chain. "I suppose I have to admit I've felt that myself, sometimes. Business used to be the only thing that interested Robert. Even a year ago I can't imagine him entrusting the devising of this new blend to Ross. He would have worked on it himself. Or if he had given it to Ross, he would never have been off the poor chap's back. But now, with that on the go and our sales under attack, he wants to run off and be a member of Parliament." His mind had gone over from concern for Fiona to the purely business track. "Another thing: he's engaging too big a staff in London. He used to do everything himself."

"Yes." She gave him a teasing look. "And do you remember you were forever scolding him for it, telling him there was more to life than work

44

and that he should have interests other than business ones? Perhaps he's decided you were right."

He smiled at the jab, accepting it in a brave silence. This sunshine seemed to make everything bearable. After a while he said, "Do you and Robert quarrel?"

"Hardly ever. And never seriously."

"Does he neglect you? Or your home?"

"Oh, no. Robert has always been very generous. Besides, I have—"

He nodded. "I know. You have money of your own."

"I've never had to use any of it."

"Then why are you giving me the impression that you are unhappy together?"

"I didn't really mean to. It's not as definite as that."

"I don't quite understand. A little while ago you said . . ." He turned to her almost impulsively, his beard very white in the sunlight, his eyes narrowed and intense in the glare. "You know, my dear, I love you at least as much as I love Robert. Robert and I have fought . . . often . . . and bitterly. But I've never had even a single passing quarrel with you. If there's any help I can give . . . or perhaps Rita. I could speak to her."

She smiled gratefully. "Thank you, Grandfather. I'll remember."

They sat on in the golden glow until at last she rose and went quietly into the house, leaving him listening with closed eyes to the rustle of her cool green dress. In a moment there was only the memory of her perfume, disappearing already into all the other sweet garden fragrances that hung over him.

Perhaps a half mile away, to the east, a carriage stopped and Gordon stepped into the mid-morning crowd of shoppers, hawkers and business people moving about Sauchiehall Street. The long thoroughfare of expensive shops was hot and dusty. As he skirted the barrows of the noisy street traders, he had to avoid a litter of cabbage leaves, chipped apples, turnip ends and withered flowers heaped along the gutter.

He bought a rose for his buttonhole from a cheerful girl in a shawl and turned into the backwater of Blythswood Street. Here, reflective citizens browsed among secondhand books displayed for sale on handcarts. He gave them hardly a glance. He was still remembering with satisfaction the neat way he had handled Andrew Paterson.

He had arrived early at the offices of King & Co., given the head clerk a fulsome if slightly tight-lipped apology for being absent the previous day, and then, when the man was still basking innocently in the pleasure

45

of having such sway over the boss's son, blandly asked if he could have the morning off. Paterson's mouth had dropped, but before he could open it wide enough to protest, Gordon said, "You'll know, I suppose, it's Sir Fergus's birthday on Friday. Mother's giving a party for him at Castle Gare. I must get a present for him, but the trouble is it's too late by the time I leave here in the evenings."

Paterson tugged carefully at his wing collar and said pointedly that the shops were all open during the King & Co. lunch break.

"I couldn't do anything in a half hour," Gordon said. "I want to get him something in silver from Aunt Gwen's shop—you know how he loves anything old. But she's at the other end of town. Of course, I should have seen about it before this. It's my own fault if you say no, but if I don't have a present for Grandfather, Mother and Father are going to be dreadfully displeased."

He waited for the head clerk to mull over the implications. It did not take long.

"Very well, Gordon," Paterson said with a trapped look. He was beaten, but perhaps some little authority could be salvaged. He raised his voice for the ears of the other clerks and said commandingly, "You'll find the message I want you to deliver lying on my desk, Gordon. You can take a penny from the petty cash box for your tram fares. Don't forget to enter it in the book, and don't be gone all day."

Gordon looked at his reflection in the window of Gwen's shop, straightened his hat and his tie and opened the door. The paintwork in Adam green was gently faded, and against it the old walnut and mahogany furniture looked comfortably at home. To a large extent the business was run now by Miss Murray, but Gwen's hours of attendance were well known to the family and to the regular customers who had come to rely on her taste.

A bell had *pinged* as he walked in, and as he closed the door Gwen came from the back shop. Before the curtain swayed into place he had a glimpse of Miss Murray sitting at a table, polishing silver. It was a scene known to him since childhood, timeless and comforting. Like all the Kings, he was strongly pulled by the past. Here, as nowhere else in Glasgow, it was perfectly evoked in a display of mellow furniture, delicate porcelain and richly lustred silver.

"How nice to see you, Gordon."

"Hello, Aunt Gwen."

"I know why you're here. I remembered what you asked me and I think I have something very suitable. I got it at the last big sale I was at." She opened a drawer in a Sheraton tea table. "And it's not too expensive. I put it in here in case Miss Murray sold it by mistake."

She was too nice, he always thought, to have a son like Jack. Her hus-

46

band must have been a terrible rascal. All the bad blood must have come from him. It always pleased him to know the shadow of the father, reformed though he might have been at the end, hung over the son even from beyond the grave. It was impossible to grow up in the family without realising everyone who knew the original Tom Hoey was aware of this. No one ever said very much, but they were all waiting and watching, slightly fearfully, wondering if there was anything there to come out.

She handed him a small silver box with an engraved lid. "What do you think of that?"

He opened it. The inside was lined with black velvet. "What is it, Aunt Gwen?"

"It's for keeping pen nibs in. Don't you think it would look nice on Grandfather's desk in his study at Ardfern?"

He turned it over, looking for the mark.

"It's an Edinburgh piece," Gwen said.

"I like it," he said. "And I'm sure Grandfather will." He hesitated. "As long as he doesn't already have one. He has most things."

"No. Just a little wooden affair. I asked Grandmother."

He took out his purse and shook it, a worried expression on his face. "Can I afford it?"

"Oh, you can pay me anytime."

He laughed. "That was just a joke. How much?"

"You can have it for what it cost me: two guineas." It had in fact cost her three.

As he handed her the two coins, the doorbell rang. He turned and found himself looking into the dark, strained eyes of Anne Dunbar. He gasped and moved blindly away, the blood of confusion hammering in his head. "I want to have a look at this clock before I go," he muttered, his hand reaching out uncertainly.

Gwen gave him a curious look and then smiled at Anne. "Good morning."

"Mrs. Hoey?" He exulted at the sound of her voice.

"Well, Mrs. Lindsay, actually."

As Gordon bent over the onyx boudoir clock he had lifted, his amazed elation at seeing the girl again so soon turned to dejection. It was humiliating that she did not recognise him. Her face, and the sweep of her shining hair, had been vividly with him all the previous night and throughout the train journey that morning from Helensburgh. And yet, already, apparently, he had disappeared from her memory. It's the city clothes, he told himself in a desperate bid for comfort. They are like a disguise. And, of course, he had walked quickly into shadow before she had time to look at him properly.

He fumbled with the clock, bending over it as if fascinated, suddenly

47

struck by a contradictory fear that if he turned, she might recognise him after all and hit him, this time with something more damaging than flowers.

Her voice, which he had been able to recall only for the anger in it, was attractively pitched. "I am here on behalf of my father," she said to Gwen. "He has been told you are the most reliable dealer in antique furniture in Glasgow."

Gordon sensed Gwen's slight embarrassment. "If people say that about me, then I am very pleased."

"Yesterday, Father was in a house on the Gareloch—a castle at Row, in fact."

He was drawn irresistibly round and found Gwen's eyes on his. "But that must have been"—she stopped as he gave an alarmed shake of his head—" . . . must have been very nice," she finished in confusion. "In such weather, I mean. I know the Gareloch well."

"Father came away from the castle very impressed with the effect created by old furniture."

"It is an effect that cannot be gained in any other way."

"He would like to achieve this effect in his own home. He lives in a large and impressive house but the furnishings are, quite frankly, indifferent. He would like you to supply him from time to time with items of first-class quality. Expense would not be a consideration."

"I would be delighted to, but what are his requirements?"

Anne smiled and looked round the shop, her eyes resting for a moment on Gordon and then passing on with a lack of interest that pierced him. The tiredness which he had glimpsed in her eyes when she came in was very marked. It gave the young face a strangely tragic quality that he had not been aware of in the confused excitement of their meeting at Row.

"I think he really needs everything, but it would be a matter of starting with the public rooms. He would be prepared—in fact, he would be delighted—to accept your advice on all matters of taste."

Gwen held her hands up in protest. "That is very flattering, but it would place quite a burden of responsibility on me."

Anne put out her hand and touched a seventeenth-century walnut chest. "When I see the beautiful things you stock, Mrs. Lindsay, I'm sure father would have absolutely no cause for complaint."

The second Anne had gone, Gwen turned quickly. "I'm dying of curiosity, Gordon. Why did you stop me from saying it was your house her father had been at? It was Castle Gare, wasn't it?"

"Yes, Aunt Gwen, I'm sorry." He came a few reluctant steps away from the window. "It was Castle Gare she was talking about, all right, but I can't go into the story now. Just believe me when I say Miss Dunbar is a young lady of ferocious temper who belongs to a family to which the name of King is like a red rag to a bull. I didn't want her to wreck your shop. I'm sure she's quite capable of it."

"I can hardly believe that. She looked very refined and, in a strange way . . . almost burdened."

"It's true. And you wouldn't have thought her burdened—whatever that means—if you had seen her yesterday."

He was watching the girl climb into her waiting carriage. It was the one she had been sitting in outside the castle. Her movements were precise and almost dainty, giving no hint of the fires that burned beneath.

"Then what happens when her father discovers I'm a King? I would be better telling her immediately."

"Probably he never will find out. Anyway, you're not a King now. You're a Lindsay." His smile was mischievous and his spirits soared recklessly as he told himself that this girl he had wanted so much must have been directed to this spot at this time as part of some heavenly plan. They must both have been brought here for some purpose greater than the purchase of silver or antique furniture.

"Don't worry about it, Aunt Gwen," he said blithely. "Take his money."

But as the carriage door closed, out on the street, he felt a choking panic. If he did not grasp this opportunity, he might never have another.

"Gordon, you look so strange. Where are you going?"

He ran up the shop, seized his hat and with a babbled apology rushed out, heedless of Gwen's astonished expression.

The carriage was turning into Bath Street before he caught up with it. He had no plan, no story prepared, only a determination that he would speak to her. He pulled the carriage door open and jumped in.

She looked at him with only mild surprise and said coolly, "Did I forget something?"

The silk-lined compartment was filled with the scent of flowers, and on the seat beside her he saw a spray of fresh roses. "The only thing you forgot is that we have met before, Miss Dunbar," he said breathlessly.

"Apart from just now in the antique shop, I can't recall . . ."

"I know. I can't be very impressive."

She straightened, lifting her head. Already he recognised it as a characteristic move. "Who are you?" The imperious note from yesterday was back in her voice.

"You must promise not to be angry when I tell you who I am."

"Oh? We will have to see about that."

He swallowed. "I am Gordon King. We met yesterday at Castle Gare, under rather unfortunate circumstances."

49

The fury his name had provoked at their first encounter was not repeated. Instead she seemed slightly disappointed, as if she had expected
something much more intriguing.

He sat stiffly in the corner he had taken, staring at the roses and letting her look at him properly for the first time.

"You seem older," she said at last. "Yesterday you were like a school-
boy." He stifled his irritation and put his hat back on. "It must have been
the holiday clothes you were wearing. I remember you appeared to have
been in the water with them on. What age did you say you were?"

Despite the unexpectedness of the question, he hardly hesitated.
"Twenty," he said, adding another year to yesterday's lie. His confidence
had returned. "Forgive me for not speaking when you were in Mrs.
Lindsay's shop, but, to be honest, I was afraid you might attack me
again."

"And aren't you afraid now?"

"No. I can see you are in a more docile mood today, but no less
beautiful."

Her eyes flashed and for a moment he thought he had annoyed her.

"You seem just as forward as ever, Mr. King." The words were accompanied by her worried smile. "May I ask why you followed me from the
shop?"

"An impulse," he said truthfully. "Something outside of myself. I can't
explain."

He was relieved to see that she seemed to regard this as reasonable.
"Then I hope we are at least going your way."

"Any way will suit me," he said gallantly, then stifled an upsurge of
alarm. Paterson would be watching the clock. The man was a power in
the office, and to antagonise him could only lead to more trouble with
his father.

She looked into the street. "Where are we?"

"Still in Bath Street, near Wellington Street."

"I am only going as far as Hope Street."

His heart sank. In a few moments the journey would be over. He sat in
squirming silence, trying to find courage to speak the only words that
mattered.

"May I see you again?" His voice almost stuck in his throat. "Perhaps
for dinner some night?" He tried to look as if he was accustomed to taking ladies to dinner.

She seemed neither surprised nor annoyed. "You asked me something
like that yesterday."

He managed to smile. "Yes. I realised later that was rather silly of me.
I don't think at that time you were in the right frame of mind for such an
invitation."

50

The carriage had turned into Hope Street and stopped.

"I am a married woman," she said, lifting her spray of roses. "I have a little son."

The words gave him an enormous sense of intimacy with her. "I know."

She appeared uninterested in how he knew. "And you still wish me to have dinner with you?" The question, although spoken softly and with no particular emphasis, seemed to him to hold a faintly mocking challenge.

"Yes." For a moment he wondered if he dared touch her hand.

"My father must never know."

A joyous mist enveloped him and he was only vaguely aware of his answer. "No. Nor mine."

As they stood on the pavement, having arranged their meeting for a week later, he saw a startled look come into her eyes. He turned and saw Douglas Dunbar striding across the street, a puzzled frown carved on his stony face. For a moment Dunbar ignored him, although Gordon felt certain he was the cause of the frown. He put a hand on his daughter's arm.

"I remembered your saying you were coming here. Something's turned up. I'm going to need Maxwell for most of the day. You can go home by cab."

"That's all right, Father."

Despite his apprehension, Gordon found himself admiring the animal bulk of the man. The suggestion of strength was overwhelming and in a way made almost more disturbing by the gold rings, the broad watch chain on which rubies glowed, the expensively blocked hat and the carefully tailored clothes. It was as if Dunbar himself was shocked by his own power and wanted to disguise and dandify it.

Was there recognition now in the pale suspicious eyes? Gordon shuffled uncomfortably under the uncompromising scrutiny. His collar felt tight and he was sure his face had gone red.

Dunbar, holding him with a brutal stare, as if daring him to move, said to Anne, "Who's this?"

Either she had anticipated the gruff question or she had a mind like quicksilver, Gordon thought as he heard her answer.

"Mr. Milne," she said promptly. She smiled innocently at Gordon. "Or is it Mr. McMillan? I'm afraid I've forgotten." Her manner was negligent and unconcerned.

"Milne," Gordon said.

"He's an assistant in the antique shop you sent me to," Anne went on brightly. "He has an urgent message to deliver somewhere near here. Since there were no cabs about, I said he could come with me."

Dunbar seemed satisfied. He stepped back a little and looked at the dress shop they had stopped at, as if assessing it for purchase. "Is this a new one you've found?" His tone was indulgent. "I don't think I've seen that name on any of your dress bills before."

"It has been well recommended to me, Father. I thought I would see what they have to offer."

He took her arm. "Come along, then. I suppose I'd better come in with you and open an account."

The fondness which had transformed his appearance disappeared as he again became aware of Gordon. He seemed offended to find him still there.

"Well, boy?" He growled. "Haven't you an urgent message to deliver for your employer?"

"Yes, sir. I must be off." He lifted his hat. "Good-bye, Miss Dunbar. And thank you."

He walked down Hope Street, engrossed in the complexities of the girl's character. Yesterday's passionate tigress was difficult to equate with this morning's adventurous young liar going demurely into the dress shop on the arm of her protective father. Only the longings she raised in him remained constant.

3

Robert spent most of that morning writing a letter to the chairman of the Whitehill branch of the Scottish Unionist Association officially accepting the invitation to be Tory candidate for the constituency.

When it was finished he sat looking at the sealed envelope for several minutes before ringing for Miller to have it posted in Helensburgh. But before the butler could answer the summons, Robert was assailed again by doubts that had been with him since he had walked out of the meeting the previous night into the gaslit streets of Glasgow. They had sat beside him in the train carrying him home through the dark Dunbartonshire countryside and then kept him awake for part of the night.

Cursing his indecision, he put the letter in a drawer, dismissed the old butler and went downstairs past the dark paintings of the previous owner's ancestors, which had come with the house and which they hadn't yet had time to replace.

It was sunny in the courtyard. He had owned the castle for less than six months and his pride still rose a little when he stood under the high central tower and felt the old whin walls about him. He paused on the last step and let the heat embrace him, blessing his father for having discovered and brought them all to this lochside village so near to Glasgow and yet on the edge of the Highlands.

Row was far enough into the Gareloch for the shipyards on the industrialised southern shore of the Firth of Clyde to be hidden. Over there were tenements, sooty factory chimneys and the clang of iron ships being built. Here were white cottages, tall trees and country mansions set a little back from a pebble shore on which clean waves broke. Perhaps a quarter of a mile out, a sturdy steamer headed for piers further up the loch, with servant girls who had sailed to Helensburgh earlier in the morning with their mistresses' shopping lists.

It was a scene he had known since his youth, timeless and yet ever changing, depending on the light and the water's mood. Northward he could see a blue haze on the Cobbler, and on the other side of the loch the white cottages of Rosneath village, where his brother James had learned to paint with the Glasgow School artists Guthrie and Walton. Perhaps twice a year he sailed over there with Fiona and the children to picnic in a shingly cove.

All his life, it seemed, he had been preparing to leave the Gareloch for some distant destination. He felt a tug of melancholy as he realised he would see even less of this place if he became a member of Parliament. It seemed that this morning everything conspired to tell him he was a fool to think of leaving all this yet again for . . . for what? He shut his mind on the unwelcome avenue of thought, trying to give himself over entirely to enjoyment of the moment.

A light breeze came from the shimmering surface of the loch, carrying with it the scent of a wood fire burning on the shore. His eyes turned from the distant view to his immediate surroundings.

In front of him, purple aubretia and snow-in-summer tumbled from a group of stone troughs.

Against the sheltered walls of the castle, by the dining-hall window, the first bud of a red rose was about to open. On either side of the studded oak door a cannon stood on the freshly raked gravel. He noted approvingly that the gardeners had sprinkled water first so as not to raise dust. He stood admiring the balance of the arched entrance to the courtyard, listening to the birds in the Virginia creeper, marvelling that this house he had coveted since youth should in the end have become his. It had required the early death of Lord Glenarden, the departure for a new life in Canada of his son and heir and the outbidding of some determined opposition, but in material things life had a habit of falling Robert King's way. It always had. Against all the odds his new blended whisky had been an immediate and sensational success. His brash calculation that it would make him a millionaire by thirty-five had been inaccurate by not much more than a year. Now, his personal fortune was more than two million pounds. Not only that: he had made a millionaire of his father. And Fiona, Gwen and James—all directors of the company—couldn't be worth much less than a quarter of a million each. The grinding fight he'd had to get it all going, the trickery and blackmail he had practised on his father, his renunciation of the girl he had loved before Fiona, the endless sacrifices to success—they all seemed so far away.

And yet, the marks of that early struggle, when the pot distillers had tried to destroy King's Royal, were on him still. The hardness, the ten-

54

dency to cold introspection that in the end marred all his relationships—these were only the more obvious legacies of those formative years.

But, of course, the fight was not yet over. Even now he could be wounded. It had been a blow to his pride when, a year ago, it had become clear that out of the cutthroat melee for business Douglas Dunbar was emerging with the biggest slice of the home market. It was a setback galling beyond anything, for, singlehandedly, Robert had created the United Kingdom's thirst for blended whisky by the sheer force of his advertising during the International Exhibition of Food and Drink, in 1876. From there, with Hutt Sons & Buist as his London agents, King's Royal had started its triumphal advance, first in the fashionable hotels and restaurants of the capital and from there spreading to all the great private houses of England.

In the wake of all this golden success had come Buchanan, Walker, the Dewars, and, almost unnoticed, Douglas Dunbar. They had grown together, with King's Royal maintaining premier place. But years of supremacy had finally created in Robert a dangerous illusion of impregnability, and with overconfidence came a slackening of effort, or, at any rate, a redirection of effort. He could see that now.

His great dream had always been of a world business. He had terrified Fergus by launching into the English market not much more than two years after the first few trial cases of King's Royal had appeared in the shops of Glasgow, in 1875. No sooner had success come in London than he was driving on to test new markets—the United States of America, Australia, South Africa. As each prospered, his vision of a world drink strengthened. He became obsessed with the need to expand. And while his eyes were on distant places, Douglas Dunbar quietly stole the lead from him at home.

The loss was more than just a knock to Robert's pride. He saw it at once as a danger to his whole campaign of world conquest. If London could be stolen from him, so could New York. In a painful and dramatic reassessment of his strategy he saw that the first need was for King & Co. to be reestablished as the leading whisky blender in Britain. London was especially vital as an outlet. The capital of the United Kingdom was the supreme showplace, and only the whisky that ruled it could rule the world.

It was by seeing his business in these urgent, almost military terms that he had been able to take it out of the riverside street in Glasgow where it had started and in less than twenty years put it into the drawing rooms of the aristocracy and make it part of the folklore of Scotland.

The great need now was for him to recapture and rekindle that crusading spirit. But could he do it? Even with the threat of Douglas Dunbar to spur him on, he doubted it. For the first time in his life his interests were dangerously divided. When he was younger he had been ruthlessly single-minded in his search for business. As Fiona had often enough told him, he had put it even before wife and family. Now, when all his restless energies should have been mobilised to smash Dunbar's challenge, he had never had less taste for the fight. It was this that had led him to make his offer to buy Dunbar's business.

It had come as a startling realisation to him that his true inclination now was for a lesser involvement in business and a new commitment in politics. Fiona's belief that his interest in the House of Commons was nonpolitical did him an injustice.

It was a sign of the growing gulf between them that she should see his decision to stand for Parliament as a striving for social recognition. For if he accepted the Tories' invitation, it would be the result of nothing less than a genuine desire to do battle with the rabble of dangerous men who had lurked in the shadows of his consciousness for years—the mob orators of socialism, the wilder trades-union agitators, the street-corner disciples of Marx and Engels who thirsted and plotted for bloody revolution. That their evil doctrine could eventually prevail if it was not opposed by every man who could see its menace had been Robert's belief for years. But until recently he had been content to leave the battle to others. Slowly an urge had grown in him to be more closely involved. Already one socialist—the miner James Keir Hardie—had fought his way into Parliament and had sat there for South West Ham until the electors had regained their senses and thrown him out again. Now Hardie was known to be nursing the Welsh constituency of Merthyr Tydfil and was expected to be sent to Parliament again for that mining seat when the next election came. Where Hardie had shown the way, others would assuredly follow. Robert, so conscious of the danger, now believed passionately that it was his duty to sound the alarm. And what better platform to speak from than that provided by the House of Commons? He had the zeal and the independence, and now that the opportunity had presented itself, he was determined to find the time, even though it would mean filching a little of it from King & Co. At least he thought he was determined. . . .

He walked slowly to the arch in the courtyard wall and stood looking down on the loch, wondering again if this new fervour was an aberration that he might live to regret. That it would be bitterly opposed by the family he did not doubt. He would talk to them tomorrow, when the board met to taste Ross's new jubilee blend. He would be accused of desertion, irresponsibility, neglect. . . . He knew all the charges, for in other circumstances he would have levelled them himself. And they would be justified, of course, if he simply went off and sat at Westminster, leaving King & Co. in the lurch. But that was not his intention. He had not given twenty-five years of his life to building a great business only to see it weakened by this bug he had now been smitten with.

The fight against Dunbar would go on. He smiled slightly as he pictured their faces tomorrow and thought how he would take their protests and turn them against them. If he could talk them into agreeing to what he had in mind, he was certain the business would not suffer. It would, he believed, flourish under a strong and novel inspiration.

He turned and hurried into the house before the resolution could leave him, took the letter of acceptance from his desk and gave it to the butler for immediate posting.

Fergus had at last gone off up the hill, to lunch with Rita at Park Place, leaving Fiona to salvage what she could of the morning and get ready for her drive with James. He called for her every Tuesday shortly after two o'clock and would sit patiently in the carriage until she came hurrying out, breathlessly calling her apologies for having kept him waiting.

Unpunctuality was one of her weaknesses. With a family of four, social and charitable commitments and a close interest in the affairs of King & Co., she had constant demands made on her time. Since she rarely refused any appeal for help, her appointments suffered, and she had the reputation of never arriving anywhere at the expected time. It was a failing she never denied, and today, she saw, was to follow the usual pattern.

Fergus had eaten into a morning she had set aside for letters, and after rousing him from his slumber in the sunny garden and seeing him out of the house, she went to a small sitting room and settled belatedly with her correspondence.

At one o'clock a maid brought her a tray. She ate absentmindedly while she worked through the twenty or so letters that had to be written. As she neared the end of her task, the maid came into the room again, closed the door quickly and said in a hesitant voice, "Mr. Lambert's asking to see you, ma'am."

Fiona waved the girl away with a preoccupied frown. "I can't see him now, Morag. Send him away."

Paul Lambert had been engaged by Robert to tutor their daughter and the two younger boys in French. The scientific engineering company in Paris of which his father was a director had in the previous year sent him to take a postgraduate course under Lord Kelvin at Glasgow University. Robert had seen his advertisement in the Glasgow *Herald* offering tuition in French. There had been an interview and terms had been agreed. M. Lambert had excellent credentials. He was cultivated and amusing and his relationship with the family gradually ceased to be formal. The children were permitted to go with him on educational forays to museums, art galleries and various places of historic interest, not only in Glasgow but in Edinburgh and in Stirling. Frequently the young man's social life touched on that of the Kings—at the theatre, at concerts and in the houses of various hostesses. On two recent occasions when they were entertaining on a large scale, Robert had suggested they include M. Lambert among the guests. Fiona had found excuses not to do so, for she had begun to suspect that the Frenchman's interest was not confined to teaching her children. There had been various bold remarks and admiring glances which separately could be put down to a Latin preoccupation with gallantry but which together suggested something more substantial. Eventually, after an embarrassing encounter in a Buchanan Street tearoom when M. Lambert leaned across the scones and pancakes, presented her with a rose and asked her to wear it close to her heart, she had no doubt the tutor was infatuated with her.

It was a romantic idea, and since he was attractive, exotic and at twenty-three almost fifteen years her junior, she was flattered. She was also careful. She saw to it that she gave him no opportunity of expressing his infatuation in any more intimate or precise way than by the lingering and devoted glances to which he now quite openly treated her.

She turned irritably from her letters as she became aware that the maid was still present.

"Didn't you hear me, Morag? This is not one of M. Lambert's days with the children. They are at school. He has no appointment."

The maid's voice was a confused and apologetic whisper. "Oh, ma'am, he's outside the door. He would follow me up."

Fiona leaned back in her chair and put down her pen in exasperation. "Really, Morag, you had no business letting him past the front door." She glanced at the clock. "Oh, dear! Very well, you may show him in. But it really is very vexing. . . ." She rose reluctantly from her desk. "I had hoped to finish these letters before leaving for my drive with Mr. James."

"Yes, ma'am," the maid said as she sidled gratefully away.

M. Lambert advanced swiftly into the room, holding out a large bouquet of roses. "Ah, madame . . ." He stopped as he saw Fiona's expression. "Madame . . ."

Her mouth and eyes were forbidding. "Please stop saying *madame* and tell me why you are here."

"I have brought you some flowers."

"I can see that, but you had no business bringing me flowers."

He stood looking at them in dejected silence.

"Oh, put them down somewhere. Here, on this table."

"Yes, madame."

"And tell me why you are here. Do you wish to see my husband? If so, you will have to come back another time. He is at Castle Gare."

"I am aware of that, madame."

"Then how dare you call, bringing flowers, when you know my husband is away? What will the servants think?" Her tone did not fit the stern words and she realised with a shock that she was coming dangerously close to flirting with him.

"I had to see you, madame." His tone was apologetic and his eyes were beseeching. She noticed that they were dark-brown eyes. "To speak . . . Soon I must return to France. Before I go I wanted to ask you—to beg of you—to have dinner with me. It would be a great honour."

It was no more than she had expected, but to hear him actually say it in his delightfully accented English sent a tremor through her. She turned away and arranged the writing set on her desk.

"Certainly not. I am a married woman. I don't know what the custom is in Paris, but in Glasgow married women do not accept dinner invitations from the tutors of their children. Do you understand?"

He hung his head a little as if ashamed of his emotions. "Ah, madame, my head understands but my heart will not listen."

"Then you must make it listen. What possible reason do you have for imagining that I might conceivably accept your absurd invitation?"

He moved a little toward her, and now his tone was earnest. "Madame, I would swear that in your eyes, in your smile, last week at the recital . . . There is a certain glance that a lady . . ."

She clasped her hands sternly in front of her, realising how wrong it was of her to carry on the conversation, for despite the frowns and reproving words it was in essence lighthearted and enjoyable. It was scandalous of her to prolong and even encourage it. But her reply was in the same slightly mocking vein.

"There was no glance, M. Lambert. Last week at the recital you must have been carried away by the music. Either that, or I was."

The last sentence was more provoking than she had intended. His expression brightened and he took another step forward. "Ah, madame, so at last you admit—"

She quickly held up her hands. "I was making a little joke, monsieur, not an admission. I am trying desperately hard not to take this intrusion too seriously."

At least that was true. She crossed to the window and pulled the curtain back. It was two o'clock and she thought she had heard James's carriage.

"You look for someone, madame?"

"I am expecting a gentleman."

She almost laughed at the conflicting expressions that moved across his face. "A gentleman that you love?"

"Must you be so ridiculous? Remember that you are in Glasgow now."

He smiled slightly. "Would it be so impossible for a Glasgow lady to love a gentleman who was not her husband?"

It was the boldest invitation she had heard in a long time, and delivered with remarkable poise. She should, she supposed, have been insulted. At the very least she should pretend to be insulted, but it did not seem worth the effort. She said, "If you must know, he is a gentleman very dear to me. He will be arriving soon. I would prefer that he did not see you. When he arrives I will go out to him, and you can leave when we have gone."

"You are not . . . entertaining him . . . here?"

"In the way I fear you mean, I am not entertaining him at all. Once a week we drive about the city quite openly in his carriage. He is my brother-in-law."

His sudden laughter was relieved and reproachful. "Ah, you have been teasing me."

The artificiality of the conversation seemed to collapse under the pressure of this honest and natural remark. She smiled at him. "You have been teasing yourself, Paul, but I feel the spell is now broken. You have come to your senses. Until a moment ago I would not have dared call you Paul. You would have taken it as a signal."

She crossed to a settee that had a gilt frame and pink velvet upholstery. "You can sit beside me here until James arrives. The window is open a little and we will hear his carriage."

He perched himself decorously at the far end of the settee. She looked at him searchingly. "Poor Paul. You look quite pale."

"I have not slept."

She sighed her sympathy. "And all for a glance that was . . . not there. When next you go to a recital, Paul, you must be more careful. You must pay more attention to the music."

"Madame is cruel to make fun of me, but I will treasure even her cruelty. Somehow I will make it into a beautiful memory."

"When do you go home?"

"In one week."

She looked at him fondly for a while and then said simply, "Perhaps it is as well."

His eyes widened with surprise and hope. "You mean . . . ?"

"Do not try to work out what I mean. Just accept what I say."

She rose as a carriage drew to a halt under the window. She looked out. "It is James. He will be surprised that for once he is not kept waiting.

60

Stay here until I have gone and then let yourself out." As she crossed the room she lifted the roses. "Thank you for bringing these. They are very beautiful. Before I leave I will give them to Morag to put in water."

As she went down the stairs she permitted herself a regretful sigh.

Less than two miles west of Claremont Row there were still stretches of the river untouched by industry, and on James's instruction the carriage began heading that way. As they reached the end of the short street, he turned to Fiona. "You are quite sure you will find that pleasant?"

She had been occupied with her hat, but it was now arranged to her satisfaction. As she gave the wide, flower-trimmed brim a last adjustment, she said, "I always find it pleasant by the river, James. Especially on a warm day. I have already been into the city today, to see my dressmaker. The streets were gay, but stifling. There should be a welcome breeze from the water."

He leaned back and let her talk, his mind still on the morning's decision to make his home on the Solway. Their relationship was relaxed enough for that. If she realised he was dreaming instead of listening, she would simply laugh and fall in with his mood.

Their weekly outings had started years ago, after Rita had scolded James for spending too much time in his studio. "He goes off for a few days' sketching," she complained with motherly concern, "and comes back with enough material to last him for months. He doesn't go out again until he needs some fresh ideas."

By that time Fiona's position in the family was firmly established. By a combination of good-natured drift on her part and manoeuvre on everyone else's she had been elevated to the status of matriarch—a reluctant but effective one. That she was almost the youngest of the adults and nearly thirty years her mother-in-law's junior had made no difference. Rita, in fact, had connived at it all. Fiona was warm and capable and that would have been enough. But there was more. She had an independent mind and could give her opinion without caring—as Rita would have cared—what the male attitude would be. If one had a problem, one eventually discussed it with Fiona. If, in the family, and sometimes even in the business, it looked like a schism were developing, somehow or other it would be left to Fiona to heal it; at the very least her opinion on how it should be healed would be sought.

Rita's fear of James's becoming an unhealthy recluse had been eased by Fiona's volunteering to be his occasional companion, although she had managed it so adroitly that James had imagined he was obliging her. Who was the benefactor and who the beneficiary soon ceased to matter, for it had become a routine they both enjoyed. Except in the worst winter weather, only holidays or illnesses were allowed to interfere with the arrangement.

What James wanted this afternoon was Fiona's opinion on his decision to get out of the city. But he was in no hurry to make his announcement. First she could exhaust her small talk about the children, about the arrangements for Fergus's birthday party, and about the Boudin painting of the *plage* at Trouville, which Alexander Reid, the West George Street dealer, had for sale and which Fergus was urging Robert to buy.

As the carriage, steady on strong, well-greased springs, followed the dusty curve of Sauchiehall Street into a bumpy stretch of Dumbarton Road, Fiona chattered on, wondering when she should startle James with her sensational news about Robert's decision to stand for Parliament. Better to lull him first with lesser things; the effect would be all the greater. She smiled to herself as a picture of M. Lambert and his flowers came to her mind. But that was something she did not dare speak about. James would not find the Frenchman's ardour or her tolerant attitude toward it amusing.

There was a long pause in their conversation as they left the village of Patrick, on which shipyard cranes were now encroaching, and cut down toward a sandy stretch of riverbank between there and Whiteinch. Then, almost to the second, they turned brightly to each other with their revelations, but it was Fiona who spoke first.

PARTICK .

"I have some news which I think will surprise you, James."

"Have you?" He stifled his own announcement. "Well, I think I have a surprise for you, Fiona, but ladies first."

She looked cool and lovely, he thought, in her green dress and gay hat. Anyone who did not know her would have difficulty in guessing her age correctly. They would almost certainly take a few years off. And yet, there was this contradictory quality of warm reliability that made them all turn to her. She was the only member of the family he had ever painted. It was just before her marriage, when she was about twenty-two, yet it had turned out in such a way that it could equally well have been the portrait of a child of fourteen. There was something elusive in Fiona, he remembered, as he heard her voice.

"Robert is going to become a member of Parliament. He has been offered the Whitehill constituency." He realised she had stopped speaking and was laughing. "Yes, you may well look surprised."

"But I didn't know Robert was interested in politics. I centainly didn't know he had political ambitions."

"Nor did I. It's either a very recent ambition or he's been keeping it well hidden."

He nursed the unlikely information for a while and then gave her a

62

quizzical look. "I assume it's a Tory seat and that Robert will be fighting it for the Tories?"

"Oh, yes. You wouldn't want him to stand as anything else, would you?"

"Not really." James was unenthusiastic. He had an uncomplimentary vision of all politicians. "I suppose they're the best of a bad bunch." He rubbed his leg gently. There were few days when he did not suffer some pain. "But won't this mean his being away from home even more than usual? How is he going to combine his duties as a member of Parliament with running the business?"

"I don't know. Nor does Grandfather. He burst in on me this morning with his coattails flying. Someone had given him the news in the street. He wasn't at all pleased."

James pushed his leg out very straight. "He'll be even less pleased when he hears my news." He stopped to consider how he would express it. "When the board meets tomorrow, I'm going to resign my directorship. I've decided to live permanently at Fleetside, in the house I bought last year."

She turned to face him. "What on earth has made you decide to do that, James?" Her eyes were wide and her voice concerned.

He saw it immediately, because he had expected it and had been watching for it.

"Who will look after you down there?"

"Oh, I'll soon find a housekeeper."

She hesitated. It was always risky to refer even indirectly to his disability. "I wasn't thinking of the house, altogether."

"No." His voice was sharp. "You were thinking the same nonsensical things mother will worry herself about when I tell her. You know, Fiona, I am thirty-seven. I'm perfectly capable of looking after myself."

She slipped her arm through his. "Of course you are. But you haven't yet told me why you want to leave us all and go and live all by yourself in the wilds of Galloway."

He glared at her. "There you go again. Fleetside is hardly the wilds. It's a pleasant little town with all the necessary amenities."

She was looking at him closely, pretending to be suspicious. "I take it you will be all alone? You haven't a little friend you want to keep hidden?"

He placed his hand over hers and squeezed it. She could always be relied upon to know when it was time to change the subject. "No, I haven't a little friend I want to keep hidden. But if I had, I wouldn't tell you about her, anyway; so you're really none the wiser, are you?"

As she smiled, waiting for him to go on, he turned and looked into a small wood they were passing. Bluebells had spread in a thick haze un-

63

der the trees. It was the sort of scene he had used as a background to scores of paintings. Today it was a painful reminder that his vision was limited and that his worth depended on an intensity of treatment that seemed to be slipping away from him.

"It really is something quite serious, Fiona," he said soberly. "For some time I haven't been happy about my work. Something has gone out of it. It's become stereotyped."

She frowned as if the suggestion was new to her. "What's wrong with painting woodland or seashore scenes?"

He couldn't decide if she genuinely didn't understand or was simply refusing to admit that she understood. "There's nothing wrong with it," he said. "It's not that I particularly want a change of subject, but I feel I must make a real effort to recapture whatever vitality there was in my earlier work. Somehow, I feel if I get away from Glasgow, some of the old freshness will come back."

There was a note of longing in his voice that touched her.

"You're being too hard on yourself, James," she protested. "Don't go by what the critics say. Your paintings are wonderful. Everyone loves them. It's every successful Glasgow man's ambition to have a James King painting hanging on his wall. How many commissions have you in hand at the moment?"

"Far too many." There was a hint of reluctant pride in his half smile.

"You see? You have more work than you can cope with. You have had for years and you always will, so long as people appreciate beauty."

"Does that mean you think I'm making a mistake in going to Fleet-side?"

She spoke carefully. "No, it doesn't. I think you're probably wise in seeking a change of scene. We all become jaded from time to time. The trouble with you, James, is that you work too hard. You have little interest in business, but in your own way you are every bit as intense as Robert and your father. I think you should go to your new house, if that is what you feel like doing, but not in any mood of depression about your work or with any sense of escaping from something. I don't have to tell you that you won't escape by running away. If you have a problem about your painting, you will have to identify it and then face up to it. And you will have to do that whether you are in Fleetside or Glasgow."

Looking at Fiona and listening to her comforting realism often made James think it would be pleasant to be married. He was not a bachelor from inclination, but the loss of his leg had made him wary of women. In their attitude to him he always sensed pity or sympathy, and he shied violently away from it. He was single now from habit, and though it meant his stubborn independence was intact, he missed the intimacy he

64

imagined must be possible in marriage—and only in marriage—with a woman like his sister-in-law. He frequently envied Robert his home and his family and cursed him as a fool for having neglected them so consistently.

His dreamy silence lasted until the carriage turned onto a grassy track leading to the river. "Hold tight," he said as they laughed and swayed together on the last bumpy stretch.

"How different the river is becoming," Fiona said as they walked past hedgerows strung with honeysuckle. "Robert first brought me here almost twenty years ago. Every time I come back, the shipyards and factories have taken over another stretch of the banking."

They found a spot with an unspoiled outlook and an almost imperceptible breeze. For an hour they sat watching ships glide slowly past, the wash curling toward them in long, unhurried waves. James, who loved the Clyde and its traffic, recognised some of the vessels and talked entertainingly of their likely destinations and cargoes, and gave Fiona the latest gossip about the families who owned them. He was reminded of the time by the appearance of the *Loch Goil* returning from its daily circuit of the piers on the firth.

"School will be coming out soon," he said.

They rose reluctantly and walked back to the carriage.

As usual on these occasions, Fiona's fifteen-year-old daughter, Florence, and the two younger King boys, Steven and Allan, were waiting when she arrived back at James's studio; their schools were only a few blocks away.

James poured two sherries, then fetched tumblers and some bottles of fruit juice from among a jumble of paints and bags of tea and sugar in a cupboard. Several partly finished canvases were on the floor, propped against walls, chairs and boxes. He looked harassed as he manoeuvred a way between them.

"And how was school today?" He was never totally at ease with his niece or his nephews. Their eyes were on him as he prepared to pour the drinks.

"Uncle James asked you a question," Fiona chided them. She looked hopefully at Steven, who was twelve.

"It was beastly," Steven said with a grin.

"That's because you're a stupid little boy," Florence said as she accepted a glass from James. "You don't know anything."

Steven struck out at her in a halfhearted way. "I'm not a swot like you, I'm glad to say."

"Take your fruit drink from Uncle James, Steven, and behave yourself." Fiona had Allan, a dark-haired, steady-eyed child of nine in front of her, straightening his tie.

"When Uncle James was at the High School, they wouldn't have let him wear his tie as untidily as this," she said.

"Steven pulled it," Allan said. "We were fighting again," he added with solemn confidentiality. "Steven said Papa doesn't love you, and I hit him. Papa does love you."

Florence's voice came out of the long silence that filled the attic room. "Of course Papa loves Mama." Her eyes were fastened anxiously on Fiona.

"He does not," Steven said defiantly. "If he did, he would live at home more often."

"Of course he loves her." Florence's voice had a very slight tremble in it and her eyes were glistening. "That's why he married her."

Fiona looked helplessly from one to the other, too surprised to think of a way of ending the embarrassment.

"He married her a long time ago," Steven said triumphantly. "People don't love each other forever."

Allan had been watching for his mother's reaction. "You've no business saying these things," he said in alarm. "You're hurting Mama. I can tell by her eyes."

Steven looked uneasy but his voice was defiant. "Mama doesn't mind, because she knows it's true."

"Be quiet, all of you," Fiona managed to say at last with as much lightness as she could summon. "You're all far too young to know what love is."

"I'm not." Allan grabbed her skirts and whined ostentatiously. "I love you, Mama."

James, not looking at anyone, said from the door, "I had some paints being delivered today. I'll see if anyone took them in for me."

His footsteps receded on the bare uneven boards of the corridor. They heard a door open and close. Steven pulled a dust sheet from an easel. There was an unfinished painting on it, and after studying it for a few moments he said to Fiona, the question of whether Robert loved her or not clearly forgotten, "Why must Uncle James always paint the same old picture, Mama?"

"It's not the same picture, Steven."

"They all look the same to me." He pointed to the canvases lying about the room. "All those silly little girls." He looked pointedly at Florence, who maintained a pose of aloof superiority as she waited for Fiona to reply.

"They're not silly little girls. And don't let Uncle James hear you say

66

that. They're sweet and beautiful and people adore them. And they're all different. Superficially they might seem the same, but you must look at the poses, the expressions and the backgrounds. And, above all, the colours. When you're older you will realise that Uncle James is a very fine artist."

Steven looked unconvinced, but at that moment James stumped back, carrying several heavy-looking boxes. He let them drop in a corner with a thud that shook the room. "I knew someone would have taken them in for me," he said breathlessly. He lifted the dust cloth Steven had taken from the easel and draped it again over the unfinished painting. He looked round them, relieved that the embarrassing conversation of a few minutes ago seemed to have ended.

"Have you all finished your drinks? Good. Then I think I should take you home. Grandmother will be waiting for you."

When Robert and Fiona were at the castle, the children stayed on in Glasgow with Rita and Fergus, so that their schooling would not be interrupted.

Half an hour later Fiona stood on the doorstep at Claremont Row and waved as the carriage turned up the hill. M. Lambert's roses had been stuck inartistically in a silver bowl by Morag. She spent a minute or two in the hall, arranging them before going to her room. She sat at the dressing table, brushing her hair and thinking sadly of her children's squabbling on their way home from school over the question of whether or not their mother and father were still in love. She did not know which disturbed her more—their subject or their precocity. She could not think it would ever have been possible for her to raise such a question with either of her own parents. Nor, she thought, had she had Steven's perception.

She went into the bathroom and turned on the hot water. Tomorrow there would be the board meeting, and a lively one it promised to be. Then a return to the castle by early train the next morning, to supervise the arrangements for Fergus's birthday party. At least this evening she could relax with a book after her letters were finished. She lay in the scented water, mentally sorting out which of the remaining invitations she would accept and which she would invent excuses for refusing.

She decided to finish her letters before dressing, with the idea that if she did not feel like going down to dinner, she need not dress at all. It was too warm to fuss when she was alone. Fergus, before leaving after his morning visit, had tried to lure her up to Park Place for dinner, but she had pleaded her neglected correspondence. She banished a twinge of guilt at having shamelessly seized the opportunity to have an evening free of children, free of Robert, free of all conversation and responsibility. She put on the coolest negligee she could find and went to her writing desk in the sitting room along the corridor.

As she started to write, there was a noise behind her. She turned and stared in disbelief at the sight of M. Lambert, coming from behind a china cabinet at the side of the window.

"Paul!" As she opened her mouth again, he put a finger to his lips as if he was afraid she was going to call out. His expression was beseeching.

"How did you get in here?" She was annoyed when she realised she had lowered her voice.

He was looking at the shining folds of satin lying smoothly about her. "I have not been away."

"I don't understand. Morag should have told me."

"She does not know I am here. No one knows."

Excitement began to rise in her. She should have been ringing for Morag or opening the door and screaming, but she did neither.

"After you left I went down and banged the outside door so that she would think I had gone. Then I came back up here . . . to wait."

"To wait . . . for what?"

"For you."

"Your presumption is monstrous. If it was not that I had a friendly affection for you, I would already have rung for assistance to . . . to have you put out. But you must not abuse my affection. I don't want to bring disgrace on you, but I will not hesitate to fetch every servant in the house if you do not take yourself out of here immediately. How dare you hide behind my furniture, waiting for hours to importune me in this manner?"

Her attempt at haughtiness was unconvincing. Her emotions were too confused. To make things worse, she knew he was coolly assessing her. There was a confident determination about him that she had not seen before. She was reminded of the transformation in their good-natured cat when it turned from lazily washing in the sun to stalking a bird. Lambert, the uncertain presenter of roses, the ridiculous hider behind furniture, had become a hunter.

She spoke quickly. "Anyway, do you seriously imagine that even if I felt like it I would risk having an affair with you? The notion is ridiculous." She wanted to sound imperious, but he made her feel gauche and vulnerable.

"There would be no affair," he said levelly. His voice was low and his tone reasonable, even businesslike. "I am leaving for France in one week. I could, if necessary, leave Glasgow even sooner. My work here is finished. I could write my farewells to the children."

Every word calmed her fears and weakened her resistance. Astonishingly, it could be made to sound reasonable. What he was proposing was a single act of abandon—daring, but almost without risk. After all, whether she liked it or not, he was here, and later, whatever happened, he would have to leave the house. If he was seen by any people who mattered, they would put their own interpretations on what they saw, whatever the true facts were. If the children had been under the same roof, it would have been inconceivable that she should have thought like this, even for a moment. But the situation left her free of almost any restraint except that of old-fashioned fidelity—and time and Robert's own record had worn that thin.

She took another look at Lambert's dark, expectant face. He seemed determined to risk her ringing for the servants, gambling on her not doing so. If she did ring, it would mean disgrace for him; servants always gossiped, and he had made many friends in Glasgow. Was she prepared to disgrace him? Was what he wanted from her as important as that?

He walked slowly across the few feet of carpet that separated them and stood looking into her eyes. "You will not be compromised," he said softly. "I promise you. I will leave Glasgow tomorrow."

Her gaze drifted to the key in the unlocked door. It was his one mistake. He should have turned it earlier. She walked quickly past him, opened the door and stepped into the corridor. The house was silent except for the thudding of her heart. She felt faint.

"Leave as quietly as you can," she said breathlessly.

She had time to notice his pallor, and against it the black rage of his eyes. Then, without another glance at her, he was gone.

4

Next day the sky was still cloudless, the air soft and the sun hot. All those who could sat under trees or picnicked in the green spaces of the city and on the banks of the broad river. Shopkeepers lowered awnings or spread newspapers over the goods in their windows to prevent fading. In the main streets watering carts laid dust while urchins ran behind, thrusting bare feet and legs into the cool spray.

Perhaps only in the offices of King & Co. was the single-mindedness essential to the amassing of great wealth unaffected by the glorious weather. There, the vision never wavered. Hard work had become a habit too ingrained to be broken by any quirk of nature, no matter how beguiling. Through international crisis and war, personal triumph and tragedy, the Kings had laboured at their business with almost mystical dedication. Today would be no different.

Andrew Paterson said as much to the new clerk who hopefully suggested they might open a window.

"And have every invoice in the place blowin' about the floor?" The smile above Paterson's wing collar was tolerant of the pale youth's ridiculous suggestion. "You'll get all the fresh air ye need when ye leave here at six o'clock the night."

Beyond the various offices was the blending hall. There, workmen knocked the bungs out of casks filled at distilleries in various parts of Scotland and splashed the gurgling contents into large blending vats. Down the centre of each vat ran a wooden shaft from which arms projected. When the vats were full, these shafts were turned manually, the arms agitating the contents to achieve an even marriage of perhaps a dozen different whiskies. From there the spirit streamed along open runs into another hall, where it was siphoned into bottles and labelled by women sitting on either side of long wooden tables.

The whole vast warehouse, to which, sixteen years earlier, the Kings had moved from the more humble riverside birthplace of King's Royal, was pervaded by the sharp tang of evaporating whisky and the sweet smell of sugar being burnt to colour the final blend before bottling.

A poetic visitor to the premises, perceiving this fragrance, had once declared himself reminded of peat smoke drifting across moorland hives filled with heather honey. Few connected with the production of King's Royal were as romantic. Fewer still noticed the aroma at all after their first few months in the drab building.

But even after almost twenty years Peter Ross was momentarily aware of it each morning as he walked down Seabank Lane to his office. It was this keen "nose" that had led Robert to put Ross in charge of the firm's blending operations. On Ross's judgement, on his selection of whiskies, depended the quality of each new batch of King's Royal. His skill was basic to the continued success of the business. Only one man could match him, and that was Robert himself. It was Robert, looking for other shoulders on which to place part of the burden, who had taken Ross out of the run-down grocer's shop he owned in the Candleriggs when he had discovered that the tall young man with the disillusioned eyes shared his feeling for whisky's future.

Now Ross's "nose" was legendary among the Glasgow whisky blenders. Normally he took his skill for granted. Only during the months he had spent working on the blend, to commemorate the queen's diamond jubilee, had he come near to doubting it. Since the board meeting at the end of the previous year, at which he had been given his instructions, he had devised literally hundreds of blends. Quality was not difficult, since he was free to draw on any distillery, no matter how expensive its whisky; character was the elusive quality. The new whisky must have individuality; otherwise they might as well use the King's Royal formula under another name.

Ross produced various blends which to his sharp senses were different, but he was realist enough to know that the subtlety would elude the ordinary drinker. One day, in depression, he began thinking how simply it had all started, with Robert's inspired idea of blending malt and grain to produce a drink instantly recognisable for its light and pleasant taste. Something sparked. Could this lightness be extended? Excitement began to rise in him. Could a new blend of "character" be created by further removing the characteristic taste of malt? The paradox thrilled him. Obviously it could, if he selected whiskies of less flavour than those used in King's Royal.

71

This was the key to the blend which Ross would today submit to the board. He was nervous about it. His own opinion was that he had produced a beautifully palatable blend without loss of body. But would the others agree? Several times in his months of experiment he had tried to get Robert's advice, but on each occasion had been told to rely on his own judgement until he was ready to let the whole board pass an opinion.

When he went into the board room only Fergus was there, but they were soon joined by Andrew McNair, from Lochbank distillery. At almost sixty McNair was the company's longest-serving employee. Fergus had never regretted his gamble in taking McNair out of the Corkcutters' Arms, a decrepit tavern King & Co. had owned in the Goosedubbs, and pitching him headfirst into distilling. McNair had risked his life putting out the fire that had destroyed the original Lochbank and then laboured for a year with the stone masons who had put up the new building.

Fergus glanced at the strong, cheerful face beneath the silvering hair. "Loch Lomond must be a picture in this weather," he said.

"Aye, a picture." McNair nodded, then looked thoughtfully into his tobacco pouch. "But I've never known the water so low. If we don't get rain soon, we'll have to stop distilling a month earlier than usual. The burns in the hills behind the distillery are running dry. I don't think the dam has a week's water left in it. I've even had to rig up pumps to use the loch water for cooling."

Fergus smiled at Ross. "Here we are, innocently enjoying the sunshine, and all it's doing is giving poor McNair headaches."

His expression changed as Robert came into the room with Fiona and Gwen. This was the first Fergus had seen of his son since being given the startling news of his political ambitions. It was bound to come up before the meeting ended. He would say then what he thought. Dear knows!

After a few minutes' informal talk Robert took his seat at the head of the table. "James will be a little late, as usual, I suppose?"

The sarcasm was softened by a note of tolerant affection.

"He wouldn't be James if he was on time," Gwen said, "but at least we know he won't hold us up once he does get here." This was a reference to James's well-known disinterest.

Robert turned to her. Although her face was unlined, her eyes were tired and her hair was completely grey. She was only two years his senior, but the tragedies of her twenties had been lastingly destructive.

He said, "Did you know Jack is going to be here?"

Gwen brightened. "No, I didn't. I thought he was at Lochbank."

"I thought it a good idea that he and Gordon should occasionally sit in on board meetings from now on. They won't speak, of course, but it will be useful for them to see how we arrive at decisions." He turned to McNair. "Where is Jack?"

McNair put down his pipe. "I don't think he'll be long, Mr. King. We travelled up together from Lochbank, but he left me at the station. There was some business he wanted to attend to."

Robert grimaced. "I would have thought this would have been the most important business he had. That's two we have to wait for now."

Gwen flushed and started to speak, then changed her mind.

"Anyway, I told Gordon to wait for him in the front office," Robert said. "They can come in together."

Fiona thought it advisable to change the subject. She looked cool and businesslike in a blue dress with slightly puffed sleeves, sashed waist and severe skirt, chosen because it was one of the least feminine outfits in her wardrobe. She had sat for a long time the previous night, overcome with revulsion at the thought of the easy prey she had almost become for M. Lambert. This morning she had been filled with a desire to suppress her femininity. It was as if, by denying her womanhood, she could atone for her weakness. Today her mind was firmly on business.

"You must be glad the long hunt for perfection is over," she said to Ross.

His smile was nervous. "I won't know if it's over until you've all tasted it, Mrs. King." His glance strayed to the decanter and the tray of glasses on a side table.

"I'm sure you have nothing to worry about," Fiona said comfortingly. "But I know the feeling you must have. I get it every time we give a dinner party, wondering how the food will turn out."

She looked round the table, conscious that she was the only one who knew there would be the surprise of James's resignation to digest on top of the whisky-tasting and the heat that would inevitably develop around Robert's political plans.

"We should get James to paint us—and himself—sitting round the table, looking purposeful," Fiona said. "Somehow or other these meetings sum up the whole of King and Company for me."

"It would be a fine thing if James could be persuaded to do that," Fergus said, taking the suggestion more seriously than it had been intended, his eyes bright at the idea. "But it would be a waste of time even to ask him. He won't paint portraits, and that's all this would be, really—a multiple portrait."

"He painted Fiona," Robert reminded him.

"Ah, yes, but that was a long time ago."

"And still you won't part with it."

Fergus looked amused and then shook his head. "But that isn't so much a portrait as a vision." He turned in his chair and looked down the table at Fiona as if he had not seen her for a long time. "I think it was James's vision of the whole of womankind. And he couldn't have had a better model," he added gallantly, then began to worry that this might be a slur on Gwen. He let his gaze pass casually across the table and was relieved to see she seemed unconcerned.

Fiona, who remembered the painting more for the good-humoured squabbles Robert and Fergus had about where it should rightly hang than for any resemblance she saw in it to herself, said, "That's a flattering thought, Grandfather. And if that was really James's intention, then I'm honoured he chose me as his model."

"Well, my dear, it's you and yet it isn't you. You had just become engaged to be married when James painted that picture, and yet you could be a schoolgirl in it. And you could belong to almost any age. The clothes he dressed you in give nothing away. Nor does the hairstyle. And the setting—*there's* another puzzle. Where is it meant to be? A great sandy infinity on the edge of a sea that you only sense to be there. It could be Scotland, or the edge of some other world." Again Fergus shook his head, pondering the riddle not only of the painting but of the painter. "No, that wasn't a portrait James was painting. It was an enigma."

"If it's such a mystery, why don't you simply ask James to explain it?" Gwen's voice might have had a slight dryness in it.

Fergus leaned forward almost eagerly. This was close to the heart of his world. "Oh, but I have, my dear. Several times. But James won't explain. 'If I have to explain it,' he said once, 'it's no use.' No, I think it will always be a puzzle. We'll never solve it."

Robert decided to give him another dig.

"And still you won't part with it, Father. A practical man like you, who hates conundrums. Come along, how much will you take for it?"

"It will hang in the hall at Ardfern for as long as I live," Fergus said with sudden seriousness. "It was painted there and I think it belongs there, but after I'm gone your mother can do what she thinks right with it. It's James's masterwork. He'll never do anything better now." He lowered his eyes as if at the foolishness of his fancy. "I don't think it's going too far to think of it as the Scottish *Mona Lisa*."

Behind him the door opened, and Gordon came in with Jack Hoey.

"Ah, the missing link!" Robert tempered the rebuke with a smile.

"Sorry I'm late, Uncle Robert," Jack said with an air of concern. "I hope I haven't held things up." He kissed his mother and then walked around the table to kiss Fiona. "Where will I sit?"

He was two years older than Gordon, slightly taller, and dressed, like McNair, in tweeds. It was a convention that although the head office required sober conformity, those concerned with the distillery were expected to dress like country gentlemen. The casual clothes increased the dash that Jack exuded as he moved confidently about the room. He had the same easy grace that most of them remembered in his father, and the way he wore his black hair, cut short and plastered flat, enhanced the resemblance.

Gordon watched him with open irritation. "There's a chair over there for you," he said loudly, nodding to a corner. "I'll take the one by the window."

Gwen cast an anxious glance at her son. The good reports Robert had given her of his progress with the company should have been reassuring, but lingering doubts still frightened her sometimes. Yet what cause had he given her for worry? He was high-spirited; but better that, surely, than Gordon's gloomy introspection. Young men were supposed to be lively. He was interested in girls, but could she complain about that? Certainly he had come home, more than once, clearly having drunk more beer than he should. But that was what young men did when they got together after rowing on the Clyde at Glasgow Green or spending the afternoon on a cross-country run. She had nothing explicit to worry about. Colin had been understanding and had said her fears were natural but, so far as he could see, unfounded. Still she had spells of uneasiness, drifting memories of the self-centred rake who had so cruelly filled all but the last months of her first marriage with pain and worry, and of whom she was reminded every time she looked at her son.

"You had no right going off on some personal matter, Jack," she said sharply, and to her own surprise.

Everyone turned to her. They had imagined the question of his unpunctuality past. Jack gave her a wounded look.

"I had to buy a birthday present for Grandfather," he said quietly. "There are no shops near the distillery. But I'm sorry if I have been thoughtless."

Gordon closed his eyes. Grandfather's birthday again! Perfect, if it hadn't been just so glib. He wondered how many of them were taken in. Probably everyone but himself. It took one to recognise one. His mind drifted. Everything going on in the room seemed unreal to him. The only reality now was his forthcoming meeting with Anne Dunbar. The scandalous daring of it thrilled and yet frightened him. Six more days to go. His mind filled with restless longings.

James kept them waiting another ten minutes and took his seat with only the barest apology. They saw at once that it was one of his bad days. His face was pale and hollowed with pain and there were tiny flecks of blood in his eyes. The rules that he had long ago imposed on them prevented anyone's sympathising with him or even enquiring, other than casually, about his health.

They listened without interruption as Ross gave them the vital technicalities—mainly the ages, prices and availability of the eleven whiskies he had chosen. But when he tried, with a mixture of enthusiasm and apprehension, to describe the blend, preparing them for what he had arrived at, Fergus interrupted with an understanding smile.

"All right, Peter. With a minimum age of twelve years, I'm sure it's old enough to speak for itself. Who's going to pour?"

Ross hurried to the decanter, put a small amount of whisky into seven crystal glasses and carried them round the table on a tray.

James looked at the frugal measure and said, "This must be precious stuff." With little more than a token sniff he swallowed the whisky greedily.

Fergus watched him rise, walk stiffly to the decanter and pour himself another measure. There had been a time when James would not drink whisky. There were times now when he seemed driven to it by the trouble his leg gave him. It had become so noticeable that in the autumn of the previous year Rita had summoned the courage to discuss with him the advisability of seeing his doctor. "I have seen him," James told her. "There's nothing can be done." He had tried to make light of it. "I'm used to it by now, you know, mother. It always has come and gone a bit."

Fergus, ridding himself of these reflections, raised his glass. He considered the bouquet for a few moments before tasting a little of the whisky. Robert, he noted with slight irritation, was going through the professional rigmarole, pouring a little whisky onto the palm of one hand, vigorously rubbing both palms together and then cupping them under his nose. The mystique had to be upheld, Fergus supposed sardonically, as he waited for someone to give an opinion.

Ross, his own glass still untouched, was watching them all expectantly. *Poor Peter*, Fergus thought. Almost as if the sympathy had communicated itself, Ross turned to him hopefully. Fergus decided to commit himself. If he couldn't honestly say what he thought at his age, then there was something far wrong.

"I like it," he said emphatically. He lifted his glass and had another sip. "You and Robert are the experts, of course, but to me it seems very smooth and more than usually palatable." Beyond that he couldn't go. It was only whisky, after all. To the ordinary nose or palate, how different could one whisky be from another? Besides, he was of the generation that remembered whisky as a crude and lowly drink, and at heart he was still a wine and brandy man. Impossible to say that, though! Even at his age. Dear knows!

76

James, who had quickly emptied his second glass, looked less drawn. Some of the customary good humour was back in his eyes.

"I agree with that," he said. "To be quite honest, I don't know exactly what finer points we're looking for, but I can't imagine a whisky being any gentler or more comforting than this. I think Peter is to be congratulated."

Fiona and Gwen, whose knowledge of the subject was almost entirely academic, made vague but emphatic noises of friendly agreement.

A look of wary pleasure began to replace the tension on Ross's face. He lifted his own glass and sipped as if to test the accuracy of some memory. McNair gave him a comradely grin and the whisky solid and forthright assent. It was left to Robert to put the seal firmly on it and, with a few complimentary remarks and searching questions, to lift from Ross the anxiety of almost half a year.

There was, to Robert, a curious sense of anticlimax about the occasion. His real desire was to reach the end of the meeting, formally announce his adoption as a Parliamentary candidate and then put to them the startling proposal that had in the last two days taken over his mind. When they had voted unanimously in favour of Ross's new blend, he looked almost anxiously round the table, impatient to unburden himself.

"If there isn't any other business, I have something . . ."

He stopped as he realised James wanted to speak.

"There is one item of business I'd like to get over with," James said hesitantly.

They waited patiently. James rarely contributed anything to their meetings. He was the one King devoid of commercial ideas. Perhaps a quarter of his riches had been the reward of his artistic talent. The rest had been thrust on him by Fergus, in the form of shares in the company.

"I want to resign my directorship. I've never been able to contribute much to the business, but at least I've been able to attend board meetings and vote. In future I won't be able to do even that, at any rate, I wouldn't be able to do it without an awful lot of inconvenience. . . ."

Fergus interrupted harshly. "What are you talking about, James?" His fingers worked worriedly at his beard.

James looked across the table at him. "I haven't told mother about this yet, and I know I should have, but I'm leaving Glasgow to live in Fleetside." It was almost a private apology to Fergus.

"That's a perfectly ridiculous idea," Fergus protested. "You can't bury yourself down there. Having a holiday house you can retreat to when you feel like it is one thing, but to move permanently to such a remote corner of the country is . . . " Fergus couldn't think what it was. "What's your mother going to say?"

77

This was the worst question he could have asked, especially with so many others present.

"I'm thirty-seven years old, Father." James's voice was defiant. He glanced at Fiona and received a message of silent support. "I don't suppose I have to remind anyone that I'm first and foremost a painter. It's not easy to explain, but my work has reached a stage where I feel I must get away from Glasgow and . . . and make a fresh start."

After the initial surprise, Robert's feeling was of annoyance. In practical terms James's resignation would mean little. It was the emotional impact that irritated him. It complicated his own position. Two upheavals was one more than he had planned for.

He heard Fergus say, "You could do all that, James, without resigning from the board."

"No, Father. I want to make a clean break."

Fergus's eyes held a mixture of concern and resentment. He had a vision of his cosy business life collapsing into some new and unfamiliar form. James off the board. Robert wasting his time with all the other meddlesome gasbags at Westminster. Both his sons gone while Douglas Dunbar swung an axe at the foundation of the business. He turned angrily on Robert.

"There seems to be an epidemic. I happen to know you'll be breaking some similar news to us."

Robert was jolted by the unexpectedness of the attack. He had wondered if the news had filtered back to Fergus. He looked across at Fiona, but she was following the various expressions at the table as they each dealt with this baffling hint of yet another shock to come.

"We haven't reached my news, yet, Father," he said quickly, "and before we do I think we should finish with the matter James has raised."

Now that he was himself under pressure, he was able to face his brother with a slight smile of understanding. "I'm every bit as surprised as Father, James, but I presume you've thought well about this?"

"Naturally, Robert."

"Of course. Then I'm sorry, because it is sad news for all of us, but having said that, I do think Father's distress is exaggerated." He ignored Fergus's frown. "After all, you'll continue to hold your shares. You'll own exactly the same slice of the company as you do now."

"That's right, Robert. There really won't be much difference at all." James welcomed Robert's attempt to diminish the breach.

But Fergus was not comforted. He shook his head and spoke almost as if to himself. "It's the idea of us all sitting here, year after year, thrashing things out, pulling together as a family. That's the important thing." His voice was hoarse. "That's what the business is to me. It's not just money. It won't be the same without James at the table."

Robert felt a twinge of pity for him. He tried to soften the blow.

"If James's mind is quite made up, I don't suppose anything we say will make him change it. Nevertheless, I propose we leave his resignation lying on the table until our next meeting. We won't accept it today."

It meant nothing, but there was a murmur of relieved approval. James gave Robert a grateful nod. Fergus would have grown accustomed to the idea by the next board meeting, and by then James would have slipped quietly off to Fleetside.

With James's resignation hardly digested, Robert's announcement was even more disconcerting than it would otherwise have been.

Fergus pounced immediately. "You can have little thought for the business if you can even contemplate abandoning it for a seat among a lot of damned useless politicians in London." His voice was bitter.

Robert spoke quietly. "I happen to think, Father, that there are forces at work that in time could destroy not just our business but our society and our country. I want to help fight these forces, and that can best be done from the House of Commons. It does not mean I am going to abandon the business. It simply means that in future I intend to give some of my time to politics. For the last twenty years I have given my whole life to this business. I'm well into middle age now. Surely I have earned the right to live a little of my life outside King and Company." He sounded like an underdog who had been press-ganged into the service of the company. The ensuing sense of unreality affected everyone at the table.

McNair and Ross, whose careers with the company had been passed with Robert at their sides, either in body or in spirit, seemed too surprised to be capable of any comment.

Gwen, with her strong practical side, was the first to speak. "What would being a member of Parliament mean in terms of absence, Robert?"

"It will mean my being in London almost all the time that Parliament is sitting. But I need only attend the House in the evenings. I can put in a full day in our London office. I won't be shirking, I assure you."

Fergus glowered and said sombrely, "This is not the time for you to be standing for Parliament."

"It might be the only chance I'll be given. If I let it go—"

"Damn it, your place is here. There might be a time when we can spare you, but not now. Douglas Dunbar is gnawing into our sales like a wild animal. King and Company has never been more in need of dedicated management."

"Sir Fergus is right," McNair said, confronting Robert across the table with an almost shame-faced expression. "And apart from Dunbar, what about this new blend? Launching it is going to involve us in the outlay of an awful lot of money. It doesna seem the time for you to go off, Mr. King, and leave us kind of . . . well"—he looked away—"kind of in the lurch."

If anything could have deflected Robert, it was this reluctant but honest opposition. His heart went out to McNair. Always, the big man had been with him, a comforting buttress. There must be a great depth of feeling there for the loyal McNair to have spoken like that. He looked like someone being abandoned. Robert stifled a groan. He must convince McNair—convince them all—that this was not so.

"I think I appreciate how you all feel," he said passionately. "I understand your resentment. I can even see it as a compliment to me that you should react in this way. But, of course, I am not indispensable. Besides, I hope you all know me better than to believe I could bear to see King and Company neglected. It's true that if I win this election, I'll only be able to concentrate on the London end of the business, and that would leave us without an ultimate authority here in our head office. But, as I said, I am not irreplaceable. Far from it." He paused and looked round the room. The moment could be delayed no longer: this was the point where he must reveal his plan. "Someone else can take charge, and without any beating about the bush, I propose Fiona."

The long, astonished silence was broken by a protest from Fiona.

"The least you could have done, Robert, was warn me that you had this in mind. It's a ridiculous suggestion, and I might have been able to stop you from making a fool of yourself."

He gave her a smile of sympathy. "I'm not making a fool of myself, Fiona. You'll see. I've thought about this very deeply."

Fergus fidgeted with his beard in a dazed way. "If you're serious, then I don't know what to say. Dear knows!" He looked to Gwen, as if he might find help there.

She seemed to be the only one considering the proposal seriously. "Do you mean that Fiona should literally move into your room and sit at your desk and simply leave your home and your children to servants?"

"Of course not. The day-to-day running of the business does not require me, so I don't see why it would require Fiona. The business goes along perfectly well when I'm travelling abroad, so Fiona needn't be too tied. She would only have to concern herself with major decisions of policy. Anyway, I won't be ten thousand miles away if she wants my advice. To be honest, I could probably remain in charge, even based in London. But I don't want to. I want to have a clear mind to concentrate on my other duties, at least for a year or two."

James, who was relieved that attention had been diverted so dramatically from his own defection, said, "Now that I'm resigning, I don't suppose I have a vote or any right to take part in this discussion, but if I had a vote, it would go to Fiona. Ross and McNair know it has to be a member of the family who takes over from Robert, so that excludes them without the slightest reflection on their abilities. I'm just a renegade painter who would never be there when he was needed and who wouldn't be able to make any decisions except, no doubt, absolutely disastrous ones. Father is at a time of life when he can't be asked to take on any more burdens. Apart from anything else, Mother wouldn't stand for it. Gwen has a husband, a son, and her antiques to look after. By a process of reduction that leaves only you, Fiona." He bowed to her. "Personally, I think you're capable of running the business as well as any man—which is the real question in everyone's mind—and as well as that, you *should* have the job since you and Robert between you own over half the shares and therefore have the most to lose."

She looked at him reproachfully. "But I don't want the job, James. It's ridiculous. Robert should never have suggested such a thing."

James leaned back as if enjoying the situation. "If Robert is determined to go into politics, someone must do the job. In a way, the whole family revolves round you, Fiona, so why not the business, too?"

Ross pushed his chair back. "Those were very small whiskies I poured. Perhaps we could all take another." As he went round to the glasses with the decanter he said to Robert, "It might have been better, right enough, if you had prepared Mrs. King for this."

Robert swirled the whisky in his glass and savoured the aroma. "No, Peter. I deliberately didn't do that because I knew Fiona's answer would then be prejudiced not only by her own real feelings but by the thought of what the rest of you would think. Likewise, I didn't sound the rest of you out because I felt there would have been too much talk, too much consultation. I wanted everyone to come right out and say what they thought without prior warning. Now, I might be misreading the situation, but my feeling is that although you are all very naturally surprised, I don't think any of you are very deeply opposed to the idea, except perhaps on the ground of prejudice against Fiona as a woman. That's only natural, but I'd like to point out that women in charge of businesses are not completely unknown in these enlightened days. I suppose the supreme example of a woman in charge is the queen, who has been at the head of the country for sixty years. To go back into history, was Britain ever greater than under Queen Elizabeth, a woman who wielded almost despotic power?"

He smiled. "You're all beginning to look a bit dazed, and I don't blame you. To come closer to home, Gwen founded her own business and has run it successfully for years, despite the initial scepticism of father and

81

myself. When Fiona was only twenty she ran Lochbank Distillery when her father was ill. It was no fault of her management that when he died, the distillery had to be sold. But when King and Company bought Lochbank, Fiona was shrewd and determined enough to agree to the sale only on condition that instead of paying her with money we pay her with a share of King and Company. That was a brilliant stroke, and not the obvious move all those years ago that it might seem now. Since then, her contributions have been invaluable. Everyone here knows that a lot of our decisions are based on views, ideas or suggestions put forward by Fiona. What none of you realise is how many of my decisions over the years have also been based on advice given me privately by Fiona—privately, I hasten to add, not because of any collusion but simply because of the normal exchange between a man and his wife. I don't think any of you will deny that Fiona is an unusually capable woman. She has the confidence of all of us. In fact, I sometimes think the phrase I hear most often, here and elsewhere, is 'I wonder what Fiona thinks?'"

Tea was brought in, pipes were lit, whiskies were poured again, as, for almost an hour, they studied the revolutionary proposal.

The unfairness of trying to thrust such a responsibility on Fiona troubled both Fergus and Gwen, but finally, under Robert's determined arguments, their fears were quelled. The possibility that she might be inadequate was raised only by herself and quickly disposed of by a volley of denials.

As the argument went on, Fiona was aware that her protests were growing more perfunctory. As her surprise subsided she began to feel flattered that Robert should think her capable of replacing him as the brain and the nerve centre of the complex and still controversial organisation that was King & Co. The prospect was undeniably tempting. Quickly she rejected the ridiculous notion that she could ever sit at his desk, perhaps having to overrule Ross, McNair or even Fergus. Yet, was it so ridiculous? Why shouldn't she be able to take command and run the business successfully? She had, as Robert said, taken charge of her father's business. Anyway, would it in essence be so very different from running a home and a family, where differences and tensions arose continually, where decisions had to be made and conflicting interests reconciled? Yes, she told herself, it would be different. Of course it would. It would be silly to pretend otherwise. And men had been better equipped by nature to face the world. And yet . . .

When finally the talking was over and they all said they supported her, she neither refused nor accepted. She asked for time to think, but in her heart she knew it was only a formality. As the discussion switched to another issue, excitement began to rise in her. She thought, *I'll show them*

82

that I can do it. I will run it and I'll run it as well as Robert or Grandfather ever did.

They were now trying to think of a name for the new blend, but she couldn't concentrate. She was vaguely aware of Gordon's watching her from his seat in the shadow at the side of the small window. His expression was difficult to read. Was it pain she saw there, or disbelief? He looks, she thought with a twinge of panic, like a boy who has lost his mother and found a new employer. She banished the fanciful idea and forced herself to listen.

"I wonder if Sir Fergus would let us use the name of his house?" Peter Ross said. "We all know it, and four generations of the family have been connected with it. I thought 'Knight of Ardfern' had a nice ring to it."

Robert, to whom it seemed they were all prepared to defer in the matter, pursed his lips. "I agree it has a nice ring, Peter, but father's a baronet, not a knight."

"But does that matter? All we want is a suitable name. I had thought of a variation: Laird of Ardfern."

Fergus smiled self-consciously as Robert wrote it down without comment. "Any other suggestions?"

"Golden Reign," McNair said, as if ashamed of it.

"That's more the line we should be thinking along," Robert said with an approving nod. "We should remember this whisky has been created to commemorate the queen's diamond jubilee. The nearer we get to conveying that in the name, the better."

Gordon moved his chair slightly, scraping the legs on the polished boards. "Can I make a suggestion, Father?"

"I wish you would. We're not doing too well over here."

"What about King's Tribute? That keeps the family name to the fore and in the advertising we could explain that it's our salute to the queen."

"I think that's very apt, indeed," Gwen said. "So apt," she added with a smile, "that I'd be ashamed now to put my pitiful offerings forward." She crumpled a scrap of paper on which she had scribbled some names. "I'm afraid they're all of the Highland Dew variety."

Fergus laughed ruefully. "It must run in the family. Mine all tend to heather and tartan. I think I'd better keep them to myself. King's Tribute seems excellent to me. It incorporates all the essentials." He looked apologetically at Ross and said in a low voice, as if no one else should hear, "Laird of Ardfern is flattering to me, Peter, but not really apt."

"Then I'll put King's Tribute at the top of the list," Robert said. "We all seem to think it the best so far."

Gordon smiled as a murmur of agreement went round the table. Then, across the room, he heard his cousin cough loudly.

83

"Hold on, Uncle Robert. I think I can beat that."

Jack's smile was confident, challenging and yet pleasant, a combination Gordon knew well. As always, it provoked in him a seething irritation.

"Our basic whisky is King's Royal. Our new blend, as Gordon said a moment ago, is intended as a salute to the queen. Surely, then, the obvious name for it is Queen's Royal."

It was so unquestionably right that Robert almost broke the silence with a cheer. The approving smiles and admiring exclamations of the others told him in an instant that the matter had been settled. Then, with a shock, he saw his son's face, masked with the surliness of a resentful child thwarted by a rival. He remembered the extraordinary reaction to his innocent remark about Jack's drawing for a new copper junction tap. He choked back his praise, ashamed that a brilliant contribution could not receive its due. The name would have to be quietly adopted later.

"Yes, Jack," he said judicially, "that's a very good suggestion, too. Very interesting. I'm delighted I brought Gordon and you into this. You've both given us something to think about."

But it was not to end there. The encouragement brought Jack walking quickly from his corner. He stopped where his mother could see him.

"I'm sure the longer you think about it the more you'll like it," he said confidently. "Think of the two bottles sitting side by side on a shelf or in a shop window—King's Royal and Queen's Royal—each helping to sell the other. It would make it not just a tribute to the queen, but"—his imagination soared, triumphing over inconvenient fact and even death—"to the king . . . I mean the prince consort . . . the late prince consort, as well." He smiled easily. "She always thought of him as king, you know. But not ony that . . ." He went quickly round the table to Fiona's side. "It's for Aunt Fiona, as well, you see. This tribute to the queen was her idea. And if she is going to head the company, then she will be our queen. It all blends together." He leaned forward and took Fiona's hand. "It would be a private tribute to Aunt Fiona as well as a public one to . . ."

Gordon waited for no more. He rose noisily and went blindly out of the room, sick with fury at the sound of Jack's persuasive enthusiasm, the sight of Gwen's pride, his father's respectful attention, his mother's slightly embarrassed pleasure.

He was in the warehouse, pacing the long, dim corridors formed by thousands of stacked whisky casks, when he heard footsteps.

"I've been looking for you," he heard Jack say. "Old Paterson told me he'd let you off the leash early."

"What the hell do you want?"

Jack's eyes narrowed. "Hello. You don't sound very friendly. And I've been thinking of your welfare all afternoon."

"What does that mean?"

"There isn't much diversion down at Lochbank, so I thought I'd put my visit to Glasgow to good use. When I ditched old McNair at the station, I nipped up to Bank Street and told Isabella she could expect to see me this evening. I took the liberty of making an appointment for you with Dorothy. I know you like her but never have the courage to visit her on your own."

Gordon felt his blood stir. Isabella and Dorothy were sisters in their twenties who provided board and lodgings for students. For a bouquet of roses or a bottle of champagne, plus a sovereign left discreetly on the hall table, they could be persuaded to cater to other youthful needs. Jack was one of their regular visitors and Gordon had twice accompanied him. He had been forced to lie about his age. Dorothy had her principles, and to entertain a boy so young would have struck her as immoral.

"Come on, what do you say?"

In the end he would probably say yes, but first he had his spleen to get rid of. He swung full round on his cousin, almost spitting.

"You're nothing but a filthy sycophant, Hoey."

Jack stiffened a little, but his lighthearted expression did not change. "That's a bit thick, isn't it? Especially for nothing."

"Queen's Royal! A tribute to Aunt Fiona! My God, you crawled to my father with your bloody copper junction tap and all that, and now he's leaving you've started licking around my mother. You make me want to vomit."

"Then please go ahead. Get it out of your system. As a matter of fact, I thought you already had. It's not many weeks since we went through all this before. Only then it was about your father. Now you've brought your mother into it."

"You're the one who's brought my mother into it. Aunt Fiona will be our queen! Holding her hand and drooling over her. You did everything but kiss her. Maybe you did even that, but I was too sickened to wait to the end of your performance."

Jack leaned his elbow on the rim of a hogshead, his expression still amused and tolerant. "Yes, you did make rather an ass of yourself. But never mind, it'll soon be forgotten."

"I doubt if your sycophantic little act will."

Jack sighed elaborately. "I do wish you wouldn't doubt my sincerity in everything, Cousin Gordon. My remarks about your mother were perfectly genuine. She deserves our tribute. Besides"—his expression became arch—"I have a special, unnephewlike feeling for her."

85

Gordon frowned, caught not only by the words but the tone in which they were spoken. "And what exactly does that mean?"

Jack grinned. "You know what we do with Isabella and Dorothy? Well, I have to confess I'd love to do exactly the same with Fiona."

"You dirty bastard!" His fist lashed out but Jack swayed away from it, caught him by the wrist and jerked his arm behind his back.

"I'm three inches taller than you and two years older," he said coldly, "and if you insist on having a thrashing, I'll give you one. But there's absolutely no need for it. I only said I'd like to go to bed with Fiona."

"My God, you swine, that's my mother!" He yelped as his struggles sent pain jabbing up his twisted arm.

"Dorothy must be about twenty-seven and is probably somebody's mother, but you don't worry about that. If you weren't such a prude, you would see there's no need for you to be so annoyed. What I said is really a compliment to Fiona. There aren't many women of that age I find attractive."

Gordon kicked him hard on the ankle, dragged his arm free and lashed out at his face. The next moment he was lying on the damp earth floor with a knee in his back.

"Calm down, you silly young brute. Keep your energy for Dorothy. She'll be delighted to have you work it off on her."

"Let me up!" His mouth was touching the earth and his words came in smothered gasps. "This floor is filthy. My clothes . . ."

"Your clothes! I thought it was your mother you were worried about. Your feelings can't be too deeply outraged, after all."

"Let me up, Jack. Please let me up."

"I'll let you up when you promise to behave. Then, when I've got my breath back, we'll go and have a pint of beer at White's. Do you promise?"

"Yes."

They were slightly drunk when they arrived at the flat in Bank Street, and although the sisters made them welcome, it was Anne Dunbar's arms Gordon imagined about him when he was in bed with Dorothy.

5

Later that week, Rita King stood with Fiona on the steps of Castle Gare in the glaring late-afternoon sunshine and watched Great-grandmother Veitch reach the top of the long drive on the arm of Jack Hoey.

"All this sunshine can be a mixed blessing," Rita said. "I can't decide if I've gone suddenly grey in the last few weeks or if it's only the sun that's bleached my hair."

"It's only the sun," Fiona assured her. "I'm quite envious of you, sometimes. I'm sure I have more grey in my hair than you have. And you look so slim and young in that dress."

Rita tried not to feel too pleased. She thought the dress, white with pink flowers and soft frills, flattered her small features and delicate colouring, but if she did not guard against a too literal belief in all the compliments Fergus and the family paid her, she could quite easily have her head turned; she was not too old for it, yet.

Her mother had seen them and was waving her stick.

"Fergus wanted her to come in the carriage with us, but she insisted on walking," Rita said wonderingly. "Can you imagine it? In this heat! You would think at eighty-nine she would have learned sense."

Despite the words, her voice was warm with pride for her mother's stamina and stubborn independence. "It was good of Jack, volunteering to accompany her. One always worries a little when she's on the road alone."

Fiona raised a hand to shield her eyes. The sun had dropped almost directly in line with the castle's hilly perch. Soon it would sink behind the ridge of the Rosneath Peninsula, and the various groups strolling or romping in the grounds would go inside. She could hear the children at some noisy game in the woods.

"Jack really seems quite attached to her," she said, as if marvelling at the rarity of such a relationship between youth and extreme age.

"Oh, yes. He sits with her at the cottage for an hour or so whenever he visits us with Gwen. Mother always did get on well with the children. Especially the boys. Fergus always said Robert and James spent more time with her than with us. It was the same when Jack was a child. Gwen used to send him down to us at Ardfern, to get the country air, but half his time would be spent with Mother. She fussed over him, of course, but there seems to be something about that little cottage of hers that appeals to children. It's so cosy and secure, I suppose, with its low ceilings and leaded windows."

They raised their parasols, went carefully down the steps and across the courtyard to meet the old lady. While regaining her breath, she had turned to admire the shimmering stretch of loch and the wide firth beyond. Close to the shore a yacht lay becalmed, its sails slack, the crew searching the blue sky for some sign of a breeze.

Jack lifted his straw hat and saluted. "One great-grandmother safely delivered," he said. "Just a little late, I think, but we sat on the rocks by the water for a few minutes before tackling the drive."

Mrs. Veitch, though slightly stooped, was almost as tall as Fiona, and although the years had softened the sharpness of her features and the barb of her tongue, there was still a forbidding glint in her clear grey eyes. She wore a mutch over tight white curls and despite the sunshine she was entirely in black. The yellow dust of the shore road clung to her skirts.

Fiona, who had always been a little in awe of the old lady's link with what seemed an incredibly distant past, said, "Welcome to Castle Gare, Mrs. Veitch. It's lovely to see you."

"Oh, but I've been here before," Mrs. Veitch said with a satisfied smile. She spoke with more of a Scottish intonation than either Rita or Fiona. "It was when the Glenardens were here." She looked about and then pointed her stick. "It was at a fete, and over there they had stalls laden with flowers and vegetables. I remember there was honey from the minister's bees and Granny Reid had sent up some of her strawberry jam. Professor Laidlaw's wife baked a whole board of her famous meringues." She shook her head. "But it rained. The heavens opened and half of the lovely stuff was ruined."

"Well, it's not going to rain today," Rita said, "but I do think perhaps we should go inside, where you can sit down out of the sun. Besides, there's someone looking forward very much to seeing you again: Fiona's Aunt May. Do you remember her?"

"I remember her fine," Mrs. Veitch said crisply as she took Rita's arm. "The last time we met was nine years ago, in Glasgow, at the christening of Fiona's youngest. She wore a ring with an enormous cluster of diamonds that must have cost a great deal of money, and I remember wondering about it, because I had heard she had only been modestly well provided for when her husband died."

She looked enquiringly at Rita, as if she might be able to supply an explanation.

"There's nothing wrong with your memory, anyway, Mother," Rita said.

"There's not. Why should there be?"

Jack grinned and offered his arm to Fiona.

"That's what I like to see," Mrs. Veitch said, her mutch bobbing forward with approval. "A young man showing good manners and respect for a lady. It's all a matter of simple consideration. There's not so much of it about as there used to be."

Fiona had also envisaged the party as a grand family gathering of a completeness that might not be possible for much longer. Fergus, at seventy-three was still vigorous. Mrs. Veitch, at almost ninety, and Aunt May, at eighty, were remarkable. By comparison, Rita, at sixty-five, was hardly past middle age. Nevertheless, with the excuse of Fergus's birthday and Robert's recent purchase of the castle, she had thought it advisable to get them all together for what could very easily be the last time. There was a long span of eighty years now separating the youngest from the oldest. It could not be stretched much further.

Even with Robert helping, it took some time to arrange them all in a group in the drawing room to have a photograph taken. The children had to be brought in from the woods and made respectable. Allan had a cut knee, and since his place was to be a prominent one, at the front, the bleeding had to be stopped and the wound disguised.

Florence was whisked upstairs and came back looking pleased with herself in a pink taffeta dress with wide embroidered skirt. When all else had been attended to, Fergus had to talk Mrs. Veitch out of a superstitious reluctance to be photographed at all. At last, Mr. Henderson, from Helensburgh, was able to go under his black velvet shroud. At a signal his spotty young assistant braced himself importantly, gave them all a warning glance and set off a pan of flash powder. Half a dozen plates were exposed, with much graoning and fidgeting from Mrs. Veitch and the children. Then the party was quickly transferred to the hall and the first-floor gallery while servants opened windows to clear the drawing room of smoke.

Mrs. Veitch tapped her chest a lot and complained that the fumes would probably be the death of her but seemed to forget the danger when Robert invited her to have a glass of sherry. "Not too sweet, dear," she cautioned him as he went off to give the butler his instructions about circulating the drinks and sweets for the children.

Colin Lindsay attempted to amuse the children with a conjuring set he had bought for the occasion in a trick shop in Argyle Street. Allan and Steven were mildly impressed, but Florence had her eyes firmly on the grown-ups.

"I hope Jack doesn't start following Mother about," she said anxiously. "Gordon said he's going to kill him if he does."

Colin tried not to look too startled at the casual revelation of this threat to his stepson. "Why should Jack follow your mother about, Florence?"

"I don't know, Uncle Colin. You're his father. Don't you know?"

"I'm his stepfather, Florence, and I don't know. But would it do any harm if he did follow your mother about?"

"It must, mustn't it? Or Gordon wouldn't say he was going to kill him if he did."

"Well, Gordon must think so, but didn't he explain?"

Florence frowned. "No. I asked him to, but he wouldn't. I suppose it must be something pretty dreadful, or Gordon wouldn't make such a mystery of it. I wondered if it could have anything to do with Jack wanting to kiss mother, or anything like that."

Colin's narrow white face twitched. He almost dropped the cards he was shuffling as he looked round to see if this worrying conversation could be overheard.

"Do you think it could have anything to do with kissing, Uncle Colin? Or . . . you know . . . touching?"

"I shouldn't think so at all, Florence." Colin was becoming more and more flustered. "I can't imagine why you should think a thing like that."

Florence's eyes widened in disbelief. "I'm sure you must, Uncle Colin. After all, kissing and touching is the usual reason for men following women about."

Steven yawned and Allan tugged at Colin's sleeve in an effort to get him to complete a trick that involved two matchboxes and a pair of dice.

"I'm sure you're absolutely wrong in this case. Your mother is Jack's aunt. Men don't have feelings like that about their aunts. Besides, your mother is twice as old as Jack."

Florence seemed to see the force in this argument. "I suppose so," she said. "But I wish I knew. If I get a chance later, I'll ask Jack if he knows what Gordon means. Or, better still, I'll ask Mother."

"No, I wouldn't trouble either of them," Colin said hurriedly, brushing aside his matchboxes and thrusting a pack of cards at Steven with a brusque invitation to him to pick one. "Not at a party. I'm sure you must have misunderstood Gordon. But whatever it is, I'm sure it's not important. I would be inclined to forget all about it. . . . Oh, look!"

He turned gratefully as a babble of voices and some hand-clapping came from the far end of the drawing room, to which most of the guests had now returned. "Aunt Gwen is going to play and Jack is going to sing."

"Show us another trick, Uncle Colin," Allan begged, preferring Colin's amateurish magic to the tedium of someone's singing.

"In a little while," Colin said, examining his stepson closely for a sign of something that he might have missed before.

"My love is fair and flower-fresh, her hair the sun, her eyes the stars," Jack sang in a good baritone.

"Soppy," Steven muttered. "I prefer the bagpipes." He nudged his brother. "Isn't it soppy?"

"I don't know," Allan said. "I'm only a child."

"Well, I enjoyed that," Mrs. Veitch said when the song was finished and the applause over. "Didn't you, Gordon?"

"Not very much, I'm afraid," Gordon said and moved off quickly from where he had been sitting on the arm of her chair.

"What strange moods Gordon takes," Mrs. Veitch said to Aunt May. "Not at all like Jack."

"His father had a good singing voice," Aunt May remembered. "Such a distinguished, soldierly man. It was all so sad."

They sat for a moment or two, recalling the troubled past.

"Gwen seems very happy now, with Colin, but I suppose she must sometimes wonder. . . ." Mrs. Veitch turned as Rita joined them. "I was just saying to Aunt May how Gwen must worry about Jack. She must watch him grow more like his father in appearance, and she wouldn't be human if she didn't wonder if he might one day be the heartbreak his father was."

She stopped, as if expecting Rita to agree with her. Instead, Rita said, "Do you find that chair quite comfortable, Mother?"

Mrs. Veitch ignored the enquiry. She was not so easily deflected. "My own belief is that Jack is a steady and upright young man. Oh, I don't doubt he'll make some hearts flutter and maybe break some. The tobacco he smokes is rather noxious, I admit, and from what I hear he rather likes the effect malted liquor has on the brain. But what of it? He will outgrow all that."

She looked challengingly at Rita and then at Aunt May. Neither spoke. Rita marvelled in silence at her mother's airy tolerance.

"I hear he's hardworking and quite brilliant at anything he's given to do," Mrs. Veitch went on. "There should be a good future for him with King and Company. I hope Robert gives him a good salary. What a pity he has no money of his own." She turned to Aunt May and lowered her voice a little. "His father left practically nothing, you know, and I don't think Gwen allows him very much. Well . . ." She sighed. "I suppose it's understandable."

"Is it?" Rita asked icily.

"Of course. Surely you must know why, my dear?"

"No, I don't know why, Mother. And I don't want to know." Rita was determined her mother wouldn't get an opening from her for one of her indiscretions. But the old lady would not be silenced.

"It's because of what we've just been talking about. Gwen's natural worry that Jack might have inherited some flaw from his father."

She paused for a moment, her pale eyes staring thoughtfully past them to where Jack stood in conversation with Fergus. "Well, I don't know. Too much money can be ruinous for a young man, but so can too little. There has to be a balance."

"He'll get Gwen's money, in time," Rita said, stung to a reply despite herself. "One day Jack will be rich."

"One day." Mrs. Veitch peered bleakly at the carpet, as if remembering the difficulties of her own early years as the wife of a struggling solicitor. "You mean one day when he is middle-aged?"

"I'm sure Jack has enough for his needs, meantime," Rita said, exasperation making her raise her voice. She collected herself with a start and turned decisively from her mother to Aunt May. "Fiona will have given you the news about Robert?"

"I was thrilled."

"Well, I wasn't," Mrs. Veitch said.

"Why ever not, Mother?"

"Well, just imagine! Robert running off at his age to make a fool of himself in Parliament."

"Really!" Rita made a note to see that the old lady had no more sherry. "How do you know he'll do that?"

Mrs. Veitch looked at her pityingly. "Well, they all do, dear, don't they?"

Aunt May leaned forward. "What absolutely fascinated me is the suggestion that Fiona should take Robert's place at the head of the business."

Mrs. Veitch craned her neck. "Fiona as head of the business?"

"Yes."

"Surely not? You must have misunderstood."

"No, Aunt May has not misunderstood," Rita said irritably. She looked quickly round the room to see where they all were. "Fergus would be very annoyed if he knew we were sitting here discussing the affairs of King and Company, but it is very probable that when Robert goes to Par-

92

liament, Fiona will take his place. The directors have asked her to assume the responsibility. It is entirely up to her whether she accepts or not. She has spoken to me about it and I have advised her that if she has the support of the board and is prepared to take on such a burden, then she should not hesitate."

Mrs. Veitch made a dismissive sound. "It won't work."

"Why will it not work?"

"She's a woman. Women do not head great businesses."

"Only because men have never been progressive enough to let them try. Well, King and Company has always been a progressive business. If the men are willing, it's ridiculous that you should scoff at the idea. It's your sort of backward attitude, Mother, that has helped men keep women under their thumbs."

Rita's eyes were sparkling, but her indignation collapsed into confusion as she saw her mother's mischievous expression.

"I must tell Fergus what you've been saying, Rita. I'm sure he will be very interested to hear your views about men."

"Oh, Mother!"

Aunt May saw her chance to remind them that Fiona came from her side of the family. "Fiona's father would have been so proud of her."

"If ever a man believed that the Almighty had created a place for women and that they should be kept there, it was your brother," Mrs. Veitch said mercilessly.

"Oh, I'm sure you are mistaken, Mrs. Veitch. We all know Roderick put Fiona in charge of Lochbank Distillery for long spells when she was hardly past twenty."

"We all know that when that happened, Roderick Fraser was flat in bed with a heart ailment. He didn't have much choice but to let Fiona sit at his desk."

"The point is that it worked," Aunt May said stoutly. "Fiona did much more than just sit at Roderick's desk." She turned abruptly to Rita. "Be all that as it may, what I've been waiting to ask you about, my dear, is this other news I've heard concerning James. Is it true he's going to bury himself in some outlandish place in the south of Scotland?"

Rita winced. This had been exactly her own description of James's plan.

"I'm afraid it is. Neither Fergus nor I approve, but nothing we say sways James in the slightest. His mind is apparently made up. He has always been very determined."

"Changes," Mrs. Veitch said. "Everywhere changes. It's a pity the boy has never seen fit to marry. I did my best to talk him out of that silly painting business when he was young. None of these artists ever lead normal, sensible domestic lives. I hope this isn't James going off to starve

93

himself in the equivalent of a garret. That's what they do abroad, apparently."

Rita struggled between alarm and irritation. The old lady really was being very trying today. James was comfortably sprawled in a chair with a whisky in one hand and his pipe in the other, deep in conversation with Gordon. *He's just an overgrown boy*, Rita thought. *He doesn't realise how he'll miss the comforts of home.* Her dismay at James's plans was suddenly uncontrollable.

"Oh, I don't know how he'll manage all on his own," she said in an anguish of worried love for her son. "He has never been away from Park Place for more than a few days at a time since his accident, and then always with friends. If he enjoyed robust health, I would not be so concerned, but there is hardly a day when he does not suffer some pain. People do not realise that." She sighed. "James imagines even I do not know. He never complains, but I do know. I am his mother. I can see. And, of course—" she shook her head— "sometimes it is so compelling the poor boy has to find some way of making it bearable. On these occasions, I'm afraid, James drinks far too much whisky. It's only a few times a year, thank goodness, but when it happens he often becomes quite unsteady. Here in Glasgow he has the sense to stay in his room or in his studio. But that is so neither Fergus nor I will see him. Down there on his own he won't have our feelings to consider. Will he be as careful? He could easily go out some day when not quite himself, and goodness knows what accident could happen to him."

She stopped as her mother prodded her with her stick. James had left Gordon and was crossing the room in their direction.

"Well, ladies, isn't this a marvellous party?" He beamed at them. "I can see by your expressions you're all enjoying yourselves tremendously. But your glasses are empty." He signalled to a maid with a tray. When they had selected drinks, he pulled over a chair. "Now, I'm going to sit down here and you must all say something to make me laugh. Then I'll get Gwen to play the piano and you can all sing 'Three Little Maids Are We.'"

"My dear!" Rita said with fond reproach, while her mother and Aunt May laughed at James's playful way of letting them know he had caught them gossiping.

Anne Dunbar inspected the lavish assortment of cream cakes that had been wheeled to their table in the Buchanan Street tearoom. She said, "Tea is such an innocent activity compared to dinner."

After much indecision she selected a sumptuous pastry layered with

94

chocolate and copiously decorated with candied angelica. Gordon slavishly chose a piece of the same confection.

He waited until the pert young waitress had trundled the creaking trolley to another table and said, "I thought dinner would have been more of an occasion."

"Oh, it would have been, but too much so," she said blithely. Cream spread richly across her plate as she stuck a fork into the flaky pastry. "Tea between a married woman and a man who is not her husband can be explained, even if with difficulty. Tea, after all, can happen by accident." She cast an astute glance round the crowded room, gay with the chatter of fashionably dressed women shoppers. "Even complete strangers are sometimes compelled to share a table for tea. Dinner, on the other hand, is a premeditated event. It is an intimate ritual with a deliberately chosen companion. Above all, tea is an end in itself; dinner, often a mere prelude to something else."

Her frankness enthralled him, but before he could speak she went on. "No. Here we are safe. But to be seen dining together . . ." Her smile caressed him with such a suggestion of secrets shared that his heart almost burst. "Even I couldn't think of a story to explain away candlelight and wine."

Gordon felt absurdly happy. Little more than a week ago she had been a dreamlike vision among the flowers on the shores of a distant loch, beyond his reach, glimpsed for a few dazzling moments and then disappearing as if forever. His longing for her had been immediate, defying all reason. The omens had been disastrously unfavourable. And yet, the barriers had all melted away. A few swift and mysterious steps had brought them miraculously together. He told himself that they had been made for each other. He was bewitched and dizzy with the wonder of it. Her astonishing transition—from virago through cool liar to worldly companion of an illicit afternoon tea—he accepted uncritically. He thought her the loveliest girl among the many in the room, the bone structure of her face perfect under the smooth skin, her shining hair carefully arranged round a scrap of a hat that matched the pale pink of her blouse. Only the strained expression that came and went from her eyes was puzzling. The odd word Gwen had used flashed into his mind. "Burdened." Superficially it could not have been less apt, but for a moment he had a glimmering of insight. Then the blanket of his own delight fell across the moment of perception.

His sense of intimacy with her was enormous. "I can hardly believe I'm really sitting here with you," he confided. "I was so afraid you wouldn't come."

She smiled at his eagerness. "I almost didn't." He shivered at the reali-

95

sation of how easily this happiness could have escaped him. "After all, it's pointless." Her quiet seriousness was in confusing contrast to her earlier poised exuberance.

"No," he said. It was a heartfelt mixture of plea and protest. A woman at the next table paused in her chatter to give him a curious glance.

Anne gave him a warning look and lowered her own voice. "But it must be."

"Then why did you come?"

She retreated into an evasive smile. "You were so very persistent."

"And you were simply rewarding my persistence?"

"You could say that." She was still smiling, but it was clear she did not want him to pursue her reasons.

During the next hour her manner underwent a series of disconcerting changes. Gaiety suddenly trailed off into moody silence. Warmth took on an edge of challenge. From being a wicked lady she became a vulnerable waif, dressed in clothes that did not belong to her, looking through haunted eyes to some scene beyond the tearoom.

He remembered his father's words: "She's said to be every bit as wayward and uncontrolled as Dunbar himself." Certainly, he had already seen a great many different Anne Dunbars. To which one should he reach out? For an instant, doubt at the wisdom of his passion for her rose in him and then was gone.

They had arrived separately, and she said it would be sensible if they left in the same way. As she made positive signs of being ready to go, he became filled with a deep sense of loss. In view of what she had said earlier, she would hardly agree to meet him again. But he must try. He couldn't just let her walk away. "Couldn't we have tea . . . just once more? Perhaps next week?"

He was baffled, but too grateful to show it, when she accepted his woebegone plea almost without hesitation.

6

It was a rough election, fought under the war clouds threatening from South Africa and, so far as one of the candidates was concerned, under the banner of socialism. Several of Robert's meetings ended in riot, with halls wrecked or in flames and speakers mauled.

By the end of the first week's campaigning he hardly had a suit of clothes that hadn't been splattered with egg yolk or rotten fruit. Fiona, as she kept coats and trousers shuttling between Claremont Row and a nearby valet service, frequently expressed wonder at this strange turn in their lives.

"Why you should want to become involved in rowdyism like this I simply can't understand," she said one morning as she stepped over another ruined garment lying on his dressing-room floor.

"It's the intervention of that damned socialist," he said. "If it had been left to the Liberal and myself, it would have been a less boisterous fight. Anyway, this sort of thing stops as soon as the campaign ends. Members of Parliament don't spend their lives dabbing egg yolk from their waistcoats."

"I'm glad to hear it."

That he enjoyed the battle was obvious. There was an elated gleam in his eyes even when the air was so full of missiles that the platform had to be evacuated. But after three weeks of it, Fiona was bored and tired. Her social round was in ruins. To have been at his side when he faced a rioting mob would at least have been stimulating, but he was careful to leave her at home when he went into areas where trouble was known to threaten. Perversely, he insisted she should be with him when he addressed gatherings of somnolent supporters in staunch Tory districts.

With one such drab occasion in prospect, she tried to be excused. He was sympathetic but said he couldn't spare her. "It's most important that the candidate's wife be there. The ladies expect to see her at his side. They like to assess her dress sense. A nice hat is worth at least five hundred votes."

"Oh, Robert, I hate being trailed round all these draughty halls, listening to the same dreary speeches and the same boring questions and answers."

"So that's what you think of my brilliant campaign?"

"Truthfully, yes. But if it's any comfort to you, the other man—the Liberal candidate—is even worse, judging by the reports of his speeches in the *Herald*." She handed him his tie. "So, you see, bored as I am, I am on your side."

"That's something, I suppose." He steered her gently toward her dressing room. "Now, please get ready, or we'll be late."

"Oh, all right. If you insist. At least it will be over and done with next week." She stopped as if another unwelcome thought had just come to her. "Then you'll spend all your time in London, leaving me to struggle with the cares of King and Company."

He took her hands and pulled her close. "Now, there's no need to pretend. I'm sure you're looking forward eagerly to the exercise of all that power. I've been watching, and I can see the idea has taken hold of you."

She coloured slightly. He was right, but it did not seem proper to admit it. "Beast," she said. "You left me with no choice. You simply dumped the whole business in my lap."

He kissed her lightly and went back to his mirror. "Anyway, you seem very sure I'll win. The battle's not over yet, by a long way."

She turned at the door of the dressing room. "Oh, you'll win, Robert, despite the eggs and the mouldy apples. It would take a miracle for the Liberal to come out on top, and neither the socialist nor that nice independent man has a chance. They'll both lose their deposits. Unless old Russell Mathieson's twenty-four thousand supporters all died with him, you can't possibly lose."

He shook his head in humorous reproof. "What a terribly cynical view you take, my dear. Not a word about my charming manner or my persuasive arguments. Not a word about all the hours I've spent. . . ."

He stopped as a hoarse shout came from the street. Next instant a brick came through the window and the room was full of broken glass and flapping curtains.

There were other incidents—including the overturning of his carriage—but close to midnight on polling day, the returning officer came to the steps of Whitehill Public Hall, where the votes had been counted, and declared Robert elected with a majority only slightly less than that of his predecessor.

Next day, after a celebration lunch in White's Chop House, he found himself facing Douglas Dunbar in the corridor outside the dining room. He tried to walk on, but Dunbar, his well-dressed frame seeming to fill the narrow space between rows of plants on marble pedestals, blocked the way, blowing cigar smoke.

"So things became too much for you, King?" There was a sneer in the deep voice.

"Too much for me?" Robert's stare was cold and blank.

"Aye." He tapped his *Herald*, with its report of Robert's victory. "You're running away, aren't you?" He made it sound self-evident.

"I've been elected to Parliament, if that's what you mean."

"That's what I said." He grinned complacently. "You're running away. Everybody in the trade knows it." He flicked cigar ash from his sleeve.

"I really don't have time to waste listening to your childish nonsense."

"You've been reduced to hiding behind your wife's skirts. I've heard all about your arrangements."

"I don't think King and Company's arrangements concern you."

"You're making yourself a laughingstock."

Robert's expression was contemptuous, but the gibe hurt. "Do you mind standing aside."

Dunbar responded by splaying his legs and tipping his hat jauntily off his brow. With his thumbs fixed in the pockets of his brocade waistcoat, his jutting elbows almost touched the pedestals on either side of the corridor. The invitation was plain.

When Robert ignored it, Dunbar pressed on. "Don't think it'll make any difference to me. I'll show her no quarter. I'll make no allowance for her being a woman."

"I'm sure you won't. But then, no one who knows you would expect you to."

Dunbar seemed to take it as a compliment. Sounds of approval rumbled out of his broad chest. "Just so long as you both know," he said, nodding comfortably.

Robert made a gesture of baffled impatience. "Why do you insist on acting as if we were waging war instead of simply earning a living?"

Dunbar put the remains of his cigar in a flower pot and leaned malevolently forward. "Because so far as I'm concerned, King, it *is* war. That's why I'd rather it was you than your pretty lady wife. I don't like crushing a woman."

Robert held down his anger. "I'll let her know," he said calmly. "It will be a comfort to her." Dunbar was clearly enjoying himself, and to let him see his taunts were having an effect would only increase his pleasure.

"And then there's this great big secret you've got up your sleeves."

"What secret?"

"Queen's Royal!"

His eyes sparkled as he watched for the effect. He guffawed triumphantly as anger flashed uncontrollably across Robert's face. "You didn't think I knew about that, did you?"

"I really hadn't given you a thought."

"Man, you hadn't a chance of keeping your precious secret. Tongues wag in this trade. Usually, I suppose, because they're so well oiled." He laughed again.

Robert felt forced to comment. "With labels and cases being made, I don't think anyone could imagine we were trying to proceed secretly." Inwardly he vowed that if either the printer or case-maker had been gossiping, they would trade no more with King & Co.

"Don't think toadying to the palace will save your neck. I'll still drive you to the wall. *Queen's Royal!*" His pose of lighthearted mockery suddenly slipped. His face twisted bitterly. "It sounds like a drink for bloody cissies." His disgust was obviously heartfelt.

Whatever the consequences, it was an opening too great to be rejected. "Then I must remember to send you a bottle," Robert said loudly. "In the meantime, I'll thank you to get out of my way."

He braced himself, ready for violence if it came, almost hoping for it.

For a long, dumbfounded interval, Dunbar eyed him murderously, hands twitching. Glasses clinked and somewhere along the corridor men laughed.

As if emerging from a trance to a frustrating realisation of where they were, Dunbar stepped ponderously aside with a shuddering sigh. He raised an iron ball of a fist as Robert pushed past. "My God, King, the sooner you're in London, out of the reach of this, the better."

The encounter filled Robert with fresh doubts. Was it fair, even safe, leaving Fiona to cope with the Black Douglas? For a long time he had been a threat, but an unseen and distant threat, waging an impersonal campaign from behind an office desk. Now his hatred seemed to be overflowing into an urge to physical violence. Everyone in the trade knew bluster was one of his weapons. Usually, much of it could be ignored, but today his words and manner had seemed to hold additional menace.

Robert was still brooding when later in the afternoon he joined Fiona, Gwen, Fergus and Rita at St. Enoch Station, to see James off on the slow journey to his new life in Fleetside.

100

"Write as soon as you arrive, so that we'll know you're safe," Rita pleaded.

"It's not America I'm going to, Mother," James protested, but he promised.

He looked thin and almost woebegone in his black clothes, among the crowds of casually dressed suntanned people returning from early holidays at resorts on the Ayrshire coast. Although he would not have admitted it, he was not looking forward to his late-night arrival at the shuttered house in the small southern town, or to the bother over the next week or so of engaging staff and turning a neglected holiday retreat into a smoothly running permanent home. Rita had accustomed him to comfort and regular meal times.

Fergus, still searching for a little comfort in the situation, said cheerfully, "At least, James, you should benefit from the change of air."

"Yes." James brightened. "I mean to work in the open whenever possible, as I used to do in the old days, at Ardfern. I've been collecting cobwebs in the studio for far too long."

"I hope you'll remember to wrap up well," Rita said anxiously. "This wonderful weather won't last forever."

They stood on the platform, waving until the train had disappeared abruptly into a tunnel.

"I'm glad James has gone," Gwen said with a sudden rush of feeling. They turned to her in surprise, for throughout the send-off she had said little.

Her next words were even more startling. "There are too many evil tongues in Glasgow. James could only have been hurt if he had stayed here."

One by one they stopped, an astonished group standing among the suitcases and barrows.

"Really, Gwen, I can't think what you mean." Fergus was eyeing her apprehensively.

Gwen cast a regretful glance at Rita. "I probably shouldn't have spoken in Mother's presence, but she has the same right to know as the rest of us." She tugged agitatedly at her gloves.

Rita's eyes were wide. "Know what, Gwen?"

"A lot of people who come into my shop are interested in paintings as well as in antiques. Some of them don't realise I'm James's sister. They say things—hurtful, even dreadful, things."

"Oh, God," Robert groaned.

Gwen turned to him. "You sound as if you know what I'm talking about, Robert?"

He gave an unhappy nod. "I have heard certain remarks."

Fergus was baffled. "What kind of remarks? Speak plainly."

101

"Wicked remarks."

"Surely not about James?"

"I'm afraid they *were* about James."

Rita, who had been looking from one to the other with growing puzzlement, interrupted. "What are people saying about James?" She tilted her chin in a little gesture of defiance. "Tell me immediately."

Robert looked away.

"It's about his painting, Mother." Gwen's voice was uncertain, and she looked now as if she regretted having raised the matter. "The subject matter of his painting, the motif that runs through all his work."

"Well? What is wrong with the motif?" She looked helplessly at Fergus, as if to be reassured that she knew what the word meant. "It's the children . . . the beautiful children he paints?"

Fergus patted her arm without looking at her. "Let Gwen go on, my dear." He was staring at his daughter with tense fascination.

"Apparently there are evil-minded people who find it . . . somehow sinister . . . that James paints only little girls."

"But"—in her relief Rita made a small laughing sound—"don't they understand James paints little girls because they are sweet and innocent, and because . . . well, because they make nice pictures posed among the flowers and the woodland blossom?"

"In the family we all understand that, Mother, and so would these people if they knew James as we do. But they don't. To them he is just a name. They don't realise—they don't care—how cruel and unjust their slanders are."

The skin under Fergus's eyes and round his nose had gone white. "What are these innuendoes?"

Gwen closed her eyes. "They seem to think James's painting betrays something obsessive and unhealthy."

"It's outrageous to say such things about James." Fergus's voice was hoarse with fury. "My God, James's work is the embodiment of innocence. Anyone who knew the boy . . . " He turned accusingly on Robert. "How long have you known about these rumours?"

Robert avoided his father's gaze, looking past him to the carefree crowds waiting for excursion trains to Gourock, where steamers lay ready to sail on evening cruises on the firth. "A year. Two years, perhaps." *Damn Gwen*, he thought, *for raising such an embarrassing business in such a place.*

"You should have told me. I had a right to know."

"I suppose so, but it was so unpleasant. I hoped it was just idle gossip that would soon stop." His mouth twisted angrily. "If only James would occasionally—just occasionally—paint something other than those damned little girls. That's what I always hoped. I even hinted at it once

102

or twice, but he never seemed to catch on. An occasional landscape or a still life or two would have given the lie to their vile stories."

Fergus jabbed his stick viciously at the paving. "My God, Robert, it almost sounds as if you have some sympathy with these rumour mongers."

"Don't be ridiculous, Father. I despise them."

"Well, the first one that opens his filthy mouth to me will find himself hauled into court." He pointed his stick accusingly. "And that's what you should have done. Put the law on them."

Robert looked about uneasily, but no one seemed interested in the tense group they formed amid the locomotive steam and the shafts of sunlight reaching down dustily from the glass roof.

"I really don't think it would, Father," he said. "Legal action would give the gossip a status it doesn't deserve. Whatever the outcome of an action for slander, people are so warped they would say there was no smoke without fire. What good would that do to James's name? It's better to ignore it. Anyway, it's all too vague, too whispered, to take legal action against."

Fergus was not satisfied, and as he mulled over the confusion of information thrust so rudely on him, a new thought came.

"You're keeping very quiet, Fiona. I hope you don't take the same view as Robert? Still lifes, indeed!" His present mood was one they knew well; he was looking for trouble.

"No, Grandfather," Fiona said quietly. "I don't see why James should paint things he doesn't want to paint just to please other people. I've been quiet because I'm so shocked. I've never heard anything so disgraceful. And James is so sensitive, so vulnerable. These rumours would injure him terribly if they were to reach him."

She caught sight of Rita's face. "Oh, now, look what we've done to Grandmother. She looks positively faint. Robert! Take your mother's other arm." She pointed. There was an entrance to St. Enoch Hotel in a corner of the station. "Let's go into the hotel and sit for a little while. We can order tea."

Robert produced his watch and compared it pointedly with the station clock. "I suppose I could just about manage tea," he said.

As they sat at a window in the hotel lounge, overlooking the church in the square, Fiona tried to be amusing, but Rita's mind was still firmly fixed on the slander of her younger son.

"Who are these people?" she asked as Fiona ended a story from Robert's election campaign. "Are they people James has perhaps offended in some way?"

"No, Mother," Gwen said. "They are people who would not know James even if they bumped into him. They are simply scandal mongers passing on lurid gossip."

When the tea came, Rita stared at the silver trays and plate stands, too bemused to pour or to help Fiona hand round the plates of dainty sandwiches and scones.

She shook her head and her voice was plaintive. "I simply don't understand. What is James supposed to have done? All he does is take simple, everyday things, like children gathering snowdrops or rolling Easter eggs, and paint them. What is being implied?"

Robert looked hopefully at Gwen, but she seemed unable or unprepared to elaborate.

"I'm damned if I know, myself, Mother," he said with an awkward glance at Fergus. "No one ever says quite what is meant. The thing is always left hanging in the air."

And clearly, from their expressions, they approved of his leaving it in the air, so far as Rita was concerned.

Fergus, who had been making a lot of noise with his cup and saucer, said, "What appals me is that these slanders could follow James to Fleetside. Small communities are notoriously prone to gossip. He could be even more vulnerable there."

Gwen disagreed. "No. That is why I am glad James has gone away. It is only people who do not know him who could harbour these terrible thoughts. In a small town James will be known to everyone. If these stories do follow him, the people will know they are lies. They will give them no credence."

A frightful thought came to Rita. "It isn't possible that James has already heard this gossip, is it? That that is why he has gone away? To hide?"

"Absolutely not." Fiona was positive. "James has gone away full of hope for his painting. I had a long talk with him about it on our last outing. He is looking forward to doing good work in Galloway. He has no other motive."

"Poor James," Rita said, still not fully understanding. "As if he hasn't misfortune enough to contend with."

7

During that month Gordon and Anne met perhaps a half dozen times, eventually becoming bold enough to forsake the safety of their tearoom for the greater risk of strolls along the shady banks of the river at Kelvingrove. Because of his work, their hours together were usually on a Saturday afternoon. The many contradictory facets of her personality fascinated and enslaved him, arousing in him a turmoil of conflicting emotions—some tender and lofty, others lustful. Physically their relationship was static. They held hands as they walked, and when they were certain no one could see, they exchanged hasty kisses. The world of their stolen meetings was too circumscribed for more.

Gradually he learned a little about her, idealising each detail of the picture that emerged. She had married when she was barely eighteen. Her son was now two years old. He had her father's middle name: Malcolm. Her husband, who was six years her senior, had been so immersed in building his practice as a stock and share broker that several nights a week from the earliest days of their marriage he had left her alone while he pursued business after office hours at the clubs or homes of his clients. Anne had been left to find what solace she could in such solitary pursuits as reading, music or sewing. Even when she returned to her father she was hardly less alone. Her mother had been dead for almost three years. Dunbar had solicitously insisted on engaging a nursemaid to help her with Malcolm. He had a houskeeper to supervise his servants. Consequently, she led a life of indolence and introspection. She had few friends.

He absorbed the facts with adoring sympathy. One day he said, "I can't imagine us ever quarrelling, Anne. Why can't you get on with your husband? Why did you fight?"

They were in a cab in the carriageway of the West End park. She was watching the swans on the river. "Because I was bored," she said, turning to him. Suddenly her eyes flashed and words were bursting from her in a petulant torrent. "Bored, bored, bored! All I did was sit by myself and think about things I wanted to forget. Day after day, week after week, it was the same. Nothing ever changed. I felt my life was over."

The outburst stopped as suddenly as it started. She sat with her hands tightly clenched in her lap. Then, with a sad, self-mocking smile, she answered his unspoken question.

"Of course, with father my life can hardly be said to be dramatically different. But at least there are no rows. From father I don't expect as much."

From him, he was certain, she expected more than she was getting. Desperately he varied the pattern of their meetings, taking her rowing on a loch in the south side of the city, even rambling in the country. But the opportunity he was seeking continued to elude him. He became almost frantic with frustration, convinced her desire was as strong as his and fearful that if he continued to fail her, she would become as bored with him as she was with her husband. The prospect filled him with desolation. The humiliating realisation of his gauche inexperience racked him.

"My God, Anne," he blurted at the end of another unsuccessful afternoon, "I don't think we'll ever manage to be alone." His face was twisted with a confused mixture of apology and self-pity.

She said simply, "It isn't easy at our age. Older men have apartments. Or they have the aplomb to book into hotels."

She wasn't taunting him, but he felt childlike and useless. He was nagged by the thought that Jack Hoey would have managed the situation better. He couldn't imagine his having wasted all these weeks drinking tea and inhaling country air with a girl who had made it clear her expectations were identical to his own.

Her voice roused him from his gloom.

"I was perfectly alone yesterday for a time. Completely cut off from the world."

Her manner was bright, but he sensed a slight embarrassment in her voice.

He said carefully, "Were you? Where?"

"In a train."

He could not hide his surprise. "A train?"

She giggled slightly. " A railway train."

A tremor went through him at the thought of what she seemed to be suggesting. He was almost shocked. "Where were you going?" He cursed himself for the inadequacy of his response.

"Paisley," she said. "I had to go there on an errand for father, and the coach wasn't available. I had a very comfortable compartment entirely to myself. Once the train leaves Glasgow, no one can get on until it stops at Paisley."

His confidence soared as he realised that he had not misread her meaning.

"I've always had an urge to travel," he said with sudden gaiety. "For years I've dreamed of seeing Paisley. They say the thread mills are beautiful by moonlight. Perhaps we could journey there together?"

Although the words were lighthearted, he watched her intently, terrified to see some sign that she was, after all, only teasing him.

"Not by moonlight," she said, smilingly playing with the ribbons of her dress. "I have to be at home long before that."

"But you will . . . come to Paisley?"

"Yes." Then, as if to dispel the sudden solemnity, she mimicked him. "The route goes through some of the most exotic places. There are wonderful glimpses to be had of secret Glasgow. The line runs alongside the docks for part of the way. I had a wonderful view yesterday of a really big ship getting ready to sail."

Nursemaids bounced babies on the grass only yards from the park bench on which they sat, but he kissed her.

"I can't guarantee you'll see anything of the docks this time," he said bravely. He looked eagerly about. "If a cab comes, we could be at the station in fifteen minutes."

She laughed at his impatience. "Not today, Gordon. You can't whisk me off to far Paisley without warning. Beside, this is the wrong time of day. The factories and shipyards will be coming out soon. The trains will be busy. The middle of the afternoon is the time. Hardly anyone is travelling then. We'll go tomorrow."

He looked crestfallen. "It'll have to be next week, Anne. I couldn't make another excuse to leave the office tomorrow."

"Then we'll have something to look forward to," she said.

When they had arranged the day and the time she told him, "I'll see you at the train. That will be safer. You get the tickets and stand at the carriage window, where I'll see you."

"First-class tickets, I suppose?"

"Of course."

He was in the station almost a half hour before the train came into the platform. He was the first through the barrier and was relieved to see only a handful of passengers. He selected a compartment and spent the next few minutes fidgeting uneasily every time someone walked up the platform, fearful that the person might join him. Then he relaxed as he realised that if this happened, all he need do was get out and move farther up the train. There were more compartments empty than occupied.

As the departure time approached, Anne not having appeared, he paced about in an agony of suspense, dashing to the window every time he heard footsteps. At last she came, her cheeks flushed from hurrying. As he helped her up the high step, the guard's whistle blew.

He stood with his arms round her. "Did you misjudge the time? My heart was missing beats."

She leaned back as if to see him better. "I had doubts about coming," she said in a subdued voice. "But I hadn't the strength to heed them."

It was her first direct and uncomplicated declaration of her feelings for him.

"I love you, Anne," he said, staggering as the train moved off jerkily. "I love you."

He thought she was going to cry. Her eyes filled, and to hide the tears she put her cheek against his. "Oh, my darling." Her arms tightened round him. "Everything is against us. Don't you know that?"

The words hardly registered. At that moment he did not want to know. That was not what they had come to this swaying, rattling box for. He began to kiss her, easing her back on the dull brown upholstery.

She took her lips away. "You must pull the window blinds," she said breathlessly.

"Oh, God. I forgot." The train was gathering speed as it left the maze of lines converging on the station. He had a confused impression of lampposts and signal masts hurrying past the window. "Another thing I forgot. How long before the train stops at Paisley?"

"Eighteen minutes," she said with a sad smile. "Almost no time at all."

8

Fiona saw Robert formally installed at the Palace of Westminster and then spent several weeks helping him plan the redecoration of the residential flat they kept on the upper floor of the house in St. James's that was the London headquarters of King & Co.

"It will be beautiful," she said when the long and tiring job of selecting colours, fabrics and carpets was completed. "We should have done this sooner."

Robert nodded. "It was all right for a few days, every now and again," he said, "but now that it's more or less going to be home for me. . . ."

He stopped as her expression changed.

"I'm sorry, Fiona. I put that rather badly. Home, of course, will always be where you and the chrildren are, but I feel I should make the most of this place."

"Of course you should. But it will be odd with you down here and the rest of us in Glasgow. You usually have been some other place for most of our marriage, but somehow it was different when you were travelling. You weren't rooted in another place. You were away, but you were still part of the household. Now it's almost as if you're going to have a separate existence." She looked round the elegant drawing room with its Adam fireplace and finely plastered ceiling, from which a large crystal chandelier hung. "And a rather stylish one at that." She crossed to the window. "There's even a tree and a bit of grass out there to remind you of home."

He came and stood beside her.

"A poor substitute for the view from Castle Gare. Nevertheless, I hope I get some time to look at it. You're carefully forgetting there's a busy office underneath this and below that a basement packed to the ceiling with cases of whisky. I'll be involved in all that by day and in the evenings I'll be at the House."

She took his arm. "I'll read the *Herald*'s Parliamentary report every day, to make sure you are. You must speak in all the debates, so that I can keep track of you."

"I'll write as often as I can."

The friends he introduced her to were staid business people, far removed from the fashionable and slightly scandalous centre of London society.

"How undeserved London's reputation for gaiety is," she said mischievously, after a boring evening of decorous singing and reciting at the home of one of his friends. "I'm sure there's much more sin in Glasgow."

He refused to be drawn, and after a few more days of sightseeing, dining out and theatregoing, she returned to Glasgow to take his place at the head of the board.

Gradually the long summer faded. The sunshine became more mellow and the smell of bonfires drifted along Garelochside. As the hills turned brown, a haze often settled on the tangle of dying bracken and twisted about the bare branches of birch trees.

Queen's Royal had been an immediate success. Its clientele had been ready-made, and numbered in the millions. With every city in Britain holding its own programme of events to celebrate the queen's jubilee, with manufacturers advertising jubilee dinner and tea sets, jubilee jewellery and silverware, jubilee souvenirs of every description, the idea of a Scotch whisky created as a tribute to the queen had exactly caught the national mood.

Almost every trade customer for King's Royal had placed an order for the new Queen's Royal. As Jack had predicted, the two bottles, with their complementary labels, soon sat on the shelves of every public house and licensed grocer's shop in the country.

Fiona could have had no more exhilarating introduction to the affairs of King & Co. Dunbar's inroads on the sales of King's Royal were almost forgotten among the more immediate problems of ensuring adequate supplies of cases, bottles and labels for the new whisky and the timely consignment of orders to agents in all the principal cities.

Fergus was delighted. As winter approached, he said, "If orders are like this now, what is it going to be like over Christmas and New Year?"

"We'll be hard put to it to meet the demand, I should think," Fiona said happily.

The words came back to her when, one day, early in the spring of

1898, Peter Ross came into her room looking tired and worried. He sat down absentmindedly without waiting for her invitation.

"I'm afraid something very odd is going on in the whisky market, Mrs. King," he said. "During the last two weeks I've written to all our usual people, or called on them personally if they were near enough, and not one of them has a single cask of twelve-year-old Aberlivet to sell."

Fiona frowned. "Why not?"

"There's been another big buyer on the market." He looked as if he could hardly believe his own explanation.

"But all the merchants and brokers we deal with must have known we would be coming back to them."

Ross looked glumly at his boots. "We had no contracts, Mrs. King." As he saw her expression, he said hurriedly, "There was no reason for us to bind ourselves to anything. Aberlivet has always been available. Of course, we knew the price would rise because of the demand we were creating, but that had to be accepted. It wouldn't have worried us."

She tried to hide her annoyance. The prudent thing would have been for them to safeguard their supply with contracts. But the whole concept of a jubilee whisky had been embraced and executed in haste, with the additional complication of Robert's departure. No one could reasonably be blamed.

She said, "You had better go back to all your contacts and buy whatever ten-year-old Aberlivet they have. I suppose it will do just as well as twelve-year-old?"

She looked at him enquiringly. She had an irreverent approach to the whisky mystique but knew an admission such as she was inviting would have to be wrung from Ross.

As he hesitated she said, "It is an emergency, after all." She watched the argument go on in his mind. Exasperation began to rise in her. "Now, Peter, I know Robert and you regard everything about whisky as sacred, but you can't seriously expect me to believe some staggering transformation takes place in Aberlivet, or in any other whisky, between the ages of ten and twelve years?"

Ross sighed and rubbed his hands unhappily together. The months he had spent perfecting that blend! Selecting, rejecting, worrying. He could see it all slipping away.

"I suppose ten-year-old might do in a pinch, Mrs. King," he said grudgingly, "but there isn't a cask of that available, either. The same buyer has taken up all the Aberlivet on the market over eight years old."

He knew from her eyes and the deliberate way she leaned forward what the next question would be.

"No, Mrs. King. We couldn't." He shook his head fiercely. "We couldn't use anything under eight years old. It would ruin the blend."

His voice was anguished. "Besides, we would have to change the label. We say there it's a blend of twelve-year-olds. It would be noticed if we changed it. An admission like that would do us terrible harm. King and Company have a reputation."

She sank back in her chair. "You don't have to remind me of that, Peter. I'm here to uphold it." She sat staring at him in silence for a few seconds. "Well, if you can't get Aberlivet of the right age, can you use some other whisky instead?"

Although—feeling it her duty to become familiar with every department of the business—she had spent hours in Ross's blending room, watching him go through the unbeautiful but vital procedure of sniffing, tasting and spitting, she still knew very little about whisky, as such. They all tasted very much the same to her—too pungent and too strong—and she frequently saddened Ross by telling him so. He despaired of her ever learning the art of blending, but she handled him skilfully, letting him know she appreciated how much of his patient experience went into every bottle of whisky they sold.

Today, Ross was too worried to give her the half-reproachful look her question would normally have earned. "I'm afraid not, Mrs. King. Aberlivet is a very distinctive whisky. It has a ripe, fruity flavour. There's nothing else quite like it, and there's so much of it in Queen's Royal that we simply must have it."

"Since there isn't any on the market, that's going to be difficult," she said tartly.

He took out his pipe and then, remembering where he was, hastily stuffed it back into his pocket. She waved her hand impatiently. "For goodness sake, smoke if you wish, Peter."

But already the idea had left him.

"There is only one thing we can do , Mrs. King. Find out who the mysterious buyer is and make him an offer."

"I shouldn't think we'll have to look very far."

"Douglas Dunbar?" He spoke the name almost fearfully.

"Who else could it be?"

"That's my own view. Whether a man like that will sell to us or not is a different matter. Aberlivet isn't one of his requirements. The only reason he could have for buying it was that he didn't want us to have it."

"He'll sell, all right," Fiona said, "but I shudder to think of the price he'll demand."

She rose angrily from her desk. "However, that's something we'll have to face some other day. What I want you to do today is find the traitor and dismiss him on the spot."

Ross was startled. "The traitor?"

"Someone must have told Dunbar Queen's Royal is based on Aberli-

112

vet. Without knowing that, there is no way he could have engineered this situation. Who, apart from yourself, knows?"

Ross tugged at his ear. "Well, in theory, quite a number of people could know. They can all see the names stencilled on the casks as they come in. But in fact only three men could be certain which whisky predominates."

"Which three?"

"The three who actually empty the casks into the blending vats. And the foreman blender, of course. But they're all just ordinary, conscientious men. I can't imagine—"

She interrupted him. "One of them betrayed the company to Dunbar. No doubt for money. I want him dismissed."

"It might not be easy to find out which one it was. I'll talk to them myself, but I hardly expect the culprit will confess."

His mind was less on retribution than on this sudden threat to his precious blend.

"He probably won't confess," Fiona said, "but his manner might give him away when you question him. If not, I suggest you leave him to his fellows."

Ross looked puzzled.

Fiona spelled it out. "Threaten to dismiss them all, the foreman included, if the guilty man isn't found. Then leave them to it. The innocent men will soon present you with the traitor."

Any reservations Ross had about her fitness to succeed Robert had soon gone. In some ways he preferred her. In the nine months since Robert had gone to London she had shown herself prepared to let them all run their departments, never interfering or questioning unless something went wrong. Even then there were no recriminations. She told them what she wanted done and left them to do it. So far, her advice had been sound. The smoothness of the change in power had been assisted by Robert's refusing to visit the office during the two short visits he had recently made to Glasgow. Fiona mixed more with the actual workmen than Robert had. Their initial shyness—or even resentment—at having a woman as "the boss" soon melted under her warm manner. Gradually they even seemed to find a certain distinction in the situation. The new feminine touch in the office section of the old building was obvious. Curtains appeared on previously bare windows and a regular Monday morning order for flowers had been placed with a small shop at the end of the lane. So far, the flowers were confined to Fiona's own room, Ross having hastily rejected her suggestion that a simple arrangement would wonderfully brighten his own rather dark office, the window of which looked upon a large expanse of soot-darkened brick.

Toward the end of the previous year she had released Gordon from

113

his bondage in the accounts department and handed him over to the blending-hall foreman. Robert's plan to have him learn distilling, with McNair, at Lochbank, had been postponed. Eventually he would go there, but by then Jack's apprenticeship should be over. To have the two of them permanently together in such an isolated place, with no distractions, seemed to Fiona a certain recipe for trouble, and an unnecessary one. Whether Gordon learned distilling before or after he learned blending was really immaterial to his education in the business. Harmony was more important.

Today, harmony seemed to be eluding her, for shortly after Ross had gone, Fergus came to see her. He was clearly upset.

"Is this true about Dunbar buying up all the available Aberlivet? I've been talking to Peter Ross." He nodded vaguely toward some part of the rambling building beyond her door, then went to a side table and poured himself a glass of sherry. She declined to accompany him.

"Someone has bought it up," she said. "We can only guess it's Dunbar."

He caught at his beard and tugged distractedly. "It takes me back twenty years to the pot distillers' boycott. Those were terrible days. I wouldn't want you to go through what Robert and I went through then."

"This is different, Grandfather. The pot distillers almost crushed King and Company. Dunbar can't do that, although he's a menace and his tactics are obviously to harass us in every possible way."

"But will he sell us the Aberlivet we need? That's the question."

"He must sell it. What good is it to him otherwise? Peter Ross says Queen's Royal will be destroyed if we can't get twelve-year-old Aberlivet. To his expert senses, that might be true. But if we really can't get Aberlivet, then obviously we will use something else, whatever Peter thinks, and whatever it does to the blend. We can't just abandon Queen's Royal. Anyway, I know it's heresy, but I don't believe the public would notice. It's only our pride that would be hurt. From what I've been told about him, Dunbar is clever enough to realise all that. If he drives us to use something else, we'll use it and leave him sitting with thousands of casks of Aberlivet he doesn't need. No, he'll hold us to ransom, but in the end he'll sell."

"It's damnable."

And very good business on the part of the Black Douglas, she thought with grudging admiration.

Fergus drank his sherry without enjoyment. "It's terribly unfair of Robert, going off and leaving you to cope with this, my dear. I'll help you all I can, of course, but I'm not as sharp as I used to be. No, not nearly as sharp." A sigh shook him. "Dear knows!"

114

His hair, she thought, was more snowy; his skin shiny and stretched tight over the bones.

"The first thing," she said, "is for Peter Ross to find out if it is Dunbar. Then we can decide how best to tackle him."

He nodded, and then his thought wandered. "How is Gordon liking his move to the blending hall?" He chuckled. "Delighted to get away from Andrew Paterson, no doubt?"

Fiona smiled. "The delight, I think, was mutual. But Gordon seems much more settled these days. The clerking job bored him. I know Robert worried about it a lot."

Fergus glowered as he put his empty glass carefully on her desk. "He didn't worry enough to stay at home and give the boy a father's support. And what's it all for? What sort of impression has he made down there in London, among the gasbags? What good is he doing either for himself or anyone else?"

It was a recurring refrain. No one had ever given him an answer, and now he no longer expected one. His mind moved on. "Rita had a letter from James this morning. He sounds well enough, but I don't know. It's difficult to tell from letters."

For fifty years large areas of his life had been blighted by doubts. They were inseparable from his introspective nature. Since Gwen's revelations of the gossip attaching to James's name, he had been unable to accept even the evidence his own ears and eyes gave him of James's well-being. In the autumn he had gone with Rita to spend a few days in Fleetside. They approved of the motherly housekeeper James had found and were enchanted with rural Galloway and the vast stretches of empty Solway shore. It was gentler than the Gareloch landscape. On both occasions James had been cheerful. Settling in had been a greater task than he had imagined, the whole house having to be redecorated, and he had been able to give little time to his work; but he was optimistic about the turn for the better his painting would take once he could get started.

Still, Fergus remained unconvinced, forever wondering if James knew what was being said about him behind his back. He never neglected an opportunity to speir for information, to make some dark, guarded remark even to comparative strangers and then watch closely for their reaction. That morning, because of an unexpected encounter, James was very much on his mind.

"On my way here I stopped in West George Street to look at the pictures in Alexander Reid's window," he said at last—tentatively, because he knew she would not approve. "I was just moving on when Reid himself came out. It must be a year since I last spoke to him. I couldn't resist asking if he had heard any of these scandalous stories about James."

Fiona's voice and expression were gently reproachful. "Really, Grandfather! I thought we all agreed the best thing to do was forget Gwen ever mentioned this unpleasantness."

"I can't forget," Fergus said simply. A shadow fell on him as the sun passed behind some chimneys on the other side of the street.

"But we agreed to try," she insisted, "in the hope that it would all die away. Personally, I'm sure it will."

"Well, I'm not. Once these things gain a hold, they have a habit of growing."

This was in fact her own fear, but she could not admit it to him. "To go about asking people, eternally fishing for information that can only be painful, isn't very wise, Grandfather." Sympathy rose in her as she saw his hands trembling. "Anyway, what did Mr. Reid say? I can see you want to tell me."

"Yes," He brightened, putting his elbows on her desk and leaning forward. "You know Reid's great reputation? No one in Scotland knows more about pictures. Some of our finest private collections have been built up through him. He was selling artists like Courbet, Daubigny and Corot in Glasgow before even the London dealers had realised their worth."

She smiled at his enthusiasm. "And didn't he give an exhibition of James's work?"

"Two," Fergus said proudly. "He was even good enough to say some of James's South Seas paintings were absolutely original. No matter how he tried, he couldn't find in them the influence of any other painter. You have no idea how great a tribute that was."

"It was no more than James deserved," she said proudly.

"It was years ago, of course, but I felt that if any man had a right to see anything unhealthy in James's later work, it was Alexander Reid. Well, I asked. And do you know what he said?" He took his elbows from her desk and sat back in his chair looking pleased.

"What did he say?"

"He said no history of Scottish painting will ever be complete without a description of the part played in its development by James."

"I'm sure it's no less than the truth, but it's wonderful to hear it from a man like Alexander Reid."

Fergus slid his empty sherry glass along the faded mahogany of her desk. For a while he sat staring at it. "I asked him outright about these stories. He admitted he had heard them." His face saddened and he rubbed his eyes in an almost childish gesture of pathetic bewilderment. "Apparently everybody knew except us, his family. Dear knows!" He leaned back for a moment, and when he spoke again, his voice was firm-

116

er. "Reid dismissed the stories and said everyone else who knows James does the same. He himself has always liked James's vision of childish innocence, limited though it is. Before we parted in George Square, he said something else that made me very proud. He compared James to Burns. He said they both found their best inspiration in the small and familiar things of the Scottish countryside—Burns in the open fields of Ayrshire, and James in the leafy lanes and shady bluebell woods of the Gareloch. Like Burns, James has shunned the pretentious. His artistic statements might all have been small ones, but he has expressed them, when he was at his best, with all the intensity Burns put into his poetry."

He lapsed into silence and sat, bent a little over his stick, uncertain whether to be worried or pleased.

Fiona lifted his glass. "Let me fetch you a little more sherry, Grandfather." She put it in front of him and then went quietly out of the room, leaving him in the chair, with his eyes closed and his mind on scenes beyond the office walls.

It took Ross a week to extract a mocking admission from Dunbar that he did "have a drop or two" of Aberlivet on his books. He had to wait another week before Dunbar grandly agreed to spare him a minute or two of his day. He was kept for a long time on a hard chair in a dim corridor and then had to suffer the farce of Dunbar's faking surprise at the idea of King & Co. wanting to buy the whisky.

"Fancy!" The affability was grotesque. "And this new whisky of yours is based on Aberlivet! I would have thought you would have had your supplies all arranged." He leaned forward on the broad table he used instead of a desk, and his eyes became confiding. "That's what I would have done. D'you know what I mean?"

Ross tried not to squirm. "The demand has taken us by surprise," he said uncomfortably.

Dunbar nodded understandingly. "These things can happen. Especially when the boss is four hundred miles away, helping to run the country instead of looking after his business." The dark face radiated good humour. "I suppose we couldn't expect a lady to be so practical as to make sure she actually had all the whisky that was needed."

Ross flushed. "It wasn't Mrs. King's fault," he said quickly. "If anybody's to blame, it's me. It was an oversight."

Dunbar's spiky eyebrows shot up, almost as if the shortcoming had been in his own business. "Some oversight! I hope the lady's not too hard on you for it. This could cost her a lot of money, you know." The gruff jocularity had started to harden. He reached back and lifted a massive

117

leather-bound ledger from a shelf as if it were a pamphlet. He turned the pages slowly. "Luckily for you, Mr. Ross, I don't seem to be too badly off for Aberlivet." He pulled at his chin as if thinking. "I could probably let you have a few casks."

As Ross stared, fascinated, at the well-tended nails and the gold rings on the otherwise brutal hands, Dunbar closed the outsized ledger with a thud and tossed it effortlessly onto its shelf. It landed with an impact that bounced various objects on to the floor. He ignored them and fixed Ross with a wolfish grin. "How many casks did the lady have in mind? Five? Ten?"

"Five or ten hundred," Ross said, summoning a shaky smile.

"My, my! This is bigger than I thought." He rubbed his hands as if at an unexpected stroke of fortune.

"I have the authority to spend a lot of money with you."

Dunbar's voice became hushed; his expression, awestruck. "Is that so?"

Ross waited despondently for the next taunt, cursing the negligence that had landed him here.

Dunbar walked to the window and appeared to study a handful of withered daffodils drooping in a box on the sill. "Couldn't you maybe use some other whisky?" he asked with sly concern. "Some other whisky you could buy an awful lot cheaper?" he added pointedly.

"We don't want to change the character of the blend."

"No." Dunbar nodded extravagant sympathy. "Especially when you're all so proud of it." His eyes twinkled.

Ross choked down his humiliation and said desperately, "Can you help us, Mr. Dunbar?"

"Now, that's a question." Dunbar seemed to ponder it. "I wonder if King and Company would help me if I was ever glaikit enough to put out a blend without making sure I had the whisky to maintain it?"

He stood over Ross with his rocky black jaw clenched and his great shadow spread menacingly across the floor and halfway up a wall. Ross felt an urge to stand, but he was pinioned to his chair with embarrassment and apprehension. Dunbar's barely restrained violence was frightening. His voice came in a foolish mumble. "I'm sure they would be pleased to do all they could to assist you."

Dunbar swayed a little as he struggled with the terrible sense of affront that suddenly filled him. He had not heard Ross's answer. In his head he had spoken his own answer, the contemptuous answer he imagined Robert would have given to any plea he made for help. He put a hand on Ross's shoulder and shook him roughly.

"What did you say? Speak up."

"I said I was sure they would do all they could to assist you if . . . if the position were reversed."

Dunbar walked quickly away, as if he could not trust his actions if he stayed too close to this emissary of the hated Kings. "You said that, did you? Well, you're either a fool or a liar." He went back to his own side of the table and his expression relaxed a little. "Or maybe you're just frightened what might happen if you told the truth. The high and mighty Mr. Robert King would laugh in my face if I ever had to go and beg him for whisky. But why should I worry? It could never happen. My pride would see I died before asking King for an obligement. Do you believe that, Mr. Ross?"

Ross nodded, but could not leave it at that. "I think, perhaps, you misjudge Mr. King. He is—"

"Never fear! I know what he is. I know what he did to me in the past and what he'd do to me in the future if he got the chance."

He sat for a few tense moments with his eyes closed, and when he opened them the honest anger had been replaced by a mocking leer. His voice was smoothly expansive again.

"Fortunately, I'm not a vindictive man. In fact, I'm a charitable kind of chiel, always ready to extend a helping hand, even to the likes of King and Company. But in a matter of this importance it's only right that principal should speak to principal." He took a cigar from a box and carefully pierced the end with a contraption in gold, which he took from a pocket of his discreetly flowered waistcoat. He pushed the box across to Ross, who shook his head.

"Away you go back and tell your lady boss that if she wants to buy my fine whisky, she'll have to come and ask me for it to my face."

Ross rose and found his hat. "Very well, Mr. Dunbar." He hesitated, and a note of entreaty came into his voice. "But is that necessary? I am a director of the company. Mrs. King has empowered me to—"

Dunbar cut short the plea. "It's what I'd have done with King himself, if he hadn't run away. And I'll do no less with his bonnie wife. I told him I'd make no allowances. If Mrs. King wants to play the tycoon, I'm afraid she's going to discover the game has rough edges."

"He insists you go to see him, Mrs. King," Ross said unhappily when he arrived back, still shaken, at Seabank Lane. "Quite honestly, I don't know if I can let you. I don't know if it's safe. There was a moment when I felt certain he was going to go for me. I'm afraid he is not a gentleman."

"If he's the devil himself, I'll have to see him," Fiona said practically, although touched and impressed by Ross's concern. "He has the whisky. We need it. It's a heaven-sent chance for him to humiliate us. We can hardly expect him to let it pass."

She went to a silver and gilt Venetian mirror she had introduced into the room. Its rococo splendour was incongruous in the otherwise functional setting. "It's unfortunate I'm not the pale and helpless type," she said, studying her robust image. "He might take pity and let me off lightly."

Ross liked the spirit with which she was facing what she must know would be an ordeal. He smiled admiringly, but shook his head in caution. "He's to be taken very seriously, Mrs. King."

"I know." She touched her hair and adjusted the collar of her dress before leaving the mirror. She hesitated. "I don't think we should speak of this meeting until it's over. Above all, not to Sir Fergus. He would probably try to forbid it or send a wire demanding Robert come home immediately."

"I'll accompany you, of course," Ross said.

Her chin came up in the way they were all beginning to recognise. "Thank you, Peter, but that would make him think I'm afraid. From what I've been told of the man, he would like that." She smoothed her dress and sat down. "No. I'll go alone. Doubtless I'll be able to bear his vulgar bullying. We can only hope King and Company will be able to bear his price."

Her first surprise was the extent of Dunbar's establishment. It covered a site of almost an acre between Argyle Street and the river. There was a gatekeeper in a small but well-built stone office. From a cobbled courtyard rose high buildings with barred windows and massive, double-padlocked doors. In the dark and damp of these fortified warehouses some of Dunbar's whisky would lie—perhaps the precious Aberlivet she had come to buy. Beyond was the cooperage, ringing with the rhythmic hammer blows of casks being hooped and the hollow rumble of empty oak barrels being rolled across the bumpy cobbles. She had first heard these ancient sounds at her father's distillery and they were as familiar and homely to her as footsteps. There was a long line of open sheds for the distinctive brown and yellow Dunbar delivery drays and a smart stable block for his team of white Clydesdales. Over all was the sharp fragrance inseparable from the distilling or maturing of whisky.

The guide provided by the gatehouse keeper pushed open a door and led her into a corridor from which she could see into a busy office. Clerks turned on their stools and stared at her. Female visitors were obviously a rarity.

Here she was handed over to a pale old man with fluffy white hair who lifted a flap in a broad mahogany counter and introduced himself as the office manager.

"I have instructions to take you to Mr. Dunbar without delay," he said with a worried twitch of welcome. "Yes, without delay," he repeated, clearly impressed.

He squeezed breathlessly past her and went up a short flight of stairs. After knocking, he opened a door, said something into the room and then stood aside with a self-effacing grimace.

All at once the courage she had summoned and clung to during the drive from Glasgow Cross began to weaken. Her heart raced uncomfortably. She had been determined to keep her mind cool and clear for lucid thought, but now all Ross's warnings flooded irresistibly into it. There had been, in Ross's estimation, no indignity—including, he had hinted, the classic one—to which she might not be invited to submit.

Determinedly she fought back panic and a sudden sensation of limpness. She walked into the room with her head high and her hands clasped in front of her in what she hoped would look like an attitude of composure.

To her confusion, he came hurrying across the wide room to meet her, all fuss and charm. He had been smoking and the place smelled of cigars and Macassar oil. It struck her as a not unpleasant combination. His bulk seemed to darken the room and his voice to shake it, vibrating against the windows and rumbling away into corners. Nothing she had been told about him, not even her own fleeting glimpse of him galloping his carriage through Row like a demon, had prepared her for the shock of what she saw now. The raw impact came not only from his appearance but from what she sensed: power emanated from him in waves; this man was primitive. A commercial office was not his proper setting; nor were these dark and slightly dandified business clothes his natural dress. Only the gold rings were in keeping with his basic barbarity—like paint on a savage.

She lowered her eyes before they could betray the disconcerting exhilaration she was beginning to feel, unaware in the shock of the moment how forcefully her own appearance had struck him.

A chair he had collected in his advance across the room dangled from his hand like a toy as he wondered where to seat her. He was surprised, and anxious not to show it. There had been a picture of her in his mind, assembled from things he had heard and others he had imagined. He had expected a disdainful, finely bred face, like Robert's. Instead, in a moment of staring, he saw a country woman with prettily flushed cheeks, candid eyes and the full, rounded figure he admired. Instead of the severe clothes worn by the new breed of emancipated business wom-

121

an, who sat at a man's desk and felt she had to dress like him, this woman wore a shimmering blue costume with flouncing skirt, lace bodice and embroidered cuffs. Her hat was pert and feathery. It sat well back on her head, revealing the deep-burnished beauty of her hair. Her expression at that moment was tinged with wariness and another quality which he could not identify.

He put the chair down with a thump. "Sit here, Mrs. King, where I can see you."

She suffered his aggressive inspection without flinching.

"It's a pity your husband's not here to do his own dirty work." His expression suggested it was a pleasantry.

She gave him a steady smile. "Not at all, Mr. Dunbar. I wouldn't have missed this opportunity of meeting you. You have a proposition to put to me, I believe?"

His eyes glinted with surprise. "It's you who has the proposition for me, Mrs. King. I've been given to understand you want to buy some of my whisky."

She felt calmer now. "Yes. I would like to buy all the Aberlivet you have over eight years old."

His charm seemed to diminish in relation to the increase in her assurance. "And suppose I don't want to sell it to people like King and Company?"

She shrugged. "Then you must keep it." She moved to rise from the chair.

He leaned forward. "Not so hasty, lass. I didn't say I wouldn't sell to you."

There was a scar on his chin that held her attention. "You have made it clear to my husband that you hate King and Company, Mr. Dunbar. In view of that, I haven't come here to play a bargaining game with you. I have told you what I want. Please give me your answer."

His voice rose. "My answer, madam, is six shillings a gallon."

It was twice the market price but no more than she had expected. He was shrewd, not pitching his demand impossibly high. He would make a killing and at the same time have the pleasure of humiliating her. For a long time to come, the profit on Queen's Royal would be meagre. But it had to be faced. And she had faced it during the lonely hours she had spent pondering the likely course of this meeting. She had made her decision then, and her mind was clear on it now. Nevertheless, she could not resist a comment.

"That, of course, is robbery."

He held his hands up as if to show that they were empty.

"So long as you can see it isn't armed robbery. I'm not asking you to stand and deliver. Just say the word and I'll walk you down to your carriage."

"I'll pay your price," she said quietly.

He grinned. "You're not only a bonnie lass, Mrs. King, you're a woman of decision. And a pleasure to do business with." He reached toward a side table. "I'll not offer you a dram, for I don't approve of it for women, but what about a wee sherry to seal the bargain?"

She ignored the offer. "I'll require a contract."

He put the decanter down. "One day you may learn Douglas Dunbar's word is his bond, Mrs. King. For most people it's enough. But if you want it all nice and legal, I don't mind. I'll leave you to have the contract drawn up."

"I will see that our lawyers are instructed immediately." She rose and stood waiting for him to escort her to the door. "Doubtless we will meet again, Mr. Dunbar." Her expression was pleasant. "The next occasion could be in my office, with my hand on the whip."

"And pigs might fly," he said crudely, still lounging in his chair.

"Please don't rise," she said pointedly.

He stared at her unabashed.

She still felt the pulse-racing exhilaration, the thrill of the climber a finger-hold from disaster.

"My husband once offered to buy your business," she said lightly, and paused to watch a baffled stillness descend on him. "His approach was perhaps untactful and you refused. I would like to renew that offer."

He went on staring at her in disbelief, his chest swelling as he took a long, noisy breath. His voice might have been stuck in his throat. "My God, you're a cool one, Mrs. King," he said at last, seeming to think it sufficient answer.

His anger was like a stimulant to her, making her more daring. "Well?" she prompted him. "Would you consider an offer from me?"

"Douglas Dunbar is not for sale," he snapped; he recognised but was unable to ignore the goading.

Her gaze was steady. "One day you may have to reconsider that answer."

"I'll never reconsider it."

"If you go on fighting me, you will eventually lose your business. I can promise you that, Mr. Dunbar."

She went out, closing the door quietly on his speechlessness.

A week or two later Dunbar contemptuously scrawled his signature to a contract. Then, in exchange for a cheque for almost fifty-thousand

123

pounds, he issued a delivery order transferrring the first desperately needed batch of Aberlivet to King & Co. Soon, the first of a long line of iron-wheeled lorries came trundling down the cobbled lane, heavily laden with casks.

Fiona, watching from her window, began for the first time to understand something of Robert's romantic attachment to this trade which he had done so much to revivify. Her sceptical attitude to the reverence accorded the blending art had been exposed as unworthy. It had been expensively demonstrated to her that one whisky simply wasn't as good as another. They were all different. Some were low and puny, lacking all attraction and character. Others were perfectly acceptable, full of worthy qualities, but quite unremarkable. And then came the giants, each glorying in some unique power or attribute so elusive it could never be analysed or duplicated.

If it had not been so, if it had been all mystique and no substance, Dunbar could have had no sway over them. It had been a painful lesson, but she was resolved to learn some humility from it. She had been too brash in her dismissal of the whisky lore. There was much she should know which she did not yet know. It was not enough to rely on Peter Ross's expertise. He was perhaps too sunk in the whisky mystery to be relied upon always to exercise simple commercial prudence, such as making sure the supply lines were secure. With a sigh she let the curtains sway back over the window as men began to manhandle the casks from the lorry and roll them into the warehouse.

At another window, Ross brightened for the first time in months as he looked down on the noisy guarantee that the sanctity of the Queen's Royal blend would be preserved, even though at a terrible price.

"It's only a reprieve," Fiona warned him later. "The standard of the blend will have to be lowered eventually if our sales go on climbing. The day must come when there simply won't be enough Aberlivet in existence to meet our demands."

She could have said he had blundered in making the blend so dependent on one distinctive whisky, but he did not deserve that. Robert should have foreseen the dangers.

"That point is several years ahead," Ross said happily, his relief at the preservation of his artistry unshaken.

"The time will soon pass. You had better use it finding substitutes for Aberlivet, so that we never again find ourselves held to ransom. I've promised Douglas Dunbar—and myself—that the next time we meet, the whip will be in my hand."

In a way it was true, but her chance came so unexpectedly, and such a world away from the affairs of business, that she could not bring herself to use it.

Dunbar appeared at her door late one blustery night, a wild-eyed, black-cloaked figure dripping rain in the gaslit street. When she came down from her room, he was pacing the hall where the frightened maid had left him.

"I didn't know your number. I've been up and down the street twice, and this is the third damned door I've been at," he said by way of explaining the scattering of water that had collected about him on the hardwood floor.

"He pushed in past me, ma'am," the maid said for the third or fourth time. "He started shouting when I said it was too late."

Fiona gave her a reassuring nod. "It's all right, Morag." She turned to Dunbar. "Why are you here?"

He glowered, started to open his mouth and then shut it without speaking. Despite his belligerent attitude, the throb of suppressed emotion gave him an odd air of vulnerability. The fuming silence, she saw, was imposed on him by the maid's presence.

She went toward a small sitting room where she had been reading earlier and which she knew would still be warm. "I can't imagine any business important enough to justify this intrusion," she said coldly, "but you can come in here for a moment."

Dunbar's face twisted and an unintelligible grunt burst through his clenched teeth. The maid scurried past him, to open the sitting-room door, her eyes bright with alarm, one hand clutching the coat she had put on over her nightclothes.

"Will I stay by you, ma'am?"

"No, thank you, Morag. I don't think you need do that. You can go back to bed. I'll be all right. I know who this gentleman is. But take his cloak before you go, and his hat. He can collect them in the hall when he is leaving."

Morag's distrustful backward glance at Dunbar as she sidled out of the room said clearly that whoever he was, he was not her idea of a gentleman. In the cold light of the gas jet he looked almost bedraggled. It took Fiona a moment to realise that the blue velvet smoking jacket revealed by the removal of his cloak was also wet, as were his trousers. His boots were muddy.

As the door closed behind the maid, Dunbar exploded. "You needn't look so high and mighty, Mrs. King. I'm here to give you a message for that son of yours. If I catch him near my daughter again, I'll break his back." His eyes glared, his chin jutted and the violence of the outburst carried him threateningly forward.

Fiona stepped nearer to a bell handle. "I don't know what you mean, but there are children asleep upstairs. You will either moderate your voice or leave."

Dunbar scowled. "I mean what I say. If you want him to stay in one piece, keep your son away from my daughter."

"I wasn't aware Gordon knew your daughter."

For a moment Dunbar's eyes rolled in anguish, then, to her surprise, he turned away, his shoulders drooping in an odd attitude of shame.

"He's"—the words seemed to be strangling him—"he's carrying on with her."

The primness that had appeared on the wild landscape of his face was so incongruous that she almost smiled. " Do you mean he has been meeting her?"

He quelled another outburst and looked at her wearily. "I've suspected for months that Anne was meeting somebody. It was only tonight I found out who it was."

She moved closer to the fire, her mind swinging between what he had actually said and what his distraught manner and his presence in her house implied. "You hate King and Company, Mr. Dunbar. You are conducting a feud against us, so I cannot say I am pleased to learn that my son has been meeting your daughter. But is it quite as desperate a business as your charging about the street, disturbing the neighbours and then bursting in here at this time of the night would suggest? This is a respectable locality." She tried to make it sound as if it would therefore be foreign territory to him.

He was staring at her, watching her lips as if he could not believe the words they formed.

"Do you not understand what I'm trying to tell you?" His voice was horrified. "Your son is carrying on with my daughter. Not just meeting her innocently: carrying on with her. He was in her room tonight." His voice rose in an agony of outrage. "The blaggard was actually hidden in my house."

His tormented shadow blackened one wall of the small room.

"Gordon is upstairs in bed," she said defiantly. "He went to his room hours ago."

For a moment Dunbar's normal aggression reasserted itself. "He's a dab hand at getting out of windows," he said sarcastically. "If you find him in bed, you can have the rest of that Aberlivet for nothing."

She hesitated, but it was a challenge she could hardly ignore. She left the room and went reluctantly up the stairs with a sick feeling at her heart. Gordon's room was empty. The bed had not been slept in. She was shivering when she returned to the sitting room. She drew a chair close to the fender and sat, bent over the embers.

"Well? Are you convinced?"

"Where is he, Mr. Dunbar?"

"I don't know." He made a sound of disgust. "He can run faster than me."

She shook her head in bewilderment. "Will you please tell me what has happened?" She saw he was looking at a tantalus sitting on a table at the side of the fireplace. "You may help yourself to a drink. It isn't locked."

He poured some whisky and gulped it down with his back to her. "Aye," he said to the wall. "The men in your family are very good at running, Mrs. King."

He turned and rubbed the palms of his hands distractedly over his wet and wrinkled jacket. "That's why I'm in this mess. I was busy working through some papers when my housekeeper came to me in a great state and said she was sure there was a man in Anne's room. I think she thought it was an intruder. And at first that's what I thought. I ran to the door of Anne's bedroom. It was locked and she refused to open it. I could hear whispering inside." His fists were clenched on the arms of his chair. "Well, I was just going to smash my way in when I heard the window being opened. I rushed down the stairs and into the garden. Anne's room is on the first floor, at the side of the house. It was dark, of course, and pouring rain, but I saw somebody slithering down a creeper that covers most of the house. When he heard me shout, he let go and jumped the last ten feet. He was either half stunned or so frightened he didn't know what to do next. He stood for a while, leaning against the house. I nearly caught him. I'd have killed him." He lifted his hands and stared at them. "But just as I went for him he bolted across the lawn and into a wood that stretches for about half a mile along the banks of the Clyde. I went after him, but it was too dark to see anything. The wood is such a tangle of brambles you can hardly get through it in daylight. It's full of fallen trees and rotten stumps. I could hear him crashing about, and once he must have fallen into the burn that flows through it. There was a splash and a shout. If wishing could have drowned him, he'd be drowned, Mrs. King, but I heard him running again. I couldn't get near him. He had the advantage of being scared. After a while, everything went quiet. I suppose he realised that if he kept still, he was safe. I hung about for a while but it was useless."

Except for her first amazement, she had until now been strangely untouched by Dunbar's story. It was a situation, she felt , in which the anguish was all his—and his daughter's. But now alarm rose in her.

"Maybe something happened to him. Perhaps that's why you didn't hear him again. He might have fallen down something. Or into the Clyde, even."

He lifted a poker and stirred the ashes of the fire. "I'd like to think he had," he said grimly. "I'd like to think he's lying down a hole in that wood with a broken neck." He put the poker down and looked at her, his face expressionless. "But I doubt it. He'll be skulking home, more likely, wondering what he'll say to his mammy about the mess he must be in."

She had a sudden, unaccountable urge to comfort him. "If all this is true, Mr. Dunbar, I'm sorry. I can understand your distress."

"It's true, all right."

"And you're sure it's Gordon?"

"I didn't see his face. I didn't know who it was till I got back to the house. Anne was still locked in. This time I did smash the door down." He rubbed his shoulder absentmindedly and she had a vision of him hurling himself across a shadowy corridor of the big house. "I made her tell me who it was." His face was twisted at the painful memory.

"I had absolutely no hint of this, I assure you. It pleases me as little as it does you."

"I doubt that," he said grimly.

"How long have they known each other?"

"Since some time last summer. They met the day I went to Castle Gare to tackle your husband about a damned impertinent telegram he sent me." For a moment he seemed overcome by the irony of it.

In the grate an unexpected flame rose for an instant from the brown ash, softly lighting her face. She put out a hand but the fire was black again.

"I remember the occasion. But surely your daughter must have known how displeased you would be at her having a relationship with a member of this family."

It was another twist of the screw, needless and unintended, and as she saw his anger begin again, she tried to cover her tactlessness. "Of course, it's possible she may not have known at first who Gordon was. I don't know the exact circumstances of their meeting."

"Oh, she knew! She knew, all right!" Dunbar cried in a loud, wild voice, his eyes wide and swimming with self-pity. "From the very first she knew. She doesna even bother to hide it. I think that's the worst of it."

Fiona thought wryly that if the daughter had been hers, this would not have been the worst of it to her mind. A man in her daughter's bedroom would have aroused in her the fear of an outcome much more tangible than wounded pride. He was here, as much as anything, she realised, in an attempt to assuage his feelings of personal outrage. Despite a mad, momentary temptation to sink the knife into him, she thought it wiser not to do so, although she had little doubt that if the situation had been reversed he would not have hesitated to torture her. She lacked his brutality.

She contented herself with saying, "Well, I suppose this will be the end of it. She won't see him again, now that you've found out."

His head jerked back. "No. You don't know her." He was almost shouting in his frustration. The admission that he lacked control over his daughter was obviously racking him, and his eyes strayed again to the whisky decanter.

"Please help yourself to another drink," she said.

He shook his head violently and rose in an attempt to contain his fury.

"She's threatening to defy me. That's why I'm here—to warn your son to keep away. I'll not miss him a second time. I'll not be responsible for what I do."

"On the contrary, Mr. Dunbar," she said icily. "I'll see you are held responsible for any harm you do my son. Nevertheless, I'll speak to Gordon. I'll forbid him to see your daughter again, if you are quite certain that is the best thing."

He looked at her as if she were mad. "My God, woman, how could it be anything else but the best thing—not only for my Anne, but for your bloody son?" He stopped and stared at her, struggling with a new thought. "Do you not know the worst of it? Is that what it is?"

She waited in baffled silence while he forced the words out. "The girl's married. She has a husband. And a son."

Fiona sank back in her chair, bemused not only by this revelation but by the fact that the possibility had not occurred to her.

"But . . . where is her husband, then? Why is it you who are here?"

He covered his face with his hands for a moment as he steeled himself for a further bout of ignominy. "Anne is living away from her husband. She's been back home with me for about a year." His humiliation was almost pathetic, and his reluctance to speak, deeper than ever.

"I'm sorry." A realisation that it was all much more serious than the young man's escapade she had been imagining was closing depressingly around her. "That would have nothing to do with Gordon, I hope?"

"So far as I know, he had nothing to do with her leaving her husband. But if it hadn't been for him carrying on with her, she might have been back where she belongs by this time."

"I really am sorry, Mr. Dunbar. What age is your grandchild?"

"He's three. Too young, fortunately, to know anything about his mother's disgrace," he added bitterly.

"I don't want to pry, but what went wrong with Anne's marriage?" The use of the girl's Christian name rose naturally from her compassion. "I mean, has it broken down completely, or is there a possibility that she can be reconciled with her husband?"

"Christ knows." Dunbar spoke in disgust and bewilderment. "They've been separated two or three times before this," he confided gloomily. "I

129

don't understand them. Peter's six years older than Anne. He's a steady enough chap, and very successful at his business. He's a stock and share broker. They lack for nothing, but . . ." He became lost for a few moments in the confusion of his thoughts. At last, casting off his indecision, he gave her a rueful, humourless smile. "It's very hard for a father to face facts about his only daughter, Mrs. King. Especially when her mother is dead. But the truth is, Anne is headstrong. Even at school she was wild. She was always getting into trouble, leading the other girls into escapades, refusing to be disciplined. Oh, there was nothing all that desperate: truancy, running away, getting lost. All the usual things. Well, that was a worry, of course, but her mother always said she would grow out of it. I think she would have, too. But a terrible thing happened." He went silent, staring sightlessly past her. "My wife was drowned," he said at last. "To add to the tragedy, Anne was there when it happened. They went out together for a ramble along the banks of the Clyde, near where we live. It was a lovely warm August day. There's an old disused pier that the three of us used to have picnics on. They went there, as usual. My wife's shoe caught in a gap between two of the old timbers. She was pitched over the edge, into the water. She could swim quite well, but she must have hit her head as she fell. There was nothing Anne could do. Her mother simply disappeared. We didn't find her for two days."

Behind him, a long case clock began to strike midnight. He sat very straight in his chair, his head a little to the side, as if he were counting the strokes. On the twelfth, he sank back, trying to smother a massive yawn of exhaustion.

"What a dreadful tragedy," Fiona said softly. "The shock to Anne must have been awful."

"She hasn't been right since," he said brokenly. "You see . . ." Again indecision gripped him. He rose slowly, pulled the heavy curtains and stood peering into the wet street. She heard rain hitting the window. There was a rattle of harnessing and the sound of hooves grinding on flints as his horses moved restlessly. She heard the coachman call some muffled reassurance.

"You see . . ." Again he faltered and moved dejectedly to the tantalus. He poured himself a drink, speaking almost as if to himself. "It happened just a week before Anne was due to be married. Ethel had taken her only that morning to have a final fitting of her wedding dress." He drank his whisky and put the glass down carefully, speaking with great precision. "The wedding took place as planned, just three days after Ethel was buried. Everybody was shocked. They thought we were callous. Even the minister protested, but the banns had been called and everything properly attended to. I held him to his duty. Some of the

130

guests—Ethel's brothers and sisters—came in ostentatious mourning as a sign of their disapproval. I don't think they realised how cruel they were being."

Fiona shivered as out of a corner of the shadowy room a macabre picture came to her—that of the young bride facing the sombre, black-veiled guests.

"It was an ordeal for everyone," Dunbar was saying. "Of course, most of all for Anne. I'm afraid the sacrilege, the mockery, of her marriage—just as much as the actual fact of seeing her mother drown—has left a terrible mark on her. She seems . . . haunted. She sleeps badly. Often she has nightmares and wakes up screaming in the middle of the night. But when you try to find out what's frightening her, she can't explain. Sometimes I worry that the poor girl's mind has . . ." He stopped and turned his eyes guiltily away as if feeling that he had revealed too much. "It can hardly have helped her marriage. I feel sorry for Peter. For both of them. And for the bairn."

Something in his manner puzzled her. As she tried to recall some of his words, he said, "Do you think it was callous to go on with the marriage?" He was seeking a reassurance that she could not honestly give him.

"It's easy to be critical," she said. "And probably unfair, especially so long after the event, when all the consequences are plain to be seen. But perhaps it might have been wiser to postpone the wedding, even if only for a few months. For Anne's sake, as well as out of respect for her mother."

He gave her a strange look, but it was gone too quickly for her to be able to interpret it. "Aye, it should have been postponed. I know that now, and I wish to God I could turn the clock back. But the arrangements were all made. Everything was ready." Suddenly he threw his head back and stared at the ceiling with tortured intensity. "It was me. I made her go on with it. She had more sense and finer feelings than me, but I forced her."

He spoke the last words with so much suppressed ferocity that she could not conceal her surprise. "I see," she said inadequately. "Well, I'm sure you acted for the best."

He rose with such violence that the big wing chair he had been sitting in almost toppled. In the white light of the gas flare he stood writhing, like some tormented monument. Words poured from him.

"No, Mrs. King. You *don't* see. You don't see at all." She had never been so close to a bitterness so profound. "I didn't act for the best. I wasn't thinking about Anne. It was the disgrace I was thinking about. It was myself—my good name—I was worried about. And Ethel's ghost."

131

His wild grief was so affecting that she rose and put a hand on his arm, trying to return him to his chair, but he was immovable.

"I don't understand, Mr. Dunbar."

His gaze had again been fastened on the ceiling, as if it were a window through which could be glimpsed some distant scene. Now he turned his savage head and looked down at her with the wide, anxious eyes of a child showing some frightening injury.

"The lass was pregnant. I wanted her safely wed and away out of my house. I didn't know what harm I was doing her. But even if I'd known, would I have cared?"

She wondered how many hundreds of times he had asked himself the same question as he watched the progress of his daughter's illness or lay in the dark of his room, listening for her cry in the night.

"I'm sure you would," she said consolingly.

But he was not to be comforted or diverted from his headlong course of self-revelation. "No. I was too warped and poisoned with selfishness. I was too afraid of the wagging tongues and the sly glances. Anne was bringing disgrace on my house and I wanted her away, out of sight, before it became obvious to every spiteful hag with a prying eye. I hoped that once she was married only the dedicated calendar watchers would realise the shame she had brought on us." He gave a rasping laugh of self-mockery. "Aye, *us.* I didn't see it as just *me.* I told myself I was protecting Ethel's memory. Of course, now—when it's too late and the harm's all done—I can see all I was doing was protecting my own pride."

She had almost forgotten the real reason for his presence in her sense of involvement in the double tragedy of these two women she had never seen—the one dead while still in her thirties and the other still having life to face with her balance perhaps fatally upset. For Dunbar she felt a deep sympathy. In a few moments of anguished confession he had been transformed from a remote tormentor into a vulnerable man racked by family calamities to which, unfortunately, her son was contributing. He was the victim of his own bitter pride, and tonight he was being made to savour the acid. An hour ago she would have revelled in the thought, deeming his troubles to be no more than his due, perhaps even picturing how she might add to the pain. Now she could draw no satisfaction from his heartbreak. She had no desire to extract, on behalf of all the Kings, the revenge they were due. In unburdening himself, Dunbar had disarmed her. She had seen behind the iron frame to the hidden man. This was the Dunbar that Ethel would have known.

He stirred in his seat and felt for his watch. A chill had filled the room.

"You had better have another whisky before you go back out into the cold in those wet clothes," she said.

He managed a pale smile. "No. It's a good pot of strong tea I'm looking forward to when I get home. I'm more of a tea jenny than a drinker."

"Then I'll ring for Morag. It's now you need it."

"Don't bother, Mrs. King. I've kept you out of bed late enough. My troubles are no fault of yours, but now that I've explained things, I know you'll do what you can."

"I will, but . . ." She moved toward the bell handle.

"Let the lass have her rest. I'll be away."

She was aware of her reluctance to see him go. "I'll make it myself," she said, "if you don't mind coming with me to the kitchen."

He hesitated, then followed her into the hall and through another door, to the back of the house. When the kettle had boiled and the tea was made, they sat at the scrubbed table, drinking it from coarse white cups.

"The last time I drank out of these," she said, "was the day we moved into this house and no one knew where anything was. All the packing cases had been wrongly numbered."

Dunbar examined his cup. "Until I was almost thirty I hardly ever drank out of anything else," he said. "Before I married I didn't care and probably didn't know any better. Then, for a long time after I was married, I couldn't spare anything from the business for needless refinements like good china." His expression clouded at the memory of his early struggles. "Poor Ethel had been used to the very best, but her first ten years with me were gey thin. I was always going to make it up to her, but I kept putting it off until it was too late." The bitterness came rushing back. "I always had some good reason for keeping everything in the business. Tomorrow, next week, next year—everything was going to be different then. But never today. Today was never the right time."

"To some extent, I suppose we are all like that," she said as she refilled his cup. "Procrastination is a very common failing."

There was a strange fascination in the spectacle of the wild animal gone so docile and sensitive. She felt irresistibly impelled to go on discovering how tame it was and how far it could be befriended. She said, "You must have married very young."

"Some thought too young. I was eighteen. Ethel was a year older. Mostly we were happy, but I often wonder, looking back, if she wasted herself on me. She might have been better married to one of her own kind. Marrying me cut her off from an awful lot. I couldn't talk to her about music or literature, and I would put up an awful fight every time

133

she wanted me to take her to a concert or to the opera. It was easier for me to suffer the art galleries and the exhibitions of paintings. There was no noise there, and I could think about other things while I walked round pretending to admire the pictures. Poor Ethel! I can see now the only thing I ever really wanted to discuss with her was business." He smiled slightly. "And yet, despite my being a Philistine, we got on so well. The only real quarrel we ever had was near the end, when she told me Anne was pregnant. I blamed it all on her, for not seeing the girl had been better prepared for the world, for having been too lenient with her, for not having kept a stricter watch on her. I was being unjust, of course, and it didn't take me long to realise it."

As he stopped speaking, an icy feeling touched Fiona's back. The front door of the house had opened and closed. It was a faint but unmistakable sound. She sat frozen with anxiety, not daring to look at Dunbar. Had he heard?

"What was that?" The words fell into the silent room like drops of cold rain. He was bent forward, alert and concentrated.

"I didn't hear anything."

"Aye, you heard, all right." He spoke quietly in his anxiety not to drown any other sound that might come from beyond the kitchen. "It's him, isn't it? Slinking back to his lair, his dirty work done." His chair swayed and clattered on the tile floor as he rose without taking his eyes from her.

She knew it was Gordon. There was no one else it could be. She should have realised this might happen. Instead of trying to prolong Dunbar's visit, enticing him with tea, prompting his reminiscences, she should have been concerned only to get him out of the house as quickly as possible. The change in him frightened her.

He stood poised now on the other side of the table, like a malevolent giant, his face suffused with outrage that had again taken possession of him. She sat staring at the door, too mesmerised to move. If it opened, Dunbar would be uncontrollable. In her heart she framed a desperate plea that Gordon should creep up to his room. But if he was in the mess Dunbar said he would be in, he might come first to the kitchen to clean himself. She sat transfixed with dread, praying that he would see the line of light beneath the door. As the seconds passed, her suffocating tension began to lessen.

"It's him, isn't it?" Dunbar said again.

The harsh words released her.

"Sit down for a moment and let him get to his room," she said firmly. "Then, please leave."

"I'll teach the young bastard a lesson he won't forget."

134

"This is my house and you won't leave this room except to go out by the front door." As she spoke, she walked between him and the door.

He moved forward. Suddenly, all she was aware of was his overpowering nearness. She could smell the dampness of his clothes mingled with the faint scent of some toilet preparation. The hands he placed roughly on her arms seemed to melt and blend with her own flesh. Her head was thrown back and her eyes closed. For long seconds there was an incredible stillness. When she opened her eyes he was looking down at her with an expression of baffled resentment. After another moment of throbbing indecision he lifted her effortlessly out of his path and put her down beside the table. But the animal reaction, the headlong rush, had been decisively interrupted.

As he stood, thwarted, she said, "Please go. I promise you I'll forbid Gordon to see your daughter again."

She watched his eyes move over her as if he had not seen her properly before. "You'd better," he said.

The threat stung her. "Your daughter won't have been a lily-white innocent in this, you know, Mr. Dunbar. Gordon is still only an impressionable boy. Your daughter is a mature married woman and a mother. She would know better than Gordon what they were doing."

His eyes filled with fury. "Are you suggesting my daughter lured your son?"

"I am saying he is not the only one to be blamed. Since she has had a vastly greater experience of life, your daughter must have entered the relationship with her eyes open."

"Keep him away from her," he snarled. There was a moment of silence and then a look of almost tearful self-pity came on his face. "He probably won't need much persuasion when he knows his skin's in danger. My poor Anne probably means nothing to your son. From what I hear, all you Kings are given to this sort of thing. You included." His eyes blazed accusingly, as if she personally had been responsible for putting some awful contamination into his family. "It means nothing to you Kings."

She almost struck him, and then she almost laughed. His blind righteousness was unbelievable.

"Mr. Dunbar," she said scathingly, "from what you have told me of your daughter's condition before her marriage, it would seem that we Kings are not the only ones given to this sort of thing."

He gaped, searching for words that would crush her, then, still speechless, he turned and rushed from the house, leaving doors open and a chill blowing in from the street. After a while she followed. She closed the front door and stood behind it, listening to his carriage rattle along the rough street.

She felt shame stir in her as she remembered the moments of melting weakness when she had been in his rough grasp. She was hatefully weak. As she remembered his final insult, tears of humiliation began to form in her eyes.

9

Most of the night she lay awake, thinking about Gordon. At the break-fast table she watched him in silence, noting his pale and unsmiling features, his brief, unseeing glance at the *Herald,* his listless spooning of the porridge which he normally relished.

She could not bring herself to lecture him on morality. Her own weaknesses would have made that an unbearable hypocrisy. Nevertheless, she had a duty to him.

After a few forced words and an evasive smile he folded his newspaper. As he rose from the table, she told him to return to his room, pack a case and report to McNair at Lochbank. He was so startled that she had to repeat the curt instruction.

As he started to protest, she said, "You should be thankful it's only Lochbank. To escape the sort of trouble you're in, some people are shipped to the colonies."

He went still and watchful, his hands tight on the back of his chair. He was standing in profile to her, but she could see the other side of his face in a convex mirror above the sideboard. "Trouble?"

"Don't bother trying to look innocent, Gordon. Anne Dunbar's father was here last night. He was after your blood. I know all about your folly."

He turned so white that she had to quell a wave of tenderness. For a moment she let her gaze wander hesitantly along the white linen table-cloth and over the gleaming silver, then steeled herself to go on.

"You were extremely lucky he didn't get hold of you. I shudder to think what he might have done. You would have been helpless against him. I have never heard of such scandalous and foolhardy behaviour. Both the girl and you must be out of your minds."

Her words engulfed him in a sense of madness—the madness of two people held by a passion that was not only crippling them emotionally but even attacking their physical health. What other word could describe the months of furtive meetings as summer drew into the fog and frost of winter? His long walks home in the middle of the night, their frantic and degrading eighteen-minute train journeys to Paisley, their brief spells of happiness snatched in shabby rooms rented by the hour from unsavoury landladies who humiliated them with their leering familiarities—it all came flooding back. And then, their frustrated desires culminating in the final unbalanced tempting of fate under Dunbar's own roof—the desperate skulking about in the bushes until Anne opened a back door to let him in, and the heart-thumping tiptoeing up creaking stairs and along corridors in which, at every step, he was certain he would bump into Dunbar himself. And on top of it all, a growing, horrified awareness that Anne was in the grip of some unnameable illness, some instability that could change her in an instant from a poised woman into a frightened child, that could transform love into a wild fury of tears and raging accusations.

Screams, sobs, murmurings of love, threats flung after him by Dunbar as they stumbled through the black wood, filled his mind so confusingly that he felt himself begin to sway. He had not shifted his awkward, sideways stance, and his eyes were turned to the floor.

"How could either of you possibly imagine this relationship could be kept secret?"

He shook his head to steady himself and to banish the demons inside. He made some weary, wordless sound.

"And what sort of person is she? Married and with a child and yet brazen enough to smuggle you into her father's house. I should think her husband is well rid of her."

Her voice came to him as from a distance, making little impression on his private nightmare. He was too conscious of anxiety for Anne to care about Fiona's feelings. "I can't go to Lochbank, Mother. Not today, anyway." His voice was pleading and his expression desperate. "Anne might need me. She might need help. If her father knows, he might . . . he might do something to her."

She clenched and unclenched her hands in exasperation, then pounded them on the table, heedless of the clattering dishes and trembling flowers.

"If he knows? You stupid boy! Of course he knows. He found you in his house, didn't he? He chased you like a common criminal until he lost you in the darkness of a wood."

He hung his head and shook it dejectedly. "Yes. But I hadn't thought he knew who I was."

She was shocked and angered again at the recklessness this revealed. "So you do appreciate it's not just what you've done that matters, but who *you* are and who *he* is? Who *we* are and who this girl is?"

His voice was suddenly distracted. "Yes, Mother, yes! I know all that. That's why I must get to Anne." His eyes were swimming.

Fiona turned away, chilled by the obvious depth of his feeling. Strangely, she had not been prepared for this. Physical attraction would have raised problems enough. Love might be unmanageable.

On the street, servant girls passed with shopping baskets and frock-coated neighbours swung sticks as they set out briskly for business. The trees across the street looked serene and remote against a clear sky. She came away from the window and looked again at her son.

He was dreadfully white and pinched compared to the picture of the healthy, suntanned young man she carried in her mind. She felt a stab of guilt. This physical deterioration could not have taken place in a few hours, whatever shock he had suffered in his flight from Dunbar's fury. This ravaging of his youth was the result of some longer process that she as his mother should have noticed. Panic fluttered in her. Was she immersed in the affairs of King & Co. to the neglect of her children? Had she become addicted already to the drugs that had ruled Robert's life—and at the very time when he seemed to have freed himself of them? She had seen their destructive effect on him. She must not allow profit and power to take over her head and heart.

"You need not fear for Anne," she said gently. "I saw for myself last night that her father's only wish is to safeguard her welfare, her health and her future. But I had to promise him that you would not see her again."

"You had no right." His voice was weak and querulous.

"I had every right. If you have no sense of your own, then I must use mine. That's why I'm sending you to Lochbank. My mind will be easier with you out of Glasgow."

"How long are you going to leave me in that godforsaken place?"

"Until I feel it safe for you to return to the city. To some extent, it will be a matter for yourself. By that I mean it will depend on how sensible you are."

"You can't make me stay there," he cried, his eyes flashing rebelliously. "I'm not a child." He walked agitatedly up the room, china rattling as he passed the table. He stopped at the empty fireplace and stood staring into it.

"You will either stay there or in some place much more distant," she said with quiet severity. "You can make your choice. Either way, you will not see Anne Dunbar again. You must forget about her. Is that understood? Do you hear me speaking to you?"

He turned his head and glared at her in silence.

"Gordon, I don't want to have to bring your father into this. Please don't make it necessary for me to do so. I don't have to tell you what his reaction would be—almost as violent as Douglas Dunbar's, I would think."

He sighed and gradually relaxed his defiant stance.

"Am I to be a replacement for Jack Hoey at Lochbank?" His voice was cold and challenging.

For a moment she considered the complication of this mysterious dislike that existed between her son and his cousin, but she was in no mood to pander to him.

"No, Gordon. Jack's training at the distillery has not yet been completed. I don't intend to cut it short to suit you. You will work alongside him. You are both quite old enough to behave yourselves. I don't know what your silly quarrelling is about, but so far as I am concerned it is trifling compared to this present business. Do you understand that?"

Gordon clenched his jaw and pushed his hands into his pockets. "I hate him," he said fiercely.

"You seem to be ruled by unbecoming passions," she said, fighting down her own anger and perplexity. "I warn you—it is time to start curbing them before they destroy your life. But quite apart from that, I don't want the efficiency of the distillery interfered with. Mr. McNair has enough to do without having to worry about the childish animosities of two young men who should know better. Besides, you are both family. You must at all times set an example to those who work for us."

He stepped toward her beseechingly. "If I could just see her one more time to . . . to . . . " His voice broke and he hid his face.

She felt dangerously weak and sympathetic toward him, remembering some of her own youthful longings. It was an effort to put authority into her voice.

"Please go up and pack your case now, Gordon."

Still he stood. "I don't know the times of the trains."

"I'm really not concerned with the times of the trains. I want you started on your way. The trains are fairly frequent. If you have to wait, you can go into the station buffet and read a magazine."

As they stood looking at each other, the door opened and Florence came in. She had grown in the last year, and despite the austere black skirt and white blouse she wore for school, she was already showing a tendency toward Fiona's well-rounded femininity. She had a small, bow-shaped mouth and dimpled cheeks. These, combined with hair drawn straight back and carefully plaited, gave an effect of demureness that was belied by the determined wilfulness of her eyes.

140

She gave them a curious glance, noting at once the tense way they faced each other and their sudden efforts to look natural.

"I thought I heard raised voices," she said, going to the sideboard and lifting the lids of various silver dishes from which they helped themselves. Only the porridge was brought directly from the kitchen by the table maid if they rang for it. She slid a fried egg onto a plate and went to the table, her remark about raised voices having reduced them both to embarrassed watchfulness.

"You should have a little bacon or a sausage with that," Fiona said automatically.

"No, thank you, Mother." She looked at her brother with a slight smile. "Has Gordon blotted his copy book again?"

As he opened his mouth angrily, Fiona gave him a warning glance. "No, Gordon hasn't blotted his copy book, whatever you mean by that. But you may take this opportunity of saying good-bye to him, Florence. You may not see each other again for a little while. Gordon is going to work at Lochbank distillery."

Florence, her suspicions confirmed, said, "I won't ask what you've done, Gordon, but I'm sorry you're going away. We won't have a man in the house at all now."

The unexpected words came to Fiona as a jolt, and to Gordon as a boost to his masculinity.

"Father's in London all the time," Florence went on, wistfully slicing her egg. "We used to see Uncle James at his studio every week, after he took Mother for a drive. That was always fun. He gave us fruit drinks and sometimes he had sweets in a tin on the mantelpiece. But he's been away for a long time. And now you're going to Lochbank, Gordon." She shook her plaited hair and gave him an accusing look.

Fiona stirred herself into cheerfulness. "I don't know, Florence, what this sudden preoccupation with the male members of the family is about, but you must know that is the way of things. Men very often have to leave home for reasons of business or to study. Besides, your father comes home whenever he can and I don't really expect Gordon will be away for all that long." She gave him a look over Florence's head, but he avoided her eyes. "At least, I'm hoping not."

But Florence was not to be diverted. She pushed her empty plate away and reached for the toast and marmalade. "And, of course, when the summer ends, Allan and Steven are going off to boarding school in England," she said, developing her theme with relish now that she saw she had their attention.

Gordon snorted witheringly. "Allan and Steven! They're hardly out of the nursery. They wouldn't make a man between them."

"They're not men yet," Florence conceded, "but they will be one day."

"Yes, they will," Fiona said, "and meantime we have them with us. Nothing is settled about their going to boarding school, but your father thinks they should have that advantage. They have both very sensibly accepted his offer and it is now a question of finding vacancies for them in a suitable school." She paused significantly. "Gordon was given the same opportunity but refused it. I hope he never regrets it."

Gordon scowled. "I won't regret it," he said grimly. All his regrets now were concentrated on one person, concerned only with the baffling, obsessive love that bound him to Anne and that he knew would go on binding him whatever the obstacles or the opposition.

Fiona opened a diamond-studded watch pinned to her dress. As usual, the time surprised her. "Off you go, then, Gordon, and pack your case," she said as brightly as she could. "I'll come up shortly to make sure you haven't forgotten anything important. But first I'll have to see why Allan and Steven aren't down. They'll be late for school if they don't hurry."

Then, satisfying herself that Florence had eaten an adequate breakfast, she left the room, brooding on the picture of shrinking family life so unexpectedly thrust into her awareness on top of the other cares that had descended on her in less than a day.

That afternoon Rita was "at home." These days she was an infrequent hostess, but the gilded, handwritten invitations she had been issuing for almost forty years were still much sought after by young wives anxious for an entrance to the fashionable female society of Glasgow.

Normally, Fiona found her mother-in-law's gatherings relaxing. Usually, she looked forward to the chatter and the exchange of gossip. Most of Rita's friends were known to her, but there were always some additions. It was amusing to watch these often ambitious newcomers vying for attention, and a little sobering to remember that in her own young-married days she had been no less keen to earn from one of the established ladies the kindly word or the promise of a future invitation that denoted acceptance.

Today, however, she was too filled with the shock of Gordon's folly to have much enthusiasm for the frivolity of afternoon tea with perhaps fifty noisy women. She walked up the hill to Park Place, preoccupied, worried and late. Even the day was dull and disheartening. The flowers on the grassy slope opposite the houses looked sooty and defeated. The floral window arrangements seemed dispirited, and some of the brass jardinieres in which they sat looked in need of polishing.

She had almost made up her mind to find a quiet moment in which to confide in Rita and seek her advice and reassurance, but the frothy waves of sound that reached her as she entered the long drawing room made her realise this was not the occasion. Rita had her duties as hostess. It would be thoughtless to unload a sombre family worry on her at such a time.

As she stood just inside the door, looking for a familiar face, she felt a hand on her arm and, turning, heard Gwen say, "Mother asked me to watch out for you, Fiona. She's just taken one or two ladies to look at Father's collection of porcelain."

Fiona cast an interested eye around the assembly of feathery hats and shimmering, high-necked afternoon gowns. Many of the women, she noted, were cruelly corseted into the grotesque new shape of tiny waist and heavy, threatening bust. She thought this fashion too unnatural and unbecoming to last. It certainly would not tempt her. She smiled.

"I always think it's as well Grandfather is safely out of the way on these occasions. I'm sure the sight of three or four large women lifting and laying his best red-anchor Chelsea would be bad for his blood pressure."

Gwen signalled for a maid to attend to Fiona. "You're right," she said. "Even in the shop I've watched him close his eyes when customers start browsing among the ornaments."

For a moment she seemed to examine Fiona's hat, but that this was not what had been in her mind was obvious when she spoke.

"Fiona, is it true you've sent Gordon to work at Lochbank?"

Fiona's hand stopped on its journey toward a tray held by a maid. Her expression was comical.

"How on earth can you possibly have heard that? It was only decided this morning, and I haven't been to the office. Even McNair doesn't know yet."

Gwen looked as if she didn't know whether to laugh or apologise. "I suppose I could pretend I've taken up mind reading, but the explanation is quite prosaic. When Marjorie Reid was taking her daughter to school, she met your Florence. Florence told her about Gordon, and Marjorie happened to mention it to me when she came into the shop."

Fiona shook her head in wonder. "Well, it's perfectly true, and, of course, there's no secret about it. It just didn't seem possible you could have heard so quickly."

Gwen took her arm and, heedless of attempts to draw them into conversation, steered her through the crush toward two chairs which had just been vacated. "You do know Jack and Gordon have a rather strained relationship?"

"I do, although I've never been able to discover the reason for it."

143

"Nor have I, but do you think it wise to throw them together in such an isolated place?" She plopped two lumps of sugar into her tea cup and stirred anxiously.

Fiona's manner became businesslike, almost brusque. "They'll just have to behave themselves. I warned Gordon before he left. Perhaps you would write and make the same thing clear to Jack. They'll have to work together. That's all there is to it. I'm not going to run King and Company on the basis of their silliness."

"Of course not." Gwen lifted a plate of cream cakes and held it out glumly. "You couldn't be expected to."

Fiona sat up very straight. "I do think Jack should set an example. After all, he is that vital year or two older than Gordon." Almost immediately she regretted the reproachful words, but to her relief, Gwen was not annoyed.

"You have no idea," Gwen said with a furtive glance toward the nearest group of laughing guests, "how those two years worry me sometimes."

"In what way?" She realised someone almost hidden under a very large hat was trying to attract her attention from the far end of the room. She was amused when she recognised the small, kindly face of Aunt May. Hats had always exerted a strange, unbalancing influence over the otherwise unsensational life Aunt May had led, most of it in widowhood. Fiona waved what she hoped would be understood as her congratulations and turned back to Gwen, who was smiling slightly at the serene old lady's spirit.

"If war comes in South Africa," Gwen said, "Gordon will be too young to go. You will be free of that worry. Whereas Jack will be just the age to fight."

Fiona put down her cup and looked across the table in surprise. "I don't understand, Gwen. Jack is not a soldier. His career is with King and Company. He takes his work extremely seriously. Why should you think of him being involved if war comes in Africa?"

Even as she asked she knew the answer: *because he is the son of Tom Hoey.* Wasn't that what came into all their minds from time to time, and usually in some context less honourable than war?

Gwen prised open a sandwich and stared at the thinly sliced cucumber. "Do you think I'm being silly? Colin does."

Fiona leaned forward helpfully, regretting again her earlier businesslike manner.

"Well, unless there's more to it than you've said, Gwen, I must say you do seem to be meeting trouble more than half way. After all, there is no war in South Africa. We all hope there never will be one. But even if war comes, do you have any real reason to think Jack would go to it?"

144

Food seemed to have become distasteful to Gwen. She handed the plate with the cucumber sandwich to a passing maid and refused to take anything else from the vast selection. "You will probably smile when I tell you." She clasped her hands as if to keep them still. "One Sunday morning a week or two ago, I remembered I had promised to look out for some things for a jumble sale one of my customers is organising. Colin had gone to church. Jack had been out to all hours and I thought he was still in bed. It seemed an ideal time to do a bit of rummaging. I went upstairs to an attic room we keep for storage. When I opened the door, Jack was standing among the trunks and boxes, wearing one of his father's old uniforms. I almost fainted. You see"—her eyes avoided Fiona's gaze—"I was so startled . . . for a moment I thought it was Tom. It sounds so ridiculous now, but at the time . . . "

Fiona nodded, her eyes wide and engrossed. "I can understand perfectly what a shock it would be."

"I had even forgotten we still had some of Tom's things. Jack, of course, didn't realise how shaken I was. He was only concerned to know if I thought military dress suited him. I'm afraid I behaved rather stupidly. I was quite sharp and told him to take the uniform off and never wear it again. He jumped to the wrong conclusion. He thought I considered he was desecrating his father's memory. He apologised for his thoughtlessness, and then, of course, I realised I had been very harsh and tried to minimize the incident." She stopped with a short, uncertain laugh. "It all sounds so trivial and yet so hideously complicated. Anyway, Jack became quite serious. He asked if Tom had worn that particular uniform when he won the Queen's Medal during the Zulu war. Of course, I didn't know. Then he started talking quite knowledgeably about this trouble in the Transvaal. To be truthful, I know very little about the situation, but he seems to be following the news very closely, almost"—she hesitated and looked away again—" . . . almost as if he had some personal interest in it. Something he said sticks in my mind: 'One of these days we might need men like Father to go back to Africa.' Then for a second or two he stood with his back very straight and his shoulders squared, looking at himself in an old cobwebbed mirror as if wondering how like his father he was."

Fiona tried not to show the surge of compassion that filled her. Gwen's life had for a long time been a tragic one. Now that she had found peace with Colin, it would be dreadful if this spectre of the son following the father should begin to haunt her.

"Quite honestly, Gwen," she said with firm sympathy, "I think you're being fanciful. Not that I'd be any different, myself, in your position. But precisely because I'm not so close to Jack, I'm sure I can see the incident in a less involved way than you. What really happened? He found one of his father's old uniforms and in an idle moment tried it on. Naturally, he's proud of his father's bravery as a soldier and wonders, as a young man will, how like the original he is. It was understandably an emotional incident for you, and I don't wonder it's preyed on your mind, but you've read more into it than was there, Gwen. I'm sure of that."

Her smiling, yet concerned reassurance cheered Gwen. She shook her head slowly, as if ashamed at being so impressionable.

"Thank you, Fiona, for listening so patiently. You've said almost word for word what Colin told me. Obviously, I've let my imagination run away with me."

She straightened in her chair and looked guiltily round the crowded room. "And what a place I've chosen to bring up such a subject. You came here to relax and enjoy yourself. I've been very selfish. We must have looked as if we were discussing a tragedy. No one has dared say a word to us or even glance too obviously in our direction. And I'm supposed to be looking after them all while Mother is out of the room."

She braced herself and then rose quickly from her seat. Fiona followed. Then, almost in unison, they turned to face the company with wide, calm smiles. Almost immediately they were drawn into the nearest group of women, to exclamations of delight.

"Fiona, my dear! How well you are looking. But I feared you weren't going to have even the teeniest word with us. It's so long since any of us have seen you. These days you seem to accept hardly any invitations. Certainly none of mine."

The speaker was Mrs. Isobel Maitland, wife of a fashionable heart consultant, a tireless hostess in her own right and a comfortable, auntlike figure on the outer fringes of Fiona's family.

"Well, of course, Fiona is a woman of affairs now, isn't she? Her time will be taken up with much more important things than the silly chatter of boring creatures like us. Isn't that so, my dear?"

Fiona glanced at the speaker. In the past she had always seemed sympathetic. "I sometimes think I have to endure more silly chatter now than ever before, Mrs. Short," she said brightly. *Especially,* she thought, *when I'm confronted with a collection of hens who suspect they might be missing something.*

"Well, we're all very proud of you," Mrs. Maitland said placidly. "I heard it said the other day you've opened a whole new world of possibilities for women."

"I've helped a little, I suppose, but Gwen is the real pioneer. She was one of the first women in Glasgow to open her own business. And that's almost twenty years ago, now."

"But Gwen only has her Miss Murray," one of the younger matrons said. "You have sway over so many men." Her eyes flashed. "I sometimes dream what I would do if I had all that power."

Fiona joined in the laughter. "Well, I might dream, too, on occasions, Emily. But I'm quite sure in reality you would do exactly as I do: get on with what has to be done and never give the power a thought."

"But surely men don't *like* working for a woman?"

"Some don't even like working for another man."

"Now, be serious, Fiona. Do you find they defer to you, or resent you?"

"If it's someone meeting me across a desk for the first time, I think they find the situation rather novel, even disconcerting. That gives me an advantage. But I can assure you they don't defer to me. I don't get anything made easy for me because I'm a woman. Of course, everyone at King and Company has accepted the situation long ago. They just don't think about it.

"It must be wonderful knowing you have the final word on your husband," a contented-looking woman said with exaggerated wistfulness. Fiona thought some of the titters that followed sounded rather forced. For most of them it would be too deep a yearning for laughter.

In relation to most of them she was, she supposed, in an extraordinarily emancipated position. Because of this she was inevitably an object of curiosity and envy. This was the price she must expect to pay for the unique status she now occupied among the women of Glasgow.

It was a realisation that helped make bearable the veiled spite she had sensed recently at gatherings like these. Even here, under a friendly roof, she felt she was going to be made to pay for being "different," for having broken out of the frustrating and often empty round that was the life ordained for most women of her age and class.

As she moved about the room, she saw the cold calculation behind some of the smiles.

"But what about your home life, my dear?"

It was the barbed question she heard more than any other.

"You must regret not being able to give your children the time they need, especially when their father isn't at home, either."

"Yes, how is dear Robert? He seems to be practically exiled in London. How busy he must be with his politics! Surely it's ages and ages since he was last home. You must miss him so."

Smilingly but resolutely she declined every invitation. She had realised some hostesses were using her as an exhibit, even as bait.

"Fiona! Has Gwen been looking after you?"

It was Rita, returned from the tour of Fergus's treasures, now regarded by some as the best collection of porcelain outside the Victoria and Albert Museum.

147

As Fiona went gratefully across the room to her mother-in-law, she surprised one or two groups too intently discussing her to notice her nearness.

"If you ask me, it's hardened her."

"But how could it be otherwise, mixing and haggling with all those men?"

"Mind you, the extraordinary thing is, I hear she's a match for any of them."

Rita's welcoming expression turned to one of concern. "Is everything all right, Fiona? You look quite . . . flustered. Are you feeling well enough?"

"I'm perfectly well, Grandmother. Just a little startled and breathless at the sharp claws some of your friends have."

Rita, who had come through life practically untainted, frowned at this puzzling remark; but Gwen, who had joined them in time to hear Fiona, nodded understandingly.

"In the last few months I suppose you'll have had to revise your opinion of who your real friends are?"

"Frequently, I'm afraid."

"Well, I can sympathise. I had to endure the same cattiness when I opened my shop. All you can do is ignore it."

Rita said, "I hope no one has been unpleasant to you in my house, Fiona? I would be terribly annoyed and disappointed."

"It's all right, Grandmother. Women just can't help being women. I suppose there have been occasions when I've said things myself I would be ashamed of now."

The room had been slowly emptying and quietening. When the last carriage had gone from the street, Rita sighed gratefully. "Entertaining is such a strain. After every 'at home' I say there will be no more." She smiled at them. "But we shall see. Meantime, I hope you can both stay for a little while. I'm going to ring for tea. I wasn't relaxed enough when the ladies were here to enjoy anything properly. Let's sit over here, by the window."

Rita's entire adult life had centred on the family. Her own children had gone off to sell whisky or antiques or to paint pictures while she had stayed at home waiting for them to return to her with their news and their problems. Age had not changed her. Now that the circle, once small and cosy, had widened to embrace in-laws and grandchildren, her interest in all their varied affairs was as passionate as ever. At the end of these social occasions she liked to settle down for a little while with someone from the family, to go over matters too trivial or too private to be raised in the presence of guests.

When the tea was brought, she dismissed the maid and poured it her-

148

self. She turned to Gwen, noticing her paleness, but thinking that perhaps today, for once, she would desist from motherly concern.

"Is Colin well?"

"Very well, Mother. He was meeting Father this afternoon to look at some furniture and paintings coming up for auction somewhere out in Lanarkshire."

Gnawing at the back of Rita's mind was the suggestion that some of her guests had made wounding remarks to Fiona. Now, the reference to paintings swung her anxiety to James.

"I don't know how people can be deliberately hurtful," she said with sudden bitterness.

Gwen, misjudging the reason for the outburst, looked significantly at Fiona and said, "I'm sure Fiona is far too sensible to let spiteful tongues upset her."

Rita lifted the teapot and sat holding it absentmindedly. "I'm not so worried about Fiona, although it was her remark earlier which has brought this into my mind. Fiona is strong and, as you say, Gwen, sensible. In any case, I'm sure the silly chatter about her is simply what we call cattiness. It can be ignored. With James it is quite different. What they are suggesting about James is evil." She put the teapot down as if it had become too heavy. "Your father tells me it's spread over half the town."

Fiona was certain that left to herself, Rita would gradually have eased what she had been told about James into some distant recess of her mind. That, however, was not Fergus's way. She said, "Surely Grandfather hasn't been going on about that again? It can do no good."

"Well, it is a terrible stain on James, and on all of us," Rita said, coming quickly to Fergus's defence, although in private she frequently begged him to put the matter from his head. "And as to its doing no good . . . well, that remains to be seen."

Gwen seized on the note of slightly mysterious defiance that had entered her mother's voice. "And what on earth do you mean by that, Mother?"

Rita seemd to consider retreating into the deeper mystery of a tantalising silence. Then, the open forthrightness of her nature asserting itself, she said, "Well, the law does offer some protection against this sort of thing, Gwen. People cannot go about making slanderous statements with impunity. Your father's intention is to surprise someone spreading this infamous gossip in front of witnesses and take him to court for it."

"Oh, dear!" Gwen sank despairingly into her chair. "Poor James! Even his father has turned against him."

Rita reared up, her eyes bright with shock and indignation. "How dare you say that, Gwen? Your father's only wish is to help James."

149

"Then skulking about Glasgow, evesdropping on conversations is the wrong way to go about it. He'll drive himself mad."

"Don't be absurd. He's not going out of his way to find a culprit. It's simply if he does hear anyone spreading these stories."

Gwen leaned across the table and took Rita's hand. "You must promise to tell us, Mother, if Father ever looks like getting anywhere with this ridiculous plan. He mustn't be allowed to go to court without us all meeting. And if he should still be determined to behave foolishly, then James himself would have to be told."

Rita shook her head impatiently. "Of course James would have to be told. Your father is not irresponsible. Please be sensible, Gwen!" After this uncharacteristic outburst she seemed to withdraw into the embrasure of the window, staring helplessly down the long room where over the years she had created her incomparable blend of elegance and homeliness. Here, she was mistress, but after so long behind these sheltering walls, she had few weapons against the monstrous injustices of the world beyond—the world that had turned against James. She had nothing to offer her son but love. She seemed now to realise it. The defiant spark had gone, leaving only an uncomprehending limpness.

"At least James doesn't know anything about it," Fiona said comfortingly. "That's a blessing."

Rita looked at her vacantly. "I suppose in a way it is a blessing," she mused. "In another way, it makes it all the more horrible. It's terrible to think of James going innocently about his work, not knowing . . . so unsuspecting."

They were sitting in silence, the tea forgotten, when a maid came to remove the tray.

150

10

James reined in his pony and the trap slowly bumped to a halt on the narrow cart track. Through the trees he could see the gleam of water, blue and welcoming. His arms were stiff after the drive and he made no immediate move to climb down. He relaxed in his seat, idly taking in the beauty of the woodland scene.

Darker than the sea, bluebells spread away under the still trees for as far as his eye would go. Beside the rutted track birch stood straight and silvery in the clear light. In the coarse grass round the exposed roots primroses gleamed. The wild flowers were past their best, for already it was early summer. A whole year gone and he could almost count the number of times he had managed to get out of Fleetside, and explore these quiet shores. He might almost have been as well staying in Glasgow. But not quite. James smiled with wry content, for the trying and sometimes irksome work of the last twelve months was at last over, and he was free now to get on with what he had come here to do.

He had spent the autumn and winter supervising alterations to his house, for as well as decorating and modernising the old rooms, he had built on a studio overlooking the garden. The chaos had been worse than he had expected and had lasted longer, the local tradesmen having a more leisurely approach to work than their aggressive city counterparts. Perhaps from their example he had found himself falling gradually into the easy tempo of rural ways.

But despite this gentle lethargy it had been an effort to restrict his painting to the completion of several important commissions he had been committed to before leaving Glasgow. He had been impatient to start some work conceived totally in these lush new pastures. Now the way was clear. On the floor of the trap his painting materials lay strapped together. Despite Fergus's efforts to persuade him otherwise, he had decided a carriage would be too ostentatious for the small town. Nor had he wanted to burden himself with a coachman. Nevertheless his disability made some form of transport necessary. He had bought the trap because he could handle it himself and because it would be easily manoeuvrable in the narrow lanes and byways to which his painting expeditions would take him.

He reached down for a lemonade bottle and drank from it with boyish pleasure, thinking that in Glasgow he would have felt a glass or at least a cup to be necessary. It was as well Fergus wasn't there to see this slide into rustic informality.

After a few more minutes of lazy reflection James climbed stiffly from the trap and lifted out what he needed. He trudged carefully down the hard-baked mud of the track under the shade of the trees. Gradually the undergrowth thinned and he emerged almost in the centre of a wide sunlit bay. The tide was out, exposing a sweeping vista of sand in the dips and hollows of which water had been trapped as the sea receded. The Solway was a distant splash of glittering blue. The air, stirring gently now that he was clear of the wood, had a keen and exhilarating tang that reminded him of the Gareloch.

Three or four hundred yards out a rocky plateau rose perhaps ten or twelve feet high from the wet sand. It was sparsely grown with tough sea-washed grass, and here and there the first sea pinks had opened their papery petals upon it. When the tide was in, it would be an island. And at very high tides it would, he surmised, be submerged. As he studied the scene, his interest quickened. It seemed to provide everything he needed as background for the carefully posed children inseparable from his work. *Providence, and not James King, must have driven the trap,* he thought happily. Certainly Providence had placed that island there so conveniently. It was the island that held his eye. Without it, the wide bay would have been too vast for his artistic needs. He wanted water, but he wanted it with a background of wooded land. In his work there were no far horizons. Sometimes he painted two-dimensionally, sacrificing perspective to secure an overall decorative effect. Painting from the shore would give him too open and empty an outlook for the intricate and cunning tapestries he had learned to weave with paint. But if he walked across the sand and set up his easel on the island, he would have a foreground on which he could pose his children. The water would not be there, of course. It would be behind him. But he could paint it in. And on the luxuriant mainland he would have the tangled pattern of shrubs, trees and flowers from which he distilled his wild colours. Through James's thin frame the restless beat of creation began to throb. The young models Mrs. Laing, his housekeeper, had promised to produce when he needed them could come later. But his first tussle with this stimulating scene could not wait. Taking a firm grip of his easel and folding chair, he limped out to the island with almost feverish impatience and began to sketch.

The impulsive walk had started pain gnawing at his leg, but the years had taught him how to suffer that. He clenched his teeth and worked with swift dedication, conscious that when the tide turned, he would have to leave his rocky vantage point. The pencil moved over the pages of his sketching pad as if propelled by some exuberant independent force. When black and white failed to satisfy him, he put a canvas on his easel and gave himself over to the excitement of oils. Colours spurted from the tubes and were transferred to the canvas in tempestuous strokes of luscious impasto, as if brush and knife were inspired.

So absorbed was he that when a voice spoke close behind him, he jumped in surprise. He turned and saw a slim girl in a lemon-coloured dress. She had black hair arranged in a neat, boyish style. Her features were small, and although her colouring was robustly healthy, these gave her an appearance of daintiness, almost of delicacy. She was perhaps twenty-five years old.

As he stared at her, still too surprised to move or speak, he realised that she had an easel and other painting equipment resting on the grass at her side. She spoke again, her tone breezy but unmistakably exasperated.

"I said you've taken my place."

James's smile was perplexed. "Your place?"

"Yes." Her eyes were challenging. "This is where I paint. Surely with the whole Stewartry of Kirkcudbright to choose from you didn't have to plank yourself down on this spot." She was holding a walking stick, and she dug it into the ground for emphasis.

"It's so beautiful," he said helplessly.

"It's the finest spot in Galloway," she said emphatically. "It's at its best, of course, when the tide is in." She put a hand up to shield her eyes and swivelled slowly round, surveying the scene with an appearance of satisfied ownership. Her eyes finally settled on James as if she expected to see him begin moving.

Reluctantly he put down his brush. "I hadn't realised it was private," he said. "I just strayed down off the main road. I'm sorry to have trespassed. If you'll give me a minute or two to get my things together."

She looked slightly guilty, but her voice was as brightly confident as ever. "It's not private. You haven't trespassed."

"Then . . . you're not the landowner?" James's voice was faintly accusing.

Her shapely chin went up defensively. "No, but I've been coming here for ages. It took me years to find this place."

This self-confident elf needs deflating, James thought. "This is my first

153

morning out," he said deliberately. "I found it right away. Couldn't we share it?"

Spots of colour appeared on her cheeks. "Why on earth should we get in each other's way by sharing this little spot?" She slid a dainty but impatient foot over the grass. "It's not much bigger than a backyard, after all. And there are so many other places round the bay."

He thought he could detect a slightly beseeching note in her voice now. As he hesitated, she said, "Look here, this is my work. I don't know what you do for a living, but how would you like it if I pushed my way in and sat down beside you in the bank or the office? It's all right for you, pottering about with paints during your holiday, but with me it's a serious business. Can't you understand that?"

Her small face was so agitated, her whole pose so indicative of a total conviction of rightness, that he laughed and pushed back his seat.

"You're absolutely right. I'll find myself another place." He was so stiff when he rose that he had to stand for a moment until he was sure of his balance. All at once the pain threatened to engulf him. He closed his eyes, summoning all his will. Soon the level would drop to the point at which he could again begin to ignore it.

When she saw his limp, her eyes widened. After a moment of transparent confusion her face clouded with almost comic embarrassment. She pointed vaguely toward his easel with her walking stick.

"I say. Have you actually started on something here?"

"It doesn't matter," he said, grimly relishing the sudden turn in the situation. "I can easily finish it somewhere else—or scrap it."

Her hand had been at her mouth, but now she put it out toward him in a gesture of dismay. He had time to notice that the fingers, although long and well shaped, showed signs of having been used for physical work. "Oh, no, you mustn't do that. You mustn't scrap it. You must finish it, and really, I suppose, this is the place to do it. I shouldn't have been so impatient."

He had already lifted his canvas from the easel, but she walked round to where he had put it on the grass and gave it a quick glance.

"Actually, you know, you're very good for an amateur. Derivative, of course; but then, amateurs always are."

Anger had been slowly rising in James since the pity he hated so much had so suddenly displaced the girl's more acceptable aggression. Now he hovered on the verge of exploding. With an effort he regained his sense of humour.

"I try hard," he said with an exaggeratedly humble expression, collapsing his easel and gathering his paints. "I do my best, but I think I've had enough of painting for today."

For a moment she stood shamefaced, her hands clasped behind her back, like a schoolgirl caught misbehaving. Then, keeping her eyes averted, she knelt down on the grass to help him with the leather belt he used to strap his folding chair and easel together.

"Where are you staying?"

"Fleetside," he said shortly.

Her guilt was making her reluctant to let him go now. "I suppose that was your pony and trap I passed on the way down?"

He nodded. The elfin quality was enhanced as she knelt beside him, the folds of her lemon dress flowing and trailing across the grass. Or was she like a flower, rising fresh and fragile from among the rocks? Determinedly he banished the fanciful ideas. She was a self-confident tomboy who should be left to stew in the juice of her well-deserved remorse. Amateur! Derivative! He seized his canvas, heedless of the wet paint, and swayed to his feet. Her abashment as she watched his unsteadiness was oddly touching. With two good legs and a less gentle nature James might have stalked off. As it was, he hesitated.

"And where do you come from?"

"Oh, Fleetside," she said, as if mildly surprised that he could have thought she was from anywhere else.

"You didn't walk, surely?" And yet he couldn't imagine her driving a trap.

"I have a bicycle," she said.

He laughed slightly. "I might have known." She looked at him enquiringly but he didn't elaborate. Again he hesitated. "Amateurish as my work is, do you think there's a chance I might improve?"

"Oh, yes," she said eagerly, grateful for the chance to make some atonement. "I'm sure you will. Just keep at it."

He smiled coldly. "But not here?" Her eyes were so pained that he regretted the teasing. He lifted his bundle. "By the way, what do you call this spot?"

"Gatekirk Bay," she said.

When he reached home, Mrs. Laing was in the hall, rosy-faced and slightly apprehensive.

"Oh, Mr. King, a gentleman called. When I told him you were out, he invited himself back for dinner." She had a nervous habit of moving her bulk from one foot to the other.

James gave her a soothing look. "Did he, indeed?" He waited, containing his surprise. He had learned that Mrs. Laing's little excitements had a way of smoothing themselves out.

It took her some rummaging among the dusters in the pockets of her floral apron before she found the caller's card. James smiled delightedly when he read the name. The visitor was his old friend James Guthrie, whose leadership had done so much to sustain the Glasgow-school artists against the outraged disbelief of the critics. Years ago, fame had overtaken Guthrie and whisked him off to London. It had also, to the despair of many, snuffed out his unique vision. He had been diverted into more conventional ways and was now one of the most fashionable portrait painters in the country.

James turned the card over, but there was no message. "I wonder what can have brought Jim Guthrie to this remote spot?"

"He has friends somewhere near," Mrs. Laing said. "He said he didna know you lived in Fleetside, but that once he found out, nothing would make him leave without seeing you. He was very nice." Her anxiety was diminishing.

James put the card on a table. "I'm afraid neither of us was ever very keen on letter writing." He looked at his watch. "Have we enough food in the house?"

"There was nothing good enough for entertaining, but I went down and saw Mr. Petrie. Now there's some very nice saddle of lamb in the oven."

James rubbed his hands. "That sounds good. I might have known you'd have everything under control."

She began to withdraw and then hesitated. "Perhaps I shouldna have said the gentleman invited himself to dinner. It was more that he sort of put me in the way of inviting him, if you know what I mean. He left me so there didna seem anything else I could rightly do."

James laughed. "That sounds just like Guthrie. London can't have changed him much."

Nor had it. That evening, after James had welcomed him warmly, Guthrie looked round the panelled hall, with its gilt Chippendale mirror reflecting an Alexander Nasmyth view of the Clyde at Dumbarton, its elegant pedestal table on which sat a flower-filled jardiniere of early Flemish brass.

"Dear, oh, dear," he said, shaking his head with mock solemnity. "This is the worst of having such wealthy friends. When I heard you were somewhere in the district, I wrote to your father for your address. His letter said you had found a rustic retreat in which you intended to live the simple life. I expected to find you in a but-and-ben. Instead of that, here you are, installed in style in a very fine house."

James put a restraining hand on his friend's arm and guided him toward the drawing room. "Now, now, Jim, you mustn't pull my leg. You know it's the only one I have."

"My dear chap, I'm not pulling your leg," Guthrie protested. "Your father's letter really did give the impression that you were roughing it for art's sake."

"You know Father well enough to have taken that with a pinch of salt.

156

He opposed my coming here, of course. So that makes it the outer darkness. And by his standards I suppose this is a small house. It would be useless for a family. But as you say, it has some style. It's all on the one floor, which suits me, and it dates back to the beginning of the eighteenth century. Of course, all these beautiful things were sent down by Mother and Father. I probably wouldn't have bothered."

"Well, the nice motherly body in the apron must have taste. Everything's well placed. And look at those flowers!"

Under Guthrie's lively and slightly sardonic humour James soon eased into a mood of happy relaxation. With the lamps lit, logs on the fire, their pipes going and a decanter between them, his pain and restlessness retreated and the slight irritation that had lingered from his encounter with the girl at Gatekirk Bay left him. Guthrie gave him news of other friends—Lavery, Walton and Henry—fine painters of the Glasgow school who had also been diverted into portraiture.

James refilled their glasses and leaned back on the antimacassar with his foot resting on the brass fender. "How the rebels have been tamed," he said with a reflective grin. "When they write in the newspapers about you chaps now, it's with respect. You've all become pillars of the Establishment. If you're not painting Lady This, it's Lord That."

Guthrie, catching the note of seriousness in the jest, wrinkled his brow. He tapped out his pipe. "I'm afraid you're right, James. There's no good denying it. We've all been seduced. We've taken the easy way and the fat commissions that go with it."

James immediately regretted the sting that had provoked this admission. "I didn't mean it quite like that. Portraiture can be every bit as demanding and satisfying as any other field of painting."

Guthrie shook his head. "We all say that, of course, but only to salve our consciences. In practice it boils down to one compromise after another. We have to please not only ourselves but our sitters and the man who signs the cheque. I wouldn't be in demand for very long if I painted portraits the subjects didn't like. No, James. You're one of the few who've stuck it out."

James smiled at the divergence between Guthrie's view of him and the view he had of himself. "The truth is, we've all been ensnared by success. I could almost draw a line where my work stopped developing. I sometimes feel I was embalmed in the year eighteen ninety-two. I'm on the same treadmill as the rest of you. That's why I came down here. To try to get off. It won't be easy. Recognition is a very heady brew." He laughed ruefully. "But I have to admit it helps make up for a lot of lost dreams."

"That's the trouble. It does. If it didn't sound too cynical, I would say there are times when recognition is almost enough."

James found himself speaking of something he had imagined he had

157

cleared from his mind years ago. "At least the rest of you have all been elected to the Academy. I must be about the only one now who's been passed over."

He realised with dismay that the dregs of old bitterness were still there and cursed whatever subterranean disturbance had brought them floating up into this pleasant evening.

Guthrie pushed himself straight in his chair. "It's a damned disgrace," he said angrily. "But it's strange you should have mentioned it. Walton and I were talking about it the last time we met." He lifted his glass and thoughtfully swirled the whisky. "None of us can understand it." He sat looking at James for a few moments and then leaned forward impulsively. "I shouldn't be telling you this, because heaven knows what the outcome will be . . . but Walton and I have nominated you for election."

For years James had pretended indifference, but to have been consistently passed over when so many lesser men had been elected to the Academy had hurt his pride more than he had ever admitted. Almost every recognition had come his way except this one, which only his fellow artists could bestow. To be elected a member of the Scottish Royal Academy would set the seal on his career. But determinedly he stifled his interest at Guthrie's revelation. There had been rumours before, hints that soon it would be his turn, but in the end there had always been disappointment.

"It's too late now, Jim," he said levelly. "If they didn't consider me good enough in the past, I certainly haven't painted anything recently that would make them change their minds."

Guthrie took the objection seriously. "We can't say that, James. We don't know what was in their minds in the past. In any case, it doesn't depend on one particular work. You have produced a body of work second to none. Personally, when I look round and see some of the people sitting in the Academy, I don't value the honour all that much. But you're entitled to it. None of us knows why you were never given it. It could just have been some . . . oversight. Anything's possible when so many hidebound old fogeys can vote. Anyway, you've been well and truly proposed now. We were too late to have you nominated this year, but if there's any justice, if Walton and I have anything to do with it, next year you'll be James King, SRA."

When James wakened next morning, it was not, despite Guthrie's news, with grand thoughts of being elected to the Academy. The creative juices were still flowing. As he bathed, shaved and dressed, the picture in his mind was of Gatekirk Bay and its island in the sand, speckled with sea pinks and the first faint haze of blue flax not yet opened.

After breakfast he collected his sketchbook and canvas from the trap, where he had left them the previous afternoon. He went to his studio, meaning to look at them, but after a few restless minutes he opened the French window and strolled moodily up the long garden, pausing here and there to note each opening bloom. He stopped at the wall separating the garden from the river. He leaned on it. There were two or three fishing boats in the small harbour. The tide was out and they were tilted over in the mud against the granite wall. That was how James felt. *Lopsided. Beached. Stranded. High and dry. Stuck in the mud.* A few more disparaging phrases ran through his mind. Yesterday, at Gatekirk Bay, he had worked so well. But so damnably briefly! He cursed the girl. That the creative fury should have been thwarted by such a cheeky, self-opinionated scrap of a thing! It was galling. It was intolerable. And yet, strangely—surely it couldn't only be her determination impressing itself on him?—she did seem to belong there.

He could not see the bay now without her somewhere in it—an integral part of the whole wonderful assembly—kneeling on the grass with the folds of her long lemon dress undulating gracefully away in a natural, almost inevitable mingling with the primroses. He frowned. Had there been primroses? He couldn't remember. Perhaps he was simply imagining them, building up his picture. He cursed her again. But when he thought of the gay fanfare of blossom that fringed the bay with entrancing patterns of colour, he saw her there, too, her small hands resting elegantly on a laden branch, her upturned face inextricably woven with the fluttering leaves and petals, peering out at him like one of his own highly tinted little models. He had a sudden, shaking longing to be there, working as he had worked yesterday. Christ! She didn't own the bay. She could have the damned island to herself. He would swallow his pride and work from the shore. All he wanted was the inspiration of nature's enchanted arrangement. Later he could work it all out in the studio.

He looked at the sky. There were clouds today, and the sun kept disappearing behind them, but the air was warm and enticing on his face. He leaned farther over the wall and shouted to attract the attention of a man sitting on a box, dreamily smoking a pipe with his back against one of the harbour sheds.

"Is it going to rain, do you think, Wattie?"

Wattie looked up slowly from the net that hung listlessly from one hand, took the pipe carefully from his mouth and gave the sky a leisurely examination.

"Dinna mention rain, Mr. King," he called at last. "If ye'd been up as early as me ye'd ken fine the sky's clearing up a treat. Ye'll no' be needin' ye're umbrella the day unless the wind changes."

James waved and then turned purposefully toward the house. He flung open the hall door. "Mrs. Laing! Are you in? Mrs. Laing!"

She came hurrying from the direction of the kitchen, her hands white with flour.

"Do you think you could get those two little girls for me today, Mrs. Laing? The ones you said would model for me? I want to do some painting at Gatekirk Bay this afternoon."

She considered, wiping her hands on her apron.

"I daresay I could, Mr. King. If you'll just let me get the baking into the oven, I'll go across the green and ask their mother."

He had a sudden, damping thought. "What about school? Won't they be at school?"

Mrs. Laing gave him a knowing look and her cheerful laughter filled the hall. "Don't tell me you dinna ken wee girls are subject to sudden indispositions, Mr. King? My goodness, Mrs. Melville would keep those two wee dears of hers off school for a week, never mind an afternoon, for the honour of havin' them painted by a famous artist like yourself."

"Well, so long as it won't get them into trouble."

"We can but ask," Mrs. Laing said reasonably. She paused on her way to the kitchen. "What was it again you said you'd give them, Mr. King? You know, so's I can tell Mrs. Melville."

"Would a shilling be all right?"

Mrs. Laing looked scandalised.

"I mean, I'll give them a shilling each," James said hastily.

Mrs. Laing's disapproval deepened. "Deed and you will not, Mr. King," she said sternly. She pursed her lips. "A sixpence will be quite adequate. Between them."

She went off with her rosy face still twitching a little with the shock of James's profligacy.

"I'll need plenty of sweets and plenty of lemonade to keep them happy," he called after her. "See what you can get when you're out."

Shortly after one o'clock, with Mrs. Laing there to smooth the way, he collected the Melville children—Meg, aged ten, and Isa, eight.

"Now, mind you both do whatever Mr. King tells you," their excited mother said as they climbed self-consciously into the trap.

Their oval-shaped faces had been washed to a shining pink and their eyes were wide and lively. Their mother, James saw, was a woman with a sense of occasion. She had dressed them in their Sunday best—long red dresses from the wide skirts of which brightly polished boots peeped. Over their dresses they wore sparkling white smocks. Their long dark hair was set off by small caps of white lace. On one side of each cap there was a rosette, and from this an embroidered ribbon fluttered.

160

James expressed his admiration to the delighted woman. The clothes had probably been made with her own hands, but the boots, he knew, were her final tribute. For normally, like the other children in the town, these little girls would go everywhere barefooted at this time of year.

As the congratulations and protestations went on among the adults, Meg and Isa arranged themselves demurely on the seat behind James's place, conscious not only of their mother's anxious scrutiny but of the curious glances of various neighbours who had at that moment found it necessary to polish door handles or scrub steps.

When their mother had given their dresses another adjustment, the need for which was discernible only to her, James handed each of them a lollipop.

"Since Meg is older," he said, "I think she should take charge of the basket."

Meg, with an important movement, tucked it in carefully at her feet, a manoeuvre which started Mrs. Melville fussing all over again.

"Now, pull your sleeves down, Meg," she instructed, casting a proud eye over them. "And, Isa, can ye not sit up straighter than that? Mr. King will think you round-shouldered. Make the best of yourself."

She was still urging and advising them as James, having assured her that she would have them home for tea, moved off. "Watch how you lick those lollipops," was her last admonition. "Don't put your tongues out so far. We don't want Mr. King painting you with your faces all sticky."

The girls were shy, and after doing what he could to put them at their ease, James left them to make their own whispered conversation. His leg was paining him, but knowing the view that women like Mrs. Melville took of men smelling of whisky in the middle of the day, he had stoically decided that the pain must be suffered until they reach the bay. Meanwhile, as the trap bumped along the rough road, he drew what comfort he could from the hard outline of the flask in his hip pocket.

Wattie's forecast had been accurate, and the day was now hot and bright. Red squirrels scampered up trees as they rattled along the road, and once they saw a roe deer bounding away through a wood, the white of its tail marking its startled progress under the shady trees. They passed a man on horseback and a gipsy caravan rattling with pots and pans.

With each diversion Meg and Isa became less tongue-tied. Once, James stopped to let them open the basket and start on the lemonade. By the time they reached Gatekirk Bay, James and the two sisters were friends.

They left the trap and went down the track, Meg carrying the basket, and Isa, James's box of paints. Almost the first thing he saw was the girl,

161

sitting at her easel on the rocky outcrop. She paused for a moment to look at them and then went on with her painting. On a hillock wild goats grazed. Across the bay sea birds called.

James unpacked his things, took a long, surreptitious drink from his flask, then explained to the children what he wanted them to do. He let them amuse themselves in their own way for a while, sketching rapidly as they fell into some interesting pose or other. Then, as they became more confident, he had them peering into imaginary birds' nests and rolling nonexistent Easter eggs. It was the way he had worked for almost fifteen years, and, the pain in his leg now soothed by the whisky, he was happy.

At last, pausing to examine his work, he saw that the tide, which had been out when they arrived, was lapping round the rocks. The girl had dismantled her easel and was preparing to leave. He watched her come across the sparkling sand.

Today she wore a blue dress, and at her neck there was a yellow silk scarf. Her smile was uncertain. "Hello," she said. "I'm glad you came back. I would have come across sooner, but I didn't want to disturb you." She nodded toward Meg and Isa, who were sitting with the basket between them, busily devouring the last of Mrs. Laing's cream cakes. "You all looked so busy."

James was disconcerted to find that the resentment he had nursed for her in retrospect did not exist now in her actual presence. In fact, seeing her again was extraordinarily pleasing.

"Well, I hope we didn't distract you. The children were a bit exuberant." He wondered if his smile was perhaps a little foolish.

"No. It was nice to see them so carefree."

She ran her fingers through her hair where the breeze ruffled it. She gave him a glance that was almost shy, then sank onto the grass in what seemed to him a movement of supreme gracefulness. He had noticed the same yielding quality in her as she crossed the sand. She swayed and willowed like a flower.

Her manner was decidedly reticent, in pleasing contrast, he thought, to yesterday's brash assault. The tomboy had gone. He was aware now only of an appealing femininity.

"I was surprised when I saw the children with you. For a moment I thought it wasn't you at all. I hope it's not an impertinent thing to say, but for some reason I hadn't thought of you as married." She leaned back on her heels as if to see him better. "You don't look married."

James was startled out of his amiable reverie. "Married?"

"Yes. You don't look it somehow."

"But I'm not," he said, half amused, half embarrassed. "These are not my children. My housekeeper knows their mother, who was good enough to let them come and pose for me."

162

"Oh, dear." She covered her face with her hands, but between the fingers he could see various parts of a smile. "I've put my foot in it again. And I did so much want to make amends for my rudeness to you yesterday. I thought about it all last night."

"You shouldn't have," James said generously. He moved slightly backward and began fumbling for his pipe, suddenly aware that his breath would be smelling of whisky.

She was watching Meg and Isa. "Are those the Melville children?"

"They are." He pulled out his watch. "And I've just remembered I promised their mother she would have them home in time for tea."

She rose with her sinuous sway and smoothed her dress. "I'll have to be going, too." She stood with the breeze touching her hair. "By the way, I'm Jessie McNee."

"My name's King," James said as he levered himself stiffly to his feet. "James King."

Her consternation was immediate. She looked quickly from his outstretched hand to the pages of his sketchbook scattered on the grass, then to yesterday's canvas lying beside his easel.

"James King?" Her face was childlike with wonder. She lifted the canvas and stared at it with growing embarrassment. "Oh, Mr. King!"

"James," he said gently. "And perhaps you'll allow me to call you Jessie?"

"Oh, Mr. King," she said again.

He was filled with a choking tenderness. "Aren't you going to let me complete the introduction?" He took her hand. It felt so small and cool. He shook it reassuringly.

She bowed her head sorrowfully. "I don't know how I could have been so blind. And I called you an amateur!"

"Yes." He laughed encouragingly. "A derivative amateur."

"How awful!"

"No," he said gallantly. "You gave me something to think about."

"But what must you have thought of me?"

He began collecting his sketches. He felt an absurd elation. "Yesterday I thought you a saucy imp," he said brightly. "I much prefer you today."

"Then you're not too annoyed with me?"

"No, Jessie, I'm not annoyed with you."

She turned and looked at the incoming water, a hand at her scarf to still the fluttering silk. Already the rocks where she had been painting were surrounded. She faced him impulsively.

"It was terrible of me to interrupt you out there. Compared to you, I am the amateur. My work isn't important."

He made sounds of protest. "Everyone's work is important if they are

163

wholehearted about it. And I'm sure you are. Otherwise, you wouldn't have been so upset at the sight of me usurping your place."

"You must have it," she said. Her eyes were eager and her voice had taken on a note of excitement. "Oh, I can visualise already the pictures you would paint from there."

"Yes, that's just the trouble," James said with a stab of acid sorrow. "I'm afraid it's all too easy to visualise what I'll paint. The same picture I painted last month, last year and for a good many years before that." His voice rose sourly as his thoughts floundered on. "I've become too damned predictable. And everyone knows it."

"Oh, but that's not what I meant." She looked deflated and resentful that her bright thought for his work should have been turned to this.

He struggled against the pain in his body and in his spirit, hastening to reassure her.

"Of course it wasn't. I'm afraid I was being self-pitying. The critics have given me some hard knocks lately."

But the whisky had worn off and his leg ached as if raw. He clenched his hands and stood very still. Above them, a lark sang and the warm perfume of young grass and wild flowers wafted by, but suddenly James found himself on the dark verge of a vast, indefinable sadness related in some way that he could not have explained to this sunlit scene, this lovely, healthy girl and the red-frocked, white-smocked Meg and Isa immersed in the innocence of creamy buns and fizzy lemonade. He closed his eyes and his tormented being reached out toward some elusive regret hazily connected with the burden of his maimed body and the longings of that other part of him that was also crippled.

"Are you all right?"

He opened his eyes and saw the girl staring at him, her gaze open and perplexed.

He bent and collected the last of his sketches. "Haven't you finished with those cakes yet? Your mother will be waiting, you know."

The children turned, surprised at the sharpness of his voice, and, with little worried glances at each other, began pushing paper bags and crumpled cake cups into Mrs. Laing's basket.

All at once a threatening shadow had entered the idyllic bay and touched all four of them. Jessie reached into a satchel.

"I'll wipe their faces, she said, "and make them presentable for their mother."

But it was at James that she cast a backward glance as she walked down to the water and dipped a handkerchief into the quietly swirling tide.

In the distance James could see high, bracken-covered hills. These mountains, where eagles soared, and which he could see from his garden, had come to represent the ultimate barrier, the one part of this corner of Scotland where he would never stand. As he stared at the great blurred shapes, there rushed back to him all the happy days of his youth when he had climbed the wall behind Ardfern with Robert and marched effortlessly up the hill to Glen Fruin—through the haunts of protesting pheasants, watched by the lovely eyes of roe deer, joyfully inhaling the scent of bog myrtle and the damp odour of moss. All of his yearnings seemed to lie in these dear memories. And Jessie, who knew nothing of his thoughts, came back from the water still puzzling over the sadness that she sensed had fallen on the lean and suddenly lonely figure that he made against the swaying trees.

"I wondered if you were feeling all right, James," she said as she passed, then hurried shyly on with her damp handkerchief, as if to escape from the worrying intimacy of this first use of his Christian name.

Her concern changed to a vague, wondering shock as, busily dabbing at the upturned faces of Meg and Isa, she saw him tilt his head and roughly empty what was left in his flask down his throat.

But when at last he turned, she saw a boyish smile, and her heart rose with relief at the passing of a crisis that she did not understand but in which, she knew, she had in some odd way played a part.

His voice was brisk and friendly again. "That's better!" He gave his lips an exaggerated wipe with the back of his hand, as if to emphasise that there was no secret to his drink. Then, impelled halfway to the explanation he knew she was due, "You were right, Jessie. I didn't feel very well, but I'm fine now." He slapped his thigh. "This leg can be the devil at times. That was the only medicine that does me any good."

"Please don't apologise. I can imagine." She sprang to her feet and took Meg and Isa by the hand.

The simple words and the understanding in them banished the last of his depression. He seemed to know her so well! In a very small part of an afternoon, much of it spent in awkwardness, a fellowship had been established, a familiarity that he felt must not be lost.

The bay was filled with water now, and only the grassy ridge of the submerged rocks still showed.

"I would like to think I could paint out there," he said carefully. "But I couldn't possibly deprive you. I'm sure there's plenty of room for both of us. Don't you think so?"

She lowered her eyes quickly as she saw the hint of a smile behind his grave expression. "We could see," she said. "If you didn't mind."

He put an arm round Meg and the other round Isa. "Then if these young ladies are ready, I'll take them home to their mother." He looked down at them. "Will you be able to take your tea afer all that guzzling?"

Meg swung the basket to show how light it was now. "If we canny we'll have to blame you," she said with a surprising burst of confidence that immediately dissolved into a shy giggle.

"The very thing," James said delightedly. "Just you put the blame on me, Meg. And on Mrs. Laing. Don't forget, those were her cream cakes. And you, too, Isa."

Isa twinkled her assent and they went laughing over the sand and the grassy fringe to the track through the trees. Jessie collected her bicycle. "Don't wait on me," she said. "I have to tie all these things together before I can start."

"No." James heaved his own easel and chair into the trap. "There's room for everything in there, including your bicycle. How you manage to cycle with all that equipment I can't imagine. It must be quite a sight."

"I do wobble a bit," she admitted.

"Then wobble up there and I'll hand you the bicycle."

When they were settled, he flicked the reins and leaned back contentedly, neither the pain in his leg nor the other, at his heart, so commanding. Jessie McNee! He made an excuse to turn and have another look at her, sitting there, seeming, in the dappled light of the droning glade, not much more than an older sister of Meg and Isa.

For a moment he remembered he was thirty-seven years old, disabled and restless. And then, in the spell that he was under, he forgot. All he knew was that from the unlikeliest of beginnings, something he wanted to treasure had sprung.

11

Despite the increasing area of once-green land now occupied by Glasgow on both banks of the river Clyde, the city was in many ways still a series of neighbouring villages.

The shipbuilders, iron smelters, boilermakers and other tradesmen lived in self-contained communities round the works that supported them. To a lesser degree, it was the same with the merchant class. Though their splendid mansions enhanced wide stretches of the West End and the South Side, their offices were clustered into little more than a square half mile of the town centre. Daily their carriages swept them about the same handful of crowded streets in which they made their business, social or charitable calls.

In this sense, Fiona and Dunbar were residents of the same village. Their ways crossed often, although until his dramatic midnight call to Claremont Row, they had publicly ignored each other. Now, something subtle had happened. After that night's baring of his troubles Dunbar began raising his hat when their carriages passed. At first it was an almost furtive gesture. He feared a rebuff but was being attacked by insidious forces. Despite his headlong rush from her house, he knew Fiona had received him reasonably and even sympathetically. Another woman might have scorned his agony. When his enquiries revealed that Gordon had been banished to Lochbank, the physical interest she had always held for him warmed suddenly into a regard which, although it made him uneasy, he could not quell. The woman was keeping her promise! The least he could do was be civil to her—if only for Anne's sake; for she could yet change her mind and recall her brat to Glasgow. After a day or two this civility cost him no effort. There was a mischievous light in her smile—surprised though it had been at first—that made it damned easy for a man to tip his hat to her. There was certainly nothing churlish or petty about *this* member of the King clan. Well, he would show her there was nothing grudging about Douglas Dunbar, either.

Soon his passing pleasantries—still so tentative and novel—began to waken in him an almost uncontrollable sense of gallantry. His restrained and half-guilty greetings grew steadily grander and more flourishing, as became his kingly nature. As he went about the town, he even began watching for her stylish carriage, with its plumed and cockaded coachman, and for all his extrovert struttings he could be a little downcast on the days when he missed it.

It was not long before there grew in Dunbar an inescapable realisation that he not only envied Robert King his empire, but also his sonsy empress. After the first shock he chortled tolerantly to himself at the devilry of it. Why not? She was one of the acknowledged beauties of Glasgow and, as everyone knew, a neglected one. And he . . . why, he was one of the prize adventurers of this city of world adventurers—still young, vital, well turned out and free. There was no doubt he had impressed himself on her. Why leave it there? To steal a man's business was one achievement, but a far more exciting enterprise would be the theft of his wife.

Dunbar's eyes glinted, then narrowed with doubt. Should a responsible man even contemplate such frivolity? It was a common enough pastime with the glossier Glasgow crowd, but he had never been a philanderer, never a seducer of other men's women. Nevertheless, the thought would not leave him. His blood was red, no question of that, even though he had kept a tight hold on its impulses. He had been as susceptible as the next man, but too dedicated to prospering his business to be led away by distracting fancies. He had preferred the quick, commercial plunge that left his mind free for more important things. Since the death of his wife, the only women in his life had been of a type he held in low regard but which he felt a robust man must patronise occasionally for the good of his health.

Now, at the height of his powers, here was a woman—dangerous, perhaps, but all the more tantalising for that—who might be a worthy prey. The challenge, with all its complexities, not only of possession but of revenge, stirred his passions and swept his imagination along ways he had thought too tangled and overgrown ever to be travelled again.

He leaned back in a corner of his carriage and stared sightlessly at the passing crowd. That he could harry his enemy on this new and entrancing front was a concept completely suited to his thrust and daring. And one, he felt, that would not be unwelcome to the lady. He had his instincts, and the memory of the look on Fiona's face when he had taken hold of her that night in Claremont Row came back to him with the force of a sudden storm. It had shaken him at the time, but he had been in the grip then of too many other perplexing emotions. No, this was something to be accomplished in detached tranquillity, with an eye on himself as well as on her.

Aye, she was a beauty—a woman he wouldn't be demeaning himself on. He saw again the bold form of her figure—so ample, and yet every line of it in perfect balance; the proud yet open face and the spark of unconcealed recklessness in the soft yet worldly eyes. She was a woman with a mind, too. One who could take a decision, as she had shown; and not, he would wager, just in the way of business.

He fell, next, to a pleasurable assessment of his own qualities. They were abounding, but above all he was a man, a man from the tips of his sharp-pointed, heavily buttoned boots to the crown of his shiny, square-blocked hat. His chest rose with satisfaction as he felt the power run in his great limbs. His muscles were still like iron, and at the Kenilworth Baths, where he went to keep fit, even the boxing professional was wary of that long, battering right-handed punch that could devastate the most bull-like opponent.

He was like a child given a new game and desperate to start playing. When he reached his office, he composed a careful note and sent it to King & Co. by hand.

For a long time Fiona sat staring at the heavy paper. It wasn't so much written on as gouged across, like a Neolithic tablet. Even ink transmitted the boundless power of the man. Or was this, she wondered with that strangely enjoyable tension that came with every sight or reminder of him, just an idea from the depth of her own emotions?

Again she read the words:

> I am not completely at ease in my mind over the matter that recently took me to your home. I trust, since our interests are identical, you will be agreeable to meeting me again for a further discussion. I would not, of course, intrude again on your privacy, but neither am I in a position to invite you to my own home. Since I do not believe private matters should be allowed to extend into business, I feel our respective offices are also debarred as possible meeting places. Would you, therefore, do me the honour of dining with me in the Central Hotel tomorrow evening at eight o'clock?

Her first impulse was to refuse. What was there to discuss? She had kept her word and sent Gordon away. What more could he want? The affair with Anne was dead, or in the process of dying. However much in love they might be, they were young. Now that they had been forcibly separated, they would quickly forget each other. These youthful passions fed on constant meetings, and once deprived of them they would begin to wither and to wander in other directions. Anne had her child to care for, a husband to whom she must at times think of returning. Gordon had his work and would surely, even at Lochbank, soon meet some other girl.

The most disconcerting knowledge that came to her after reading the note was that she was bored and lonely away from Seabank Lane. The demands of King & Co. had forced her to resign most of her charitable activities, and she had been surprised at the extent to which she missed the entertaining gossip and chatter that had accompanied them.

Occasional dinners with Fergus and Rita, or, more often, long hours alone at home after the children had gone to bed, were an insufficient stimulus to her active nature. Whatever Dunbar wanted to talk about, an evening in his company should be interesting, even if infuriating.

There was in any case an undeniable fascination in the idea of another encounter with him. The wild strength of his personality was a challenge. He had the same lure of danger about him that made people climb mountains or sail boats in rough water. Besides, she didn't want him to think she was afraid of him, either as business rival or as man, if the two could be separated. He had humiliated her with his sly cornering of the Aberlivet market, and one day she was determined to land a crashing blow on him. The more she knew about him, the more she understood his crafty animal nature, the better armed she would be.

After another few moments of tingling speculation she took a sheet of notepaper and wrote:

I cannot pretend that your note came as other than a surprise, but I have no objection to meeting you for a discussion about Gordon and Anne if you think this is necessary. However, I have a prior engagement tomorrow but will be free the evening after that.

Fiona had an open and matter-of-fact nature. To be furtive or underhand was distasteful to her. Her annoyance with herself was immense, therefore, when she found she was incapable of telling anyone she had a dinner appointment with Douglas Dunbar. What was there to hide? He had asked her to discuss a matter of family importance. That was all. In the end she eased her conscience by deciding the secrecy was for Gordon's protection. No one knew of his foolishness.

On the day they were to meet, she made an excuse for not going to business. Instead she spent the afternoon with her hairdresser. For the children she invented a hostess too important to be ignored. But as she dressed, Florence's glances made her uneasy. *That young lady,* she thought, *has too much insight for her age.*

She chose an elaborate gown of white satin she had last worn when being entertained with Robert at an excessively formal evening in London. At the last minute, perhaps because of what she was reading into Florence's expression, she decided the décolletage was unsuitable for the occasion and had to call on Morag to stitch a modesty border of tulle to the bodice.

As she drove across the city, along streets tranquil and golden in the afterglow, she felt guilty at having taken so much trouble. But she was well repaid by the confidence she felt as she crossed the fashionable foyer and saw the shock of appreciation in Dunbar's eyes as he rose to greet her. That involuntary spark, spirited out of the innermost man, told her more about him than she would have learned in hours of talk. As he bent over her hand, the visor that hid him from the world came down again, but with a transparency now even he did not suspect.

Formal clothes suited him, softening a little the monumental outline and veneering with an elegant patina the weathered masonry of his mediaeval face.

That he was known in the hotel was obvious from the fawning attention he received. An under manager showed them to a table by a window in the little room where people gathered for drinks before dining. She was no sooner seated than a spray of red roses was brought to her and a fan with a silver handle and gilded lacework placed at her hand.

Dunbar watched the poise with which she accepted these attentions. She said she would take a glass of sherry and was startled when he told the waiter to bring him a glass of Queen's Royal whisky.

She laughed and shook her head. "That really isn't necessary, you know."

His smile was almost boyish. "I was hoping they might not stock it."

"Then you should have managed the thing properly by bribing the waiter beforehand to say they didn't have any."

He looked at her admiringly. "I didn't even think of that." He leaned slightly forward and his glance became direct and serious. "I am really more concerned with demonstrating that tonight we have a truce."

She lifted the roses and looked into the cluster of gently opening buds. "As to that, you must speak for yourself, Mr. Dunbar."

He ignored the mockery. "Those roses are from my own garden. There isn't a blemish on them." His pride in the perfection of the flowers turned into the inevitable boastfulness. "You'll get nothing like those from any florist."

"They're beautifully perfumed."

"Aye"—he nodded and smiled—"they're good old-fashioned stock, like me."

He handled the long scarlet and gold menu and wine list with confidence and ordered carefully for both of them.

Here, she thought, *was another twist to puzzle and fascinate; another contradiction to put beside the gold rings, the ruby shirt buttons and the scented hair oil.*

When they rose from the table at the window, the sun had gone, and in the gloaming the street was lively with the cries of vendors of hot pies and roast chestnuts, with cabs rattling between theatres and restaurants.

The crowded dining room was lit entirely by candles, some in crystal chandeliers, others in candelabra. The mirrored walls reflected a thousand points of flickering light. From a gallery in the shadows stringed music crept softly about the elegant room. Their table was decorated with another lavish arrangement of roses from Dunbar's garden. As the aroma of his cigar drifted across the flowers, Fiona felt a spell was being cast, a dreamlike mood being created to which it was her inclination to submit.

Suddenly, something in his expression annoyed her—some combination of self-satisfaction and amused watchfulness.

"This is all exceedingly pleasant, Mr. Dunbar," she said abruptly, "but your letter suggested you had something serious to discuss. Could we, perhaps, come to that point now?"

"Of course." He waved his cigar. "Certainly." But his surprise and hesitance were not concealed from her. "As I indicated, the matter concerning me is the unfortunate business of my daughter and your son."

"I do realise that, but what more is there to say?"

"I wanted to know exactly what restraint you have placed on your son."

"I wonder if that concerns you, so long as he does not see your daughter again."

"As I said in my letter, my mind is not completely at ease. Knowing would help to put it at ease."

"And that is all you want to know?"

She was interested to see he had the sensitivity to look slightly foolish. "Yes," he said, avoiding her steady gaze.

"Then I'm surprised you have found it necessary to go to so much trouble and expense. I would have thought a few enquiries about town—"

He seized the chance to be amiably indignant. "I am not a man to skulk about back doors, Mrs. King." The reproving growl had an almost musical quality.

172

"I have sent Gordon to work at Lochbank distillery," she said quietly. "I felt it best to get him out of Glasgow."

He nodded approvingly, as if the information was new to him. As she watched, certain he was acting a well-considered part, her mood lightened. She was not bored. He was not being unpleasant. The food and the surroundings were of the highest quality. She shielded her eyes slightly with the golden fan.

"I can hardly believe that is the only point in our meeting," she said.

His eyes narrowed as he struggled to assess her mood. "It seemed important enough to me," he said uncertainly.

"Then I am delighted I have been able to set your mind at rest."

He leaned impulsively forward, his wide, craggy smile softened by cigar smoke and candle glow.

"All right, I have given you only part of the reason." He spread his big hands. "I admit it."

"Indeed! And what was the other part?"

"I was curious."

"May I ask about what?"

"I was curious to know more about the lady who runs King and Company. Lots of people in Glasgow are, you know."

"I'm flattered to be the centre of so much attention. I had not realised until recently people were taking such an interest in me."

"What do you expect, if you take on a man's job? But never mind other people. What about me? Have I annoyed you?"

She kept him waiting, appearing to tussle with the possibility. "Do you care that you may have?"

"It was not my intention. It's my hope that I have not."

She smiled at the quaint formality. "I am quite prepared to regard this as a social evening, if that is how you planned it." Was this too big a concession?

She saw his face harden almost imperceptibly, the lines round his eyes whiten slightly as they drew more closely together. "Mind you, it won't soften me toward King and Company."

The unexpected brutishness shocked her, but she pretended only an amused surprise. "I hadn't imagined it would."

"Maybe not." His eyes half closed. "But most women would."

"May I ask if we still have a truce?" Her eyes were bright with a confusion of complicated emotions. He looked into them with an intensity that sent a cold shiver through her.

"Oh, aye. We have a truce, you and me." He shook his head fiercely. "But from King and Company I expect nought but blows. And that's all they'll ever get from me."

173

She looked at him pityingly. "Don't you ever forget your hatred of King and Company?"

"Never." He was glaring past her, to a gallery where a string orchestra played Viennese waltzes. Gradually the tension went out of his body and his head sank forward almost regretfully. "At least—"

"Well?"

"When I'm in your company, maybe I could."

It was an amazing confession, and she did not know how to react to it. He was too big a jumble of aggression and sudden softness. As she looked at him, she saw he was already retreating from the defenceless- ness of his position. She hastened to reassure him.

"Thank you for the compliment."

His relief that the admission had not been turned against him was al- most embarrassing. He leaned gratefully across the table, and for a mo- ment she thought he was going to take her hand.

"Thank you for accepting it."

Throughout the remainder of the meal he was cheerful but subdued. He drank moderately and made no effort to detain her when at ten thirty she said she must go home. It seemed almost an afterthought when he asked if he could travel in her carriage as far as Claremont Row, leaving his own to follow.

A large moon hung over the city. Against its light the tall buildings of the commercial district made patterns expressive of more romantic things than insurance, accountancy or trade. Dunbar hardly spoke, al- though the jogging box was filled with the immensity of his presence.

When the silence became oppressive, Fiona said, "Part of your way home will lie along the river. Tonight it will be very beautiful."

The silk drapings muffled his voice. "I'll probably sleep."

"What a waste," she said, wondering if this was another of his strange, almost automatic rebuffs.

To her surprise she heard a deep sigh. "No. When you sleep you sometimes dream."

Claremont Row was dotted with the yellow of gas flares, and the gently swaying trees cast thin shadows along the house fronts. Here and there silhouettes moved at curtained windows and the smoke of bedroom fires rose to the moonlit sky.

Immediately the carriage stopped and Dunbar jumped out. He walked her to the door and, with his hat in his hand, bade her a brief and curiously stilted good-night. As she climbed the stairs to her room, she wrestled with a sense of disappointment. Vaguely, she knew she had ex- pected more of him. But what? Conduct less gentlemanly, perhaps? Some remark or proposal in keeping with his outrageous reputation?

174

She felt her face grow hot at the confused naiveté of her expectations. The truth was, she had been certain he would make some advance, however crude or hesitant. Anything less had seemed out of character. And yet, there hadn't been anything even remotely flirtatious, not a hint of any of the improprieties that might have been expected from such a violent and untamed nature. The brute had left her without a trace of an indelicacy to cherish! She was ashamed as she saw the full juvenile stupidity of her attitude. She had gone to meet him filled with the gauche fantasies of a girl on her first rendezvous. She had seen herself, like the heroine in some of the novels she had been reading lately, as the lady besieged by the attractive ruffian. She had been eager to contrast his behaviour with that of a gentleman. Her whole approach to the meeting had been unworthy of anyone over the age of seventeen. While he . . . he had conducted himself with irreproachable decorum.

Her eyes began to sting as she saw that once again she had been humiliated—this time by her own absurd romanticism. When she reached her room, she realised she was still holding the roses he had brought her from his garden. Their fragrance spread about her as she stood at the dark window, listening to his carriage rumble off into the still summer night. It would be after midnight when he reached home—that great house by the water which she had seen only through the trees, from a train.

She opened the window and leaned over the iron balcony until she saw the side lanterns of his carriage swaying faintly in the distance. Suddenly, on a breeze made sweet by recently cut grass, there came to her the most wounding possibility of all. Perhaps he found her uninteresting. A rush of shame went through her. She retreated abruptly into the room and closed the curtains with a vicious pull on the silk cord.

Half a mile away, as his carriage headed westward, cutting down toward the broad silver ribbon of the moonlit river, Dunbar lit a cigar and hunched forward to the open window. Inside the carriage there was hardly any movement of air, and where her clothes had touched his a faint perfume still lingered. Out of it he conjured a picture of soft hair and smooth lips. He saw the sweep of breasts too bountiful to be disguised by a little flurry of tulle melting into white satin. Had she been flaunting herself at him? He couldn't believe it, despite the provocation that seemed always to lurk in her eyes. He leaned back with a baffled sigh. All that must lie inside his own head. Far from trying to provoke him, she had left him without the slightest opening. No, it was his own conduct that needed pondering. Had he been too forward, despite the curb he had tried to place on himself? Had his admiration—perhaps even his intentions—shown too obviously, too insultingly?

175

Lights moved on the river, and as he looked into the silvery midnight, he saw a ship with tall masts moving slowly toward the distant firth and the open sea beyond.

It seemed ages since he had written the note asking her to dine with him, full of his own devilry and the certainty that some understanding, however veiled, would come out of their meeting. The speed with which she had accepted had reinforced his belief.

A faint haze now lay in the sandy hollows along the side of the road nearest the river. Dampness rose from the water and from the fields. There was a foggy smell. He reached for the leather strap and pulled the window up. Slowly, in the enclosed space, her perfume became insistent again. In the darkness his face twisted into a slightly pained smile. His uncrushable confidence began to rise. There would be other meetings. He was certain he had discovered at least that much about her.

For weeks, memories of the strange evening she had spent with Dunbar flitted disturbingly through Fiona's busy mind. She waited, with an odd mixture of anticipation and uneasiness, for his next move. But there was no sequel. Candlelit dinner and moonlit drive endured in her memory as a solitary flirtation with unreality, a worrying reminder of her frailty. From her carriage she still saw him—flowered cravat, dark, unfathomable eyes, raised hat—passing like a massive wraith as she attended to the more solid certainties of her daily existence.

King & Co. was now almost all-absorbing, but with the management of its affairs she skilfully combined what remained of her family and social life. She missed her drives with James but wrote to him regularly. She had been intrigued to find in his recent letters a recurring name—Jessie McNee, of whom little was said but much could be surmised.

"Yesterday Jessie and I painted all morning and most of the afternoon at Gatekirk Bay." "On Saturday I'm going with Jessie McNee for a picnic in Glen Fleet." "Jessie's painting is beginning to be too much influenced by mine. I must caution her about this, for she has a delicate style of her own that does not need strong colour."

From such snippets Fiona began to construct a picture of what she happily thought of as James's Galloway idyll. The romance she scented added zest to the fresh summer days and compensated a little for her increasing restlessness. Gordon, at Lochbank, was a loss and a continual drag on her mind, but against this she prudently weighed the more positive worry of having him at home, within reach of Anne Dunbar.

To Robert's absence the years had accustomed her, but now it had taken on a more piquant quality. That year his visits home had become increasingly less frequent. Now his excuses failed to convince. It seemed that when Parliament recessed, the London affairs of King & Co. were always pressing, but not too compelling for him to miss trips to Paris and Vienna as a Parliamentary delegate. To the fact that her husband now had a life outside the business and the family Fiona was resigned.

To the challenges of King & Co. she brought an unconventional mind that on occasion had Ross, the traditionalist, mourning the loss of Robert, his fellow devotee of the old whisky faith.

Blending still surged forward on a seemingly endless boom and frequently outpaced the capacity of ancillary trades not yet strung to the same nervous pitch. As one crisis was mastered, another reared. The current worry was a shortage of sherry casks into which new whisky could be filled for maturing. Sherry wood was originally chosen by the trade because it was cheap and available—thousands of casks lying unwanted all over the country after the wine shippers had emptied them. But over the years casks that had originally held sherry came to be endowed in the minds of men like Peter Ross with almost mystical qualities.

"I've been in touch with every cooperage we've ever dealt with," Ross lamented one morning as he came into Fiona's room carrying a thick batch of letters. "These are the replies. Even threats haven't produced anything like the number of casks we need. All most of them can offer us is plain wood. The distilleries are producing so fast these days there just aren't enough sherry casks being imported to go round." He sat down on a hard chair.

"Why don't you just accept the plain wood they're offering?" Fiona asked with the freshness of approach that was one of Ross's nightmares.

He coiled his long legs under the chair and stared balefully at her flowers and frilled curtains. These were the symbols of the new era and he sometimes longed for the old drabness.

"I wouldn't like to be responsible for the result, Mrs. King," he said, his eyes gloomy and his cheeks puffed portentously.

Fiona recognised the onset of another tussle for what was left of Ross's soul. "Why don't you light your pipe, Peter, and take a more comfortable chair? I've just sent for tea."

This homeliness, so natural and uncalculated, was one of her most potent weapons. It wasn't business, he thought, as he moved to a buttoned velvet chair with a small wine table at the side. It was too feminine for him to get to grips with. As the tea was brought in and another cup sent for he sat fidgeting with his pipe and thinking of the awful advantage she had over him. If only she wasn't so nice. If only he hadn't such a deep liking for her. He thought wistfully of all the man-to-man rows he'd had with Robert.

"These biscuits are rather nice. They have honey in them," She held out the plate.

177

He took one.

"Now tell me, Peter, what is so magical about sherry wood?"

Ross bit manfully on his biscuit, seeing another sacred bastion of his religion under assault—he had already seen so many crumble. He drank his tea and tried to put a cheerful authority into his voice.

"Well, no one can really know, of course, but the belief is that whisky matures better as a result of the small amount of sherry it absorbs from the staves."

"It's no more than a belief, then?"

"A very well founded one, in my opinion," he said stubbornly.

"All that happens is that our whisky ends up with a little sherry in it?"

"Yes. As I say, it's believed to make it smoother and rounder."

Fiona's expression was helpful and her voice casual. "Then why don't we simply pour some sherry into our whisky? Sherry casks might be scarce, but sherry isn't."

Ross was at first staggered and then scandalised. "But we couldn't do that, Mrs. King."

She held out the plate of biscuits. "Why not?"

"It wouldn't be right. It wouldn't be right, at all." The biscuit crumbled between his fingers. Crumbs fell in his lap and scattered on the floor.

"I don't think it's a question of right or wrong. Surely there's no law about it? It's a matter of whether or not it would have the desired effect."

But she was wrong. There was a law—or, at any rate, a regulation.

Ross carried it into her room like a trophy when they resumed the discussion a few days later.

"I've gone into that matter, Mrs. King, and I'm afraid the excisemen won't let us add sherry to our whisky. Technically it would no longer be whisky if you added even a minute quantity of sherry. It would be a compound."

"But we only want to do what takes place, anyway."

"That is not how they see it." His gaze was on the ceiling. "They have their rule books."

"Oh, blow their rule books! They always have something tucked away to stop people doing what they want to do." Then she rose smiling from her desk and went to the gilt mirror. "And don't bother trying to hide your relief, Peter. I know you're on their side."

He rubbed his face to hide a smile. "Well, we did try."

She brightened. "We did, didn't we?"

But next morning she was in his room before her carriage had left the lane. She pulled off her gloves and waved them at him.

"Just as I was falling asleep last night, Peter, the answer came to me about those sherry casks. If they won't let us put sherry into the blending vats, we'll put it into the plain empty casks before we send them to the distilleries. What do you think of that?"

To her surprise Ross put his hands flat on his desk and gave a laugh of almost mischievous resignation.

"I wondered when you would think of that, Mrs. King."

"Do you mean you had already thought of it?"

"Yes."

She clasped her hands behind her back and swayed a little in front of him. "Good. Our minds are becoming attuned."

He leaned forward brightly, all his resentment of the previous days gone. During the night he had come to terms with his conscience. Pouring sherry into whisky would have been sacrilege, but there was no real surrendering of principle in this treating of the wood. And it would mean he could stop worrying about where to get these dratted sherry casks. He had also admitted to himself that without Fiona's original thinking they would never have arrived at this decision.

"Mind you," he said, glad to be able to interject some residual doubts, "if they knew, they wouldn't like it. They would say it was an evasion of the rules."

"They're so stupid they probably would," Fiona agreed. "But never mind. The new casks will have absorbed the sherry we put in long before they reach the distilleries and come under excise supervision."

There was a thoughtful silence, as of conspirators considering the details of a plot for possible flaws.

"It's really just another trick of the trade, I suppose," Ross said with a slight return of orthodoxy.

"That's all," Fiona soothed him, "But we'll make a little secret of it. Get it done by someone you can trust." She stopped at the door and added casually, "I wouldn't even tell him it was sherry. Just say it's something to sweeten the wood."

In the dam behind Lochbank, lilies floated. The delicate pink blooms sent out a sweet fragrance which mingled, when the air was still, with the sharp and flowery tang of peat reek from the distillery chimney. Beyond the birch trees on the edge of the rough road small boats sailed on Loch Lomond, their wash lapping quietly at the pebble shore.

From out there the distillery looked like a collection of whitewashed farm buildings huddled under a hill down which clear water ran from the mountains beyond. Only the distinctive pagoda-topped ventilator shaft above the kiln distinguished Lochbank from the farms that lay a little distance on either side. Once it, too, had been a farm, and Fiona's great-grandfather the farmer. It was he who had built the first still to make use of the barley he could not sell. Even the great fire of 1880 had not changed the basic appearance. For so great was the superstition proliferating in the trade, so strong the mystique, that Robert and McNair had decided the new distillery must be as near a replica of the original as could be managed. So devoted was McNair to this concept that he made the coppersmiths work from photographs as they constructed the great gleaming heart of the rearisen Lochbank. And in secret, like an alchemist, not even telling Robert, McNair had gone over the shining new retort with a hammer, faithfully knocking into it every dent that he could discern in the photographs.

McNair had come late to whisky, from Fergus's slum tavern in the Goosedubbs, but its mysteries had no more zealous guardian. That move from the Corkcutters' Arms to this lovely place had been the luck of his life. It had taken him from a rickety tenement in a polluted district to a sturdy stone cottage a few dusty steps along the road from the distillery. It had given his children a wild glen to grow up in, a clean, uncrowded schoolhouse, with roses at the door and heather in the playground, to be educated in. With a seat on the board and kingship of the distillery the sawdust of the barroom was an age away. The only cloud in McNair's life, these days, was Gordon.

"The lad's a right mystery," he told his wife, puzzling over the latest incident as he filled his pipe by the open door of the cottage. "Nothing I show him seems of any interest. Jack Hoey, now. I need only tell him once. You would think *he* was heir to it all not Gordon."

Mrs. McNair, a round, grey-haired woman who had grasped this second chance at life with the same gratitude as her husband, looked up with a smile from the sock she was darning.

"Och, he's only a boy, Alec. Maybe you're expecting too much of him. He likely finds it a shade too quiet here, after the city."

There were times when the brawny and conscientious McNair felt like a nursemaid, taking as seriously as he did Fiona's written plea that he keep a fatherly watch over Gordon.

He drew comfortingly on his pipe. "I daresay. But he worries me, sometimes. He doesna seem . . . happy."

It was puzzling and hurtful to McNair that Gordon had not taken to the wonderful business of producing whisky. To him it was all excitement and romance, from the smell of the barley malting to the sound of the new spirit gurgling into casks and then being rolled away to the dark, damp warehouses to lie maturing for years.

That morning they had run off the first whisky made from a barley they had never used before. For McNair it was a tense moment. Any departure was a risk, a journey into uncertainty. He had carried the beaker to a shaft of light slanting from a high slit in the undressed stone of the stillhouse wall. Anxiously, slightly averted from the watching men, he held it to his nose. When he turned he was smiling.

"Grand," was all he said.

Gordon had given the colourless liquid a cursory sniff, turned up his nose and said, "It reminds me of sour vinegar."

McNair had stifled an angry rebuke. In silence he passed the beaker to Jack Hoey. Gordon watched darkly as his cousin gave the whisky elaborate consideration. He laughed acidly at Jack's businesslike approval.

"How on earth would you know whether it's good or bad?"

Jack's moderate reply had pleased McNair.

"You get to know after a while. You begin to develop a sense about it. There's a slight difference between each distillation. That's why blending is so important."

McNair was still wrestling with the niggling undertones of the incident as he tapped out his pipe and got ready to leave again for the distillery. He would have been even more troubled if he had known what had happened when he left the stillhouse to take the sample of new whisky to his office.

Gordon had turned on his cousin in a fury of resentment. "Sneak," he said viciously.

Jack's expression was calm and pitying. "Fool," he replied.

"You just can't help creeping."

"Perhaps when you grow up you'll learn the difference between creeping and not rubbing people the wrong way."

"I don't have to care what McNair thinks."

"I wouldn't be too sure about that."

"Why? He's only an employee."

"He's a director of the company."

"A director of my father's company."

Jack's grin faded. "Oh, for God's sake, stop waving the silver spoon."

This, Gordon knew, was painful ground. "That's something you don't like to think about," he sneered.

"You're pathetic, and I haven't time to waste on you. Now, start getting the numbers stencilled on those casks. I want them finished before McNair comes back."

"You want!"

Jack gave him a push. "Yes, I want. Now, get on with it. The men can't move the casks till you've stencilled them."

"My God, Hoey, one day I'll be in charge of this company. I'll be giving the orders."

"One day, Cousin Gordon, but not today. Today I'm giving the orders. Today you do what McNair tells me to give you to do. Today you're only a labourer, and a bloody stupid one at that."

"Just wait. You'll suffer for this. One day I'll make you crawl."

Since Gordon's first bleak day at the distillery, all his anguish and resentment at being parted from Anne had found an outlet in brawling quarrels. His cousin's enthusiasm intensified his heavy-hearted bitterness. And any thoughts he'd held of striving for a pretence at harmony had died at Jack's first crude joke.

"The first thing we'll have to do is show you the place," McNair had said, handing him over to Jack. "I've a couple of things to do first, but I'll catch up with you."

They walked across the cobbled yard to a shed where barley was stored in sacks.

"I can never get over the fact that this is our only raw material," Jack said, plunging his hand into an open sack and letting the grains trickle through his fingers. "Whisky is made from barley, water and absolutely nothing else. It's miraculous when you think of it: all those bottles all over the world; all those people raising glasses and saying *Slainte*! And it starts here or someplace like this at the foot of a glen, done with a bag of barley and some water from a mountain stream."

Gordon glanced up in surprise. The note of fascination in Jack's voice was too obviously genuine to be doubted. His estimation of his cousin as a lickspittle had not allowed for the possibility of his enthusiasm for the affairs of King & Co. being real. It was a novel thought. For a moment he envied him this satisfaction in his work.

"You seem to have been smitten by McNair," he said.

Jack kicked at a sack of barley, his eyes lowered in a way that suggested he realised he had revealed more of himself than was wise. "Trust you to make it sound like a disease," he said. "But it is catching. You'll end up the same way."

"I doubt it. This was mother's wish, not mine."

Even as he stood in the sunshine, staring into the dusty, cobwebbed dimness of the shed, he saw Anne as she had been in the candlelit bedroom on that last night, her face thinner and more strained than ever, yet still beautiful; her eyes flooding him with love one minute, and the next filling with a dread of something she could not explain. It seemed so long ago. Jack made some remark about supplies of local barley being inadequate for their needs, but it was Anne's voice Gordon heard. His mother was mistaken if she thought that simply by sending him here she could keep them apart. They were together now. She was in everything. Her walk was there in the slight sway of harebells in a hollow between the trees at the foot of the hill, and the brightness of her eyes in the clear streams that sparkled into the dam and set the lilies swirling. But the metaphysical was not enough. Nothing would keep him from the reality—certainly not sixteen or seventeen miles of country crossed by roads and railway lines, dotted with clachans where a horse or a wagonette could be hired. Already he had a plan half made.

"Dammit, are you listening to what I'm telling you?"

"I'm hanging on your every word."

As they stood glaring at each other, an old man approached with a creaking wheelbarrow. He collected some sacks of barley and with a nod moved off unsteadily toward the main building.

They followed him through a wide door into the gloom that seemed to prevail in all the distillery interiors. It was ten years since Gordon had been here, but a slight memory stirred of steam drifting in the cavelike recesses formed by the wooden pillars that loomed about the place.

"This is the malthouse," Jack said. He beckoned Gordon to follow. "They soak the barley in these tanks for about sixty hours, then spread it on the floor to germinate. Part of the maltman's skill is in knowing when the germination has gone far enough. It takes between eight and eleven days. After that it is malt." In a corner a furnace glowed. Beside it lay a stack of cut peat. "The malt is taken up to the next floor and dried over that furnace. Some of the smoke from the peat rises and flavours the malt. It all goes toward the taste of the final whisky."

As he talked, the maltman moved rhythmically in the shadows, turning the sprouting barley with a long wooden shovel. The man with the wheelbarrow had trundled off for another load.

Gordon looked after the bent figure. "Are these the only two in here?"

"Yes. Although distilling is a twenty-four-hour process, we employ only twelve men. I told you it was a miraculous business."

It was primitive, unmechanised work that had changed little since the earliest days. Therein lay its attraction for the unhurried men who were drawn to it. They took what power they needed from a waterwheel. Nature called the tune, for when the mountain burns ran dry and the dam water fell, distilling had to stop. Although there were rules, instinct was more important. Speed was impossible. Patience was part of the training. The whisky they made today would not be ready for drinking for perhaps five years.

But Gordon, in his unhappiness, saw only a damp, shrouded barn filled with an acrid smell and a floor that was partly of bare earth. The smell thickened as they approached several tall vats which reached up to the wooden ceiling and disappeared through it. They climbed a ladder to the second floor. Here, in bins along a wall, dry malted barley was stored.

"First it goes into this mash tun, to be mixed with hot water," Jack said.

He stopped at the first vat. The wide top was about three feet above the level of the rough wooden floor. Steam drifted from it. Gordon saw a thick malodorous mess that looked like brown porridge. "The water in this mash turns into wort, which is run off into washbacks for fermentation. The tun is refilled with hot water and the mashing is repeated until only draff—spent malt—is left."

The area was lit only by skylights. In the other two vats the liquid was dark brown in colour. This was wort, the wash from the mash tun. The surface moved with a sluggish, volcanic life. Bubbles rose and burst.

"That's it fermenting," Jack said as he saw Gordon staring. "That's the biggest miracle of all. It turns into something like beer in these vats. From there pipes take it through that wall into the stillhouse. There are two stills, although before the original distillery was burned down they worked with only one. Anyway, this fermented wash goes into the first still and condenses out as a low-grade spirit. The second still turns these low wines, as they're called, into whisky. Do you think you'll remember all that?"

Gordon shrugged. "As much as I'll need, I suppose. I won't be required to sit a written paper, will I?"

Jack rubbed his chin. His eyes were thoughtful. "There's something here that'll help impress it on you. It's rather like being baptised or kissing the Blarney stone. Just come and take a look at this fermenting wort."

"The level seems much lower than it was."

"They must have started running it off, but there's still time. Just look inside the vat and tell me what you see."

The liquid appeared blacker now that it had receded from the light. Bubbles still plopped, releasing small spurts of steam. Gordon put his hands on the edge of the vat and leaned over. Next instant he felt his nose had been hit by a hammer. Molten metal seemed to enter his lungs. He staggered back with a cry of pain that suffocated halfway out. As he reeled away from the vat, gasping for breath, he had a glimpse of Jack laughing. Then he saw McNair hurrying toward him. A strong arm went round his shoulder and a heavy hand began thumping him on the back.

Gradually his breath returned. "My God," he gasped, "what was that?"

McNair was glaring at Jack. "I imagine it was a practical joke that went too far," he said.

"But what was it?"

"Carbon dioxide. You always get it from fermenting wort."

"Did he know?"

Jack had an eye on McNair. "I knew, but I didn't tell you to go and eat the stuff."

"You bastard, you didn't tell me anything."

McNair, who thought he had left this sort of language behind in the Goosedubbs, was startled. He wasn't sure how to react. The ways of these educated striplings were beyond him. He tried to think how Fergus would respond. Immediately he felt on surer ground.

"There's no need for that, Gordon," he said sternly. "It was a rough joke, but I'm sure Jack didn't mean any harm."

Gordon dabbed his running eyes with a handkerchief. "I wish I could believe that," he croaked, trying to stifle another attack of breathless coughing. "How dangerous is carbon dioxide?"

Again McNair hesitated, trying to get both of them into view. The baffling undercurrents of the relationship between these two privileged young men who were "family" made him uneasy and anxious to get back to the known quantities of whisky distilling.

"It's very dangerous," he said. "It's a poisonous gas." As he saw Gordon's fists clench and his distorted face jerk round toward Jack, he added hastily. "But only in a confined place."

"A confined place such as the inside of that vat?"

"I suppose so."

Jack, who had been standing with a hand in his jacket pocket and the other rubbing restlessly up and down one of the wooden pillars, came forward a pace, his eyes widening in protest. "I say, don't encourage him, Mr. McNair. He knows it was only a bit of fun."

"It might help if you told him you were sorry."

For a moment it looked as if Jack would refuse, almost as if he was going to stalk unrepentantly away. He half turned, his eyes cold. Then, as if suddenly seeing the justice of Gordon's anger, he relaxed, his dark face twisting into a grin.

"I tell you what. I'll take him down to Ma Cameron's tonight. He's become very fond of her beer. It will be my treat, of course." He turned impetuously to Gordon, his face bright and eager with the easy charm that reminded so many of his father. "What do you say? Will you come?"

McNair laughed encouragingly as he felt the tension ease. "That sounds a practical enough apology, Gordon. If Jack's hand is going to be in his pocket, I might even join you. What do you think?"

Gordon brightened despite himself. McNair's fatherly way was hard to resist. He kicked at the floor. "Well, if he's paying, and if you're coming . . ."

He could bear the quarrelling and the routine—even the unexpected discovery that under happier circumstances he might enjoy this work which he had been prepared to resent. It was so much more varied and less restricting than clerking on a high stool under Paterson's watchful eye. What he could not endure was the separation from Anne, and after another two weeks of it he began seeing her again.

The clandestine meetings went on all summer, but attended now by an even greater sense of guilt and anxiety. At times the strain—not only of the secrecy but of the distance to be covered—became almost unbearable. He managed the seventeen miles that separated them partly by train. But the gap between Lochbank and the railway at Alexandria had to be travelled by bicycle or on a horse hired from a stable at Drymen. Sometimes it was the middle of the night when he fell, worn out and troubled, into his bed in the farmhouse where he lodged near the distillery. On these occasions his exhaustion was impossible to hide from the curious eyes of his cousin when he had to turn out for work a few hours later. He countered the prying and the teasing with sulky silences.

As happens with children, the relationship between Gordon and Jack was constantly changing. Despite the underlying animosity they had days of companionship, supping beer and playing dominoes at Ma Cameron's or rowing a dinghy on the loch. Often, at weekends, Jack went home, but usually by way of the Gareloch. The complicated journey puzzled Gordon.

"It seems a long way round," he said suspiciously one Friday night as he watched Jack prepare to leave.

Jack snapped the lock on his valise and tipped his straw hat to an angle that Gordon considered common and typical of his cousin's rakish ways.

"I like to look in on Great-grandmother Veitch," he said. "She's a character and she doesn't get many visitors when the family are in Glasgow. She gives me her gossip and I give her mine."

Gordon laughed but his expression was disbelieving. "Tell that to your mother," he said. "I know you too well. They tell me some of the girls at the yacht club over there have the reputation of being sports."

Jack gave his hat an adjustment. "So I've heard," he said with an inscrutable smile.

Gordon watched with a pang of envy as he went down the stony path to the road, swinging his bag and whistling. His cousin's carefree life was in painful contrast to his own labyrinthine journey. As he went about his work, he was laden with an oppressive realisation of Anne's deteriorating health and increasing unhappiness. Every time they met she seemed more pathetically strained and lost. He saw with alarm and a feeling of panic that threads of grey had grown into her lovely hair.

Almost all their meetings were in the open, along empty stretches of the riverbank near her home. Foxgloves swayed in the breeze and honeysuckle trailed from the hedgerows, but however tranquil the scene, peace eluded them.

One day she came running down a woodland path to meet him with her eyes red from recent weeping. "They're both at me," she cried hysterically when he questioned her. "Father and Peter. Peter wants me back and father is on his side. I've told them I'll kill myself if they don't leave me alone." She turned away from him and stared desolately into the silent river with agonised eyes. "I've told them I'll put myself in the water, where mother went. And I would, if it wasn't for Malcolm." Her eyes went suddenly wild. "I would if it wasn't for my little son."

She collapsed sobbing in his arms. He clung to her in a torment of bewildered tenderness and fright, trying to remember her as she had been that first day on the Gareloch. Memories choked him so that he could hardly speak.

"No, we'll run away," he gasped, scarcely knowing what he said or how it could be done. "It wouldn't matter where we went. If we were away from them all, we would be happy."

He felt her stiffen in his arms, and when she looked up she seemed to be smiling through the tears. Her hair had loosened and wet strands streaked her face.

"No, my poor darling. Never. I wouldn't do that to you. Oh, if only you knew how often I lie awake thinking that one day we might. I lie wondering what it would be like if we were married. And then I cry, for it's only a dream. We've made our own unhappiness. I've wasted my own life and now I'm wasting yours. We can't escape. I'm married. There's Malcolm. We couldn't take him and I couldn't leave him."

He pulled himself gently away from her, looking down the river to a horizon that had become blurred and depressing with the setting of the sun. For the first time he appreciated how real his mother's fears had been. The sudden knowledge tore at his heart.

"Does that mean you think we should . . . ?" His voice faltered into an aching silence.

"Yes." Her tears began again. "We must. There's nothing for us, Gordon."

It was hardly more than a moment of reality, and as they lay huddled to each other in the gathering twilight, resolution died.

It was ten days before he saw her again. They both had excuses to be in Glasgow and they met in an unfashionable tearoom in Sauchiehall Street. A sign creaking above the door said: MISS FRAME'S—HOME BAKING A SPECIALITY.

The tables sat on an uneven floor covered with worn linoleum. The faded floral wallpaper was hung with inferior watercolours which a hopeful notice said could be purchased.

Anne watched him examine the drab room and its clientele of women shoppers. "I thought in a place like this we were less likely to meet anyone we knew," she said.

He nodded, watching the elderly waitresses with their rattling trays of battered teapots. "I wonder which one is Miss Frame? Perhaps that stout lady in bombazine at the cash desk. All she needs is a lorgnette and she would look like a duchess."

Here, to a table near the bead curtain that shielded some inner place, his father had come a long time ago with another girl who had aroused family disapproval. Little had changed. Perhaps only the watercolours and one or two of the waitresses.

Anne was examining the cake stand with its laden willow pattern plates. "Everything looks very fresh," she said encouragingly.

A subtle change in her appearance caught his attention. Her eyes were calm and her colour better. She looked more rested and relaxed than he had seen her for many months. In the shabby room among the dark homespun frocks and coats she looked startlingly young and untainted. She wore a highnecked dress of pink silk with a delicate pattern of flowers embroidered on the bodice and sleeves. Her little hat was sewn with pearls and sat confidently on top of a feathery, swept-up hairstyle. Across the tea bread and cream cakes there drifted the sharp bouquet of an expensive French perfume he had bought for her, with much embarrassment, in a shop where the assistants had painted faces and disdainful expressions.

As he looked at her, an inexpressible hope and happiness rose in him. He leaned forward. "You look so well, Anne."

She touched the brooch on her breast with a quick gesture of pleasure. Her head tilted with some of the old poise that he had almost forgotten.

"Is it so obvious?"

"Wonderfully obvious."

She lifted a potato scone and buttered it carefully. "I have quite a lot to tell you. You know I haven't felt well for a long time?"

Her smile had become less certain and she spoke with a suggestion almost of formality, as if making a confession.

"Yes." He nodded.

"Well, last week father took me to see a doctor someone told him about. I didn't want to go, but he insisted, and now I'm glad. This man—Durande is his name—specialises in nervous disorders. In a way his appearance is rather frightening. He has strange dark eyes and a little sharp black beard. He was trained in some mysterious clinic in France and came to Glasgow only recently. The questions he asked! Some were embarrassing and others distressing. Especially the ones about mother and how she died and the awful dreams I have sometimes."

He watched uneasily as the haunted shadows he knew so well began to gather in her eyes. His voice was abrupt with disappointment at the sudden collapse of a meeting that had started so well.

"What has all that got to do with you not feeling well? Didn't he examine you?"

With great concentration she rolled the potato scone and sliced it. Then she answered, "He listened to my heart and took my pulse but mainly he just sat looking at me with his extraordinary eyes, asking these very personal questions. I had the feeling he was trying to see right inside me." She sat twisting her napkin and staring into a corner of the room where a castor-oil plant and some neglected aspidistras reached palely for the light.

"He became more and more intimate in his interrogation. I could see Father starting to fidget and glower. I think he was beginning to regret having brought me, although I don't know if it was the questioning he resented or my response to it. You see, some of it made me cry, because of what seemed to lie behind it."

Gordon had a sudden sense of sitting with a stranger beset and isolated behind some terrible invisible barrier. He longed to be able to touch her, to give her the knowledge of another caring presence. Words were inadequate.

Presently she shuddered. "I asked him if he thought I was going mad. I asked him if he thought that was what it was." Her hands were raised in front of her as if she were keeping something at bay. "That's what I've often wondered. Have you ever thought that about me?"

A butterfly with red wings hovered about a posy of sweet peas at an open window. Pigeons basked on a ledge of the building opposite. But Gordon felt cold. He waited until a passing waitress creaked away, out of hearing, with her trolley of cakes and scones.

"No, of course I haven't." The smile he managed was little more than a worried grimace. "Darling, what a terrible thing to ask."

"I know. Even to ask it makes me think I must be going . . . peculiar. Father was outraged and told me to stop being hysterical. Dr. Durande was very abrupt with him. He told him he must be quiet or leave the room, that it was better for me to say exactly what I felt. He said these things are better understood now, and can be treated. There was a time, not all that long ago, when doctors didn't feel competent to deal with anything they couldn't see. That sort of thing was left to the Church."

"The Church!"

A woman rose from the next table and went out carrying parcels printed with Glasgow names he knew well. Some of the watercolours depicted streets he recognised. But he felt himself in unknown and hostile territory. Where was she going? Where was she taking him?

"Yes. Irrational fears, as Dr. Durande calls them, used to be regarded as the work of the devil. Some sick people were believed to be possessed by evil spirits. The priests, or whoever they were, tried to drive the demons out with crucifixes and burning candles. They chanted in Latin, rang bells and burned incense. It must have been awful."

"But that was insanity!" The word burned in his mouth. "What's he bringing all that up for? You're only run down. You probably need a tonic. Didn't he give you a bottle?"

She leaned back. Calmness seemed to enfold her again, as if the reliving of her consultation with the strange doctor was over.

"Now I've made *you* look ill, Gordon. I've frightened you, but I told you some of it was disturbing. There's no need to worry, though. In the end it was a wonderful relief. I left feeling so much better. It was as if I had been carrying a burden and he had lifted it away." Gwen's flash of insight and odd choice of word came back to him. "And, of course, he did give me some medicine. It's colourless, and I take a teaspoonful of it in water three times a day. It's quite tasteless. I don't know what it is, but he said it would calm me."

"Whatever it is, it seems to work," he said, relief growing in him at the returning naturalness of her appearance.

"Father refers to it as my 'dope.' He's very pleased with himself. I suppose it must be some sort of sedative. I've slept well since I started taking it."

Outside, cabs and carts rattled. Hawkers called, young and shrill or rough and dehumanised after years in contest with the traffic's grind. Shadows, disembodied and without cares, hurried across the heavy net curtains. Beyond the window it was life as usual. And yet, across the table, around this beautiful girl to whom he was bound, darkness yawned.

"Of course, the medicine won't cure me by itself." Her cheeks were flushed and her voice quick. She ignored the tongs and lifted a flaky, cream-filled pastry between two dainty fingers which he thought trembled. "I must go into Dr. Durande's nursing home for more intensive treatment."

"Oh." He leaned forward and bit on a fingernail to hide the extent of his concern. "That's rather a shock. I hadn't thought of anything like that."

"Nor had I." She broke her pastry with a fork. "It took me a day or two to get used to the idea. But if it's going to help me . . . I'm to be admitted on Thursday afternoon."

The sun went behind some obstruction and the room lost even the garish gaiety of the watercolours. Nursing homes were almost as far outside his experience as priests with bells and candles. He could not remember any of the family ever having been ill, except with coughs and

190

sneezes. Health for the Kings had never been interrupted by more than an occasional mustard foot bath.

"How long will you be gone?"

She smiled a little. "Don't make it sound so far away, Gordon. I'll only be a mile or so across the river. He has a big house set in extensive grounds."

"And what is this intensive treatment?"

"Father asked that, but Dr. Durande said he wouldn't know exactly until he had me under observation for a few days."

"You haven't told me how long you'll be in this nursing home."

She pushed a crumb about the table. "It depends on the progress I make. I don't suppose he could be expected to say more than that."

"No." He felt avenues closing, increasing the distance between them and happiness.

"I'll be lost and lonely. I don't suppose I'll dare visit you."

"Oh, no. I'm not to be allowed visitors, not even Father. He's had to sign some kind of admittance form."

He shrank from this reminder that, for all his love, so far as the world was concerned, he owned no part of her.

12

July was a dull and sultry month broken by thunderstorms and drizzling rain. The restless throb of the expanding city was muffled and the streets were heavy with dejection. Awnings sagged and trees dripped. Clerks crouched lethargically in airless offices, and in the gardens of the big houses roses gathered mildew and paths crept green with moss.

Factory smoke of many poisonous hues swirled drearily over the roof-tops, casting turbulent shadows to match those that had invaded the mind of Douglas Dunbar. Alarming reports reached his riverside domain. King's Royal was ascending again. Worse. Far from being the short-lived novelty that he had prophesied, Queen's Royal had emerged from the jubilee festivities as an established favourite among people prepared to pay for extra quality.

Instead of having one red rag in front of him Dunbar now had two.

No morbid midnight juggling of figures, no loud haranguing of quaking sales representatives lined up in the heavy morning light, could clear from his mind the bitter fact that his campaign of price-cutting had failed. He had cut until he could cut no more. Other prongs of his onslaught flagged. He had run out of stealthy slanders to be spread about King & Co. and of brazen claims to be made for his own whisky. It was all recoiling on him. He had heard the sniggers in White's Chop House and seen the sly smiles as he stood at the bar emptying a mid-day glass of whisky. He had soon crushed the furtive titters with a threatening glare or a challenging growl. He could manage that puny crowd of smug strugglers but the setback to his dream of domination was cruel. The sacrifices he had made! And to be thwarted by a woman! It was ruinous to his pride.

Even his pursuit of Fiona had lost momentum. For all his ingenuity he could not think of an excuse to approach her again. It was frustrating, but instinct told him finesse was all essential. Crudeness would be a fatal blunder. He consoled himself with the thought that it was a long, unhurried game he was playing. The opportunity would come. Meantime, he had worries enough.

However often he sat down with his ledgers, grimly determined to find a way of continuing the fight against King & Co., he ended with the same sense of humiliation. For the first time in his life he was afflicted by a knowledge of helplessness. Robert's words came ringing back to him from that furious afternoon at Castle Gare. *You're cutting your price so recklessly you're in danger of leaving yourself with nothing.* It was true; he had known it even then. He was baulked by a force that even he could not master—the immutable economic law that ruled every business. His percentage of profit was now derisory and below it he could not go. He had run out of gunpowder.

His only comfort was the certainty that King & Co. must have had a year every bit as lean. They had their fat overseas profits, of course, which he could not touch and which Robert had so gallingly waved in his face. But against that was to be weighed the telling financial blow he had struck at Queen's Royal. His price war had been fought only against King's Royal. Their other damned fraud was a blatantly expensive whisky in a category in which there was no competition. But, oh, that cornering of the Aberlivet market which he had engineered had cost them dear. He dwelt lovingly on that early victory over Fiona.

As he agonised his way through the damp and sulphurous days, avoiding his usual haunts, it was to this crafty stroke that he kept returning. The memory of it eased the pangs and made the long clammy days more tolerable.

Only with that triumph in mind did business retain some savour. He clung to it steadfastly, for if business lost its lure, what had he? He looked round the brown room, with its framed letters signed by illustrious customers, its sample bottles filled with the malty produce of distant glens, its inadequate window which nevertheless showed too much of the griminess beyond. It wasn't much; certainly, he could see now, it wasn't enough, but away from here there was . . . nothing. Ethel dead. Anne lying in that fellow's nursing home, being treated for God alone knew what. He didn't know. She didn't know. Did Durande—for all his silly, French-bearded presumption—did Durande know?

What a foolish, headstrong girl she had been, he thought sadly: pregnant before marriage; separated from her husband; carrying on with, of all men, the son of his enemy. He had put an end to that, but there were times when it was almost too much for him to believe or forgive. And yet, he could not deny the source of so much of Anne's trouble. The qualities which drove her came from him. His was the impatience, the determination, the daring that was heedless and wholehearted. But what was the source of the fatal flaw of which he was so mercifully free? It all crowded in on him, and what lay ahead in that direction he dare not think. Much as he loved her, he was pitifully inadequate to deal with this crisis in her life. She needed her own home and a husband who could strengthen her out of his own devotion.

He frowned at the reproachful emptiness of his table—usually impressive with the signs of his industry—then, with a choking sigh of self-pity, reached listlessly behind him for the massive ledger in which were recorded the battle honours of his remarkable career. Soon he was immersed. He went through the columns of neat figures as another man might have read a diary of his youth, remembering the thrills and the heartbeats behind the dead symbols. The dark hills and dales of his primeval face were lit by a wavering sunshine as he relived the heroic foray he had made against Reid & McMillan, the epic rotting of McSorley and the slaying of that foolhardy ass Henderson, who hadn't known what was happening to him until the dirk went in and his guts were revealed to the whole of Glasgow. He twisted the broad gold rings on his fingers with satisfaction as he lingered over the brief purchase and sale prices that signified his besting of Fiona in the Aberlivet deal.

And suddenly, as if written there on the page, he saw another deal, a possibility so stupendous that it almost frightened him. He pushed back his chair, closed his eyes and let his mind cautiously circle the audacious idea. After a few minutes he rose and pulled the bell cord. A clerk answered the jangling summons and was sent running for various files and trade statistics. For the rest of the morning he worked furiously, darkening the room with cigar smoke, opening the door and shouting for more information, throwing himself down at the table to make feverish calculations.

At last he was satisfied. He seized his hat and, with his coat negligently open to reveal the flowered pattern of his green brocade waistcoat, went striding up the street. Labourers squatting on the pavement against the walls of warehouses put down their cans of tea to stare after him, grinning knowingly at each other as men stepped aside at his approach. *He's a man, that one*, their expressions said.

For the first time in a week Dunbar marched boldly into the lunchtime swarm at White's Chop House, quelling with a proud sweep of his eyes the stir of interest that went round the crowded bar. He collected a glass of whisky and pushed his way carelessly to a table where the whisky contingent met. They made way for him with sounds of welcome, watching

194

each other's reactions. *He's perked up,* their veiled glances said, for his depression had been the cause of much gloating speculation.

The hearty rumble of his voice confirmed their quick analysis. They had all known him so long, since the days when he had come about their offices a raw bumpkin in rough country clothes and with a humbler manner they now had difficulty in remembering. That he had so far out-stripped them was still the cause, among the more thoughtful of them, of much heart-searching and grudging respect.

Dunbar gave them a large smile. He saw them with a certain affection, like souvenirs of his past. They were the human measures against which his progress could be comfortingly assessed, and he still did business with most of them.

"And how are things?" he said, the tilt of his hat and his relaxed way with the glass of whisky clearly indicating that with him they were very good. He listened to their answers with placid or congratulatory nods.

Sandy Whyte was still on the point of invading America and Jimmy Crawford was negotiating, as he had been for months, a deal which, when concluded, would mean his having to think about bigger premises. Some of them were fading a little and growing ragged at the edges, but it was all interesting to Dunbar, for he had never, unlike some people he could think of, forgotten his own less affluent days. No, he was still just one of the boys. And to prove it he raised a lordly hand and commanded that their glasses be refilled.

"And what about you, Douglas?" said Maxwell, a lean, bold man with a stiff wing collar and a sound connection with all the leading hotels. "Still wiping the floor with the opposition?"

Dunbar's benevolence clouded a little, but only momentarily.

"What does opposition matter in this business?" he said, tipping the remains of his drink over his throat with a flourish of rings. "There's more than enough for all of us."

They chorused their agreement, happy to be reminded that the road they were on was of seemingly untarnishable gold. This prosperous city was rightly proud of what they did down there in their blending halls on the banks of the Clyde.

Those who had heard rumours spread them with malicious winks or sympathetic murmurs, depending on whom they referred to. They managed to cover most of the trade without once naming King & Co. They knew the boundaries to his affability.

"You'll be coming to the summer ball next week, Douglas?" someone asked, referring to one of the trade's two big annual functions.

Dunbar nodded ponderously. "It's a duty, isn't it? But I'll be without my partner this year. Anne hasn't been very well, lately. She's had to go into a nursing home to rest."

They were sympathetic but not too enquiring. There had been talk, dangerous talk, but this was one rumour none of them had the inclination to investigate.

"What age," Dunbar asked suddenly, looking round them invitingly as for expert opinion, "would you say was the minimum for the top dressing in the average blend?"

He listened intently to their answers. "Oh, eight years," someone said. "Without a doubt. You couldn't get by with less."

Blandly he ignored their curiosity, called abruptly for a plate of pigs' trotters to be brought to the table, and, when he had eaten it, soaking up the gravy with crusty bread, left as grandly as he had come.

His next call was at the head Glasgow office of the Bank of Scotland. They had handled his account for fifteen years, and although he didn't have an appointment, Finlay, the general manager, was immediately available.

Finlay's room was hung with paintings of the Glasgow School and furnished with what Dunbar, since his purchases from Gwen, now recognised as antiques. Every time he visited it he left resolved to transform his own office. So far these artistic impulses had not survived the more pressing demands of business.

For all his ostentation of dress and his occasional bombast, Dunbar was the kind of customer Finlay liked. His account, if it went out of credit, was unfailingly back in credit by the promised date. He ran his business on his own money. This appealed to Finlay's ingrained prudence. When the inspectors came round, Dunbar's account was never one of his worries. The pattern had not varied in fifteen years. It was against this background that the old man's surprise grew as he listened to what Dunbar had to say.

The outline was clear enough in Dunbar's mind, but in this temple of caution the enormity he contemplated made him nervous. He began at the beginning.

"Earlier this year," he said, moderating his language to the level of seemliness that he knew worked best with Finlay, "I did a very lucrative bit of business. I picked up all the available supplies of a certain whisky."

As he paused, Finlay's speckled beard parted in a slight smile. "You cornered the market?"

"So it turned out," Dunbar said modestly. "As it happened, a well-known company needed this particular whisky and offered me a lot of cash for it. I doubled my money in a few months."

Finlay's response was encouraging. He admired commercial cupidity, even though he had no scope for it himself. These adventurers could be

196

relied on to bring a little spice into the routine of his life. "Very nice," he murmured.

Dunbar leaned forward. His hand covered a large area of the well-polished desk. "It was damned nice," he agreed, "and it's given me an idea. Every blender uses quite a high proportion of top quality malts in his whisky. Even the ones who save money by basing their blends on lower-grade malts still have to use some tops. In the trade its known as 'top dressing.' Now, there aren't all that many distilleries in this top category. Maybe four or five. That means that with the demand there is these days, there isn't all that much of these particular whiskies about. Another thing, they don't really reach perfection until they're about eight years old. Now, if someone owned all the surplus of these whiskies above, say, five years old, he would be in a very strong position."

Finlay, whose beard had been pointed at the cut-glass chandelier, brought his eyes down to Dunbar's level and said, "In a strong position to do what, Mr. Dunbar?"

"To put his own price on them."

"If they are surplus, who would want them?"

Dunbar stifled a harsh reply to this ignorance. "They're only surplus until they're needed," he said.

Finlay still needed some clarification. "But don't blenders fill all the whisky they're going to need direct from the distilleries when it's new?"

"They fill all the whisky they *think* they're going to need," Dunbar said triumphantly. "But remember, you don't use the whisky I'm talking about until eight years after it's distilled. That means you have to try to think eight years ahead. It used to be reasonably easy, but with the boom in whisky, nobody ever lays down enough. Sales keep going up faster than anyone expects. We all have to go to the open market and buy fully matured whisky to make up the deficit we didn't budget for. So much of this goes on that there are brokers now who deal in nothing but whisky. This is why people invest in whisky. They know if they hold it for a few years, they can make a nice profit by selling to blenders who're short. But if one man held all this surplus—"

"He'd have cornered the market," Finlay finished for him.

Although the banker's eyes were twinkling, Dunbar felt suddenly defensive. He stuck his thumbs in his waistcoat pockets. "It's done with other things: tea, coffee, tin, copper, pepper. All sorts of things. I don't have to tell you that. No one's thought yet of doing it with whisky. It's only the boom that came with blending that makes it a practical proposition. There used to be more whisky of all ages lying about than could ever be used. These days that's not the case."

"This would require one to be a very rich man," Finlay said, looking past Dunbar to a calm pastoral scene by James Guthrie. The paintings had all been picked for qualities of restfulness; sometimes the adventurers could be a little unsettling. "How much money would be needed to buy all this whisky?"

So fixed was the old man's gaze that Dunbar turned slightly to see what he was looking at. He saw fields with trees and sheep in sunlit tones that were unusually soft and veiled. Nothing had much detail to it, yet there was an undeniable distinction to the picture. He was almost grateful for the diversion, for like Finlay he was unsettled. They had reached the frightening part of his vision. He took a sheet of paper from his coat and sat staring at it in silence. When he could bring himself to look up, his expression was almost as distant as Finlay's. He was struggling with a sense of unreality.

"Three million," he said quietly. "It's not possible to calculate exactly, but it would take something like that. If three million didn't buy it all, there wouldn't be enough left to make any difference. Whoever held the rest would reap the benefit as well. And good luck to them."

Finlay's movements became brisk and his posture businesslike as he reached for a pen and a scribbling pad. Figures, even very large figures, were reassuring to him. He wrote them down and began calculating the interest and wondering about the security. "And you would like the bank to accommodate you to the extent of three million pounds, Mr. Dunbar?"

To hear the sum articulated in Finlay's professionally forbidding way sent a shiver through Dunbar. "Well . . . not all at once."

"No." Finlay's face twisted as if the grip he had taken of his beard were painful. "It's an exciting idea, all right, but isn't it too big for you?"

Even though this was the thought that was disturbing him, he resented anyone else's entertaining it. "Too big!" He waved his page of figures as if parrying Finlay's sword play, then, ignoring the rebuff, repeated his argument. "Look at these." He leaned across the desk to give Finlay a glimpse of his calculations. "Every year for twenty years the sales of Scotch whisky have risen. Whoever controls the whisky stocks names his price. There's a fortune to be made."

Finlay put down his pen and pushed away the pad. "You have a sound business, Mr. Dunbar, but I don't think you could provide the security the bank would ask for such a sum."

Dunbar had foreseen this difficulty and was pleased with his solution to it.

"You could have the whisky itself as security," he said, watching closely for the reaction. "As soon as I bought a parcel, I would sign it over to the bank. Then the bank would lend me money to buy the next parcel, and so on."

Finlay could not hide an admiring smile. "That's very ingenious," he said, "but I'm afraid the bank would not consider whisky as gilt-edged."

Dunbar clenched his hands and restrained a sudden desire to lean across the desk and get a grip on Finlay's beard. His voice rose. "What could be more gilt-edged than whisky? It increases in value every year."

"Every year so far, perhaps," Finlay conceded. "But there's no guarantee that will continue."

"Of course it'll continue."

"It may well do, but the bank would not take that risk. They might accommodate you to a third the value of the whisky. Perhaps even half. But that would still leave you to find half the money yourself."

"A third or a half!" Dunbar snarled. "My God, that's playing safe."

"Quite. The bank does not believe in taking risks." The banker's voice, although smooth, had a sharp edge to it. "Now, could you find two thirds or even half of three million pounds from your own resources?"

"You know bloody well I couldn't."

As Dunbar struggled with his resentment, Finlay, his supremacy established, raised his hands in a gesture of sympathy. "I told you I thought it too big for one man. And by that I mean any one man. Now, that doesn't mean I wouldn't like to help. If only the load could be spread, if there were others involved, the bank might well be disposed to take a more favourable view."

"Others?" Dunbar was puzzled. "What others?"

"Well, if there was a syndicate."

Dunbar floundered. He had never worked with other men. He had always been too jealous of his independence, too certain of his rightness, too impatient of other opinions.

"I don't know any other men," he said gruffly.

"Perhaps in that respect the bank could assist. We have a number of customers with large resources who are accustomed to taking risks. They are always on the lookout for tempting speculations. Risks do not deter them if the rewards are great."

"Are you saying you know people who would lend me this money but at a high rate of interest?" Usury he might be able to stomach.

But Finlay dashed this faint hope. "No. They would want to come in with you."

Dunbar swallowed. The thought of sharing the rewards of his great inspiration was a bitter one. But he forced himself to face it. Forced himself to remember it wasn't just money he was playing for. The blending trade was to be held to ransom, no doubt about that. But there was the greater lure of what was to be done to King & Co. They were to be denied supplies at any price—or only at a price synonymous with ruin. He

199

could see Finlay watching him. Damn the old fool's faint heart. To suggest saddling him—a man like him—with partners! He couldn't do it. He couldn't work with other men for mere money. But to net a fortune and at last cripple—perhaps even smash—his enemy . . . oh, for that, he could put up with anything.

"Who are these other people?" His eyes were baleful with the sense of surrender.

Finlay refused to give names. "I would have to consult them first."

"But you think they'll be interested?" Already he was desperate not to lose them.

"I think they well might be." Finlay leaned forward with a friendly smile. "Despite my necessary caution, I think your scheme is an excellent one. Don't be too disappointed that the bank can't entertain it from an individual."

Dunbar rose with a resigned grin. "All right. I'll hold myself available for any meeting you can arrange." He held out his hand. "And the sooner the better."

Four days later the syndicate for the destruction of King & Co. was formed.

13

Fiona surprised Fergus by asking him to escort her to the summer ball.

He held a match over his pipe, his eyes closed to the clouds of smoke. "Surely that was never one of Robert's engagements?"

"Perhaps not, but it's one of the grand trade functions of the year and a very good place, I should think, for getting to know people."

He smiled quizzically, using his matchbox to tap down the newly lit tobacco. "Whom do you expect to meet?"

She was annoyed when Dunbar's was the only trade name that came to her. He seemed to have taken over a small but important part of her mind. Didn't she know any other whisky people? "I couldn't tell you," she said firmly. "That's exactly the point. I'm still a stranger in this trade."

Fergus stroked his beard reflectively. "And so am I, Fiona. Even after almost fifty years. But it doesn't worry me." Then, as if regretting the mild rebuke, he bowed with the gallant smile she could always win from him. "But as you wish, my dear. And, of course, in Robert's absence I'll be delighted to escort you."

Fiona took his hand and gave it a grateful squeeze. "Thank you, Grandfather. Actually, there's more to it than I've said. I had arranged a little surprise. . . ."

Fergus was always wary of surprises; life had sprung too many on him. He looked at her suspiciously.

"I have persuaded James to attend the ball."

"Dear knows!" He smoothed his hair energetically but seemed unable to find a question.

"And that isn't all."

"Isn't it?" He puffed his cheeks and waited, vaguely wondering why neither Rita nor he knew James was coming to Glasgow. Or had he simply forgotten? The thought of James always raised a painful confusion in him these days.

"No. He is bringing a young lady."

His reaction was a sad and unexpected reminder to her that he was no longer young, or as resilient as he had been even a year ago. She had expected him to be startled, amused, even skittish. Instead, he became plaintive.

"Fiona, what is all this mystery about?"

"Oh, there's no mystery," she reassured him. "James mentioned in a letter he would soon be visiting Glasgow to see the Institute of Fine Arts people about some paintings he has ready for exhibiting. The date he gave coincided with the ball. I wrote asking him to be my guest and suggested he bring with him a certain Miss Jessie McNee. To my surprise, he accepted. I must say I'm delighted. I think he must want to show her off."

Fergus seemed unable to keep his pipe lit. He struck another match. "Who is Miss Jessie McNee?"

"I gather she's a young lady artist James has become friendly with in Fleetside."

He frowned elaborately at the troublesome pipe and, through it, at all those involved in this vaguely upsetting situation. "He's never told Rita anything about her." He cupped his hands and sighed into them with a noise like the sea on a lonely shore.

"You know what James is like. He probably feels shy about the girl. I'm sure there's a romance in the air."

He seemed amazed at the possibility. "Romance? How can you tell that?"

She laughed. "Call it woman's intuition. Also, I can read between the lines of his letters."

"I don't know what his mother will say."

"Grandfather!" She slapped his wrist in playful reproof. "James is thirty-nine now."

Fergus persisted in his uncertainty. "I don't think the boy's ever had a ladyfriend. I can't remember one."

"There you are! That's why I thought it would be a lovely surprise. But, of course, now you must tell Grandmother. Tell her James will spend two nights in Glasgow. Because it was supposed to be a surprise, I invited him to stay the first night with me. I reserved a room for Miss McNee in the St. Enoch Hotel. That is the station they will arrive at. No doubt Grandmother will want James to spend the second night at Park

Place." She hesitated. "Perhaps she might even want to invite Miss McNee."

"We'll have to see about that," Fergus said dourly.

But by the night of the ball he had become accustomed to the idea that James would be in the company of a young lady. He had even persuaded himself—and Rita—that benefit could be derived from the situation. It had occurred to him often, as he brooded over the gossip about James, that it was his son's bachelor status that gave credence to the slanders. If James had been married, the mischief would never have started. There were times when Fergus almost wished his son a philanderer, a rake— anything that would give the lie to these damnable innuendoes. Now, suddenly, he saw Jessie McNee as the possible salvation of James's good name. He clung to the hopeful idea, elaborating on it to Rita and refusing to be downcast when she, more practical, said, "But Fergus, dear, no more than perhaps two hundred people will see James with this young lady at the ball. What is that out of so many hundreds of thousands?"

"It will be a healthy sight," Fergus persisted. "It will be some sort of antidote to all this wickedness."

He saw Rita was half convinced and his spirits were still buoyant when he collected Fiona from Claremont Row.

"James left just a few minutes ago to meet Miss McNee at her hotel," she told him. He nodded agreeably and settled back in a corner of the carriage with a good view of the busy evening scene.

When they arrived at the Central Hotel, the nearby streets were dense with sightseers loitering round the gleaming carriages of the whisky barons. As they edged their way across the crowded lobby, Fiona thought guiltily of her last visit. The little room where she had sat with Dunbar was gay with flowers and chintz covers. Their table by the window was occupied by a young man and a girl with the unmistakably tender look of lovers. The sight filled her with an unaccountable sadness.

"Sir Fergus King and Mrs. Fiona King." The names carried clearly despite the hubbub in the glittering suite.

Dunbar reared up in surprise over the heads of the men and women who had gathered round him—mainly the whisky crowd from White's Chop House, and their wives. He saw Fiona in a gown of pale blue, her hair held high in an exquisite arrangement of loose waves perfectly suited to her aura of exuberant good health.

There was about her, he thought, *a haze of warm summer beauty.* He laboured for some poetic simile more worthy of what he saw. None came, and from the lyrical his thoughts collapsed into a form more natural to him. *And I came here thinking I was going to be bored!*

Exultantly, his hand went out and lifted a large glass of whisky from a passing tray. "I don't remember any member of that great family ever before honouring us with their presence," he said, concealing his elation with sarcasm.

"They're under new management now," Sandy Whyte reminded him, with an appreciative smile and a significant nod in the direction of Fiona.

"Oh, that's right, I remember now," Dunbar said with huge playfulness, the whisky swirling carelessly in his glass, his dark eyes ferreting jovially round them to see if they were enjoying the joke. "Things became too hectic up here for that Mr. Robert King who used to be the boss. He had to run away and hide in London."

He stifled a noisy guffaw by biting on his cigar with large white teeth. His elbow dug roguishly into Sandy's ribs. "What do you think of the new gaffer?"

"She's a bonnie lass," Sandy said with conviction.

"Aye, she is that." Dunbar's agreement was heartfelt and unconcealed. Almost immediately he wondered if he had been indiscreet in the presence of perceptive men. With a leer he added, "What a pity she had to go and spoil it by taking a name like King."

Mrs. Jimmy Crawford said, "Is that the famous Mrs. King we've all heard so much about? Her gown is cut far too low."

Dunbar was affronted but limited himself to an eloquent inspection of the lady's own narrow shoulders and meagre, well-concealed chest, and the mild remark, "There's some it suits."

"Surely that isn't her husband," another of the wives said.

"It's her father-in-law," Dunbar said, emptying his brimming glass in the heroic way that always provoked surprise and admiration. "The lady's husband is in London, helping to run the country." He grinned. "At least, that's what *he* says."

He put down his empty glass and, disengaging himself, entered the crush of medal ribbons, cummerbunds, sparkling jewellery and gowns made in London and Paris.

Fiona watched him approach with a feeling almost of panic. Surely he wouldn't embarrass her by letting Fergus see they knew each other socially. He had been so circumspect when there had been less need for it. In two or three heart-pounding seconds she regretted having foolishly compromised herself by dining with him, regretted having wilfully come to a ball at which she should have known he would be present, regretted the whole naive and ridiculous illogicality of her attitude toward him.

She was not afraid of him, but he made her nervous. Under his influence she felt not only his but her own behaviour to be unpredictable. He became too easily boorish or hectoring, but in his presence she felt vague, unsettling stirrings unknown since the days of her unconventional youth. He was dangerous, yet the power and mystery out of which he

204

was constructed fascinated her, striking a response from some wild chord buried deep in the untamed part of her nature.

She tried to look away but her gaze was drawn back. That this was not one of Dunbar's nights for circumspection seemed alarmingly clear from the determined way he was elbowing himself forward, his eyes fixed on hers and his face set in a reckless smile.

Didn't he recognise Fergus? Wasn't he aware of the gossip that would sweep the trade and then the whole city if they were seen exchanging a civil word? Her thoughts became frantic. She felt her lace handkerchief tear between agitated fingers. He was drunk! There could be no doubt of it. It was the only explanation. She felt hot and weak. Fergus was speaking but his words were lost in the turmoil that unbalanced her and reduced the wide room to a narrow corridor down which Dunbar stalked her. She had awareness enough left to realise, disconcertingly, that if her life had been different, it would have been exciting to see him hurrying toward her so singlemindedly. It was as if, so far as he was concerned, they were the only two people in the room.

She began to marvel at the remarkable change dress wear made in him. The flattering, well-cut black cloth seemed to draw the crudity from his features and the excessive bulk from his frame. Why had she ever thought of him as lumbering and ungainly? He was lithe and light-footed, crossing the room with the effortless step of a dancer. And for the first time she saw beneath the pirate mask to a face of elusive sensitivity. It was on the mirror of this previously undetected refinement, she realised, that his many moods were reflected, in the same way that a mountain slope switched from harsh to beckoning as it registered the sky's changing light.

She was aware of the same spell that had gathered about her when they dined together.

"Look, Fiona. James is here. And that must be Miss McNee."

The excitement in Fergus's voice ended her drifting journey. She waved and sent a flustered smile to James, then turned back imploringly to Dunbar. She saw him hesitate at the strength of the pleading in her eyes. Her lips formed a single, silent word: "Later." For an instant their wills clashed; then she smiled. What the smile denoted she could not have said. But the space separating them was vibrant with the knowledge that between them a bond existed. Their lives had touched and were now strangely intertwined. It had been inevitable from the moment she accepted his dinner invitation. Now her whispered "later" had sealed that early promise.

"Douglas! You old ruffian!"

She heard the exclamation come from somewhere to his left. He turned irritably. There was a moment of indecision before he smiled.

Then, carefully clutching what he had wrung from her, he joined the man who had called his name.

She heard Fergus whisper, "What a charming girl." Jessie's unspoiled simplicity had appealed immediately to his love of the wholesome.

She replied with a slightly distracted smile.

Champagne was brought to the table, but James insisted on having whisky. "I like my medicine strong," he said, and according to their various understandings of him, they took from the words what they thought he meant.

Even when dancing an energetic polka with Fiona, Fergus puzzled over what he saw in his son's face. The lines of pain around James's eyes had deepened, and yet the eyes themselves were contradictorily bright and happy. If Jessie had not been there, Fergus might have cynically ascribed this mystery to the whisky. After the polka he sat for a while in a withdrawn silence, seeking to disentangle the real James from his involved speculations about him.

Fiona, quicker and more intuitive, saw the romance she had prophesied amply confirmed in the almost timorously tender glances that passed between James and Jessie. Normally, this would have taken up all her attention, but tonight she was too preoccupied.

From where she sat, Dunbar, despite the many mirrors, was unseen, but the room—or her mind—was heavy with his presence. "Later" was what she had said, not fully knowing what she meant. How soon would he expect "later" to be? With his impulsive nature, not long. Soon she must keep her rash promise. But not yet. He could wait. She turned determinedly to Jessie and spoke brightly of the fashions on display.

Balloons hung from chandeliers and streamers were looped round mirrors. Everywhere there was colour and light, and on the long buffet tables silver shone discreetly among massed arrangements of exotic delicacies.

It was a convention that each table be laden with the blender's own brand of whisky. Fergus shook his head wonderingly at the vast assortment. "Dear knows!" he muttered. "Twenty years ago King's Royal was the only blend. Now look at them! They seem to spring up overnight, like mushrooms."

At that moment a trolley stopped beside him and a waiter placed a bottle of whisky on the table. Fergus lifted it in surprise and almost dropped it when he read the label: DUNBAR'S SPECIAL. He returned the bottle to the trolley with a noisy thump. "We didn't ask for this. Take it away."

"There's one for each table, sir."

"Don't argue with me. Take it away. We have our own whisky."

Fiona leaned hurriedly forward. "Grandfather, is it worth making a fuss? If there's one for every table, he hasn't singled us out. He wouldn't know we were coming."

Fergus hesitated, then gave the waiter a surly nod. "All right. Put it down. We'll accept it. Dear knows!"

He hastily turned the bottle until he couldn't see the label. "Flamboyant fool," he said. "I'm told he does this at every function he attends. It must make quite a hole in his pocket."

"I suppose it gets him talked about," James said uncaringly. "Keep his name to the fore. He's a bit of a showman. I've even heard it said half his bombast is for effect."

"More than one man who's thought that has ended up with his jaw practically broken," Fergus said impatiently.

James shrugged and asked for the cork on Dunbar's whisky to be pulled. After a careful sip he made an approving face and said, "Very good." He held the bottle up invitingly, but Fergus quickly put a hand over his glass. "Not for me, James. I think I would choke."

James casually refilled his own glass, but not without a flickering, sideways glance at Jessie. He had never made excuses for his occasional overdrinking and Fiona was amused to hear him come near to one now.

"If I'm to attempt a dance after all these years, I must have a little lubrication," he said.

Good for Jessie, Fiona thought. *She's taking him in hand already.*

"It doesn't seem a year since you left Glasgow, James," she said. "Is Galloway all you hoped it would be?"

James leaned back in his chair. "All, and more besides," he said expansively. "It's a different world down there. It's a unique corner of Scotland. Some of the big estates actually have tropical gardens. I've seen bamboo growing by the acre."

"I was wondering more about your work." Fiona's tone was gently pointed.

"Oh, it's all right," James said with a negligence that did not deceive her. "There's more to life than work, you know."

"He works far too hard," Jessie said, giving James a fond glance that nevertheless had an edge of challenge to it.

Fergus looked across the table at Fiona and laughed drily. "It's a family failing, I'm afraid."

"But he's never satisfied with anything he does." Jessie persisted. "I've watched him paint until he's exhausted and still not pleased. And he sits out at his easel in all weathers. I thought I was obsessive until I met James." She turned and looked with warm appraisal at the pale, sensitive face, her eyes narrowing as if with the concentration of trying to read something puzzling that eluded her. She sighed. "I suppose that's what being a real artist involves. It's not just a hobby with James, or even a job. He's on some sort of endless quest."

"Talking about endless quests," James said with a bland smile to Fiona, "how is Robert?" He was clearly determined to change the subject and untroubled by the irrelevance of his interruption.

"He's very well, so far as one can judge." Her voice suggested she disclaimed all responsibility for how Robert was. Fergus glanced at her sharply.

"I get the *Herald* every day," James went on, "but I haven't noticed his name in it recently. Has he given up warning us about the Marxist peril?"

"I'm sure he hasn't. It's simply that Parliament is in recess until October."

"Then why isn't he here with us tonight, or at least home in Glasgow?"

"The London affairs of King and Company require his attention. Remember, James, it's not just King's Royal now. Queen's Royal has a very fast-growing market, too."

"I suppose so," James said. And then, aware of his own new dependence on Jessie, "But don't you miss him?"

Fiona almost choked on her answer. Dunbar's reflection, clearly cut and oddly magnified by its isolation, had come looming into a mirror on the pillar behind James. He was speaking to someone she could not see, but his gaze seemed to be fixed intently on her. She looked quickly away. After a few moments of nervous indecision she excused herself and went to the ladies' rest room.

When she came out, Dunbar was leaning against the corridor wall, blowing smoke at the ornate plasterwork of the ceiling. She pretended to be surprised. "Hello, Mr. Dunbar. Thank you for the bottle of whisky."

He ignored the stumbling remark. "Well," he said, his complacent smile widening, "I didn't give you away."

"No, but you frightened me," she said severely. "Surely you must appreciate my position."

"Oh, I do. You've got a guilty conscience."

"I don't know what you're suggesting, but I don't have a guilty conscience. What do you want?"

His eyes widened into his favourite expression of exaggerated surprise. "A dance, of course. That's all. Just a wee dance."

She stared anxiously past him, but to her relief the entrance to the ballroom was out of view. "That's impossible. I shouldn't even be talking to you. I'm here in the company of my father-in-law and my brother-in-law."

His eyes sparkled. "That must be dull."

"I hadn't noticed that it was, but it does mean I can't dance with you."

"Then what's this for?"

She looked down and saw she was holding her dance card. He took it gently from her hand. "Don't tell me you're carrying this by accident?"

She coloured slightly at the mocking insinuation. "I suppose I picked it up without thinking." His insolent grin maddened her. "I certainly didn't bring it to lure you, Mr. Dunbar."

He laughed almost as if to provoke her. "Say that again. Your eyes shine beautifully when you're annoyed."

"I'd rather you kept your personal remarks to yourself," she said, pivoting a little on one foot and her vanity case beginning to swing.

His good humour turned to sarcasm in his annoyance at the continuing flat coldness of her voice. "Dear me! And I thought we were personal friends. After all, I'm here by invitation."

Her temper flared. "What invitation? You conceited man!"

She had the brief pleasure of seeing his mouth begin to sag and a half-smoked cigar fly from his hand and land in a metal tray on the floor in a shower of sparks. Then he braced himself and his chin jutted.

"Don't bother playing the great lady with me, bonnie lass. I may not be your idea of a gentleman, but my wife was a lady." His threatening stance relaxed abruptly and his eyes brightened as if he had begun again to relish the situation. "My father-in-law even ended up with a title, so there's not a lot to choose between us."

The accuracy of this statement was infuriating, and it had the effect of making her manner even more imperious. "I asked you, what invitation?"

"Yours. Back there. . . ." He nodded to the function room without turning his head. "You distinctly said, 'Later.' What's a gentleman to think? As far as I'm concerned, this little assignation was your idea."

"Don't twist things, Mr. Dunbar," she said indignantly. "I intended no assignation. I had to stop you speaking to me as best I could. You would have caused me trouble with my father-in-law."

He pondered. "Are you sure he knows me? We've never met, you know."

"You must have been pointed out to him about town at some time or other." Despite herself she smiled slightly. "You're rather an outstanding figure."

Their eyes met. "I'd rather you kept your personal remarks to yourself, Mrs. King," he said solemnly. Her lips parted as for a moment she stared in consternation at his unsmiling face. Then she began to laugh, naturally and openly, her colour rising prettily and the normal liveliness of her features breaking through the strained nervousness.

"That's better," he said, stepping back briskly and bending slightly to take a beaming, proprietorial look at her. "But what a pity it took you so long." He glanced quickly in the direction of the ballroom. "They might be starting to worry about you in there."

She nodded, wondering at this sudden consideration. He really was a very unpredictable man. "Yes. I must go back."

He fumbled a disreputable stump of pencil from a pocket of his splendid coat. "One dance won't ruin your good name," he said coaxingly. "If they say anything, you can tell them you had to agree to avoid a scene. That's the sort of thing they'll understand. I don't mind what you say. Put all the blame on me."

She felt bent and pliable. All her resistance had been pitifully useless. She shook her head in protesting submission. "Make no mistake," she said. "That's exactly what I'll do."

He wrote his name next to GAVOTTE and returned her card.

Jessie and Fergus had been to the buffet and a heaped plate of cold grouse, pheasant, venison and quail was waiting for her. She looked at it in dismay.

"This is magnificent," she said, "but I'm afraid I won't be able to eat half of it."

"No." James shook his head in disapproval. "But no doubt like Jessie you'll be able to do more than justice to the fancy sweet things."

"We'll see," she said vaguely, leaving him speculating about her uncharacteristic mood. Her mind was too full of the encounter with Dunbar and of the dance yet to come. It had turned out to be a disastrous evening. It was even an effort for her to smile at Jessie's amusing stories about the worthies of Fleetside. Without relish she spooned the sumptuous assortment of jellies, mousses and cream that Fergus insisted on fetching when she left her plate of cold meats almost untouched.

Only the sight of James manfully dancing a minuet with Jessie cheered her a little. "When did you last see James look so happy?" she asked.

Fergus smiled. "It's a pity his mother isn't with us to see him."

"I have a feeling," Fiona said, forcing her own cares into the background, "that his work has not improved in Galloway as much as he had hoped."

Fergus tried not to see the typical James King painting that immediately sprang to life in his mind. If only the boy would turn for a little while to landscape, portraiture or still life.

He cringed a little as he remembered how he had berated Robert for treachery when he had revealed similar thoughts.

Fiona was still speaking. "But I'm sure James's move has been worthwhile, if for Jessie alone."

Fergus nodded vigorously as if to banish his disloyal reflections.

The dance Dunbar had chosen was almost the last of the evening, and as the time for it approached, she made a plan for minimising the embarrassment she was certain must come. The earlier stiff formality of the occasion had long since dissolved, and people wandered from table to table, greeting friends. Fergus and James were as mellow and relaxed as she could have wished.

"I came here to meet the trade," she said, looking about the room, "but our own little party has been so enjoyable the evening has gone like lightning. I'm no wiser about who's who in the trade than when I arrived."

"They're a dull lot," Fergus said placidly, ignoring all the noisy indications to the contrary.

"I suppose so, but there is someone I must speak to. I've had my eye on her all night—Janey Mason, at that long table in the far corner. She hasn't seen me, but I can't let the evening pass without saying hello."

She was gone before either Fergus or James could struggle to his feet.

Dunbar was at her side, taking her hand, as the lively music started. "I tried to think what you would do," he said. "I was sure you wouldn't let me come to the table for you."

"I wonder if you would have had the nerve?"

It was a question that had been raising doubts in his own mind for the past half hour, but he could not admit it. "Of course I would have," he said, leading her lightly through the pattern of the dance. "Do you like the gavotte?"

"Under normal circumstances."

He laughed. "Its great virtue from your point of view tonight is that we can dance it here. We needn't move round the room. If we keep to this corner, your in-laws won't know you've disgraced yourself."

"But plenty of other people will," she said, her eyes sweeping nervously over the multitude of faces.

"Damn other people."

An additional worry for her had been the thought that by this stage of the evening he might be drunk; a great many of the men were. It was a relief that he seemed quite sober. His capacity was either very great or overindulgence was not one of his vices.

They danced in silence until he said, "I would value your opinion on something, Mrs. King."

She looked at him suspiciously but his expression was serious.

"If you have something to ask me, I will answer as best I can."

"Good. Could you spare me an afternoon of your time later this week?"

"Mr. Dunbar!"

"It's a serious question."

"Yes, it is. And my answer is, *No, I can't.*"

His hand tightened slightly on her waist. "Do you dislike me?"

211

It annoyed her that the answer came evasively. "I am a married woman."

He tilted his head and showed his teeth in a taunting smile. "There's damned little evidence of that, these days."

She flushed. "That is no concern of yours."

"Maybe not, but it does occur to me at times."

"I would have thought you had more important matters to occupy you."

She realised with alarm that he had danced her out of their secluded corner. "Please don't go any farther that way," she said in a sudden panic.

He looked about, as if surprised to see where they were.

"I was carried away," he said, blandly dancing her back to the security of their corner. He watched her look anxiously about the room. He said, "I haven't told you what it is I wanted your opinion on."

She looked at him sceptically. "No, you haven't."

"I'm thinking of buying a motor. A lot of people have them now. The suppliers are going to give me one for a day, to try it. If you allowed me to take you for a drive in the country, you could let me have your opinion on it. Women are better than men at judging comfort and colour, and things like that."

Nothing could have appealed more to her. For years she had wanted a motor and a telephone, but for all her pleas, Robert had refused to have anything to do with either. "Novelties" was his disparaging word for both.

From her quick intake of breath and the hesitation she could not conceal, he knew he had her attention. "What do you say? We could go to the Trossachs."

"I'm sorry, but I daren't." She was staggered at her attitude of submissive apology. She felt herself colouring, and all at once the room seemed oppressively hot and smoky.

"Why? Can't you trust yourself?"

"Really, Mr. Dunbar, your conceit is absurd. I can trust myself very well, especially with anyone as unattractively self-centred as you."

He put back his head and laughed deep in his chest, swinging her out of the corner as if on a surge of careless energy.

"Please," she cried, her fingers digging into him.

"Please what?"

"Please don't take me down that way."

"There are only two ways we can go."

She tried to hang back, heedless of the exhibition she was sure they were making of themselves.

212

"Two ways," he said with a mad laugh that made her think she might after all have underestimated his intake of alcohol. "We can go this way. Or we can go to the Trossachs."

The thought of Fergus seeing her with him now, and of the explanation she would have to manufacture at this late stage of a nerve-wracking evening, was more than she could face.

"It's disgraceful of you," she said breathlessly, "but all right."

"You promise?"

She could see the table where Fergus sat. He was hunched forward, talking to Jessie. James seemed to be contemplating the whisky bottle. At any moment one of them might turn.

"Yes," she said frantically.

Deftly he reversed the direction of their dancing, but she was almost too limp to follow.

"This is a despicable way to behave," she said with a sob in her voice. "How *can* you be so ruthless?"

"It's no trouble to me."

"You have no honour."

"None at all," he said, looking down at her with blatant triumph. "But I'm sure you have enough for both of us."

The promise she had given him, she told herself, as she lay twisting restlessly in bed, was not binding. It had been wrung from her. It had no possible validity. The man was an opportunist, a quick-witted, unprincipled bully. Her pledge, having served its purpose, should be promptly forgotten. There would be no drive in the country, no advice from her about the colour or comfort of his motor. No doubt he had more pliable ladyfriends who could be enlisted to provide this service.

After lying wide-eyed for another ten minutes she lit the candle on her bedside table and looked at the clock. Almost three. On the drive home from the hotel she had acted so strangely—fits of agitation alternating with long silences—that Fergus had remarked on it. "I'll be all right," she assured him. "I'm just overtired."

Now, almost two hours later, her mind was still too active. She went to the window and pulled the curtains. The street was wet and around the gas jets she saw rain. A lone cat came out of the bushes opposite and hurried toward one of the houses. She pulled on her robe and went down to the kitchen. She was sitting at the scrubbed table, drinking tea, when the door creaked slowly open and Florence peered hesitantly round it.

"I thought I'd find you here, Mama," she said, blinking in the light. "I heard your bedroom door open and close. Are you all right?"

213

Fiona stifled a yawn and pushed back her falling hair. "I couldn't sleep, darling. That's all. I thought a cup of tea might help. You shouldn't have come down. You have to get up for school in the morning."

"I didn't like to think of you down here on your own."

"That was sweet of you. I'll be glad of your company while I drink this tea. Would you like a cup?"

"No, thank you." She went over and stood by the long black range for warmth. "You're alone an awful lot now, Mama. Most of the time, in fact."

Fiona swung round to face her, smiling a denial. "Oh, no, Florence. I have just come home from a wonderful evening at the whisky trade ball. Most days I am at King and Company, surrounded by people, and in the evenings I have you and the boys. . . ."

Florence shook her head with certainty. "We're not company. Not proper company. Papa should be here."

"You know Papa is fully occupied in London. He has business affairs as well as his Parliamentary duties to attend to. You will understand better about that when you are older."

"He should be here with you. Then if you couldn't sleep you would have him to talk to instead of sitting down here all alone in the middle of the night."

"One night, Florence. Don't make it sound like a life sentence." She stretched her hand out and smiled invitingly. "Come here, darling." Florence edged closer and let the warm, motherly arm encircle her waist. Fiona leaned her head against the girl. "Surely it wouldn't be right of us to expect Papa to give up his career in Parliament so that he could be here the one night I can't sleep? Would that be fair?"

Florence allowed a smile to be coaxed from her little bow lips. "I suppose not. But you do seem so lonely, sometimes."

"You imagine things, darling." She spread her hands. "Oh, perhaps, just occasionally, I do weary a little, but we are a very fortunate family, you know. We have so much. There is always something we can do."

Florence's concern became slightly scornful, as if the situation was being distorted more than she could allow.

"You don't do much. You would think you didn't have a husband. What's the good of a husband if he's not there to take you to concerts and things?"

"Marriage isn't about going to concerts and gadding about," Fiona said gently. "It's about making a home and rearing a happy family. That's what I meant when I said we have so much. We have two beautiful homes. Papa provided those for us. It's not just houses, you understand. Houses, as such, are not awfully important. It's the warmth, the security and love people manage to create inside them, that matters."

Her arm tightened round the girl's waist. "You're happy, aren't you, Florence? Papa is not here as often as any of us would like, but I try to make up to you all for that. There's nothing you want, is there? Nothing I haven't given you?"

There was a long silence, which she listened to almost fearfully. At last a tear fell on her lap, then another—two small dark blobs which spread raggedly as the material of her robe absorbed them. She didn't look up. Her own eyes were too moist.

"Don't cry, dear. It's far too late for us to be sitting here. We must get back to bed."

"I'd be happier," Florence sniffled, "if you were happier."

Fiona became businesslike. She lifted her cup and held it out. "Put that in the sink, dear. Mrs. Lauder gets annoyed if her kitchen is upset." Her voice softened. "And you musn't worry about me. I know you're a young lady now and feel I need looking after, but really, there's no need for it. I'm perfectly happy. As happy as anyone can expect to be."

They went up the stairs holding hands. Florence tumbled into bed and smiled with her eyes closed as her mother tucked the clothes round her. "I'm glad I came down," she said sleepily.

"So am I," Fiona whispered as she kissed her.

But despite the disconcerting diversion, Dunbar was still in her thoughts. She lay again in the dark with the events of the night going through her mind like clattering footsteps.

"I'll collect you at noon outside the Botanic Gardens the day after to-morrow," he had said, as if issuing instructions to an employee.

"If you are serious about this, you will call for me at my home," she had said resolutely. "I am doing nothing wrong. You will not make me act furtively."

"Nor would I want to, lass," he had said as if delighted with her independence. "You've too much spirit, too much pride, for that."

Tears had come into her eyes. "Not enough pride, or you would not be able to force me to do this."

But, of course, he could not force her. He would never be able to force her to do anything, for she would never see him again. It was her last thought before falling asleep.

It was still in her mind when she wakened and it endured all day without sway or waver. By mid-morning the exact manner of his rejection was clear in her head. At first she had thought of writing to tell him not to call. But why should she extend him even this small courtesy? He deserved to be humiliated. He could call, in his silly motor, as he said he

215

would, and she would not be at home. He would be left standing in the street like a knotless thread. That would put a dent—a well-deserved dent—in his arrogance.

The decision gave her such a feeling of elation that after lunch she put on her most frivolous hat and walked all the way to the bottom of Buchanan Street, window shopping as she went.

When she wakened next morning, birds were singing in the trees and a bee droned among the bright blooms in her window box. It was a perfect summer day, with the noises of the city seemingly far distant from that favoured street. After breakfast on the terrace she went to the little garden behind the house and forked the weeds from around her best shrub roses. It was warm to work, and when she had finished she went to her favourite seat in the shade of an old apple tree close to the house. Here, all the perfumes of the garden seemed to meet and mingle. She leaned back with her face turned to the sun. *It was weather for the Gareloch rather than Glasgow,* she thought. *Or the . . . the*—despite herself, she spoke the word in her mind—*Trossachs.* Angrily she banished the thought and the picture it conjured of Dunbar and his motor. If she wanted a breath of country air, all she need do was order the carriage round. She opened her watch. It was still only ten o'clock—plenty of time for her to dress and be gone before he arrived. But gone where to? Gone to what pleasure? Whom to turn to? Whom to speak to? Once there had been James. Once, although that was so long ago she could hardly remember it, there had even been Robert. Florence's melancholy words came back to her. *You're alone an awful lot now, Mama. Most of the time, in fact.*

Ah, well, she wouldn't be alone at King & Co., which was probably where she would go presently—and needlessly. She sighed a little for the beautiful day that would be wasted. And not only *her* day. His, too. He was probably driving into the city now to collect his motor. Was it fair, what she had planned? She had promised to go with him. If she broke her word, was she not simply lowering herself to his level? He had played the game according to his rough rules. In a way his behaviour could be interpreted as a compliment. He had gone to great lengths to engineer a day in her company. Of course, he had stooped to trickery. There was no use trying to deny that. But mightn't it be better just to accept that she had been outwitted and pay the price? Hardly a terrible one on such a day.

She continued sunning herself, nodding dreamily when Morag suggested she bring her tea tray to the garden. She was dressing when she heard his motor arrive in the street, its engine panting noisily under her window. She looked at the clock. It was only half past eleven. She wondered, comfortably, if she had been outwitted again? Had he suspected she might leave before he was due to arrive and decided to forestall her? She lifted an atomiser and released a spray of her most ethereal perfume. The sense of unreality induced by her indolence in the garden persisted. He was here. There seemed little she could do but go down and join him.

But not immediately. Noon was the time. He could wait. She went to her desk and started work on the correspondence that never seemed to diminish no matter how many letters she wrote. A few minutes later the front-door bell jangled. Presently Morag came.

"There's a man here says he's got an appointment with ye, ma'am, but he'll not give me his name."

"A gentleman, Morag?"

The girl hesitated. "No, ma'am. A man. I told him the tradesman's entrance was down the back lane."

Fiona lifted a letter to hide her smile. "And how did he react to that?"

Morag's eyes widened with indignation. "If looks could kill, ma'am, I wouldn't be standing here now."

"Tell him his appointment is for twelve o'clock and that I will see him then. At the tradesman's entrance. He has come to demonstrate a motor I may consider buying. Perhaps such people do not have names."

She stifled her mirth until the mystified maid had gone; then, leaning back in her chair, she laughed softly until she became slightly alarmed. She was behaving like an irresponsible adolescent. What should have been a sobering thought merely reminded her of carefree preparations for school outings, and it was with the same sense of careless unreality that she left the house and strolled unhurriedly through the garden to where she could hear the motor snorting impatiently in the back lane.

Despite her curiosity about the vehicle, she had kept well away from the windows rather than give him the satisfaction of seeing her looking. It was only now that she understood Morag's disapproval of Dunbar and her failure to recognise him from his previous visit. He was enveloped from his chin to his boots in a shapeless black coat roughly pulled in at the waist with a shabby leather belt. On his head there was an old cloth cap, worn back to front, with the skip pulled well down on his neck. His hands were encased in leather gauntlets reaching almost to his elbows. His eyes were covered by goggles which he pushed up onto his forehead as she opened the gate in the brick boundary wall. He looked like some great statue over which a tarpaulin had been carelessly thrown while repairs were being carried out.

217

As she looked at him, her astonishment dissolved into another fit of the feckless merriment that seemed to have replaced her normal common sense.

"What is there to laugh at?" he asked with a bad-tempered glare. The heat, the maid's disdain and the fact of being made to wait at the back entrance had outraged him.

"You," she shouted delightedly above the rattling and occasional banging of the motor. "No wonder Morag sent you round here."

"I'm delighted to find you in such a carefree mood," he said with mild sarcasm. "But aren't you afraid of what your Morag might think?"

"Not now." Her laughter was not yet under control and she had to turn slightly away. "I told her you were a mechanic. Now that I've seen you, I don't think she'll doubt it."

Her high spirits were infectious as well as unexpected.

"All right," he said with a slow grin. "So that's what you think of me. But what about the motor? What do you think of it? It's a Benz, made in Germany."

She walked round it. "It's rather like an outsize perambulator," she said unfeelingly, "minus the baby and the handle to push it. It even has bigger wheels at the back than at the front." She smiled innocently. "This is the front, I suppose?"

"Oh, yes," he said tolerantly. "You can tell because the driver's seat is pointing that way."

"It's making an awful noise. Can't you turn it off?"

He hesitated and then gave an almost shamefaced laugh. "I could, but there's always the risk it wouldn't start again. If you stop the engine, you're advised to do it when you're pointing downhill."

She walked round it in the opposite direction. "Where do you keep the coal? In this box at the back?"

"This isn't a steam one," he said. "It runs on petrol. The drums with extra supplies are in that box."

"It's awfully greasy in places. I hope I'm not going to spoil my new dress."

It was a simple, clinging garment in a summery shade of yellow, with a blouse effect at the neck.

"If it was a tennis party we were going to, you would turn every head," he said admiringly. "But you can't go on a motoring expedition in a wisp of a thing like that."

He put a large gauntleted hand on the shining dark-green coachwork of the Benz. "This machine can go at speeds up to fifteen miles an hour, you know. Once we get out of the city we'll be raising the dust. Anyway, you would be cold sitting up there in dress like that, even on a warm day like this."

218

"I'd better go back and fetch a coat, then."

He shook his head. "You wouldn't have anything old enough." He lifted the lid at the back of the spindly vehicle. "I came prepared." He dragged out a huge leather coat. "Here." He handed it to her and went under the lid again. "Try this first." He waved something grey and shapeless in front of her. It was a floppy, wide-brimmed felt bonnet fitted with a broad ribbon for tying under the chin.

She pulled it on reluctantly over her carefully brushed hair. He smiled at the collapse of her elegance.

"There's a men's smoke room in town with a picture on the wall called *The Goose Girl*. You look like her grandmother in that." His laughter rebounded from the walls of the narrow lane, and for all her feeling of freedom she was glad trees screened them from the windows of neighbouring houses.

His competitive nature made it inevitable that he should seem to find her funnier than she had found him. He leaned against the motor with one hand, his knees bent and his head thrown back in the classic attitude of hilarity. "Oh, my," he chortled. "If I'd known you were going to look like this, I wouldn't have bothered asking you."

He straightened, lifted the voluminous coat and held it up for her. She pushed her hands down long, unyielding tunnels of leather. He dropped it on her shoulders and stepped back, leaving her drooping under the weight, the cuffs reaching almost to her knees.

He went into another fit of laughter. "What's happened to your hands?" he gasped. "Have you lost them?"

"They're up here somewhere," she said, peering into the sleeves.

He helped her turn back the cuffs until her hands showed. She climbed comically into the motor and sat mourning the disappearance of her lovely dress. "Somehow," she said, "I don't think this fashion flatters me."

He stepped up beside her and pulled his goggles down. "It does something better," he said. "It disguises you. Your own mother wouldn't recognise you now."

"I'm thankful for that," she said, sobering for a moment as she thought of the exposed journey ahead through public streets.

She needn't have worried. Perhaps he had more heed for her reputation than had seemed likely. His knowledge of back streets and lanes would have done credit to a cab driver, and they left the city by ways she had never travelled before.

When she remarked on this he smiled reflectively and said without elaboration, "I had more than one job before I came into the whisky trade."

The road toward the mountains was rough and the journey uncom-

219

fortable, but there was an exhilaration in the effortless speed that compensated for the bumping. The clean, rushing air massaged her face till it tingled as if after a beauty treatment.

They drove north by way of the clachan of Bearsden and not far beyond broke onto a landscape almost worthy of the Highlands. A golden glow had spread across the sky, and in it larks sang above meadows fragrant with wild flowers.

In the town, children had shouted and run after them. Here, from wayside cottages, people waved and an occasional old man or woman, mystified and frightened by the noise and the black fumes belching from the machine, scurried behind a wall or a water butt.

Ahead the brightness was undimmed by their dusty progress, and in its intensity the mountains looked blue and strangely fragile. Around moorland lochs wild iris pointed yellow spears at the sky and heather rolled away in low waves of shaggy purple from which startled grouse whirred at their approach.

Conversation was difficult, but once, thrilled and excited by the grandeur of the scene, she shouted, "Isn't this incredibly wild and beautiful to be only a few miles from the city?"

He rubbed the grime from his goggles and looked about as if surprised. Then, with an absentminded nod, he quickly returned his concentration to the steering tiller and the variety of levers and handles which needed constant pulling and adjusting as the gradient of the road changed.

Once they stopped briefly by the side of a lochan, where, watched by long-haired Highland cattle, he filled an enamel jug with water. He carried it back to the motor, lifted a flap and emptied the water into an opening beside the engine. "It has to be kept cool," he explained.

"Where did you learn so much about it? You seem to control it very well."

He was pleased. "You think I'm a good driver? You aren't frightened?"

"Not in the least, but it is exciting going fast down the hills. It's as if it was going to fly. It's as well there's a rail to hold on to."

"I took an hour or so's instruction," he said negligently. "It's perfectly simple."

He climbed back to his seat. "These machines are going to open up country like this to people who've never seen it before," he said.

"I hope they don't spoil it."

"Do you know why it's called the Trossachs?"

"I don't."

"It's a Gaelic word that means 'bristling country'—bristling, I suppose, with mountains and trees."

"And all these beautiful little lochs," she said. "They're like precious stones sprinkled among the heather."

"We'll have a picnic later by one of them. Mrs. Prentice, my housekeeper, made me up a hamper. It's under your seat. But I want to get up into the Rob Roy country first."

"My mother's people were MacGregors," she said. "I might be a descendant of Rob Roy. And, of course, the Kings are a sept of the Clan MacGregor."

He couldn't resist a jab. "So, wed or unwed, you've been related to a gang of outlaws from the start," he mused, with one eye watching for her reactions.

It was interesting, she thought, *how he seemed able to separate her from his all-embracing hatred of the Kings.* She was still speculating on this when they went through Aberfoyle Village shortly before two o'clock and took the precipitous road leading to the Duke's Pass. Dunbar adjusted his goggles as if challenges lay ahead.

"It's a steep climb to the top," he said. "I hope I don't have to ask you to get out and push."

But he did. The motor was defeated by the last bend before the summit. It had been a slow, labouring climb up the stony track between encroaching trees. Now the Benz began steaming and shuddering. In his excitement Dunbar rose to his feet and began shouting as if urging horses to a last effort.

There was an outbreak of violent vibration and the machine grated to a halt. He sank slowly back onto his seat, pulled on the brake and sat cursing till his humour returned.

"This is the sort of thing that makes it a bit of an adventure," he said philosophically. "You never know what's going to happen or where you'll end up. I don't suppose you'll believe me, but I was joking when I talked about your having to get out and push. I'd never have attempted this road if I'd thought this might happen. The suppliers said wherever a road went, it would go. Damned liars!"

"Don't worry," she said. Then, looking doubtfully at the hairpin bend, "But what happens if it won't go any farther, even with a push?"

"We'll just have to turn and go back the way we came."

She looked round the machine with more attention than she had given it so far. A new thought seemed to have come to her. "What does this thing weigh?"

"Oh, maybe round about half a ton."

"And what do you weigh?"

"Sixteen stones."

She nodded briskly. "I think we should just go back the way we came."

He laughed. "Where's that fighting spirit? You're surely not going to

221

let a little mountain beat us? Besides, we'll be missing a lot if we're forced to turn. What I'm hoping to do is get over the pass and go back to Aberfoyle in a circle, by way of Callendar. Now, if you get out, I'll run backward for a bit and start off on a more level stretch. You stay here, and when I come back, get behind and push for all you're worth. Are you game?"

She pretended to spit on her hands. "I can see now that getting me to come with you was an even bigger trick than I thought. You just didn't want to be without a donkey if anything went wrong."

"If you could drive, I could have pushed," he said breezily as he let the brake off. The Benz rolled slowly back until it disappeared round a pot-holed bend. From somewhere farther down a raw sound, as of grinding metal, jarred through the still air.

When at last the motor came forging up the hill, he was again standing, urging on his invisible horses. "Now," he shouted as he drew level, "shove like hell, bonnie lass. It won't take much. She's making a better show of it this time with only one of us on board."

There was less resistance than she had imagined. With the flints flying, the dust rising in a suffocating cloud, her slithering behind, the machine stuttered round the last few yards of the bend and shot suddenly forward on the more level ground at the top.

She fell on her knees behind it and stayed there, gasping and laughing inside her leather coat until he came running back and lifted her. Her hands were greasy and her face smudged. The hair she had spent so much time dressing tumbled untidily from under the hag's bonnet.

"Beauty spots," he said grandly as she sat on the grass verge under the trees, lamenting the oil on her cheeks. "A drop of petrol will soon get rid of those when we stop for our picnic." He held out his hand. "Are you ready? We'll run on another few miles and then look for a good place to stop."

Living life at a gallop, is right, she thought, as she remembered Robert's reference to Dunbar's burning impatience.

"You're sure you'll have time for a picnic?" she enquired.

He looked at her suspiciously but, apparently unable to fathom her expression, set the motor rolling with a muttered, "It's early yet."

"Look, there's a lovely sandy cove," she shouted as, a few miles further on, they began to wind along the shores of a tranquil loch. He stopped, but sat with his goggles raised looking uncertainly at the road.

"I'll have to switch the engine off to save petrol," he said, "but we're not facing downhill. I hope she starts all right."

She jumped down, determined that here they would picnic. "Risk it," she said. "If need be, the donkey will give you another push."

Gratefully she threw off the ugly bonnet and discarded the heavy-weight coat. She felt and looked transformed. Her dress was crushed, but in the clean warm air it looked fresh and flowerlike.

She walked to the edge of the loch and stood on the white sand of the rock-fringed inlet studying her reflection in the crystalline water. She adjusted the collar of her dress and did what she could to repair her hair.

When she turned, Dunbar was standing on the verge of the road, watching her, the thumb of one hand tucked characteristically into a pocket of his waistcoat, his face fixed in a fascinated smile. He came out of his admiring reverie only when she moved across the sand and sat on the edge of a rock.

"Now I can see again why I invited you."

"Why?" she asked, clasping her hands on her knees and listening to the brazen invitation as if she were not responsible for it.

His expression became surprisingly gentle, more so than she would have thought the rugged nature of his face would allow. "Because you're beautiful," he said, so softly that if she had not seen him standing there, solid against the silvery blue foliage of the tall trees, she would not have recognised the voice as his.

"Thank you." She bowed neatly and tried to look unconcerned, as if his compliment were without complications.

His voice hoarsened a little. "You're a picture in that yellow dress, but"—his face twisted with the effort of trying to express what he felt— "not like a picture on a wall. In even the loveliest picture there's always something missing. It's never real, because there's no heart in it. It's remote, like so many beautiful women are remote. It's meant to be looked at always from a slight distance, and never touched." He put a foot upon a rock and looked intently at his boot. "You're not like that."

They stood in a world gone very small and silent, the easy swaying of the trees and lapping of the water now outside their intensely concentrated attention. Each avoided the other's gaze, she waiting with a tight breathlessness to hear if he would go on to say what she *was* like, and he sadly regretting his inability to find the words he needed.

She walked round the rock and said, "Should we get the hamper out now?"

"In a minute." He took a folded handkerchief from his pocket and lifted the box lid at the back of the motor. He screwed the top from one of the drums and splashed petrol on the handkerchief. He held it out. "This will take the oily marks from your face. You don't want to get them on your dress. Have you a mirror?"

"I haven't."

223

"Will I do it for you?"

She nodded and came close to him, standing like a child with her eyes closed and her face turned up while he rubbed the black smudges away. There was a vague scent from him. She heard his watch chain jingle and his linen shirt rustle. For a few brief and possibly imagined seconds she thought she felt his breath on her cheek. Would he kiss her? Her eyelids began to flicker, but with an effort she kept them closed. Her heartbeat quickened and her face began to burn. Almost furtively she ran the tip of her tongue over lips gone suddenly dry.

All at once she felt he was no longer there. From some distance away his voice came.

"That's it—all off—but it might be better if you splashed some water on your face in case the petrol irritates your skin."

She walked slowly to the edge of the loch feeling dazed and foolish. She was greedily grateful for the cold, cleansing touch of the water, gulping some of it in and letting it trickle soothingly over her throat.

By the time she had dried her face, Dunbar had opened the hamper and spread a cloth on the border of grass between the road and the sand. They ate chicken, ham and hard-boiled eggs with buttered bread and glasses of creamy milk. The rocks were warm against their backs and the sun comforting on their faces. Around the mountains a few wispy grey clouds had gathered, their shadow darkening the gullies down which streams tumbled to feed the loch.

Fiona pushed her empty plate away. "Why don't any of these things taste half as good when you eat them at home?" she asked, moving from her rocky support and leaning back on the grass on her elbows.

Dunbar shook his head. "I wonder. The greatest treat of all, of course, is tea brewed in a can over a wood fire. It's a pity I didn't come better prepared."

Before she realised what was happening he had crossed over the grass and was lying on his back at right angles to her with his head on her lap.

Although she was not displeased, she stiffened with the shock of his boldness. Her hands felt awkward lying so dangerously close to his wavy black hair. She moved them quickly away.

"You don't mind me making myself comfortable?"

She recognised the tension behind the casual words. He was barefaced and presumptuous, but he was well aware of the boundaries. When he stormed them, he knew exactly what he was doing. If she did not rebuff him now, it was another milestone reached in their tortuously evolving relationship, another hurdle crossed on the road from antipathy to . . . where?

224

His eyes were closed as he waited for her response. It came in a carefully neutral voice, halfway between acceptance and rejection.

"You believe in making yourself at home, Mr. Dunbar."

After two decades of dealing and negotiating he knew an open door when he saw one. "I would feel even more at home if you called me Douglas. Everyone else in the whisky trade does."

"And do you treat everyone else in the whisky trade to this sort of familiarity?"

He opened one dark and well-satisfied eye. "I would if they looked like you."

Perhaps a quarter of a mile out a breeze ruffled the surface of the loch, but in their cove among the rocks the water remained glassily tranquil. On the far shore trees waved anxiously under the shadow of clouds gone more black than grey. She was reminded that Scotland endured some of the most erratic weather in the world. In an hour the temperature could soar deliriously or plunge disastrously and the sun could be driven from the sky by rain rushing in from nowhere. Mountaineers swore that on some of the Highland peaks conditions were more treacherous than in the Himalayas.

The parallels with Dunbar were so obvious she wondered if the thoughts were as chance as they seemed. Perhaps they were a warning. Her position was uncomfortable, but when she tried to straighten, his weight made it difficult. He ignored her tentative strivings.

"I hope there isn't a change coming," she said, sinking back resignedly.

"I hope not. Those clouds certainly weren't there when we arrived. If it rains on the way back, there's a hood I can put up."

"That will make it look even more like a perambulator."

He was staring at the sky with such a fixed expression she wondered if he had heard. She was able to study him without seeming to. In full sunlight his swarthiness was less marked and in a way quite Latin and romantic, she thought. It could even be seen as natural to the glowing vitality of his eyes. In repose there was a sensitive, even susceptible curve to his mouth that did not show when he was bargaining loudly from behind his great cluttered table or throwing out one of his boastful challenges. She saw this as confirmation of her old belief that despite the overwhelming iron aspect, there were undoubted gaps in his armour through which pain could be inflicted. Not that it mattered, for she had no desire now to take advantage of any vulnerability.

He was so still and quiet she thought he had fallen asleep. Around them there was hardly a breath or rustle. The sun moved slowly over the peaks. Her senses were drifting when he lifted his head from her lap and sat up, half turned to her, with his hands splayed behind him for support. For several seconds his silent appraisal was so frank that one hand moved involuntarily to her bare throat in an odd little gesture of modesty.

When he spoke his voice was slightly distorted, as if he were listening intently to each word.

"I don't want to dig up bones better left buried, but if it's any comfort to you, I don't feel so bitter now about your son."

It was so unexpected and the way he said it so stilted she could find no adequate answer.

"Naturally, I'm very pleased to hear that," she said hesitantly, "but . . . has something happened I don't know about?"

"No."

He lifted a handful of warm sand and sat watching the grains trickle from his tightly clenched fist. He seemed to draw inspiration from the sight.

"There are some things you can't hold on to," he said enigmatically.

Bitterness, she thought, *was surely one thing he had demonstrated he was capable of cherishing, apparently forever.* She waited for him to go on.

"In fact, I can almost sympathise with him."

Her expression became openly sceptical but she controlled the urge to interrupt.

"It's true," he said. "It's possible to be drawn into a situation that all reason tells you to avoid. There are some things that in the end you can't be held responsible for."

"And you think that's what happened with Gordon? I'm sure you're right."

"It can happen to any man when he's faced with an attractive woman."

The insinuation was crystal clear and she hardly hoped her pretended obtuseness would divert him. "Yes, I've heard Anne is very beautiful."

"Any man," he repeated. A sigh escaped him. "Even a man like me." He said it not only as though his superiority were self-evident but as though there could be no greater illustration of the indiscriminate workings of fate.

She knew she should sidetrack into some wide, even if ridiculous, detour. Instead, she heard herself blurting, "In what way?"

He lifted a stone, weighed it for a moment, then threw it thoughtfully into the loch. "Do I have to explain?"

She tried to return to safer ground. "I'm afraid you would have to," she said, and added hastily, "but not now, please."

Her emotions were far too hopelessly confused for her to deal sanely with a situation that was developing faster than she had expected. She

226

was drawn to him. His attentions enticed and excited her. They opened vistas down which she dare not do more than glance hurriedly before retreating. To abandon herself to the sweet and seductive temptation he inspired in her would be madness. What *was* his baleful attraction? He was rough, arrogant and piratical in manner, as well as appearance—a wild, unpredictable giant whose natural instinct for selfish brutality had obviously to be kept constantly in check. Despite all this, he lured her. Or did he lure her *because* of all that? Did the primitive in him correspond to some need deep in her nature—perhaps deep in the nature of every woman—a need which in the normal, humdrum way of life would never be aroused and, even if aroused, would rarely be satisfied?

She started to rise, but his arm went across her, pinioning her lightly to the grass.

She gasped with surprise but stifled any further reaction. He had managed to make the movement seem casual, even unintentional, effectively robbing her of the chance to protest without seeming prudish or revealing how nervously unsure she was of herself.

"Besides, I would never have got to know you like this if it hadn't been for your son."

"Is that so important to you?"

"I have a feeling it's important for both of us."

She felt a spark of irritation. His presumption really was insufferable. She tried to lift his arm but it was as immovable as a fence post. He watched her struggle with it.

"Can't you see I want to get up?"

"Aye," he said in a preoccupied voice. Then, seeming to come to a decision, he moved his arm until his hand was on her back.

She felt herself being moved gently forward until her mouth was pressed unresistingly against his. His other hand seemed to have become entangled with her hair, and from where his fingers touched the back of her neck a tingling sensation shivered down her spine. Her hands rose to his shoulders and then, caressingly, to his face. It was an uncomfortable, toothy, dry-lipped failure of a kiss, but like the sun glowing behind a morning mist, it banished the artificiality and pretence that had until then shrouded the light of their true feelings.

Now that it had happened her fear of it seemed unreasonable; all the fencing and parrying that had gone before, mere futile posturing. She was vaguely disappointed when he made no effort to prolong the embrace. He looked at her for a few devouring moments, then rose and held out his hand to help her. They walked contentedly toward the water, hands clasped, and, like children, languidly kicked up small spurts of sand as they went.

227

They stood listening to the ripples lap the rocks. He tilted his head until his face was against her hair. "I was almost too nervous to do that," he said, as if still struck with wonder.

She saw their reflections intertwined in the water. "I must have lost my reason," she said breathlessly, "but I'm glad you did."

As they encased themselves again in their heavy coats, Dunbar was clearly nervous about restarting the motor. "Send up a prayer," he said as he gripped the handle. At the first turn the engine sparked to life, with a splutter and then a roar. Their elation was complete and he let out a loud cheer.

As he grasped the steering tiller, she put a hand on his arm and shouted, "Could I drive it for a little way? It seems so simple."

He hardly hesitated. It was a day for boldness. "Why not? You can steer and brake, and I'll handle the gears for you."

He jumped down so that she could move over. "It's just like steering a boat. You move the tiller in the opposite direction to the way you want the motor to go. And when you want to slow or stop, you brake with this lever, here. That other one is the throttle, and it controls the speed. But leave it to me."

They moved off at a creep, with Fiona holding her breath and the car veering erratically about the road. "You're moving the tiller too much," he explained. "Easy does it. That's better."

The road ran straight for about a mile. Toward the end of this stretch her arms were sore, but she felt she had gained reasonable control of the steering.

"Slow for the bend," he cautioned.

She went round it smoothly, her arms taut and her tongue out a little with concentration. She turned her head to see if he approved. Next second her heart gave a fearful jump. From being level, the road plunged steeply. The changing contour of the land had been hidden from them by the tall trees on either side.

Immediately, from having mastered the steering, she found it impossible to keep the Benz going straight. The wheels seemed to find a suicidal life of their own. As they went shooting across the road, toward the trees, Dunbar seized the tiller with one massive hand.

"Start braking," he shouted, correcting their disastrous course. "I can hold the tiller, meantime."

But the brake required physical strength. On a level road she could have applied it successfully. With the motor gathering impetus, the effect was imperceptible. She turned from the dizzy spectacle of the road rushing toward them and began tugging desperately again at the lever.

228

"My God," she cried in panic, "nothing's happening. What will I do?"

He had put the vehicle into its lowest gear while she took the bend. It was still in it. They were gaining speed against the maximum braking power of the engine.

To her astonishment, he seemed to be laughing. His mouth was twisted open and his lips curled back in a grimace over teeth parted as if ready to bite. His eyes were alight with the challenge of the situation.

"You could try praying again," he cried, reaching with furious zest for the brake. "It seemed to work last time."

But long as it was, his reach was inadequate. For another two seconds he debated their chances of gaining the bottom of the long descent in safety with the brake out of use and him trying to steer the hysterical machine with one hand from the wrong seat. Alone, he would have fought on. But he was not alone.

"Hang on to the rail with both hands," he shouted.

When he was satisfied she was secure, he took a deep breath and deliberately steered the Benz off the road, running it in a shallow angle toward the ditch. The front wheels hit the rough grass verge without too much protest.

He had abandoned everything else and was now clinging to the tiller with both hands. The next thudding shock as the motor struck the ditch almost tore it from his grasp. For a moment the Benz canted over on two wheels, hung for a moment as if suspended and then righted itself, clearing the ditch and heading for the trees beyond.

But the headlong rush was over, ended by the dive into the ditch and the near impossibility of the buckled front wheels' continuing to turn. Dunbar let out a whoop of triumph. He was still wrestling with the useless tiller as if demanding that it respond to his will.

Trees were now all round them. A branch dipped into the careening motor and knocked his cap off. "Hold tight," he shouted, and flung himself over her as the Benz hit a beech tree almost as wide as itself. The impact, although not great, was enough to throw them from the mangled machine into a springy tangle of bracken and moss.

It was gloomy even on the edge of the forest, and when he struggled to his feet he could not see her. Steam rose from the wrecked Benz and drifted over the bracken in a melancholy haze.

"Douglas!"

A few yards away an arm came through the bracken, then a floppy bonnet.

"Fiona!"

He stumbled gratefully to her through a maze of clinging bramble briar and pulled her gently into a sitting position against the base of a tree. "Are you all right? Are you hurt?"

229

She spat moss from her mouth and tore off the hated bonnet. "I don't think so. The ground is like a cushion. Are you all right?"

"Yes."

"Then we've been lucky." She shook her head and her hair tumbled down over her shoulders in a cascade of shining brown.

"My God," he said hoarsely, "you look like a little lost girl." He was down on the bracken beside her, kissing her until, murmuring and gasping for breath, she pushed him gently away.

The Benz was hissing pitifully. "Your poor motor," she said. "I'm sorry. I'll pay for it. When we started running down that hill, I just didn't know what I was doing."

"Don't worry." He gave the wreckage an affectionate salute. "After all, it was only a glorified perambulator. And the suppliers have it insured."

"How are we going to get home? What time is it?"

The lid of his gold watch was dented, and when he prised it open, pieces of broken glass fell out. The hands had stopped at seven minutes to four o'clock. He looked about as if taking directions.

"I don't see anything else for it. We'll have to walk back to Aberfoyle. From there I'll be able to hire a wagonette to take us to Glasgow." He took off his cumbersome coat. "At least I don't need this now." He threw it over the crumpled seat of the Benz. He helped her out of her encumbering leather garment and dropped it on top of his own.

She put out a foot to show a flimsy summer slipper. "At least I'll know the road. Through these shoes I'll feel every stone on it. How many miles is it to Aberfoyle?"

"Seven or eight, I suppose."

"Perhaps we'll meet another motor," she said hopefully. "Or even someone with a horse and cart."

"It's possible, but not likely."

He led her to the roadside and stood looking at the mountains with a hand shielding his eyes against the sun. It was lower in the sky now and the shadows it cast were longer. Part of the loch had already gone dark and unfriendly.

"I think we should go that way," he said, pointing to the hills. "That's the direct way. We would save maybe three miles, and you wouldn't be walking on stones with those silly shoes."

She stared aghast at the massive ridges. "You're not seriously suggesting I should climb over those?"

He shook his head with a hint of impatience. "We would go over the shoulder of that lower slope. You won't be called on to do any mountaineering. It will hardly be more than a moorland walk."

As she continued to hesitate, his irritation became acute. "If you prefer crippling yourself on the road in the hope of meeting help, I don't mind. But I'll go the short way." His exasperated laugh hardly took the sting from the cruel words.

Her eyes flashed. "You brute! I believe you would."

He saw how close she was to real anger and cursed the ugly streak in him. He made a blustering retreat. "You know I wouldn't leave you. Surely you don't believe that?"

Her smile nevertheless was chiding. "I suppose it is more sensible to go over the hills than follow a road that wanders halfway round Perthshire."

Although the slope was gradual, it was warm work climbing in the sun. They were glad of the cooling breeze that swayed the heather. When they turned and looked down on the road, now hundreds of feet below, they caught a glimpse of the Benz—or of its brasswork—gleaming in a shaft of sunlight that pierced the forest.

Soon the gradient levelled and walking became almost effortless. Moss and heather cushioned their feet, and air like pure oxygen wafted them along as if they were weightless.

Little streams trickled quietly over rocky beds, and one, wider than the others, was crossed by a humpbacked bridge denoting, according to Dunbar, the route of some ancient drove road. Bees from some wayside hive worked industriously in the purple haze carpeting the moor. When they encountered marshy ground, the fragrance of bog myrtle and apple ringy compensated for wet feet. Occasionally a deer reared a startled head above the bracken before loping gracefully away. Anxious curlews swooped over them threateningly when they strayed near nests hidden in the heather.

"We wouldn't have seen any of this if we'd stuck to the road," Dunbar said in a satisfied voice.

Once, a great bird, which they thought could only be an eagle, rose from a cluster of boulders and soared toward the remote world of craggy peaks. Here and there they had to scramble over rocky shelves or push their way through thickets of gnarled and stunted trees to avoid detouring. Eventually Fiona's dress was torn in several places. Her hair became tangled and windswept.

Although she insisted she was not tired, Dunbar ruled that they should stop regularly to let her rest.

They chattered incessantly and inconsequentially, except when they ran out of breath, and although this rather fevered lightheartedness was a result of their changed relationship, no direct reference was made to it. It had happened, and for the moment that was enough.

Less than two hours after starting to walk, they saw smoke rising above trees in a long valley through which a river flowed.

"That must be Aberfoyle," Dunbar said.

"Already?"

"I told you it wouldn't be much more than a ramble."

"I enjoyed it." Her face and her bare arms tingled. "Have I caught the sun?"

"You're as brown as a berry."

She was delighted. "I take it very quickly, and the mountain air would help."

Their only mishap came when they walked into another marsh at the foot of the hill. Fiona came out of it without her shoes. He had to carry her the last three or four hundred yards, depositing her on a bench in the village street while he went to arrange the hire of a wagonette.

He was back in ten minutes. "There's one available," he said, "but I'll have to take it myself. They haven't a man they can give me. It's a bit of a nuisance. I'll have to get it delivered back to them tomorrow."

"I'm sorry I've caused you all this trouble."

He sat on the bench beside her and draped his arm over the back rail. The air about them was drowsy with the gentle scents of village life. "There is an alternative."

"What is that?"

"We could stay the night at the inn and go back to Glasgow in the morning. They could give me a driver then." His voice was casual and his attention seemed fixed on the birds singing in the tree above them. "I looked in. It's old-fashioned, of course, but it seems cheerful and comfortable."

It was the sort of call to adventure which until today she had never thought to hear again. She felt her blood respond as if, despite the years, some magical remnant of her irresponsible youth lingered still.

"I must get back to the children," she said quickly, wondering what her answer would have been without the excuse.

"Of course." He sank back on the bench and closed his eyes. "Well, it'll be pleasant just sitting here until they get the horses fed and harnessed."

Within half an hour they were cantering back toward Glasgow. "The road looks so different from behind two horses," Fiona said.

He inspected her torn dress, straggling hair and stockinged feet. "So do you. You can't go home like that."

Incredibly, it had not occurred to her. Now, in a ferment, she wondered how she could explain being in such a state. At least it would be late when she reached Claremont Row. The children would be in bed. But Morag would wait up for her, and although she was discreet, the less she saw to set her wondering, the better. Gossiping servants were the greatest worry of any household with a secret to keep.

"What on earth can I do? The shops will be closed by the time we reach Glasgow."

He kept his eye on the horses, jingling the reins slightly to encourage them. "We can stop at my house. It's on the way into town. You can clean yourself up there. There must be shoes lying about that will fit you, and a dress if you want one."

Before she could reply he said, "Can you sing?"

"Not very melodiously. Why?"

"We could have a few choruses. It makes the time pass."

She clasped her hands. "All right," she said gaily. "If I know the words."

"Ah." His face went solemn and his voice was sad. "But you probably won't. My songs won't be your songs." He gave her a quick glance, as if he could hardly spare it from the road. "I don't suppose you ever go to the music hall."

"No," she said, wondering why the admission should make her feel vaguely guilty.

"I thought not. It'll be too low for you, I suppose?"

"Not at all." She hoped he couldn't see her defensive expression. "I've been to the halls on quite a number of occasions. But not recently."

He gave a rough laugh. "Not since you entered high society?"

She became impatient of his teasing, which was too close to the truth for comfort. She turned on him haughtily. "Are you going to sing or not?"

"Certainly, I am."

His singing voice was not as deep as she would have expected, but it had a coarse quality and an emotional sob in it well suited to the words of his song. "Rather common" was how she would have described it if she had been listening to it coming from the stage of the Queen's, the Britannia or one of the other Glasgow halls.

Yes! Let me like a sol-dier fall,
Up-on some o-pen plain,
This breast ex-pand-ing for the ball
To blot out ev'-ry stain
Brave man-ly hearts con-fer my doom
That gent-ler one may tell
How-e'er for-got, un-known my tomb,
I like a sol-dier fell.

His rendering was so realistic she could almost see a defiant figure posturing in the cold limelight of a darkened stage. He had reached the end before she began to suspect he was acting a part.

E-nough they mur-mur o'er my grave
He like a sol-dier fell,
He like a sol-dier fell.

As he finished, with his head thrown back and the last note vibrating deep in his chest, the singing dissolved into loud, self-mocking laughter.

"Could Mr. Kenny Stewart himself have done better?"

"Mr. Kenny Stewart?"

"Don't tell me you haven't heard of Scotland's Own Gentleman of the Ballad? If you're not careful, I'll give you his *Dear Mother, I've Come Home to Die.*"

"Please do. You sing really well."

"The sign of a misspent youth, I'm afraid, with too many Saturday nights wasted at tavern singsongs."

It was now almost eight o'clock. Long summer shadows crept across meadows spread with mellow light. Lochans which had been blue and cheerful on their outward journey were now grey and mysterious. On the banks of one of them, tinkers camped by a fragrant fire. The sun still sent out golden rays from low in the sky and the only clouds were those they had left far behind above the mountains.

Bees still droned in the hedgerows, and on tangles of briar along the roadside a few early brambles shone with the richness of dark wine. The only noises were the sound of their voices and the steady trundle of the wagonette. When they stopped to water the horses, the peace was almost as tangible as the faint haze beginning to form along the low banks of the stream.

From the songs he chose she discovered he was a sentimental man. *Ring the Bell Softly. The Last Rose of Summer. Saved by a Child.* The more maudlin the words, the more he seemed to relish them. Gentleness, she realised, as he touched her hand or her hair, was another contradiction to be added to all the others in his baffling nature.

During the journey through the countryside's gathering shadows they sat close, swaying happily together to the movement of the simple carriage. On the outskirts of the city they moved apart. Fiona found a rug under one of the seats. She draped it over her head and pulled it round her shoulders like a peasant shawl.

Soon, as houses became more frequent and the road busier with strolling people, they hardly spoke; but the silence was richly laden. She felt she had known him for years. Apart from the clandestine nature of the outing, so many things had happened during it to create a bond.

Even with the shawl hiding part of her face, Dunbar felt he could now read all her expressions. Her eyes would never again hold secrets from him; nor would the unspoken message of her lips puzzle and frustrate him. For all his high spirits it had been a bewildering day. He could hardly doubt any longer that he loved her. The chase on which he had set out so cynically had taken an incredible turn. He, the coldblooded hunter, was enmeshed in the tender trap of her unaffected, almost

234

homespun attractions. For all the correctness of his behaviour on the last stages of the journey, he ached to touch her—not, as earlier, like an uncertain boy, but with the intimacy natural to his maturity. He sensed she was aware of this desire and he was almost certain she shared it. From her eyes he was convinced she had been over all the arguments even before they were put and had arrived at answers to questions not yet asked.

In this he was wrong, led astray again by his presumption. With Fiona the debate was not over. She had not yet submitted, even in her mind. But her defences were in disarray. At the very least she was gloriously infatuated with him, her resistance ruinously weakened by the sheer novelty of his appearance and his ways. She wanted him with a disgraceful and unbelievable urgency. For this the stage seemed set, whether by chance or by his cunning contrivance she was not sure. What she did know was that she was recklessly allowing him to drive her to his house after a long, intimate day together. On her subsequent behaviour there could be little restraint. For all practical purposes Robert had abandoned her. Their lives, loosely interwoven even in the early years of marriage, were now almost completely disentangled.

She was startled when Dunbar spoke.

"This is it," he said as he turned the wagonette into a well-tended drive lined with ornamental trees and shrubs. They drove down it mainly in silence. She was uncomfortably aware of her breathing and noticed his hands were tightly clenched on slack reins. They rounded a bend and her heart quickened at the first glimpse of his house. It was a long, two-storeyed rectangle built in the Georgian style and finished in grey harling. Creeper grew over the walls in homely profusion and from some of it large purple flowers which she took to be clematis shone richly in the dusk. On a circle of grass in the centre of the forecourt a large white-painted stone cherub stood with hands outstretched to the first faint stars. Some way beyond she caught sight of the river, dark and, to her imagination when she thought of his wife's having died there, sinister in the gloaming.

Despite the approach of darkness, the only light showing at the front of the house was in a large window beside the door. So this was where he came alone at nights—to work on after the city closed, to brood over King & Co., to worry about his daughter. She would not have recognised it as the house she had fleetingly seen through the trees from the Helensburgh train. It looked friendlier and less lonely, set in a natural garden of closely cut grass and well-placed evergreen trees. From the train it had appeared to sit on a bleak, untended stretch of the river bank.

As the wagonette crunched onto the ornamental chipped stones of the forecourt, all her doubts rose urgently. What would happen if she went in there with him—not immediately after she went in (that, if she had

235

read him, and herself, correctly, was hardly in doubt) but rather, after she came out, when all the complications would have to be faced?

She felt his hand come over hers, and the simple clasping and intertwining of warm fingers seemed to suspend all rational thought. Suddenly, she didn't care. The years fell away, and with them all her responsibilities. She was again the untamed girl of the Gareloch that Robert had first known, revelling in her scandalous contempt of convention. All the old, almost forgotten wildness came rushing back, and she was shaken by a trembling eagerness to rebel against the dreary years of conforming respectability to which life had led her; against all the sedate afternoons she had spent perched on the edge of hard settees, drinking tea with complacent ladies who appeared never to have known temptation or the terrible pleasure of yielding to it.

He jumped from the wagonette and walked round it to stand in front of her, holding out his arms. "You can't walk over these chippings without shoes."

She felt amazingly serene as he lifted her and walked to the house. At the top of the steps, in the shelter of the porch, he kissed her, making no attempt to put her down.

She tightened her arms about his neck. "Aren't you worried about the servants?"

"They're well trained," he said. "They come when I ring for them. Otherwise they keep out of my way, especially at night."

He stooped to let her turn the door handle. The hall was lit by several well-spaced lamps, and in the homely glow she saw panelled walls, a scattering of Persian rugs, a walnut tallboy, a long-case clock and a wide staircase with a curving balustrade of carved wood. *All bought from Gwen's*, she thought, and wondered if he knew Gwen was a King.

He pushed the door shut behind him with his foot. She turned in his arms. "Let me down," she whispered.

In the lamplight his eyes looked deep and dark as the lochans they had passed on the moorland road. His lips were parted in a slight smile.

"Not after getting you this far," he said with soft determination.

She clung to him unprotestingly as he carried her toward the staircase, his boots ringing purposefully on the tiled floor.

"Father!"

She felt his arms slacken and thought he was going to let her fall. He swung clumsily round to face the voice.

"Who is that woman?"

As he let her slide slowly from his arms, she saw a wild-eyed figure standing in an open doorway near the fireplace. Behind it, firelight flickered on a wall lined with books.

"Anne! What are you doing here?"

His voice was distorted with guilt and astonishment. Despite her own heart-thumping confusion, Fiona could feel him trembling. She edged away from him, watching spellbound as the girl stepped further into the hall. A lamp on a nearby table threw her into sudden relief. On her head there was a cheap, frilly dust cap of the type worn by working women. From under this her hair straggled in lank strands over sunken cheeks. Apart from her eyes, which were shining with a fierce life, her face was a frozen mask. She wore a loose, sacklike dress of cheap grey flannel, too featureless even to have been suitable for a servant.

She ignored her father's question and repeated her own in a voice pitched almost to screaming. "Who is that woman?"

"She's . . . she's a Mrs. Currie." He turned slightly toward Fiona with an expression of embarrassed desperation. "She's been in an accident up on the road with her motor. I brought her down here to see if Mrs. Prentice could help. Cuthbertson will take her home in the carriage."

Anne still faced them suspiciously; but her voice was less violent. "Why were you carrying her?"

He twisted his huge hands in silence for a moment. "She lost her shoes in the accident and seems to have twisted one of her ankles. Her dress is torn. I thought Mrs. Prentice could look out some things she might wear until she gets home."

The girl seemed to accept this. As he saw her relax, his confidence rose. "You haven't told me what you're doing here, Anne."

"I've escaped." The mask split open as she spat the words at him.

"Escaped?" He was puzzled and scandalised. "You make it sound as if you've been in prison, or the madhouse."

"It was the madhouse." Her voice rose in fury. "You knew that's what it was when you sent me there. You tricked me. You plotted with that fiend Durande to put me away." Her hands worked like claws at the rough material of her dress. "But you won't do it a second time. I'll never go back. If he comes here after me, I'll kill him. I'll get him with something." She looked excitedly round the hall as if for a weapon.

Dunbar went slowly toward her, his face tense with horror and disbelief. "Stop it," he shouted taking her arm and shaking her. "Stop talking like that in front of a stranger. She'll think you're mad. You went into a nursing home of your own free will because we both felt the treatment would help you."

She tore herself from him in a passion of rage. "Does a nursing home have bars on the windows? Do they keep all the doors locked? Do the patients scream from morning till night? Do they take away your own clothes and give you these terrible rags?" She held out the skirt of her dress for him to see her shame. "It's a madhouse. That's why I couldn't write letters and you couldn't visit me." She stamped her foot on the

237

floor and stood quivering with hysteria. "I'll never forgive you, Father, for what that man did to me in there."

His eyes were glaring and baffled. "If he did anything to you, he'll be sorry for it." He shook his head and said almost pleadingly, "But he's a doctor, Anne. He wouldn't do anything he shouldn't. Didn't you like the treatment?"

"It wasn't treatment. It was torture. I should have known when I first saw those queer eyes of his. So should you, but you didn't care what happened to me. You just wanted rid of me." She ran to the window and threw it open. "If it wasn't for my little Malcolm, I would never have come back to you." She leaned forward to the dark square at which creeper waved and there entered the slightly damp chill peculiar to the Scottish twilight. "I would have gone on down there to the river. I would have put myself in the Clyde. If it wasn't for my lovely little son, I'd gone now, the same way Mother went."

Hysteria choked her and she stumbled back from the window, coughing. She collapsed into a chair, pouring out a flood of tears.

Dunbar's hands hung helplessly at his sides. His shoulders drooped and his eyes were unashamedly wet. He turned to Fiona with an expression of bewildered apology. She walked past him with a little gesture of sympathy and knelt beside the weeping girl. She put a hand on her shaking shoulders.

"Whatever's happened, Anne, I'm sure it isn't your father's fault. I don't know either of you"—she was surprised, even in the intensity of her desire to comfort the girl, how easily the lie came—"but I'm sure your father's only concern is for your welfare."

She heard Dunbar's voice. "It's Anne, Mrs. Prentice. She's come home in an awful state." As a tall grey-haired woman walked forward and knelt beside Fiona, his voice wandered aimlessly on. "This lady was in an accident up on the road. If you can give her a pair of shoes and another dress, Cuthbertson will take her home."

The elderly woman cradled Anne's head against her shiny black dress. "There, there, dear. It's sleep you need. I didn't know you were here. We'll get you up to your room."

The girl's sobbing became subdued and she did not resist when Dunbar lifted her from the chair and carried her up the stairs as so recently he had almost carried Fiona.

They followed, and as they helped the girl into bed, he said, "I'll go down and turn Cuthbertson out with the carriage."

When he returned, Anne was sleeping, still wearing the dust cap she had refused to let them remove. "She's worn out, poor little lady," the housekeeper said. "But I think I should sit in here with her till morning."

"No. I'll do that," Dunbar said. "Will you take this lady and find some things for her to wear?"

When they came back, they stopped at the open door.

Dunbar looked up. "I'll take you down to Cuthbertson," he said listlessly.

"No." Fiona put up her hand and gave him a lingering look in which more confused emotions were combined than she could have explained. "Mrs. Prentice has offered to do that."

When she turned away, he was hunched forward over the bed with a hand lying on the pillow beside Anne's neglected hair.

14

It was almost half past eleven when Dunbar's carriage deposited Fiona under the hissing gas jets of Claremont Row.

It had been a day too long, too eventful and too momentous. Her body was stiff and aching, but whether from tiredness or as a consequence of the accident with the Benz, she did not know. Her head throbbed slightly. Her mind was exhausted and her emotions shredded. Gordon's entanglement with Anne Dunbar had been worrying enough before, but the frightening revelation of the girl's unbalanced state added an element of horror.

During the lonely drive home, along the misted river, she had been haunted by memories of the harrowing confrontation between the girl and her father. It overshadowed in her mind even the thought of her own involvement with Dunbar. That, of course, would have to be faced, but not tonight. She was too weary and downcast, as well as being physically uncomfortable in a dress and shoes too tight for her.

A cold breeze rattled through the trees and made the street lights flicker. Most of the houses were in darkness. Another light went out as she stood watching the departing carriage. She yawned and shivered as she crossed the pavement. A little sigh of gratitude escaped her when she stepped into the house and felt the presence of familiar objects. As she closed the door, she felt she was shutting out some of her problems. With a sense of relief enfolding her she went quietly along the hall and up the stairs, putting out lamps as she went; but the endless day was not over.

She stopped in surprise with her bedroom door half open. Florence, Steven and Allan stood in a self-conscious row at the foot of her bed.

The canopy of pink satin draped from an ormolu coronet on the ceiling isolated them from the rest of the room like a frame. They were in their nightclothes and they faced her with expressions of guilty defiance.

She closed the door. "Why aren't the children in bed, Florence?" It was a recent concession to Florence's rapidly blooming womanhood that she now enjoyed a semiadult status. The disadvantage was that she could be held to some extent accountable for the actions and behaviour of her brothers. "And you, too? Is there something wrong?"

For a second Florence's silent aggression looked as if it might crumble; then, with her eyes brightly challenging, she stepped determinedly forward. "Where have you been?"

The loud, uncompromising tone and the angry expression stung Fiona. Her feeling of guilt vanished in the face of this insubordination. She threw her soiled gloves and dented vanity case onto a chair.

"I don't think that's any concern of yours, young lady. You are being impertinent. Now, answer my question. Why are you all here in my bedroom at this time of night?"

Their eyes became evasive as her authority threatened the revolt, but before any of them could reply there was a hesitant knocking at the door.

"Yes?"

Morag peered in, her round face frightened and stained with signs of recent crying. She leaned heavily on the handle.

"Oh, Ma'am, it's no' my fault. They defied me. They woudny go to their beds. Isn't that the truth, Miss Florence?"

Florence gave her an icy glare. "I told you quite clearly I would take the responsibility, Morag. I will see that you don't bear any blame."

Fiona nodded to the maid. "All right, Morag. Don't distress yourself. Make yourself a cup of tea and go to bed. I will attend to this." As she spoke, she could see Florence intently examining the dress Dunbar's housekeeper had given her. The girl's face was flushed.

"Those aren't your clothes," she cried accusingly the moment the door had closed behind the maid. "The buttons don't even fasten properly. What have you been doing?"

Fiona put a hand to the straining bodice of the dress. She had forgotten she was wearing borrowed clothes.

"I was in an accident," she said with a return of guilt, "but I have no intention of explaining that to you tonight, especially in view of the rebellious mood you are in. Now, go to bed. All of you. You won't be able to rise for school in the morning."

No one moved. Allan and Steven, who while Fiona was speaking had edged closer together and taken hands, were watching Florence as if for signs of submission. Fiona noted their worried expressions.

241

"I'll hold you responsible for this when we talk tomorrow, Florence. I can see it is you who are behind it. You have kept these boys in here instead of seeing they were in bed at a respectable hour."

Florence gave them a quick glance to judge if she still had their support and, deciding she had, resumed the attack, "You had no right leaving us here all night, none of us knowing where you were," she said, her excitement mounting toward fury.

"I agree that was unfortunate," Fiona said with dignity. "I would have sent word if I could, but the accident took place in the country. You are lucky to see me here in one piece. I was extremely fortunate not to have been injured." She was alarmed at being so easily forced to the defensive.

Florence, sensing her advantage, gave full vent to her rage. "You're every bit as bad as Papa. He should be here, not in London. And you should be at home instead of always being at King and Company. You care much more about all that old whisky than you do about us. When we come home from school, you're still out at business. Most of the time we're left with servants. But today you haven't even *been* at business." Her voice rose hysterically. "Where have you been till this time of night?"

"How dare you interrogate me like this, Florence?" She took the girl's shoulder and shook her till her plaits swayed. "Nor will I have you dictate to me about what I should do or should not do."

Allan began to wail and Steven's eyes grew bright with frightened tears.

"I hate you," Florence screamed. "I was sorry for you that other night when you were all alone in the kitchen, but now I hate you. I hate you! You don't care about us at all."

Allan could stand no more. He tore his hand from Steven's and shot forward, burying his face in Fiona's skirts. "You care about me, Mama," he yelled. "I know you do. You love me and I love you."

She bent and swept him up into her arms. "Of course I do, darling." Tears burned in her eyes. She was half blinded. "I love you all. Whatever Florence says; you must know that. If I've been neglecting you, I'm sorry. I didn't mean to, and you must forgive me."

Steven hurled himself at her, his arms tightly encircling her waist and his face pressing hard against her.

"It was Florence," he howled. "She made us do it. She told us you didn't love us or you wouldn't stay out so late, and we believed her. We were lonely."

Fiona shook the tears from her eyes. "And now you must both be terribly tired," she said. "I'm going to take you along to your rooms."

"What are you going to do to us?" Allan sobbed.

242

"I'm going to tuck you into bed. That's all."

"Aren't you going to punish us?"

"No."

At this, Steven showed his face. "And what about Florence? Will you write to Papa about her?"

"Why should Florence be any different from you two?' I think we've all been very upset tonight. We're none of us really ourselves."

As she took them from the room, she turned. Florence still stood in her original stance at the foot of the bed, very vulnerable now that she had been deserted by her allies. Her face was white but the fury had left it. She was staring at the carpet as if she could not trust herself to meet the eyes of any of them.

"I won't be long, Florence."

Fiona's voice was not quite steady, and it was difficult to know whether she meant the content of the words to be taken as an order or an invitation.

When she returned a few minutes later, Florence was sprawled face down across the bed. Her shoulders rose and fell with convulsive sobbing. Fiona stood watching in silence for a moment, then went over and sat beside her on the bed. She placed a hand softly on her arm.

"Do you really hate me, Florence?"

With a loud, racking cry of regret Florence twisted round until her face was buried in her mother's lap. "Oh, Mama. I don't. You know I don't. Forgive me."

"Hush, my baby. There's nothing to forgive. You didn't mean it."

Normally she thought of her bedroom as a homely place. Tonight, despite the shades of pink, it felt cold and desolate. For a long time she sat soothing the girl's guilt, knowing her own was a greater guilt and that for it there was no one she could turn to for forgiveness.

Next morning a kindly veil had settled over the events of the previous midnight. In sleep her guilt had been lifted away. Her confrontation with the children seemed to have taken place in a dream. Dunbar was the shining reality and there was no shame in her for it. Her attitude and her reasoning had become that of a woman without husband, responsibilities or morals. In the end, seen against Anne's anguish, their intention last night had been made to look shabby. In an instant the magic had been swept away. As a consequence they had parted like strangers and her last glimpse of him had shown a worried man cast down by sorrow and the sudden frustration of desire. The strutting dealer of the city and the singing motorist of the countryside might both have been creations of her imagination. But in a strange way the revealing moment, the

243

shattering collapse of the wonderful day, had heightened her sense of intimacy with him. And so, she was sure, it would be with him this morning when the harrowing encounter with Anne had fallen into perspective.

She heard across the corridor the door of Florence's room open and close and then the girl's footsteps on the stair, but she sat on at the window, dreamily brushing her hair. She sang quietly to herself as she went about the bedroom, unafraid of the spell that was on her. She was scarcely aware of the bruised stiffness of her body. What she remembered in every detail was the sudden passion of his relief at finding her unhurt after the smashing of the Benz. In those moments, as he clung to her in the dark-green gloom of the wood, restraint had been cast away and his emotions revealed without disguise or calculation.

When she heard Steven and Allan pass her door, she went down to breakfast. They were all subdued and uncertain of her until they saw her smile and realised she had not regretted or reversed her forgiveness of the night before. When she saw them off at the front door, Florence kissed her more warmly and Allan clung to her for a fraction longer than normal. As she watched them go up the street, the boys nudging each other, Florence keeping a little way apart, a fingertip of doubt touched her and then withdrew.

When she reached Seabank Lane, there was a note from Dunbar on her desk. She was unsurprised. In this mood she would have regarded anything less as neglect. She lingered over the heavy pokerwork lettering, imagining all the agitation of heart that would lie behind his brief question. He wanted her to have luncheon with him and named a solid but unfashionable hotel once famous for its mutton stew and sheep's-head broth and mainly patronised now by elderly people, in from the country, who remembered the place from more glorious days.

She smiled slightly at his choice. His discretion was reassuring. They were unlikely to be recognised in such a faded place. Oddly, the possibility of discovery troubled her less now, even though there was so much more to hide. Her mind was too occupied with the wonder of her feelings, operating at too rarefied an altitude, to be able to concern itself with any unpleasantness, perhaps even catastrophe, that might later occur. Wherever she looked, there was a beckoning prospect.

Everything conspired to maintain and even increase her exaltation. A report on sales for the previous month showed both King's Royal and Queen's Royal accelerating their upward climb. Negotiations had been successfully concluded with the Foreign Office to have both whiskies on the wine list at all British embassies throughout the world. There could be no better shop window than a grand diplomatic function, and it was a market King & Co. had cultivated with care. New agencies she had personally negotiated in various parts of the country had all contributed to the story of continuing success. And for once their planning had not been overtaken by the unforeseen. These last few weeks had been blessedly free of crisis. Stocks—not only of whisky, but of casks, bottles, labels and cases—were good, and their deliveries were once again the speediest in the trade after a much-needed reorganisation of the dispatch and transport departments which she had initiated despite some mild objection from Fergus.

When things went well, she never failed to thank or congratulate Ross and expected him to pass the good cheer downward. When she stopped at his open door to tell him how pleased she was with the sales position, he was cursing over a cork that had disintegrated as he tried to pull it from a bottle of Queen's Royal. He held it up to let her see the fragments floating in the whisky.

She was reminded of a thought that had come to her a few weeks previously. She stepped into the room.

"Is there any special reason, Peter, why whisky is corked in that way?" she asked.

"In what way, Mrs. King?" He had lifted a decanter and was trying to pour the contents of the bottle into it without letting the particles of broken cork follow.

"With those wine corks that are mechanically rammed down the neck of the bottle until they're flush with the lip."

He shrugged slightly. "What else is there?"

"I don't know, but once you take a cork like that out, it's finished. You can't put it back in the bottle."

"Who would want to?" He laughed. "There's not much in a bottle, you know. Anyway, surely the sooner it's finished and another bottle opened, the better it suits us?"

"Joking apart, Peter, not everyone wants to finish a bottle of whisky at one sitting. It's getting so expensive I'm sure a lot of our customers can't afford to, even if they felt so inclined."

"Of course, but people like that can put it into a decanter."

"We have to remember decanters are not standard equipment in every household. Besides, it would suit us if the whisky remained in the bottle until it was finished. People can see the label and know it's our whisky. I'm sure many people would prefer to leave the whisky in the bottle and let their friends see they are serving a quality brand. Decanting was all right in the days before blending, when whisky was simply whisky. People rarely knew or cared where it came from or who the proprietors were. Don't forget, one reason for Robert's success was that he marketed whisky with a name, so that people could ask for it again if they liked it."

At the mention of Robert, who was rapidly becoming little more than a

245

memory here at the headquarters of the great business he had built, Ross seemed to become more attentive, as if some weight had been added to Fiona's words.

"That's so," he said.

"After all, decanters are for wine. The whole idea of decanting is to leave the dregs in the bottle so that what goes into the drinking glass is attractively clear. Isn't that right?"

He nodded, feeling no more was required of him.

"Well, there are no dregs in whisky. It doesn't have to be decanted, and if the cork could be replaced, I think a lot of people would leave it in the bottle for reasons of convenience, and even snobbery."

He put his decanter on a tray and the empty bottle in a waste bucket. "Should we encourage snobbery?"

"Yes, when it encourages the sales of our whisky, we should," she said, ignoring his levity.

It fascinated her that she could keep one half of her mind on a business problem while the other half concerned itself with images of Dunbar.

Ross was looking at her doubtfully. "You're not thinking, surely, that we should use the type of cork that goes into a medicine bottle? That would look ugly and makeshift."

"I'm not thinking of any known type of cork. It would have to be specially designed. What I visualise is a cork with a circular head on it that would act as a sort of crown to the bottle and also provide something for the fingers to grip so that it could be pulled out by hand and pushed back in again."

She took a pencil and drew it for him. He studied the rough sketch, then lifted the empty bottle from his waste bucket and looked at it thoughtfully.

"A stopper like that could certainly be removed without a corkscrew," he agreed. "And it could be re-placed in the bottle. The objection I see is that it could be removed far too easily. What guarantee would the customer have that the whisky hadn't been tampered with—diluted, perhaps? The bottle could be opened, the whisky contaminated in some way and the cork replaced without any trace being left. At the moment, no one can interfere with the whisky because no one can re-cork the bottle without a machine."

"Yes. I hadn't thought of that. There would have to be some sort of seal, I suppose."

"Wax?" He frowned and shook his head as he visualised what this would mean in the bottling and labelling hall. "That would be a very slow and troublesome process. I think we'd regret it."

She lifted her sketch and walked with it to the window. Somewhere out there, beyond the grimy wall that formed Ross's only view, was Dunbar. Doubtless he, too, would seem to be attending to business in the normal way. Additionally, he would have Anne on his mind and the motor company would have to be informed of the accident. Already she was involved in his private affairs.

She turned back to Ross. "If the crown of the cork could be made attractive in some way, possibly coated with something to give it a colour, it would enhance the appearance of the bottle. We could simply put a strip of printed paper over it as a seal. The bottle couldn't be opened without the paper being torn. Or, better still, we could use a strip of ribbon. That would be less likely to tear accidentally. How would that do?"

A ribbon, to Ross, was something pink and feminine that hung from a bonnet to be tied under a pretty chin. It was not in tune with his conception of whisky as a masculine drink, and he said so.

For a moment Fiona agreed. Then, "I know! A tartan ribbon! There's nothing feminine about tartan, and it would be very apt. The Kings are a sept of the MacGregors. We could use their tartan."

Now that he'd had time to consider the advantages of the idea, Ross shared her enthusiasm. "I'll call on the corkcutters tomorrow and discuss it with them," he promised. "It's such a simple idea, I don't think it should present them any problems."

"It's certainly worth serious thought," Fiona said. "It would make a good selling feature in our advertising. *King's—The Only Whisky With The New Replaceable Cork.* It's a pity it's not the sort of thing we could patent. If it's successful, all the blenders will go over to replaceable corks. Still, we would be the first."

Soon her carriage arrived, as she had earlier ordered, and she drove away to meet Dunbar.

15

The hotel was overpoweringly shabby, its clientele more outdated than she could have imagined, its food even more attuned to bygone tastes than she had expected. The soup was so stodgy with barley that she left most of it. Dunbar tackled his with customary energy.

"You don't know what's good for you," he reproached her as he tilted his plate to spoon the last drops.

For a while an uneasy shadow from the previous night hung over them, but after a brief and nervous reference to Anne, his manner became rapidly more lighthearted and flirtatious. She surrendered eagerly to the change of mood. Only once, as she glanced at the other staid patrons, did reality intrude again. Momentarily her exaltation faltered as she saw beyond his charm and her own infatuation to the madness of her behaviour. But swiftly the last trace of prudence disappeared.

The troublesome fact that he was a ruthless business competitor was buried beneath the actuality of his powerful presence, though even this seemed more subdued and manageable than previously. She felt she knew him so well. In a single, unforgettable day she had shared many moods with him and seen him in many lights.

As she sat watching a sunbeam creep across the dark hair on the back of his hands, part of her attention was on his lively conversation and the other engaged with her own drifting thoughts. Her heart quickened as she contemplated the future as she felt it must be. A doubt rose, instantly to be quelled. It was inescapable. They would go on together down the path that had opened for them yesterday and from which at the last moment they had been turned. How could it be otherwise? They had been drawn to each other, if not from the very first day, then certainly from the fateful night in Claremont Row when she had glimpsed the vulnerable and complex man behind the iron exterior. Looking back, everything that had happened since had been ordained, given his determination and her susceptibility.

The sheer novelty of the man enthralled and excited her. His nearness raised expectations in her, as would the sound of familiar music unexpectedly heard after a long interval.

The table between them almost ceased to exist for her as her mind caressed the physical memory of him—the kisses and embraces that would have seemed a scandalous impossibility if they had somehow been suggested to her when she sat only a day ago amid the innocent scents of the garden, telling herself she would not go with him in his motor. Now they signified only pleasure, heedless, interrupted and incomplete; pleasure yet to come.

She was recalled by the laughter that marked the end of the story he had been telling. The incongruity, against the drab surroundings, of their almost adolescent gaiety only heightened its headiness.

"I feel I should sing something to you," he said exuberantly as he pushed away another empty plate. The glance he sent round the somnolent room was so recklessly challenging that she took him half seriously. There was a hint of alarm in her smile.

He noticed it and spread his hands. "Alas! I might wake these good people."

"And that would never do," she said. "Much better they don't notice us."

He leaned closer. "They may be sleepy," he said earnestly, "but every head turned when you arrived. And so they might. You're even lovelier, dear Fiona, than you were yesterday."

She accepted the compliment and the endearment in the same unembarrassed way that he spoke them. Yesterday, all the preliminaries had been gone through.

"Aye," he said thoughtfully, "yesterday you were . . . wary. Today you look as if you really wanted to be here." His smile became momentarily concerned. "You do want to be here?" Quickly he answered the question himself. "But you must. This time I didn't trick you into it."

"I do want to be here," she said softly.

He looked at her admiringly, taking it as the final brave acknowledgement that their preoccupations were identical. "That's good." Impetuously he pushed his chair back. "I can see you're not too taken with the food here. I think we should go." He beckoned to a waiter. "Somewhere more private."

"But where?" She could not stifle the nervous catch in her voice.

"I have a place," he said quietly. "It isn't far, but we'll take a cab."

Uncertainty rose in her. "I can't risk driving about town with you."

"No." His brow wrinkled. "You can follow in another cab." He gave her the address.

As they stood in the foyer while the doorman summoned cabs, she asked only one hesitant question. "You're quite sure I won't be seen?"

He pressed her arm reassuringly. "We won't be seen together. Which is all that matters."

It was a furnished flat he had rented in a tenement near the university. The parlour window had a view of the Kelvin. "It's the best I could do in the time," he said, as he saw her glancing about.

She had come too far with him to resent the presumption the remark revealed. It was in any case too well justified for comment.

"I did have time to lay these in, though." He opened a cupboard to reveal some bottles.

She shook her head. After a moment's hesitation he poured himself some whisky and drank it quickly.

She made a last effort at rational thought, but her mind slid down erotic avenues. At a time when life might have had no further adventures for her she had been presented with the chance of one more rich experience—the thought gripped her with longing. It seemed to her that there was no real choice to make. It was either the excitement of an affair with Dunbar or the continuance of her gradual slide into a lonely and loveless middle age, her children leaving her for work or school, her husband already gone. Her mind was turned to such an extent that the possible consequences hardly troubled her.

She tried to make him sit a little while in the ugly parlour, but he was impatient and determined, and the mood of abandon he had induced in her was too strong to be resisted. Her eagerness matched his. After the first kiss he started unbuttoning her dress and within minutes they were in the bedroom.

It was like a continuation of the previous night. The rapturous spell conjured out of their day in the country might never have been shattered by Anne. Her mind floated. Anne, Florence, Steven, Allan, and all they signified had receded to a limbo where they no longer troubled her. The consuming reality of this suspended moment was the reawakening of her profound sensuality, deadened for so long by an unsatisfactory marriage and a pattern of life which family and society had imposed on her. Now she was aware only of her flesh, and of his. Then she could no longer think of it as his, or hers. It was their flesh, one and the same, like the rhythm of their breathing and the delirious beating of their hearts. As his hands touched her face she kissed them, pressing them fiercely to

250

her mouth. For so long, what she had accepted as life had been shadow. A vision from the previous day came to her. She was with him again in the Benz, at the top of a high hill, poised on the edge of an unsustainable joy. Suddenly they were spiralling over the brink, the long, startled cry of her rebirth filling the room.

For Dunbar, after they parted, there was a quick return to business. He had to wait until Fiona was out of the street. He stood impatiently at a window until she turned a corner that would take her home by way of the park. Then he went leaping down the bare stone stair of the tenement and ran to the nearest cab rank.

Desire had been satisfied, and now it was back to work. If asked, Fiona might have surmised as much, but never could she have guessed the nature of the business that took her ardent and considerate lover of a few minutes ago hurrying toward a small conference room in the Central Hotel.

She had forgotten the man she held in her arms was the same man who schemed against her business. She had forgotten that for Dunbar, selling his own whisky was not enough, that he had to stop King & Co. from selling theirs. If it had occurred to her to consider the matter, she would almost certainly have taken it for granted that his attitude had now changed. How, she would have asked herself, could it *not* have changed after what had taken place? But such was the strength of Dunbar's fixation that even a passionate and loving afternoon with one King did not make him forget his sworn aim of destroying the others. How Fiona was to be spared in the general holocaust he could not have explained, for he had not considered it. Somehow, his mind had conveniently separated her from the others. Somehow, although she controlled its affairs, she was not part of King & Co. He had a mind that could believe anything that suited him, and it was one reason for his success.

In his original plan of striking at Robert by stealing his wife, none of this would have been a consideration. He had visualised a calculated but loveless seduction, for the gratification of his senses alone, in which Fiona would be bent to his will and Robert publicly humiliated. Then, following a few weeks or months of dalliance, the lady would be discarded, a wiser, though sorrier, woman.

He could see now that his plan had been too simply conceived. For a start, Fiona must be protected. He was too fond of her to hurt her. The relationship would have to be kept secret, and what Robert didn't know couldn't humiliate him. Secondly, he hadn't made allowance enough for the potency of her attractions. Was his attachment to her already too deep?

251

He sat well back in the cab as it rattled him toward his appointment, letting his mind roam back. Even in retrospect it was exciting. She had been everything he had thought she would be—and more! She wasn't like some he'd known who had provoked and promised but couldn't deliver. He looked up at the new office buildings as the cab went down Bath Street. In most of them were men who knew him. He felt like jumping out and telling them what he'd been up to. The triumph of having had Robert King's wife in bed was almost too heady to be savoured in secret. Such knowledge should have bells rung for it. If it were known, there wasn't a red-blooded man in Glasgow who wouldn't envy him—or, even better, snigger behind King's back. That was *really* what he wanted! He closed his eyes and sighed with regret because it could not be.

They were all there at the long table in the first-floor room when he arrived, some of them glancing ostentatiously at their watches to let him see he was late. He looked at them with the resentment a man reserves for those who have helped him with their money.

In his proud case, the bitterness was twice distilled. He had never wanted them. They had been foisted on him because the bank was too timid to support him with its own money—a man like him, who in twenty years had never troubled them for more than a few miserable thousand and always repaid on the dot! His chest could still rise in a sudden blaze at the thought of this betrayal. He hadn't forgiven it, nor would he ever. As he had told old Finlay, he had never worked with others. Nature had designed him to fight alone, not to trim his style to suit the paltry outlook of lesser men. Especially these!

He looked round at them with a forced smile as he sorted his papers. None of them would know a distillery from a glue factory. Aye! and he had told them as much when one or two had the gall to object to something they knew nothing about. There were seven of them and, apart from Laird and Hutchinson, who were in coal and iron, respectively, not a practical man among them. The others, so far as he gathered—for he wouldn't deign to ask—spent their time plunging in and out of rubber or sugar or some other foreign commodity forever at the mercy of the weather and the darkie. The God-given nature of good Scotch whisky and the ways of those who lived by it were mysterious territory to them. Some of them, wine snobs, he suspected, had hardly known the taste of it. But they would recognise it now! For in a warped effort to relieve his contempt, he had lured and bullied these innocents into a "tasting session" and sent them home swaying like the heather and babbling like burns. He smiled at the memory.

Of course, at the first uneasy meeting, when the banker had brought them together, he had made his conditions forcefully enough. It might be a syndicate, but there was to be no doubting who ran it. If they chose to put their money beside his, it must be with the knowledge that he would spend it. All whisky purchases would be made at his direction. He would say when and how stocks would be sold. They were required simply for the provision of capital and the docile stamping of his decisions. In return they would scoop rich profits. And they, forewarned by Finlay of what they might expect, had swallowed their astonished wrath and agreed, because in Glasgow his reputation as a moneymaker stood high and his interests were—or appeared to be—identical with their own.

Today he scorned them more than ever. Never had their bearded greyness of appearance, their nervous caution, their mean suspicion of mind, so irked him or stood out in such offensive contrast to his own grand spirit. *He wasn't like them.* He was an eagle and they were pigeons. He addressed them as if there were other things he would rather have been doing. A man like him, his manner said, had other interests which distinguished him from such a collection of narrow, money-grubbing squeaks.

He had to stifle a mad urge to raise them off their seats with a detailed description of what he'd been about while they were tamely at their desks. If he hadn't had to break off to come here and pander to them, he could have been doing it still.

They watched and listened to his antics with the same fascination as would have been inspired in them by the bravura performance of a great ham actor. He was larger than life and just as cruel, but then, so was his scheme, and they thoroughly approved of that. Hadn't they already, in the first few months of discreet operation, collectively backed his judgement to the tune of almost two million pounds? There could be no greater demonstration of their faith in him. To the surprise of some of them, the first inklings of understanding of his nature were beginning to form, and even—although they recoiled shyly from it—a little liking. Grudging respect they already had. He was straight. He was gifted. And despite his deplorable lack of grace, they felt their money was safe with him. Nothing could be more important than that.

"Since we last met, I have placed orders for tops worth three hundred thousand pounds," he said in a casual murmur, "and I'm on the track of parcels worth as much again."

He knew the jargon annoyed them because it robbed them of the feeling that they were "in whisky," which was what everybody seemed to want to be in, these days. For this reason he made exaggerated use of it.

In silence he passed round some typewritten sheets which gave the details of his purchases. They took them eagerly, for this was practically all they ever saw for their money. The whisky itself remained in casks

253

locked away in distilleries all over Speyside, where it had been since it first gurgled hot and clear from the stills and where it would remain in dark bondage till consigned to Glasgow or to Leith for blending.

But that would be for other men to do—once they had paid the ransom. Until then, all the syndicate would have to ponder was an unspectacular bundle of delivery orders transferring the whisky to them, and the memory of some resounding names Dunbar rumbled to them at these meetings: Glen Grant, Highland Park, Glenlivet, Cragganmore, Linkwood, Dallas Dhu, Mortlach, Bunnahabhain, Glenmorangie, Caol Ila, Macallan, Glenfarclas, Bruichladdich. Of course, not all worth buying, he warned them. Not all good enough for their high purpose, but names, nevertheless, that held not only the essence of whisky but of Scotland itself—names, he emphasised loudly as the lyricist in him expanded, to lift the heart.

"I see," Livingstone Frame said respectfully, fluttering Dunbar's typed sheet almost apologetically, "you paid sixpence a gallon more for this latest purchase of Macallan than you did for the last one."

Dunbar nodded. "And if you look farther down, you'll see I had to pay eightpence a gallon more to get the Mortlach. This is what we can expect. The more we buy of these good whiskies, the scarcer they become. The price must go up." He tapped the table with a broad finger. "But don't forget, the whisky we've already bought increases in value to this new level. We're already showing a profit." He looked down one side of the table and up the other as if to be sure they all appreciated what he was doing for them.

Denholm, whose family was using the profits of its Shanghai trading company to open up China with railways, caught his eye.

"Some of these purchases are from your own company, Mr. Dunbar."

"They are."

"You feel justified in charging the syndicate the increased price?" The words were spoken mildly and accompanied by an enquiring smile.

"The syndicate must pay the market price."

"Yes, but if you had sold to us a month ago, the price would have been lower."

It was a legitimate point, and Dunbar did not object. "That was my good luck, Mr. Denholm," he said, returning the cool smile. "And if I'd decided not to sell for another month, the price would have been higher still. The truth is, a month ago I didn't know that particular whisky was surplus to my own blending requirements. A month ago I wasn't even certain about the morality of selling private stock to the syndicate and making a profit on it. I've sold now because I was more worried about the morality of holding on to the whisky and seeing it appreciate further in value through the activities of the syndicate. I'm perfectly willing to take it back."

Denholm smiled and shook his head. As an afterthought he looked round the table. They all nodded to indicate they were satisfied. "Thank you, Mr. Dunbar."

There was talk of warehouse rents and a discussion of whether or not it would be cheaper for them to build their own bonded premises. In all of them there was the sense of an empire growing. A decision was taken to increase stock insurance.

Finally Dunbar returned to the question of rising values. "As I've said, the law of the market means the price will go up, anyway, the more we buy. But it will go up a hell of a lot faster if what we're up to gets about. Secrecy is now one of our most valuable assets. That's why I'm buying slowly. If we rush at it, we give the game away. The brokers would see right away it was organised. Of course, eventually they'll see anyway, but the darker we keep it, meantime, the cheaper we get the whisky. As soon as it gets out there's a syndicate operating, the price will go through the ceiling. The whole blending trade will start scrambling like maniacs for what's left." He grinned. "With luck, there won't be much. We'll have it all locked up. After that, we sit on it until they start screaming. Then we hammer them."

His fist came down with a thump that lifted a decanter of water an inch off the table.

And the ones we'll hammer hardest, he told himself, without a thought of Fiona, *will be the bloody high and mighty Kings. We'll hammer the Kings so bloody hard they'll never get off their knees again.*

Next afternoon Fiona walked from Seabank Lane to Glasgow Cross and hired a cab from the rank under the Tron Steeple.

Twenty minutes later she paid the fare in a quiet street and started walking through the park toward the flat near the university. Ducks came out of the Kelvin and waddled across her path. On Gilmorehill the university clock struck one. The scene was sylvan, but she hardly noticed it. Her perceptions were all inward. She was physically elated at the prospect of soon being with Dunbar again, and yet she felt furtive and unattractive.

With this second meeting in mind she had left home in the morning dressed in clothes she felt would draw the least attention to her. Yesterday, her dress had been too striking. Today she had hunted through the house until she found a hat that shielded her face. It was wildly unsuitable for business wear, and she had noticed Ross and one or two of the workers glancing at it with amusement. Even in the park it was incongruous on a day without sun. It was, she supposed, silly as an effort at secrecy, and now she would not be looking her best for him! Perhaps he would think her plain. Perhaps, after the abandon with which she had given herself to him, he would not even be there. She had sensed his surprise. Or, in her endless going over of it all, had she only invented it?

She walked more quickly, too eager to get to him even to pause at the various picturesque corners where normally she would have lingered a little to admire the miniature splendours of this leafy grove, enclosed now by the city, but still not of it.

The tenement block was of grey stone, not yet dimmed by the grime of industrial prosperity. She recognised the flat from a distance by the empty brass plant-pot sitting on a high table at the oriel window between partly drawn chenille curtains.

As she crossed the street, hordes of untidy students tumbled from a tram that had just reached the terminus at the foot of University Avenue. They went chasing noisily up the hill to afternoon classes, swinging satchels and biting at thick bread "pieces." She realised why people living in the area had opposed the university's being moved here from the old High Street site.

It was a superior close, with wall tiles forming a pattern of blue sailing ships on a cream ground. In less favoured tenements the closes were simply painted, usually in drab shades of brown. She went up the stairs quickly, fumbling in her handbag for the key. It turned easily in the lock, and when she pushed the door open, he was standing in the hall. She rushed into his arms, her lips raised to his. At last he released her, looking down at her with a tenderness she knew few people could ever have seen.

"I thought you might not come," he said breathlessly.

"How could I not come?" she murmured happily, the anxieties of her walk through the park swept away by the love she felt in his embrace.

"You could have changed your mind; you could have thought better of it."

She smiled at the uncharacteristic humility. He had been as worried as she had been! But it was too emotional a moment for coquetry. "I haven't thought better of it," she said simply.

He stood back, as if to see her better, and she thought it was her inelegant clothes he was inspecting. But as he spoke she realised he hadn't noticed them.

"I was watching from the window. Even after I saw you coming there was a moment when I wondered. You looked . . . worried."

When he kissed her the wide hat had been pushed back on her head. Now she pulled it off. "I was worried that someone might see me," she

256

said. "That's why I came in this disguise. After all, we're not far off the main road here, and I live just on the other side of the park."

He unbuttoned her cape and put his hands round her waist. "Even if you were seen, surely no one would attach any special significance to it. They would simply assume you were visiting a friend."

"Yes. It was silly of me to be apprehensive. But I'm all right now."

He lifted her as if she were weightless. "Are you going to prove it to me?"

She ruffled his hair and snuggled against him. "I'll try."

Again she had the melting conviction that in the act of love they were not two people. They were not even a miraculously matched pair. In the flood of sensuality they released in each other they became a unity. Even when he relaxed into drowsiness, she clung to him, feeling that for the first time she understood the mystical meaning of the marriage vow. She was married now to Douglas as completely as she had ever been married to Robert. She had experienced with Douglas a joy more intense than she had known even at the height of her love for her husband. It was this that should not be put asunder. And yet it was unsustainable. It could only be repeated. *As often as possible,* she thought with a drowsy smile. She turned to kiss him and found he was asleep.

She had little memory of the room from the previous day. It had an unaired smell. She felt the window should be thrown open and masses of flowers brought in. She was watching a cobweb dangling from the dusty cornice when he wakened. He seemed able to read her thoughts.

"I explained yesterday that I rented the place in a rush. I know it's not very great, but we couldn't risk a hotel." His terrible sarcasm broke through, although softened by a teasing smile. "You'll have to forget you come from a castle."

"I'm not being critical," she said tolerantly. "But it does tend a little to make me feel I shouldn't speak above a whisper."

"I like hearing you whisper. It does something to me."

"Really? I wonder what." She leaned over him and put her lips close to his ear.

For a moment or two he lay grinning with his eyes closed, and then slowly his arms wrapped round her. "I've never heard such a disgraceful suggestion from a lady in all my life."

"It was only a stray thought. I didn't think you would hear."

They were surprised when the university clock struck four. She left ahead of him, convinced, as she went down the stairs, that a record of the last few hours must be written on her face. When she was clear of the street, she slowed. The emotions he had aroused must be given time to subside before she reached home. She stopped by the massive stone pillars and iron gates at the entrance to the park.

257

When she was sure there was no one to see her, she pulled off the camouflaging hat and shook out her hair with a slow, luxurious movement. She was safe now. To be seen from this point on would not matter. Her step became effortless and the hat swung happily at her side, as, flushed and shining-eyed, she went down a riverside path under the trailing branches of a weeping willow.

16

Next morning Gordon found a letter from Anne propped against his eggcup on the kitchen table when he came down the steep and narrow stairs from his attic room.

He tried to hide his eagerness from Jack, who watched with unconcealed curiosity from the other side of the table. There were less than a dozen lines, and the writing, unlike the address on the envelope, with which she must have taken care, was almost unrecognisable. It looked as if it had been scrawled frantically. He sensed her distress before reading a word. His expectation of a happy report foundered among the badly formed sentences and broken letters. A blur stood between him and the anguished page. Dear God! He bent over it, peering with an emotion he had forgotten he did not want to show.

She was home. The nursing home had been a nightmare. She had escaped after being hunted through the grounds like a convict. Durande was a sadist. The ordeal had exhausted her. She knew now there would never be any betterness for her. She would be better dead. But she loved him dearly. He was the only person in the world she loved, apart from little Malcolm, and she was desperate for the comfort of seeing him again. She would go to Miss Frame's tearoom the following day at lunchtime and hoped he would allow nothing to stop his being there.

His eyes blinked and his hands trembled as he pushed the gold-rimmed page into a pocket without refolding it. Through the haze he was aware of being watched. He made a belated effort to look unconcerned but Jack was not deceived.

"Bad news from the lady?"

The certainty in his voice was startling. "Who said it was from a lady?"

"The writing has that certain delicacy about it. Then, there's the daffodil-tinted paper. I can't see a man laying his pen to anything as flowery as that." He tapped his teaspoon against the cup as if enumerating the points. The rhythmic tinkle, though musical, jarred through Gordon's unhappiness.

"You have a talent for jumping to the wrong conclusions," he said as crushingly as he could.

Jack continued undeterred. "Above all, of course, the game's really given away by your lovesick expression. It is from a lady, isn't it? Come along, you may as well admit it. You never know, I might be able to give you some advice."

"Just mind your own bloody business."

He jumped from the table. "I'm going to work."

It was not yet eight o'clock and the air still had the nip of the mountains in it. A translucent haze lay on the glassy surface of the loch. Clear water lapped almost imperceptibly at the shingled shore, and an occasional silent ripple spread widely as drops of dewy moisture fell from the pale serrated leaves and the red berries of overhanging rowan trees. Above the shoulder of a rocky hillock, steam drifted from the distillery's pagoda top, then, mixing with peat reek, swirled away in fragrant wisps to the fading heather and feathery bracken.

They trudged the winding road in an uncompanionable silence, one slightly in front of the other, till Jack said, "What do you imagine will happen in Africa?"

Despite his agonised preoccupation with the bewildering contents of Anne's letter, Gordon was surprised enough to turn and stare at him. "In Africa?" His heart and his mind were in a foreign land, but one much nearer.

"Yes. With the Boers."

"I don't know. Why?"

"I just wondered if you thought it would come to war."

"How should I know?"

"Presumably you read the reports and form some opinion."

He hadn't read a newspaper since being banished to Lochbank, but he did not admit this.

"Lots of people seem to think it's inevitable," he said. He pretended to brighten, as if at a pleasant thought. "Is there some likelihood of your going out there if the worst happens?"

There was no reply, except the sound of the stone that a second or two later shot calculatedly close to his head and splashed into the loch, startling a heron from its stance in a patch of reeds and bullrushes.

Next morning, having asked McNair for the day off, Gordon reached Miss Frame's early and sat in a small alcove at one of the windows. It was not busy, and as he looked down the long room, he saw his first judgement of the place had been too harsh. Despite the shabbiness, a pleasant air was created by the smiles of the motherly waitresses and the floury smell of newly baked teabread. The unpretentious atmosphere soothed his uneasiness a little, but his first sight of Anne as she came through the rattling bead curtain at the top of the stairs shocked him into a state of anxiety that he had to struggle to conceal.

She was smartly dressed in a dark-blue suit with the pearl buttons of the three-quarter-length jacket continued down one side of the skirt. It was the bloodless pallor of her small face that held his aching gaze. Her skin was waxen on hollowed cheeks and her eyes flat and lifeless. Her wonderful hair, so burnished when she was well, had lost all vitality. The sinuously youthful sway of her body had gone, and she came round the tables toward him with the stilted walk of someone recovering from an accident.

He forced a smile and rose with a deliberate fussiness behind which his distress could hide. He took her gamp and hooked it over the back of a vacant chair. His heart shrank further when he saw the pathetic flicker that was all the response she could summon.

Until their waitress had departed, after bringing a large pot of tea, they spoke inconsequentially, their eyes meeting with a sad longing for the privacy and intimacy they craved but had not yet found. When he was sure they could not be overheard, Gordon said, "What's happened? I've been frantic since I got your letter. What went wrong in the nursing home?"

For the first time, her face became animated with an ugly hatred she seemed almost to have been waiting to unleash; that she had brought with her especially for him to see.

"It isn't a nursing home. It's a private asylum for rich lunatics. It's a place where people with money can get rid of awkward relatives without putting the stigma of the madhouse on them or on the family."

He raised a warning hand, not only to caution her about the indiscreet pitch of her voice but to stop the furious flow of words.

"I don't understand. What about Dr. Durande? He had been recommended to your father, hadn't he?"

"That's the most awful bit of it. Father must have known. He swears he didn't, but he isn't a fool. What it amounted to was that he was paying Durande to hold me prisoner."

She faced him with her eyes flaring, her appearance of instability more frightening than the previous deadness. She seemed to think that

261

in uttering the terrible accusation she was in some measure triumphing over the forces that encroached on her.

Gordon hesitated. For all he had heard of Dunbar he could not believe this of him.

"Why should your father do that to you, Anne? What had he to gain by it?"

Her face twisted in exasperation. "He's tired of me, that's why! I haven't been well for a long time. Men have no patience with illness. He was always at me to go back to Peter. Can't you remember my telling you that?"

"Yes, I do." He nodded emphatically, realising she was watching him as if even his loyalty were suspect.

"He wanted rid of me. I was a nuisance and a distraction from more important things. All he cares about is his precious whisky."

"But Durande gave you medicine that helped. You were quite hopeful about his treatment."

She seemed almost to grind her teeth. "Durande's a fiend. I don't believe he's a a doctor at all. Oh, Gordon"—she leaned toward him as if for protection from things that could not be seen—"I can hardly bear to think about him or his madhouse. But if I don't tell you, you'll think I'm raving."

"I won't think you're raving, but you must tell me."

"Well, the house is like a castle, and just as gloomy and forbidding. The moment Father left I was handed over to Miss Craig, the matron—a fat, cruel woman who's more like a jailer than a nurse."

She bowed her head and covered her eyes with her hands, but as he made embarrassed sounds of comfort, she recovered and went on. "She was my first shock. The second was that away from the more public part of the house, every door was locked. The stairs and corridors were cold and dark. The floors creaked and they didn't even have waxcloth on them. My room was tiny, like a cell, and the only furniture was a bed and a battered old chest. I don't know what the chest was for—they took all my clothes away and gave me a dress a scullery maid wouldn't have worn. But the really frightening thing was that they locked me in.

"There was a bell I could ring if I wanted anything, but they took hours to come. When the place quietened at night, I heard screams and cries coming from some far part of the house. When I looked out in the morning, I saw some of the windows were barred. If I hadn't been on the second floor, I would have smashed the window and run away there and then. Durande came to me that afternoon and and spoke to me for five or ten minutes. When I complained about the door being locked, he said it was necessary because patients with nervous disorders sometimes wandered and frightened other patients. It was best for everyone's sake that the rooms be kept locked. When I told him I wanted to go home, he said he had my father's authority to treat me and that I would soon settle. When I demanded to be allowed to write to Father, he reminded me I had agreed there would be no letters. Then I pleaded with him at least to give me some of the medicine I'd been taking before I went in, so that I could sleep. But he refused. He said he wanted to study me under normal conditions. Normal! In that place!"

"My God, Anne, it's no wonder you look ill. They've made you worse in there. Wasn't there any treatment?"

"Not for the first week, because I was supposed to be under observation. Oh, God"—she threw her head high and turned away so that her face could not be seen from the other tables—"when it did start it was hideous, but a lot happened before that. The food was almost inedible, and after two days with nothing I threw a plate of cold soup over the matron. After that they wouldn't answer the bell when I rang. I kicked and hammered at the door, and when that didn't bring anyone, I smashed the window. After that they moved me to a room with wooden shutters on the window. They wouldn't give me a lamp because they said I might set the place on fire, so I was in darkness except when Durande or the matron looked in."

He closed his eyes in a surge of helpless rage. "It's unbelievable! Monstrous! If I'd known, I'd have got you out of there if I'd had to tear the place apart."

"One day the matron and a nurse took me down to what they call the theatre. It's really just part of the cellar where there aren't any windows and no one can hear when you scream. The floor and the walls are tiled and there's a big sort of operating table in the middle of the room. They made me lie on it and then strapped my hands and feet. I thought they were going to murder me. It might have been better if they had. They"—she stopped as the waitress hovered over them for a moment to enquire if they wanted more tea—"they shaved my head, Gordon." She bit her lip to stifle a sob. "Here"—she put her hand up—"at the crown. There's a patch there now. I have to wear a hat all the time—even indoors."

He was shaking with anger. "What kind of treatment is that?"

"That wasn't the treatment. The treatment was much worse. After they had shaved my head, the matron brought an enamel bowl to the table and stuck it in front of me. I was almost sick when I looked inside. It was full of horrible, writhing things, like worms. They were about two inches long. She said they were leeches and they would suck the bad blood away from my brain. I screamed and struggled, but with my hands

263

and feet strapped it was useless. They put the awful things on my head and went away and left me. I cried and cried until I was too weak to make a sound. I turned and twisted to try and shake the things off. I could feel them moving, but it was even worse imagining them slithering about and boring into my brain. When the matron came back and took the slimy things off and showed them to me, I vomited. They were bloated with the blood they had sucked. My blood. I had to endure that every day. Can you imagine?"

"My darling, I can't. If it had helped you, it would have been bad enough, but at least you would have gone through it all to some purpose." He saw hysteria trembling in her again and hurriedly placed a reassuring hand on her arm. "Anne! Don't! Please don't. You had to tell me so that I would know what you've been through, but you mustn't dwell on it."

"Dwell on it!" she cried, as if amazed and resentful at his lack of feeling. "My God, how can I help dwelling on it? Wouldn't you dwell on it? Would you be able to put it out of your head as if it were nothing?"

"That's not what I meant."

Despite his efforts to calm her and her own awareness of where they were, people at the other tables were turning and staring.

"You don't know what I suffered, Gordon. If they had been trying to drive me mad, they couldn't have gone about it more cunningly. I can see now that's why Durande questioned me so closely. It wasn't to help me, it was to discover my weaknesses and worries, so that he could exploit them to destroy me. He's inhuman!"

If they had been alone in some private place where she could have given full rein to her distress, it would have been harrowing enough, but to watch her pouring out her agony in short, smothered bursts, mindful of the watchers, added a piercing bitterness to it that he could hardly bear. He had to quell a mounting urge to knock aside the table and take her in his arms, regardless of who saw or of what they thought. They should never have met in this restricting place. In her affliction she cried out for comfort and he could not give it. His life was inextricably mingled with hers, yet they had to sit there pretending, behaving like mere friends having an animated conversation.

The outward situation seemed to typify what was going on inside him. He was overpoweringly drawn to her, yet tormented by a nagging sense of disloyalty. A black tide of doubt was running through him. What was their future? In health, bleak enough, separated as they were by a bitter family feud and the demands of respectable society. But far greater than the unreasoning hatred that lay between their fathers, more implacable than all the social conventions or moral ordinances, was the terrible bur-

264

den nature had placed on the girl. For all his reluctance to face the grim truth, he was beginning to realise this. She could not live with her husband, or, it seemed now, with her father. Even if it could be accomplished, could she live with him? For how much longer could she even go on living with herself? He banished the poisonous thought and the vista of unbearable possibilities it suddenly threw open to his horrified gaze. She could be cured! Durande had been a disastrous mistake; a rogue, or, at best, a well-intentioned but dangerous meddler. But there were plenty of other doctors. Among them there must be a man who could lift the cloud from her. It shouldn't be so very difficult. She was still young. Life—the tragic loss of her mother, an unsuccessful marriage, a love that had to be practised in secret—had proved too much for her. The strains had worn down her defences. What she needed was a period of tranquillity during which she could recuperate—away from her father, away from a house that must be filled with painful memories of her mother and reminders of happier days. It was so simple. And so naive! He knew it even as the random thoughts raced through his mind.

"They even tried to drown me," she said.

As he stared at the worn beauty of her face, she retracted. "Well, not really, I suppose, but it seemed like that when it was going on. In another part of the cellar there was a sort of pit dug in the floor which they could fill with water. The first time they took me down there I thought it was for the usual treatment with the leeches. It was early in the morning and I was hardly awake. I was shivering in my nightdress and an old coat they had given me. I began to feel relieved when we passed the usual room, but almost immediately I became more scared than ever wondering where they were taking me and what they were going to do to me.

"They took me into a dimly lit room and told me to take my coat and nightdress off. If it had happened during my first few days in the place, I would have defied them, but after ten days there I knew the nurses would simply use force, so I did what they said. Then they took me to the far end of the room and for the first time I saw the pit filled with water. It was black and frightening. They told me it wasn't deep and that I was to jump into it.

"Of course, I was panic-stricken. I can't swim, and I couldn't bring myself to do it. I was convinced it was bottomless and that I would be sucked down into some underground river. I told them Mother had been drowned and that I was terrified of water. I pleaded with them. I begged them not to make me do it. I even promised them money. I pointed out that neither Durande nor the matron would know, but they were too afraid of losing their jobs. It seems incredible, but I realise now it's all just honest work to them. They spend their days torturing the poor people trapped in that awful place. I suppose as far as they are concerned, it's simply treatment prescribed by a doctor. The longer they carry it out, the more callous they become, until it won't mean much more to them than giving reluctant patients medicine by holding their noses to make them open their mouths.

"Of course, in the end they simply took hold of me and pushed me in. The water was freezing and the shock was terrible, I screamed and screamed. My mouth filled with water and I began to choke. I was demented at the thought that this was what had happened to Mother. Suddenly, I felt completely paralyzed and was convinced I was dying. Just then the nurses pulled me out. It was hours before I realised I had been standing on the bottom most of the time. The water didn't come as high as my shoulders."

Gordon felt bereft of sympathetic words. The phrases that came to his mind seemed too inadequate a match for the horror of her revelations. "You must be right about Durande," he said. "He can't be a proper doctor at all. It makes you wonder if he's even human. How could any doctor prescribe treatment like that for you when he knew your mother had been drowned, that you had actually seen it happen and had been plagued with nightmares ever since?"

He was surprised to see her summon a faint, wry smile. "Oh, he has an answer for everything. He said the whole idea of the water treatment was that the mind should be subjected to a shock that might act as a counter—a kind of antidote—to the shock that had originally disturbed it. Apparently all the patients receive this barbaric treatment.

"When I taxed and threatened him about it, he actually seemed quite proud of it. He had the nerve to say he was particularly pleased to be able to use it on me. As he saw it, the fact that Mother had been drowned was almost a bonus, since it would make the shock all the more fundamental with me."

Gordon put a hand to his head and leaned against it. The rage against Durande that had earlier energised him had exhausted itself. Now he merely felt baffled and weary.

"I'm so stupefied, Anne," he said, "I doubt if I'm taking in the full horror of all this. How often did they make you go into the water?"

"Every second morning. They came for me at five o'clock and took me straight out of bed. I dreaded it every bit as much as I did the leeches, and I was never able to sleep the night before. I just lay in the dark, waiting to hear their footsteps."

"And how did you get away from the place?"

"It was surprisingly easy. One afternoon when Durande was visiting me an awful commotion broke out in another room. It sounded as if one

266

of the nurses was being attacked. Durande went to help. He closed my door but forgot to lock it. I hardly hesitated for a second. While the row was still going on, I ran down the stairs and out the front door.

"Someone must have seen me crossing the lawn, for soon the warning bell began tolling. Within seconds there was a terrible racket and people seemed to be shouting from all directions. I could hear them crashing through the bushes behind me, but I had a good start. I just kept running and by luck came into the open at a spot where the boundary wall ended in a privet hedge. I was able to push my way through without very much difficulty and came out in a field full of cattle. Another hedge separated the field from the public road. I just followed it till I came to a gate. By the time I had climbed over it I couldn't have gone farther, but at the first corner I came to a woman who had just got out of a cab and was paying her fare. I jumped in and told the man to take me home."

"When you told your father all this, what happened? Did he go to see Durande?"

"He didn't have to. Late that same night, Durande arrived at our house. Father was in my room when Mrs. Prentice, our housekeeper, came to tell him. I insisted on going down. Durande was full of apologies for not being there earlier! His audacity is breathtaking. He said he had been delayed because the police had to be called after a patient attacked the matron.

"I was delighted to hear it was she and that she was quite seriously injured. Of course, I'm sure he was only using that as an excuse. He was late in arriving because it had taken him a long time to summon the courage. You see, if Father was in league with him, he would be angry that I had escaped. If he wasn't in league with him, he would be furious at the treatment I'd received. Either way, Durande had reason to be afraid of Father's reaction. But being such a barefaced scoundrel, he had finally decided it would look best if he faced the lion of his own free will."

Gordon felt a twinge of pity as he listened to the convoluted reasoning, delivered with quiet conviction.

"Father put on a great display of being furious with Durande, even threatening to report him to the police. But I think he was doing it for my benefit and to put himself in a good light. If he had really been serious, Durande wouldn't have taken it all so calmly—because that's what he did. He just sat there as cool as could be and said the treatment I'd been given was in line with the very latest theories about nervous ill-health and that it was being carried out in various countries by some of the world's leading specialists." Her manner became less certain, and for a moment or two she hesitated. "You know, Gordon," she said with be-

267

wilderment in her voice, "after a time I found I was almost believing him myself. And I could see Father had a baffled expression, but, of course, that could have been part of his pretence at innocence. . . ."

He interrupted almost pleadingly. "But don't you think, Anne, your father might have been quite genuinely taken in by Durande? After all, if the man's as plausible as you say. . . ."

He waited for her to be resentful again, but to his relief she merely looked perplexed and immensely vulnerable.

"To tell you the truth, Gordon, I don't know what to believe," she said desperately. "If I'm not mad already, I feel I'm being driven mad. Sometimes I'm prepared to believe Father did act for the best. And for a little while, as I've said, I even found myself doubting Durande's wickedness. He made it all sound so reasonable. He seemed to talk for hours, with his strange, hypnotic eyes holding my attention no matter how much I wanted to look away. Oh, he was masterly! Wheedling, specious, ingratiating—anything and everything that would confuse the situation. The human mind and nervous system are among the last unexplored regions on earth, he said. He painted a great picture of himself as some sort of hero, courageously venturing into places too dark and dangerous for the ordinary doctor.

"Some of the treatment might be considered drastic, he said, but so was the illness. He even had the audacity to ask me to go back with him and continue the treatment. When I saw Father was half in agreement, I almost fled from the house. If I had, I think I really would have thrown myself in the river." All at once her voice became calm and her expression almost reflective. "It's strange, isn't it, how that's the solution that keeps coming to me, despite the fact that water petrifies me? It repels me and lures me at the same time. At least, the thought of it lures me when I'm dejected, and yet the reality in the nursing home when they forced me into it was so dreadful, so evil, that I don't know how the certainty keeps coming to me that some day I'll follow Mother; that it's ordained and written down somewhere."

"Please, Anne. Don't speak like that. You mustn't. This is a passing thing. I'm sure of it. You'll be well again. You're needed and wanted. Malcolm needs you and I need you. *I love you.* These are the thoughts you must hold on to."

For the first time her features brightened into a reasonable semblance of the face he had first fallen in love with. Her smile had a tenderness in it that gave him hope.

"I know," she said in a voice of longing. "I must try. Oh, I want to, and I will try so that one day—"

"One day . . . what?"

She shook her head and narrowed her eyes as if striving after something infinitely elusive.

"I don't know. It was a glimpse of something, a picture of us together in a setting of wonderful peace, the sort of place you see in old paintings, something so fleeting it was gone before I could grasp it."

She had been staring past him as she tried to recapture and describe the fragile vision. When she turned to him again, there was in her eyes a light of inexpressible yearning.

"Do you think we'll ever be able to sit by a stream, Gordon, or under the shade of a tree in the happy way other people do? And not . . . and not feel hunted, or haunted?"

The gossamer moment she had created enveloped him in such a delicate magic he felt anything was attainable if his heart demanded it with enough insistence. He heard himself speaking phrases he had never before used in his life and whose content he would until recently have scorned.

"If we prayed for it, Anne, it could happen. If we prayed hard enough, everything would change for us."

He could not have explained what meaning the words had for him, but the earnestness with which he spoke them was undoubted.

"You really believe that," she said, as if struck by the wonder of his faith.

At that moment he could believe anything that made the future look less hostile. "I do. There's a way for us. There must be."

"Then perhaps I have taken the first step toward our happy land."

"Why, what have you done?"

"Father's been going on at me again to go back to Peter. Of course, I refused. In the first place, I couldn't bear it, not even for Malcolm's sake. In the second place, Peter probably wouldn't have me now. I have heard he has found other feminine company. Equally, I have no intention of staying with Father after what he did to me. So, I have taken the lease of a flat in West Regent Street. It's quite commodious and very well situated."

He felt a thrill of expectancy at the idea of her having a place where he could visit her. He was pleased, too, at this evidence that despite her ordeal and the apparent worsening of her condition, she had not lost interest in life. The comforting thought came to him that with Dunbar's blood in her veins, she would fight.

"You must have been busy," he said with an encouraging smile. "I mean, it's only a few days since you came home."

Her expression became almost eager. "It was all done on impulse. The first agent I called on had this particular flat on his books. The situation appealed to me immediately, and once I had inspected it, I didn't look at any others. Father says I was too impetuous, which is a strange accusation coming from him, but I know I wouldn't have found anything more suitable."

He still could not accept the dire suspicions she had of her father. He said, "Did you encounter much opposition?"

"Oddly enough, the opposition wasn't as fierce as I had expected." Her face wrinkled, as if by intense concentration she might solve a puzzle. "Father seems to have something else on his mind these days. Something very pleasant. He goes about singing to himself and seems more ready to listen to anything I have to say. He's altogether more tolerant. I'm beginning to think he has found a ladyfriend. Actually, the night I came home he had a woman in the house. She was supposed to be someone he was helping after a road accident, but looking back, I can see the expression of horrified guilt on his face when I surprised them."

Gordon had not thought of Dunbar as a lady's man. He was sure by the time he reached that age he would have got all that out of his system. He smiled faintly. "I don't suppose you mind what it is, so long as it softens him up."

Her cheeks, which had appeared almost transparent when she arrived, had taken on a delicate tint, strengthening his hopeful conviction that, freed of the unseen stresses that plagued her, she could be restored to health.

They sat watching the lunchtime surge of traffic and a newspaper seller waving placards headlining the news of another Boer raid in South Africa. A breeze swirled litter along the gutters.

The calm that had come to them seemed to have communicated itself to the rest of the room. They were no longer being watched so intently, and the old waitresses smiled again as they went past with their heavy trays.

17

Despite the distractions, longings, worries and separations that afflicted them, business and work went on as usual for the Kings. It was the way of life they all knew, and in it, in their various ways, they found uplift and release.

One night at dinner in the House of Commons, Robert learned that Princess Alexandra's fund for the aged, launched to collect fifty thousand pounds in commemoration of the queen's jubilee, had been disastrously undersubscribed. More than a year after the event less than twenty-five thousand pounds had been donated, and the princess faced humiliation.

His guest was Ian Hutt, who as chairman of Hutt Sons & Buist had introduced King's Royal to all the great houses of England. The company had long since been absorbed into the King empire. Hutt had retired from business and now, as Sir Ian, was lord mayor of London.

When he saw Robert's deepening interest, he withdrew slightly, for he was a circumspect man mellowed only a little by the Nuits-Saint-Georges.

"Needless to say, Robert, this is in the strictest confidence. The princess is desolate and His Royal Highness, as you might imagine, is furious."

"Not with Alexandra, surely?"

"Yes, I'm afraid so."

Robert tilted his head. "Disappointment at the poor response I can understand, but anger with her seems rather unreasonable."

Sir Ian lowered his voice. He did not trust this place. There were too many liberals in it. Even the food was undistinguished, these days.

"Despite his rather frivolous ways, Edward is an intensely practical man. And surprisingly sensitive to the public mood. He is well aware that the monarchy is in the doldrums. He knows it can't afford to have fiascoes. And I agree with him. Unfortunately, he blames Alexandra for having given her name to what has turned out to be an embarrassing failure. It's a damned unhappy business for both of them."

Robert had been a guest of the Prince of Wales on several occasions, having at last fulfilled one of Fergus's darkest apprehensions. He had even, during a boisterous night in Marlborough House, endured the pleasure of having a decanter of very pale old brandy poured over his head by the royal hand. His ear was well attuned to the malicious gossip of London, and he had little difficulty in imagining the gibes that would be directed at Edward when the inevitable revelation of his wife's debacle finally became public. That an antagonistic and often scurrilous press would report them he did not doubt.

He lit a cigar and drew on it thoughtfully. "But might not the donations pick up?"

Sir Ian finished his Clanrana liqueur and frowned into the empty glass. "There isn't the slightest chance of it. The dratted thing has lost all momentum. I'm chairman of the trustees and I had the unpleasant task yesterday of telling the dear lady that it's finished."

"It's damned unfair she should have to bear the brunt of it."

"Well, even her own view is that she has somehow been at fault. She's taking it personally." He shrugged and then smiled wryly. "I find her very lovable, and strangely vulnerable. She made no secret of what Edward feels." His thin clergyman's face puckered sadly. "But I'm afraid we're soon going to be forced into an announcement. You see, the money that has been collected must be disbursed. It's dragged on far too long. Some of the newspapers are already asking awkward questions. They scent something distasteful—which, of course, is the breath of life to them."

Next morning Robert wrote a cheque for twenty-five thousand pounds and sent it by messenger, along with a note addressed personally to Alexandra. His motives were complex and he made no effort to analyse them. Undoubtedly, sympathy for a lady he had liked immediately was a powerful factor. But he could not have denied that somewhere in the impulse his feeling for a good investment lurked beside his instinct for the beau geste. How benefit could accrue to him or to King & Co. from this particular gesture he could not imagine, especially since he asked in the note that his name be withheld. If it did, it would be a bonus, and one that might be a long time coming. He was, he thought as he left his flat to go down to his office, becoming uncommonly philosophical.

272

But the luck that had blessed all his ventures, that had so often baffled and even infuriated Fergus, was still in attendance, though on this occasion it advanced in a tortuous way.

A week after he made the gift a paragraph appeared in one of the newspapers. "Princess Alexandra's seemingly ill-fated jubilee fund," it said, "has been rescued at the eleventh hour by a mysterious donation of £25,000."

Next morning there were headlines in all the newspapers. "Who is the mystery man?" they asked.

All week it went on. Marlborough House kept aloof and silent, whetting the public interest and intensifying the probings of the more adventurous newspapers. Speculation was feverish, for the sum was vast and the mystery tantalising. The names of various well-known philanthropists were dangled, only to be followed by denials.

And then a report that left Robert stupefied appeared in the *Daily Sun* under the jubilant headline, SUN NAMES MYSTERY MAN:

Following a week of energetic investigation the Daily Sun can state that the benefactor who saved the Royal Jubilee Fund from disaster and Princess Alexandra from considerable personal mortification is a Scottish whisky millionaire. Because of his stipulation that the donation remain anonymous there can be no official confirmation of our discovery, but the generous tycoon is almost certainly Mr. Douglas Dunbar, proprietor of the famous Dunbar's Special Scotch Whisky.

The newspaper almost slid from Robert's trembling hands. Dazedly he read on.

Yesterday our correspondent in Glasgow traced Mr. Dunbar to his imposing mansion on the shores of the River Clyde. However, so self-effacing is this pillar of the Scotch Whisky trade that our correspondent had great difficulty in meeting him face-to-face. Even when Mr. Dunbar consented to see our correspondent he maintained an inscrutable discretion and reluctance. He would say little more than, "I do, of course, contribute to various charities but always anonymously. This is a pledge I have with myself and with them and I have no intention of breaking it now to satisfy vulgar curiosity." When our correspondent pressed for an answer to his questions Mr. Dunbar added, "My final answer to your question is that I am not telling you. I refuse to either confirm or deny your belief."

273

Robert's fury at last broke through his bewilderment. He rose, white-faced and cursing loudly, from the breakfast table and tore the newspaper to shreds, scattering the pieces about the room.

Dunbar's staggering nerve was matched only by his diabolical cunning. With hardly a word said that could be held against him he had drawn to himself the glory that was rightly Robert's—and at not a penny's cost.

But what, *what, what*, Robert agonised, could he do about it? He was trapped by his own stupid request for anonymity. In his mind he bitterly reconstructed the probable course of events that had led to the *Sun's* "scoop." He saw some venal—or possibly just foolishly self-important—official of the fund being seduced into revealing part of the truth to a persistent and persuasive journalist. The twenty-five thousand pounds had come from a Glasgow whisky millionaire. Wonderful! The newspaper's correspondent in Glasgow would have been unleashed immediately. His task would not have been a daunting one. There weren't so many possibilities. Whisky "millionaires" were rare. A few enquiries would produce two names: Robert King, Douglas Dunbar. Robert King was not in Glasgow to be interviewed. Very well, what had Mr. Douglas Dunbar to say? Could the correspondent or his editor be blamed for reading into Dunbar's quick-witted exploitation of the situation exactly the message Dunbar intended? What an unprincipled opportunist! And yet, even in his fury, Robert could not quite quell a faint stirring of admiration for such monumental gall. A second later he had recoiled from his contemplation of Dunbar's warped brilliance and thrown himself into an armchair in a ferment of corrosive self-pity. A picture came to him of his adversary, strutting jauntily through an admiring Glasgow, displaying himself to the business community in White's Chop House with his hat tipped cockily and his thumbs tucked in his waistcoat pockets. Like a child he buried his face in the upholstery to blot out the unbearable scene.

And then he heard the wild recriminations of all the other Kings. Oh, they wouldn't miss him! The invective would be murderous, for they had been disapproving from the start. Fiona's letter, when he told them what he had done, had expressed surprise and an unmistakable resentment at the lack of consultation. Fergus, the pages of his passionate letter sprayed and blobbed with ink in a way that suggested an infuriated use of the pen, had clearly been aghast. He had concluded with a wounding accusation that Robert had used company money to further his own trumpery social ambitions. How, now, could he ever explain the tangle of impulses that had made him issue the blasted cheque? He could no longer even justify them to himself. At best he had been recklessly soft-hearted and that, he saw with a flash of painful insight, was altogether far too sympathetic an interpretation. He had gone galloping with more gallantry than sense to the rescue of his future queen—a reckless white knight lured from the narrow path of commercial prudence. And for his pains, as Fergus might have said, he had come up covered in mud—a pathetic sight. For a long time he cringed in his chair before going down to the day's work. The thought of that night's debate in the House, for which he had some well-cut aphorisms prepared, filled him now with disinterest.

In Glasgow the storm burst first from Fergus as he hurried wide-eyed into Fiona's room and excitedly dropped a copy of the *Daily Sun* on her desk, almost knocking over a posy bowl.

"Grandfather!" she reproached him as she reached for the scattered blooms.

"Never mind your flowers, my dear," he spluttered. "Just read that." He jabbed at the newspaper. "God help me," he moaned as she stared at the report in frozen disbelief. "I never thought to see the day when King and Company would spend twenty-five thousand pounds to turn its sworn enemy into a public hero."

He went to a side table and with shaking hands poured himself a drink, dribbling sherry all over the silver tray in his agitation, and then banging the decanter down. He swallowed the wine in an angry gulp.

"I knew no good would come from Robert's besotted interest in royalty. Dear knows! My own son responsible for a situation that allows Douglas Dunbar to pose as a public benefactor—*with our money!*"

He stopped to stare at her with a puzzled frown. "Haven't you anything to say, my dear? It's all very well being loyal to Robert, but you can hardly deny his idiotic efforts at social advancement have become too damned expensive, and made fools of us all besides."

She rose slowly, struggling with the bewildered fury that hung like a muffling blanket between her and almost everything he had said. Methodically she crumpled the newspaper and threw it to the floor with a gesture half vicious, half petulant. *Douglas!* A wave of vexation rose to mist her eyes as his name rang out in the bemused recesses of her mind. How could he do such a thing to her? Everything people said about him was true. Shallow, unprincipled, treacherous—she could see it all now. He had proved the case against himself by this violation of her trust. She closed her eyes in an agony of shame. She had given him her love, almost thrown herself at him. A smothering sense of humiliation engulfed her as she remembered all the passion and tenderness she had lavished on him in their hour together the previous day. He had seemed so affectionate, so genuinely loving, and yet he must have come to her straight

275

from this barefaced interview with the *Sun*. Such behaviour was incomprehensible to her. The acclaim rightly belonged to King & Co. If he loved her, how could he so coolly divert it to himself? In no circumstance could she have acted in such a way against him.

"It's scandalous," she said, bitterly.

"Dreadful," Fergus agreed, with emphasis.

"I don't understand him."

"It's easy enough to understand, my dear. He was out to get a clap on the back from this libertine Bertie. Perhaps an invitation to spend Christmas at Sandringham." He snorted. "Now it's all gone wrong."

"Not Robert!" she said loudly, stifling her tears, shaking her head impatiently. "Douglas Dunbar. What a low trick to play."

Fergus grimaced. His eyes, in which the blue seemed recently to have faded, became fixed and introspective. "Robert's the one I'm angry with. Dunbar was simply clever enough to see an opening and jump in."

She turned on him irritably, detecting in the words the faint admiration of one campaigner for another.

"Really, Grandfather! I don't think you should be making excuses for Douglas Dunbar."

"Maybe not." Fergus walked bleakly to the door. "Anyway, I'm having nothing to do with it. It's Robert's shambles. But later, I'll make it my business to see he refunds every penny of that money to the company out of his private resources."

When he had gone, Fiona sank down despondently at her desk. Her anger had subsided into a stifling self-pity. She could mean little to him. Well, better to have had her eyes opened to that now, however painfully, before the situation became irretrievable.

She'd had a month of glorious madness. And madness it had certainly been. Sometimes she had hardly been able to believe it was really happening, that she was really doing it. When, in quiet moments, she had allowed herself to consider the possibilities, she had been appalled. But the spell had been so overpowering she hadn't even tried to break it. She had been in total thrall to him, a pitiful prisoner of her own carnality. Well, now he had set her free. It was probably the best thing that could have happened. They had arranged to meet at the flat in the early afternoon, but she would not be there. She would never be there again.

She clung to her decision despite the pictures of him that came to torment and lure her as she picked without interest at the luncheon tray that was brought to her desk.

Fergus, passing her open door, stopped in surprise. "Aren't you going out, Fiona?"

"No. There's rather a lot to be seen to." She managed a grim smile.

She worked steadily through the afternoon and at five o'clock sent a boy to the steeple to fetch a cab. Shortly afterward she was in Trongate, in a stream of west-moving traffic. If she had met him as arranged, she would probably have been leaving the flat at about this time to walk home through the park. Despite herself, regret rose, and her blood stirred as she pictured the afternoon lost.

She lowered the window and looked out impatiently into the street. It was congested with handcarts and delivery lorries returning to their quarters for the night. It was an hour when she usually managed to avoid travelling in the city. In her emotional state the crawl to which the cab was reduced was especially irksome. After the hours of heart-searching she felt drained and worn. She was desperately anxious to be safely behind her own walls, among familiar things. As she sank back with a frustrated sigh, the door opened and Dunbar jumped in.

Her eyes widened and her heart thumped wildly but she could not speak.

"What happened, Fiona?" His voice was concerned but wary.

She moved violently away from him with a little cry that might have been of horror. "I don't want to speak to you."

"But I must speak to you. Why didn't you come to the flat this afternoon?"

He was sitting on a corner of her skirt and she tugged it from under him before answering. "You know perfectly well why."

"If it's this business about the damned jubilee fund—"

"I don't want to speak to you, Douglas." She was aware of a faint note of hysteria. "Please go."

"I want to explain."

She moved her hand as he reached for it. "There can be no acceptable explanation."

"You can at least listen. I've been sitting in a cab at the end of Seabank Lane for hours, waiting for you to come out. Come with me to the flat, where we can have some privacy."

"Certainly not!"

His eyes hardened. "I'm going to sit here until you agree."

"Please! Someone could see us." She twisted her gloves, and her eyes, which had been forbidding, were now almost pleading. "We're going through the busiest part of the city. Have you no thought for me?"

He became very still. "I think of you night and day. Sometimes I yearn for you so much I can't sleep or work."

There was such feeling in his voice that for a moment she almost responded. She had to force coldness into her reply.

"Yesterday I could have believed that."

"You must believe it today."

"I will not."

277

He shrugged and leaned back in his corner, folding his arms.

She reached for the door. "I'll get out and walk."

He sat up with a slight smile that deepened her sense of helplessness. "Yes, a walk would be rather pleasant. I'll accompany you."

She clasped her hands and bowed her head submissively. "You blackmailed me like this once before, Douglas." If she had hoped to wring sympathy from him or to shame him, she was disappointed. She tried again. "My children are expecting me."

"We must speak," he said, his voice roughening for the first time. "And we can't do it here. Your children are not infants. They must know you are a woman of affairs who could be detained for many reasons."

"How cruel you can be."

She let him give the driver new instructions. She left the cab near the flat and went to it while he drove to another street and then walked back.

When he arrived, she was standing in the hall, still holding her handbag—an indication, she hoped, that her stay would be brief and formal. He observed the signs and walked round her to the cupboard where he had put his stock of bottles.

She shook her head coldly to his invitation. "I am here at your insistence simply to hear whatever explanation you have to offer for that disgraceful report in the *Daily Sun*."

His smile was nervous and evasive. "My darling, don't you think you're taking it too seriously?"

"It is serious when you steal the credit for a fortune that King and Company—or my husband, it doesn't matter which—donated to charity. In fact, it's despicable."

"I didn't say I had donated the money."

"No, but you might as well have." She struggled with the intensity of her distress. "Anyway, it's not the money I'm concerned about. It's what this incident reveals about you, Douglas . . . about us. You must have known that in giving that twisted interview you were striking at me."

"No!" The cry came as if torn from him. His eyes were darkly scandalised. They held her gaze so unwaveringly that she did not notice his hands until they had folded themselves round her own. "Won't you believe me, Fiona, when I tell you I didn't think of you at all when that newspaperman came to see me? All I saw was a man I don't like, and a chance to get at him. All I thought of was King and Company."

Her subsiding temper flared again and she pulled her hands away. "I *am* King and Company now more than Robert is. If you strike at King and Company you strike at me—not him. You must have known that. You just didn't care."

"You don't realise how much I care, Fiona. If I had known you would

278

be so hurt, I swear I wouldn't have said what I did." His eyes closed in the fervour of his search for words to placate her. "I just can't see you as part of that crowd, but I'll admit I should have. I'm sorry."

The last word came oddly from him, she realised, not because he was being insincere but because he meant it. She wondered when he had last been able to bring himself to use it. That he *had* used it meant a lot. At least he wasn't being defiant or trying to browbeat her into an acceptance of his behaviour, as he once would have done.

"I'm going to London soon," she heard him say. "Why don't you come with me?"

She tried not to show that suddenly all her resentment had gone. "I daren't." Even that, she thought, was too great a concession.

"If you loved me, you would come."

Her head came up. "*If* I loved you?" Her eyes flashed with a wild variety of emotions. "My God, Douglas, how can you doubt it? Don't you know what I'm risking for you? Have you ever really thought about it? Husband, children, respectability—even the challenge of running King and Company—I'll lose them all, I'll be an outcast if what I've been doing becomes known."

To have catalogued it while standing there in a drab hall surrounded by someone else's ugly furniture made her realise again the desperate illegality of the feelings he had kindled in her. He had induced in her an abandon matched only by his own tempestuousness. Momentarily, she shuddered for her future, and then he was leading her away again in the sensuous dance that only a few hours ago she had sworn to end.

"We *must* get away together, Fiona. This place is all right, but it's too restricting, and you're always having to rush home. I want to sleep with you, darling. Really sleep with you—to wake in the morning and find you beside me. I want to breathe good fresh air with you and see the sky with you, other than through these dusty windows. I'd like to walk down a lane holding your hand without being ready to turn and run if someone appears on the horizon."

He stopped and looked at her with a shamefaced boyish grin, as if half embarrassed. Her eyes were closed and when she opened them their expression was wistful.

"Those are lovely pictures, Douglas, but you're only dreaming. It wouldn't matter where we went or what hotel we stayed in or what cottage we rented, we would always be afraid of being recognised if we tried to behave normally for even a few days. At any rate, I would. We would have to find a desert island."

He took her into his arms, sensing the crisis had passed. "Then I'll *find* a desert island. Meantime, we'll have to make the best of this little nest, poor as it is."

279

She let him kiss her without protest and her resistance was gone as he lifted her. "Am I forgiven?"

She replied by sinking her teeth into his ear and keeping them there until she was certain his howl of pain was genuine.

Next afternoon Robert was sitting unhappily at his desk when the office manager came into his room. He held an envelope and spoke excitedly.

"A message, Mr. King, from the residence of His Royal Highness, the Prince of Wales."

Then he stood bent slightly forward with an expectant expression on his white face as if hopeful that this gold-crested communication might be the means of restoring the harmony lost since Dunbar had stolen Robert's thunder.

The single sentence, written by Edward's personal secretary, asked Robert to call at Marlborough House at his earliest convenience. Smiling for the first time in days, he hurried upstairs to his apartment, changed into his most formal clothes, and within thirty minutes was in the secretarial suite at the big red brick house that Wren had built at the western end of Pall Mall for the first Duke of Marlborough almost two hundred years before. He was given tea which he could hardly drink for excitement, and fifteen minutes later was taken to where the prince waited in a sitting-room overlooking the rose garden.

Compared to more public parts of the house, which were dominated by crystal chandeliers and French furniture laden with ormulu, this room was restrained and mellow almost to homeliness. The tables and chests were of faded mahogany made by English craftsmen during the previous century.

As he crossed the room a floorboard creaked reassuringly and the drops on a wall sconce tinkled musically in the air from an open window. Here, Fergus could have been comfortable. The thought was not irrelevant, for Edward's imposing girth always reminded Robert of his father. It was a resemblance he found useful for keeping his awe under control. His nerves were further calmed by the prince's informal appearance. The slight flamboyance that distinguished him on public—and even on social—occasions was today entirely absent. He wore a green suit of very heavy tweed. His trousers were baggy at the knees and his boots dusty.

"I've been doing a little gardening," he said with a twinkle, noting Robert's furtive inspection. "We like to give some time to the roses ourselves. Come and look at this."

Robert followed him to the open window.

"Have you ever seen such a blaze of colour? This year our efforts have

280

been well rewarded. Some of the newer varieties have done exceptionally well." He gave Robert an interested look. "Are you a gardener, Mr. King?"

"A very infrequent amateur, sir. On the Gareloch, where we have a house, we specialise in rhododendrons and azaleas. Even magnolia and camellia do well, but your roses, I'm afraid, put ours to shame."

Edward looked pleased. He nodded toward a group of colourfully dressed women seated in an arbour. Their voices carried gently through the leaves fluttering against the sun. "You will recognise my wife, of course. We will go down to her before you leave, but first I wanted to see you alone."

He crossed to a table and lifted a copy of the *Daily Sun*. "You'll have seen this damned nonsense, I suppose?"

"Yes, sir. I saw it."

Above the pointed beard the blue eyes were watching him closely. "Well, what do you think of it?"

"I can only hope their other reports are more accurate."

Edward laughed. "That's far too restrained a response. But then, the Scots are noted for their canniness." His eyes hardened and he pulled tetchily at his carefully trimmed moustache. "It's a damned poor return for your generosity, and I'm not going to allow it. It was bad enough, their speculating, but when they start giving the credit to the wrong man"—he shook his head determinedly—"it's too unfair. I'm not going to have it. My wife and I were very distressed when it was shown to us."

A sense of vindication, almost of triumph, began to rise in Robert. "Well, I did ask not to be named," he said moderately.

Edward's mobile features became openly admiring. "Of course you did, and I understand and respect the motives behind such a request. Apart from personal fastidiousness there's the practical consideration of being plagued by every other charity in the land if you become known for such munificence."

He sank down abruptly into a brocade-covered armchair and pointed to another for Robert. His gardening boots were incongruous on the silk Persian rug. He clasped his hands over the bulging tweed and seemed to inspect Robert's sober propriety.

"But, Mr. King, we must put this thing properly to rest. My wife and I are deeply indebted to you. Without going into the details, for I'm sure you know them as well as I do, you rescued us from a very embarrassing situation." He thumped the arm of his chair and his voice rose. "I won't have you cheated of the credit." He looked angrily about the room. "If I ever discover how all this got out, there'll be trouble for someone. But apart from that, this nonsense about this other fellow—what's his name?—Dunbar, still leaves the matter open enough for anyone who

281

prefers to leave it open. Do you know, it's even being said in some quarters that I put the money in myself to save face? This"—he pointed to the *Daily Sun*—"won't have extinguished that particular story. No, the only satisfactory thing now is for you to admit you made the donation. Will you authorise the fund to issue a statement?"

Robert felt that some show of continuing reluctance was only seemly.

"It's not what I wanted," he said hesitantly.

Edward took the protest lightly. "Of course it's not. But, surely, as things have worked out, there is no other way. After all, there's nothing shameful about giving money to charity. Now, have I your permission?"

Robert submitted with a resigned smile and a slight bow. "If Your Royal Highness thinks it the best thing to do."

Edward left his chair with surprising nimbleness. "Good. My secretary will attend to it. Now, before we go down to the garden I have something to tell you that may be more pleasing. We dined in the palace with Her Majesty last night. In her sitting room she treated us to some of your very excellent Queen's Royal. I am happy to tell you that particular tribute caught her imagination and gave her more pleasure than most of the pomp and ceremony that went on all last year. She is a great admirer of everything Scottish."

Robert's heart soared. "I am delighted to know that, sir."

"Has it been a successful enterprise? You must have put a lot of money at risk."

"The response has been very good."

"Would my patronage help it along, do you think?"

"Oh, without a doubt."

"Then in future I will ask for it wherever I go. It may serve in some little way to repay our debt to you."

Next morning Robert's reward burst across the pages of all the English and Scottish newspapers. Most of them, taking a perverse delight in refuting the upstart *Daily Sun*'s "irresponsible revelations," gave even more space to the affair than they might otherwise have done. In twenty-four hours he was transformed from a mystery man into a national hero. Special writers came to his flat, to his office and to the library of the House of Commons to interview him. His philanthropy was not enough for them: his riches had to be explained; his inventing of blended whisky and the remarkable triumph of Queen's Royal, his secret blend of rare old whiskies which in less than a year had become the envy and inspiration of every whisky company in the land.

If he had written the articles himself, he would not have dared use the words Queen's Royal half as often. The effect was magical. An endless convoy of laden carts trundled out of the courtyard behind the depot in St. James's. In two days the warehouse was empty. From every part of the country, agents and wholesalers telegraphed for supplies.

At the end of the week Robert put a thick wad of newspaper cuttings into an envelope and sent them to Glasgow with a succinct note to Fergus. "At present rates the enclosed advertising would have cost us upwards of fifty thousand pounds. The advantage to our sales will be continuing and incalculable."

A few days later a wooden case containing a dozen bottles of Queen's Royal lay in a corner of Douglas Dunbar's office. Dunbar himself sat at his big table, staring malevolently at a card that read, For services rendered.

18

The routine of Fiona's previous life—the family evenings, the weekly visits to Rita and Fergus, the letters and reports placed on her desk—had taken second place to her passion for Douglas Dunbar. Against her consuming ardour for him everything else was now measured, and to it all her other responsibilities were subordinated.

She was gripped by a restless desire to see him as often as possible. With hardly a qualm she broke important appointments to be with him, brazenly lying her way out of any resulting awkwardness. It was not uncommon for dinner at Claremont Row to be spoiled or eaten without her as she snatched a few fevered hours with him at the end of a day in which—even with her new recklessness—she had found it impossible to desert King & Co.

Intellectually she saw the upheaval that had taken place in her, but emotionally she could not resist it. She took comfort from the fact that despite her constant preoccupation with Dunbar, the outward form of her other relationships had subtly improved.

Where before she might have been irritated at some thoughtless remark by Ross or one of the children, she now took care not to be. This was not difficult, for her natural tolerance and affection seemed to have deepened. Her love for Dunbar overflowed in many directions. What Douglas had inspired in her was benign and beautiful, she told herself. It had not even diluted the considerable feeling she still had for Robert. Only once, in a brief moment of insight, did she wonder if she might not be compensating for her infidelity. Was the increased sunniness of a nature always noted for its warmth merely a distorted form of guilt? The tangled thought soon drifted away in the beguiling prospect of another afternoon in the flat, which she was almost beginning to think of as her real home. Only there, it seemed, could she behave completely naturally, without continually guarding her tongue. Even her expression must be controlled, for twice she had caught Ross glancing at her curiously as she sat at her desk thinking of Dunbar. Only behind the green door with its tarnished brass handle and name plate could she find the physical and emotional fulfillment that had become indispensable to the stability of her daily existence.

In this drugged state her days went by, the rhythm alternating from the dreamy expectation of his company to the fevered reality of their stolen hours.

Whatever she was doing, thoughts of him distracted her. He had first call on her mind and on her imagination. She wanted constantly to see and touch him, and on days when they could not meet she had to seek substitutes for his presence. She would go into the city and buy a gift for him. It was as if by means of cuff links or a cravat pin a mystical link were established.

But it was only after he left for a three-week business visit to London—still begging her to accompany him—that she discovered the full depth of her craving. Denied his presence, robbed of the customary knowledge that even when she could not see him he was near, she found the hours leaden. They dragged vacantly as she sat reading to the children or listening to Florence play some of her favourite music. Even the affairs of King & Co. failed to satisfy. In her more philosophical moments she pondered how incredible it was that the routine of a life so recently content should have become intolerable because a man she had not known a few months ago was four hundred miles away. At nights, when she could not sleep, she repeated his name as if the sounding of it would somehow unite them, like the cuff links or cravat pin. But the gulf was far too great. She had asked him to write, and then, seeing his surprised and wary expression, had said no, he mustn't, it was silly of her even to suggest it. It was one of the things they had agreed not to do. Instead, she tried to construct her own letters from him, imagining how he would describe the ache of this first parting, selecting the words she felt he might choose to tell her of his love.

Partly to fill the void, partly to atone for her neglect, in the evenings she took the children out to dine, or to a carnival, an opera, an exhibition, a recital, a concert, until she realised that in Florence, at least, all this attention, all the capsizing of accustomed behaviour, was arousing an enquiring wonder amounting almost to suspicion. She parried the girl's probing questions, ignored her puzzled surveillance and quickly allowed the hectic round to subside into normality.

Somehow time passed.

She knew the day and the hour of Dunbar's return and was in the flat waiting for him as they had arranged. He looked irresistibly attractive to her in his well-cut travelling clothes of grey tweed. In his absence she seemed to have seen only dull men in dark businesswear, and beside these he had the exciting look of a soldier or an explorer, an adventurer of some kind. She realised that despite everything he was still a foreigner to her, a man from a world that had never been hers. Could it ever really be her world? The darkness of his skin enhanced the faint air of exotic mystery. The ways of Glasgow and of respectable commerce seemed merely to have been uneasily superimposed on him. Beneath the whisky baron there still lurked, she knew, a creature not quite tame or domesticated. She could see it in his gaze, imperious yet watchful; in his walk, confident but slightly menacing. It was all as familiar to her now as the characteristics of any of her own children.

"How I missed you," she said as they lay contentedly together, her longing for him assuaged at last.

He ran his fingertips lightly through her hair. "You could have been with me. You must come next time."

She smiled, but her tone was stubborn. "No, I still have some discretion left. You must find that desert island."

"Don't think I haven't." He laughed at her surprise. "A thought came to me when I was away. There is a place where we could be completely alone and surrounded by water."

"Where?" She watched him sceptically, half suspecting he was elaborating one of his jokes.

"On a boat. We could go sailing for a week or two in the Western Isles. Early September is often the best time of the summer in the Hebrides. Could you make an excuse to get away?"

Her interest had risen, but now it sank back. "A boat would be no different from a hotel, Douglas. It could even be worse. If there was anyone on board who knew either of us, there would be no escape."

"I don't mean a passenger ship. I mean we should literally go sailing, just the two of us, on a yacht."

Her face brightened again, and then she shook her head. "It's a romantic thought, but I'd be afraid that somehow or other something might get out through the crew."

His voice rose and she felt him brace himself in a familiar gesture of impatience. "My God, aren't you listening to what I'm saying, Fiona? There wouldn't *be* a crew. There would be the two of us and no one else. I would sail the damned boat myself."

The claim surprised her, for he had never talked of sailing.

"I don't want to go to a watery grave, even with you beside me." She

286

could have bitten her tongue as she remembered how his wife had died, but he seemed unperturbed.

"I wouldn't ask you to. You would be quite safe."

"Can you really sail a boat?"

Her insistence stung him to boastfulness.

"Of course I can. And for your information I can ride, run, box and swim with the best of them. I have climbed high mountains and when I was younger I could kick a football hard enough to tear a hole in the net."

"You lovely, modest man!" She lay back with a gurgling laugh. "Douglas, you're wonderful! Your humility is irresistible. I adore it."

"I'm only speaking the truth."

He grinned and attuned to her mood, lapsing gradually into the skittishness that had surprised her so much the first time she heard it. "You love me," he told her, reverting, she suspected, to the playful talk of some previous affair, perhaps even of his marriage.

"And you love me," she said, taking his hand and kissing it and then pressing it to her breast. "I mean so much to you."

His eyes closed. "I want to sleep," he murmured. "Just for a little while. Will you stay till I waken?"

She looked to the table where his watch lay. "The children will be—" And then she remembered how in the last weeks she had yearned for him. She kissed his eyes. "Go to sleep, my tired giant. I'll watch over you."

He tackled the holiday as if it were a military adventure, baffling her with Gaelic names, admiralty charts and *Glasgow Herald* weather predictions, which previously he had always scorned. After a week of energetic planning and enquiring he selected the West Highland resort of Oban, on the Argyllshire coast, as their port of departure.

This fishing and holiday town ninety miles northwest of Glasgow not only lay close to the Inner Hebrides but was a noted summer haven for yachtsmen. Dunbar knew from other holidays that even so late in the season there would be dozens of small boats moored in the bay. Through the secretary of the local sailing club he found one available for charter, but mindful of Fiona's preoccupation with secrecy, he left his solicitor to negotiate with the owner and sign the contract.

"Everything's arranged," he told her jubilantly a few days later. "Have you made your excuses?"

Her keenness for the adventure had waned a little in the welter of elaborate lies she had told Ross and Fergus the previous afternoon. She was also troubled at the conscienceless way she had arranged for Florence, Steven and Allan to be boarded with Rita. But now, under the spell of his infectious zeal, she responded cheerfully.

"I just said I'm going to visit some of the Speyside distilleries to discuss discounts."

He smiled reflectively. "That should appeal to the skinflint in old Fergus."

Having to listen to even occasional snide remarks about the Kings filled Fiona with a depressing sense of disloyalty. He was sensitive enough to know these gibes caused her pain but too bitter to be able to stifle them. Now, regretting the shadow he had cast, he retracted. "Just pretend I didn't say that."

He hurried on to soothe her with an account of the discreet way he had hired the yacht.

"We don't even need to travel together to Oban," he said. "We could sit in different compartments of the same train, of course, but I have a better idea."

Two companies ran trains to Oban, taking different routes out of Glasgow before converging on a mutual line some forty miles farther north. It was decided that Dunbar would travel London, Midland and Scottish, while Fiona would take the more scenic London and North Eastern way.

It was evening when she arrived in Oban, and they went like conspirators through dark streets to a dinghy tied to a wooden jetty. She could smell fresh fish and seaweed, and the perfume of burning oak chips still hung about the nearby curing sheds.

Claremont Row seemed to belong to another world, and to another woman. "I feel like a pirate or a smuggler," she whispered.

"You look much more like a princess," he said as he untied the mooring rope. He held out his hand. "Careful how you step."

He pushed the dinghy into the darkness of the bay and pulled lightly on the oars.

The night was filled with sounds—creaking timbers, lapping water, the cry of disturbed seagulls—that brought memories to her of distant days on the Gareloch. All about them, mast lights rose and fell. She had a vague sense of houses rising in terraces to the sky and, in another direction, of mountains and open sea.

It was next morning before she had any clear picture of the boat. It was a thirty-foot carvel-built ketch of a kind her father had once sailed on the firth of Clyde.

"It's a fair size," she said doubtfully, shielding her eyes to look up at the two masts.

He caught her expression and laughed. "Wait till you see it with the sails up. We could sail the Atlantic in this." He put an arm round her and pulled her close. "How would that appeal to you? We need never come back."

The still, sunlit air, the feeling of freedom, the beauty of the setting—already they were all affecting her strongly. "I'd prefer the South Seas. The Atlantic can be terribly cold."

"Have you brought your grass skirt?"

She raised her face appreciatively to the sun. "I should have. It's going to be hot enough for one." She threw herself impulsively onto the deck and dangled her hand in the water. "How perfect everything is. I've never known air so soft and clean or seen water with so many wonderful colours."

"It's the magic of the Hebrides," he said with a pleased smile, her enchantment bringing on his proprietorial manner. "But this is nothing. Wait till we reach the islands."

The heather was smoky purple on the hills of Morven as they left Kerrera behind and moved gently into the firth of Lorne. Peat smoke from crofting cottages drifted over the island of Lismore, and from among the rocks in a placid inlet a heron watched them pass.

Dunbar handled the boat with skill, explaining each move to her. The years fell away again as she heard the once-familiar phrases. Luffing, bearing away, wind abeam—they all came back so vividly she could almost picture occasions long forgotten.

The ketch had three sails—jib, main and mizzen—and the leisurely flap of the canvas was mesmeric. It added to her sense of having been transported not just to another part of her own country but to another world.

"I used to be quite good at tacking," she told him dreamily, idly dipping her hand in the sea and wetting her face and arms to speed the suntan that suited her so well. She had expected him to fret at the lack of wind, but the pervasive peace had soothed away even his ingrained impatience. He was content to let the mild breeze drift them along, his huge frame overflowing from the cramped cockpit. Once, when she asked the time, he took his pipe from his mouth and looked reproving.

"Out here time doesn't exist," he said. "The sun rises and sets. That's all. What matters is that we've got almost two weeks together, and we needn't see or speak to another soul if we don't want to."

289

"Do you think you could forget about eating, too?" she asked hopefully. "I don't know how I'll manage on that little cooking stove."

"Now's the time to find out." He put out a bare foot and pointed her
gently toward the galley with it. "I'm hungry. I put up with a slice of
bread and butter for breakfast, but you're not going to get off as lightly
as that all the time."

By afternoon, as they slid past Duart Castle on its isolated cliff on the
isle of Mull, her feeling of detachment was complete. This balmy voyage
might have been the only life, and Dunbar the only man, she had ever
known. Her skin tingled with health, her lungs felt clean and her mind
tiptoed in wonder across a vast plateau of content as scenes of ever-
increasing beauty unfolded.

The course he steered was inshore, giving them close glimpses of eme-
rald water breaking gently on white sand, of waterfalls splashing down
boulder-strewn mountain slopes and of wild flowers speckling tough,
sea-washed grass.

She had come, despite his optimistic predictions, prepared for cold
and rain or at the least for a buffeting from bracing winds. The unexpectedly drowsy, almost droning charm of their poetic progress had induced in her an expectant happiness not known since childhood. It
seemed that within a few hours they had ceased to be the two serious
business people who drove stiffly about Glasgow in formal carriages in
an endless quest for more and more money.

She had changed from a heavy, sensible dress into a flowery summer
skirt and sleeveless blouse. He, stripped to the waist, his face free of its
dark city strains, seemed almost to have stepped from one generation
into another—even, she thought, as she lay back and watched his deft
handling of the ketch, from another age.

In the early evening they rowed the dinghy into a sandy cove near
Craignure and set up camp with pots and pans, a hamper of food and a
bottle of wine. They laughed, ran, sang and made love in the gloaming,
but later, as they lay wrapped in blankets by a fire of driftwood—the
ketch anchored in a lagoon made silvery by the stars—a sudden, almost
physical coldness touched Fiona.

He felt her shiver and misunderstood. "We could sleep in the boat if
you would prefer it," he said. "It would be warmer."

"It's not that, Douglas. I'm really quite warm."

There was a catch in her voice that made him look at her anxiously,
turning back the blankets to let the fire light her face.

"Then what is it?"

"I don't know. For a moment I felt . . . almost frightened."

Despite her seriousness, he tried to make a joke of it. "Frightened?
With me here?"

She tightened her grip on him and pressed her face to his chest to hide a tear she felt trickling down the side of her nose.

"It's too perfect, Douglas," she said in an inexplicable rush of panic. "Too perfect."

He kissed her. "My silly darling."

"And all day I've been so wonderfully happy."

"You're a funny thing," he said gently. "But tomorrow you'll be even happier."

"Yes. I'm sorry to be so foolish."

A log fell in the fire, and when she looked about, the cove was cosy with the fire's glow flickering on the encircling rocks and sheltering trees. The exact impact of the passing fear was already too elusive to be recalled. A few minutes later she was asleep, and next morning it was as if the shadow had never been.

Sunlit days passed into nights of undisturbed content, some of them spent under the sky, if they found a suitable shore, others with them boxed up separately, and less comfortably, belowdecks in the ketch.

As the miraculous succession of burnished days and ardent nights continued, Fiona became convinced their holiday had been blessed. She could almost see it as some kind of Providential approval, a sign that what she was doing was not wrong, that love sanctified her actions. Their happiness, their good luck, could not easily be explained in any other way.

Nothing came to disturb the ecstatic mood. The same warm breeze that had wafted them gently out of Oban Bay took them on a leisurely odyssey. They stood silent and awestruck at the mysterious majesty of Fingal's Cave, on the island of Staffa. At Tobermory they peered into depths where lay the treasure-laden wreck of a galleon of the Spanish Armada. On the gemlike island of Iona they picnicked in the monastic ruins and swam naked in water that swirled warmly about them in translucent shades of green, blue and purple.

Each day they felt they had experienced the ultimate in happiness, only to discover a few hours later that still higher spheres existed. As they sailed from one island to another, their blissful harmony became more luxuriant. As they grew ever more finely attuned to each other, the scope and nature of their lovemaking became more imaginative and the quality more joyful. In Glasgow the furtive nature of their meetings had made them tense, even frantic. Here they discovered laughter.

As the holiday went into its final phase, they reached a bay on the south end of Mull so sheltered and sunny that they decided to moor the ketch there until it was time to return to Oban. Fiona read or sunbathed. Dunbar's restless energy took him swimming or climbing. He was tireless and could refer to a swift race up a two-thousand-foot peak as "just a bit of hill walking."

As the hours shortened, the time he had said did not exist became more precious. "Soon all this will just be memories." He was gazing wistfully across smooth water to rocky mountains softened by a haze which, for the first time, had a hint of autumn in it.

She put down her book. "I don't suppose we've seen more than twenty people since we left Oban, yet all those crowded Glasgow streets are waiting for us just a couple of days away."

"I wonder if eventually we'd get bored with this?"

"We'll never know."

He rose with a slight sigh. "I'm going out to the boat. If we're leaving tomorrow, I must look up the charts."

An hour or so later there was a splash, and when she looked up from her book, she saw him swimming from the boat. He came out of the water and crossed the sand toward her with the golden light glinting on his dripping skin. There was something in his smile that caused desire to rise in her instantly as she stared at the ripple of hard muscle, the tigerish spring of his walk, the perfect symmetry of his body against the sky.

As he knelt in front of her, she ran her hands along his shoulders to brush the water away. She felt his fingers at the buttons of her dress. "Breathe in," he said.

Her eyes became exaggeratedly wide. "What are you going to do?"

"What they did in the Garden of Eden."

"Then shouldn't we go out to the boat?"

"No. We might never get a place like this under such a sky again."

"Isn't that rather a pagan thought?"

"The old ways are best, they say." He smothered her laughter with a kiss, then lifted the dress carefully over her head and dropped it neatly on the sand. "No whalebone?"

"Hadn't you noticed before? I've never needed it."

She began to caress and kiss his wet skin as he rolled down her stockings and unfastened her bodice.

"In the Garden of Eden there was no chance of being seen," she said in a quick whisper. "We'll go to jail if we're found like this."

"I'll try to make the risk worthwhile." He drew the bodice gently away and put his face against her brown skin. "Shouldn't you be wearing a slip of some kind?"

"It's not necessary in such warm weather, but you're very knowledgeable You should have included undressing ladies with your boxing, riding and mountaineering skills."

"I'll soon stop your giggling."

"Don't be too long." She listened to her own happiness as if the voice

292

belonged to a stranger. She felt wildly carefree and abandoned. She had an urge to spread her limbs in all directions, luring him on to deeds for which she had no names and only hazy pictures.

She heard him laugh at his own clumsiness as his fingers fumbled with the elastic at her waist. A marvellous elation suffused her. "Are you going to take those down, too?"

He was gripped by the same mood of erotic hilarity. "Only if you say please."

"Please." She wriggled a little and arched her back to assist him with his tugging. "You're managing to make me feel I'm being seduced for the first time."

Two nights later, as she sat alone in a train already half way back to Glasgow, she felt the rest of her life would be spent trying to recapture the sweet mystery of all the idyllic moments that had made up the previous two weeks.

19

Three days later Robert walked into the dining room in Claremont Row at breakfast time, unannounced.

She could hardly smile or speak when she saw him. She could think only of Dunbar. The touch of his lips and of his hands was suddenly, suffocatingly, close.

She had not seen him since he had put her on the train at Oban and had been living in a glow of remembered pleasure. Now, with Robert standing there, still in his travelling coat, her mind began to swim. Her hands trembled and the cutlery rattled loudly against her plate as she put it down. She was alarmed to the point of panic. Her thoughts were erratic and uncontrolled. Had he somehow found out? Perhaps someone had seen them and written to him in London. Her mind raced along all the paths. She looked along the table to where Steven and Allan sat. If there was going to be a scene, she must get them out of the room.

She waited, lost in anxiety, until Robert spoke again.

"I knew this would be a surprise, Fiona, but there's no need to look as if you've seen a ghost."

His tone was sardonic, but in recent years they had adopted banter as a defence. It had become their substitute for emotion. Now, it told her little. He kissed her lightly and turned his attention to Steven and Allan. Their greetings were subdued.

"Well, I'm blowed," he said ruefully as he threw off his coat and walked across the silent room to the array of silver dishes on the sideboard. "I must say, I'm not generating much excitement. I'm reminded of the scene in the Commons when I get up to speak."

He couldn't know. He wouldn't joke like that if he did. With a resolute return of brightness she rose quickly from her half-finished breakfast. We're all surprised, Robert. I don't think any of us knows what to say. You didn't write, did you? I haven't had a letter."

"No." He looked appreciatively round the rich homeliness of the room. "It was a last-minute decision. By the time the office closed last night I swore I couldn't stand London for another day. It's been a long, stifling summer down there. I was lucky enough to get a sleeper compartment. There had been a cancellation."

She took the plate he had lifted. "I'll do that. You sit down. But don't you want porridge first? I'll ring for it."

"I don't think so." He made a face. "I've rather been put off porridge in London. They simply have no idea how it should be made. It always ends up lumpy, and if you don't watch them, they put sugar in it instead of salt. I'll have some bacon and eggs."

She watched in the convex mirror as he returned, slightly distorted, to the table and stood between Steven and Allan. He put an affectionate but elongated hand on each of them. She thought of Douglas's strong hands.

"And how have you two vagabonds been behaving yourselves?"

They had recovered from their embarrassment at seeing him so unexpectedly. "Impeccably, Papa," Steven said, turning a little to see if Fiona could hear.

"Ho-ho. I'll have to get confirmation of a claim like that." He bent over Allan. Is that the truth, Allan?"

"Oh, yes, Papa."

"I'm glad to hear it, for I have a pleasant surprise for you. We're all going on holiday to Castle Gare. When I've had breakfast, I'll write a note and have it delivered to your headmaster, telling him you'll both be off school for a week."

Their jubilant cries banished the dregs of Fiona's uneasiness, but she still felt a need to divert attention from herself.

"Now, Steven," she said as she put Robert's bacon and eggs at the head of the table, "isn't this your chance to tell Papa how you all hate him spending so much time away from home?"

Steven was surprised and hurt by this inexplicable treachery. When she saw his expression, she felt mean and unscrupulous. Robert gave her a quick glance. It was a heart cry he had heard often enough before. In a way, it had been the theme of their marriage, and always Fiona had been the musician. Was his family going to start singing the same song?

"Don't you like my being a Member of Parliament?" he asked Steven.

"It's all right, I suppose," Steven said carefully, "but it would be nicer if you could do it without being away all the time."

"Surely this is my fourth visit home this year?"

"They were very short visits, Papa," Allan pointed out, encouraged by Steven's boldness.

Robert ruffled the child's hair. "I hadn't realised I was missed so much." He looked along the table to the place set for his daughter. "Where's Florence?"

"She should be down any minute. She's taking much more trouble with her appearance these days. She's become quite self-conscious."

"She's a woman now, of course. She won't be going to school for very much longer. That's another note I'll have to write—to her headmistress—and another to McNair, asking if he can spare Gordon. I want this to be a real family holiday."

Fiona walked slowly to the window, carrying her teacup, an informality for which Robert had often enough upbraided her. Today he either did not notice or felt she was incorrigible. A sodden mist which had been close to her room when she wakened still hovered over the area. It had thinned a little in the last half hour, but the spire of Trinity Church was still lost in it.

She said, "I see some of the leaves are turning brown. Autumn has come in a single day."

He joined her, looking across to the grassy strip of shrubs and old trees that gave the house a country aspect. "Yes, the air is quite sharp. The Gareloch should be invigorating. I think I like it almost as much in autumn as in spring. A week down there, out of the city, will be a tonic." He turned to her, seeming to inspect first her hair and then her face. "I don't suppose any of you have been in the country recently, although I must say, Fiona, you are looking exceptionally well."

Again guilt stirred in her. Could the words be as innocent as his casual way with them suggested? Tension made her take a deep, uncomfortable breath. "We haven't," she said, "unless you count a business tour of Speyside. I'm not long back, you know." She waited nervously for him to pounce.

He merely said, looking back at the table, "Aren't you going to finish your breakfast? I hope I haven't spoiled it for you." He went to his place and started eating. "By the way—" his brow furrowed as he reached for the toast—"I hope going to Castle Gare won't interfere with any of your own arrangements?"

Her heart turned over. Would she suspect traps everywhere until he had gone back to London? Was this the awful price that had to be paid?

"Socially, there's nothing that matters," she said, listening to the strain in her voice and wondering if it was apparent to him. "And Peter Ross can cope perfectly adequately with anything that needs attention at King and Company. When you go in, you can tell him I'll be away for a week."

296

He put his teacup forward to where she could fill it. "I won't be going in," he said. "You can drop him a note."

She was so surprised she looked at him properly for the first time since he had walked into the room. "But you always go in."

"Ah," he laughed, "but you were only a probationer then. Now you've passed your exams. I'm quite sure no one along there ever thinks of me now. They've learned to look to you, and I don't want to deflect them from that."

She went out of the room to hurry Florence, marvelling at the depth of disinterest his words revealed. His life was clearly rooted in London, even more firmly than she had thought. He was like a fond relative willing to keep in touch but determined not to get too involved. Apart from appearances, would he care so very deeply if he knew of her involvement with Dunbar?

On their third day at Castle Gare a very solemn Fergus walked along from Ardfern in the middle of the morning to tell them Great-grandmother Veitch was dead. She had gone to bed the previous night apparently in her usual health. A maid found her when she carried in her morning tea. She was lying as if still peacefully asleep and had obviously passed away without a twinge of pain or uneasiness.

"God rest her," Fergus said with unusual piety, "and may we all go as easily."

Among the papers on her bedside table, he told them, there had been a scribbled line taken from Tennyson:

But still I think it can't be long before I find release.

He recited it to them with a slightly shamefaced expression and then said, that of course no significance could be attached to it; some of the papers went back fifty years; the line could have been written a long time ago.

By the following evening the whole family, including James, had gathered at one or other of the houses on the Gareloch. The morning after that, in keeping with the old lady's eccentric wish, the coffin was drawn slowly along the dusty shore road in a simple spring cart. The mourners walked behind, a long line of family and locals straggling by the side of the grey loch. The captain of the *Marquis of Ailsa* kept his vessel motionless at the pier until the procession passed and went up the lane that led between mossy verges to the old churchyard. And as the coffin was lowered into a grave under the yew trees, the steamer sounded a farewell

297

that echoed sadly between the cloud-shrouded hills on either side of the loch.

The will was read in the parlour of her cottage at the bottom of the rose garden at Ardfern, in the presence of the entire family. The other mourners, many of whom had travelled considerable distances, had dispersed after being given the traditional meal of "funeral ham" at the local inn.

There was no sun, but the light had that peculiar quality in which colours are seen at their best. Under its pearly gleam the last burst of rose blooms stood out in vibrant contrast to the autumn tints already creeping over the surrounding greenery.

The Kings—reduced now to three generations—made a drab assembly as they came down the garden path and crushed into the small house. Their ugly black clothes extinguished the bright touches the old lady had cultivated wherever there was a flat surface: the flowers by the window, still standing as she had arranged them; the fragile Meissen ladies, which the servants were not allowed to dust; the crimson and blue decanters carefully locked into the silver tantalus. *What a hunt there would be now to find where she kept the key hidden,* James thought with wry fondness. Rita stifled a tear as Fergus guided her round the familiar objects to a chair at the side of the empty grate.

There were only two or three tapestry-covered chairs and a neat, gilt-framed settee in the uncluttered room, a reminder to Fergus's roving eye that Mrs. Veitch's early influences had come from the Georgians. With an inward smile he remembered some of the tart lessons in taste his mother-in-law had given him when he courted Rita. With hand chairs carried from the dining room they seated themselves as well as they could, conscious that after their walk in the cemetery and in the garden their boots and shoes might not be as clean as in life the stern old lady would have insisted they should be.

Her will was as clear and to the point as she had always been herself. It was read by a melancholy old man whom Fergus introduced as Mr. Pearson, of Veitch, Baptie and Pearson. Having looked after his client's affairs for more than fifty years, Mr. Pearson had insisted on coming from Glasgow to officiate at the end, although he was now almost eighty and in virtual retirement. This gallant gesture was a tribute not only to Mrs. Veitch but to her late husband, who had been senior partner in the firm when he joined it.

Although the slightly wavering voice coming from the corner in which Mr. Pearson had stationed himself belonged to the lawyer, the words were clearly from the sharp tongue of Mrs. Veitch.

Fergus, Rita, Gwen, Fiona, Robert, James and Colin were rich, and to these, as mementoes, she left her jewellery, paintings and more important pieces of furniture. Gordon, Florence, Steven and Allan would doubtless be provided for to the standard their father thought fitting, and this was as it should be. Nevertheless, to these, as an expression of her love and as a test of their characters, she bequeathed the sum of two thousand pounds each, this to be immediately deposited in their own names for them to do with as they wished, "although it is my hope that they will heed any advice their parents may give them."

Hardly an eye moved from the floor until Mr. Pearson reached the last sentence of the testament. "Money can never compensate for the loss of a father, but to my great-grandson John Hoey, I bequeath the residue of my estate, because, of all the family, his need I judge to be the greatest."

Fergus's head came up with an involuntary jerk, for he alone realised the significance of this last bequest. Mr. Pearson removed his glasses and began a symbolic gathering together of his papers.

Jack's voice broke the solemn silence. "Sir, is it possible to say what that means, exactly?"

Mr. Pearson peered at him from red-rimmed eyes. "Means, sir?"

"Yes." Jack's smile was open and unembarrassed. "What exactly is the residue I've been left—in money terms?"

Gwen's shock was so great she could not quell an exclamation of dismay. "Jack!" she cried, turning in her chair to face him.

He looked at her in surprise and then swung back to Mr. Pearson as the old man found his voice. "You are asking me, sir, if I know what the residue of your great-grandmother's estate will amount to?"

"Well, I was, but Mother seems to think—"

Mr. Pearson quavered coldly on, as if he had not heard. "And you wish me to divulge that information to you here, in the presence of these others?"

Jack's grin of good-natured hesitation went here and there in the room, as if inviting their views. "Well, yes, if it's all right. I mean, I don't mind. After all, I know what everyone else is getting. Why shouldn't they know about me? We're all family."

"Very well." Mr. Pearson put his glasses back on and scraped about for a while among his papers; but when he spoke it was without consulting them. "When all disbursements and adjustments have been made, the sum will be"—he unfolded a sheet of foolscap and glanced at it—"speaking roundly, of course, in the region of forty thousand pounds."

Apart from someone's coughing, the only sound came from Jack. "My God," he said.

Fergus controlled his agitation until he was alone with Rita in the sitting room at Ardfern where they took tea in the afternoons before he went off to spend an hour with his paintings. Then he also said, "My God!"

She had been waiting for him to explode. Her calm silence irked him a little, and he looked at her accusingly over his raised cup. "I really think Grandmother might have had more consideration. For Gwen, I mean. What a worry this will be to her. Forty thousand pounds to a boy barely twenty-one!"

He caught a straggling corner of his beard and tugged at it, watching her with increased sharpness. "I take it you knew nothing of this in advance, my dear? Grandmother never mentioned it to you?"

"Of course not, Fergus," she said with a worried frown. "If she had, I would have tried to persuade her to give Jack the money in some less worrying way. Perhaps by putting it in trust for him." She closed her eyes and ran her fingers back and forth across her forehead, as if trying to conjure some memory from the past. "But looking back—"

"Well?" He was impatient at the faraway note that had come into her voice. "Looking back to what?"

"To the party Robert and Fiona gave for your birthday at Castle Gare last year. Looking back to that I might have guessed, knowing how contrary she could be. Jack seemed to be on her mind that day. You know, he visited her regularly. They were excellent friends. Well, she went on and on to Aunt May about Jack's poor financial position in relation to the rest of the family. What a pity it was, she said, that Tom Hoey had died a penniless soldier. I tried to chastise her, but you know how terribly headstrong she was." She paused for a moment and then her voice became more animated. "Some of her actual words are coming back to me now. 'Too much money can be ruinous for a young man, but so can too little. There has to be a balance.' She thought it unfair, even a cruel stroke of fate, that in the normal course of events Jack would be middle-aged before he inherited Gwen's money. If I'd been sharper, I might have guessed she was considering leaving her money to him. Or am I simply being wise after the event?"

Her expression had become doubtful, and it was a relief to her when Fergus nodded. "I think so, my dear. You couldn't have guessed. No one could have guessed such a sensible woman could be so irresponsible. It wasn't as if she didn't care if Jack went off the rails. She would have been as vexed as any of us. After all, she was a stickler for all the proprieties—at any rate, in others, although she could ignore them easily enough herself when it suited her."

Irritation overcame him again. "Damn it all, she was as aware as any of us that Jack might have inherited more of his father's blood than would be good for him."

Rita lifted the teapot and put it down again slowly as another memory came back to her. "Mother was certainly aware that Gwen had reason to worry about Jack in view of his father's record, but I distinctly remember her saying she considered him a steady and responsible young man."

Fergus motioned impatiently to her to pour him another cup of tea. "So he is, damn it. We know that in the business, my dear. But we want him to stay that way. We none of us know how he would react in the face of strong temptation. Forty-thousand at his age could easily lead him astray. Gwen will spend sleepless nights over this, I'm sure."

"She certainly didn't look very happy when she left," Rita agreed. Her expression became abstracted. "But, Fergus, it came as a shock to me to learn Mother was so wealthy. I had no idea. Father left her less than ten thousand, and that was over thirty years ago. Of course"—she shrugged to indicate she realised there was no reason why she should have known—"it was her own business. We never discussed money."

A pleasurable gleam came into Fergus's eyes.

"I'm rather proud of the way I was able to help her with her investments," he said quietly. "It was quite a responsibility, but she trusted me."

He rose from his seat, sighing heavily, and walked to the window. The loch was grey and ruffled. A small boat with brown sails dipped to the tune of an easterly breeze. Through the trees he could see part of Mrs. Veitch's cottage. The leaded windows looked black and the rambling rose at the door seemed to droop. For almost thirty years the old lady had lived there. Never again would they see her look up from her weeding and wave in welcome as they arrived from Glasgow.

Fergus sighed again and turned back to Rita.

"It's ironic that my advice made the money for her, yet she didn't consult me before engaging in this rash and thoughtless bequest."

Rita opened her watch and rang for a maid to take away the tea things.

"Well, Fergus," she said, "we can only hope for Gwen's sake that our fears are groundless. There's nothing else to be done. We've all been watching Jack and wondering about him for a long time. We'll just have to wait and see."

The worry Rita had noted in Gwen when they parted at Ardfern increased steadily during the train journey back to Glasgow. Over dinner she was withdrawn and preoccupied. Colin, who had married her knowing part of her dwelt permanently in the past, kept up a bright monologue throughout the meal. Afterward, in the drawing room, he went to the piano and softly played some of her favourite music.

Their house was part of a grey terrace near Charing Cross and, in Fer-

301

gus's view, unsuitable to their money or station because of its exposure to the noise of traffic converging on the western shopping end of the city. They had bought it mainly because the back garden was exquisitely landscaped in the Japanese manner. The drawing room overlooked it, and from his seat at the piano Colin could see the maple tree had shed some of its scarlet autumn leaves.

Soon the familiar outlines became indistinct as shadows gathered at the window.

"Gwen!"

She looked up with a start. "Yes, dear?"

"Aren't you going to ring for Hannah to light the lamps? I soon won't be able to see the keyboard."

Her smile came slowly. "I'm sorry, Colin." She reached out and tugged at a silken bellpull. "I've been miles away. You play so soothingly."

A girl appeared within seconds, for they were well, if unpretentiously, staffed. Like all the family, they employed only maids, considering butlers ostentatious for people engaged in trade. The old man at Castle Gare had been inherited from the previous owner and kept on out of charity as caretaker rather than butler. Similarly, no King had ever gone to a boarding school. In Glasgow there was no tradition of public-school education, even among the most prosperous families. There were a variety of excellent day schools, and these had, until now, been adequate for the Kings. When Steven and Allan started at Rugby in October, as Robert had arranged they should, it would be a break with family custom. When Fergus was told, he had nodded and murmured, "It's time, I suppose." *At least,* he thought, *no one can say we've rushed at it.*

The lamps threw up a homely circle of red carpet and well-polished brass. "Build up the fire, Hannah," Gwen said. "I haven't warmed all day. It was so cold at the cemetery."

"Yes, ma'am."

When the girl had gone, Colin left the piano, took one of Gwen's hands and held it between his own. "You are cold, my dear. I think we should have a glass of Madeira."

When he went to get the wine, she held her hands to the fire. "Colin . . . ?"

He turned to her with a decanter in his hand, his lean, poet's face cast like a sculpture in the pale beam of one of the lamps.

"What do you think of Great-grandmother's leaving all that money to Jack?"

It was her first direct reference to it, but he'd had little doubt this was what was occupying her.

"He's a very fortunate young man," he said brightly, putting a glass of Madeira on the wine table beside her chair.

302

"Of course he is," she said quickly, "but you must know that's not what I meant."

He sat down opposite her and drank some of his wine. "Well," he said reluctantly, "I suppose I have to confess I did get a bit of a shock when I heard that old lawyer chap read it out. To tell you the truth, for a second or two I didn't quite catch on. He managed to make it sound like a bag of broken biscuits instead of a fortune."

She seized on the admission. "So it did worry you, too?"

"Well"—he spread his hands in a gesture of helplessness and twined one thin leg round the other—"only because of you, my dear. Only because I knew perfectly well what you would be thinking."

"But don't you see, Colin, the thought would never have come to you at all if you didn't share my feelings in some degree."

"I'm sorry, Gwen," he said airily. "I simply don't accept that."

"You just don't think my alarm is justified?"

"I don't. I never have, and nothing's happened to make me change my mind."

She moved her chair. "My goodness, that fire has suddenly come to life," she said, pulling a pole screen into position to protect her face from the blaze.

He tried to extend the diversion, but she returned determinedely to the subject in her mind. "Great-grandmother must have known it would worry me—Jack's getting all that money. And I must say his behaviour in front of the entire family did nothing to soothe my fears. What did you think of the exhibition he made of himself? I prayed for the floor to open and swallow me. He sounded so heartlessly mercenary. It was as if he couldn't wait to get his hands on the money."

He nodded. "It was tactless of him. But he's young."

She pulled the pole screen closer. "Not young enough to justify a scene like that."

He clenched his long jaw stubbornly and reached for a pipe in the rack at the side of the fireplace. "I'm still not convinced you're right, Gwen. Part of Jack's trouble is that he's too frank. He has an open nature and doesn't realise how easy it is to be misunderstood. I don't think he's aware how keenly the eyes of the family are trained on him. Anyway, I prefer to judge him by his behaviour rather than by his words."

He leaned forward to put a taper to the flames. When it was lit, he held it over his pipe and puffed clouds of smoke. "Can you remember how worried you were when Jack started work with King and Company? You were convinced it would be the start of some awful deterioration. It wasn't, but that didn't stop your thinking it was the end of the world when Robert said he was sending him to Lochbank. You were certain that once he was free of home restraints, he would run amok. Of course, he did nothing of the kind. Instead, he became engrossed in distilling. But still you worry that there's some taint in him just waiting to break loose. Now it's this money."

"Money's the great corrupter," she said, as if none of them had any.

"Well, I'm afraid, Gwen, you'll just have to resign yourself to it. It's been left to him, and in due course it will be handed over to him to do with as he pleases. There's absolutely nothing you can do about it."

The curtains had not been drawn, and through the leaves of the maple tree she could see lights shining from another house. She wondered what the problems were over there.

"There is nothing I can do about it, Colin. You're quite right. But there is something you could do." Her voice sank. "If you would."

He put his pipe in his mouth and bit hard on the stem because he knew it gave him a forbidding expression. "And what might that be?"

"You could speak to him."

"Speak to him about what?"

"About what he might do with the money. What he might invest it in. I feel if it was locked away somewhere, it would be less likely to do him harm."

He waited until she was finished, then took the pipe from his mouth and shook it at her. "Oh, no, Gwen. You're not going to get me to do that."

"But why not? I can't do it. There would almost certainly be a row. He would resent it from me."

"And he might just as well resent it from me."

"Oh, you could approach it on a man-to-man basis," she said coaxingly.

"Gwen, I'm not Jack's father, but it has made me very happy that he has treated me almost as if I were. I have tried to treat him as a complete equal, as a chum. For this reason we've never quarrelled, and I don't want to start now. I'm not prepared to put our relationship to the test until I have to. I don't want to risk squandering the regard that exists between us. We might need it for something important later on."

"This is important."

"Not important enough."

They were smiling slightly at each other now, each realising that in the last seconds the discussion had ceased to be completely serious. She could see—and she accepted—that he would not be persuaded.

"What are you holding yourself in reserve for?" she said.

"I don't know. Some crisis could arise in the lad's life about . . . anything. About a girl, perhaps."

"A girl!" She laughed softly and teasingly. "And what, pray, could you tell him about girls?"

He rose. "Perhaps more than you think, my dear. You don't imagine you were the only wild dark beauty in my life, do you?"

"I was a wild *fair* beauty," she said in a petted voice, "except that I wasn't wild and not at all beautiful. Don't you even remember that?"

He put his hands on her shoulders and bent over her. "I never forget anything about you, Gwen," he said softly. "I remember everything: the night we first met, at a dinner party at Ardfern; the colour not only of your hair but of the dress you wore. You were a married woman then, but it didn't stop me from falling in love with you on the spot."

She put a hand over his and pressed it in happy silence. He kissed her on the forehead. "And now I must go and do a little work before bed-time."

She sat on alone at the fire for a few minutes. They had risen early for the journey to Row. The long day and the heat of the room combined to make her sleepy. She collected a stole and went into the garden.

There was a miniature stone bridge over a goldfish pool, and she liked to stand by it in the dark listening to the myriad sounds of the night. In daylight the garden was irresistibly reminiscent of a willow-patterned plate. In the evenings it was pleasantly perfumed. Tonight a chill rose from under the dwarf trees and evergreen azaleas. She strolled across a strip of grass and leaned for a few moments against the maple tree, staring at the stars. When she looked back at the house, she could see Colin moving about in his study. In the light from the windows she was surprised to see her footprints on the grass. It would be a damp night and a dewy dawn. The city lay only a little way over the rooftops, but she felt she could have been in the country. What she missed most in town was a view of water. Fergus had spoiled them from childhood with his week-end house on the Gareloch.

But it was another scene, another stretch of water, she pictured as she walked slowly back to the house. She saw the tree-fringed bay in front of Lochbank distillery, the moonlit mountains behind and, a short way along the twisting road, the little house where Jack lived.

The death of Mrs. Veitch threw a blight over the holiday from which it never recovered.

Robert, after taking them rambling in Glen Fruin one day and sailing over to Rosneath another, seemed to lose interest. He moved between the library and his study, emerging only for meals. When he did appear among them, kissing Fiona on the cheek, tousling the hair of the younger boys, it was with slightly guilty references to the high wind, the nearness of rain or some other twist of the weather which made his seclusion seem more excusable.

305

When Fiona remonstrated with him, he gave her what she called his "parliamentary smile" and said, "I'm gathering notes for some major speeches I plan to make in the House next session. It's important to set things in the correct historical context."

"I thought you had brought us here on holiday," she said mildly—hoping for some diversion from her longing for the sight and touch of a different man.

He frowned absentmindedly as he turned back to his books. "My dear, you are on holiday." As she began closing the door she heard him calling as if in apology. "Perhaps I am a bit absorbed, Fiona, but to tell you the truth, I've been given a job—a very minor job—in the government, and it's rather important that I do well next session. There's no telling what it might lead to. Perhaps a junior ministry."

She came back into the room. "Why on earth are you only telling me this now, Robert?"

He shrugged. "Well, you're not all that interested in parliamentary affairs, are you?"

"I'm interested in anything that happens to you. What is the job?"

"I'm the new PPS to Hicks Beach."

"Robert, you're back in Scotland! What is a PPS and who is Hicks Beach?"

"Good God! He's the Chancellor of the Exchequer and I'm his new parliamentary private secretary."

"That's wonderful news."

His eyes began to stray.

"Well, it's the bottom of the ladder, but it shows they've noticed me. Now, why don't you all go over the Black Hill without me and have a picnic on Loch Lomond?"

Twice Gordon pushed the dinghy out and rowed up and down the loch in a desultory way, but the view to the shore reminded him too much of Anne as she had been when he first saw her. When he told Fiona that McNair could do with him for the start of the new distilling season on Monday, and that, in any case, he would as soon be working, she nodded understandingly.

On Sunday night he went to the library to say good-bye, since he would be leaving early next morning. Robert looked up, hesitated, then decisively pushed his books and notes away. He reached for his pipe and pointed invitingly to a chair. "Make yourself comfortable, Gordon." They chatted for a half hour.

"I knew you would take to distilling," Robert said. "It's in your blood, after all. On your mother's side you're the fifth generation to work at Lochbank. I'm glad she sent you there as soon as she did, although I'll admit I was surprised. I was sure she would hang on to you at home until she ran out of excuses for keeping you there."

He suddenly lifted his pen and pulled a book forward. "Well, we should all be proud of her," he said, turning a page. "She's a remarkable woman. She's running the business every bit as capably as I ever did."

He had resumed his engrossed note-taking before Gordon reached the door, but the turning of the handle recalled him briefly.

"Tell Grant I've authorised you to take the carriage. It's an awkward journey otherwise. But tell him I want to see him back here as near to noon as possible."

Gordon was early out in the courtyard next morning. The breeze from the loch was cold, and on the hills the bracken was falling over in sad tangles. The heather was fading to russet and the mountains had lost their purple veil. From the direction of the stables he could hear the clinking of harnessing and horse brasses as the coachman readied the carriage. He walked to the parapet to wait. The turrets of Ardfern rose above the trees and two or three of the chimneys showed smoke. Fergus and Rita were still in residence. They would probably stay on until the end of the month, before locking up the house until the following spring.

To Gordon, there was an aura of unreality about everything these days. He seemed to see through stone and round corners. The sight of Mrs. Veitch's house, empty now except for servants, increased his sense of impermanence and insubstantiality. The little garden she had tended so faithfully would never bloom as well again, for no one would give it the love she had shown.

He turned with a bleak sigh and walked across the grey courtyard to the front steps of the castle as he heard the wheels of the carriage turning on the gravel. He directed the coachman to go through Helensburgh, because he wanted to buy tobacco. The front was deserted except for some seagulls and an old man in a frock coat and tall hat taking his constitutional. The tide was out and the sand was littered with seaweed, as if it had been stormy on the firth during the night. From there the route lay over the Black Hill and along the western bank of Loch Lomond.

Layers of white vapour hung low over the water, shrouding the far shore, on which the distillery stood. About a mile out, trees growing on the island of Inchmurrin pierced the fleecy mist. Their foliage appeared to lie on it like giant springs of parsley. Over everything, tinted with all the shades of encroaching autumn, towered the great buttressing shoulder of Ben Nevis. The sharp black peak itself was not visible.

At the village of Balloch several wayside houses displayed notices proclaiming that teas were sold inside, an indication of the area's growing popularity among Glasgow's voracious—and some thought despoiling—hordes. Here, the road swung away from the loch, through farming country, to Gartocharn and Drymen. Shortly, on the Balmaha road, which skirted the eastern shore of the loch, he had his first sight of the telltale wisps of steam which forever drifted above the small glen at the entrance to which Lochbank stood.

All at once the subject that had been in the background of his mind since the day of the funeral was clamantly in the foreground. Jack, whom he had left here less than a week ago, a dependent worker, the most humble of the family, was now a wealthy man. Forty thousand pounds! It was almost too great a sum to grasp. It made his own quite substantial bequest of two thousand seem paltry. With forty thousand a man could do as he wished. He was his own master. He needn't take orders from McNair. He needn't be beholden to the Kings. He needn't work at all. On the income from a fortune like that he could lead the leisured life of a gentleman. Of course, Jack, being a Hoey, wouldn't. He would squander the money as his father had squandered his fortune—on horses, drink and women. And no one would be able to stop him! Jack was free now! Free to go to hell in his own way!

Gordon sat back in the carriage and closed his eyes as a stab of envy went through him—not for the money as such, but for what it meant. For the freedom, the blessed freedom! It was something he had never known, he thought sadly. There hadn't been a single day of his life he could remember when he felt free. He had felt trapped even in the nursery, more so at school, and now, above all, in the business. And not alone in the business. There was that other tugging, nightmarish side of his life.

Others of his age and background went from one woman to another, sampling all the flowers before, perhaps at twenty-four or twenty-five, settling on one. But his heart was imprisoned already, almost before he had started to live. And although he loved Anne, he resented his loving her. He ground the knuckles of one hand into the palm of the other in an involuntary gesture of violence. My God, how he resented it! His beaten mind raved on. Why should this have happened to him? Why couldn't she have been ugly that first day he saw her on the Gareloch shore? Or healthy? Or in love with someone else and so out of his reach? The mad irreconcilability of his extreme attitudes to her inflamed him even further. He clenched his fists and gritted his teeth to stop himself from throwing the window open and crying out to the wilderness at the weird unfairness of his fate.

He dismounted at his lodgings and arranged that the coachman be given refreshment before setting out on the return journey. After changing out of his holiday clothes he walked almost eagerly to the distillery, anxious for the salve of physical work.

McNair was surprised to see him. "Can't you bear to stay away from the place?" he asked cheerfully. "I didn't expect you for at least another two or three days."

"With Great-grandmother dying, the holiday was a bit of a failure," Gordon said. "I knew you would be busy here, so I decided to come back."

"I'm glad you did, lad. The start of every new season brings its problems, and this one is no exception. The silent months are supposed to be used to bring everything up to the mark, but it never works out like that."

Gordon, who during the last two nondistilling months had whitewashed warehouse walls, greased various mechanical parts, crawled inside cold furnaces, as well as attending to his office work, gave McNair a puzzled frown.

"I didn't think there was a corner of the distillery you didn't have us bend our backs to."

"Oh, we were thorough, but there's always something that doesn't work as it should when we light the furnaces again. This morning we've got an air lock between the washbacks and the stillhouse. The maintenance man's ill, but Jack volunteered to see what he could do about it."

"And what does he know about plumbing?"

McNair chuckled. "It's amazing what Jack can turn his hand to. He probably wouldn't tackle a dripping tap at home, but because this has to do with whisky, he sees it as a challenge. He's up there now. You'd better see if he needs a labourer. Till that's fixed, everything else will go at half speed."

Gordon went out and walked slowly across the cobbles and round the cosy huddle of whitewashed buildings. He was less anxious for work now that the task he had been given meant the close company of his cousin. It was unlikely they would be working together for much longer. Once Jack was in receipt of his inheritance, he would be off to enjoy himself. It seemed all the more important, therefore, that these last days, or weeks, should pass without trouble. The less they saw of each other, the more easily this could be accomplished.

He delayed his journey to the upper floor of the malthouse by pausing occasionally for a word with one of the men, or to savour the sharp tang

309

of whisky evaporating from the dark depths of the long, windowless warehouses.

Evaporation through the staves of the casks was inseparable from the maturing process. It was a loss—estimated at millions of proof gallons annually—that tore at the heart of every Scot who knew about it. An ocean of the precious stuff silently disappearing into thin air every year! It was almost too terrible a thought to be contemplated, and for generations the distillers had been putting it out of their heads. But whisky had been taken out of the glens in the way that Robert King had shown. It was big business now. And the blenders, a more cost-conscious breed than the distillers, were worrying about the evaporation problem. If it could be mastered, millions of pounds would be added to the industry's yearly profits without extra effort. A fortune awaited the man who solved it.

"But they'll never stop it," McNair had prophesied as they discussed it one morning over their mugs of tea. "They'll no more stop the whisky going up than they'll stop the rain coming down. If you stop the evaporation, you stop the maturing. It's as simple as that. Damn it, all you have to do to stop whisky evaporating is store it in metal or glass containers instead of in oak casks. But do that and it comes out as rough as when you put it in, even if you keep it there ten years."

Today, in his resentful mood, the twisted thought that came to Gordon as he sniffed the richly laden air was, *Has this intractable problem been referred yet to Mr. Jack Hoey? A man of his many wondrous talents should be able to solve it in a jiff.*

He went through the shadowy vault of the malthouse, past the man with the long wooden shovel bent over the sprouting barley and up the rough wooden stair to the floor above, where the mash tun and the washbacks gently steamed and plopped, the air heavy with their pungent vapours.

Jack knelt on the floor surrounded by wrenches of various sizes. The boards were sodden. When he saw Gordon looking at the mess, he said, "I had to bleed off every copper pipe in the place to get rid of an air lock. It was the devil of a job finding it."

"McNair told me. I hadn't realised that on top of everything else you were a plumber as well."

"I'm not. But I've fixed it."

His satisfaction at his success stung Gordon further. "Naturally."

Jack raised his eyebrows but ignored the sarcasm. "What are you doing back so soon?"

Bitterness rose in him. "My sense of loyalty to the company brought me here on winged feet. I didn't think you would still be working for us."

Jack paused in his loading of the plumbing tools into a canvas bag. "Why not?" His puzzlement seemed genuine.

"Well, you're of independent means now."

"Oh, that." He smiled into the greasy depths of the bag. "It will be some time before the estate is settled. I had a chat about it with old Pearson once mother was out of the way."

"A few weeks, even a couple of months, but why should that delay you? On the strength of Great-grandmother's will I'm sure your bank manager will be very willing to help with an advance."

"He may well be, but I haven't asked him."

Gordon walked round the bent and work-stained figure. Jack's refusal to reveal his plans was infuriating, but typical; he was such a slippery rascal. Suddenly, all he wanted to do was strike. Jack's apparently equitable progress through life unbearably highlighted his own frustrations.

"At least," he jeered, "we now have the explanation of all those visits to see Great-grandmother Veitch, all that concern for her health and her loneliness."

"What do you mean?"

"Don't bother looking so innocent, Cousin Jack. You know, I never really believed you on all those occasions when you said you were going over to the Gareloch to see Great-grandmother. It didn't seem in keeping with what I knew about your usual pastimes. I couldn't picture you sitting having an enjoyable chat with an old lady when the world is full of so many young ladies. I always imagined you had another Dorothy or Isabella over there who was willing to lie on her back for you."

Jack was listening with an expression of precarious tolerance. "That just shows what a filthy, suspicious mind you have." His voice had a hint of his habitual mockery but his eyes were not amused. "How could you possibly think such a thing about me?"

"It was easy, for I know what a liar you are. But my mind wasn't nearly filthy or suspicious enough." His voice rose. "My God, it takes a rank bastard to go sucking around an old woman of ninety, wheedling her money out of her. Only you would be low enough to go wallowing around in that sort of sewer. No wonder you're so good with those plumbing tools."

In the steamy, slightly throat-catching dimness Jack had gone pale. For a silent moment he stood frozen in his crouching position over the tool bag.

"So that's what you think?"

It was too mild a response for Gordon, too much the answer of a man hurt or startled rather than guilty. The docility was a goad to his fury.

311

"It's what the whole family thinks," he said, his eyes enraged and accusing.

"That's a lie!"

"Oh, is it? And what else could they think? It's all so obvious." Suddenly, he hardly knew what he was saying. "It's all so much in character. It's what everybody's been waiting for all these years. At last you've lived up to their expectations. Your father was an unprincipled scoundrel who broke your mother's heart. How could you be anything else with his blood in your veins? The whole family's been watching for the rot to show up in you. You've been the skeleton in the King cupboard, Hoey. They've all been waiting for you to rattle your rotten bones. They didn't know you like I knew you. They didn't know you were doing it all the time behind their backs. They were taken in by your act. They were beginning to believe you really were Eager Jack. They were beginning to breathe easy. They thought the Hoey decadence had passed you by. Well, now they know it hasn't. It's all out in the open now. You've shown them you're tarred with the same dirty brush as your father."

Jack was staring at him in disbelieving silence.

"What do you know about my father? He was dead before you were born."

"So was Napoleon."

All at once, the way ahead looked too dark and pitlike. He wanted to retreat. He had said enough. He turned and began to walk away, but he had hardly clumped three paces over the bare wood before he felt Jack's hand tight on his arm.

"I asked you a question." The voice was low but it throbbed with a complexity of emotions.

"I don't think you would like an answer."

"I want to know what you were hinting at about my father. What do you know about him?"

The brief interval of reason departed as abruptly as it had arrived, and again a deranged hatred rose in Gordon.

"More than you do," he shouted, tearing his arm free. "They kept it hidden from you, but I've picked it all up over the years. They hadn't the same guard on their tongues when I was about, especially when they thought I was too young to know what they were talking about or simply couldn't hear them." Jack was ominously silent. "Your father was a dissolute blot on the family. He gambled away a fortune and practically drank himself into the gutter. Above all, he betrayed your mother. He had women all over the place and he finally deserted her for one of them. She was almost killed because of him. I don't know all the details about that, but it was when she was pregnant and went running through Glas-

312

gow in a storm trying to stop him from leaving her. She lost her baby through that."

The tumbling words were as acrid in his mouth as the fumes from the mash tun and the fermenting wort that floated about them. In a strange way they pained him, but he was driven on by the cruel effect the terrible revelation was having on Jack.

"Oh, yes, you can stare. You didn't know that, did you? You thought you were your mother's only child. Well, Cousin, you have a dead sister. She was born in a railway station after your mother had a fall when she was trying to find your father. She lived for only a few minutes. Your father killed her. Although he was on a train heading for London with a tenth-rate music-hall singer at the time, he was morally responsible for the death of his own daughter. How's that for a family skeleton? And that's only part of it. He was a thief. He stole books from Grandfather's library at Ardfern and sold them to get money for drink and gambling. It was almost a relief to some of the family when he ran away with his singer. Of course, for Aunt Gwen it was a tragedy. She was a lonely, abandoned woman for years. She sold the house they had and went to live by herself in a rented flat. She opened her antique shop to give her life some purpose. Hadn't you ever wondered why your mother had a shop, a woman with plenty of money from a family like ours? Eventually, your father came crawling back. His type always does. To everyone's horror your mother forgave him. He hadn't been back all that long when he left her again for the army. I can tell you, a lot of them thought it was just as well when he was killed. They weren't convinced he was reformed. Oh, he won a medal, all right. He covered himself with glory in Zululand and came home a bloody hero, but how long would it have lasted? That's what worried them all. Some of them didn't think it would be very long before he went off the rails again. A leopard can't change its spots and it always passes on its bad blood. That's why you've been such a worry to them. They saw themselves as having got rid of one incubus only to be saddled with another. And when I say *them* I include your mother. Perhaps most of all your mother. Can you imagine the bad dreams she must have had about you? And now you've turned the nightmare into reality."

When he stopped he was gasping for breath and shivering as if from cold or exhaustion. Jack, who had listened to the torrent of words as if transfixed, was the calmer of the two.

There was still a need in Gordon to taunt him. "I don't suppose you believe me. Well, why not ask your mother? See what she says."

Jack gave a strangely vicious shake of his head.

"The trouble is, I do believe you." His voice was low and distorted with

313

intensity and his gaze was fixed piercingly on Gordon, as if to prevent him from moving. "Geographically, Glasgow is a big city. But in our particular circle it's still not much more than a village. Stories spread. People hear things they're not meant to hear. I've heard things about my father, but always in some quarter where I could dismiss them as evil or distorted rumour. Damn you for a poisonous bastard for confirming them! You're a twisted bloody misfit and I couldn't wish anything more fitting on you than Anne Dunbar."

It was his turn now to gloat at Gordon's surprise. "There's more than one skeleton in the family cupboard, isn't there?" he jeered.

"What do you know about Anne Dunbar?"

The name sounded hollowly in his head. It rumbled round the rambling wooden loft as if about the inside of an empty cask.

"Quite enough. You should take more care not to leave her letters lying around. My God, I really am sorry for you! What a disaster to get mixed up with, apart from all the family and business considerations! She's half off her head and known to more than one lad-about-town as a sport. She made quite a number of them happy until they dropped her as too big a worry. Only an innocent like you would fall in love with her. You couldn't have done worse for yourself if you'd scoured the gutters and madhouses of Glasgow. She's every bit as much a tart as Dorothy or Isabella and crazy into the bargain."

Gordon's fist landed hard on Jack's mouth, splitting his upper lip and knocking out two of his teeth. He reeled backward, spraying blood. One of the wooden pillars stopped him. He sank to the floor with one of his arms round it, half stunned. Gordon shot forward and snatched an eighteen-inch wrench from the canvas tool bag. Then, cursing incoherently, he hurled himself across the bumpy flooring with the wrench raised murderously above his head.

Jack swayed to his feet. "Put that down, you raving idiot!"

"I'm going to kill you, Hoey."

"Come on, then! You can bloody well try!"

As the wrench came down at him he caught Gordon by the wrist with both hands and bent his arm back until there was a shriek of pain and the rusty tool clattered to the floor. Next second Gordon's free hand was driven into Jack's throat with terrific force. Jack went staggering back again, choking for breath, his face smeared with blood.

Almost two years had passed since their last fight, among the racks of whisky casks in King & Co.'s Glasgow warehouse. Then it had been an easy victory for Jack. In the interval, Gordon had matured. He had grown not only taller but heavier. Psychologically he had also changed. He had stepped from little more than boyhood into embittered man-

314

hood. Previously, even when he struck the first blow, he had been handicapped by an attitude that was basically defensive. He had been hampered by an awareness that Jack was his senior in years and his physical superior. Now he was the aggressor, free of any sense of inferiority. Above all, he was filled with a manic resentment against forces which, for reasons he could not have explained, Jack symbolised.

Gordon closed the gap between them in a headlong rush, insanely inspired by his obvious victory over this cousin who in the past had so often and so easily inflicted humiliation on him. The blow to the throat had crippled Jack. He was bent forward, his breath coming in rattling gulps as he swayed and tottered on legs hardly able to hold him.

At any other time Gordon, observing the rules as applied by Jack in their previous encounters, would have floored him and held him there until defeat had been conceded. Today, such a course did not occur to him. His instinct was to kill. His blood thundered as he went quickly behind the dazed figure and locked an arm round his neck. Then, half pushing, half carrying, he manoeuvred him across the loft to the nearest washback. With a deft movement he transferred his grip to the back of Jack's neck and began pushing his head over the edge of the washback toward the dark, bubbling surface of the fermenting wort.

"Don't!" It was a little more than a bruised croak, but vibrant with Jack's sudden panic as he realised he was helpless.

One arm was twisted behind his back. The other was trapped in front of him between his body and the washback. He tried to kick, but their bodies were too close together.

"Don't!" The word disintegrated into a tortured cry as the invisible carbon dioxide gas entered his respiratory system. His body was galvanised with pain and terror, but Gordon clung on with mad-eyed determination, pushing his head steadily forward.

Jack gave another cry of agony and then went silent, his body writhing, but with decreasing energy. After a while he went limp. Still Gordon's death lust was not satisfied. With blind, unthinking hatred he kept pressing the inert body over the great vat. He was aware only of the spread of black liquid, broken here and there by bubbles which burst and released spurts of steam.

The smell was sickening and his head began to float, but the fingers of his left hand bit ever more viciously into Jack's neck. A weird, almost gibbering sound burst from him as he felt his cousin's feet leave the ground. He changed his grip, the better to find a point of balance that would allow him to heave the unconscious body over the edge of the vat into the wort.

He was so diabolically engrossed that he did not hear the clatter of boots on the wooden floor. Only when McNair's urgent cry was against his ear did he hear it. Then he felt hands on his shoulders. He was being dragged back from the vat. Still he clung frenziedly to Jack, as if his purpose might yet be accomplished.

His fingers only went limp when McNair put a hand under his chin and began pushing upward with a desperate warning shout, "Let him go, Gordon. Let him go or I'll break your neck."

His neck was at snapping point before the fit dissolved, and McNair and another worker were able to prise him away from Jack. He slithered to the floor and lay there in a semiconscious heap with his teeth still grimly clenched. He was dimly aware of figures gathering round Jack. He saw the long frame being lifted by the feet and shoulders and heard McNair urging, "Get him down into the open air as quick as you can; then we'll give him artificial respiration." There was a pause and then a shout. "Hughie, take the gig and fetch Dr. Hamilton."

As the men began manoeuvring Jack down the awkward steps, Gordon rose slowly to his feet. He stood unsteadily, staring after them, his heart pounding now with a sick fear. No one seemed interested in him. He hurried after them and caught McNair by the arm. "Is he all right?"

"All right!" The big open face was masked with concern and anger. "I'd say he's at least two-thirds dead. What the hell did you think you were doing?" As Gordon started to speak, McNair silenced him with an impatient gesture. "Never mind, just now. You can tell me later." He added threateningly, "You'll be lucky if you don't have to tell more than me. Do you realise you'd have killed him if one of the men hadn't heard the rammy and come running for me?" As he went down the steps, his voice came back sombrely. "For all I know, you *have* killed him."

Once they were outside the malthouse the men quickly threw off jackets and overalls and spread them on the cobbles. They stretched Jack out face down and McNair knelt astride him with his hands spread flat on his back. Another man had once been trained in first aid, and between them they applied a crude artificial respiration.

To Gordon's almost tearful relief, signs of returning life showed quickly, but it was fifteen minutes before a perspiring and breathless McNair felt the treatment could stop.

"Take him home and see that he goes to bed. I'll be along presently and sit with him till the doctor comes."

He put a reassuring arm across Jack's shoulder. "You'll be all right, lad, but by the look of your lip, it'll need stitching."

Jack insisted on walking to the cart. When it had rattled out of the yard, McNair turned to Gordon and said gruffly, "I want to see you." The usual slight deference was totally absent. In his office he turned angrily. "This is too serious to be kept quiet, Gordon. I don't know what's going on between Jack and you, but I've had enough of it. I'm running a distillery, not a prison for young offenders. Do you realise you'll be up on an attempted murder charge if Jack goes to the police?"

"He won't do that."

"I don't suppose he will. For your sake, I hope not."

"I'm sorry to have caused you this worry."

"I don't doubt that, but when I said I've had enough of it, I meant it. One or other of you will have to go. It'll be up to your mother which one. I'll have to put it all in front of her."

"I'll go." A door seemed to open as he said it. "I started it. It was entirely my fault."

A shade of relief passed across McNair's worried face. He reached for his pipe. There could be no doubt which of the two he preferred to keep. "I'm afraid this'll be a real worry to your mother, especially with your father in London, but I must tell her."

"I understand that, Mr. McNair. There's nothing else you can do. If the doctor says Jack's all right, I'll leave this afternoon."

McNair put down his pipe, his brow creasing. "You'd better wait till I've told Mrs. King. One of you will have to go. I don't go back on that. But she can decide who it is. She may want you here and Jack in Glasgow."

"It doesn't matter what Mother wants." His voice was controlled and unemotional. "Jack says I'm a misfit. Well, he's right. I don't fit into the whisky business, that's certain. When I leave here, I'm leaving not just the distillery but King and Company."

McNair shook his head decisively. "Your mother won't stand for that, Gordon."

"I'm afraid she'll have to. I've decided to leave home as well. I may as well be thorough when I'm at it. I can take furnished rooms in Glasgow. Great-grandmother has left me some money, enough to make me independent for a few years."

"I'm sure Mrs. Veitch wouldn't have left you a penny if she'd thought that's what you'd do with it," McNair said impatiently. These family affairs were too harrassing for him. He understood the family less, the larger it grew. Thank God he'd be retired before this generation took over. "My advice to you, Gordon, is to do nothing hasty."

"It's something I've often thought of, Mr. McNair, in a hazy sort of way. But now it's all come to a head. I know my own mind."

317

20

James wakened slowly, gazing vacantly at the ceiling for a time before sitting up with a guilty start. The bedroom was filled with October sunshine. The leafless branch of an old apple tree swayed gently at the window, and beyond that he could see the curving river tinted to a mellow gold. There was little water in the harbour and the boats leaned against the granite wall. Men worked at nets or fish boxes, watched by seagulls and small boys.

It was a scene he knew well, but he had not been aware of it, or of very much else, for several days. He had been either drunk or too ill from the effects of drink to be conscious of his surroundings. He fixed his eyes on the activity at the harbour and tried not to think of this latest bout in a drinking pattern that had been developing in his life since the beginning of the summer. The whisky that had for so many years helped him combat pain had now also become an antidote to the frequent fits of depression that assailed him.

For despite his discovery of Jessie and the brightness she radiated into his life, disillusion had entered deeply into James's artistic being. The high expectations he had held for his work under the influence of the Galloway landscape had collapsed. He knew now he would never recover the fresh intensity of his early days. It had been a naive aspiration in a man of his age. His work was still unique; it was as charming and as popular as ever, but the flame of his bygone greatness had gone, never to be recaptured. As if to confirm his acceptance of this, he had started taking commissions again. The number of these available was flattering and, as Jessie pointed out, in no way interfered with his inspirations or his integrity.

"They're not commissions at all, really," she comforted him. "Not in the usual sense, where the client says what he wants. You paint what you please. What it really means is that in order to get one of your pictures people are willing to bind themselves to buy whatever you paint before you even put the canvas on the easel. I think that's a great tribute to you, James."

James could only agree, and for a time after one of these discussions he would paint quite happily. Usually Jessie worked nearby at one of her own canvasses, and his child models—grown now from the original Isa and Meg to a little band of four or five—posed among the seashore flowers while the swans and wild goats watched from a distance.

Jessie did not always accompany him on his outdoor expeditions, for the illustrations she did for magazines published in Edinburgh involved her in much detailed work which could best be done at home. Without her cheering presence James's spirit slumped more readily, especially on days when his leg was troublesome. It was then that he drank unwisely, often to an extent that marred his work. Frequently he fell asleep and returned home in the evening with a throbbing head and an empty canvas. Even when Jessie was there, his intake sometimes made him drowsy, and when she noticed him nodding, she prodded him with her stick, sometimes till his ribs were bruised.

If he did not arrive home when expected, Mrs. Laing would come worriedly to her door. Jessie would mount her bicycle and go off to search the countryside. She had roused James from slumbers in the heather and even found him curled up beside his easel on the rocky islet in Gatekirk Bay.

In the course of the summer their relationship had deepened and in some ways grown to resemble that of people married for many years. Her personality was more aggressive than his, and she bullied him when he flagged at his work. In discussions he often deferred to her rather than argue. They were in love, but it was a word neither of them used. Even in his own head James shunned the word. He tried to think only of friendship. His disability had over the years stamped his attitude to women with an almost insuperable hesitance. Although they held hands when they sat on the shore or jogged along in the trap, they seldom kissed, and then only tenderly. What James prized was the companionship. Marriage was to him a distant goal that would be reached only when many difficult psychological barriers had been surmounted.

Anyway, did Jessie *want* to marry him? Had such a thought ever entered her pretty head? Surely not! She couldn't possibly love a man as disabled as he was. He had catalogued all his disadvantages, making himself as unprepossessing as possible. His walk was ungainly, even ugly, and his stance, even when stationary, slightly lopsided. He carried the

319

burden of frequent pain, which in turn drove him to drink too much. He could be desperately irritable and moody, not only because of his pain but because of the many frustrating restrictions his one-leggedness placed on him, not least with regard to this dear Jessie, who was rarely out of his thoughts. Could he, in view of all this, be considered even remotely suitable as a husband for a girl young and still carefree? Was it right that he should be stealing these precious months from her? He shied away from the unbearable alternative. He could not face that, but at least he must not weigh her with a declaration of his love; and he must not encourage love in her. Friendship was sufficient.

This morning, James's sense of guilt was particularly heavy. He never became accustomed to his lapses. He was ashamed of his weakness. Pain did not excuse his behaviour. Drink did not help. In fact, often it deepened his plight. So it was on this occasion. Before lunch, the wife of an important local farmer would be calling to collect a commissioned painting that should have been ready almost a month earlier. James had written advancing the date until today. But still the painting was uncompleted and there was no way now of stopping the woman from calling.

He put his head back and groaned in self-disgust. He had no excuse. The painting was unfinished because he had been drunk when he should have been working on it. Even in his befuddled state a sense of responsibility had risen in him, and yesterday he had made a last-minute effort to meet his commitment. He had taken no drink, but he had been too ill to work. He had spent the day in bed, recovering from the excesses of the previous half week.

Today he felt physically well. He was ready to start painting again, but this would be little comfort to the woman after her journey from ten miles away.

After breakfast he walked worriedly up the twisting garden path to the low wall. He leaned over it for a long time, watching the tide swirl in over the glazed mud and the stranded fishing boats right themselves in the rising water. He rehearsed his apologies for the wife of the important farmer.

There was an hour to spare before she was due, but little could be done in that time. The painting required a full day's work. He sighed and went down a path toward his studio. In a neglected patch near the boundary hedge wasps worked noisily among a tangle of briar on which glistening black brambles clustered. Where the sun had not yet reached, cobwebs strung with dew formed silver traceries against an old wall and over the arc of a rose bower.

When he entered his studio, he left the glass door wide. He had worked so many years in the open he liked, even when inside, to hear the birds sing and smell the scented country air. He had left the picture on an easel. He went to it. At least he could minimise his disgrace. He could be working on the canvas when the woman arrived. That might placate her. He took away the dust sheet and stepped back to assess what had yet to be done. After a few moments a puzzled expression came on his lean face. His eyes narrowed. He bent forward uncertainly, then retreated again.

His heart began to beat faster and a sense of unease rose in him. The picture was finished in every detail. It was even signed and dated. After another spell of baffled inspection he put a finger on the paint. The varnish was dry.

Was his brain so affected by alcohol that his memory no longer functioned properly? It was a well-known phenomenon, but he had not believed himself at that stage of degradation. His alarm increased as he studied the painting further. There was a lack of expertise to be detected in various parts of it. The drawing of the hands, he saw, was not up to his usual standard. They would not have had that slight malformation if he had been sober when he painted them. And the cherry blossom reflected in the shining hair of one of the children had too much red in it. His keen eye soon found other telltale touches of a hand not truly his.

No one else would notice, of course, but it was amazing! Try as he would, he could not recall the slightest memory of the work's completion. He had not been in the studio yesterday. Of that he was certain. He had been ill, but he had been lucid. Of the previous days he could construct only a hazy record. Scenes—some of them almost too painful to be gazed on—reared out of the mist. Somewhere in the dark intervals he had somehow managed to finish the picture without ruining it. As he gazed at it in wonder, there was a sound that made him turn. Jessie was standing at the open door, watching him.

She made a movement of greeting with her stick. "Good morning, James." Her voice was slightly withdrawn and her gaze suspicious, but when she saw he was sober, she smiled. "How are you feeling?"

"Worried," he said, looking at her sheepishly.

Her head went up. She had the quick, uncalculated movements of an alert child. "What are you worried about?"

He stepped forward impulsively and, taking her hand, drew her into the studio. He led her to a settee and sat beside her.

"Jessie, I'm sorry for my awful behaviour. I start off simply trying to make things more bearable, but it runs away with me." He lifted her hand and kissed it. "Do you forgive me?"

She appeared to consider. "Yes, James," she said at last. "I forgive you. But do you forgive yourself?"

He shook his head. "No. I never do that. My weakness is deplorable. I can't think why you bother with me."

Her eyes softened. "Someone has to bother with you."

"I'll have to stop it," he said. "I'm getting worse. I've read about the long-term effects of too much drinking. A stage is reached where part of the brain ceases to function. A man can walk about doing things and talking to people and have absolutely no knowledge of it. The next step is permanent brain damage. The worrying thing is, I think it's started happening to me."

"Oh, James!" She took his hand. "Why should you think that? What's happened?"

"Look there." He pointed to the easel. "I finished that painting without knowing anything about it. I might have ruined six week's work. It was unfinished on Sunday when I started drinking. It was the first thing I thought of when I wakened this morning, that I would have to tell Mrs. Houston I had let her down again. Later I came in here and found it finished. Now, I was sober yesterday, Jessie. You know that. I didn't do it then, so it could only have been when I was drunk. The worrying thing is, if I can paint when I'm drunk without knowing it, what else might I be doing?"

Her small face had gone pale and her eyes were as worried as his. They sat looking at each other in silence until she bowed her head and said, "James, it was I. I did it. I wasn't going to tell you, because after I'd done it I was frightened, but I can see now that I must. When I did it I was silly enough to think you would imagine you had finished it yourself before you started drinking. I hadn't allowed for your thinking your mind was going. I can't let you think that."

"You, Jessie!" He was incredulous. "You did it? You finished my picture?"

"I'm sorry, James. Don't be angry with me. I thought I was helping you." He rose, muttering to himself, and stood in front of the easel—bending, peering and touching as she went on with her confession. "I knew you should have had it finished a month ago and that the Houstons were anxious to get it. I knew Mrs. Houston was coming specially today to collect it, and I could see you were in no condition to finish it. At first I was going to put her off, and then I thought, oh, no, I can't; that would be the second time. I was afraid of the bad name you would get if you kept disappointing important people like that."

James turned slightly from his rapt examination of her forgery. "Bad name?"

"I mean, I thought you would get a reputation for unreliability, and if that happened, you could lose a lot of clients."

"I don't need clients," he said with a gruff, uncharacteristic bravado. "I don't need their money."

Jessie, who had to work hard for a fraction of what he could com-

322

mand, shook her head cannily. "It never does to turn away money, James."

He turned and her heart lifted when she saw his teasing smile. "I forgot what a great respect you have for the bawbees, Jessie."

"They've never come to me easily," she reproved him.

"Ye're quite richt, lass," he said, putting on a music-hall accent. "We maun look efter the siller."

Despite the gentle mockery, he was filled with enormous tenderness for her. Her explanation of how the finishing touches had been put to the picture had come as a great relief to him. At least his mind was not going.

"And so you decided to help me, Jessie."

"Yes, James." She came and stood with him in front of the picture, emboldened and heartened by the lightening of his mood. "What do you think of it?" She bent to scrutinise her handiwork more closely.

"I can hardly tell the difference."

She made a challenging expression. "What do you mean 'hardly'?"

He put an arm round her. "Well, you're very good, Jessie; you've been an apt pupil, although I didn't want you as one and warned you often enough about letting my style influence yours. But . . . you haven't got it quite right."

She pouted sceptically. "Well, of course, you've got to say that, James. It wouldn't do to admit too much, would it?" Her eyes glinted with mischievous satisfaction as she saw him rise to the bait.

"If you think that, Jessie, I'm perfectly willing to go over the whole canvas, pointing out the bits you did. But do I have to do that? After all, some of it's so crude—especially the hands—I thought I'd done it when I was in a drunken trance."

"You're a cruel beast," she said, lifting her stick and threatening him with it. "And absolutely devoid of gratitude."

He put a hand on either side of her face and gave her a tender peck. "I am grateful, Jessie. And touched. It was a kind act, and I repeat—I can hardly tell the difference." He took his hands quickly away from her face as he caught sight of a clock almost buried under a jumble of rags and brushes. "But now we must clean it all off before Mrs. Houston comes; otherwise she'll want to take it away with her. Good heavens, she'll be here any minute. Ah, well, it won't take long." His voice grew cheerful at the prospect of action. "It's only touch dry. Did you know, Jessie, paint doesn't dry out completely for about twenty years?"

She watched in consternation as he crossed purposefully to a table and busied himself, collecting clean rags and a bottle of turpentine. Her lips were tightly compressed, but as he approached the picture, splashing the solvent onto a rag, a cry of dismay burst from her.

323

"Oh, no, James! No! You're not going to do that, surely. Not after all my work? Mrs. Houston will still be made furious. Your name will still become mud. I might as well not have bothered. You're very pig-headed!"

He lowered the sodden rag as he turned to her in astonishment. "Surely Mrs. Houston would be even more furious, Jessie, if she discovered part of a picture she's paying me one hundred and fifty pounds for had been painted by you?"

She jabbed her stick impatiently at the floor, her eyes flaring expressively at his stupidity. "But she won't know. You've said twice you can hardly tell the difference yourself. Who else will ever be able to tell?"

His voice censured her for her lack of understanding. "It's a question of artistic integrity . . . of my integrity. Surely you can appreciate that."

"If you're so worried about your integrity, you should stay sober," she said cruelly. "If you hadn't been drunk when you should have been working, you could have finished the blessed thing yourself."

"You little shrew!" He brandished the spirit-soaked rag, and for a moment it looked as if he would throw it at her. Then, collecting himself, he closed his eyes and took a deep, steadying breath. "Jessie! It wouldn't be honest." His voice had become pleading, and as he asked for her understanding, he shook his head at her with the beginning of a sadly reproachful smile.

"Of course it's honest, James." Her disdain had lessened, but her desire to convince him was just as intense. "You composed the pictue. You drew it and decided on the colours. Yours is the original and unique inspiration. That's what counts. All I did was a labouring job on a few insignificant parts of a very large canvas."

He laughed at the unscrupulous enthusiasm with which she moulded the situation to her advantage. "Jessie, you're delightful. Only a moment or two ago I thought you wanted me to applaud you for a major contribution."

"This is not the time for joking," she said, compounding her perversity.

"Well . . ." Although his resistance had been undermined a little, his stance was determined and his voice stubborn. "I can't really pretend the hands are an insignificant part, especially of this particular composition."

"Hands!" she said, her scorn rising again. "Do you not know, James, that when the fashionable of the land were queing to have their portraits done by Allan Ramsay, he had a youth in his London studio who did nothing but paint hands? His place was like a factory, with various talented pupils painting in the things they were best at."

He walked to the open door and pulled down a branch of the rose that rambled over the back wall of the house. It was clustered with small green buds tipped with the apricot tint of the bloom. Even in this sheltered place it was unlikely they would open now. Here was another hope never to be fulfilled, another striving all in vain. Life was laden with them. He let go of the branch and watched it spring back into place. With an effort he remembered Jessie's last blandishment.

"I doubt if Mrs. Houston would be impressed by that argument," he said over his shoulder. "I would question if she could even tell you who Allan Ramsay was."

Jessie shrugged. "I am not responsible for Mrs. Houston's ignorance," she said grandly, "but I suppose she knows who Leonardo, Michelangelo, Rembrandt and Rubens were? They all employed helpers to work on their paintings. Why, you know as well as I do, James, that even the greatest experts can hardly tell us of a single old master completed in its entirety by the master himself. It simply wasn't thought necessary in those days. Painting was regarded as just another job. The masters were not expected to spare time for details. But no one suggests they were dishonest."

"I suppose not." It was a reluctant concession.

"Then why should you be any different?"

He turned from his gloomy survey of the dying garden, the falling leaves, the fading colours.

"My God, woman, you can construct a persuasive argument. I'll say that for you."

"I am merely stating facts, James."

"Then stop stating them, before you corrupt me," he said, walking determinedly to the picture and pouring more turpentine on the rag which had gone dry as they argued.

There was knock at the door, and Mrs. Laing came in, smoothing her floral wrap-round apron. "There's a Mrs. Houston called to see you," she said, surreptitiously examining James to see if he was still sober. Her life, like Jessie's, had in recent months been turned devotedly to protecting him from the public gaze and from the worst consequences of his sad excesses.

"Show her in, Mrs. Laing," Jessie said quickly.

"No!" James's voice was almost a shout. "Not just yet, a minute."

Mrs. Laing looked from one to the other with a placid smile of enquiry. She was becoming accustomed to the unpredictable ways of these artistic bodies. She even felt it added a certain distinction to her own status, setting her interestingly aside from those unexcitingly employed in more humdrum households. *At least I'll never weary,* she always told herself when some new crisis arose.

"You can't clean it off now," Jessie said quietly. "There isn't time. And if you tell her it's not finished she's bound to ask to see how far it's advanced."

"I could refuse," James said with a distracted grimace.

"That would hardly be courteous, especially since you've involved the lady in a long journey."

He was worriedly aware of Mrs. Laing. "Tell the lady I'll see her presently."

As soon as they were alone, he whirled on Jessie. "It's monstrous that you should have landed me in this predicament."

"The predicament is of your making. I tried to save you from it." She nodded calmly to the picture. "What are you going to do about it? The woman's waiting."

He took a long, agonised look at it. "I couldn't possibly charge her the full price. I'd have to give her it cheap."

"I can't think that's very complimentary to me, James, but I won't object."

He rubbed his hands on the front of his Norfolk jacket. "I suppose for once it wouldn't do all that much harm," he said, going back to the picture to assess once more the quality of her work. "In relation to the whole canvas, it really amounts to very little. It would certainly save me from having to give an embarrassing excuse."

He caught her glinting smile of victory. "Get out," he said, giving her a gentle push toward the garden door. "I'm not going to have you here, watching the woman's face—or mine—when I unveil it. Which reminds me . . ." He snatched the dust sheet from a chair and hurriedly threw it over the painting.

"I'm glad you've decided to be sensible, James," she said from the door.

"Out," he repeated. "Begone! And don't ever do it again."

21

The city took on a bleak, secretive look as the mellow mists and red sunsets of autumn gave way to black fog and freezing mud in November and December. Ships edged carefully up and down the shivering river, calling startled warnings to each other as their shrouded shapes loomed out of the yellow gloom. Heavier curtains were hung in the houses and closely pulled for cosiness. The streets emptied as soon as the shops closed and the clop of horses sounded mournfully in the long, gas-lit darkness. As New Year approached, the shops became cheerful with colourfully wrapped cherry and sultana cake. Cotton wool was stuck on windows and bottles of ginger wine and fruit cordials were entwined with holly and mistletoe.

People danced at Glasgow Cross for a brief hour as they gathered to hear the last year of the century rung in on the Tron bells. Bottles of King's Royal, Queen's Royal, Dunbar's Special, Black and White, Johnnie Walker and other popular whisky blends were brandished, passed from one mouth to another and finally smashed against the old stone steeple.

Soon the revellers dispersed, most of them unsteadily, to join thousands of others on the annual mission of "first-footing." Superstitious householders laughingly but insistently barred all others until a dark-haired man carrying a lump of coal had first put his foot across the step. By breakfast time, all but the strongest had collapsed from a combination of exhaustion and drink, and the streets were dead.

For the holiday it had been cold but fine. Now, winter settled in again with showers of icy rain and sleet. The sullen river lapped its despoiled banks with Arctic greyness, and men working on the skeletons of iron ships froze.

In these first bitter days of the new year a flame of alarm suddenly swept the blending industry. For months, almost to the neglect of his own business, Dunbar had worked obsessively toward the goal of the syndicate. So cleverly had he moved, so labyrinthine were his purchasing deals—made in many names and from a multitude of addresses—that his mission was accomplished almost before the blenders realised what was happening.

Within days, the syndicate's masterstroke was the admiration of the financial world. Investors everywhere applauded and wished they'd been in on it. Such cunning as was gradually revealed could only be admired and envied. Only the whisky blenders, who now faced astronomical prices for top-class malts, could not appreciate the stealthy skill with which the operation had been carried out. To their frustrated fury was added the derision of others scornful of their sleepy simplicity.

That it had been allowed to happen was now almost unbelievable. That there had been a pattern of rising prices was obvious. But that there could be a malign intellect behind this, no one dreamed. In a trade where no shortage of supplies had ever been known, where the common memory was of huge unsaleable surpluses, the idea of the market's being cornered had occurred to no one. After all, were not one hundred and sixty distilleries now busily producing a yearly torrent of malt and grain whisky approaching the forty-million-gallon mark? Amid such plenty, who so pessimistic or suspicious as to think of drought? Admittedly, the open-market price for matured top-class malts had risen in the year by almost fifty percent. Everyone knew it, but few wondered why. After all, top-class malts represented only a very small fraction of the total market.

Hardly anyone remembered just how vital that fraction was. The trend was seen almost everywhere in the trade as some sort of fluctuation that would right itself in due course. In a booming new industry full of complacent self-satisfaction, there were no precedents that men could recall with alarm. Whenever a slightly anxious voice was raised in White's at lunchtime, Dunbar quelled it with such good-humoured scorn that the whisky crowd slept on, hypnotised by the confident and persuasive sway of his whisky glass. A few canny men, motivated by some perception beyond ordinary reason, began buying all the top malts they could afford, even at the new high prices. But even they saw the situation as a merely puzzling quirk of the market against which wise precaution must be taken, but without alarm.

Nowhere were the sinister implications realised until too late. Only as men crouched over their office fires in these raw days of early January— when plans were traditionally made for buying the next twelve months' requirements—did they discover the market was practically bare. By the middle of the month panic raged in the blending houses along the north side of the river and in the warehouses lining the slum streets leading up to the city. In the scramble for what little top-class malt the syndicate had not cornered the price quickly doubled again.

Dunbar, anxious to avoid his stunned and duped cronies, kept clear of the usual meeting places. But in the street, if he saw any colleagues approaching, he affected the same worried expression as was everywhere common, while inside he listened gleefully to the familiar lament.

"Well," he would say sombrely when he had tired of hearing them, "I suppose we've never died a winter yet. It's bound to come back on the market sometime, and we'll just have to pay the going price." And he would walk off with a swagger that belied the lugubrious hang of his lip.

He was careful to maintain this grave pose, for contemptuous as he was of his competitors as individuals, the thought of their combined wrath raised faint tremors of anxiety even in his massive arrogance. But, most of all, his fear was that his part in the conspiracy might reach Fiona. Having engineered a situation in which, at last, he had King & Co. at his mercy, how to explain it to her? It was the one hurdle he had failed to surmount, and at which cunning had failed him. He could think of no way in which the act could be made to appear compatible with his love.

Only when reporting to his backers did he feel able to indulge himself. It had been his plot, brilliantly conceived in his brain and triumphantly executed by him. It had worked gloriously and he had done it single-handed. All this collection of rabbits had contributed was a little money. Facing them in the hotel room where they still met, he basked and postured as never before. He was determined—all the more because of the secrecy he had to keep elsewhere—to extract the full tribute. And they, knowing well, now, the part they had to play, plied him with flattery until their smiles became rigid with weariness. He was insatiable. He was unconvinced that they realised the full extent of what he had done for them—a man like him, who had been saddled with them by the damned bank! As he emptied glass after glass of whisky, his loathing of them mounted. He contemplated, with a terrible sense of being plundered, the vast profit that must go to them because old Finlay had been too yellow-livered to give him the backing that had been his due. It could all have been his, the whole bloody lot, all the millions of ransom the blenders would have to start doling out because he was smarter than the whole pitiful trade put together.

Suddenly, words came to him from nearby, and he whirled on Livingstone Laing, spitting brutal disdain on the man's mild musings as to when they might start converting their golden assets back into money.

"Just you keep sitting on your fat arse and leave that to me," he

329

roared, blind to their horror at his savage intensity. But the gasps of outrage that followed his outburst reached him, and he remembered he had to work with them still.

"Let them scrape awhile for what's left," he ruled in a calmer voice. "The longer they scrape, the more they'll appreciate it when we're ready to sell."

"I wonder if Dunbar's behind this?" Ross said as he sat with Fiona, compiling the list of top-class malts they would need for blending in both King's Royal and Queen's Royal later in the year.

She kept her eyes on a stock ledger she was consulting. "Why should you think of him?"

"I'm remembering how he bought up all the twelve-year-old Aberlivet we needed."

"That was years ago," she said. "Besides, this isn't directed against King and Company. Every blender will have to pay inflated prices when these whiskies come back on the market. The talk is that it's a syndicate of financiers."

"I wonder what their price will be?"

She shrugged. "If it's too much, the price of a bottle of whisky will have to go up. We'll all be in the same boat."

But that night, Ross's suspicion was still in her mind when she met Dunbar. She told him what had been said, making it sound ridiculous.

His heart thumped, and for a moment he almost confessed. But if he told her the truth, how could he continue with his headlong assault on King & Co.? And yet, if he went on with it, wouldn't he be ruining her as well? At last he had been forced to accept that she *was* King & Co., as much as—and these days perhaps even more than—Robert. The dilemma was with him night and day, but he could not resolve it. If he smashed what he hated, he would maim what he loved. If he protected what he loved, he would be sparing what he had sworn to destroy. He shuddered and then smiled quickly, realising she was watching him.

"Your Mr. Ross must have a high opinion of my business sense," he said lightly. "And an inflated notion of how much money I have. You can tell him I'm not guilty."

He felt a stab of shame when he saw how trustingly she accepted the lie.

Throughout January and into February the bitter weather continued. April, when spring must come and colour return to the earth, seemed a long way off.

330

During these iron months they met at least once a week. He arranged things in his military manner, renting a new flat every few weeks, moving from one part of the city to another, altering the days they met, even varying the hours. The nomadic pattern forced on them by the need for secrecy was not confined to his relay system with the flats. Under the cloak of a merciless winter in which few moved needlessly, they made frequent day trips in empty trains and steamers to various small resorts on the Clyde coat—Ayr, Largs, Dunoon, Arran—revelling in their isolation on desolate beaches and in the intimacy of meals served in front of leaping fires at inns where they were the only travellers.

Emboldened by their long success in avoiding detection they went in February to Edinburgh, where for five days they stayed in a hotel as "Mr. and Mrs. Deans," Fiona having the excuse of business calls and Florence, the only one of the family still at home, being looked after by Fergus and Rita. This was their happiest adventure since the yachting holiday. The time of the last train need not be remembered, the hours need not be counted in ones or twos, nor the next striking of the clock be awaited with dread as the signal for parting.

The Capital, swept by east winds, was even colder than Glasgow and, at this time of year, deserted of visitors. They had the public sections of the Castle and the Palace of Holyroodhouse to themselves. With arms linked they walked the frosted cobbles of the Royal Mile, which separated the two, heedless of the cutting blast that scoured the historic street.

Wrapped in furs and scarves they climbed Arthur's Seat and looked down on the Queen's Park, the breweries, the reeking chimneys of the vennels and the bell tower of St. Giles's Cathedral. Dunbar pointed out the dwarfed carriages turning off Princes Street for the grey terraces and open squares of Georgian Edinburgh. On an afternoon they deserted the historic Old Town for the more sedate atmosphere of the residential New Town with its views across the Forth to the distant shores of Fife.

While others crept about, bent and huddled by the fierce chill, their enjoyment was unconfined. On a dire night they bribed a reluctant and shivering cabbie to drive them down forsaken roads to Queensferry where, after a candle-lit dinner in the Hawes Inn—much as Fiona had imagined it from Stevenson's reference to it in *Kidnapped*—they clung to each other on the water's edge, gazing up at the massive girders and soaring spans of the Forth Bridge glistening under a brilliant moon, as happy as if they beheld the Great Pyramid.

Behind them a row of whitewashed cottages stood stark in the ghostly glare. At one window the curtains had not been drawn. As they passed they had a glimpse of burning logs and a single lamp illuminating a room containing only necessities. A man and a woman sat contentedly on either side of the fire and between them a dog sprawled, cocking its ears at their footsteps.

In that moment, if it could have been done, Fiona would have exchanged all her possessions and her position for the life she imagined such people led. The demands of King & Co. were usually insistent and, when not, boring. Family problems persisted. Gordon, in his lodgings, was a worry, not simply because he was living away from home and therefore giving rise to gossip but because his attitude to life was feckless. He was like no other King. There was a great business which one day he should rightfully head, but apparently the traditions of the family meant nothing to him. If his disinterest—like James's in an earlier generation—had been the result of a desire to shape his life in some other worthy direction, the situation could have been accepted. But he seemed devoid of ambition, of direction. His shameless intention seemed to be to live a life of total indolence until the money he had inherited was spent. And then? He had been unable to tell her, and gave no sign he cared. If he had been another woman's son, she would have stamped him a wastrel. Robert had already done so, reminding her of various escapades in the past when Gordon had shown he preferred sailing, rambling or simply lazing in the sun to working. The black shock of his murderous attack on Jack had reverberated round the family and the business for weeks. No one could understand it, and despite all demands for an explanation, the lips of the two had remained tightly closed.

Other names and faces came to her. James and Jessie had been in Glasgow for the New Year. In a disgraceful scene in Fergus's Bath Street club a drunken member had challenged James to give some decent explanation of his preoccupation with "all those damned little girls." When James had stared uncomprehendingly, the man had hurled a glass of whisky over his head at a massive James King picture on the smoke-room wall. The drunk had been dragged away, still shouting innuendoes which James, who was quietly drunk himself, had seemed to find merely ridiculous and which, judging by his lack of reference to them in sobriety next day, had been forgotten or had at least left no mark.

The man had his membership withdrawn at a special meeting of the club's management committee next morning. The painting, which had been slightly damaged by broken glass, was taken down and sent for repair. Apologies and a report of the action taken were sent to James and Fergus by special messenger. After reading them Fergus nodded grimly, went to his study and wrote his letter of resignation. He had been a member for thirty-eight years and served on all the committees. Next day, although still fuming, he finally accepted his solicitor's advice that any action in the courts would be a reckless gamble which could as easily damage James as it would his slanderer.

332

Jessie had revealed the depth of James's disillusion at his failure to attain in his work the old dimension which he had so hopefully pursued and imagined lay just a little way over the Galloway horizon. But she also told them of the efforts being made to have him elected at last to the Academy. His old friends Guthrie and Walton were campaigning behind the scenes. Support, she told them, was growing. Several members of the Academy had always thought it unfair that James had been denied the honour, and Guthrie hoped to put their indignation to good use. In Jessie's opinion election to the Academy would be the greatest imaginable boost not only to the sagging spirit of James's self-respect but also to the future course of his work. Under this great new impetus, all the more powerful for its long delay, what might not James achieve? she asked, her eyes glowing with a loyalty and affection for which all present silently blessed her.

Anne. In Fiona's head it sounded like a name from some distant period of time. So much had happened to her own life since the night in Claremont Row when she had first heard the name, even since the more recent night in Dunbar's house when the girl had stepped from the shadows of the library and thrown them into a panic of guilt. And yet, but for Anne she would not be here now with Dunbar, fifty miles from home on a piercing east-coast shore, her passionate blood already tingling at the prospect of returning as "Mrs. Deans" to the sumptuous hotel room with its flock walls, coal fire and canopied bed.

She tightened her grip on his arm as the road became icy, and said gently, "Don't speak of it if you don't want to, Douglas, but I've been wondering how Anne is now?"

The slight apprehension that had been in her at the raising of this delicate subject subsided as she realised he was prepared to talk about the girl.

"It's difficult to know, now that she's not under my roof, but the last time I saw her in Glasgow she seemed more her old self. She's still a worry though. I know how suddenly things can change for her." He shook his head. "It's not right, that little boy Malcolm being reared without a father."

An enormous pity for the girl rose in her. She was so young and beautiful to be so tragically afflicted.

"I often wonder what happened between her and Gordon . . . whether they really stopped meeting or not. I've never asked. I felt I had done all I could."

It was a measure of their intimacy that she could say it without provoking an outburst. But she had taken at face value his declaration, during their day out in the Benz, that he no longer held the same anger for Gordon.

333

"Nor have I. But like you, I often wonder." She felt him turn to her, and in the light of the moon she saw he was smiling with an expression of wry tolerance. "Although we're hardly in any position now to complain about them." She brushed her head affectionately against his arm. "Mind you!" His voice rose a little and she detected at once the odd mixture of challenge and defensiveness in it. Clearly, despite the weakness of his position, he intended to pontificate and felt embarrassed about it. "She should be back with Peter. There's no two ways about it. They should make another attempt at patching things up."

"Hasn't it got past that?"

He shook his head fiercely but did not speak immediately. In the silence she heard waves running coldly on the sand. When he spoke, it was almost as if to convince himself. "How can anyone know if they don't try?" He muttered something incoherent and then, sorrowfully, "It probably is too late. But for the boy's sake, if not for their own, they should try again. It hasn't done Peter any good, you know. From being too involved with his business he swung the other way and neglected it for too much playing about. Now it's collapsed."

"That won't make it any easier for them to come together again."

"Oddly enough, I've been wondering if it might not be the making of them," he said musingly. "He's been at me for help to start up again. He knows I don't blame him for their troubles—not all of them, anyway. He was a sorry sight. He's lost weight and by the look of him he'll not have a hair on his head by the time he's thirty. But I think he's wiser. I've thought it over well and he'll get the money he wants only if he can make a home with Anne again. It's up to him to persuade her."

Ahead of them there was a rattle of wheels and the sound of a horse. Their cab was nosing erratically along the shore of the firth, facing into the wind. When he saw them, the cabbie waved his whip and let out a mutinous cry. "Ah thocht ye were loast. This is nae a nicht for winchin' or loiterin'."

He was hanging in a disconnected way, as if he did not have control of his muscles. He was so muffled in hat, scarves and blankets that only his eyes could be seen.

Dunbar put a hand on the reins. "What's happened to that flask of rum I bought for you at the inn?"

"It's feenished," the cabbie said, making an effort to straighten. "A wee bit refreshment like that doesna go faur in sich a nicht. Are you twa no' fur hame yet?"

Dunbar, catching Fiona's expression, laughed. "You're a disrespectful old rascal. I wouldn't have thought it of you, but we'll say it's the rum talking." He opened the cab door. "I hope your horse can see the road, for I doubt if you can."

* * *

Soon the winds stopped blowing. The city went still. Early blossom opened and the trees wore green veils. The days lengthened, spreading the streets with light and colour but filling Anne, it seemed, with a new restlessness.

Since the move from her father's house into her own flat, she had regained some stability, interesting herself in supervising the running of the household, a therapeutic chore that had previously been denied her because Dunbar had servants for everything.

With Gordon in lodgings only a street or two away they had built up over the winter a sense almost of domesticity. To flout the conventions and live openly together hardly occurred to them. But they spent several evenings a week with each other, dining at a small table set close to the fire after Malcolm had been put to bed and the cook had gone home. The single maid Anne employed was discreet, and often it was after midnight when Gordon went quietly down the stone stair and through the silence of the mixed commercial and residential district to his rooms.

Their relationship had assumed a pattern and tempo that took little account of the future beyond the following week. They had no vision of an ordered life stretching enticingly ahead, with children arriving, possessions being amassed, position gained and the nucleus of another prosperous middle-class family forming. This was the dream of other young lovers of their social level in this most Victorian of cities. This was the rock on which their—and its—contented solidity was based.

Gordon hardly even considered how he would live when his money was spent. Although he frequented some of the clubs that provided gambling and drinking pleasures for the gentlemanly young of the city, he still had funds to last another two years at least. After that? The thought aroused no panic in him. Anne's illness had taught him to be happy when it was possible. The last inclination he had was to anticipate events that might never happen. Was it, he sometimes idly wondered, the philosophy of a wastrel, as his father had declared, or a kind of unfashionable wisdom?

For a year it had kept him content enough, but as he sensed another change in Anne, he felt his own durability threatened. Could he stand a return to the wear and worry of watching her live through another disintegrating bout of mental turmoil, if that's what was coming? With growing dread he listened to her fret about Malcolm. He was at an age now, she lamented, when his memories of adult behaviour would begin to form. What would he remember of this period of childhood? A home without a father, to which a man he was hardly ever allowed to meet came to spend evenings with his mother? It wasn't good enough, she would cry. And turning her tragic eyes on him, she would challenge him to deny it. "Well, is it, Gordon? Is it, honestly?" Bewilderedly he would agree that it might not be, and cautiously enquire how she felt the situation could be improved. Did she want him to stop coming? And then she would sob, "I don't know what I want, but it isn't that."

There had been no further treatment from Durande, or even talk of him. That had been too racking a period for either of them to want to recall it. As the long months of improvement had followed her flight from the nursing home, Gordon had even found himself wondering if in some bizarre way the cruelty inflicted on her had been beneficial, perhaps forcing her "to take a grip on herself," as he thought of it, now that she had been given a glimpse of the awful alternative.

Cautiously he remarked on her paleness and suggested she might need a tonic after the grim winter. To his astonishment she replied by throwing herself into the chair beside him and resting her head, weeping, against his face. At last her voice came in painful gulps.

"Are you tired of me, Gordon? Is that what it is? Do you want rid of me, too?"

He was stung to cruelty. "When I'm tired of you, all I have to do is walk out through that door and never see you again."

She leaned back so that she could see his face, her tears checked by the sharp reality of his answer. A gasp shook her and her eyes were alarmed. "Yes, I'd almost forgotten that. You're not tied to me in any way."

"Only by the damned fact that I love you," he said harshly, all his old resentment at the injustice of his strange passion for her rushing blindingly in on him.

A shade of a sad smile formed round her mouth. "I've ruined your life, Gordon, haven't I?" she said softly. "Almost as thoroughly as my own."

He didn't deny it. "I love you, Anne," he repeated.

"If only I didn't love you."

"My God," he said, his exasperation rising again. "What does that mean?"

"If I didn't love you so much, I could be cruel to you, and in the end that would be the kindness you would remember me by."

"I'm not in the mood for riddles," he said.

"Surely it isn't much of a riddle."

He pressed her head gently to his chest. "Once—it seems a lifetime ago—I wanted us to go away and start life all over again where no one would know who we were. We could still do that."

"Less than ever," she said with a certainty that surprised him. He looked down quickly and saw her gaze was fixed on a photograph of Malcolm which had been taken on his fifth birthday.

336

"If we were determined enough we could arrange things so that—in the end—we would be quite . . . respectable." His voice faltered on the last word.

"How?"

"Surely after all this time Peter would divorce you? We could be properly married. In time people would forget you'd had another husband."

She looked at him in wonder. "You would have me as your wife?"

"You're my wife now," he said in anguish. "My only wife."

"No!" It was a shrill cry of regret. "It would be too great a scandal. In Glasgow, people like us don't get divorced. We're too bound up with family ties. If it were just the two of us . . . but . . . "

He saw she was looking at the photograph again. "I know," he said, unable to keep the vinegar from his voice. "Little Malcolm."

She ignored the bitterness. "And my father. And your people."

"You could leave my people to me. And I wouldn't have thought you cared about your father after your belief that he plotted against you with Durande."

"Perhaps I was wrong. Anyway . . . Peter wouldn't divorce me."

All at once he saw the truth, and his voice rose almost to a shout. "That's who's upset you. You've seen him recently, haven't you?"

"Yes." She leaned toward the fire, as if she had become suddenly cold. "He wants me to go back to him."

"It's Peter who's put all this in your head about Malcolm."

She stretched her hands toward the flames, nodding her head. "He said we should try again, for Malcolm's sake. He said it might be the last chance to give him a normal upbringing. I've never seen him so anxious. He was pleading."

Gordon was hardly listening. "After your being so well, he's knocked you sideways again. Didn't the fool realise the harm he was doing?"

"I'll be all right, Gordon. Perhaps, as you suggested, I need a tonic."

"What answer did you give him?"

"The same old one. I refused. But . . . he's been through a lot, too, you know. He's suffered. His business has gone. He looked desperate."

He glanced round the room with something like horror. "Was he in here?"

"Yes." Her attitude had become defiant. "He has called several times."

"He's being very persistent."

She shrugged. "Legally he is still my husband."

An unbearable thought came to him and his face twisted with pain and suspicion. "My God, I hope he hasn't been . . . You don't let him . . . ?" His eyes were moving over the outstretched lines of her body.

She straightened quickly in the chair. "Of course not."

He banished the surly mood that was threatening him. "Has he accepted your refusal?"

"I made it plain enough."

The quarrel that had been so near retreated, but when he left, she looked worn and her eyes held an expression he had hoped never to see again.

Fergus did not respond to these first soft days of spring. He looked from the open windows of Park Place to a grassy banking nodding with daffodils, but he saw only winter. He was haunted still by the memory of the terrible night in his club when in drink there had tumbled from the mouth of a man he had always considered decent the dark suspicions which in sobriety could not be mentioned. He remembered James's baffled but unworried expression. It had been the face of an innocent man. But he remembered also the expressions of several members, even among those who had dragged the drunk away. They had not been baffled. They had been outraged and desperate to silence the man, but they had known what he was raving about. They had heard the gossip. It must be oozing over the city like sewage trickling from a cesspool.

Fergus sat in his study, going over it all for the hundredth time. If he'd been allowed his way, he'd have brought it all out into the open then and put an end to it. But those blasted lawyers had baulked him! They never came up with the advice you wanted. For more than a year he had waited to catch someone slandering James in front of witnesses. But the moment he was in a position to nail the foul lie in court, old Taylor and his sycophantic younger partner had funked it. He remembered with contempt the lawyer's final words: "I will accept your instructions, of course, but the shortest, cheapest and best advice any lawyer can give a client is —*never litigate*." And with contempt for his own weakness he remembered how he had allowed himself to be persuaded.

He leaned back in his chair and glowered at the ceiling. He no longer kept office hours. There had been no interesting auctions recently, and, deprived now of his club, he had too much time to put in.

The house was quiet. The servants had completed their morning routine and Rita was in town helping a friend shop for an evening fan or some other silly, frilly falderal. He couldn't remember. *They* never had any difficulty putting their time in.

He rose, collected his hat and stick and walked down toward the city, pausing at Charing Cross to watch the windows of the Grand Hotel being painted. Beyond this, on the same side of Sauchiehall Street, were the fine terrace houses of Albany Place. There was some talk of pulling them down to make way for an extension of the shopping area or, alternatively, to build shops in front of them. He didn't suppose he would live to see it. He could remember when this had been the edge of the country. His lifespan had seen Glasgow bound forward into the forefront of the world's industrial cities. His had been a generation with vision.

All at once he felt immensely sad. And, for the first time, old. His two gods—hard work and respectability—were everywhere under attack. He sometimes felt a stranger in this land he had helped build. Dear knows! He shook himself. This gloom would never do. It was cast, he knew, mainly by the cruel cloud hanging over James. It was strange how he, who had all his life fled in terror from the slightest hint of scandal, had, paradoxically, been afflicted by more than his share of it. Tom Hoey had been a blot, until in the last year or so of his life he had redeemed himself. At least he had atoned and died a credit to them. Robert had given them years of crushing anxiety—first by almost marrying a Catholic and then by landing them in court, charged with defrauding the public by selling their new King's Royal blend of malt and grain under the name of whisky. They had been exonerated, of course, and Robert had gone on to make King & Co. the foremost name in whisky.

Now it was all starting up again. There was Gordon—refusing to work and living alone in rooms barely a mile from his parents' home. What must people think? And how was young Hoey going to cope with all that money?

Above all, here was poor James being traduced for his simple scenes of childhood. How ironic that such innocence should be evilly twisted. Fergus cursed whatever warped mind had first distilled the poison. The only gleam he could see was the prospect of James's being elected to the Academy. That should help put a halter on the gossiping tongues, for there was no more respectable body in Scotland. But, of course, the elusive accolade had yet to come. The present had still to be made bearable.

His walk had taken him as far as West George Street. His heart lifted a little, as it always did, when he stood on one of these vantage points and looked down on the great city, split by the life-giving river. A cab stopped down the hill, and he saw Alexander Reid step out of it and go into his gallery. Fergus stopped at the door.

There were two easels in the window. On one there sat a woodland scene by Corot and on the other a river landscape by Daubigny. The Glasgow shipbuilder, coal owner or ironmaster who prospered to the point of being able to indulge his artistic taste had been educated by Reid to buy these fine Barbizon painters long before their value had been realised by the London dealers. Fergus felt Reid was one of the city's assets. He followed him into the gallery with an idea beginning to form sketchily in his mind.

After walking round the colourful display Fergus returned and stood in front of a picture by James. It was one he had not seen before, but without looking at the date he could tell from the vigorous movement and intensity of colour that it was an early work.

Behind him he heard Reid's voice: "I bought that under the hammer about a month ago." He turned and saw Reid's sharp beard and bright, discerning eyes. "I think it can take its place with any of these others." He indicated the French and Dutch paintings.

Fergus warmed. "It's good to know someone still has a good word for James."

To his surprise, Reid put a hand on his shoulder and shook it slightly, as if to impart something too heartfelt for words. His voice was intense. "I heard about that awful business in the club. I was disgusted. I almost followed you out."

Fergus was suddenly too choked to speak.

"I felt I should make some gesture," Reid said, "but, possibly to my shame, I let them talk me out of it. They want you back, you know. The committee plan to meet specially and put it to you formally."

Fergus blew noisily into his beard. "They won't get me back. Not that I'm blaming the club. The committee acted promptly. I just feel I couldn't sit there in peace any longer, knowing what some of them would be thinking." He nodded to the painting. "That's the sort of gesture James needs most: a man like you hanging his pictures is a declaration that there is no evil behind them." His hands clenched on the head of his cane and his voice thickened with bewildered anger. "You know, Reid, I've heard some people have actually taken James's paintings off their walls."

The dealer's mouth twisted in exasperation. "They must be fools, and there can't be many of them. James's work is still in great demand. I paid quite a stiff price for that." He paused. "None of this scurrilous nonsense has reached him, I hope. He's still painting?"

There was a settee behind Fergus and he sat on it heavily.

"So far as we know, James is not aware of it. Even that scene in the club didn't seem to leave a mark. Although you would have thought it would have set something working in his mind." Fergus shook his head wonderingly.

"Perhaps not." Reid tapped the frame of James's picture. "These paintings are filled with innocence. People recognise it in them. That's why they prize them. They see there, captured in paint, emotions they remember with fondness. In a King painting they see themselves as they can never be again, in a world that's gone. Only a man wonderfully innocent himself could paint pictures like that. I don't think James has the mind that could understand what is being hinted at. His innocence will shield him."

"It shouldn't have to!" The protest was torn from Fergus, and realising the pitch of his voice, he looked worriedly about the gallery. They were alone. "Forgive me, Reid. It's so unfair. I get outside myself, sometimes." Determinedly he forced a more cheerful note into his voice. "There's one bright spot: James had been put forward for election to the Academy."

Reid frowned and made a sound of impatience. "That's another scandal. He should have been elected years ago. But better late than never, and if there's anything I can do behind the scenes, I'll do it."

Fergus looked interested. "Would you? I'd appreciate that."

"I don't mean anything improper, of course," Reid said hastily. "But there aren't many of them I don't know. There won't be any harm in letting them know what I think of James, not simply as an artist but as a man. I might have a little influence."

Fergus was struggling with his courage. He did not like asking favours, but there could be no better moment to voice the vague thought that had brought him in. "There's something you could do quite publicly." He watched carefully for signs of Reid's withdrawing. He did not want to embarrass the dealer, or himself. But the slightly grizzled face was expectant and open. "You could put on a full-scale exhibition of James's work. Nothing would redound more to his credit." He hesitated as he saw Reid's protesting smile. "It's an audacious request, I know, but I feel . . . it's my duty . . . to get support for James wherever I can. He needs it so damned badly."

"Do you know how much work there is in mounting an exhibition of the kind I think you're visualising?"

Clearly Fergus did not.

"At the very least, six months," Reid said. "For any exhibition truly representative of James's work, pictures would have to be borrowed from private collectors and public galleries, some of them not in this country. It's the sort of thing not normally tackled by a dealer. It's a different matter when the artist is fairly unknown and simply supplies the dealer out of his own studio."

"I could put the resources of King and Company at your disposal for all correspondence," Fergus said hopefully.

Reid rubbed his beard. "Is James still turning out the pictures? Any exhibition would have to contain a good proportion of work for sale. The public would expect that. After all, he's still very much alive. Besides"—his eyes twinkled—"I have to cover my expenses here. They couldn't all be loan pictures."

With anyone else, Fergus might have interpreted this as a hint. With Reid, he knew that any attempt at financial inducement, however well phrased or disguised, would be a fatal mistake. He contented himself with saying, "James is still working. I'm sure he'd be more than delighted to set pictures aside for you."

"I hope he kept a record of where the best ones went. I sold some myself, of course. I've kept on good terms with most of my clients. I don't think any will refuse."

Fergus kept his elation concealed. "You'll do it, then?"

Reid's laugh was rueful. "I've an idea I've let myself be talked into it." He looked round the gallery as if seeing a challenge. "Anyway, it's been too long since I gave the whole gallery over to a Scottish artist."

Suddenly Fergus remembered they were talking of an event that would be many months ahead. "I hadn't realised an exhibition took so long to organise," he said, slightly deflated. "It was silly of me. A moment's thought, and it's obvious."

"Actually, it could be an advantage," Reid said shrewdly. "Elections to the Academy are made in November. If we had the exhibition coinciding with that, everyone concerned would have James very much in mind. The papers and periodicals would be writing about him. The whole glory of his work over twenty years would be assembled here for them all to see."

Suddenly, each catching the other's rapt expression, they laughed.

22

It was now not unusual for Jessie to finish pictures for James. He always protested and threatened, but each time with less conviction. The solution would have been for him to stop accepting commissions, for it was only when there was someone waiting for a painting already unforgivably late that Jessie "interfered," as James referred to it. When he was painting for himself, time did not matter. If the work was interrupted, it simply lay until he could return to it. Unfortunately, whatever resolutions he made, James could rarely refuse a request. They usually came from important local people, introduced by those for whom he had already painted, or from friends of collectors who had supported him when he was unknown.

In this respect the news of Alexander Reid's plan came like a prescription for a return to self-respect. "No more commissions," he said excitedly, showing the letter to Jessie. "Here is the perfect excuse. I'll have to hold all my work for Reid until his exhibition is over."

The news made Jessie happier than she could have said. There were few men less vain than James, but she knew that what he desperately needed to carry him through this difficult period of his life was nourishment for his self-esteem. Election to the Academy would provide this, but he needed encouragement now. The flattering attention that preparations for an exhibition would generate must provide a valuable interim boost.

Of this Jessie was convinced. And the lift, she realised, would be for her troubled spirit as well.

In the last year she had watched dark phantoms creep up on James and squat in the shadows about him. Some came from within, from his failure so far to come to terms with his artistic limitations. Others were external. His leg troubled him with increasing severity and a specialist she had driven him to consult had hinted it would eventually need surgical attention. But more menacing was the incredible web of gossip which had slowly been spun around him.

It seemed there was hardly a soul in Fleetside who had not heard the whispers that had followed James from Glasgow. Jessie was racked by the injustice of remarks she overhead, glances she was not meant to see, an awareness of tongues being hastily bitten in the middle of unthinking sentences. The certain knowledge that no one who knew James treated the rumours as other than cruelly false provided limited comfort. Some mud always stuck. There was proof of this, she felt, in the way that in recent months various of the little girls who modelled for him had become unavailable, sometimes with elaborate explanations from their mothers, sometimes with none.

At first she had imagined the gossip to have started in Fleetside, but when she timidly confided her unhappiness to Fiona, she learned the origins were older.

It had taken her months to comprehend exactly what was being implied against James. Not only did she have a naturally innocent mind but she had been on so many of his sketching expeditions she knew better than anyone the fond, kindly and totally blameless nature of his relationship with the children he painted.

When realisation came, she at first recoiled with numb sorrow from this blind wronging of a man already wounded enough by life. Then she had been seized by a violent impulse to turn on the callous gossips, challenging them to substantiate the horrible defamation or withdraw, perhaps even threatening them with legal action. But when she made a secret visit to a lawyer in another town and presented him with a hypothetical case, she had, like Fergus, had her eyes opened to the possibility of James's being further damaged by the publicity that would inevitably follow any resort to the courts.

She had cycled furiously back to Fleetside, fuming. After months of lonely railing at the injustice of it all she had slumped into a state of frustrated helplessness. Eventually she became aware of what seemed to be a lessening of the gossip. Her heart rose. The calumny, she thought, had at last been seen for what it was and was now in the process of dying away.

Then, hard-headedness reasserting itself, she decided this was too optimistic an interpretation of what was happening. Tongues no longer wagged so often in her hearing because her closeness to James was now well known. People were simply being more careful. Often, when she should have been painting, she sat at a window looking angrily across the green and along the cobbled streets radiating from it. At these times she hated the town.

Slowly the brooding passed, and in fairness to the good-hearted majority of townspeople she encouraged in herself the conviction that very often the gossip was retailed with a sense of scandal not so much at James's supposed obsession but at the very idea of such wicked things being said about him.

This, in fact, was true, but poor consolation for the greater injury.

Throughout this period James painted on, succumbing every few months to an excess of drink, but apparently unaware that his artistic vision had given rise to so much gloating, shocked or worried speculation.

Now, in the long summer days, Jessie dared hope that a new era might have dawned. Under a powerful impetus inspired by the prospect of Reid's exhibition, James painted with absorbed steadiness. Dire events in the world beyond the leafy lanes and fresh shores of Galloway hardly touched his consciousness.

In June the Bloemfontein Conference collapsed, bringing open war in South Africa another stride nearer. In September the Boer republics, confident of their armed strength, issued an ultimatum. If their demands were not met by October 11, they would consider themselves to be officially at war. Within days, ten thousand troops sailed for Cape Town to reinforce the tiny British force already there.

James was hardly aware of these developments. He worked incessantly, giving way to only one outbreak of drinking severe enough to earn Jessie's disapproval—and even then the exasperated proddings she gave him with her stick were restrained and even sympathetic.

By the beginning of autumn he had almost twenty paintings ready for exhibition. Each, when completed, had been locked away in a storeroom, seen by no one but himself. Despite Jessie's curiosity, he refused to bring any of them out. "I want them to be a surprise," he said. She considered it too simple an explanation. Into these pictures, she was certain, had gone so much of James's hope that he was almost afraid to have them judged.

But one October afternoon when she came through the garden door, the studio was ablaze. There were pictures on every wall and propped against all the tables and chairs.

"I can't say any of them are inspired," James said, "but at least they're all up to standard." His voice was casual, but she felt he was watching anxiously for her reaction. "I don't think Reid will have any complaints." His face, which had grown paler and more gaunt under the stress of pain and his ceaseless work throughout the summer, broke into a self-mocking grin. "If he has, I certainly won't be able to blame anyone but myself."

This reference to her "interference" swept Jessie with a sudden, un-characteristic humility. All at once, confronted with the great array of paintings, any one of which would have been far beyond her capabilities, she realised the full enormity of her presumption. Some of these pic-tures must rank with James's best work. At least, since coming to Fleet-side, he had done nothing better.

Her eyes filled with tears of regret for the deceit he had become in-volved in because of her rash and arrogant self-confidence. She was not worthy to paint the smallest petal of a primrose or seashore rose onto one of his canvasses.

"James, forgive me." Her voice was muffled and unsteady. "I'll never again be so unfeeling. It was awful of me to finish those paintings. It's only when I see all these wonderful pictures that I realise how terrible it was of me . . . how unfair to you and to the people who bought them. It was wicked. I had no right."

He put an arm round her. "What about Rembrandt and Michelan-gelo?" he said, drawing her close.

She looked up in dismay at his teasing. Her eyes were beseeching. "Don't remind me!"

He gave her a long hug of forgiveness, and when she became cheerful again, they walked round the paintings. The colours had a fresh intensi-ty she had not seen except in his gallery work. As a student she had visit-ed most of the public collections. She had not known him then, but she remembered how she had stood and marvelled.

"I'm glad you think they'll do," James said. "If nothing else, they rep-resent a lot of hard work."

"They represent an awful lot more than that," she said.

Next morning James stopped his trap outside Jessie's cottage on the green. He was on his way to Gatekirk Bay with Meg and Isa and an older girl, Helen Marshall, who had only recently joined his troop.

Helen was fourteen, a paler, lankier version of the robust Melville sis-ters. She was one of the girls James used for what Jessie called his "young coquette" pictures. In these, the figures were still of children, but in more elegant poses, the dresses more adult and the features in refined and ladylike contrast to those of his more usual pink-cheeked country girls. Although the background was always what his admirers expected, the restrained attitudes in these studies suggested the good behaviour of the drawing room rather than the exuberance of play in the woods or on the edge of the sea.

Of all the children, Helen Marshall was the one Jessie liked least. With the others, it was all fun. Their pleasure was unfeigned. They were una-ware of what it was James was watching for. Helen knew—she was the only one who struck conscious poses. And she always started, Jessie felt, from the moment she climbed into James's trap.

There! She's at it now, Jessie thought with amusement as she watched the girl over James's shoulder. Helen's expression, as other children passed in the street, indicated a clear belief that being in a trap was socially better than walking. Additionally, she sat a little way apart and aloof from Meg and Isa, perhaps to emphasise her superior age.

It was arranged that Jessie would have tea with James at his house at four o'clock. Then, with the children laughing and the horse eager for the country ways it now knew well, they went round the green at a trot. Jessie waved as James raised his hat before the trap disappeared along Abbeyside.

She closed her door, thinking how cold and pinched he had looked in the October sunlight. There was hardly anything of him, of course, under the thick tweeds. She went to the room at the back of the house where she worked, still musing on his worrying appearance. His spirits were high after the long and successful output of the summer, but although he rarely complained, she knew he was dragged continually by pain. It was a miracle how he managed to work as steadily as he did. The strength of will under the youthful smile was a constant surprise to her. She could usually persuade and manipulate him to her purposes without trouble, because toward others he was good-natured and easygoing, but in the control of his own faculties James was a grim and heartless master.

When she went to his house in the afternoon, Mrs. Laing showed her into the sitting room overlooking the garden and the river. Smoke trailed across the narrow plot from a bonfire of leaves on the other bank. Already the garden had taken on a desolate look. Roses still flowered but the blooms were small. A clematis blossomed on a wall but the petals had a pale and precarious appearance. Brown leaves lay in heaps where the wind had blown them, for James's gardener came only twice a week. A faint haze hung over the boats in the harbour, and on the wall a fire crackled as water was boiled to scald fish boxes. The sun was red and low in the sky and soon the light would go. Jessie turned from the view and its memories of a summer gone. It was cold by the window and she went gratefully to the fire.

It was almost half past four when James arrived. He looked worried and dishevelled as he slumped heavily into a chair on the other side of the hearth rug. He smelled faintly of whisky and his smile seemed forced.

She leaned toward him with a concerned and inviting smile. "Are you all right, James? Is there something wrong?"

Before he could reply there was a knock at the door and Mrs. Laing,

347

who had been watching for him with the kettle boiling, carried in a tea tray.

"There's been a right nip in the air the day, despite the sun," she said. "If you're going to be painting in this weather, Mr. King, I'll have to see you wrap up well."

James nodded absently. "I have a good woollen scarf somewhere about, if you can find it, Mrs. Laing." His courtesy to her was unfailing. It triumphed over pain, disillusion and inebriation.

"I'll find it, I suppose," she said, her tolerant tone suggesting it wouldn't be easy, the way he kept his things, but she'd manage. She went out, smiling at them and wondering when they would marry. Immediately Jessie's concerned expression returned. "You look quite exhausted, James."

He sighed heavily and rubbed both hands wearily over his face. "Pour me a cup of tea, Jessie, and I'll tell you." His eyes strayed to the decanter as if he would have preferred her to pour from that. "The day started so happily, but it ended up a bit of a disaster." He shook his head as if at events beyond his understanding. "This morning I worked so well. The bay was beautiful, with the tide in and the water sparkling. I hardly stopped to eat my sandwiches." He looked at her guiltily. "I had some whisky. Not very much, and I diluted it well with water from the stream."

"James! You promised me you would only take whisky if your leg was really very bad."

"It was nothing more than a refreshment, Jessie. And to get my blood going. I had been sitting all morning. Anyway, not very long after that I got off my stool. I don't know what it was—perhaps the ground was uneven, or maybe it was because I was so stiff from sitting in the cold—but I stumbled. I fell headlong on top of Helen. I didn't hurt myself and I was sure she was all right. You know how cushioned the ground is with grass and moss. Well, you wouldn't believe the scene she made. She bounced up, holding her arm. She stood looking at me for a moment—I was still sprawled flat on the ground—and then she started screaming. I got up and went toward her to see what was wrong. She just kept backing away. Next thing, she had taken to her heels and was running up through the trees to the road, still screaming as if all the fiends were after her."

Jessie felt her brow go hot and then clammily cold. "Perhaps she'd fallen on a rock." There was no conviction in her voice.

James snorted. "There wasn't a rock in sight. Anyway, she seemed to have forgotten her arm when she ran away. I noticed she was able to push the bushes aside with it."

"What about Meg and Isa? What did they do?"

"They were as dumbfounded as I was. They just stood staring after her; then they helped me get my things together and up to the trap. I heard Meg muttering, 'Silly thing.'

"We bowled back along the road as fast as we could, looking everywhere for Helen. By the time we reached Fleetside I was in a panic. I was sure she'd got lost or fallen down a hole. But I might as well not have been so bothered. The little tinker was home before us. She must have got a lift from someone."

"Don't you know how she got home?" Jessie's voice was sharp. "Is she all right?"

"I suppose so, but I don't know. I didn't see her." He looked baffled. "Her mother slammed the door on me. She said I should be ashamed of myself. They must be a very strange family. After all . . . " He leaned forward. "Are you all right, Jessie? You look very white."

She shook her head impatiently and ignored his question. "Was that all Mrs. Marshall said?"

"No." His voice dropped. "I can't understand it. She said she was going to send for the police. I was thunderstruck. I told her not to be silly. That's when she shut the door in my face. I knocked and tried to get her to open it again, but she wouldn't. She shouted something again through the letter box about getting the police. It was only then I realised my breath would be smelling of drink."

He stopped when he saw her dazed and worried expression.

"I swear I wasn't drunk, Jessie," he said, misunderstanding her concern. He pulled his flask from a pocket and shook it. "Listen! The damned thing's still more than half full."

Despite efforts to talk about other things, they both kept going back to the incident, she with veiled and fearful questions, he with exclamations of fresh puzzlement. For distraction they spent an hour in the studio, labelling the new paintings for Reid and taking measurements for the frame maker. Afterward, subdued, they had dinner. A wind had risen, dispersing the autumn haze and whipping dark clouds across the moon. The dining room was small, and even at night, James insisted on the curtains' being left open. From the table they could see the changing patterns of the sky.

From there they went to the drawing room and sat listening to the wind rumbling in the chimney. Jessie was preparing to go home when Mrs. Laing came in and said there was policeman asking to see James.

"The wicked, scheming little vixen!"

The words burst from Jessie, turning Mrs. Laing's curiosity into astonishment.

"It's Alec Mason, the policeman," she repeated, as if perhaps they had misheard her.

349

"Yes. Show him in." James fumbled nervously for his pipe.

Constable Mason was in his middle twenties but looked even younger with his helmet off. He was best known to James for the amazing speed at which he could pedal his bicycle along the country roads. There had been a complaint from Mrs. Marshall, Mason explained diffidently, and he had been sent to get a statement. He seemed enormously broad amid the delicate finery of the drawing room, and when James made him sit, he looked even more awkward. He cast a worried glance at Jessie.

"It might be better if we spoke alone, sir," he said with a tense smile.

Jessie shook her head vigorously behind his back.

"I'd prefer Miss McNee to be present, if that's all right." James said.

Mason took out a notebook and pencil in a way that made obvious his reluctance to start.

In the end James had to prompt him. "What exactly is Mrs. Marshall complaining about, and what is it you want to know?"

"It's kind of delicate, sir, and if Miss McNee's going to stay, she'll have to excuse me. I'm only doing my job."

"We appreciate that."

"The complaint we have received, sir, is that you behaved in an improper way with this girl, Helen Marshall, and put her into a state of fear."

James was exasperated. "Improper? What in God's name does that mean?"

"Improper, sir," Mason repeated with a sideways glance to see where Jessie was.

"I asked you to be clear."

"The girl says you interfered with her," the policeman blurted.

James sank back in his chair. "Oh, my God." The words might have been meant only for himself. "So that's what it was."

"Do you know this girl, Mr. King?"

"Not as well as I thought." James spoke with effort, and it might still have been for himself. "Or maybe it's her mother. . . ."

"Did she go with you this morning to Gatekirk Bay?"

"Yes."

Mason wriggled to the edge of his chair. His gaze was fixed on his feet and he cleared his throat repeatedly before speaking. "The complaint we have states you knocked her to the ground and placed your hand on a private part."

"The evil child! Oh, the wickedness!" The cry came from Jessie.

Mason kept his eyes down but turned his head half toward her. "I did try to spare you this, miss. Well, sir?"

James's voice was strangled with incomprehension. "I can't believe it! It's diabolically untrue. Well . . . it's partly true. I did knock her to the ground, but it was an accident. I only have one leg, you know. I had been sitting all morning on a stool, painting. It wasn't warm, and when I got up I was badly cramped. I simply fell over, or perhaps I stumbled; I don't know which. I lurched against Helen and we both toppled onto the grass. But she was up on her feet in a second."

"Did you touch her, sir?"

"Certainly not—at least, not in the way you mean, or if I did, I wasn't aware of it."

"The girl's lying, then, sir?"

"She's either lying or mistaken."

Mason was writing it all down, and as a consequence the conversation was proceeding as if between idiots.

"She's lying." Jessie spoke with such conviction that the man turned and looked at her directly for the first time. Jessie sighed. "I've never been keen on that child. She is too . . . aware of herself for her age."

Mason hesitated, started to put it down, then, changing his mind, scored out what he had written with long, deliberate strokes.

James lurched up and went stiffly to the fire, where he stood chewing at the stem of his unlit pipe. The accusation was so numbing that the awful possibilities were dawning on him only gradually. Until now he had innocently imagined Mason was there only for some facts that would clear the matter up. Now he had an overwhelming sense of being trapped. The horror showed in his eyes as, moving a little toward the policeman, he came more directly into the light spread by a lamp on a table in the middle of the room.

"No one believes this disgusting nonsense, do they?" In the silence his voice rose. "Well, do they? Surely *you* don't?"

Mason shook his head, not in denial but as an embarrassed indication of his neutrality. "That's no' for me to say, sir. I've been sent just to take your statement."

James's temper began to flare. A raw nagging was eating at his leg. "Hell's name, you have my statement. There's nothing more I can say. You must have an opinion."

"I'm no' allowed to express an opinion," Mason said uncomfortably.

"Then you must be a damned ninny," James shouted, realising even as the fury broke the wild unreasonableness of the attack. "What right have you to come in here with a disgusting pack of lies or imaginings from a child of fourteen, and, after I've explained to you what happened, sit there and as good as tell me I'm a liar?"

A stolid look had come on Mason's young face, as if he had remembered he'd been trained to endure this sort of thing.

"James!" Jessie walked quickly between them and took James's arm. "You know it has nothing to do with the constable."

351

James closed his eyes and, his whole body drooping, went limply back to his chair with a resigned sigh. "Is there any more?"

"Yes, sir. Had you anything to drink when the incident took place?"

"Oh, God, Jessie, everything's being twisted." It was little more than a dejected moan. He raised his face to her as if pleading for her help. Before she could speak he had turned back to the policeman. "I had taken a little whisky. It deadens the pain in my leg. Why are you asking?"

"The statement of complaint we have alleges you were drunk, sir."

"Then it's a lying statement. I wasn't drunk. I was completely sober and my mind was perfectly clear. I can recall the incident in quite a detailed way, and the complaint you have is so much damned rubbish. You should be at the Marshall house finding out why it was ever made."

"I suppose it's being taken into account that there were other children there?" The two men swung toward Jessie in surprise. Even in the flattering oil light she looked haggard. "It's hardly the sort of thing that would be done in front of witnesses."

"I'd forgotten that, Jessie." James leaned eagerly toward the policeman. "Does the statement you have mention the Melville children were there?"

"We have that information, sir, and I spoke to the Melville children before coming here."

"Well?"

Mason hesitated. When he spoke his voice was sympathetic. "They can't help. They didn't see what happened. They had their backs to you when the incident occurred. The first they knew of it was when they heard Helen Marshall screaming."

He closed his notebook and turned to look for his helmet. James had a perverse desire to keep him there, to go on talking about it.

"Can I offer you a whisky?"

"Thank you, sir, but I'll have to get back to the station."

"Then, what happens now?"

"I'll make out a report for the sergeant. It'll be up to him to decide."

"To decide whether I'm innocent or guilty?" In James's head the words sounded unreal.

"That's not our job, sir. All we have to do is see whether there's enough evidence to justify a charge."

The word struck James like a hammer blow. "When will I know?"

"It'll likely be the morrow, sir."

James saw him out and stood by the door watching him cycle along the moonlit street, bent to the wind and pedalling slowly, as if in recognition of the dazed misery he was leaving.

Next day the constable returned to the house with his sergeant. In the

352

studio, among paintings for some of which the Marshall girl had modelled, James was formally charged.

Mason, who kept glancing at his notebook to remind himself of the legal formula, was no happier than on the previous night. The sergeant, who arrived seemingly determined to display a brusque detachment, possibly to impress his subordinate, gradually acquired a tinge of awkward sympathy when confronted with James's distress.

As they left, he even spoke what was clearly meant to be a small piece of comfort. "This doesna mean there's bound to be a prosecution, sir. I'm glad to say that's not for the police to decide. It's a matter for the procurator fiscal."

James seized on the scrap. "You mean, when it gets to him, he might decide there's nothing to take to court?"

"Exactly, sir. It's possible."

But two weeks later a summons was delivered decreeing that James must answer the charge before the sheriff at Dumfries.

"I can't believe it," he said to Jessie a hundred times. "How could a thing like this happen to me? Why should the girl make up such an awful lie?"

"Out of badness," was Jessie's bitter explanation. "Some of these little maids are schemers from the word go. The worst of it is, by this time she'll have convinced herself it's true."

Mrs. Laing's outrage when James falteringly told her what had happened came from the heart. "Oh, it's not true, Mr. King," she cried. "It's not true and not a body in Fleetside will credit it. The wicked little beesom that she is! May she be struck down for her badness."

Despite this comforting faith in him and the assurance about the townspeople, James was too miserably self-conscious to leave the house except for short spells in the garden, when he would walk numbly to the river wall and back, seeing nothing. If he heard voices from the harbour, he would go abruptly inside. He had a terrible sense of being hunted.

After nights of sleepless indecision Jessie made up her mind that he must be told the background to the accusation. She would have to tell him about the rumour-laden atmosphere from which Helen Marshall's lie had sprung. Undoubtedly it was this which had influenced the local policemen, leading them, however reluctantly, to place more weight on the girl's allegation than they would otherwise have done. The fiscal, resident in another town, and knowing nothing of James as a person, would have his mind even more coloured by the gossip. In court he would inevitably strive to create some link between the alleged assault and James's work. In the depressing loneliness of the night Jessie imagined a court scene in which the idea of artistic vision would be scorned, in which the

353

fiscal would ask, with a contemptuous glance at James in the dock, "When does a vision become an unhealthy obsession? Your lordship might ask himself that when considering his verdict."

No! Jessie shook the nightmare tableau of gowned and wigged figures from her mind. James must not hear of the evil speculation for the first time from the mouth of a hostile lawyer, in the unnerving atmosphere of a court of law. The experience would be harrowing enough without that. She would have to tell him herself of the cruel taint to his name.

She waited and chose a time when he plunged once more into tormented speculation with the standard cry, "Why Jessie? Why?"

When she had finished explaining, her heart ached.

James walked in silence to the garden door of the studio and stood for a long time staring blindly into the damp afternoon. It seemed to him, in his terrible despair, that his whole life had been a preparation for this final, heartless stroke of fate. Long ago, his boyhood had been clouded by a knowledge of his oddness in a family born to business. Then there had been the long years of adjusting to the loss of his leg. For a brief spell his talent as a painter had soared and then hung on the edge of the limitless sky, its tantalising suspension filling him with restlessness. Then had come Jessie—dear, dear Jessie!—and the awful discovery that his physical disability had crippled him emotionally, too, so that the normal development of their relationship was thwarted and might forever remain so. *Must forever remain so, now,* James thought with a tearing pain, for how could any man so afflicted—a limping cripple accused of this foulness—continue to contaminate the life of this sweet girl?

He turned to her with dull, wet eyes. "Why have they picked on me, Jessie? There are other artists who put children in almost all their paintings . . . Hornel, Macgeorge and Blacklock at Kirkcudbright . . . Gemmell Hutchison. Why me?"

"I don't know, James."

"How long have you known about this?"

She walked past him and closed the glass door against the dripping chill. "For almost as long as I've known you."

"Why didn't you shun me, for your own sake?"

"Because I love you." Suddenly she was in his arms, sobbing against his chest. "Oh, James, why do you have to ask? Don't you know? Can't you tell that I love you?"

For a long time he stood numbly distant from her; then all the emotion that should have come from him long ago was released in a heartfelt torrent.

"Jessie! Dear Jessie! You shouldn't. I didn't want you to love me. I'm too pitiful a man for you, Jessie. More than ever now you shouldn't love me, and more than ever now I want you to."

He laughed with a breathless joy that he had not known in his life before, except in his work. "I'll have to sit down," he gasped. "If I don't, I'll fall." They went, still clinging to each other, to the settee. "Oh, but I'm a pitiful thing," he said uncaringly as he sank down.

"No," she said, her eyes alight, her thin, childlike face happy now behind the tears. "You're James. Just James." She kissed him and her voice became slightly petted. "The same old James who hasn't told me whether he loves me or not."

"My sweet, darling girl, I do. I do love you, Jessie."

She put her hands on either side of his face and looked steadily into his eyes. "And nothing else matters, James. Everything else will pass. We must remember that."

That such happiness could have followed so quickly on despair seemed impossible. He felt unbelievably buoyant and boyish again, as if his burdens had been lifted away by this beautiful and intensely sensible girl. But was that what he should be feeling? Wasn't that a selfish reaction? Surely love should be giving, not taking. What did he have to give her?

"What do I have to give you, Jessie?" he cried aloud in a stabbing agony of doubt.

"Yourself, James," she soothed him. "Just yourself. I want nothing else."

He sat drawing strength from her, all at once realising it wasn't selfish of him; it wasn't the negation of love but the warm, glowing heart of it. This was what love was for. Today, in his need, he took from Jessie, and tomorrow, when Jessie's need was greater, she would take from him. And suddenly James felt that one day he would rise from the morass into which he had been cast to a position of strength. The awful trouble that beset him now would pass, and although it would never be forgotten, with Jessie's help it would be conquered. Already he felt better able to face it. He had been filled with a new and mysterious hope.

Almost without effort, the question, the very thought, which had until now been so far beyond him, seemed easy and natural. When he spoke, his voice was firm and certain.

"Jessie, when all this incredible business is over, will you marry me?"

"Oh, yes, James." The remnants of her tears sparkled in eyes flooded now with happiness. "Even now, before it's over, if you want."

"No." His joy clouded a little. "I think it should be afterward." He eased himself away so that he could see her properly. "And you won't mind having me . . . the way I am? How words could be used, he thought, to hide so much infirmity of body and character.

"I can only have you the way you are." And then, lest this might be interpreted as placing some qualification on her love, she added, "I wouldn't want anything about you changed, James."

For a long time they sat huddled together on the settee until the studio became dark except for the firelight flickering on the face of Helen Marshall, amid the tangled blossom of a summer now gone, a summer that had produced work more rapturous than he had done for years, work perhaps never to be repeated. Would he ever paint again? For the first time in his life the thought did not frighten James. With Jessie beside him, supporting him with her loving faith, he felt he could face anything—even the end of his work.

Across the river, from behind a ridge of distant hills, the edge of the moon appeared, the silver purity of its light catching strangely at some deep part of his sensitive being. But as he strained toward the elusive moment, it was gone.

They heard Mrs. Laing and her daily servant girl moving about the house, lighting lamps and rattling coal into fires. The sounds reminded James of the other world still waiting beyond the warm security of Jessie's presence.

"We won't tell anyone," he said, "until this other thing is over."

"If you think it best not to."

"I'm sure it's best."

"But, James . . . about the other thing. You'll really have to tell your people soon. You can't risk having them hear about it in some way that would make it even more painful for them."

"No, I daren't let that happen. It will be dreadful enough for them. God knows what it will do to Father. It could kill him."

"He may take it better than you think." She felt it her duty, almost her mission, to comfort him at all times.

"No, Jessie, you don't know him as I do. Father spent the first half of his life achieving a sound position in decent society, and he's been cherishing it ever since. I believe respectability means more to him than all his possessions. I don't know how I'll ever be able to face him with anything as terrible as this. And yet, I can't simply write to him. That would be too cruel and cowardly, even for me."

He sensed her shock and distress at his rambling evasion of what was his simple duty. "You'll have to face him," she said with a harshness that was startling so soon after the sympathetic understanding. In the darkness he could not see her expression. But from what she said next he realised she was impatient with him only because he had lost sight of his own innocence. She was determined that his courage would not falter. "There's no reason on earth why your head shouldn't be high, James. You haven't done anything. That's what you must remember."

356

"But will Father believe it?" Despite her effort to bolster him, he could not keep the plaintive note from his voice. "You're telling me the air's been thick with rumours about me for years, and that he has heard the slander. Now comes an accusation that would seem to substantiate all the gossip. People—and perhaps Father among them— are bound to say, 'After all the talk it's too much to believe that a child should have made up this particular story about this particular man purely by coincidence?"

He felt the exasperated shake of her head.

"Can't you understand, James! It's *not* coincidence. She made it up because she'd heard the gossip. She's a schemer. Don't imagine such a thing is beyond her because she's only fourteen. Far from it. The police will know that. So will the sheriff, when it comes to the court. Girls of that age—or, at any rate, some of them—know a lot more about all kinds of unmentionable things than adults care to admit."

"But people are bound to ask why she should invent a lie like that even if she did know the gossip."

"Yes, they will. And a lot of them will know the answer well enough. She invented it out of sheer badness and a thirst for notoriety."

Twistedness of that kind was outside James's experience, and he was only half convinced. "Could a child crave notoriety to that extent?"

"Yes!" There was no room for doubt in Jessie. "There are perverted minds that will get attention one way if not another." She straightened as if, while huddled against him, she could not put enough emphasis into her conviction. "Oh, James, you have too good and kind a mind to understand that such wickedness *can* exist behind a smile like Helen Marshall's." Another thought came from the back of her mind, and she plunged on as if no switch of ideas had taken place. "Tomorrow I would like you to take me a drive along High Street in the trap." She felt him stiffen and rushed on. "You haven't been out since this thing started. I can understand that, but it mustn't go on. You could easily become a recluse. Shunning people could become a habit. You must face them. Will you have the trap ready if I call at about half past ten?"

"Not tomorrow, Jessie," he pleaded. "Some other day. You're perfectly right, but not tomorrow."

"Tomorrow," she insisted. "The longer you leave, it the more of an ordeal it will be."

He sighed in the darkness and rose from the settee. She saw him at the mantelpiece against the glow of the fire. He bent to the coals and a spill flared. "For such a scrap of a thing, there's no end to your bossiness," he reproached her as he touched off the lamp on a table at her side.

She was wearing a striking feathered hat when she walked round the

357

house next morning and came in by the studio door, which lay wide as usual despite the frost on the grass and the hungry piping of the birds on the bare trees. To her surprise he was smiling and excited, as if the prospect of the outing pleased him. But as they drove off along the street, he turned to her with a catch in his voice. "If you weren't here beside me, Jessie, I couldn't do this."

He drove slowly, resisting the inclination to speed the trap over the cobbles and get it over with. At first, he could discern no reaction among the people they passed. A few heads were inclined or hats lifted as usual. Then, the deeper they penetrated into the congested centre of the town, the more aware he became of the signs he had feared and had spent a restless night imagining.

Heads were deliberately and pointedly turned away. He saw faces shocked, smirking or cold.

Here, where they were in full view of so many other disapproving townspeople, those loyal or bold enough to give signs of friendly recognition did so in a restrained and sometimes almost furtive way, as if anxious not to draw to themselves the wrath of their more righteous neighbours. Though most went no further than pretending not to notice them, others flaunted their disapproval with challenging stares.

James was trembling when he reined the trap to a halt at the busiest part of High Street. He saw people pause on their way into shops, some turning to stare openly, others watching more discreetly the scene reflected in the windows. The street seemed to go unnaturally quiet. He turned to Jessie almost for the first time since they left the house and saw her face white and pinched with nervous strain.

"It was your suggestion," he reminded her with a tense smile.

She nodded. "But why have you stopped?"

He pointed to the nearest shop. "We're going in there." In the window there was a display of watches and jewellery.

"Have you something to collect?"

"I'm going to buy you an engagement ring, Jessie. I thought there should be more point to our drive than simple defiance."

She looked down at her gloved hands, and he realised for the first time that the only jewellery he had ever seen her wear was an inexpensive gold brooch that had belonged to her mother. "If you do that, it will be all over the town by noon."

"That's part of the idea."

"But I thought you wanted our engagement to be a secret, meantime."

"I've changed my mind. I think we should give them something additional to talk about. Come along. I'm going to buy you the finest ring

358

Beattie has in his shop, but first I'm going to have him empty his window so they all realise out here what's happening."

Next day, now that she had broken his dread of being seen, she suggested he should visit Mr. Robertson, of Dean, Baxter and Robertson, Solicitors. "Mother always consulted him," she said. "Of course, if you preferred it, we could go to a stranger," she added, remembering the earlier legal visit she had made on his behalf.

James, although knowing he would need a lawyer, had delayed this final recognition of his plight, not only because the idea of discussing it with a stranger was distasteful to him but because he feared hearing a dispassionate professional assessment of the likely outcome.

He nodded reluctantly. "Mr. Robertson will suit me perfectly, if you know him, but won't it be an embarrassment to you?"

"Not in the least," she said staunchly.

The first sight of the lawyer's ascetic face and formal clothes was depressing, but his manner was kindly and helpful as he prompted James through a painful recital of the facts. At the end he closed his eyes, leaving James to stare at the dented deed boxes lying in a corner and the letters scattered about the floor.

"I wouldn't despair," Mr. Robertson said at last, almost as if he were still partly in a trance. "No, I wouldn't despair at all, Mr. King. Not at all. I'll have to get a sight of the prosecution's case, of course, but from what you say they have no proper evidence. No proper evidence. To accept the uncorroborated testimony of a girl of fourteen against the word of a gentleman of blameless character would be very dangerous. Very dangerous, indeed. I can't see the sheriff doing it. What else have they? I don't know, but from what you tell me, nothing. Nothing of any weight. There is the additional improbability of any man doing such a thing with another two children present. I will advance that in due course as supporting your version of the events. Yes."

James refused to be too swayed by this unexpected optimism. "Surely neither the police nor the procurator fiscal can see it quite in the same light, or things wouldn't have gone this far?" he said cautiously.

The lawyer rubbed his sharp chin carefully and stared for a few moments at James as if inspecting his dress and general appearance. "Well, they're in rather a difficult position." He smiled slightly as if to temper any suggestion that he was favouring the opposition. "Quite a difficult position. Yes." He gave James another quick inspection. "People look at a man like you, Mr. King, and say you are privileged. Well, in my experience privilege can rebound. The authorities—who are more anxious than ever these restless days to appear impartial—might well have taken the view that if they didn't prosecute, it could be imagined they had been influenced by your social position. They would not want to be accused of that."

James was shocked. "If that's the case, it's a scandalous reason for dragging me into court on such a ruinously unsavoury charge."

Mr. Robertson's silence and his faraway expression seemed to indicate that in his experience of the world such sad things happened, scandalous or not.

23

In Glasgow another scandal was engrossing the business community and the enclave of fashionable society which centred on the long, curving stone terraces of the Park district. In White's, and in the various other chophouses and smoke rooms, it rivalled the South African war as the most frequent topic of conversation.

The Boer ultimatum had expired, followed immediately by the news that Ladysmith, Kimberley and Mafeking were all under siege. But this drama was taking place in a remote country, as the result of events that few understood. More luridly real and close was the shocking love affair of Fiona King and Douglas Dunbar, conducted as it was in surroundings known to all and in defiance of standards observed by all but the most shameless.

The first hint of trouble came to Fiona when two women she knew well turned pointedly away at her smiling approach and crossed disdainfully to the other side of the street. After more than a year of daring and successful duplicity, her secret was known. And once known, people could not wait to spread it. Ripples ran about the respectable grey city with a speed that the eminence of the characters involved made inevitable. The names alone were enough to feed and inflame the imagination. Even people who had never met Dunbar or a single member of the King dynasty felt they knew them. The high points of countless lives had been celebrated over the last twenty years either with Dunbar whisky or King whisky. A generation had grown up with these household names staring at them from shop windows, placards and newspaper advertisements.

To realise that such names were being disgraced sent tremors through circumspect society. It was a scandal that came complete in almost every detail. Rumour could not be improved on. Embroidery was unnecessary, almost impossible. With the involvement of two rival whisky millionaires, a beautiful pioneer of women's emancipation and a titled patriarch in the background, even the most avid were satisfied. At first, no one could understand a woman in Fiona's position so compromising herself. Dunbar's upstart flamboyance was contrasted with Robert's sober-minded dedication to national affairs. But soon, as the facts were further considered, everyone was agreeing that once a woman had been liberated to the dangerous degree that Fiona had achieved, it was only a matter of time before she did something disgraceful. One outraged hostess, on being given the news, summed up the general feeling: "Put a woman in a man's job and you can expect her to start behaving like a man," she declared, as she tore up an invitation she had written that morning to Fiona.

Fiona's fearful suspicions became certainty as the weeks passed and she could no longer doubt she was being ostracised. Two women crossing to the other side of Buchanan Street with their noses in the air could be explained in various ways, but the message of a dozen heads turned haughtily away and an almost complete cessation of invitations was unmistakable.

A year of successful subterfuge had lulled her into a belief that she would never be found out, that somehow she would be able to go on enjoying the fruits of two worlds—the clandestine world of passionate meetings with a secret lover and the world of douce social and commercial routine in which she enjoyed the prestige accorded a respectable matron of high family and unique status. The suddenness of exposure and the knowledge that she was being shunned by this privileged society in which for so many years she had played a major role was shattering to her sense of security. If so many knew of her relationship with Dunbar, it could not be long before the Kings were informed.

She went to her next meeting with Dunbar in a panic and was dashed by his lack of sympathy. He seemed not to understand her fears. The rendezvous was in a cottage he had rented on a rustic stretch of the river Cart. The view was of woods and open fields, yet the city centre was less than four miles away. He stood in the tiny porch among the last blooms on geraniums and begonias which she had watered faithfully on all their visits.

"It had to happen sooner or later," he said, gently enough, but clearly surprised that she could have imagined their secret would endure forever.

"But what are we going to do? I have a husband, and children. I have to think of them."

He bent to come under the low lintel of the doorway into the living room. "If it's out, you're too late in thinking of them," he said. Then, putting his arms around her as if to counter this bluntness, "Surely you must have prepared yourself for this possibility. I know we haven't spoken much about it, but you must have considered the risks."

She stared sightlessly past him to the tranquil pastoral scene beyond the small panes of a window roughly hewn from a wall two feet thick, too absorbed in her ferment to answer.

"After all," he said, frowning at her pale, faraway expressssion, "it was always on the cards we would be found out. We took all the care we could, but it's a wonder we got away with it for so long. Glasgow's a big place, but we're both well known people. Eventually, someone was bound to recognise us somewhere, under circumstances that would set tongues wagging. It had to happen."

"You knew that, Douglas?"

His eyes widened, for it sounded almost like an accusation. His voice hardened a little at the naive illogicality of her attitude. "Of course I knew it. And, my God, Fiona, so must you. You're a sensible, far-seeing woman. Don't start pretending I led you astray."

A bitter little smile crossed her face as she shook her head in denial. "That's not what I feel, Douglas. It just seems incredible now that I could have been so blind—so blinded. Oh, to begin with, I was terrified. I can remember it clearly. I knew it would be the end of everything if I was found out. But I couldn't help myself. I loved you and wanted you and that was stronger than the fear I had of the consequences. I suppose it's the same with everyone who does what we've done. Then, as time went on and nothing happened, it all began to seem quite safe and normal. Almost . . . I began to believe I was entitled to have you and all the other things as well."

His values were so different that he could not hide his impatience. To him, the news that their relationship was known had a liberating quality. It was what he had subconsciously wanted. In the last months he had found the furtive journeys and skulking meetings increasingly frustrating. His nature was such that he wanted to proclaim his passion for Fiona, and to have it known that she returned it. He longed to be seen with her. Instead, he had been compelled to slink. A dozen times his proud spirit had almost rebelled against the demeaning imposition. Secrecy defeated the retributive part of his plan, for although he was in love with her, she was still his instrument of revenge on Robert. Possessing her was not enough. To complete the triumph she had to be seen to be possessed. He did not shrink from the thought of the notoriety. Nothing would change for him. In the city he was not liked, only feared or respected for his vigour and skill in business. He had no social position to lose, for he had steadfastly steered his life in another direction. His business would not be affected. He had thought on numerous occasions that if it hadn't been for the need to protect Fiona, he could even have gloried in the notoriety. Aye, *gloried* in it, for what he wanted was for the whole city to see that although King's Royal and Queen's Royal still flourished, he had struck a deadly blow deep into the heart of the King dynasty.

And now, at last, without his breaking faith with her, despite every effort to keep the secret, it was all out in the open. According to what she told him the streets were awash with it. All at once her worry seemed churlish, almost insulting.

"It's not murder you've done," he said reproachfully. "It's not just any Tom, Dick or Harry you've taken up with, either. Douglas Dunbar is not a man to be ashamed of." He seemed to grow in all directions at the sound of his own name. "Christ," he cried unreasonably as the mood grew in him, "you've mixed so long, my lass, with all those high-and-mighty Kings, your mind's been turned like theirs. You've been gulled like everybody else by their bloody upstart airs and graces."

It was shattering to her that at such a critical time for her his uppermost thought should be one of hatred for the Kings.

"Douglas, Douglas! It's not that at all," she protested. "I'm not ashamed of you. If I'm ashamed, it's of myself."

"You needn't be," he said. "King had deserted you in everything but name. He's been using you to run his business and look after his children while he followed a fancy new career among fancy new people. Do you think his behaviour in London will have been so innocent? You told me he'd hurt you often enough. Well, now it's *his* turn. You don't love him now. Let him look after himself. The old people will be scandalised for a while, but if he divorces you, they'll feel the family honour has been avenged. That leaves the children, but they're not tots any longer. Once we're married they can live with us if they want to."

His voice and manner had become matter-of-fact, as if he was dealing with some minor points of business policy. For him it was cut and dried. They were only names to him, but as he spoke she saw each face. *Divorce!* For someone like her it was a calamity, yet he made it sound like a technicality. But she was so deeply in thrall to him that, as usual, she felt herself being swept along. Their entire relationship had been like that. During the last year she had become more and more dependent on him. All her life, it seemed, she had carried people, starting at the age of twenty by deputising for her ailing father in the management of Lochbank distillery. Then came the Kings and her own children. They had all leaned on her. She had received little support from Robert, obsessed during the crucial years in his business.

Part of Dunbar's allure had lain in the contrast he offered to all that had gone before. He did not lean; he lifted and carried. He never sought advice; his own conviction burned too bright for that. She had been glad to relax, to surrender, to let him lead. It had been a luxury. But now she had a frightening awareness of being rushed along too quickly, perhaps in a direction she did not want to take. For her, divorce and remarriage were awesome to contemplate, events which fell into almost the same categories as birth and death. It was too soon to talk of them. There was a simpler and more obvious move that must be made first, but not one, she realised, that would ever occur to him. They could retreat in the hope that the danger ahead might be avoided.

"We must stop seeing each other," she said. "At least for a time, until we can judge better what's happening. People may not know about us with all that much certainty. How can they? We've been very careful. Someone must have seen us, I suppose, but for most people it can't be more than gossip and rumour. We've never appeared in public together."

He shook his head. "It's too late, Fiona. You're clutching at straws. Your marriage is finished."

She gasped at the brutal statement and her eyes filled with tears. "Then I will clutch at them" she said determinedly.

"You told me it was me you loved now." His eyes were accusing, but he sounded as if he was asking for reassurance.

She struggled against the gathering confusion. "I do love you, Douglas, but at the very least I must have time to think. For a while I must try to brazen it out."

For a long time after she had gone he stood at the cottage door, staring down the road she had taken, stricken by a different pang from the one that rent her. He was still agonising over the impossible dilemma of how to sunder King & Co. while leaving her unscathed. But, oh, Christ, she *was* King & Co.! He knew it more painfully every time he turned aside from gloating over the deadly grip he had on them. He loved her. But he hated Robert. To which side did the scale tilt? Having achieved the mastery he had striven toward for years—had almost wrecked his business for—could he now let even Fiona stand in his way? For a moment he glimpsed the awful destructiveness of his obsession, and then the vengeful mists closed in again. This concern for her had already warped his judgement. He had been vacillating—casting about for an answer that did not seem to exist—when he should have been acting. If the whisky was withheld too long from the desperate blenders, the affair could become a public scandal. Even the rabbits of the syndicate were becoming mutinous. When he met them that evening, he would have to bow to their clamour.

He drove grimly into the city, still telling himself that somehow, at the end, he would save her. How? He did not know. But he *would* save her. Then *how? He could not shut out the tormenting voice.* Unnerved, he turned to more immediate, practical considerations. His original plan of depriving King & Co. of stocks except at ruinous prices must now be abandoned. If King & Co. were asked for a higher price than the other blenders, it would be clear they had been selected for especially vindictive treatment. It would be realised immediately that he was involved. Fiona must never know that.

The way to do it, he decided as his carriage rattled over the Jamaica Bridge, was to have a list of applicants for whisky, with King & Co. permanently at the end of the queue, forever waiting, never receiving—never, ever to receive—the whisky they needed.

A little cheer went up in the hotel room when he told them that next day he would put the first parcels on the market to see what sort of money they would draw.

As the days went by, Fiona's hopes received another blow.

At King & Co. she felt Ross was looking at her with a curious intensity, as if seeking an answer to something that troubled him. It could, she knew, simply be her guilty conscience, or even his preoccupation with the crisis that loomed as their stocks of top malts ran dry. There was no way of knowing. But a day or two later, at her dressmaker's, she had to endure a humiliation of cruel directness.

She did not have an appointment and was shown into a waiting room. Euphemia Martin & Walker was the most fashionable dressmaking firm in that part of Glasgow, and Fiona had patronised it for almost twenty years. After a few minutes Mrs. Martin herself came into the waiting room, fumbling nervously with the scissors that hung from a cord round her waist. After some stumbling and breathless pleasantries she told Fiona she could not accept any more business from her and asked her to leave. Throughout, Fiona sat in a cloud of blackness, hearing, as if from some distant place, a succession of disconnected phrases: ". . . valued client for many years . . . but unfortunate and no doubt malicious gossip . . . however, business had to be considered . . . of course, not presuming to judge, but feelings of other clients have to be considered . . . any taint of scandal and they might well withdraw their custom. . . ."

She rose, unable to find a single defensive word or to summon the slightest spark of outrage to turn the erratic flow of Mrs. Martin's flustered monologue. She left, hardly able to grasp what was happening to her. Would all doors close to her? She walked in the direction she was facing, turning corners as she came to them without thought, not knowing or caring where she was going. The awful picture of the dressmaker's fat face, her hair plaited and drawn back into a bun, would not leave her. In the past she had always been kindly, managing to be almost motherly in her attitude without ever being presumptuous. That such a woman felt public sensitivity required her to act in such a way brought home to Fiona as never before the enormity of what she had done. She had made a sacrilegious assault on the rock on which the whole edifice of respectable living was based, and she must suffer the consequences. If she was truly unmasked, neither money nor position would save her from the wrath of society, any more than they could have staved off the consequences of an act of murder. Indeed, her position would ensure that society would apply its sanctions with double severity. The penalty exacted from her would be immeasurably more harsh than anything inflicted on a servant girl guilty of the same transgression. In her circle there were no advanced coteries in which notoriety carried cachet. So long as she lived in Glasgow, she would never be forgiven or forgotten.

As she walked blindly on, her pace became faster and her mind more agitated. Several times she had to draw back to the pavement from hurrying traffic she had neither seen nor heard until almost too late. She was aware of other people about her only vaguely and kept her eyes steadfastly averted. On the occasions when her gaze did inadvertently meet another eye she realised she was being closely scrutinised. A woman of her dress and appearance hurrying as if pursued would have been a spectacle anywhere, but especially in the district of tenements and small dockside factories into which she had strayed. In her shocked state she misinterpreted the reason for the interest she was arousing, fancying, irrationally, that it had to do with ignominy.

With an effort she worked out where she was. Ahead, she saw the outline of tall cranes against a murky sky. Through a gap in a line of grey buildings a stretch of dark-brown water impressed itself on her. She had walked almost to the river. Smoke drifted across the street, blotting out the busy industrial scene. For the first time she became aware of the din that characterised this area in the way the sedate tread of well-groomed horses hallmarked the streets around her own house. The tall double doors of some of the factories yawned open directly onto the street, and inside, machinery moved deafeningly. Hammering and banging seemed to come from the dark reaches of every tenement close, for in the backyards of this congested area small workshops were situated. But overall was the majestic sound of the river, its traffic and its shipyards. Here and there were high brick walls into the top of which broken glass had been cemented to prevent the men from climbing out during working hours. Behind one wall a clocktower rose. It was almost four o'clock. She turned and began walking back up a cobbled hill.

Eventually she reached familiar streets in the commercial district. Although she was weary, she ignored the cabs loitering for business. She crossed St. Vincent Street, Bothwell Street and West George Street, going up a long, badly paved incline. Dusk was thickening when she reached Blythswood Square, but nursemaids still pushed prams round the gravel paths of the gardens. She opened a gate and crossed to a bench under a leafless tree. A lifetime ago, when she had been forced to endure six months of strict mourning for her father, she had escaped when she could from Aunt May's house, in Pitt Street, and met Robert secretly in this secluded glade. Little had changed.

There was the same sense of being in an oasis above the city. Trees and shrubs deadened the traffic noises and it was possible to forget the bustle only a block or two away. Almost every day for months after her father died she had sat here for a little while listening to piano music drifting from one of the houses. Which one? Somehow it seemed important. She looked anxiously along the terraces of yellow stone, but memory failed her. What had happened to the girl who had played so beautifully? Was her touch as light, or had life made it leaden? Her thoughts were irrelevant and trivial compared to her problem. Her mind sought refuge in them rather than confrontation with the dreadful prospect.

As lights began to appear in the windows she felt someone come and stand beside her. "Are you all right, Mother?"

She looked up with a start. "Gordon!"

"Why are you sitting here, Mother?"

"I was tired," she said. "I thought this a pleasant and familiar place to rest for a little while."

He sat down, looking at her curiously. "Are you all right?" he repeated. "You look . . . odd."

"I had an upset, earlier, but I'm feeling better now." She shook off the smothering lassitude. "But what are you doing here?"

"I followed you. I recognised you ahead of me, farther down the hill, but you were walking very quickly." He lifted some pebbles from the path and began flicking them toward a wire wastebasket fixed to a tree. "What was the upset?"

"Oh"—she shook her head while she thought—"just a silly quarrel with a lady."

"A lady?" His eyes were fixed on a pebble as it arched toward the wastebasket, overshooting it by an inch.

Was there knowledge in the intonation he gave the word, or was this just a part of the continual guilty wondering she must suffer now? "Yes. Someone you don't know." She managed a slight, uneasy smile. "It would sound like nothing if I told you about it. It was one of those bitter things that flare up on committees every so often."

368

The last pebble landed in the wire basket and he straightened as if satisfied. He put his hands in his pockets. "It's chilly now," he said, leaning back on the bench with a glance at her unbuttoned coat. She had thrown it open uncaringly during her rush through the streets.

"Yes." She fumbled with the buttons. "A garden becomes suddenly damp at the end of the day at this time of year."

Although he was still in lodgings, she saw him perhaps once a month. He refused to call either at Claremont Row or at Seabank Lane. Usually she took him to lunch. Each time they met he seemed older than should have been possible in a few weeks. His face was leaner and his eyes never still. There was about him the same air of irresolute discontent that seemed to stretch back to his early childhood.

Sometimes, when she looked at him, she saw not her son but a stranger standing at a point where many roads met, wondering about each but unable to decide which to take. He was always correctly and neatly dressed. His clothes, he told her, were regularly valeted. Always—although almost automatically now—she asked him to come home and to resume his work in the business.Today a thought she had not had for a long time came to her and she asked a different question.

"Do you still see Anne Dunbar?" It was the first time she had mentioned the girl to him since the day she had sent him to Lochbank.

"From time to time," he said calmly.

"I've often wondered." She might have been enquiring about strangers. *It was his life,* she thought vaguely. The joy and the pain were his and they would come to him, whatever she said. He was that kind of person. Besides, she had lost the right to moralise or advise. Soon—if he didn't already know—he would hear about her association with Dunbar. Perhaps, although he was so young, he would have more understanding than those already outraged. Or—her heart sank lower at the thought— would he deride her, too, in revenge for her attempt to separate him from Anne? She had a sudden urge to tell him, at least to warn him so that the shock would be less terrible. As she tried to find words, a nursemaid passed with two noisy children. He rose.

"If we don't go, we may find ourselves locked in," he said. "It's getting dark and these gardens are supposed to be private to the residents of the square. All these nursemaids have keys."

They stood for a few moments at the corner of West George Street, listening to starlings gathering on the ledges of the buildings.

"I hope your landlady will have good fires going in your rooms," Fiona said. "I hadn't realised just how cold it is."

"She's very attentive," he said, putting his hand up to stop a cab turning out of the square. An extending necklace of lights was appearing on either side of the hill that ran down to the centre of the city as men touched the gas lamps with carbide torches.

369

He stood with his hat in his hand as she settled herself in the cab. As it headed down Douglas Street toward the teatime hubbub in Sauchiehall Street, she turned and saw him still standing there, bareheaded, as if he had no place to go.

When she reached Claremont Row, Florence was crouched over a blazing fire in the small sitting room off the hall.

"You'll burn your face," Fiona said. "Move your chair or use the pole screen."

The girl lifted her head a little but did not move back. "I don't care."

"You'll care if you end up with a blotchy complexion," Fiona said as she pulled a bell cord. When Morag came she told her to bring tea.

Florence had left school at the end of the summer term. Apart from her embroidery and advanced tuition in music, which she took at home twice a week, she had little now to occupy her. It was a fate she did not question, since it applied to all girls of her social position. She was at "the awkward age," which would last until she was eighteen, when she would be permitted to take up more adult pursuits. These would be restricted mainly to engagements centring round the activities of her own parents or those of approved and trusted friends.

"You look bored," Fiona said sympathetically, remembering the long days of her own adolescence in Helensburgh. "Haven't you been out at all?" Here, within the walls of her own house, it was slightly easier to believe that everything might yet be all right, that Mrs. Martin's reaction to the gossip had been eccentric and exaggerated.

Florence shrugged and hung her head over a buttered scone selected from the large variety Morag had carried in. She watched her mother open a lacquered tea box and spoon leaves from the various pewter containers into the wooden blending bowl. Today, as she stirred the mixture, the soothing ritual seemed particularly important to Fiona. It seemed the only homely activity she had engaged in for a long time, and one associated with a lifetime of pleasant afternoons. The silver kettle on the spirit stove began to steam. Only when she had infused the tea did she turn to Florence.

"I asked if you had been out today, Florence. I'm not sure what your answer was, if you even deigned to give one."

A plate fell from the table and clattered against the leg of a chair as the girl sprang to her feet. "How can you sit there, calmly blending tea, as if everything was normal?" Her voice was shrill and her eyes tearful. "You must be completely without shame. I daren't go out. I'm a prisoner here."

The outburst was so unexpected Fiona froze with the teapot poised over a cup. Suddenly it became enormously heavy, and she put it down with a trembling hand. She stared at the girl through eyes blurred with guilt. Desperately, she willed some authority into her manner. "Sit down, immediately, Florence, and explain yourself. And control your voice while you're about it."

Instead of sitting, Florence gave the nearest chair a violent push and sent it banging against a sewing table which swayed wildly, sending bobbins of thread rolling about the floor.

"You wicked girl! What's wrong with you? Why daren't you go out?"

"Because you're the most notorious woman in Glasgow, Mother. I feel everyone's staring at me and saying horrible things behind my back."

Fiona held out a hand, hardly knowing what it was appealing for. "Who told you that, Florence?"

"Josephine Anderson. She says everyone knows."

"Knows what?"

Florence's little mouth trembled on the edge of the unmentionable, her bow lips contorting as she struggled with growing hysteria. At last her defiance broke out in a tearing sob.

"About the man you've been carrying on with. I thought it was only strangers who did that. I never would have believed it of my own mother. Josephine heard her mother talking about it."

"It's not true." Fiona's voice had risen to a note of anguished pleading. "You don't believe anything like that about me, Florence?"

For a moment the girl stood with a hand moving distractedly over her tear-stained face. Then, straightening, her eyes blazing, she yelled at the top of her voice. "Yes, Mother, I do believe it, because it's true. I *know* it's true. You've been behaving peculiarly for a long time. You're hardly ever here now. You never mention Father. You wouldn't care if you never saw him again. You don't miss Steven and Allan. You don't care about anything except this man. I can see that now. I'm not a child. You're disgracing us, and I can't stand it. I won't stand it. Gordon did the right thing when he left home and got away from you. And that's what I'm going to do. Then you can devote all your time to this man. You'll even be able to invite him here, because there'll be nobody but you."

"Calm yourself, child. And be sensible. You can't leave home. You're far too young."

"Don't worry. I'll be quite safe. I wasn't out today, but I went to school yesterday to see Miss Pirie. I got an address from her of a finishing school I'd heard her talk about once—a convent school near Paris. Just wait and I'll get it."

She ran from the room. Upstairs a door slammed twice, then she came thudding back down the stairs.

"Here you are!" She held out an envelope as she burst back into the room. "You once asked me if I wanted to go to a finishing school, Mother. I didn't, because I was quite happy, then. Well, now I'm going. I'd go anywhere to get away from here."

Fiona stared at the writing on the envelope. "This is a Catholic school," she said foolishly.

"I don't care what it is. Are you afraid they may convert me?"

"Your father might not approve."

"Do you think he'll approve of what you're doing when the news reaches him?"

"They may not have a vacancy."

"Miss Pirie says they always have vacancies, but you can telegraph."

"It's not as urgent as that. But if you are interested in this school, I'll write."

"Telegraph!" Florence screamed, her hands clenched in front of her.

Fiona walked to the window, forcing herself to be calm. "You won't know anyone there. Paris is a long way away. You'll be all alone."

"Yes." The small mouth twisted, then the bow lips compressed themselves into a thin, bitter line. "That's what I want. A place where no one will know me. Far away from you, Mother."

A mile away, Gordon stood in the shadow of an office doorway watching a window two floors above the street. After leaving Fiona he had walked to Exchange Square to buy pipe tobacco. On his way back up the hill a man had come out of Douglas Street and turned into West Regent Street. His erratic behaviour attracted Gordon's attention. He began to cross the street, then stepped back on to the pavement and stood under a lamp, looking up at the window Gordon was now watching.

It was the window of Anne's flat and Gordon had been able to see enough of the man to recognise him as her husband. He had stopped at the next corner to watch. He had derived a warped satisfaction from seeing the man light a cigarette. These insubstantial weeds, although frequently seen in clubs and drinking places, were regarded as rakish in solid society and shunned as insolent novelties. For all his fecklessness, Gordon still preferred gentlemen to others.

As he waited, he tried to remember the man's surname. It was Anne's surname, too, but early in their relationship he had put it out of his head. He had not wanted to think of her as another man's appendage. Nor did he want now to think of this man as "Peter"; it implied a friendliness that did not exist. But after these years of suppressing the name it had gone from his mind, and to his annoyance he had to continue thinking of an enemy in Christian terms.

He saw nothing absurd in regarding a man he had never met as a foe.

He was even able to see him as an intruder, a fellow with no rights who was "pushing himself in." This was the man who had contributed to Anne's mysterious affliction—perhaps even initiated it. He was as ruinous to her as her father had been. It was since she had abandoned them both that her health had improved. And it was since this "Peter" had returned to the scene that her health had again deteriorated. It was too clear to need further elaboration. The man under the lamp was a wrecker.

He was in the middle of this bitter resentment when Peter threw down his cigarette, crossed the street and went up the stair leading to Anne's flat. He had been there now for well over an hour.

The street had become increasingly quiet. The offices were all closed. Only here and there, where the houses were still residences, did lights show. The damp that had come down when he sat with Fiona in the nearby gardens had thickened into a misty haze. He was chilled, and his earlier anger had turned to a baffled dejection. Why was he spying on Anne like this? What could he gain by it? Her windows were heavily draped and high above the street. He realised there were men who earned their living in this way. Policemen. Confidential-enquiry agents. No doubt there were others. He pitied them for their lonely, cold and demeaning jobs.

Then, with a penetrating glimpse of his own vagabond existence, he saw the absurdity of his pretensions. He was as big a misfit, as much an outcast—even though his exile was self-imposed—as any in the city. This furtive loitering in the shadows of a deserted street while his paramour met with her husband was ample proof of it. He had a sudden vision of his father in the debating chamber of the House of Commons, in the company of great men; of his grandfather wrapped in the glory of his baronetcy. Could this skulking wraith of the darkened city really have been born to inherit one day that title and all that went with it? Perhaps the blood of the Kings had passed him by and his nature had come largely from his mother; for she, it seemed, was capable of folly, too.

When hints of it had come to him, he had at first been disbelieving, then astonished, and finally incredulous when the man involved had been revealed as Douglas Dunbar. Even now, when he did not want to believe her capable of such behaviour, he was able to find plausible reasons for not doing so. If she was meeting Dunbar, it was on behalf of King & Co. After all, although they were enemies, his father had on occasion met Dunbar. Dunbar had even forced his way into Castle Gare on a purely business matter. What misconstruction might not have been put on that visit by malicious tongues if his mother had at the time been head of the business and his father, living in London?

On these occasions of willing—even anxious—disbelief he had a second line of defence. If his mother and Dunbar were meeting, and if it was not for business reasons, then it was because of *his* relationship with Anne. Again there was the instance of Dunbar's bursting into Claremont Row late at night when Fiona was alone. Anne and he were meeting now without any particular attempt at secrecy. They were content to maintain a little discretion. Their affair must be widely known. His mother and Dunbar probably knew of it. This could account for their seeing each other. When he discussed the rumours with Anne, her attitude was less tortuous. "I know my father is perfectly capable of it," she said. "Is your mother?" When he had conceded that anything was possible, she went on, "Then it's probably true . . . to some extent. Gossip always has some basis to it."

He had seized on this as substantiating his own reasoning. "Exactly. They may be meeting, but only they can know why."

To his annoyance, she had laughed. "Wouldn't it be priceless if it's true? I mean, when you think how determined they were to keep us apart." And then, with a bright cynicism that had jolted him further, she added, "Well, they say there's no fool like an old fool."

He drew back in his doorway as across the street footsteps sounded and his enemy appeared and walked quickly down the hill. His lodgings beckoned. The fires would be well stocked and the previous day he'd had a parcel of the latest novels delivered. But the lure on the other side of the street was stronger. He crossed, full of curiosity and quiet indignation.

Anne was startled when he walked into her sitting room, for although he had a key, she always knew when to expect him. It was an odd formality that had survived all their intimacies. She was crouched by the fire, strained and worried, as he had come again to expect, these days. After her instant of surprise she looked confused, as if thinking perhaps she should have been expecting him.

As he read her expression, he was daunted to realise it was still possible to violate her privacy. A picture came to him of two stars swirling helplessly in the coldness of space, approaching each other for a little while and then being torn apart by an irresistible gravity.

He sat down opposite her and said, "What did he want this time?"

She apparently had not connected his unannounced appearance with the visit of her husband, for now her head came up indignantly."Are you spying on me, Gordon?"

"No."

"Then how did you know Peter had been here?"

"I was passing and saw him leave. I'll ask again. . . . What did he want this time?"

374

"I don't think you should question me in that tone of voice."

The distracted expression that had been absent from her eyes for so long was back. She looked pathetically vulnerable. He shouldn't have come. He could only increase her pain.

"I suppose it was about Malcolm again," he said with sudden sympathy. It wasn't even a question. He intended it as the beginning of a retreat, but her response was aggressive.

"Your attitude to Malcolm is juvenile and immature," she said loudly. "If he was your child, you would have more understanding of the feelings involved."

The rebuke stung all the more because of its accuracy. He turned away to hide the wound and to ponder out of her gaze the terrible confusion of emotions looming about them. He felt her pass him. A moment later he saw her hurrying along the narrow hall, buttoning on a coat. She was hatless. "I'm going out," she said.

"At this time?"

"I couldn't stay here another minute. You all go on at me till I feel frantic." Her eyes at once appealed to him and rejected him.

He moved toward the chair on which he had thrown his coat and hat.

"No," she said shrilly, walking quickly to the outside door. "I want to think. I don't want you with me. I don't want to see you anymore tonight."

It was such a childish cry that his heart filled with tenderness for her. He cursed his clumsiness in bringing on this distress. "Anne!"

She hesitated, as if deflected by the ardent pleading in his voice, then, without turning, went out on to the dimly lit landing. He stood at the open door, listening dejectedly to the sound of her steps ringing on the stone stairs, and then, briefly, from the empty street.

It was after ten o'clock when she returned, tired but apparently composed. She did not seem surprised that he was still there. She stood inside the sitting-room looking at him without speaking. He went to her and took her hands.

"I'm sorry I upset you, Anne. It's just that I hate the thought of his being around you again. What's he about? If his business has failed, he couldn't even support you."

She drew her hands away. "Father has said he will help him to start again . . . if—"

"If you go back to him?" His voice was hushed.

"Yes."

He waved his hands in exasperation. "Then, can't you see that's why he's so keen to get you back? Don't you see that's what it is?"

375

She looked down as if engrossed in unbuttoning her coat. "I suppose it might be."

"Then how can you entertain him!"

"You don't understand, Gordon." She shook her head wearily and stood fumbling with the ribbons inside her coat. She closed her eyes and threw her head back in an attitude of submission. "I'm going to have a baby."

From out of the shock, one horrifying thought came leaping at him. "Whose baby?"

She straightened, seeming almost to recoil physically from the assault in his voice; then a light that could have been of defiance came into her dark eyes. "Whose baby do you think?"

"That isn't an answer." All he could think of was the slow change in her over the last months and his discovery that her husband had been visiting her. His voice rose. "Is it his?"

The shining quality in her eyes came now from tears. As she spoke, they trickled brightly down her face. "Is that what you think?"

"Is it his?" He shook her by the shoulders.

She gave a smothered gasp and, turning from him, sank down sobbing into a chair.

"My God!" He felt a burning sickness rise in his throat. "Do you mean it could be?"

Her voice was so distorted he could hardly make out the words. "I can make him think it is."

"You slut. You filthy slut."

"I'm going back to him, Gordon. It's the only thing. It's best for both of us . . . all of us."

"Slut!" He shouted as he went dementedly to the door and tore it open. "Crazy slut! I was warned about you. I should have paid attention. Go back to him. And to your father. Between them they'll soon have you put away again. And maybe this time you won't escape so easily."

The terrible words repeated themselves in his head as he clattered down the stairs and went running blindly up the street.

He left his lodgings early next morning and began to wander aimlessly. At Stockwell Bridge he boarded a Clutha, paid the penny fare and sat staring moodily at the debris in the water as the small steamer moved out from the quay. The three-and-a-half-mile sail passed in a haze, and when he stepped ashore at the Whiteinch landing stage forty-five minutes later, he could not recall any of the ten other stops the ferry had made.

He immediately began walking back along the river toward Glasgow. The restless dockland scene corresponded to something in his nature. The activity round the busy wharves as ships were loaded or unloaded

376

suggested to him a freedom that was not only enviable but which now, at last, might be within his reach.

In her terrible betrayal, had Anne freed him? If so, he had a curious reluctance to cast off the loosened bonds. The manner of his liberation was too terrible. All night he had lain awake trying to grapple with the unthinkable development.

He stopped to watch a puffer being loaded for its journey up the west coast and to the islands beyond. But as coal and an assortment of ugly industrial cargo were slung onto the dirty, low-lying vessel, unbearable pictures tortured him.

He passed exhaustedly on, climbing fences, detouring across fields when the way was blocked. Despite the cold, he fell asleep in a weedy corner sheltered by the gable end of two sheds. It was afternoon when the clatter of nearby winches wakened him. Steam and smoke drifted across the busy river from a dozen noisy sources as he rose stiffly from the wooden box on which he had been perched. He walked to the edge of the dock with a dominant new thought pulsing in his head. He had been aware of it the instant he wakened, even before, looking bewilderedly about, he had remembered where he was. *Whose?* he had asked brutally when Anne told him she was going to have a baby. The impression she had given—the one he had almost forced on her—was that her husband was the father. *But she hadn't said that.* Again the whole scene flashed through his mind, and nowhere in it did she say her husband was the father. That had been *his* thought, and for some reason it had suited her to let him think it. Or was he being too kind to her? Although she had not said Peter was the father, that did not mean he was not. Of course, the most likely father was himself. But if so, why hadn't she simply said that?

He stood for a long time looking down at the brown water lapping twelve feet below him. The one thing he could be absolutely certain about was that she had not said who the father was. She had said, referring to Peter, "I can make him think it's his." And he had damned her for it, concluding that it *could* have been Peter's. But she might only have meant she could make Peter think it was his if she went back to him soon.

As his mind started to churn again through the perplexing jumble of possibilities, he turned and began walking quickly to the nearest stage where he could board a Clutha to take him back up the river.

It was after five and already dark when he arrived in the city. Frost was glistening under the gas jets in the quieter sidestreets. He crossed West Regent Street and went bounding noisily up the stairs to Anne's flat. If it was his child, he wanted to be told it was his. He didn't want to be tricked or let down lightly or whatever it was she was up to. He had ruined his life for her already. How dare she decide now that another

377

man would be a better father to her children. For that, he felt, must be her devious intention. She was pregnant by him but weighing him, had found him lacking as a father, especially when she had another one conveniently at hand, one to whom she was respectably married, one more suitable for little Malcolm.

When there was no reply he opened the door with his key. It was black inside. He found a lamp and lit it. Immediately, the hall struck him as having a deserted look. There was no carpet on the floor. The coat stand had gone. He went into the sitting room. The few tables and chairs with which she had furnished it had been taken away. He went round the denuded rooms. In the kitchen some bottles had been left on a cupboard top. Among them was one with some brandy in it. He swallowed a mouthful before going back to the sitting room. He stood by the window feeling the warmth of the spirit spread. In the centre of the gentle glow a seed of comfort sprouted. He began to see her desertion in a different light. It didn't mean she didn't love him. It didn't mean that all they had been to each other was now so much dust and ashes. She was a married woman, a mother struggling against ill health. She had at long last settled for what she thought life was prepared to give her. She had simply, in the face of all the forces bearing on her, accepted what she saw as her responsibilities and gone off to face them. Was that it? Or was that a romanticised and gilded view of one more shabby defeat of the human spirit? He could not tell. He could no longer be sure of anything.

He put out the lamp and left. As he walked down the street he felt oddly unencumbered. Free, useless and unwanted. Even desolate. The newsvendors called the latest humiliating war news. He bought a newspaper. Kimberley, Ladysmith and Mafeking were still under siege despite all the optimistic forecasts of their early relief. Lord Roberts would sail soon to take command in the Dark Continent.

In St. Vincent Street there was a shop with a flag fluttering above the doorway and a window plastered with patriotic posters. When he went in, a sergeant in a red tunic looked up from a plain wooden table spread with papers. "Well, lad?" his expression, although unsmiling, was inviting.

"I want to go to Africa," Gordon said.

The sergeant rose, walked round his table and inspected him appreciatively. They were accepting almost anybody, but he preferred them like this—tall, broad and neatly dressed; soldierly; men who would not disgrace the uniform. "Good, lad," he said. "Regular or Volunteers?"

"It doesn't matter."

"Maybe not, but you've got to say which." As he saw Gordon hesitate and look uncertainly round at the posters and regimental literature pinned to the walls, he said comfortably, "To me you look like a Volunteer."

An officer came out of a back room and began looking through the papers on the table. The sergeant drew himself up very tall. His voice became loud and slightly inhuman. "I'll repeat the question, lad: Regulars or Volunteers?"

"Volunteers," Gordon said uncaringly.

In Claremont Row the rest of the week passed in a daze in which neither Fiona nor Florence left the house. A message was telegraphed to the convent school after another furious scene in which the girl's baleful will dominated.

"If they can take you, I'll see you're out of here and on the first available train," Fiona threatened. A day later word came back that there was a vacancy. Florence already had a trunk packed. So unreal was the situation that until now Fiona could hardly believe it was happening. She had not consulted Robert. There was no way she could do so without giving him the reason. Further threats or pleas would clearly be useless. All her authority over Florence had gone. She was at an age when there was no real sanction that could be applied against her. And in the background, unmentioned, was the two thousand pounds she had inherited from Mrs. Veitch. She would have to be allowed to go. By this time, there was a part of Fiona that almost welcomed the prospect. When the storm finally struck the family itself it would be easier to make decisions if the children were all being cared for elsewhere. For their own sakes they would be better out of Glasgow. Steven and Allan were safely at school in England. It was not unreasonable that Florence should finish her education in France. It was only the disorderly manner of her going that was so distressing. What would Robert say when he was told? How could it be explained to Fergus and Rita?

"Christmas is not so far away," she said. "You'll come home then."

"I might never come home again," Florence said with unrelenting bitterness. On a Saturday night, with a sheet of instructions prepared by a travel agent, she climbed into a train at a dim and draughty platform of the Central Station, still sullenly unforgiving.

Fiona was at her desk, vainly trying to concentrate on her weekly letters to Steven and Allan, when Gordon arrived and told her he had enlisted.

All her emotions were released in a flood of bitter tears. "You silly

379

boy," she sobbed. "You don't know what you've done. You haven't been home here for a year, and the first time you come it's to tell me this."

Gordon, who had never seen her cry, almost gave way to the mood of doubt that had set in since his rash visit to the recruiting office. His lips quivered on an appeal for advice, then, remembering the dominance she had once exerted over him, he pulled himself up. "I've only done what everyone else my age is doing," he said stiffly.

She pulled a tiny handkerchief from her sleeve and dabbed at her eyes. "Not people in our position."

"Do you mean people in our position aren't patriotic?"

"You know perfectly well what I mean," she said, her anger rising at his folly. "They have other responsibilities." And then all her resentment collapsed as an unbearable thought came. Was it because of her? Was he going to his death because, like Florence, he had heard what she had done and couldn't bear the shame?

She seized his hands and looked up beseechingly, all the caution that had grown in her in the last year gone. "It's not because of me, is it, Gordon?"

He went warily round the surprising question, looking for possibilities not immediately obvious to him. Vaguely he knew that the emphasis of the interview had undergone a drastic change. Reproach had turned to something he could not quite grasp. The subtleties eluded him because of his own turmoil.

He was struck by how young she looked. Her hair, usually so immaculately dressed, appeared windswept, almost untidy. Her lips were pale and her eyes kept looking about the room as if trying to follow a disorderly confusion of thought. He was reminded, disconcertingly but irresistibly, of Anne. Tenderness flooded him. He bent and kissed her forehead.

"No, Mother, it's not because of you. You haven't been as bad as that to me." He hugged her till she smiled.

"You'll be an officer, of course."

"No. Just an ordinary private soldier."

"Oh, but you should be . . . Your father could have arranged it. He could have spoken—"

He stopped her with a gentle shake. "No, Mother."

She pushed back her chair and rose from the desk. "You'll be handsome in uniform. I haven't even asked you what regiment it is."

"I don't think it's any regiment. I don't know much about it. I've to report to a special serving company of the Volunteers at Stirling Castle tomorrow morning. I'll train there for a few weeks and we'll sail for Africa in February."

At this mention of his eventual destination her tears started again. "I hope it's all over before you get there,"she said. "It might be. The newspapers don't think it will last much longer."

"It'll soon finish once I get there," he said with more jauntiness than he felt.

She allowed him to coax her into a mood of resigned cheerfulness.

"You must stay for lunch."

"Yes. It might be my last decent meal for some time."

They sat for a little while in the afternoon reading the latest bulletins in the *Citizen*. The news was brighter, and by the time he was ready to go, she had it worked out that if he sailed in February, it would be May at the earliest before he could be in the fighting area. It must be over by then. He readily agreed with her, and when she was alone again, Florence soon became her more immediate preoccupation.

Next morning, with a thumping heart, she called at Park Place with word of Gordon's enlistment and a concocted story of a sudden opportunity that had arisen for Florence. Fergus and Rita received the news of their grandson with a mixture of pride and concern. The sudden departure of their granddaughter, without a word of farewell, left them bemused, but they accepted the involved explanation without suspicion. Clearly, no one had yet dared tell them of the hideous massing of events.

With what he imagined was circumspection, Fergus extracted from Fiona an admission that the school to which Florence had gone was run by Roman Catholic nuns. The noises he made into his beard were indicative of a state of shock which would normally have worried her. Today she had little sympathy with his bigotry and silenced his disapproval by telling him that half the great titled Protestant families of England sent their daughters to the same school. This massive lie robbed Fergus of all further ground of protest.

"'I suppose Robert and you went well into things," was his last speculative reference to the matter. But it went on puzzling him until searing illumination came with the first sleet showers of another winter, toward the end of the following week.

Fergus stopped in the entrance to Gwen's shop and shook the clinging flakes from his coat and hat before entering. He had spent an hour prowling about Morrison McChlery's and had word of some fine pieces of furniture she might buy at a forthcoming sale. Gwen appeared to listen to his enthusiastic description of a painted satinwood table with less attention than he thought it deserved. Important pieces were rare and worth getting excited about. As he expounded on the quality of the wood and the intricacy of the design, he saw her gaze wander and realised her mind was on something else.

He quelled his irritation. *She had her worries, poor girl!* These last months must have been a particular strain on her. As war fever racked the country, it had become obvious her attention was fixed anxiously on Jack. She was clearly remembering another war and another man who had gone off to fight in it. Now that the battle had started, Jack's mind must be filled with dangerous thoughts of his father and of his campaign a generation ago in another part of Africa. The hysteria was almost inescapable. Street-corner orators passionately denounced Kruger, the Boer leader, and Smuts, his underling. Urchins played soldiers under the wheels of the traffic. And now, of course—above all—there was the example of recklessness set by Gordon.

At least, Fergus thought, *Jack is still safely tucked away at Lochbank, and with a bit of luck might not be infected by the general loss of reason.* What a waste it was, all those raw boys abandoning their careers and going off to face such a treacherous foe in so dangerous a land. Only that morning he had stood in the Central Station watching a company of them load their packs and guns into a troop train. They hadn't looked half trained to him. Dear knows! It would be better to leave the fighting to professional soldiers. When, like this, Fergus allowed himself to dwell on events, he was aware of an unrest greater than could be explained by the war alone. The country was changing. He was intensely grateful that his life had been lived in an era of stability and leisure, under the umbrella of the old queen. She had reigned so long and with such steadiness that the nation's life had assumed the same reassuring tempo. He remembered so clearly the day when, as acting Lord Provost of the city, he had driven through Glasgow with her at his side in an open landau. Now, her time neared its end, forces which had been checked by her mere presence were massing to surge forward when the defences were weakened at her going. When it happened, ruin would assuredly follow, for her son symbolised nothing but self-indulgence.

"I may well buy that table myself," he said abruptly, suddenly stung, despite himself, by Gwen's disinterest, his sympathy dissolving into peevishness. "It's probably far too good for you."

Her eyes widened at the change in his manner.

"After all, you'd put hardly any profit on, as usual, and let it go to someone who didn't appreciate it. Dear knows!"

He turned his back on her and lifted a plate with a lacework rim, taking it nearer the light to peer at the mark. To his surprise, she didn't follow, as she would normally have done, sensing she had offended him and anxious to make amends. Instead, he heard her walk to the back shop, where, as he came in, he had glimpsed Miss Murray bent to some task behind the bead curtaining. The beads rattled and Gwen was beside him again.

"Give me your coat, Father. It looks quite wet. I've asked Miss Murray to make tea for us before she goes to collect some little silver boxes that have been away for repair."

There was something in her tone that made him look at her sharply. Surely the boy hadn't . . . hadn't . . . Fergus shook his head and blew noisily. Like Gwen and all the other Kings, he had no idea what it was he was waiting for Jack to do.

"Is Jack all right?"

He saw the question took her by surprise and knew that whatever her preoccupation, it did not concern Jack. He was pleased to see a slow smile liven the characteristic sadness of her eyes.

"As fascinated as ever by distilling," she said. "He could have come back to Glasgow last month if he had wanted to, but he asked to be allowed to stay on at Lochbank. He says he still has a lot to learn from McNair. Quite often he doesn't even come home at weekends. He takes a train north and spends Saturday and Sunday walking in the Highlands."

"Hill-walking?"

"No. He tramps round the distilleries on Speyside. He knows all about them. He can tell you who the owners are and the characteristics of each whisky and where the various distilleries draw their water from."

The unexpected innocence of his grandson's activities drew a smile from Fergus. Then he frowned thoughtfully. "We mustn't let him hang on too long at Lochbank. His future is in Seabank Lane." He glanced toward the back shop and lowered his voice. "By the way, you needn't worry that the boy's being silly with the money Great-grandmother left him."

It *was* one of Gwen's worries, and she looked at him expectantly, her other commanding thought temporarily overshadowed.

"The last time I was in the bank I twisted old Montgomery's moustaches. He told me how Jack's account stands. He's dipped into the money hardly at all."

"Are you sure?"

"Montgomery was too worried at talking for there to be any question about it. Mind you, I'd rather he had it in something that brought him a better return. But perhaps later we can turn him round to that."

The bead curtain rattled as Miss Murray came from the back shop. She put a tray set with teapot and cups on a table in front of the fire. This part of the shop was shielded from passing window-gazers by a large gilt screen. After she had left on her errand Fegus settled heavily into a chair, his eyes feasting on the mellow glow of old wood and the delicate lustre of fine silver.

How he had opposed Gwen opening this shop all those years ago! And how he had come to love it! His pleasure was ruined by the sight of

Gwen's hand as she poured the tea. It was shaking. As she saw him watching, her face became agitated and apprehensive.

"My dear!" He leaned toward her. "Is there something wrong? Are you quite well?"

She replaced the teapot on the tray and turned her anxious eyes on him. "Now that Miss Murray has gone out, there is something I must tell you, Father. Something very upsetting. I hardly know how to begin."

He jerked back in alarm, as all his life he had done at the first whisper of trouble.

"It's about Fiona." She put an extra emphasis of regret into the word, for she knew how he loved Fiona.

He sat, numbly rubbing the palms of his hands together as she told him, in sentences broken with pained embarrassment.

"Douglas Dunbar!" The horror in his soul trembled round the small shop. "Fiona! I spoke to her only yesterday." She could have been dead, so pitiful was his anguish.

"Colin first told me of the rumours perhaps two months ago," Gwen said. "I waited to tell you until there could be no doubt. If one looks back there are things—little things—that take on a new significance."

"Yes." He rose with an odd lethargy and stood facing the street. He had come in so blithely, filled with the beauty of the satinwood table he wanted her to buy.

She tried not to think of the effort it would be for him now to walk these familiar streets again. There had never been a man more sensitive to public scorn.

He turned to her helplessly, his face very old and drawn. "What's to be done?"

"I'm sure Robert can't know. It will have to come from you, Father. I'm sorry." She took his arm and stood close to him.

"I'll have to see Fiona first."

Her concern deepened. "Must you do that? You're hurt enough now."

A slight flicker of impatience crossed the stony blankness of his face.

"I can't simply . . . I must be sure it's true."

"I'm not sure that's required of you, Father. That's for Robert, after you've told him what's being said. After all, will she admit anything so terrible?"

His hair and his beard had never looked so white, nor his shoulders so rounded. All at once she saw him as the sort of old man who might have to be helped across the street, and in her heart a cold resentment rose against Fiona.

"I'll know," Fergus said as he went dazedly toward his coat. He opened the door and then slowly withdrew into the shop again. "I wonder, my dear, if you would give that boy there a copper to find me a cab. I don't feel like walking anymore today."

He waited until early evening before going down the hill to Claremont Row in the sodden but sheltering darkness. At every footstep he pulled his head deeper into the upturned fur collar of his coat. Huge flakes of sleet fluttered past the gas jets in another of the showers that had carried the city so abruptly into winter. The drear prospect matched the desolation of his spirit.

She was at home, and in tears she told him it was true. After the awful initial question he asked her nothing, and when she was finished he rose without a word. But at the door he turned, looking at her as if he might never again see the wonderful attributes of face and figure which over the years had given him so much joy.

"I loved you, Fiona," he said with a quaver in his voice she had never heard before. "Perhaps even more than I loved my own children."

It was as near as he could come to reproaching her, but the heartbroken restraint tore at her more woundingly than fury.

"Grandfather . . . " She could find no words to express her yearning that things could be as before. But even in the moment of longing, a confused and half-blind honesty intruded, and she knew she did not truly want just her old life. She wanted it with the addition of Dunbar. As she stood at the open door, watching Fergus cross to the black shadow of the dripping trees, she realised with an additional stab that for all the gloss on her life, her emotions were as banal as a housemaid's.

As she closed the door, a cab slowed in the street, hesitated, then resumed a steady trot. It passed Fergus's bowed and muffled figure. As he reached the top of the hill and turned into Park Place, he saw it had stopped outside his own house.

It was James, come at last to face the moment which for weeks he had been dreading.

24

Even with all that must be done Fergus was too cast down to leave the house next day, even at night. Rita was almost as distraught and disbelieving. That so much blackness had come into their lives in the course of a day seemed impossible. In the ordinary way, they would have run to Fiona with James's dreadful news, for her calm and sensible advice. That this pillar of their lives should have crumbled, and been turned into another instrument of pain for them, was almost more than they could credit.

James, unable to bear their grief, and himself stunned by their word of Fiona, had crept out of the house before seven o'clock that morning to catch the first train home. Fergus could find no escape in any of his usual activities. The only thing that mattered was the family and the happiness of its individual members. Never could he recall so many of them being struck by such appalling and intensely personal trouble as now. The awful events just revealed left none of them untouched. The entire family unit was threatened as never before. It could easily be destroyed. What respect could the Kings command in Glasgow in the midst of two such scandals? One they might have survived, but two!

"Two!" he cried to Rita in his despair when she came into his study in the middle of the afternoon. "How could two tragedies like these fall on us at once?"

She stood over him, stroking his hair, until he calmed. Her own eyes were heavy with baffled tears. "You must tell Robert," she said for the dozenth time.

Next morning, before the city stirred, he crossed it and caught an early train to London. He arrived in the middle of the afternoon and took a cab to St. James's, past walls chalked with war slogans—HANG KRUGER, MAFEKING WILL NOT FALL—his ears ringing with the sombre cries of news-vendors selling the latest casualty lists.

It was so long since he had last been there that no one in the public office recognised him. He stood waiting like an awkward stranger. A few minutes later Robert's exclamations of surprise and his own initial evasions faltered away. He began blurting what he had come to say. The words came in an agony of sympathy. Whatever their bitter disagreements in the past, this was a terrible moment. No man could be given worse news of his wife. *Death itself,* Fergus thought, *might be borne more easily.*

Suddenly, all he was aware of was his own distress. It stood out among the mahogany, gilt and crystal of the elegant office like an embarrassing weakness, for apart from a slight paleness Robert was apparently unmoved.

As he saw Fergus's pain grow more acute and heard his voice stumble, he stepped forward and took his arm, guiding him to a chair by the window. "There's no need to go on, Father," he said softly. "I've known about Fiona for months."

Fergus's lip trembled. "Then . . . why haven't you acted?"

"What can I do?"

"She's your wife. You must stop her dishonouring you—and us."

"I've been hoping it would end of its own accord."

They were strange words from a man who had always moulded life to his own requirement, and they only added to Fergus's confusion.

In the little park opposite the house gardeners swept shrivelled leaves. The peaceful sound of their brooms on the gravel was in contrast to the turbulence hanging in the room.

"I'm sorry you had to make such a tiring journey," Robert said. "I'll book you into Stone's for a day or two. You used to find it very comfortable. I'm told the food is first-class these days."

The gaping expression left Fergus's face as he moved forward on his chair, certain at last that he had not misunderstood. "Damn Stone's," he said. "That's not what I came all this way to talk about. Can't you understand? Glasgow's seething with this scandal. How can you tolerate it?"

"Because I can't afford to act rashly." Robert's fingers worked irritably at his watch chain. "If I do the wrong thing, it could be the finish of me in politics."

"Politics," Fergus moaned. "What I want is to be able to hold my head up."

Robert left the window and went to the farthest chair in the room, touching the furniture as he went, as if he had never seen it before.

"This job I have with Hicks Beach—the chancellor—is a small step,

387

but an important one. I don't want to jeopardise my chances. If I threaten Fiona, she may defy me. I would then have little option but to divorce her. If I'm forced to go to the courts, it could be the end of me at Westminster."

"If you can't threaten her, then you'll have to appeal to her, but you must do something. " Fergus's voice grew shrill with self-pity. "If you could hear the gossip in Glasgow. It's terrible!" A thin beam of wintry sunshine filtered through the net curtaining, showing his eyes to be full of unshed tears.

Robert rose and carried his chair a little nearer. There had always been a gulf between them, but the long stretch of polished floor made it too palpable. His voice remained distant.

"I am not in Glasgow. To people here, Glasgow is a remote provincial city in another country, almost in another world. Nothing that Fiona does in Glasgow can harm me here unless I allow it to do so by acting foolishly."

A furious resentment swept Fergus as he saw that even in such an apparently straightforward matter as dealing with a faithless wife, his son's attitude was bafflingly beyond him. Thirty years of his life had been marked by conflicts with Robert. Was he to be tormented all the way to the grave?

"My God, Robert," he said, "you think of no one but yourself. Your mother and I have to live in Glasgow." He scowled his disgust. "Politics is the right place for you. You never had two principles you could rub together and you still haven't." He looked fiercely round the room, recognising even in his anger the influence of Rita, as passed on through Fiona. Momentarily he was sidetracked. The subtle continuity of family life had always fascinated and pleased him. Now, here, it was being shattered, and his efforts to preserve it, being spurned. "You may think you're safe in this other world you've created for yourself, but I'll see you suffer as much as the rest of us." He couldn't have explained the threat, except as relief for his tortured feelings. "You're the one really responsible for this state of affairs. I blame you more than I blame Fiona."

"Naturally." Instantly, Robert regretted the sarcasm, with its evocation of so much bygone acrimony, but before he could retract, Fergus had rushed on.

"You pushed Fiona out of the security of her home into the affairs of King and Company. You exposed her to every kind of worldly strain and temptation so that you could escape down here and swank with a lot of fancy new people. You didn't care what happened to her."

Robert's arm swept the accusation violently aside. "Of course I cared. And what a melodramatic picture you paint. You make King and Company sound like a hellhole of iniquity and Fiona a little girl who had nev-

388

er been out alone before. All our married life I've been away for long periods. And it *was* the family business I talked her into, not a brothel in Bombay."

Fergus rose with a sound of despair and walked heavily to a table in the middle of the room. He poured a glass of whisky and then put it down untouched.

"Don't you see? Always before, no matter how long you were away, your home was with her. You ended all that when you came to London. After a while it became clear enough to the rest of us, so how do you think she felt? If you had stayed in Glasgow and run your business, leaving Fiona to conduct your home, this would never have happened."

"I'm not so sure." For the first time, Robert's voice was harsh and the words biting. "Once a sport, always a sport. It might not even be the first time she's done this."

He turned quickly away from the sight of Fergus's shock. But the façade of self-control, having cracked, widened. "What a dreadful mess." His words sighed miserably across the room. The intensity in them touched Fergus almost hearteningly. Anything was better than the previous, cold indifference.

His voice softened. "I'm trying to appreciate your dilemma, but you really can't ignore what's happening."

Robert groaned. "I suppose I can't. Especially after this." He lifted a letter from his desk and after glancing at it let it drop.

"Florence is at a convent school in France, and I didn't even know about it until this came from her yesterday." He lifted the letter again. "Fortunately, she seems to like it."

Fergus shook his head. "I suspected Fiona hadn't consulted you, but I thought she would at least have informed you afterward. I suppose events have started moving too fast for her now."

"Ideally, what would you like to see happen?"

Fergus walked to the window and stood watching the gardeners. "I can't see inside you, Robert. I don't know if you'll ever be able to forgive her. But if you can, come home and live with her and shut the gossiping mouths."

"But my future is in London."

"Then bring her here with you, away from that man."

"And who will run the business?"

Fergus stared at him, his anger rising again. "My God, Robert, no one has been more dedicated to business than me, but it is incredible you should think of that now. Ross could take over in Glasgow. You could make London the head office."

"I don't intend ever again to give all my time to business. I can manage this as a branch but not as our headquarters." He sank wearily into a chair and closed his eyes. "I've turned this over in my head hundreds of times, and I still don't know what to do. You're right, though. I'll have to see Fiona. But it won't be this week, and possibly not next week, either. Hicks Beach is a demanding master." As he saw Fergus gather himself to protest, he said quickly, "I know what you're going to say, Father, but this has been going on so long, another couple of weeks isn't going to make any difference."

"I hope not." Fergus rose and in two quick gulps emptied the glass of whisky he had poured earlier. He needed a bracer, dear knows! He still had to give the awful news about James. As he stood trying to find words, Robert's voice came again.

"There's one thing we've left out of account in all this."

"What?"

"Fiona's feelings. She may not be prepared to come meekly to me in London. It may have suited her until now to keep up the pose of being my wife. She was having the best of two worlds. But now that it's all started tumbling round her, she may go off with Dunbar." His mouth twisted into a warped smile. "To put it quite crudely, it may not be just a fling she's having. She may actually prefer Dunbar."

25

Two days later James left Park Place to drive to the opening of the exhibition of his paintings at Alexander Reid's gallery. Fergus sat at his side, braced for his first daylight appearance since the day of Gwen's shattering revelation.

They sat in silence, James clutching a bag of breadcrumbs which he had held up as he left the house as an indication to the coachman that they should go by way of the park to feed the ducks.

It was a still morning, and as they went down the hill into the frosted dell, the city sounds seemed more distant than usual. There was no sun and the light was tinged yellow with a threat of fog. All the grassy nooks were snowy with rime, and in the shrubberies rhododendron leaves drooped inside a thin powdering of sugary ice. The chimes of a clock drifted through the bare trees and along the cold river as the carriage stopped by a bridge under which generations of ducks had gathered to be fed, thousands of them with crusts from Rita's kitchen.

As James pushed the door open Fergus tugged his watch out. "Ten fifteen," he said worriedly. "Can't Paton take those crusts?"

"Come along, Father. It's years since I've done this. The air will do us good. Reid isn't expecting us for another half hour. His people are probably still running about, sticking labels on the pictures. These exhibitions are always chaotic until the final minutes before they let the public in."

After the last crumb had been emptied from the bag, and the ducks returned to the frosted grass of the riverbank, they continued to lean over the bridge, soothed by the slow swirl of the water. It was difficult, in this placid place, to credit the reality of the events that crowded their minds. James could not resist another reference to those that concerned him most clearly.

"At least this is going to be a week in which I won't weary," he said. "Today the exhibition, two days later my appointment with the sheriff at Dumfries, two days after that the elections to the Academy. Everything nicely spaced out."

Since James's arrival at Park Place the previous afternoon, Fergus had been struck by his bouyancy. He had at first assumed it to be bravado. Then he had put it down to the excitement of the exhibition and the prospect of at last receiving his due from the Academy. It was only when they had settled in the library with a decanter after dinner that he discovered James's optimism stemmed from an absolute conviction that the trial would go in his favour.

"Mr. Robertson is completely certain of it," James said.

Fergus, who knew that black despair would have been his own mood at the approach of such an ordeal, smiled cautiously into his glass. "I hope he's a good man, James."

"That's what makes his confidence so heartening, Father. He's the old sort of safe-as-houses family lawyer who really cares what he's about. He wouldn't raise my hopes lightly."

"My boy . . ." The words were wrung from Fergus now as he relived that hour by the fire. The unexpected sound of his own voice, echoing away over the misted river, brought him out of his reverie in a flurry of embarrassment.

"Yes, Father?" James was looking at him curiously. "Are you all right?"

"My boy . . . we're going to be late if we hang over this bridge all morning," Fergus stammered as he backed away in confusion toward the carriage. "And remember, Paton has to go back and fetch your mother and Jessie."

Rita had not wanted to be there in the first few formal minutes of the opening and had said she and Jessie would arrive about noon, in time for Fergus to take them all to lunch after they had looked at the pictures.

James and Alexander Reid greeted the invited guests while Fergus remained in the background, as far from the entrance door as he could get, his eyes steadfastly fixed on the paintings and his mind on the other, imagined, scenes in a drab courtroom.

"I can't tell you how much I appreciate your courage in keeping this exhibition going in view of these court proceedings," he said thickly when Reid appeared for a moment at his side.

"To have cancelled would have been like pronouncing James guilty," Reid said. "I couldn't have done that."

"If there's any loss, I'll be responsible for it," Fergus said. "I talked you into this."

Reid's smile indicated his sympathy, his gratitude and not only his refusal of the offer but his belief that it was unnecessary. "Keep your eye on those paintings, King," he said as he moved away. "James's innocence looks out at you from every one of them."

Fergus turned again to face the wall, bent and misty-eyed. A moment later he heard James's voice behind him. "Let me get you a sherry, Father. It's not like you to be empty-handed in a room full of glasses." He waved his catalogue to attract a waitress, and when Fergus had been provided with a drink, he said with quiet elation, "It couldn't have got off to a better start, Father. I hope it is an omen for my luck the day after tomorrow. Reid tells me he's sold three pictures already." He looked round the noisy groups of people. "I must still have some friends and admirers. Everyone's come who was invited. All except"—Fergus's head jerked up—" . . . except Fiona," James finished lamely. When he saw Fergus's expression he said, "I'm sorry, Father. It was thoughtless of me to . . . "

Fergus's attempt at indifference was a pitiful failure. It collapsed almost instantly into a bitter outburst that James found equally unconvincing. "Perhaps she'll come yet. She seems to have the nerve for anything." His voice, despite the harshness of the words, was unsteady.

"No." James shook his head. "She won't come. I knew perfectly well she wouldn't, but I wasn't . . . I wasn't able to leave her out."

Fergus turned quickly away, and after watching him sympathetically for a few moments, James went to where James Guthrie stood inspecting the paintings with open admiration.

"They're breathtaking," Guthrie said exuberantly. "I'd almost forgotten what a marvellous painter you are." His eyes narrowed as he scanned them. His smile was wondering. "Every time I see an example of your best work, I'm baffled all over again. I've never known where it came from. Your vision is unique."

His voice dropped, and, taking James's arm, he led him to a corner. "Will you be at home on Friday?"

My God, I hope so, James thought fervently, his confidence in the outcome of his trail suddenly wavering. He nodded.

"Then I'll send you a telegram from Edinburgh. Otherwise it could be days before you know the result of the elections. The secretary of the Academy would simply send you a leisurely letter. I'm afraid they are rather lacking in human understanding." He grinned. "I sometimes wonder if they know very much about painting, either." He became aware of James's withdrawn expression. "Cheer up, old man! I've sounded out quite a number of the members. Perhaps it's wrong of me to raise your hopes, but it's my belief only the most awful luck can stop your being elected this time."

James's smile of gratitude disappeared in a sudden torrent of guilt. Guthrie knew nothing of the charge hanging over him. He should have told him instead of letting him go on working for his election, unaware that he would first be judged by a far more awesome court. Several times he had tried to write a letter, but it had been beyond him to commit the awful accusation to paper. There was no way it could be made to look other than sickening. Desperately, as he faced his friend, James tried to find the courage he needed. But he quailed and retreated from the vision that came to him of the bewildered uncertainty that would gather in the keen blue eyes. The whole business was too foul to be mentioned, except after days of emotional anguish. He felt himself trembling and reached quickly for a glass from a passing tray. Then, his hand still shaking, he put it down on a table, untouched. He had promised Jessie. . . .

Guthrie, watching the performance with amused surprise, said, "I suppose you prefer the family poison?"

James nodded dumbly. For a long time after Guthrie had gone there was a lump of regret in his throat. It had been despicably weak of him to leave his friend in ignorance.

It was the only blot on a successful day, and by evening James had recovered his high spirits sufficiently to insist that they all dine out. No one was keen. Rita pleaded tiredness. Jessie protested that the gown she had with her was too homely. Fergus shrank from the ordeal of another public appearance, especially when he heard the place James had in mind was the St. Enoch Hotel. It was invariably busy. But after a quick refusal he retracted, anxious that the buoyancy his son would so desperately need should not be destroyed by him. Together, they overcame the objections of Rita and Jessie.

"I had a reason for wanting this little gathering," James said as they sat self-consciously in the hotel lounge with their drinks, surrounded by beautifully gowned women and well-tailored men gathering for functions in the various suites.

"I hope it's a good one," Jessie said reproachfully, even more conscious, in the midst of such splendour, of her homespun appearance.

"It's the best," James said mischievously, his humour heightened by several whiskies.

Fergus watched and listened with a vague sense of unease. All this lightheartedness seemed so out of place. In his douce view it was unnatural and suspect. He felt it was too brittle in the face of what had yet to come. It was almost as if James had been drugged against a reality everyone else could see. And yet, there was no question of its being a mood induced by alcohol. James had been genuinely convinced by his lawyer that he had nothing to worry about. But surely the mere fact of having to appear in court on such a charge, whatever the outcome . . . Fergus disguised a shudder by emptying his glass energetically. He said almost testily, "Well, tell us what we're here to celebrate, James."

"The engagement of your youngest son to Miss Jessie McNee, spinster, of the parish of Fleetside."

Jessie's blushes enhanced her elfin prettiness. "You might have warned me you were going to do this, James." She looked quickly at her future parents-in-law and was relieved to see two faces bright with surprised but welcoming smiles. "After all, it was supposed to be a secret."

"My dear"—Rita leaned across the table and kissed her—"it can still be a secret with us, if you wish it. But I'm so glad James has told us." She could see Fergus's moist eyes. "We are both so very happy for you. James could not have found a better girl to be his wife. You are what he has needed all these years."

Fergus was swept with so many emotions, his mind crowded with so many pictures, that he could only take Jessie's hand. "Jessie." He repeated it several times in a choking voice. "If only James had found you sooner." And then his eyes could hold the tears no longer. He tried to struggle from his seat, but Rita put a hand gently on his arm.

"There's no need for you to go anywhere, my dear. Just sit back. I'm sure we all understand."

Although James's summons to appear before the sheriff had been timed for ten o'clock in the morning, several cases were heard before his. It was half past three before his name was called. With Mr. Robertson hurrying ahead, James limped along an echoing stone corridor. Inside the courtroom he went to a wooden enclosure indicated by a policeman.

Along the ledge of this dock there was an iron rail about a foot high. Through the space between the ledge and the iron bar James, with thumping heart, saw an elevated bench with a very large padded chair behind it. That was where the sheriff would sit. To his left, along one side of the well of the court, there was a long enclosure filled with bench seats. That, he supposed, was where the jurors sat in jury trials. The complaint against him, Mr. Robertson had explained, would be heard by the sheriff alone.

He turned slightly and with a shock his eyes met Jessie's. She was sitting a few feet behind, as close to him as it was possible for her to be. To his relief, the public benches were only moderately filled. Even those most antagonistic to him had desisted from making him a spectacle. These country people had a reticence unknown in the city. Their sense of seemliness had kept them from crowding here to glory in his humiliation.

"Court stand!"

The usher's booming voice reverberated round the bare white walls and disappeared upward, toward the high, dusty windows. There was a clattering of feet and scraping of chairs as everyone rose for the sheriff's entrance.

Oh, my God, James thought, in a sudden iciness of spirit, as he saw an immobile white face under a wig. *He looks a real old hanging devil.*

It was the last lucid thought he had in the next bewildering hour.

Fergus and Rita had stayed in Glasgow at James's insistence. He wanted only Jessie there to see and hear what happened to him.

"But we must know the outcome," Rita had said.

"Then I'll telephone," James had promised. "And . . . if for any reason I can't, Jessie will."

"But we have no telephone."

"Father will have to wait by the telephone in Seabank Lane. We will make a time. Five thirty. It must be over by then."

"You know perfectly well your father won't speak on the telephone."

"Then you must go to Seabank Lane with him, Mother."

Fergus had not been to Seabank Lane since the day Gwen had told him about Fiona. He assumed she was still going there daily, since otherwise he would have heard from Peter Ross.

The thought of meeting her was unbearable, and Fergus waited until after five o'clock—when he knew she would be gone for the day—before arriving with Rita. It was after six o'clock, with the warehouse closed and the offices empty except for the cleaners, before the telephone rang.

"It's James himself," Rita whispered excitedly. Fergus waited in a fidgeting torment for the first sign from her. He did not have long to wait. Her voice rose to an even higher note of excitement.

"That's wonderful, James. I'm so relieved I could cry." As she spoke, she was telling Fergus with her eyes that everything was all right.

But despite the clear message of her words and her ecstatic expression, he had to be certain. "Not guilty?" he asked desperately.

Rita turned a little from the mouthpiece. "Case dismissed," she said.

Later, Fergus, who in his years as a magistrate had presided in a police court, explained. "It's even better than a verdict of not guilty," he said happily. "It means the sheriff threw the whole thing out because he didn't think there was any case for James to answer. This is what James's lawyer had more or less said, although I don't think even he was optimistic enough to think the case would be dismissed. He would have been satisfied with simply a verdict of not guilty."

"Oh, and James said the sheriff rebuked the fiscal quite strongly for having wasted the court's time," Rita remembered.

Fergus had risen and was striding elatedly about the room, his back straighter than Rita had seen it for a long time.

"James could probably sue," he said, taking a fierce grip of his beard as he pondered the possibility of redress. "It was monstrous that he should have been subjected to such an ordeal for reasons so flimsy that even the sheriff was annoyed."

Rita, looking alarmed, held up a hand to stop him. "I'm sure James won't want to become involved in anything like that. He'll want to forget the whole dreadful episode."

Fergus frowned at her from his corner and then chuckled as he crossed the room to stand at her side. "Perhaps you're right," he admitted. "But it's such a victory for James." He hesitated. "It could almost be a blessing in disguise. Surely when this appears in the papers, it will help lay all those rumours."

Rita put a hand on his arm. "It won't be in the newspapers, Fergus?"

"I'm afraid it's bound to be, my dear. James is a well-known painter. All the newspapers will have had correspondents in court. They would be hopeful of a scandal. As it is, all they will be able to print is the charge and the fact that the sheriff ruled, in effect, that there should never have been a charge. Any of the so-called evidence that led the sheriff to that decision would be given to him in private, with the public cleared from the court."

"It will be so distasteful," Rita said.

"But think what it could have been! Up until now I've hardly faced the thought of what they might have been printing tomorrow. As I said, in a strange way—if it had to happen at all—this may have worked in James's favour. And then, if he's elected to the Academy . . . " He stopped as a new thought came. "When are they announcing their engagement?"

"It will be in the *Herald* next week, I think."

"Good." Fergus saw the disconnected events almost as steps in a planned campaign to clear the hideous slander that had for so long besmirched James's name. "And then, when do they plan to get married? I've been so worried I don't think I even asked."

"They haven't set the exact date, but it will be before the end of December." She smiled. "Don't you remember the joke James made of it? He said they didn't want to wait until the following century."

Next morning, four men carrying placards began picketing the entrance to Alexander Reid's gallery. Newspaper reports referring to James's court appearance were pasted to the placards under glaring slogans: KING PAINTINGS ARE TAINTED, BOYCOTT KING PAINTINGS, PROTECT OUR CHILDREN, THE CASE IS NOT DISMISSED.

From the considerable section of Glasgow society which believed all art was suspect, the response was remarkable. Soon the four men were joined by several score other outraged citizens.

After all the years of whispering, a positive outlet had been provided for the moral incense raised in the righteous by James's supposed sins. For once, the often frustrated impulses of the Puritan, the Philistine and the *unco guid* could be aired publicly with no great loss of respectability. The crowd were not unruly, nor were they undesirables. They were well dressed, and articulate—able and eager to explain their motivation to puzzled passersby. These were the only slightly eccentric watchdogs of public purity—well-doing citizens of impeccable behaviour, given to charitable works and regular church attendance.

Gradually they were joined by the exhibitionists and the generally unstable who rejoice in any public demonstration, whatever the cause. By early afternoon the pavements on both sides of West George Street were blocked. Only the efforts of a contingent of mounted policemen kept the road itself clear for traffic.

Without the presence of James the aggression building up in the crowd was thwarted. It needed a target. Gradually, James's admirers— who until now had merely been subjected to good-natured heckling as they went in to see the paintings—became surrogates for the artist himself. Banners were roughly thrust in the windows of their carriages as they drew up, puzzled but unsuspecting, outside the gallery. Insults were spat at them if they dared dismount. Despite the presence of the police, they were jostled if they tried to cross the pavement. Only the very determined persisted. Mostly, clutching hats and bent against the shouts and waving banners, they retreated from the fury and were driven away.

Several times Reid tried to reason with those nearest the door. When this failed, he appealed to the police to clear the street. The stolid lieutenant in charge, influenced perhaps by all the good coats, hats and gamps he could see, said blandly that he would not do this unless the public peace was threatened. So far as he was concerned, it was still an orderly demonstration. Tolerance, he said philosophically, kept these things within bounds. Provocation was always unwise.

At last Reid sent a messenger to Fergus, who arrived a half hour later, bowed from the insults of the crowd.

"My God, Reid, this is dreadful," he sobbed. "What are the police coming to?"

"Possibly they don't like painters, or perhaps they don't like to hear of cases being dismissed, even in distant parts of the country," Reid said cynically. "But there's no doubt whose side they're on."

"This business will finish me," Fergus said pitifully. "They're out to crucify us." He was not referring to the crowd as such but to the dark cosmic forces they represented in the confused turmoil of his mind.

"Well, I'm going to close for the day and see if that will placate them," Reid said. "But I didn't want to do it until you'd seen what I'm facing."

Fergus nodded his assent, looking round the empty, darkened gallery. "You might as well," he muttered.

Reid marshalled his staff and they all left together, the doors being elaborately barred and locked as a symbolic act of submission.

As he drove away, Fergus, the ex-magistrate, found himself sympathising a little with the police view. It was not the crowd but James and his paintings which posed the threat to society. Fergus was honest enough to admit to himself that under different circumstances he could have nodded blind approval of their attitude.

Early in the evening he turned out Paton and drove back into the city, drawn irresistibly to the scene of the disturbance. He left the coach in Bath Street and walked toward West George Street. A cold wind came from the north, swirling in the basement areas of the old houses and causing the gas jets to hiss and flicker on their posts. The lonely tap of his cane in the darkness was matched by the occasional sad groan of a ship feeling its way down the dark river to the firth.

He turned a corner that would give him a view of Reid's gallery. The street was empty. Now that the offices and shops were closed, no one came here. The main routes to theatres, restaurants and public houses skirted this locality. Farther on there was the noise of traffic and the lights of passing transport. He stopped at the gallery window. In the waning glow of a nearby lamp he saw two paintings on easels and recognised the unmistakable colours, arrangements and figures—at once the ingredients of James's fame and the spur to his persecutors. Wondering at the insistent uneasiness that had brought him here, he moved on, heading back by another route to where his carriage waited.

He went to bed before ten without his customary tea and digestive biscuit, without even the interest to make his usual round of the public rooms to see that the fires were safe. He wakened to what sounded like the front door's being kicked and battered. He fumbled for the matches and lit a candle. It was not yet midnight. Rita was first to the window. A few dark shapes seemed to move in the street and then disappear. Among the shrubs and ornamental trees on the grassy stretch opposite the house, a small flame wavered. With a chill sense of disaster, Fergus threw on his dressing gown. "I must see what's happening," he said breathlessly.

"I'll come, too," Rita said, and in his excitement he forgot to forbid it. When they reached the hall, two or three of the staff were already opening the door. As it swung back, a lurid orange light struck them. The uncertain flame across the street had become an inferno.

"It's a bonfire," Fergus heard one of the maids say.

By its glare, the street looked empty. Whoever had battered at the door had gone. Fergus was within a few yards of the fire before he saw its purpose. Gilt glinted in the fierce glow. There was a strong smell of burning paint. Picture frames warped in his gaze and burst into flame, their canvasses already gone. He could not see the paintings, for at the side of the bonfire from which he approached the fire was at its hottest, but he knew they were James's. With a hoarse cry he rushed forward, skirting the pyre, looking for an opening from which something could be snatched. His hands were scorched and he could smell the singeing of his own hair before someone pulled him away empty-handed.

Neighbours from the adjoining houses had tumbled into the street and stood in sleepy, puzzled groups.

As Fergus watched, a young man with a military overcoat pulled on over his nightclothes dashed forward, grasped a frame and hauled it free in a storm of sparks that showered over the watchers. The canvas had not caught alight, but when Fergus bent to look at it, all he saw was a congealed mass of blistered paint.

Someone took his arm. When he turned, he saw Rita, her eyes wet and baffled. Occasionally, as the mountain of paintings collapsed, an unscathed canvas would appear momentarily, and then, the flames reaching it, they would have a horrifying glimpse of children's faces melting into grotesque travesties. In seconds, sweet smiles degenerated into obscene leers before disappearing in explosions of blue and orange flame. In a few minutes the bonfire had burned itself out, leaving only a glowing heap of ashes.

In the middle of the night Alexander Reid arrived, accompanied by two policemen. He was almost as numbed as Fergus.

"They went in through the window and stripped the entire gallery," he said. "There isn't a single painting left on the walls. The police assume they had a waggon waiting to bring them up here. I can't tell you how sorry I am about this, King. It's a tragedy."

Fergus nodded brokenly. "But why here?"

"I suppose this was as near as they could get to James."

"God knows how James will take it."

One of the policemen had been standing with an open notebook. His matter-of-fact voice broke the silence. "How minny pictures were there, sir?"

"Over a hundred," Reid said.

"The cream of my son's life's work." Fergus spoke guiltily into a corner of the cold and shadowy room. "They were collected from the ends of the country. And it was my idea it should be done."

26

Reid insisted on accompanying Fergus when he set out next morning for Fleetside. They sat huddled in silence as the train edged its way south through the fields of Ayshire. Cold sunlight cast shadows from frosted bushes and leafless trees onto land over which a few hardy cattle not yet taken in for the winter foraged with steaming breath. At Dumfries they changed to a branch line that cut into more remote country. The productive fields petered out into brown moorland and the gentle rise of the country became more pronounced.

Soon they saw the high Galloway hills and the blue Solway glittering coldly through a scattering of gnarled trees. For part of the way the line followed the firth.

They had not telegraphed James and there was alarm in his quick, welcoming smile. Fergus was too choked to speak and Reid had to tell the story.

When he finished, James rose. He walked carefully through a litter of canvasses and frames to the studio door. Although the clock had just struck one, it looked as if it would soon be dark. The garden dripped in a foggy haze. There were footprints in the grass where Mrs. Laing had crossed it to hang some kitchen cloths on a line.

He spoke over his shoulder. "Do you remember a picture I did called *A Field of Poppies?* It was in the exhibition, wasn't it?"

"Yes."

They could not see his face, but they heard pain in his voice. "It was the best thing I ever did. I often wished I'd never sold it."

When he turned, Fergus was shocked to see a sneering smile distorting his pinched features.

"You never really liked them, did you, Father? You must really be glad that so much evidence of my decadence has gone."

"James . . . " Fergus was too confused to defend himself.

Reid came between them.

"Your father has always been one of your greatest admirers," he said severely. "He persuaded me to hold this exhibition in your support." His voice drifted away as he remembered the dreadful consequences.

But James's mind was on another line. "I wonder, was it in my support or in his own?" he asked with heartless insight.

Reid, with a sympathetic shake of his head to Fergus, resolutely turned the talk to the practical matter of preparing insurance claims.

Throughout the afternoon, James's manner remained one of numb bitterness. Their efforts at sympathy were repelled with snideness. As they left the studio to take tea in the sitting room, there was a clatter. They turned and saw James's stony face. Behind him, an easel lay on the floor on top of a canvas on which he had been working.

At last the shock passed. James rose from the chair in which he was slumped and, crossing to Fergus, put a hand hesitantly on his shoulder. "I'm sorry, Father, I don't know what made me take it like that." He turned. "And I owe you an apology, too, Mr. Reid. It was kind of you, coming, and I've been very ungrateful."

Fergus looked blearily at his watch. "It's after six o'clock, James. Would it be safe for us all to have a drink now?"

James went to the decanter. "You would have thought this was the first thing I'd have made for, wouldn't you." When he had poured the drinks, he said, "I thought I would have had a telegram from James Guthrie by this time. Although I have little doubt what the Academy will have decided. The sheriff at Dumfries might have cleared my name, but the voice of public opinion will ring louder for the electors."

They were at dinner when Guthrie arrived to confirm James's despondent expectations.

"I couldn't send you a telegram with news like that," he said. "I had to come myself."

James's mind was almost too battered to absorb further pain. "I've lived until now without initials after my name," he said, "so I suppose I can go on."

"My God, James," Guthrie said in a surge of regretful frustration. "You should have told me what was happening. If I'd known that court case was coming up, I'd have advised you to withdraw your name. You would have lived to fight another day. The Academy shrinks from the faintest breath of anything . . . unpleasant. Even with the court's verdict in your favour they were in a quandary. But, of course, that rabble in Glasgow put the tin lid on things."

When James gave Jessie the news next day, she was at once broken and scandalised. "All your lovely pictures," she cried. "I can't take it in." The Academicians in Edinburgh were a more tangible target. "It's shocking they should have reacted so badly," she said, her eyes sparkling with anger. "You would have thought that as artists themselves they would have rallied behind you and elected you almost as a gesture of defiance to the ignorant mob." She looked into his despairing eyes and her fury turned to tenderness. "Even out of sympathy," she said as she kissed him.

James's shock at this final rejection was submerged in the greater suffering of the burning of his pictures. And despite Jessie's outrage at what she saw as the Academy's spinelessness, it was on the loss of his work that his mind was fixed.

"Oddly enough, it's not so much the ones I painted this year I dwell on," he said. "They were good, but I can hardly remember them. It's those others, the ones Reid went to so much trouble borrowing from public galleries and private collections. Most of them were painted in the days before the world had got on top of me. I sold them all years ago, and I hadn't seen a single one of them since, but I knew they still existed. It's strange how an artist feels the process of creation hasn't been completed until the work is sold. Someone else has to put the final stamp on it with money. I've often thought it degrading, but it seems to be how it works. The sale is the closing of the circle. In a strange way, all those paintings were still a part of my life. Now they're all gone. It's as if I'd had children who had gone to live in other parts of the world and I'd been told they had all died."

"You must paint them all again, James," she said, realising the absurdity of the suggestion but her spirit rising in her anxiety to defend him against the awful shades she sensed to be gathering in his mind.

They were at the end of the garden and his eyes remained on a bleak stretch of mud on which seagulls sat waiting for the return of the tide.

"Or we could advertise that we want to buy any James King paintings still in private hands," she said with determined brightness. "There must still be some about. We could buy them and keep them ourselves no matter how much people asked for them. I haven't much money, James, but they could have it all so that the remaining paintings could be in our care."

"What rot you talk, Jessie," he said crushingly.

Guthrie left that afternoon for London, and Reid, next morning for Glasgow. Fergus stayed another nine days, during which he realised he had given James all the support he could. With thoughts of Rita alone at Park Place and other worries beckoning, he announced on a Sunday night that he would go home next morning. They saw him off in a downpour of icy rain. "We'll see you on the twenty-sixth," he said. It was the day fixed for their wedding.

That night, James cheered a little.

"If it's dry tomorrow, I think I'll go sketching," he said.

A picture came to Jessie of a forbidding December landscape denuded of the lushness inseparable from his work. But, anxious not to discourage him, she said, "So long as you wrap up well, James."

He nodded.

"Where will you go?"

"Gatekirk Bay."

"I would come with you, but I have so many things to do. I have miles of stitching still to do on the train for my dress."

"With so little time, you should have had it made," he said.

She smiled tolerantly. "You don't understand, James. I wanted to make it myself. But it would have been nice if I'd had a sister, or if Mother had still been alive to help me with some of the arrangements."

He shook his head. "We agreed it would be a very quiet and simple wedding, Jessie."

"That's what we agreed, James, but now I know there's no such thing. Not, at any rate, when you're the bride."

"Then I could stay and help you instead of going sketching," he said. When he saw her expression, he laughed. "But perhaps I've kept you back enough this last week."

It was dry next morning, and he stopped outside her cottage shortly after nine o'clock.

"I thought I'd let you see all my scarves and rugs," he said. "Mrs. Laing fussed so much, I thought I'd never get away."

"What about a flask?" she said after inspecting him. "You'll need something besides tea to keep your blood circulating."

He hesitated. "I haven't brought one. I'm surprising even myself with my abstemiousness these days."

"There's a time for everything," she said. "I still have that bottle of King's Royal you gave me. I'll fetch it." When she had pushed it down beside his hamper, she looked doubtfully at the iron sky. "This is awfully silly of you, James. Are you sure you want to go sketching in such grim weather?"

His smile was a mirthless one uncharacteristic of his real nature. "I've never felt less like it, but I feel if I don't make the effort, I'm finished."

She watched him drive round the green with a feeling of apprehension that remained with her vaguely all morning.

Shortly after noon the light failed so badly that she had to put away her sewing. She tried to engage herself with other things in an attempt to dispel the persistent uneasiness that depressed her. Every sound of a horse or a rattling wheel in the street took her to the window.

At half past two there was a knock on the door. Her anxiety rose when she saw Mrs. Laing.

"Mr. King hasna come home," the housekeeper said, almost apologetically. "I was hoping he might be here. It's an awful long time for him to be gone on sich a day."

"He might be sheltering," Jessie said, quelling her imagination. "It's not all that late."

"No, but I really expected him by now. He said he might even be back in time to take a late lunch." There was now no doubting the depth of Mrs. Laing's concern.

"I'll get out my bicycle," Jessie said decisively. "At least we know where he went. I'll probably meet him on the road."

It was almost dark under the dripping trees when she left the deserted road and went down through the woods to Gatekirk Bay. Where the cart track petered out, she saw James's trap in its usual place. The shivering horse nuzzled her miserably as she hurried fearfully past.

As she broke through the barrier of brooding trees, the scene lightened. She saw a hazy stretch of sand and, perhaps a hundred yards below high-water mark, the leaden lip of a sullen sea pitted with rain. She had a quick impression of overwhelming desolation, and then all she was aware of was James. Almost in the same instant he saw her, and his cry floated across the water, mingling forlornly with the screeching of gulls. He was marooned on the rocky islet where they had first met, and across the last visible stretches of which heavy grey ripples were already creeping.

As she stood rooted with horror, his voice came faintly. "Go for help. . . . "

She was paralysed with sudden memories of stories known to everyone who lived on the Solway shores. The firth was notorious for its great rise and fall of water and for sinister tides that came racing in silently and unexpectedly from miles out. Every summer some unwary visitor was trapped in the sand and drowned by the sea's treacherous rush.

His voice came again. "Go for help. . . . "

She turned her head frantically in the direction of the road. The nearest house she could think of was several miles away. Before she could get there and back with help, James would have been washed from his rapidly shrinking perch. The smoothness of the sea's approach was frightening. There was no wind. No waves broke. The bay was like some great vessel being silently and speedily filled from an unseen underground source. On the road itself, of course, she might find help—a passing cart, or a farm labourer on his way home. But if she did not, it would be precious time wasted. There was no time to spare. The rocky outcrop had now vanished completely. James appeared to be standing on the surface of the water. She saw him cup his hands.

"I'll have to try and splash ashore before it gets any deeper."

She heard the fear in his voice and saw panic grip him. He seemed to be trying unsuccessfully to take off his coat with fingers presumably too numbed to work.

"Don't move," she shouted. "Stay where you are. I'll try to find a boat."

At nights men fished in the bay, and she had sometimes seen their dinghies pulled up and beached in the undergrowth above the high-water line. She ran along the fringe of the bay, tearing at the brown tangle of collapsed bracken. Almost immediately she found a boat. Her heart rose and then sank as she saw there were no oars. Whoever owned the boat would have taken them with him, a sensible and obvious precaution against theft that would apply to any boat she found.

With a sob of panic she ran back along the sand and down to the edge of the water. It had advanced startlingly and was now about a foot deep where James was trapped. He was bent, and seemed to be clinging to something under the water—probably a rock. With only one leg to brace him he would soon be floated off into deep water.

Jessie waited no longer. She had noticed a wide plank of wood wedged between some rocks. It was the next best thing to the unwieldy, oarless boat. She dragged it to the water's edge and threw off her coat and boots. Then, pushing the plank in front of her, she waded into the freezing sea.

When James saw her intention, he began thrashing about excitedly. "Go back, Jessie. Don't come out here."

Her concentration was such that she hardly heard him. Her feet had now left the bottom. She was floating quite easily. With the plank in front of her for buoyancy she began kicking her way toward James. Her heart was hammering but her head was clear. The water was quite still. She was a fair swimmer. If she tired on the way out, she need only cling to the plank until her strength came back. The return journey, with the tide working in their favour, should not be too difficult. All her common sense, allied with the strength of her love for James, was focussed on the desperate endeavour. Above all she must not panic. The pull of the in-rushing tide was strong, but immensely comforting was the thought of its soon carrying them both safely ashore. The plank was cumbersome. It took all her strength to keep manoeuvring it in the right direction. Occasionally her gaze took in James. He seemed to be watching now with a wonder amounting to calmness. Even when she had almost reached him, he remained silent, as if fearful that the sound of his voice would somehow act against her. Only when she was standing beside him, gasping for breath, did a flood of words come.

"I'm sorry, Jessie. I drank almost all the whisky you gave me and fell asleep. When I wakened, the rock was surrounded with water. If I'd had the sense to try to leave then I might have been able to wade ashore. But it looked so deep. I've never been able to swim."

"Never mind all that now, James. We'll need all our strength to get back."

He was numbed and shivering, and while he clung to the plank with one hand, to keep it from drifting away, she helped him out of his sodden coat. The rock they stood on was now so deeply submerged they were almost afloat. The greyness had advanced to darkness and the shore was a frighteningly distant line of scarcely visible sand.

"All we do is take an end of the plank each and hold tight," she said. His long wait on the rock had undermined his nerve, and his fear of surrendering the last remnant of solidity still under him was obvious.

She forced her voice to be matter-of-fact. "So long as we hold on to this plank, nothing can go wrong, James. In fact, the tide will wash us ashore. We will help by kicking a little—but gently, without any panic."

Her quiet confidence gave him courage.

He nodded, and a second or two later they allowed themselves to be washed off the rock. There was none of the sensation of sinking that James had feared. His body, already so cold that he was hardly aware of it, seemed to become completely weightless. His only difficulty was in keeping his leaden fingers on the plank.

"Kick just a little, James," he heard Jessie say.

Now that they were actually on the way, she felt astonishingly calm. She even had the presence of mind to realise that because James had only one leg, they would turn in circles unless she kicked only half as often as he did.

After what seemed a very short time James saw with a surge of relief that the dark blot of the wood fringing the bay had become less solid. He had a vague sense of individual trees.

"We're getting nearer," he gasped.

Several more minutes passed, during which objects on the shore became steadily clearer.

Jessie was the first to feel the sandy bottom of the bay under her feet. "Don't let go yet," she warned him.

They clung to the plank until their knees touched bottom and they were able to crawl exhaustedly beyond the water's reach before collapsing into a sobbing huddle of relief.

"I'm so cold and stiff," James said when at last they stumbled to their feet.

She shouldered him over the sand and through the wood, then bundled him into the trap. The horse neighed pitifully and moved off with steps as faltering as their own. The first house they reached was occupied by an old man. He was too unsteady to help except by boiling a kettle for tea while Jessie helped James into the house. After a mug of tea in front of a good fire he recovered enough to take off his wet clothes and collapse into the old man's bed.

"If I go now, I should catch Dr. Douglas at his surgery," Jessie said worriedly. Even in the warm glow of the firelight James looked pitiful. His long exposure would have been worsened, she knew, by the depressant effect of the whisky. She was hardly aware of her own shivering. The grass outside the cottage was stiffening with frost when she left with a tattered blanket over her wet clothes.

The elderly doctor's first act, despite her protests, was to order her home immediately, to a warm bed and as many hot drinks as she felt like taking. She was drained by the ordeal and was asleep when later in the evening he let himself into the house.

"I arranged for Mr. King to stay where he is tonight," he said. "He's exhausted, of course, but he doesn't really seem any the worse for his experience. I'll see him again in the morning, and if he's as right as I think he'll be, he can come home."

"I'll fetch him back in his trap," Jessie said, stifling a sneeze.

"Only if I let you," he said, popping a thermometer into her mouth as she opened it to proclaim her fitness. "And I don't think I'm going to," he muttered when he saw the reading. "Maybe we've had enough heroics from you, Jessie, for a day or two. I'll look in on you tomorrow morning as well. But there's something I want you to take tonight." He inclined his head a little, indicating the house beyond the room. "You've no one here with you, have you?"

"No."

"Then I'll come back myself with these powders I want you to take." As he went to the door, the loneliness of her position seemed to strike him. "I should tell you, Mr. King was almost delirious with praise for your bravery, Jessie. I'm sure he'll be your friend for life."

Her eyes sparkled in the lamplight and against the white pillows her cheeks were marked with a delicate flush. "I hope so, Doctor. We're going to be married the day after Christmas."

After a moment of surprise he took her hand and shook it delightedly. "Congratulations, Jessie. And you must excuse my ignorance. No one tells me anything except their symptoms." He went out still laughing.

Next afternoon James arrived home in a hired coach. His court appearence, the burning of his paintings, his rejection by the Academy, seemed events of a long time ago. His thoughts were now only of Jessie.

409

"I'm keeping her in bed, meantime," Dr. Douglas had said. "As a wise precaution. But, of course, you can visit her."

His clothes, which had dried in front of the old cottager's fire, were stiff and discoloured with salt water. After a bath and a change he left for Jessie's. Since she was alone and in bed, he took Mrs. Laing with him.

"We don't want any more gossip," he said.

They found her bright-eyed, red-cheeked and with a harsh cough. "I'm afraid I've taken a cold," she said, shivering. She pointed to a jug on her bedside table. "Pour me a glass of water, please, James. My mouth feels so dry."

Her hand, when he held it, was very hot. Several times, as they talked, her eyes closed and they thought she had fallen asleep. But each time she started up and apologised with a drowsy smile. "I've tired myself coughing," she said weakly.

Early that evening, when James had returned home, leaving Jessie asleep, Dr. Douglas called to see him.

"I'm not very happy about Jessie being alone," he said. "She needs nursing. I can get a trained woman, but not until tomorrow. Besides, two will be needed. I want someone with her all the time. Have you anyone who could help?"

James felt suddenly sick at the gravity of the old man's manner. "I'm sure Mrs. Laing, my housekeeper, will be willing to do anything she can."

"Can she go over there tonight, and stay?"

"Is Jessie's cold worse?" James stumbled in his anxiety to reach a bell-pull.

"Her condition has developed quite worryingly, despite all the medication she's had." He hesitated and looked keenly at James. "Since she has no family, I must regard you as her nearest, Mr. King." His voice dropped. "I'm afraid Jessie has pneumonia of both lungs. Her temperature has gone very high."

The quiet, careful voice so discouraged overreaction that seconds passed before James's anxiety burst out. "Oh, God. Poor Jessie. That cough . . . I should have known. Mrs. Laing didn't like the sound of it. We shouldn't have left her. But she was so cheerful, Doctor!"

The doctor nodded slowly. "She still is. She has great spirit."

There was a knock at the door and Mrs. Laing came in. "The poor mite," she said, without surprise, when given the news. "Of course I'll go to her. I'll just get some things."

Logs crackled in the fire, but to James the room had gone cold and cheerless. The window rattled in its frame, and the heavy curtains swayed in a draught that he had previously not noticed. *Pneumonia.* The awful word struck in his head like the solemn tolling of a great bell.

He leaned over the back of a chair in an attitude of stifled fury. "Why Jessie, Doctor? Why Jessie, when I haven't even got a sniffle?"

The slight contortion of Dr. Douglas's lips seemed to indicate that the cruel and baffling inconsistencies of Providence were hardly even to be pondered.

"You were lucky, Mr. King." He stroked his trim grey beard. "And you heard what your housekeeper said. Jessie's just a mite—a dainty little scrap of a thing. Apart altogether from the exposure, the physical effort of what she did must have taken a lot out of her. And then, afterward, when she came to fetch me, there was that long drive in freezing weather in wet clothes. She had a temperature that same night, but I was hoping I had caught it in time."

The boom of the awesome bell reverberated again in the confusion of James's mind. He felt dizzy and afraid. *Pneumonia.* He had been so immersed in worry. Now, in the face of the dreaded illness, everything except Jessie's continued existence was reduced to puny insignificance.

"We're going to be married on the twenty-sixth of the month," he said.

The doctor turned from a picture he had been idly inspecting. "Don't worry, Mr. King. Jessie hasn't forgotten. I had to go into one of her rooms for something. Her wedding dress was lying over a chair. Apparently she had been working at it the day of your accident. She got me to hang it up with a dust sheet over it." His smile widened. "She was quite cross when I had some difficulty in finding a hanger. She's a strong-willed little girl. You'll have to stand up for yourself when you're married."

"So long as she gets better," James said. All at once, the weight of guilt became insupportable. A distracted cry burst from him. "You know it's my fault, Doctor. I'm responsible for her being ill. You must tell me if she'll be all right."

"She'll have all the attention I can give her."

It was too evasive an answer.

"Will she be all right? Is she going to get better?"

The harsh insistence surprised the old man into a quick gesture of helplessness. "I don't have to tell you pneumonia is a grave illness," he said softly. "But there is no immediate cause for alarm."

The window in the room where Jessie lay was closed against draughts and the fire stoked high. Mrs. Laing and the nurse moved about on tiptoe, and often the only sound during the unending hours James spent at the bedside was Jessie's rapid struggling for breath. His sense of responsibility was terrible.

Was this what he had been sent to Galloway to accomplish? Had it

411

been preordained since that first day, when he had looked up to see her standing imperiously over him with the breeze fluttering through the graceful folds of her dress? Had the answer to that first demand—*With the whole Stewartry of Kirkcudbright to choose from, did you have to pick this little spot?*—been a resounding yes? Had all the joy and the final unifying worry of their brief time together been leading only to this? It all came crowding back—the shrewish scoldings and proddings with her stick when he got drunk and couldn't work, her outrageous forging of his paintings to protect him from the consequences of his awful irresponsibility, her defiant public support of him when the accusations were at their most hideous, and that great-hearted swim into the bay to snatch him from where he would have been better left to drown.

Sulphur candles, lit against the spread of infection, polluted what little air there was and made the sickroom eerie with their chill blue flames.

In her intervals of lucid wakefulness Jessie lay turned toward James as, from his sorrow, he struggled to radiate cheerfulness. Mostly she slept restlessly, so weakened by the raging fever and the pain of her inflamed lungs that even the effort of taking a few sips of beef tea drained her. She was poulticed continually and dosed with a variety of medicines, none of which she responded to, and the prescribing of which seemed to James to have become acts almost of desperation. Frequently she was delirious, her painful ramblings concentrated on their recent ordeals or their coming marriage. "Did you remember to post all those invitations we wrote last night, James?" she asked once. "I don't think we've forgotten anyone. It will really be a very quiet wedding." And James, fighting to control his bursting heart, gave her an elaborate description of an imaginary journey to the post box.

He had in fact spent the previous day cancelling all the wedding arrangements on the advice of Dr. Douglas.

"Even if the fever burned itself out today, she would still be convalescent at the end of the year," the doctor said.

For the first time, James had allowed himself to ask the awful question. "And if it doesn't?"

"We mustn't think of that."

"But how long can this go on?"

"It could go on for eleven days, but I don't think it will. This is the sixth day. I would expect the crisis to come in the next forty-eight hours."

It still had not come on the night of the seventh day. James was in the suffocating room when the doctor arrived for his evening visit. Jessie was barely conscious and her breathing was frighteningly loud. The doctor signalled for James to follow him out.

"The crisis is very close," he said as he shut the bedroom door behind him. "I'll come back later tonight, but I've done everything I can. And so

412

have those two wonderful women," he added as he saw one of them pass.

The narrow lobby seemed desperately cold after the stifling atmosphere of the sickroom. James shivered. For a week he had hardly slept, spending up to ten hours every day sitting practically motionless on the chair by Jessie's bed.

The old man looked at him with concern. "I should be sending you home to bed, but . . . perhaps you could make yourself comfortable here in an armchair, with a couple of blankets over you."

"All night?"

"I think it would be better."

"But is she going to . . . ?"

"I've been a doctor for a long time, Mr. King, and I still can't tell. All I can tell you is we won't have long to wait. She's at the point where it can't go on like this for many more hours. Either her temperature begins to drop and her blood pressure to rise, or . . . "

James felt himself swaying. He moved back against the wall. "But there is still some chance?"

"All I can say is this"—his hand went out and rested on James's shoulder—"if determination has anything to do with it, Jessie will live. I don't think I've ever seen such a fight." His voice dropped and his hand tightened as if in an attempt to stiffen James's spirit. "She's desperate not to leave you, Mr. King."

At two o'clock in the morning the nurse came into the little parlour and roused James from a cramped sleep. His body ached as he straightened in the chair.

"Can you come ben?"

He rose in an icy trance, trying to fathom her expression.

A stillness had descended on Jessie. For more than a week she had been racked by coughing and tossed by the consuming fever. Now she lay motionless, the bedclothes neatly about her. Her eyes were closed and her hair seemed to have been combed.

"I think she's easier." It was a barely audible whisper.

He turned almost incredulously.

"I'm going to fetch Dr. Douglas," she said from the door. "That's why I needed you here. He said I'd to get him if there was any change."

When she had gone, the quiet of the house was almost palpable. Even now it was impossible to associate this awful hush with the radiant girl of not much more than a week ago. The shrouded room, deprived of fresh air and denuded of flowers, would have been hateful to her. He pulled a chair to the bedside and gently buried his face in the pillow, burrowing close to the ravaged cheek, hardly daring to entertain the flickering hope the nurse had raised.

The dry burning had subsided! He was certain of it. He lifted his head to look at her, and suddenly the fragrance of a hundred leafy walks they had taken hand in hand rose from the herbs inside the pillow slip.

Behind him the door opened, and hurriedly he moved from the bed to make way. The examination seemed interminable, but when the doctor turned, his expression had lightened into a thankful smile.

"She's turned the corner," he said.

James's answer was too choked to be intelligible.

The old man put a comforting hand on his arm. "Believe me, I know something of what you've been through, Mr. King. I was there when Jessie was born. I helped her into this world."

"And I almost helped her out of it." For a long time James stood struggling with the tormenting thought. Others came, and he saw again the agonising events of the last terrible months. And then, all he was aware of, all he cared about, was Jessie. It seemed to him that even in the deep worn sleep that had now claimed her, her face had assumed a little of the old pert impudence that never failed to cheer and sustain him. At last, joy and gratitude flooded through him and he sank, trembling, into a chair.

"Oh, thank God. Thank God, Doctor."

It was hardly more than a whisper, but its vibrance filled the room.

27

Robert sat alone by a misted window as the train struck north toward Glasgow. A vague physical unease accentuated his dread of the meeting with Fiona that could hardly be delayed for many more hours. He had shirked it for weeks. In the artificial worlds of Westminster and Mayfair, the scandal had seemed a distant, almost unreal threat. Now, back in his own country, where values were stern and unchanging, the charade had been stripped. As he gazed on its bones he was affected as he hadn't been even when the news first reached him. How could she? And with Dunbar! Without a thought for what her faithlessness would do to him or to the children! The heartless bitch! And then, fairness asserted itself. Almost despite himself, he began to see the justification for Fergus's accusation that he had struck the first weakening blow by moving to London without her.

But had he really used her as uncaringly as Fergus implied? From the start the pattern of life forced on them by the business had led almost inevitably to drifting apart. In the end there had been little left but an appearance of marriage. But the appearance had been valuable. To him it was still necessary. Perhaps it was cold and calculating of him, but he meant to cling to it. Love in its original sense had left them and was beyond recapture, but on another level they still needed each other. There was an outward form to life that was important, too. Especially, he thought bitterly, if it was all you had. The fragile shell depended on their remaining together.

He closed his eyes and leaned back, swaying to the movement of the train. It was all so desperately material! And yet, to survive in this world, one had to be practical. Being practical, then—being fair and sensible—

it was difficult to grudge her a lover. His time in London had not been entirely innocent. There was the apartment he kept in another name. Had he any thoughts of giving that up? Fewer than ever! Of course, he was a man, working within a different set of rules. Then he remembered this had been part of Fergus's excuse for Fiona. Fergus saw her as having been lured from her rightful place in the home into the world where men operated their double standards. If that was the case, then she would only need a talking to, a scolding . . . just like a man who had wandered a bit. It could be made to sound reasonably plausible. Last night he had believed it.

Now, as he turned to the window again and watched locomotive smoke drift over bare fields lit with cold sunshine, it was suspect. Fiona was a woman. There would be nothing casual about her relationship with Dunbar. There would be little likelihood of his finding her conveniently disposed to being practical. Since she was financially independent, what sanctions could he apply?

His thoughts were as entangled as ever when he left the train at Glasgow and joined another that would take him part of the way to Lochbank. For almost a year McNair had been arguing the case for improvements to the distillery. Fiona had considered the proposals too technical for her. Robert had sidestepped all pleas that he should give a decision. Now a visit to Lochbank was a welcome excuse for another few hours' procrastination. He had telegraphed McNair to meet him with transport at Croftamie.

Memories swept him as they drove along empty roads toward the mountains. So much of his life had been centred on this area when he was still fighting to make his way. There had been his dash here in an abortive attempt to borrow money from old Roderick Fraser, Fiona's father, when Fergus had refused to finance his new blended whisky; his journeys to Lochbank when Fraser had gone on staunchly supplying them in secret when every other distillery in Scotland had been boycotting them; the happy days sailing with Fiona on the loch or climbing the ben. Did McNair know what it had all come to? It was impossible to tell. The big man seemed as serenely open as ever as they jogged along the stony road in the distillery wagonette. Robert managed a smile at the informality of the conveyance. McNair believed in keeping the expenses down.

Once he would have been impatient to reach the distillery, give a decision on the proposals and get back to Glasgow. Now it was with surprise that he saw the whitewashed buildings as they rounded a bend.

"I must have been dreaming," he said. "I hadn't realised we were so near."

"I suppose you'll have a lot on your mind," McNair said sympathetically. "These are worrying days. It's good of you, sparing me the time."

Robert caught his breath, but McNair's next words showed that their preoccupations were different.

"If this damned syndicate keeps its grip on the trade, these alterations might be worth their weight in gold. They should increase our capacity by twenty percent for a comparatively modest outlay."

Robert frowned at the mention of this other crisis. Worrying as it was, it had been subordinate to his more personal anxieties.

Instinct had told him Dunbar's must be the mind behind the syndicate. The strangely endless wait for supplies that King & Co. was having to endure was the vital indicator. But he had accepted almost eagerly the reports from Glasgow that there was no evidence of Dunbar's involvement, discounting the fact that the information came from Fiona. That Dunbar should have been able to construct such a brilliant weapon while he was stealing Fiona was a horror Robert felt he could not gaze upon. But eventually the mystery had been more than he could stand. Using the resources of the Treasury, to which he now had access, he had asked for enquiries to be made. The humiliating answers had started arriving on his desk a day or two before he left London.

They goaded him now into brusqueness. "I can't see the connection," he said. "It's top-class Highland malts we'll soon be crying out for. Lowlands like Lochbank hardly come into the picture."

"How are we going to manage, Mr. King? I hear we haven't been able to get a single cask out of these people." McNair's voice was angry.

Robert gave him an evasive look. "I suppose we'll survive somehow," he said.

After he had tramped from one shadowy building to another he readily approved the plans. "It's all worth doing," he said almost apologetically. "I should have been here sooner."

When he had taken tea by the log fire in McNair's office he sent for Jack, who had asked to see him.

"It's odd you should have come this week, of all weeks," Jack said. "You haven't been at Lochbank since you sent me here. You went to Parliament shortly afterward."

"That's right," Robert said, wondering what significance the visit could hold for his nephew. "I had forgotten you had been here so long."

Jack moved from the window, away from the view across the courtyard to the stillhouse. "That's really why I asked to see you, Uncle Robert. Since you were here, and since it was you who sent me here, I thought it only right that I should tell you personally that I'm . . . that I'll be leaving."

417

Robert misunderstood. "I suppose it's time you were back at Seabank Lane."

Jack leaned eagerly across the shabby old desk that separated them. "Uncle Robert, I've bought my own distillery."

The words and the expression on Jack's face took Robert back twenty-five years, to a picture of himself filled with an enthusiasm for work that had worried even Fergus. Here was another adventurer. The image was unmistakable. He had a fleeting sense of regret that this was not his son.

"Glendhu," Jack was elaborating. "I wanted to use Great-grandmother Veitch's money wisely. I hope I have. It's a fine whisky. Oh"—he turned animatedly to the window—"it's not a modern distillery, like Lochbank. In fact, it's rather decrepit and tumbledown. Old Mr. Kerr was a bit of an eccentric. He plodded on in the old ways, taking advice from no one—"

Robert held up a hand to stem the excited flood. "And he produced a Highland malt second to none." He laughed and, leaning across the desk, took Jack's hand. "Decrepit or not, if you now own the Glendhu distillery, you are to be congratulated. I didn't even know it was for sale."

"It was never publicly advertised," Jack said. "Mr. Kerr died two months ago. I bought it from his widow. I've been going north every weekend, nursing the deal along. I was terrified someone would get in ahead of me." He smiled. "I think the old lady took a liking to me. In the end she overruled her lawyer, who wanted to invite offers." Jack began pulling paper from his pockets. "If you're interested, I've got all the details here. The bargain was concluded only yesterday, when my bank transferred the money to her bank." He made a face. "It's cost me every penny of forty thousand pounds."

Robert could not hide a frown. A fear for Jack's impetuousness began to rise in him. "Isn't that an awful lot for what everyone knows to be a very old-fashioned distillery? Did you have proper advice?"

Jack smiled slowly and combed his hair flat with his fingers. "It wasn't just for the distillery. I was after something much more valuable. I got all the stock of matured whisky as well. The warehouses are full of them." He began pushing his papers about the desk. "Look at these! I don't think the old man could have known what he had lying there. Or maybe he didn't care. He was an autocrat, apparently. He wouldn't sell his whisky to anyone unless he liked them. It was the actual distilling that interested him, rather than the money he made from the whisky."

Robert whistled as he flipped rapidly through the papers. "Most of this whisky is ten and twelve years old."

Jack's stance was proud, and again Robert was reminded of incidents in his own youth and the joy of clever things done. "I know," Jack said. "That's why I said I don't think he could have known he had it. And, of

418

course, no one else would know. He managed the distillery himself. It was an odd way to live. Their house is hardly more than a glorified cottage. If you saw Mrs. Kerr pottering in the little garden, you would never dream she was a wealthy woman."

Robert was still immersed in the papers. "I can't understand how you could get so much matured whisky plus the distillery for forty thousand pounds. Unless I'm not reading this properly . . ."

"I got the whisky at probate," Jack said exultantly. The consternation of a man as experienced in business as Robert was a high compliment to Jack's astuteness. "The old lady's interest in the distillery was mainly a sentimental one. Her main concern was that it should go to someone who would appreciate its great tradition. She was impressed and pleased that I knew so much about distilling. She said I reminded her of her husband as a young man, and I think she saw me as someone who would carry on his work."

Robert looked up with a slight smile. "And will you?"

"Of course. So far as is possible. But, of course, improvements will have to come eventually."

Robert laughed as another thought came to him. "You know, Jack, as you have been applying yourself sensibly and profitably to business, your mother's fear was that you were about to go off to the South African war."

"The war! How on earth did she get a silly idea like that?" His expression changed. "I say, Uncle Robert, that's tactless of me. I'd forgotten about Gordon's enlisting. I didn't mean it was silly to go and fight in the war. I only meant it was silly of Mother thinking I would go. I mean, I'm not the type." His expression became understanding. "I suppose she was remembering Father fought out there."

"Possibly. But I'm quite sure this will be a great relief to her." Robert lifted the papers again, still marvelling at what they revealed. "If you don't mind my asking, what probate value had they put on this whisky?"

"It was all down at cost."

"Are you telling me you got all this at the price it was filled for ten years ago?"

"Every drop."

"Does the old lady know Glendhu is one of the whiskies this syndicate has cornered—or thought it had cornered?"

Jack lifted the papers and folded them. "I don't know, Uncle. It was never mentioned."

For a moment Robert had a glimpse of something he did not think he should like, a drive even more determined than his own had once been. Almost immediately he dismissed the thought as too harsh. Jack could not be judged by the same standards as the rest of them. His upbringing and his parentage had meant that he could never take anything for granted. He had always had to prove himself. "Men pass their lives dreaming of a deal like this! These stocks are worth at least a hundred thousand pounds."

Jack pondered, and then said moderately, "I suppose they could be. It's difficult to know until the whisky has all been regauged. You have to remember, there will have been a lot of evaporation."

Fiona's attempt to "brazen things out" had been helped by Fergus's avoidance of Seabank Lane. She continued to work hard, not only because of the darkening nightmare of dwindling stocks, but because of a guilty need for some form of atonement. She arrived early and usually went home late, hardly leaving her room and seeing no one except Ross.

Had Fergus told Robert? From all she knew of him, he must have. And yet, what sign was there that Robert knew? She scanned his letters, searching for some telltale phrase. There was nothing in the bland sentences. It was eerie and unnerving. Was it a deliberate form of torture? The avalanche must descend. But when? The uncertainty gnawed at her until she almost prayed for the onslaught to begin. At nights she lay awake in the big house at Claremont Row, alone except for Morag, asking herself why she was waiting under this roof. Dunbar wanted her. She wanted him.

Her attempt to stop seeing him had collapsed at his first approach after less than a week. He pressed her continually to live openly with him and became infuriated with her stubborn return each night to Claremont Row. Why was she clinging to the remains of a life that was gone, going through the motions of still being a King? Sometimes he taunted her with the glaring inconsistencies. She could find no satisfactory answer, either for herself or for him.

She still dreaded the final disgrace of a public admission. She wanted the lie of the last year to go on. She still wanted to be Mrs. Robert King, retaining the public appearance of all that had once meant while continuing to enjoy the excitement of a double life.

She knew it couldn't be, but was she capable of making a choice? Or would she finally be pushed humiliatingly in whatever direction life lay for her now? At this point in her tortured reasoning she sometimes came to tears. How had it all happened? What had it all been for? Surely not just for the physical gratification? And yet . . . she was no happier now than previously. Indeed, she had lost many of the old advantages. They might not have been "living," but hadn't they been a reasonable substitute for it, a substitute for which most women of her class were willing to settle, if not with gratitude then at least with sensible resignation? Robert hadn't been all loss, and she still had a strong affection for him. Through him and around him she had achieved an existence most women would have regarded as enviable. There were her children, who for a time had seemed enough. There were her parents-in-law, with whom she had known a long and comradely relationship. There had been the fascinating machinery of King & Co., trustingly put in her care.

Why had it all suddenly gone dull? Or had it been dull for a long time and she had only noticed when she had been offered an exciting comparison? How easily the comparison had become an alternative!

Only in efforts to acquire the whisky they would soon need had she been able to find distraction. The files for several years back were turned out and searched for offers that had been made to them of top-class malts. Not all had come from brokers or merchants. Some had been from private investors. In the hope that some of these people might still hold stocks, all were contacted. Only in three or four cases were the replies positive. And in only one instance was the holding substantial. It was available only because the owner had been abroad and out of touch with the market. The final bargain was a hard one—King & Co. paying sixpence a gallon more than the syndicate's known price. But the haul of more than a thousand casks would postpone the crisis by several months.

Every effort Ross made to discover from the syndicate when King & Co.'s order would be met produced the same reply: there was a waiting list. Why there should be a waiting list was never explained. Their position on it was never revealed. The address for the syndicate was care of a solicitor's office. No one could be approached for discussion.

"It beats me what they gain by being so mysterious," Ross fumed when he realised he was being deliberately kept at a distance. "It's more like a conspiracy than a syndicate."

"Unless the people behind it are prominent in other circles," Fiona said, "and feel they can't afford to be publicly involved. After all, they've been very clever, but it *is* rather unsavoury."

Ross, who could not now bring himself to mention Dunbar's name, had to content himself with a sceptical shrug. It pained her to see him growing away from her, the friendship she had won from him warping into long, enigmatic silences. He, too, she realised, was waiting for the inevitable to happen.

She was in the same downcast mood when Robert arrived from Lochbank. He was contained in front of the maid, his remarks little different from what they would normally have been. She realised the advantage was entirely his. She went trembling back into the room where she had been sitting, saying as he followed, "Haven't you any luggage?"

"I sent the cab up to Park Place with it." He looked round the room as if he had never seen it before—or as if he might never see it again. "I'll be staying up there tonight." He paused in his inspection of the room. "I take it you're alone? Perhaps I should have warned you I was coming."

She turned away. At least there could be no doubt now. "I'm alone, Robert," she said quietly.

"It's a pity you hadn't been alone more often."

Now that it was actually happening, the confused and elaborate denials she had rehearsed were revealed to her as pitiful. For a moment the defiance she had considered echoed grotesquely in her head and then was gone. She was left with only a sense of her absolute vulnerability. She sat down submissively on a hard chair in a corner of the room.

Aggression had almost left him in the months of hesitant pondering. Now, an odd sympathy rose in him at her meek and silent acceptance of his sarcasm. She seemed to carry even her shame with dignity. Somehow, if it didn't exactly lessen her crime, it suggested there must have been some justification for it. She was too sensible and considerate by nature to have stooped wantonly. She must have been pushed. Dear God, was his father right? Had *he* pushed her into it? Memories dazed him as he remembered their early happiness in a more leisurely world that seemed to have gone in only twenty years. How quickly the spirited rebel had matured into the warm and responsible guardian cherished by the whole family. And now . . . he was startled to hear her speaking.

"How long have you known?"

"So long that I thought I'd grown used to the idea. But now, back in my own house . . ." His voice was as leaden as his gaze.

"I'm sorry, Robert. I haven't wanted to hurt you."

His mouth opened in a short, bitter laugh and the dregs of his anger stirred. "I suppose that's why you chose Dunbar!"

"I didn't choose him. It . . . happened."

"Are you still meeting him?"

A clock in the corner whirred and she waited until it had struck nine times before she answered.

"Yes."

"I needn't tell you how seriously I view your behaviour. I'm here to ask how serious it all is to you. How do you see your future?"

She had not expected such calmness. It was somehow more threatening than the fury she had imagined and dreaded for weeks. And yet, it seemed to invite her honesty.

"I'm too worried and confused to know what I want," she said.

"The possibilities are rather limited, I'm afraid." The room was small, but the positions they had taken and the tone of his voice conspired to create an illusion of distance between them. The lamps, which she had always considered adequate, seemed to leave too many areas of shadow.

422

"Perhaps it would help if I told you what my hope is." He stopped as if expecting an answer.

She nodded.

"You may be rather surprised at what I have to say. Our marriage, of course, can no longer have any real meaning, but it would be convenient for me if we could keep up an appearance. I could divorce you for what you've done, but that would almost certainly have repercussions on my political future. The fact that I am the innocent party would be forgotten. They don't like scandal at Westminster. It doesn't seem sensible that I should suffer twice over. It would suit me that we continue legally as man and wife. Whether it would suit you must be your decision, and we will come to that later. If we continue together, there would be certain conditions. First, of course, your relationship with Dunbar would have to end. Second, this house would be sold and we would live in London, retaining Castle Gare for holidays. In London we would be unknown. There would be no gossip. I would require nothing of you except absolute discretion and, very occasionally, a little entertaining."

He was thinner than when she had last seen him, and the lean immobility of his features added to his air of tired detachment. The lack of recrimination, almost of emotion, was strangely insulting.

And yet, he was offering her more than she could have expected; more, perhaps, than she deserved. She could have everything except what she needed most. Her resentment burst out in a little cry. "You could always take the cold, sensible view of things, Robert."

For the first time he was almost stung to passion. She sensed him waiting until he had control before answering. "It's a pity you hadn't been able to do the same." He left his position by the curtained window and stood staring into the fire, his head bowed toward the marble surround. "Of course, whatever happens, you'll have to resign as managing director of King and Company."

A spark of pride flickered in her as she remembered all she had achieved. But the need to debase herself was stronger. She said, "I'm sorry your bold experiment in emancipation has turned out such a sad failure."

He turned, half expecting—almost wishing—to see the smile of affectionate mockery that had always been one of her weapons. It wasn't there.

"On a business level, it was far from a failure," he said. "During a difficult time you didn't just hold the business together—you kept it forging ahead. You established a strong market for Queen's Royal. Thanks to you, we will move into the twentieth century with two popular brands."

From the very start it was King & Co. that had stolen their possibility of happiness. She had a vision of an entity more enduring than either of them. Even now, it was important to know what would happen to it. "Who will take control?"

"I will propose we put Ross in charge and give him an assistant."

"And who would the assistant be?"

"Jack Hoey."

The name startled her out of her preoccupation with her own problems. "But that will alienate Gordon even further."

"I don't think we can afford to consider that. Gordon has taken himself out of King and Company. He is completely without interest in it."

She had never abandoned the hope that one day Gordon would come back. Often, when she passed the indicator board in the entrance at Seabank Lane, she imagined his name there in gilt and the slide moved to reveal the word IN. Even his enlistment had not extinguished the hope. The war would not last long.

She said, "I know Jack is eager and hard-working, but isn't he too young to be given so much responsibility? He is clearly fascinated with the process of distilling, but do we know if he has any real business instinct?"

"I don't think we need worry about that. Jack has just turned the money Great-grandmother Veitch left him into a fortune of over a hundred thousand pounds. He's managed to buy Glendhu distillery and all its stocks of matured whisky at a knock-down price. If that's not business instinct , I don't know what is."

"How do you know all this? He hasn't told me. And he can't have told McNair, or I would know."

It seemed to her typical of their entire marriage that the talk had somehow become dominated by considerations of business.

"I spent this afternoon at Lochbank," he said. "It all came out when Jack told me he was resigning. I've talked him out of that. The idea of being Ross's assistant appeals to him. He can see perfectly well what the next step could be."

"What about his distillery?"

"It will run perfectly well without his being there all the time."

Her smile was bemused. "And to think how Gwen has tortured herself for years worrying about him."

"Yes. It is rather ironic. Especially when you think of the mess Gordon is making of his life." He walked to the window and pulled the curtain aside, staring moodily into the dank street. "It shows how very little we really know about each other." His shoulders heaved in a dry laugh. "As if we weren't aware of that already!"

She struggled to understand his attitude. Did he care for her at all?

424

Was his coldness a pose? The only thing she could be certain of was that their meeting had been infinitely less dreadful than she had feared. She was glad, but not grateful. Relief made her feel less guilty.

"Apart from ability," Robert was saying, "Jack almost deserves the job as a reward. He has offered to let us buy his entire stock of Glendhu at substantially less than the price this damned syndicate is demanding. That shows his loyalty to King and Company. He could make himself a pot more money if he sold it on the open market."

On this level she felt she could face him with confidence. "Ross and I have been moving heaven and earth to buy whatever top malts the syndicate might have missed."

He walked restlessly across the room. "That's the only bit I can't understand," he said, in a tone which could have indicated sarcasm or mild sorrow. "Where your pride has gone. How can your attachment to your gentleman friend survive the fact that his syndicate is willing to sell whisky to anyone but you?"

"It isn't his syndicate," she said breathlessly. "He's being held to ransom like the rest of us."

He looked at her keenly, shaking his head slightly. "You really believe that?"

"Of course. Ross thought like you, but I asked—"

"And he told you a lie. You must be very blinded by him not to see what's staring the rest of us in the face."

His air of quiet certainty was frightening. "It's not true," she said falteringly. "It couldn't be true."

"It's entirely up to you what you believe," he said with every appearance of not caring. "So far as King and Company is concerned, it doesn't really matter who is behind the syndicate. And thanks to Jack, even the syndicate itself has lost its importance."

"I don't understand." Her mind was still worrying over his clear conviction that Dunbar was responsible for their troubles.

It seemed that he might not explain. Then, with emphasis, he said, "The Glendhu Jack is selling us will tide us over until Mr. Dunbar and his syndicate receive a very nasty surprise in the spring and we can all buy as much whisky as we want again at reasonable prices."

Her eyes widened. It was not her reading of the likely progress of events, whoever controlled the syndicate. "And what miracle is going to happen in the spring?"

His air of doubt returned. He walked worriedly about the room, then, for the first time since his arrival, he sat down. He leaned toward her. "I'm going to take it for granted you still have some loyalty to me, for if this ever gets out, my political career is finished." He sat back and stared at the ceiling as if swithering if his trust in her was wise. When he spoke his voice was low. "In the next budget, as an emergency war measure, Hicks Beach plans to increase the excise duty on whisky by at least sixpence, and possibly as much as a shilling a gallon. It will be the greatest blow whisky has ever suffered. Sales are bound to tumble catastrophically, and it could be years before they recover. After such a long boom, I suppose a slump—for whatever reason—was inevitable. The swing of the pendulum . . . it's inescapable. In this case, there's a ruinously expensive war that has to be paid for. Your Mr. Dunbar is suddenly going to find the blenders don't need his whisky—certainly, not nearly so much of it. He'll be left holding enormous stocks he can't sell, and rent and insurance to pay on them still."

She looked at him suspiciously. "How could a Tory chancellor possibly do that? The Tories don't believe in taxing spirits."

"The war has changed a lot of things."

As resentment of such an impost rose in her, she saw what a creature of business she had become—a perfect King, apparently always capable of being sidetracked into some commercial byway.

"But it would be monstrous," she protested. "It would harm the whisky trade dreadfully. How could he justify it? Everyone agrees the present excise duty of eleven shillings a gallon is punitive. The public wouldn't stand for any more."

For a moment the strength of her reaction surprised him. Then he shrugged. "I'm afraid they'll have to. Hicks Beach is set on it."

She leaned back and covered her face with her hands, struck by a strange, comic vision of the perversity of events. He was disconcerted to see her laugh.

"Oh, my God," she said. "Do you mean these people have spent all those millions cornering the market in top malts, and now they're going to be left with them? They were so cunning! They thought of everything. Everything except a budget that would slash the demand for whisky."

He stood in a patch of shadow, watching her unstable amusement with disapproval. Business failures—even other people's—weren't funny.

"They won't be left holding everything, of course," he said. "They'll do very well until the spring. Fortunately, thanks to Jack, we now have stocks that will last until after the budget has knocked the feet from them. We are very fortunate they had us so far down their waiting list. It has saved us money."

He went on elaborating, but although she could hear his voice, the words did not register. All at once she knew he was right about Dunbar's being the brain and the hand behind the syndicate. It couldn't be otherwise, given the fact that no matter how hard King & Co. tried they could not buy the whisky they were able and ready to pay for.

Douglas! The pained protest reverberated bewilderingly in her head. He had lied to her, and she had trustingly accepted his lie. That he had been able to keep his secret from the trade in general was understandable, considering the tortuous precautions he had taken. But to her, as a King, it should have been shining clear. She had been blinded. Now she could see—as certainly as Robert, as certainly as Ross—even though there was no proof.

Again her hands went over her face, but this time to hide the tears. She heard Robert rise and walk about the room, as if to leave her with her thoughts. That he had read them correctly seemed certain when he spoke from behind her chair.

"I need you, Fiona, for the reasons already stated. They are, frankly, selfish reasons. Whether you go or stay is a matter for you. I can't tell the strength of your passion for Dunbar." He made it sound like a disease. "But whatever it is, you should weigh against it the fact that your only hope of a normal family life in decent society lies with me. If you go to him, you will always be an outcast. At the moment your domestic life is in ruins, but perhaps it could be rebuilt. At any rate, partially.

"You would have to win your children back—especially Florence—but it shouldn't be impossible. Another thing you should consider well is the complication of your business interests. You own a very large part of King and Company. How long would you be able to stand the machinations of a man dedicated to the destruction of a business substantially owned by you? Your relationship would be rent with a continual conflict of interests."

She turned impulsively to face him, searching the rigid mould of his features for a hint of some feeling. "You make it sound so simple, Robert. So obvious. You manage to take all the emotion out of it. To strip it down to the irreducible facts. That's how you've always manipulated everything to suit yourself. Beside you, the rest of us are children."

"Not at all," he demurred, but a faint smile creased his face, as if in the words he detected a bleak compliment. He added another twist. "Remember, he'll be a very different man by the time all this is over. His arrogant conceit took him above himself, and he'll fall hard. He'll go on posturing, and threatening us, I suppose, so long as he has a case of whisky to his name, but he'll only be pathetic. His price-cutting has burned itself out. His syndicate is heading for catastrophe. As far as King and Company is concerned, he really no longer exists." For the first time, his control slipped. "It's really a case of good riddance to bad rubbish," he said viciously.

She rose, unable to bear the pictures in her mind. In the lamplight her paleness did not show. Apart from the hunted expression in her eyes, she still presented the same picture of robust and wholesome beauty that seemed hardly to have altered in twenty years. He watched her without bitterness, almost with sympathy. He would have cut the entangling strands for her if he could.

"I have a dreadful headache," she said.

"Then I'll let you get to bed."

As he moved towards the door she said, "Can you tell me how James is? And Jessie? I haven't seen anyone for a while."

"I broke my journey and detoured to Fleetside on the way up from London. Jessie is recovering well. James . . ." He sighed. "Well, James is a different matter, but I think with Jessie beside him he'll come through. They've set a new date for their wedding sometime early in February."

"I pray for them both," she said.

He stood holding the handle of the door, looking at her in silence. "When do you think you might let me know?" he said at last.

She saw him in a blur. "I can't think tonight, Robert," she said pleadingly. She looked about almost desperately. "I don't know if I can think at all in this house now. Perhaps I could go down to Castle Gare for a day or two."

In his surprise he moved back a little way into the room. "In December? But it will be freezing."

"I don't care. I could think there."

"There's no one there but old Miller, and he'll be in the cottage. He wouldn't be prepared for you. You couldn't possibly spend New Year there."

"I could take Morag. If you're going to stay at Park Place, this house can be closed."

He seemed to lose interest. "I'm returning to London tomorrow. There will have to be a special board meeting soon, but I'll travel back for that."

She was hardly aware of his going.

28

On the last day of December a gig came rocking along the bumpy shore road and turned into the steep driveway leading to Castle Gare. Fiona watched from a rattling first-floor window as it wound slowly up from the lochside between tall coniferous trees which flailed noisily at the darkening sky.

As the small vehicle came round the last bend, she saw from its colours that it belonged to a Helensburgh hiring firm. Then, with a shock, she recognised Dunbar, hunched in massive impatience over the labouring horse, the folds of his Inverness cape flapping and billowing as the stormy wind swept about him.

It was an afternoon in which the stark scene matched the restless desolation of her spirit. A high black tide covered the rocks by the roadside, and every so often the road itself was deluged in icy spray. Slender branches snapped from trees and sailed past the windows. Already the gloaming had obliterated the mountains behind Arrochar and tinged the heaving loch a dismal grey. Across the Gareloch a line of rough white water denoted the shores of the Rosneath Peninsula.

In a strange way the bleakness of outlook had sustained her since her arrival two days before. It reminded her that everything changed. The last time she had been here there had been butterflies in the rose garden and swallows darting about the eaves. Now, everything was cold and wet. But on one of her solitary walks she had seen the first pale hint of snowdrops round the base of a beech tree. After the snowdrops, crocus would come, and then primroses. The barren months would pass.

So let it be with me, she prayed, as she went disconsolately along twisting flagstoned paths or wandered empty rooms and corridors, past portraits of people she had never known, glimpsing from little windows unexpected views that she might never see again. *So let it be for us all*, she found herself saying beeseechingly, and in the heavy silence of the castle her voice carried so that Morag cast curious glances at her when they passed. So let it be for Florence, in Paris. For Robert, in London. For Steven and Allan, at Rugby. For Gordon, in Stirling. For Douglas, in Glasgow. In different ways, she told herself when she reached the end of the distracted litany, she loved them all. Yet she must leave them all.

When she spoke these last words to herself, it was a true intention. A silent disappearance in which she renounced everything seemed the best solution to her dilemma. And then, reason and common sense would reassert themselves and tell her along which path her future must lie. The way indicated was always the same. But still she hesitated, for it would lead to a life weighted—perhaps forever—with regret. She would always be looking back, wondering what would have unfolded for her if she had chosen the other way. But this afternoon, sitting by the window, she had at last made her choice. And now, in this state, it seemed to her as she looked down on Dunbar that he must have been directed there providentially, before her resolution wavered once more.

As he threw down the reins and jumped from the gig, she hurried to a bellpull. The wind drowned the sound of his steps on the gravel, but as she stood waiting, she pictured him leaping impulsively up the steps. She heard the heavy door-knocker strike four times. Almost at the same moment Morag came into the room, looking flustered.

"You rang, ma'am, but there's somebody at the front door," she said breathlessly, with a quick glance backward, to the landing. She was not at ease in the castle.

"Yes. I saw a gig arrive a moment ago. That's why I rang. I don't want to see anyone. Tell whoever it is that I can't receive them."

"Yes, ma'am." As Morag turned to go, the knocker struck another succession of heavy blows, causing her to start.

"Tell whoever it is," Fiona said, her hands clenched and her eyes closed, her back to the maid, "that I am preparing for a journey. Tell them I am leaving tomorrow to join my husband in London."

When the girl had gone, she crossed the room again and stood back a little from the window. She saw the courtyard and the gig as through a mist. She imagined she heard voices carried on the bounding wind: one rough, insistent and querulous. *Douglas!* The word sounded passionately in her mind. Then there was a crash, as if the door had been torn from Morag's grip and slammed in his face.

She watched him come into view, retreating from the house in a baffled way, with backward glances and an outraged expression. He mounted the gig and sat for a few moments, glowering up at the windows as if

430

still unable to believe the rebuff. Then, his pride seeming to rear, he seized the reins, swung the gig quickly round and urged the horse across the courtyard in a shower of flying gravel. As he went under the arch, the wind struck him hard. His hat soared from his head and went spinning into the dark trees. With hardly a glance after it he plunged heedlessly onward, into the twilight and out of her sight.

Out of her life, she thought with a sob as she turned from the window and the now empty view. It was too stark and final a concept to be properly grasped, especially with such a turmoil of doubt in her heart. The full meaning of what she had lost would only come to her in tranquillity. Her thoughts were almost irrelevant. His exit had been completely characteristic of him. Nothing but a proud, headlong rush would have done.

A tear ran down her cheek, and the bemused reflection turned slowly to anxiety as she remembered what lay ahead of him if Robert's information was accurate. Almost immediately, the concern hardened. Hell mend him! He deserved to be rolled in the mire. He was a treacherous brute. But as she walked to the fire and threw herself into a chair, all the virulence went out of her again, and she remembered only that she had loved him and that he, in his own wild way—she was sure of it—had loved her.

She sat sobbing until the room was black and Morag knocked timorously at the door and asked if she should light the lamps.

"It's warmer in the downstairs sitting room," Fiona said, thankful for the muffling darkness and hoping her voice did not betray her. "Light them there."

If it had been less stormy, she would have set out for Glasgow immediately, but in her dispirited state the thought of the long journey on such a night was too daunting. Rain had come at last, lashing in from the loch and striking the windows like hail. It was impossible to escape from it. It seemed almost to have entered the house. The curtains had all been taken down for washing at the end of the summer and had not been rehung. Even with walls almost three feet thick the castle seemed vulnerable.

After a makeshift dinner, which she helped Morag prepare in the vaulted chill of the great kitchens, she tried to read by a fire heaped high with birch logs. Raindrops came down the wide chimney and hissed in the blaze. As a clock struck eight she closed her book and sat staring listlessly about the room. In every shadowed corner she saw Dunbar. Even in her unhappiness she could not renounce her year with him, despite having to regret its consequences on those she loved.

In honesty, she could not see the scale as other than almost evenly balanced. She well understood now how women could abandon everything and go off to a life of social rejection. If it hadn't been for Robert's open-

431

ing her eyes, would she have been different from those other women? She would never know, for he *had* betrayed her, and it was better to have been faced with this now than later. It had made it easier for her to point herself toward true duty. With the decision taken, there was a strange lure even in self-sacrifice. It beckoned impatiently. She should have gone tonight, despite the storm. With an effort she could even have caught the sleeper train south. Tomorrow she must leave early, and by night she would be in London, beginning another life. Somehow she would overcome the emotional emptiness. She would suffer the penalty of Robert's increased coldness. After all, she was responsible for it. Perhaps in time it would thaw a little. Above all, she must strive to create a new, secure home for her children.

The book she had been reading fell from her hand as she realised with a shock that what she had just seen at the uncurtained window was not a memory of Dunbar, but Dunbar himself. He had been peering in at her, still hatless, the rain plastering his hair flat and streaming down his face.

As she stood, undecided what to do, the iron knocker crashed on the door like a hammer. Again and again it fell, seemingly with all his strength behind it. When she went into the corridor, the din still thundered round the dark recesses of the hall.

She saw Morag standing at the foot of the stairs, holding a lamp and staring at the quivering door.

"Don't open it," she called, hurrying toward the frightened girl.

There was a short silence, in which she heard her own excited heartbeats and then a roar: "Aye, she'll open it. She'll open it, all right, or I'll smash it in."

At least he couldn't do that, she thought, looking with relief at the massive iron-studded timbers from which the door was constructed.

"Oh, ma'am," Morag whispered. "When I shut the door on him this afternoon, he was in a mood fit to kill."

"Can you hear me, Fiona? Open the damned door." The thick slab of oak shook as he kicked it.

She went forward and shouted pleadingly. "Stop it, Douglas. The door will not be opened." She signalled to Morag to follow her. As they reached the room where she had been sitting, there was a splintering crash and a sudden rush of cold air. They looked back in terror, but the door was intact. It was the glass and the woodwork of the sitting-room window that had been shattered.

Morag screamed as Dunbar stepped through the ragged gap, still clutching a cast-iron garden chair from the terrace. His cloak was sodden and shapeless. Water sprayed about the room as he shook broken glass out of the shaggy tweed.

Then he stood gasping for breath, his chest and shoulders heaving un-

432

der the enveloping cape. He looked at the wreckage as if astonished at what he had done.

"Murder!" Morag shrieked, clinging to Fiona. "I'll get the police, ma'am."

Dunbar dropped the iron chair with a clatter and held up a hand from which blood trickled. It was intended as a gesture of reassurance, but Morag interpreted it as a prelude to assault. "Murder!" she screamed again.

Dunbar ignored her. "You should have opened the door," he said to Fiona with an expression which, she thought, could only be described as ashamed.

Fiona was too choked with a combination of alarm and anger to be able to answer.

"I'm not drunk," he said, elaborating his defence, "though I'll admit to having had a dram. Now, quieten the girl." He looked almost sorrowfully at the ruined window. Rain had gathered on the waxed floor and was trickling under a rug. "I'll pay for the damage," he said.

Fiona put a comforting hand on the maid's trembling shoulder, turning her toward the door. "You can leave us, Morag," she said. "You needn't be frightened."

"But, ma'am—"

"I'll be all right."

When the door had closed, she turned to him. "This is disgraceful. What do you want?"

The coldness of her voice completed his discomfiture.

Rage had possessed him as he stood morbidly swilling whisky among the Hogmanay revellers in a Helensburgh pub, staring murderously at a bottle of Queen's Royal on the gantry. Rage had impelled him to buy the offending bottle and then, to the publican's astonishment, to slosh the contents over the sawdust floor before barging out with a force that almost tore the frosted-glass doors from their hinges. Rage had brought him galloping along the shore road on a borrowed horse.

Only in the mad violence of his entry had his fury subsided. He hardly knew now why he had come. He moved awkwardly to the fire, an apology hovering on his lips, and then retreating, as a memory of his earlier visit returned.

"I don't like being dismissed by servants," he said truculently. "If you've done with me, I want to hear it from you." A light almost of pleading came into his eyes as he mopped his wet face with a handkerchief that came out of his pocket still sparkling white. "Surely I deserve at least that."

She bridled, her courage rising at his deflation. "You deserve very little consideration, Douglas. You lied to me. You deceived me."

"Lied to you!" He looked shocked.

"Yes. You needn't pretend. I know now you are behind the whisky syndicate."

An expression strangely mingling relief with cunning gathered in his eyes. "But that was only business. It wasn't about us."

She stared at him in disbelief. "Of course it was about us. You told me you loved me and all the time you were plotting against me."

"Oh, Christ." He covered his face with his hands, and when he took them away, his cheeks were streaked with blood from his cut finger.

"How could you possibly love me and do that? How could you possibly do that if you loved me?"

"I don't know, but I did," he said, his dejection illuminated with a hint of fervour that gave his claim an odd credibility. He began to move toward her with his hands out-stretched.

"Keep away," she said. "You shouldn't have come back. I'm leaving for London tomorrow."

He stopped and gave a bleak nod. "Aye, your girl told me."

"Then why have you come smashing your way into my house?"

"I told you. I wanted to hear it from you."

"Well, now that you have heard it, Douglas, please go." All her will was concentrated on preserving an appearance of cold determination.

He turned toward the window.

"You can leave by the door."

"I'll go the way I came." He hesitated and spoke with his head bowed. "I'm sorry for what I did about the whisky."

"I'm not concerned about that now."

"In future, I'll see you get as much as you need."

As he reached the shattered window, her hand went trembling toward him. "Don't go just yet."

He turned hopefully.

"It is wrong of me to tell you this," she said unsteadily, "and after your behaviour you don't really deserve to know, but . . ."

He stood motionless, almost as if not even breathing, as she told him of the coming disastrous whisky tax. She listened to her voice with a feeling of amazement and distaste. Were all the emotional moments of her life doomed to degenerate into business discussions? Then the thought left her and she knew that despite the outward form, it wasn't business she was talking. It was love.

"If long ago King and Company did you some wrong," she said, "perhaps this information will help even the score."

She watched him grappling with the implications. At last the sodden cape flapped, as he moved his hands in a gesture of hopelessness.

"How can I use it?" he asked. "If the syndicate starts unloading, your husband will guess you've told me. What then?"

"He will not be very pleased with me."

His perplexity deepened. "You would have been better not telling me."

The room had become very cold. She moved away from the draught coming in through the broken window. "I suppose I couldn't bear to think of you suffering when a word from me could help you."

He stared at her intently as she bent to the fire. "It doesn't make sense, Fiona. If I use this information, your life with King could be ruined, yet you're leaving me because you prefer the life with him."

She stared past him. The rain seemed to have stopped and the wind quietened. "My responsibilities are there," she said shortly.

"If the syndicate starts dumping, he may not let you continue with your responsibilities."

"I'll risk that." She whirled round to face him, her eyes intense and her voice ardent. "Can't you understand? Is it beyond you? I'm telling you because I love you still." Her voice broke with emotion. "To my shame, Douglas—or perhaps it's to my sorrow—I love you still."

Despite the passionate words, there was something in her manner that forbade his touching her. What she was talking about transcended the physical. He stared at her in wonder, his mind buffeted by a fury of regret for what he now saw as his terrible unworthiness. She had given him her love and in return he had tried to ruin her. At the time, he had deluded himself that it was otherwise, pretending that somehow she would be spared. Now he saw it clearly for the heartless betrayal it had been. And yet, still she was risking what remained of her family life to give him information that could save him from ruin. In his anguish he doubted if he knew what love was. Did he really love her? Had he ever loved anyone? Even Ethel?

In a sudden, desperate need for some self-sacrifice that would match hers, he cried across the room, "I won't tell the syndicate. I'll put what you've told me out of my head."

Even in her wretchedness her heart rose, but grimly she clung to her resolve.

"I can't tell you what to do, Douglas, and I put no condition on what I've told you, but I suppose the worst you would have to face would be the failure of the syndicate, the continued flourishing of King and Company and the fact that all your plotting had been for nothing. I can't think it's any more than you deserve."

"No." His gaze was fastened on her, but he was seeing something far away, perhaps a younger, poorer Douglas Dunbar. "It's worse than that.

435

If the syndicate goes down, I go with it. I committed everything I had to that scheme. I borrowed to the hilt."

"If it's a matter of everything going, you must do as you wish."

"Aye!" He nodded as if to himself. "But if to tell the syndicate is the only way of saving myself, then it can all go." He closed his eyes and his head shook as if with some tremendous concentration of thought. "But maybe there's some other way. I could maybe get out on my own without the others. Maybe I could sell my share to them. Denholm's a greedy devil, for one. I could spin them a tale about the bank calling in my overdraft or about the money being needed to expand my own business. They would never suspect there was something up. We would still be getting the high prices. They wouldn't see any reason for my getting out."

When he looked up, he was alone.

From a darkened room Fiona watched him go. Now that the rain had stopped a faint light shone through the thinning clouds. For a few moments he was framed in the archway in silhouette and then the courtyard was empty.

She waited for several minutes and then, putting on a heavy coat, went out. The wind was harmless now, and mild. Against the castle walls creeper rustled. Between her and the water dark trees swayed. Suddenly, from the loch and the wide river estuary beyond, there came a clamour of ship's horns. Nearer, bells began to ring from the church at Row. As she stood alone in the lee of the castle, her hands resting on the stone parapet on the edge of the hillside, she pictured people raising glasses to welcome not just a new year but a new century.

From a tree at the side of the road an owl screeched. Above her, bats flitted as they had not done for several nights. From a tangle of shrubbery a nightjar called as if in relief at the end of the storm.

Somewhere in the reserves of her undrainable nature something hopeful stirred. She was reminded again that everything changed. Only that morning, amid the bareness of the garden, she had noticed buds on a jasmine bush by the dining-room window. In another month pale-yellow blooms would open and soon spring would come again.

She remembered her prayer. *So let it be for me.* As she walked back to the castle, she whispered it longingly to a sky in which the clouds had at last broken and a star or two shone.